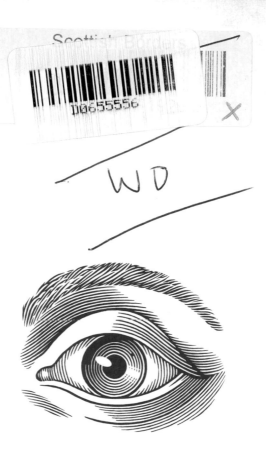

Never Sleeping

The Manual

of

Detection

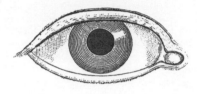

The Manual

of

Detection

JEDEDIAH BERRY

WILLIAM HEINEMANN: LONDON

Published by William Heinemann 2009

2 4 6 8 10 9 7 5 3 1

Copyright © Jedediah Berry 2009

Jedediah Berry has asserted his right under the Copyright, Designs
and Patents Act, 1988, to be identified as the author of this work

First published in the United States in 2009 by The Penguin Press,
a member of Penguin Group (USA) Inc.

First published in Great Britain in 2009 by
William Heinemann
Random House, 20 Vauxhall Bridge Road,
London SW1V 2SA

www.rbooks.co.uk

Addresses for companies within The Random House Group Limited
can be found at: www.randomhouse.co.uk/offices.htm

The Random House Group Limited Reg. No. 954009

A CIP catalogue record for this book
is available from the British Library

ISBN: 9780434019458 (Hardback)
ISBN: 9780434019465 (Trade Paperback)

The Random House Group Limited supports The Forest Stewardship
Council (FSC), the leading international forest certification organisation.
All our titles that are printed on Greenpeace approved FSC certified paper
carry the FSC logo. Our paper procurement policy can be found at:
www.rbooks.co.uk/environment

Mixed Sources
Product group from well-managed
forests and other controlled sources
FSC   www.fsc.org Cert no. TT-COC-2139
© 1996 Forest Stewardship Council

Designed by Meighan Cavanaugh

Printed and bound in Great Britain by
Clays Ltd, St Ives Plc

Contents

The Manual

of

Detection

On Shadowing

The expert detective's pursuit will go unnoticed, but not because he is unremarkable. Rather, like the suspect's shadow, he will appear as though he is meant to be there.

Lest details be mistaken for clues, note that Mr. Charles Unwin, lifetime resident of this city, rode his bicycle to work every day, even when it was raining. He had contrived a method to keep his umbrella open while pedaling, by hooking the umbrella's handle around the bicycle's handlebar. This method made the bicycle less maneuverable and reduced the scope of Unwin's vision, but if his daily schedule was to accommodate an unofficial trip to Central Terminal for unofficial reasons, then certain risks were to be expected.

Though inconspicuous by nature, as a bicyclist and an umbrellist Unwin was severely evident. Crowds of pedestrians parted before the ringing of his little bell, mothers hugged their children near, and the children gaped at the magnificence of his passing. At intersections he avoided eye contact with the drivers of motor vehicles, so as not to give the impression he might yield to them. Today he was behind schedule. He had scorched his oatmeal, and tied the wrong tie, and nearly forgotten his wristwatch,

all because of a dream that had come to him in the moments before waking, a dream that still troubled and distracted him. Now his socks were
getting wet, so he pedaled even faster.

He dismounted on the sidewalk outside the west entrance of Central Terminal and chained his bicycle to a lamppost. The revolving
doors spun ceaselessly, shunting travelers out into the rain, their black
umbrellas blooming in rapid succession. He collapsed his own umbrella and slipped inside, checking the time as he emerged into the
concourse.

His wristwatch, a gift from the Agency in recognition of twenty
years of faithful service, never needed winding and was set to match—
to the very second—the time reported by the four-faced clock above
the information booth at the heart of Central Terminal. It was twenty-
three minutes after seven in the morning. That gave him three minutes
exactly before the woman in the plaid coat, her hair pinned tightly
under a gray cap, would appear at the south entrance of the terminal.

He went to stand in line at the breakfast cart, and the man at the
front of the line ordered a coffee, two sugars, no cream.

"Slow today, isn't it?" Unwin said, but the man in front of him did
not respond, suspecting, perhaps, a ruse to trick him out of his spot.

In any case it was better that Unwin avoid conversation. If someone
were to ask why he had started coming to Central Terminal every
morning when his office was just seven blocks from his apartment, he
would say he came for the coffee. But that would be a lie, and he hoped
he never had to tell it.

The tired-looking boy entrusted with the steaming machines of the
breakfast cart—Neville, according to his name tag—stirred sugar into
the cup one spoonful at a time. The man waiting for his coffee, two
sugars, no cream, glanced at his watch, and Unwin knew without looking that the woman in the plaid coat would be here, or rather there, at
the south end of the concourse, in less than a minute. He did not even
want the coffee. But what if someone were to ask why he came to Cen-

tral Terminal every morning at the same time, and he said he came for the coffee, but he had no coffee in his hand? Worse than a lie is a lie that no one believes.

When it was Unwin's turn to place his order, Neville asked him if he wanted cream or sugar.

"Just coffee. And hurry, please."

Neville poured the coffee with great care and with greater care fitted the lid onto the cup, then wrapped it in a paper napkin. Unwin took it and left before the boy could produce his change.

Droves of morning commuters sleepwalked to a murmur of station announcements and newspaper rustle. Unwin checked his ever-wound, ever-winding watch, and hot coffee seeped under the lid and over his fingers. Other torments ensued. His briefcase knocked against his knees, his umbrella began to slip from under his arm, the soles of his shoes squeaked on the marble floor. But nothing could divert him. He had never been late for her. Here now was the lofty arch of Gate Fourteen, the time twenty-six minutes after seven. And the woman in the plaid coat, her hair pinned tightly under a gray cap, tumbled through the revolving doors and into the heavy green light of a Central Terminal morning.

She shook water from her umbrella and gazed up at the vaulted ceiling, as though at a sky that threatened more rain. She sneezed, twice, into a gloved hand, and Unwin noted this variation on her arrival with the fervency of an archivist presented with newly disclosed documents. Her passage across the terminal was unswerving. Thirty-nine steps (it was never fewer than thirty-eight, never more than forty) delivered her to her usual spot, several paces from the gate. Her cheeks were flushed, her grip on her umbrella very tight. Unwin drew a worn train schedule from his coat pocket. He feigned an interest in the schedule while together (alone) they waited.

How many mornings before the first that he saw her had she stood there? And whose face did she hope to find among the disembarking host? She was beautiful, in the quiet way that lonely, unnoticed people are beautiful to those who notice them. Had someone broken a promise to her? Willfully, or due to unexpected misfortune? As an Agency clerk, it was not for Unwin to question too deeply, nor to conduct anything resembling an investigation. Eight days ago he had gone to Central Terminal, had even purchased a ticket because he thought he might like to leave town for a while. But when he saw the woman in the plaid coat, he stayed. The sight of her had made him wonder, and now he found he could not stop wondering. These were unofficial trips, and she was his unofficial reason; that was all.

A subterranean breeze blew up from the tracks, ruffling the hem of her coat. The seven twenty-seven train, one minute late as usual, arrived at the terminal. A pause, a hiss: the gleaming doors slid open. A hundred and more black raincoats poured all at once from the train and up through the gate. The stream parted as it met her. She stood on her toes, looking left and right.

The last of the raincoats rushed past. Not one of them had stopped for her.

Unwin returned the schedule to his pocket, put his umbrella under his arm, picked up his briefcase, his coffee. The woman's solitude had gone undisturbed: should he have felt guilty for being relieved? So long as no one stopped for her, her visits to Central Terminal would continue, and so would his. Now, as she began her walk back to the revolving doors, he followed, matching his pace to hers so he would pass only a few steps behind her on his way to his bicycle.

He could see the wisps of brown hair that had escaped from under her cap. He could count the freckles on the back of her neck, but the numbers meant nothing; all was mystery. As he had the previous morning, and the seven mornings before that, Unwin willed with all the power in his lanky soul that time, like the train at the end of its track, would stop.

This morning it did. The woman in the plaid coat dropped her umbrella. She turned and looked at him. Her eyes—he had never seen them so close—were the clouded silver of old mirrors. The numbered panels on the arrival and departure boards froze. The station announcements ceased. The four second hands on the four faces of the clock trembled between numbers. The insides of Unwin's ever-wound wristwatch seized.

He looked down. Her umbrella lay on the floor between them. But his hands were full, and the floor was so far away.

Someone behind him said, "Mr. Charles Unwin?"

The timetables came back to life, the clocks remembered themselves, the station resumed its murmuring. A plump man in a herringbone suit was staring at him with green-yellow eyes. He danced the big fingers of his right hand over the brim of a hat held in his left. "Mr. Charles Unwin," he said again, not a question this time.

The woman in the plaid coat snatched up her umbrella and walked away. The man in the herringbone suit was still waiting.

"The coffee," Unwin began to explain.

The man ignored him. "This way, Mr. Unwin," he said, and gestured with his hat toward the north end of the terminal. Unwin glanced back, but the woman was already lost to the revolving doors.

What could he do but follow? This man knew his name—he might also know his secrets, know he was making unofficial trips for unofficial reasons. He escorted Unwin down a long corridor where men in iron chairs read newspapers while nimble boys shined their shoes.

"Where are we going?"

"Someplace we can talk in private."

"I'll be late for work."

The man in the herringbone suit flipped open his wallet to reveal an Agency badge identifying him as Samuel Pith, Detective. "You're on the job," Pith said, "starting this moment. That makes you a half hour early, Mr. Unwin."

They came to a second corridor, dimmer than the first, blocked by a row of signs warning of wet floors. Beyond, a man in gray coveralls slid a grimy-looking mop over the marble in slow, indeliberate arcs. The floor was covered with red and orange oak leaves, tracked in, probably, by a passenger who had arrived on one of the earlier trains from the country.

Detective Pith cleared his throat, and the custodian shuffled over to them, pushed one of the signs out of the way, and allowed the two to pass.

The floor was perfectly dry. Unwin glanced into the custodian's bucket. It was empty.

"Listen carefully, now," said Detective Pith. He emphasized the words by tapping his hat brim against Unwin's chest. "You're an odd little fellow. You've got peculiar habits. Every morning this week, same time, there's Charles Unwin, back at Central Terminal. Not for a train, though. His apartment is just seven blocks from the office."

"I come for the—"

"Damn it, Unwin, don't tell me. We like our operatives to keep a few mysteries of their own. Page ninety-six of the *Manual*."

"I'm no operative, sir. I'm a clerk, fourteenth floor. And I'm sorry you've had to waste your time. We're both behind schedule now."

"I told you," Pith growled, "you're already on the job. Forget the fourteenth floor. Report to Room 2919. You've been promoted." From his coat pocket Pith drew a slim hardcover volume, green with gold lettering: *The Manual of Detection.* "Standard issue," he said. "It's saved my life more than once."

Unwin's hands were still full, so Pith slipped the book into his briefcase.

"This is a mistake," Unwin said.

"For better or worse, somebody has noticed you. And there's no way now to get yourself unnoticed." He stared at Unwin a long moment. His substantial black eyebrows gathered downward, and his lips went stiff and frowning. But when he spoke, his voice was quieter, even kind. "I'm supposed to keep this simple, but listen. Your first case should be an easy one. Hell, mine was. But you're in this thing a little deeper, Unwin. Maybe because you've been with the Agency so long. Or maybe you've got some friends, or some enemies. It's none of my business, really. The point is—"

"Please," said Unwin, checking his watch. It was seven thirty-four.

Detective Pith waved one hand, as though to clear smoke from the air. "I've already said more than I should have. The point is, Unwin, you're going to need a new hat."

The green trilby was Unwin's only hat. He could not imagine wearing anything else on his head.

Pith donned his own fedora and tipped it forward. "If you ever see me again, you don't know me. Got it?" He snapped a finger at the custodian and said, "See you later, Artie." Then the herringbone suit disappeared around the corner.

The custodian had resumed his work, mopping the dry floor with his dry mop, moving piles of oak leaves from one end of the corridor to the other. In the reports Unwin received each week from Detective Sivart, he had often read of those who, without being in the employ of the Agency, were nonetheless aware of one or more aspects of a case—who were, as the detective might write, "in on it." Could the custodian be one of those?

His name tag was stitched with red, curving letters.

"Mr. Arthur, sir?"

Arthur continued working, and Unwin had to hop backward to escape the wide sweep of his mop. The custodian's eyes were closed, his mouth slightly open. And he was making a peculiar sound, low and whispery. Unwin leaned closer, trying to understand the words.

But there were no words, there was nothing to understand. The custodian was snoring.

OUTSIDE, UNWIN DROPPED HIS coffee in a trash can and glanced downtown toward the Agency's gray, monolithic headquarters, its uppermost stories obscured by the rain. Years ago he had admitted to himself that he did not like the look of the building: its shadow was too long, the stone of its walls cold and somehow like that of a tomb. Better, he thought, to work inside a place like that than to glimpse it throughout the day.

To make up for lost time, he risked a shortcut down an alleyway he knew was barely wide enough to accommodate his open umbrella. The umbrella's metal nubs scraped against both walls as the bicycle bumped and jangled over old cobblestone.

He had already begun drafting in his mind the report that would best characterize his promotion, and in this draft the word "promotion" appeared always between quotation marks, for to let it stand without qualification would be to honor it with too much validity. Errors were something of a rarity at the Agency. It was a large organization, however, composed of a great many bureaus and departments, most of them beyond Unwin's purview. In one of those bureaus or departments, it was clear, an error had been committed, overlooked, and worst of all, disseminated.

He slowed his pace to navigate some broken bottles left strewn across the alley, the ribs of his umbrella bending against the walls as he turned. He expected at any moment to hear the fateful hiss of a popped tire, but he and his bicycle passed unscathed.

This error that Pith had brought with him to Central Terminal—it was Unwin's burden now. He accepted it, if not gladly, then encouraged by the knowledge that he, one of the most experienced clerks of the fourteenth floor, was best prepared to cope with such a calamity. Every page of his report would intimate the fact. The superior who reviewed the final version, upon finishing, would sit back in his chair and say to himself, "Thank goodness it was Mr. Charles Unwin, and not some frailer fellow, to whom this task fell."

Unwin pedaled hard to keep from swerving and shot from the other end of the alley, a clutch of pigeons bursting with him into the rain.

In all his days of employment with the Agency, he had never encountered a problem without a solution. This morning's episode, though unusual, would be no exception. He felt certain the entire matter would be settled before lunchtime.

But even with such responsibilities before him, Unwin found himself thinking of the dream he had dreamed before waking, the one that had rattled and distracted him, causing him to scorch his oatmeal and nearly miss the woman in the plaid coat.

He was by nature a meticulous dreamer, capable of sorting his nocturnal reveries with a lucidity he understood to be rare. He was unaccustomed to the shock of such an intrusive vision, one that seemed not at all of his making, and more like an official communiqué.

In this dream he had risen from bed and gone to take a bath, only to find the bathtub occupied by a stranger, naked except for his hat, reclining in a thick heap of soap bubbles. The bubbles were stained gray around his chest by the ashes from his cigar. His flesh was gray, too, like smudged newsprint, and a bulky gray coat was draped over the shower curtain. Only the ember of the stranger's cigar possessed color, and it burned so hot it made the steam above the tub glow red.

Unwin stood in the doorway, a fresh towel over his arm, his robe cinched tight around his waist. Why, he wondered, would someone go through all the trouble of breaking in to his apartment, just to get caught taking a bath?

The stranger said nothing. He lifted one foot out of the water and scrubbed it with a long-handled brush. When he was done, he soaped the bristles, slowly working the suds into a lather. Then he scrubbed the other foot.

Unwin bent down for a better look at the face under the hat brim and saw the heavy, unshaven jaw he knew only from newspaper photographs. It was the Agency operative whose case files were his particular responsibility.

"Detective Sivart," Unwin said, "what are you doing in my bathtub?"

Sivart let the brush fall into the water and took the cigar from his teeth. "No names," he said. "Not mine anyway. Don't know who might be listening in." He relaxed deeper into the bubbles. "You have no idea how difficult it was to arrange this meeting, Unwin. Did you know they don't tell us detectives who our clerks are? All these years I've been sending my reports to the fourteenth floor. To you, it turns out. And you forget things."

Unwin put up his hands to protest, but Sivart waved his cigar at him and said, "When Enoch Hoffmann stole November twelfth, and you looked at the morning paper and saw that Monday had gone straight into Wednesday, you forgot Tuesday like all the rest of them."

"Even the restaurants skipped their Tuesday specials," Unwin said.

Sivart's ember burned hotter, and more steam rose from the tub. "You forgot my birthday, too," he said. "No card, no nothing."

"Nobody knows your birthday."

"You could have figured it out. Anyway, you know my cases better than anyone. You know I was wrong about her, all wrong. So you're the best chance I've got. Try this time, would you? Try to remember something. Remember this: Chapter Eighteen. Got it?"

"Yes."

"Say it back to me: Chapter Eighteen."

"Chapter Elephant," Unwin said, in spite of himself.

"Hopeless," Sivart muttered.

Normally Unwin never could have said "Elephant" when he meant to say "Eighteen," not even in his sleep. Hurt by Sivart's accusations, he had blurted the wrong word because, in some dusty file drawer of his mind, he had long ago deposited the fact that elephants never forget.

"The girl," Sivart was saying, and Unwin had the impression that the detective was getting ready to explain something important. "I was wrong about her."

Then, as though summoned to life by Unwin's own error, there came trumpeting, high and full—the unmistakable decree of an elephant.

"No time!" Sivart said. He drew back the shower curtain behind the tub. Instead of a tiled wall, Unwin saw the whirling lights of carnival rides and striped pavilions beneath which broad shapes hunkered and leapt. There were shooting galleries out there, and a wheel of fortune, and animal cages, and a carousel, all moving, all turning under turning stars. The elephant trumpeted again, only this time the sound was shrill and staccato, and Unwin had to switch off his alarm clock to make it stop.

On Evidence

Objects have memory, too. The doorknob remembers
who turned it, the telephone who answered it. The gun
remembers when it was last fired, and by whom. It is for
the detective to learn the language of these things, so that
he might hear them when they have something to say.

Unwin's damp socks squelched in his shoes as he dismounted in
front of the broad granite facade of the Agency's office building.
The tallest structure for blocks around, it stood like a watchtower between the gridded downtown district and the crooked streets of the old
port town.

South of the Agency offices Unwin rarely dared to travel. He knew
enough from Sivart's reports of what went on in the cramped taverns
and winding back lanes of the old port's innumerable little neighbor-
hoods to satisfy his curiosity. Occasionally, when the wind was right,
he would catch a scent on the air that left him mystified and a little
frightened, and tugged at him in a way he could not easily have explained. He felt as though a trapdoor had opened at his feet, revealing
a view onto something bottomless and unknowable—a secret that
would remain a secret even at the end of the world. A moment would
pass before he could place it, before he knew where the scent had come

from. Then he would shake his head and chide himself. Seeing it so rarely, he often forgot that it was there: the sea.

He brought his bicycle with him into the Agency lobby, where the doorman allowed him to keep it on rainy days. He could not bear to look at the clock on the wall behind the front desk. His lateness, Unwin knew, would necessitate a second report for the benefit of his supervisor. It was Mr. Duden, after all, who had only recently filed for the presentation of the wristwatch—and did Mr. Duden not expect him to continue to exhibit the virtues that the wristwatch both acknowledged and embodied?

As for this so-called *Manual of Detection,* good sense dictated that he refrain from reading any part of it, including the page ninety-six to which Detective Pith alluded. Whatever secrets the *Manual* contained were not intended for Charles Unwin.

Only one dilemma remained. How to explain his presence at Central Terminal that morning? The coffee story would not do: a blatant falsification, brought to dwell perpetually in the Agency archives, a stain in the shape of words! Yet the truth was hardly appropriate for an official report. Best, perhaps, to write around that hole in the story and hope no one noticed.

The elevator attendant was a white-haired man whose spotted hands shook when he moved the lever. He brought the elevator to a halt without glancing at the needle over the door. "Floor fourteen," he said.

On the fourteenth floor were three columns of twenty-one desks each, separated by clusters of filing cabinets and shelving. On each desk a telephone, a typewriter, a green-shaded lamp, and a letter tray. The Agency neither prohibited nor encouraged the use of personal decorative flourishes, and some of these desks flaunted a small vase of flowers, a photograph, a child's drawing. Unwin's desk, the tenth in the east row, was free of any such clutter.

He was, after all, the clerk responsible for the cases of Detective Travis T. Sivart. Some argued, though never too loudly, that without

Detective Sivart there was no Agency. The point was perhaps only somewhat overstated. For in bars and barbershops all over town, in clubs and parlors of every grade, few topics could generate more speculation than Sivart's latest case.

The clerks themselves were by no means immune to this fervor. Indeed, their devotion was of a more personal, indwelling nature. In newspapers Sivart was "the detective's detective," but on the fourteenth floor he was one of their own. And they did not need the newspapers for their morsels of information, because they had their Unwin. During the processing period, his fellow clerks would quietly note the drawers he frequented, the indices to which he referred. The bolder among them would even inquire into his progress, though he was always certain to give some vague and tantalizing reply.

Some of those files—in particular The Oldest Murdered Man and The Three Deaths of Colonel Baker—were discussed in clerical circles as paragons of the form. Even Mr. Duden alluded to them, most often when scolding someone for sloppy work. "You like to think your files stand up to Unwin's," he would proclaim, "and you don't even know the difference between a dagger and a stiletto?" Often he simply asked, "What if Unwin had handled The Oldest Murdered Man that way?"

The theft of that three-thousand-year-old mummy was one of Unwin's first cases. He remembered the day, more than fifteen years earlier, that a messenger delivered Sivart's initial report in the series. It was early December and snowing; the office had fallen into a hush that seemed to him expectant, watchful. He was still the newest employee on the floor, and his hands trembled as he turned Sivart's hurriedly typed pages. The detective had been waiting for his big break, and Unwin had silently waited along with him. Now here it was. A high-profile crime, a heist. Front-page news.

Unwin had sharpened pencils to steady himself, and sorted according to size all the paper clips and rubber bands in his desk drawer.

Then he filled his pen with ink and emptied the hole punch of its little paper moons.

When he finally set to work, he moved with a certainty of purpose he now considered reckless. He tweaked organizational rubrics to accommodate the particulars of the case, integrated subsequent reports on the fly, and casually set down for the first time the identities of suspects whose names would recur in Agency files as certain bad dreams recur: Jasper and Josiah Rook, Cleopatra Greenwood, the nefarious biloquist Enoch Hoffmann.

Did Unwin sleep at all that week? It seemed to him that Sivart's progress on the case depended on his ability to document it, that the next clue would remain obscured until the previous was properly classified. The detective produced notes, fragments, threads of suspicion; it was the clerk's job to catalog them all, then to excise everything that proved immaterial, leaving only the one filament, that glowing silver thread connecting the mystery to its only conceivable solution.

Now he could remember nothing of his daily existence in those weeks except the accumulation of pages beside his typewriter and of snow on the windowsills, then the surprise of a fellow clerk's hand on his shoulder at the end of the day, when all the desk lamps but his own had been extinguished.

Unwin disliked hearing mention of his old cases, this one in particular. The Oldest Murdered Man had grown into something beyond him, beyond Sivart, beyond even Enoch Hoffmann, the former stage magician whose mad will had been the cause of it all. Every time someone spoke of the case, it became less the thing it was: a mystery put to rest.

For twenty years Unwin had served as Sivart's clerk, sequencing his reports, making sense of his notes, building proper case files out of them. He had so many questions for the man, questions about his philosophies of detection and the finer points of his methods. And he especially wanted to know more about The Man Who Stole November Twelfth. That case represented the end of an era, yet the detective's notes on it were unusually reticent. How exactly had Sivart seen through Hoffmann's ruse? How had he known it was Tuesday and not Wednesday, when all others in the city trusted their newspapers and radios?

If Unwin had ever passed the detective by chance in the halls of the Agency offices or stood beside him in the elevator, he did not know it. In newspaper photographs, Sivart appeared usually at the edge of a crime scene, a raincoat and hat hung in the gloom, his cigar casting light on nothing.

UNWIN WAS SOOTHED BY the harmonies of an office astir. Here a typewriter rang the end of a line, a telephone buzzed, file drawers rumbled open and closed. Sheaves of paper were tapped to evenness against desktops, and from all quarters came the percussive clamor of words being committed eternally to crisp white expanses.

How superb, that diligence, that zeal! And how essential. For none but the loyal clerks were permitted to dispatch those files to their place of rest, the archives, where mysteries dwelled side by side in stark beauty, categorized and classified—mysteries parsed, their secret hearts laid bare by photographs, wiretaps and ciphers, fingerprints and depositions. At least this was how Unwin imagined the archives to be. He had never actually seen them, because only the underclerks were permitted access to those regions.

He removed his hat. On the rack by his desk, however, another hat was already set to hang. It was a plain gray cap, and beneath it a plaid coat.

She was seated in his chair. The woman in the plaid coat (she was not, at that moment, in the plaid coat, yet somehow, astonishingly, she was no less she) was seated in his chair, at his desk, using his typewriter by the light of his green-shaded lamp. She looked up as though from a dream, forefinger paused over the Y key.

"Why?" Unwin wanted to ask, but then her eyes were on him and he could not speak; his hat was glued to his hand, his briefcase filled with lead. That feeling seized him—the feeling that a trapdoor had opened at his feet and that the slightest of winds could push him in. But it was not the sea that dizzied him; it was the clouded silver of her eyes, and something on the other side of them, just out of sight.

He walked on. Past his desk, past the clerks whose typewriters went silent in midsentence at his approach. He knew how he must appear to them—addled, shaky, unsure: not the Unwin they knew, but a stranger with Unwin's hat in his hand.

He did not know his destination until he saw it. Few besides Mr. Duden himself ever approached the door to the overclerk's office. The glass window, of the opaque kind, was uncommonly so. Before today Unwin had only glimpsed the door from afar. Now he set his briefcase down and raised his fist to knock.

Before he could, the door swung inward and Mr. Duden, a round-headed man with colorless hair, said quickly, "Pardon me, sir, there seems to have been a mistake."

Unwin had never been "sir." He had always been "Unwin," and nothing more.

"Yes, begging your pardon, Mr. Duden, there has been a mistake. I arrived several minutes late today. I shall spare you the details, since all of them will go into my report, which I would like to begin writing immediately. From this I am prevented, however, by the presence of another person at my desk, using my typewriter. Measures had to be taken, no doubt, because I am so late to work."

"No, begging your pardon, sir, you aren't late at all. You just don't . . . That is, I was informed that—how to put it?—that you'd been promoted. And while of course we're pleased that you'd think to come down here to visit your old colleagues, sir, it is against Agency policy for . . .

well, for a detective, you know, to communicate directly with a clerk, without the intercession of a messenger."

"Agency policy. Of course." Already this was the longest conversation he had ever had with his supervisor, except for an exchange of memoranda regarding the allotment of shelf space among the occupants of the east row that had transpired some three years earlier, but that was not, strictly speaking, a conversation at all. So it was with great hesitation that Unwin asked, "But you and I may speak freely, may we not?"

Mr. Duden glanced about the room. No one was typing. Somewhere a phone rang unheeded, then succumbed to the general silence. Mr. Duden said, "Actually, though I am the supervisor of the fourteenth floor, I, too, am—technically speaking, that is—a clerk. So this conversation is, you see, against Agency policy."

"Then I suppose," said Unwin, "that we should terminate the exchange, in keeping with policy?"

Mr. Duden nodded with relief.

"And I'm to find my new desk elsewhere in the building?"

It pained Mr. Duden to say, "On the twenty-ninth floor, perhaps. Room 2919, according to the memo I received."

Of course, an interoffice communication! With such a missive as his guide, Unwin could follow the trail back to its source and settle the matter in person. Though to ask for a memo directed to his superior would be rather unorthodox, Mr. Duden believed that Unwin outranked him now, so he could not refuse the request. But then, to take advantage of his superior's confusion would be to employ the very misunderstanding he wished to dispel. Imagine the report he would have to write to explain his actions: the addenda and codicils, the footnotes, the footnotes to footnotes. The more Unwin fed that report, the greater would grow its demands, until stacks of paper massed into walls, corridors: a devouring labyrinth with Unwin at its center, spools of exhausted typewriter ribbon piled all around.

Mr. Duden saved him from that fate, however, when he produced the memo for Unwin's perusal without being asked.

To: O. Duden, Overclerk, Floor 14
From: Lamech, Watcher, Floor 36

An employee under your Supervision, Mister Charles Unwin, is hereby promoted to the rank of Detective, with all the Rights, Privileges, and Responsibilities that position entails. Please forward his Personal Effects to Room 2919, and proceed according to Protocol in all regards.

The bottom of the memo was adorned by the Agency's official seal, a single open eye floating above the words "Never Sleeping."

Unwin folded the paper in half and slipped it into his coat pocket. He saw that Mr. Duden wanted it back, to keep it for his records, but the overclerk could not bring himself to ask for it. It was better this way—Unwin would need to incorporate the memo into his report. "I assume that the woman at my desk," he said, "whose name I have not learned, will carry on with my work, the work I have been doing for the last twenty years, seven months, and some-odd days."

Mr. Duden smiled and nodded some more. He would not say her name.

Unwin returned the way he had come, avoiding the eyes of his co-workers, especially those of the woman seated in his chair. He could not help glimpsing the plaid coat, however, hanging where his own coat should have been.

IN THE ELEVATOR three men in nice suits (black, green, and navy blue) were speaking quietly among themselves. They regarded Unwin's arrival with scrupulous indifference. These were bona fide detectives, and Unwin did not have to be a detective himself to recognize the fact. He stood with his back to them, and the elevator attendant hopped off his three-legged stool and closed the door. "Going up," he announced. "Next stop, floor twenty-nine."

Unwin mumbled his request for the thirty-sixth floor.

"You're going to have to speak up," the attendant said, tapping his own ear. "What floor is it that you want?"

The three detectives were silent now.

Unwin leaned closer and repeated, "Thirty-six, please."

The attendant shrugged and threw the lever. No one spoke as the needle rose past fifteen, sixteen, seventeen, but Unwin knew the detectives were watching him. Were these three in communication with Detective Pith? He had been watching Unwin for some time, long enough to know that he went every morning to Central Terminal. And if he were watching, others could be watching, too—and not just while he was at the office. Unwin felt as though the Agency's unblinking eye had turned upon him, and now there was no escaping its gaze.

It might have been watching that morning eight days before, when Unwin first saw the woman in the plaid coat. He had woken early, then dressed and eaten and left for work, failing to realize until he had descended to the street and gone partway to work that most of the city was still sleeping. He could not continue to the office—it would be hours yet before the doorman would arrive with his ring of keys—so Unwin had wandered in the near dark while delivery trucks idled at storefronts, and streetlamps winked out overhead, and a few seasoned carousers shuffled home, arms over one another's shoulders.

It seemed like a dream now: his passage through the revolving doors of Central Terminal, the cup of coffee from the breakfast cart, the schedule plucked from the racks by the information booth. All those trains, all those routes: he could purchase a ticket for any one of them, he thought, and let himself be borne from the city, let the reports pile up on his desk forever. The mysteries assigned to Sivart now were hollow compared to those of earlier years. The Rook brothers had gone into hiding after November twelfth, and Cleopatra Greenwood had fled the city, and Enoch Hoffmann had performed with quiet precision the cardinal feat of magicianship and caused himself to disappear. The city thought it still needed Sivart, but Unwin knew the truth: Sivart was just a shadow, and he himself a shadow's shadow.

So it was that he found himself standing at Gate Fourteen with a ticket for the next train into the country, no clear plan to return, checking his wristwatch against the four-faced clock above the information booth. Even to him his behavior seemed suspicious: a clerk rising early, acting on whims, purchasing a ticket for a train out of the city. What kind of motive would anyone from the Agency assign to such behavior? They must have pegged him as a spy or a double agent.

Perhaps this promotion was not an error, then, but a test of some kind. If so, he would prove himself above suspicion by maintaining that it was an error, could only be an error. He would prove that he wanted his job, that he was nothing if not a clerk.

He had not boarded the train that morning after all, had not gone into the country. The sight of the woman in the plaid coat had stopped him. She was a mystery to him, and mystery enough to keep him from leaving. So long as she was there each morning, he would wait with her, and so long as no one appeared to meet her, he would return to work: that was the unspoken bargain he had struck with her.

Still, these detectives in the elevator were watching him—intently, he felt. He tapped his umbrella against the floor while humming a few bars of a tune he knew from the radio, but this must have looked too calculated, since humming and umbrella-tapping were not among his usual habits. So instead of tapping, he used his umbrella as a cane by gently and repeatedly shifting his weight onto it and off it again. This was a habit Unwin could call genuine. But employed as a distraction, it seemed even to him a very suspicious-looking contrivance. He had not read a word of *The Manual of Detection*, while these detectives probably knew it front to back, knew even the rationale behind Samuel Pith's assertion that operatives must have secrets of their own.

The attendant brought the elevator to a halt at floor twenty-nine, and the three detectives brushed past, then turned. The one in the black suit scratched a rash above his collar, glaring at Unwin as though he were somehow the cause of it. The one in green hunched bulkily, a dull, mean look in his half-lidded eyes. Navy blue stood in front, his mustache a crooked line over his lip. "That's no hat to wear to the thirty-sixth floor," he said.

The other two chuckled and shook their heads.

The attendant closed the door on the detective's thin scowl, and again the needle climbed upward. From above came the creaking of machinery; steadily the sound grew louder. When the door was opened at last, a chill wind escaped from the elevator shaft to play about Unwin's ankles. His socks were still damp.

The corridor was lit by yellow light fixtures shaped like upended tulips, and between them were doors without transoms. At the opposite end of the hall, a single window permitted a rectangle of gray, rain-ribboned light.

"Thirty-six," the attendant said.

In the memo Lamech had identified himself as a watcher. That title was unfamiliar to Unwin, but the intricacies of Agency hierarchy could not be entrusted to just any employee. There were clerks innumerable, with underclerks beneath them and overclerks above, and then the detectives, those knights-errant upon whose work so much depended, while everywhere at once scurried the messengers, lower in status, perhaps, than even the underclerks but entrusted with special privileges of passage, for their words, on any particular day, could originate in the highest halls of the Agency offices. And dwelling in those halls? What shrewd powers, with what titles? On that, Unwin did not care to speculate, nor do we now, except to this extent: on the thirty-sixth floor, behind doors marked by bronze placards bearing their names, the watchers performed what duties were entrusted to them.

The seventh door on the right (Unwin counted thirteen to a side) bore the name he was looking for. Unlike all the others, this door was ajar. He knocked gently and called through the opening. "Mr. Lamech?"

No response. He knocked harder, and the door swung inward. The room was dark, but in the column of light from the hall Unwin saw a broad maroon rug, shelves of thick books with blue and brown spines, a pair of cushioned chairs angled toward a desk at the back. To one side was a great dark globe, and before the window loomed a bald and massive globelike head. On the desk a telephone, a typewriter, and a lamp, unlit.

"Mr. Lamech," Unwin said again, crossing the threshold, "I am sorry to have to bother you, sir. It's Charles Unwin, clerk, floor fourteen. I've come about the matter of the promotion. I believe there may have been some kind of error."

Lamech said nothing. Maybe he did not wish to speak with the door open. Unwin closed it and approached. As his eyes adjusted, he began to discern a heavy-featured face, shoulders wide as the wide-backed chair, big unmoving hands folded over the desk.

"Not your error, of course," Unwin amended. "Probably a transcriptionist's typo or a bad connection on one of the older lines. You know how things get when it rains, sir. Fits of static, the occasional disconnect."

Lamech regarded him wordlessly.

"And it has been raining on and off for days now. Fourteen days, in fact. More rain than we've had in quite some time."

Unwin stood before the desk. "It's a matter of poor drainage, sir. Bound to interfere with the lines."

He saw that Lamech's telephone was in fact unplugged, the cord left dangling over the edge of the desk. The watcher said nothing. The only sound was the rain against the window—the cause, Unwin supposed, for all his talk about the weather.

"Unless you protest," Unwin hazarded, "I'll just switch on your desk lamp for you. That way I can show you some identification, which I'm sure you want to see before bothering with any of this. Wouldn't want to waste your time. And you can't trust anyone these days, isn't that right?"

He tugged the cord. The lamp, identical to the one on Unwin's own desk twenty-two floors below, made a puddle of pale green light over the desktop, over Unwin's outstretched hand, over the seated man's gray crisscrossed fingers, and over his heavy gray face, from which a pair of bloated, red-flooded eyes glared out at nothing.

Corpses were nothing new to Unwin. Hundreds of them populated the reports entrusted to his care over the years, reports in which no detail was spared. People poisoned, shot, gutted, hanged, sliced to ribbons by industrial machinery, crushed between slabs of cement, clobbered with skillets, defenestrated, eviscerated, burned or buried alive, held underwater for lengthy intervals, thrown down stairs, or simply kicked and pummeled out of being—the minutiae surrounding such incidents were daily fare, so to speak, to a clerk of the fourteenth floor. Whole indices, in fact, were organized according to cause of death, and Unwin himself had from time to time contributed new headings and subheadings when an innovative murder necessitated an addition or expansion: "strangulation, unattended boa snake," was one of his, as was "muffins, poisonous berry."

A man so thoroughly versed in the varieties of dispatchment might, then, regard with unusual ease the result of an actual murder, in this case a man whose neck had been bruised by strangulatory measures, tongue emitted as a result of smotheration, eyes bulged almost clear of the skull, result of the same.

Unwin yanked his hand from the light and took several steps backward, tripped over the edge of the rug, and fell into one of the thickly cushioned chairs, the softness of which did nothing to diminish his revulsion. In each dark corner, Unwin could almost see a killer crouched, waiting for an opportunity to strike. To move from where he sat would have brought him closer to at least one of them.

So he remained motionless, briefcase clutched in his lap, seated as for a proper meeting with Mr. Lamech. This meeting went on for some time, with only the weather having anything to say, and the weather spoke only of itself.

THREE

On Corpses

Many cases begin with one—this can be disconcerting,
but at least you know where you stand. Worse is the corpse
that appears partway into your investigation, complicating
everything. Best to proceed, therefore, with the vigilance
of one who assumes that a corpse is always around the next
corner. That way it is less likely to be your own.

A knock at the door shook Unwin from his stupor. How long had
he been sitting there? Long enough for his eyes to adjust to the
light, for him to see that he was quite alone with Lamech's corpse.
If someone were going to leap out and kill him, he would have done
it by now.

A second knock at the door, louder this time. He should have left
as soon as he saw the corpse, should have cried out, or even run into
the hall and fainted. That would have made his role in the matter obvious: he was the unlucky discoverer of a horrendous crime. But what
would they think when he answered the door and said, "Please, come
right in. And look, there's a dead man at the desk. Strange, isn't it?"

He could squeeze himself behind the end of the bookshelf, but that
would make for a poor hiding place. When he was found cowering there,
the suspicion against him would only increase. If he waited a little longer,
maybe, the person at the door would give up and go away.

Unwin waited. There was no more knocking, but he heard the sound of a woman's voice. "Mr. Lamech?"

The body, then. He would have to do something with the body. He went to stand behind Lamech's chair and gazed down at the broad, blank scalp. From this angle it looked as though there was nothing wrong with the man. He was only very tired, had eased back into his chair for a brief nap. He did not even smell as Unwin imagined a corpse would smell. He smelled like aftershave.

Still, Unwin could not bring himself to touch the dead man. He took hold of the chair and rolled it slowly backward. Lamech's big hands drifted apart as they slid over the surface of the desk, but his fingers stayed rigid. Then the arms dropped suddenly, and the upper half of the body fell forward. Unwin had to yank the chair back to keep the man's head from striking the edge of the desk. The chair creaked under the slumped weight of the corpse.

The woman knocked again, so loudly this time that everyone on the floor must have heard.

"One moment!" Unwin shouted, and the woman let out a little *oh!* as though she had not really expected an answer.

With his foot on one leg of the chair to keep it in place, Unwin heaved against the body with both hands. It bowed deeper and the spine emitted a series of popping sounds that made him recoil. He closed his eyes, held his breath, and pushed again. This time the body slid off the chair and tumbled soundlessly into the dark beneath the desk.

In the most commanding tone he could muster, Unwin called for Lamech's visitor to enter.

The woman wore a black dress with white lace around the collar and cuffs. The dress was very fine, but of a style Unwin had not seen worn in the city for ten years or more. In her hands she clutched a small purse, also strangely old-fashioned. Her hair was bound up in a black lace cap, still damp from the rain. She was perhaps ten years older than Unwin, and very beautiful—*a real stunner,* Sivart might have written.

She was also the most tired-looking woman Unwin had ever seen. She gazed warily into the room, the shadows beneath her eyes so dark that Unwin mistook them at first for an exotic sort of makeup.

"Please come in," he said.

She came forward with dreamlike hesitancy, always about to stumble, somehow remaining miraculously on her feet.

"Mr. Lamech," she said.

He sat down, relieved that she did not know the watcher by sight, but the tip of his left shoe made contact with the body under the desk, and he had to cough to conceal his alarm.

"I know this isn't how things are done here," she said.

Unwin's stomach tightened. Had he given himself away so quickly?

"I know I'm supposed to request an appointment," the woman went on, "and then someone informs me who will be handling my case. But I couldn't wait, and I couldn't see just anyone. I had to see you."

So it was she who had broken the rules. Unwin cleared his throat and gave her a stern look. Then, to demonstrate his generosity, he gestured for her to sit.

She gazed at the thick cushion, her eyelids drooping. "I mustn't," she said. "I would fall asleep in an instant." Just the thought of sitting down appeared to overwhelm her; she squeezed her purse and closed her eyes for a long moment.

Unwin rose from his seat, thinking he might have to catch her. But she steadied herself, blinked several times, and said, "I'm something of a detective myself, you see. I figured out that you are Sivart's watcher."

Unwin knew as she said it that she was right. Lamech had been Sivart's watcher, just as he was Sivart's clerk. Now he was all three of them at once: clerk by appointment, detective by promotion, watcher by mistake.

"My name is Vera Truesdale," she said, "and I'm the victim of a terrible mystery."

Unwin sat down again, knowing he would have to play along for now. He had left his briefcase beside the other chair, so he opened the uppermost desk drawer and found what he was looking for: a pad of notepaper. He set this in front of him and took up a pencil.

"Proceed," he said.

"I arrived from out of town about three weeks ago," Miss Truesdale said. "I'm staying at the Gilbert Hotel, Room 202. I have repeatedly asked to be moved to a room on a higher floor."

Unwin resorted to shorthand to get it all down. "Why do you want to be moved?" he asked.

"Because of the mystery," Miss Truesdale said. Her voice had taken on an impatient edge. "If I were staying in a room on a higher floor, they might not be able to get in."

"Who might not be able to get in?"

"I don't know!" Miss Truesdale nearly shouted. She began to pace the short width of the room. "Every morning I wake up surrounded by . . . odds and ends. Empty champagne glasses, bits of confetti, roses. Things of that nature. They're scattered over the floor, over *my bed*. It's as though someone has thrown a party in my room. I sleep through it, but I don't feel that I do. I feel as though I haven't slept in years."

"Champagne glasses, confetti, and . . ."

"Long-stemmed roses."

". . . and roses, long-stemmed. Is that all?"

"No, that isn't all," she said. "The window is open, and the room is freezing cold. There's a dampness to everything, a terrible, cold dampness. I can hardly stand it any longer. I'm sure I'll lose my mind if this continues." She opened her eyes very wide. "Maybe I already have lost my mind. Is that possible, Mr. Lamech?"

Unwin ignored her question—surely Lamech would not have known the answer either. "I'm certain we'll be able to help you," he said, but then set down his pencil and pushed the notepad away. He was already out of his depth. What more was a watcher expected to do?

"You'll send him, then," Miss Truesdale said.

At a loss, Unwin opened the appointment book on Lamech's desk. He flipped through the pages until he found the present date. There Unwin's own name was penciled in for a ten o'clock meeting. He glanced at his watch. Lamech had intended to speak with him in just a few minutes.

Miss Truesdale was still waiting for an answer.

"We'll send someone," he said.

She did not seem content with that, and her knuckles turned white as she squeezed her purse again. She was about to speak but was interrupted by a creaking sound that came out of the wall beside the bookshelf. She and Unwin both followed it with their eyes. He imagined a monstrous rat crawling up behind the wainscoting, led by its infallible nose toward the enormous cadaver that Unwin had hidden under the desk. The creaking sound rose nearly to the ceiling, then stopped, and a little bell on Lamech's desk chimed twice.

"Aren't you going to get that?" Miss Truesdale asked.

Unwin raised his shoulders as Mr. Duden often did in moments of displeasure. "I'm afraid I must ask you to leave now," he said. "I have an appointment, one that was scheduled in the usual way."

She nodded as though she had expected this all along. "The Gilbert, Room 202. You won't forget, will you?"

He wrote that down at the top of the notepad, repeating aloud, "The Gilbert, Room 202. Now, you try to get some rest, Miss Truesdale." He rose and showed her to the door. She went willingly, though she seemed to have more to say. He avoided her eyes and closed the door before she could speak again, then waited, listening. He heard her sigh, heard her irregular footsteps retreat down the hall, then the rush of air as the elevator door opened and closed.

The bell rang again.

He went to the wall and felt it with the palm of his hand. The surface was cool to the touch. He put an ear against it and held his breath. From the building's unseen recesses came a low keening sound, as of wind trapped in a tunnel or air shaft. What could be hidden there? Unwin recalled something Sivart had written about the manor of Colonel Baker, in the case reports chronicling that wretched man's three deaths: *It's more secret passageways than real passageways, and every looking glass is a two-way mirror. I had to shake the hand of a suit of armor, if you can believe it, to open the door to the library. The old guys are suckers for the classic stuff.*

Could the same be said of Mr. Lamech? Unwin went to the bookshelf and began to search. The books were identified only by roman numerals and alphabetical ranges; reference works, perhaps, for some vast and intricate discipline. He did not need to comprehend the subject to find what he was looking for: one volume, the spine worn at the top from frequent handling. He pulled it forward, and immediately a panel in the wall flew open, revealing something like a miniature elevator car. Inside was an envelope of brown paper, about a foot square, with a note attached.

Taking it, Unwin felt he was crossing a boundary that had long separated him from the world that was the subject of his work. But here was a note, so brief that he read it in the instant he saw it.

Edward,

Here is your special order. I didn't peek. But if you want my advice, you'll let sleeping corpses lie.

Kisses
Miss P.

That the Agency should employ a dumbwaiter came as a surprise. It was his understanding that every communication, no matter how trivial, was to be conveyed by messenger. The operator of the switchboard could not even connect one employee to another—Agency bylaws dictated that the telephones were for external calls only. So what manner of special order could this be, to have arrived in the office of a dead man by such extraordinary means?

The envelope was heavy, unbending, and unsealed. Might Lamech have been planning to present this to him when they met? Unwin slid one finger under the flap of the envelope and tilted it open.

Inside was a phonograph record. Unlike those he had seen for sale in music shops, it was pale white, almost translucent, and at its center was the Agency's open-eyed insignia, the spindle hole serving as pupil. Looking closer, he saw a series of letters and numbers imprinted between the groove of the lead-out. The three-letter prefix, TTS, was one he had seen on every report to cross his desk in twenty years, seven months, and some-odd days. It stood for Travis T. Sivart.

The bell rang again, and the dumbwaiter sank toward the place from which it had come. Unwin closed the panel. He felt he was a clerk again: composed, prepared to carry on, engrossed by the facts of the thing and not the thing itself. He returned to Lamech's desk, tore off the page of notes from his meeting with Miss Truesdale, and put that in his pocket.

He glanced at the telephone. Why had the cord been left unplugged? Unwin reinserted it into the base of the phone, then switched off the green-shaded lamp.

The phonograph record, he knew, was evidence from the scene of a crime, and to take it would be to commit another. But a moment later Lamech's door was closed, the elevator on its way back to the thirty-sixth floor, and the record inside Unwin's briefcase, snug beside his copy of *The Manual of Detection*.

How to account for this splendid misconduct?

When it came to Sivart's cases, it should not surprise us to learn that Unwin's sense of stewardship might extend even to covetousness. If the chosen clerk of "the detective's detective" is to come upon a file—however strange in form—that is by all rights his to review, register, and archive, is he to leave it and walk away, as though Sivart's latest case never existed? Another file, perhaps, Unwin could have forsaken. But even that minor report would have come to haunt him, in those moments before dusk when the city is enveloped in shadow.

Unwin had known few such evenings; he hoped for no more. When the elevator arrived, he told the attendant to take him to the twenty-ninth floor. He wanted to inspect his new office.

ON THE TWENTY-NINTH FLOOR, another long hall, another lone window at its end. But in place of the carpeting of the thirty-sixth, here was a buffed surface of dark wood, so spotless and smooth it shone with liquid brilliance. The floor gave Unwin pause. It was his personal curse that his shoes squeaked on polished floors. The type of shoes he wore made no difference, nor did it matter whether the soles were wet or dry. If the shoes contained Unwin's feet and were directed along well-polished routes, they would without fail sound their joyless noise for all to hear.

At home he went about in his socks. That way he could avoid disturbing the neighbors and also indulge in the occasional shoeless swoop across the room, as when one is preparing a breakfast of oatmeal and the oatmeal wants raisins and brown sugar, which are in the cupboard at the other end of the room. To glide with sock-swaddled feet over a world of glossy planes: that would be a wondrous thing! But Unwin's apartment was smallish at best, and the world is unkind to the shoeless and frolicsome.

He could not remove his shoes with the elevator attendant looking on. Unwin's two extra trips this morning were suspicious enough, though the little man gave no indication that he thought anything of it. So Unwin walked resolutely from the elevator and pretended not to hear the commotion for which he was responsible.

The doors here were more numerous and more narrow than on the thirty-sixth, and in the absence of plaques, names were painted in black over opaque glass windows. From within the offices came the steady patter of typewriters, while here and there voices muttered hushed inscrutables. Was it only Unwin's imagination that the voices quieted at his advance?

Room 2919, halfway down the hall, was not unoccupied—the window glowed with amber light. Unwin touched the glass. The name inscribed there had been scraped away, and only recently: black flecks of paint still clung to the frame.

He became suddenly aware of a spatial concurrence. His new office, at the middle of the east side of the twenty-ninth floor, was situated directly above his old desk on the fourteenth and directly below Lamech's office on the thirty-sixth. If a hole were drilled vertically down the building, a penny pushed off Lamech's desk would, on its descent toward Unwin's desk twenty-two floors below, fall straight through Room 2919.

He was still standing there when the door behind him opened and the detective with the thin mustache and navy blue suit stepped into the hall. He was about to light a cigarette, but when he saw Unwin, his pale lips went taut with a smirk. "I told you they wouldn't go for that hat on the thirty-sixth floor," he said. "Actually, it isn't well regarded here either."

"I'm sorry," was all Unwin could think to say.

"Okay, you're sorry. But who are you?"

Unwin's identification was in his coat pocket, but it was the identification of a clerk who did not belong on this floor. So along with the badge, he presented the memo from Lamech. The detective snatched them both, glanced at the badge, jabbed that back at Unwin, then read the memo slowly. "This isn't addressed to you," he said, and stuffed it into his own pocket. "I better confirm it with Lamech."

"I believe that Mr. Lamech doesn't wish to be disturbed."

"Not by some kidney-foot clerk, maybe." The detective snickered. "And this is the guy they got to replace Travis."

Unwin opened his mouth to protest but closed it once he understood what the detective had said. He, Unwin, was replacing Detective Sivart? He had neither the training nor the disposition required for the job. He was a clerk—a fine one, to be sure, and respected among his peers for his shrewd demeanor, his discerning eye, his encyclopedic knowledge of the elements of a case. He was tenacious in his way, insightful when he needed to be—but only into things already written down. He was no Sivart. And what had happened to Sivart, that he could need replacing?

The detective pointed at him with his unlit cigarette. "I'll be watching you, neighbor," he said. He removed the handkerchief from his jacket pocket and used it to polish the outer knob of his office door, then the inner knob, too. When he realized that Unwin was watching him, he snapped, "I am an enemy to messiness in all its forms," then stuffed the handkerchief back into his pocket. He threw the door closed behind him. The name on the glass was Benjamin Screed.

Unwin tucked his umbrella under his arm and turned back to 2919. So this had been Sivart's office, and now he was meant to occupy it. Meanwhile, the woman in the plaid coat had taken his place on the fourteenth floor. Did that make her his clerk? How would she busy herself until he filed his first report? At this rate she could be waiting for a very long time.

FOUR

On Clues

Most everything can be divided into two categories:
details and clues. Knowing one from the other is more
important than knowing your left shoe from your right.

R oom 2919 was small and windowless. At the center of the office
was a desk, its surface covered with balled-up sheets of typing
paper. The lamp was on. Seated with her head slumped over the back
of the chair was a round-faced young woman, thick red hair bound up
with a pin at the top of her head. Crooked small teeth were just visible
between her parted lips. Her plump, short-fingered hands were limp
across the keyboard of the typewriter.

Was it Unwin's fate to go from one office to another discovering a
fresh corpse in each of them? No—this woman was not dead. He saw
now the soft rise and fall of her shoulders, heard the sound of her snoring. Unwin cleared his throat, but the woman did not stir. He drew
closer, peering over the desk to see what she had been typing.

Don't fall asleep. Don't fall asleep. Don't fall asleep. Don't fall asleep.
Don't fall asleep. Don't fall asleep.

The phrase was repeated over half the page, but at last she had written:

Don't fall asleep. Don't fall asleep. Don't fall

Unwin removed his hat and cleared his throat again.

The woman twisted in her chair and shifted her head from her left shoulder to her right. Her hair tumbled free of the pin that held it in place, and a few strands stuck to her lipstick. The light from the desk lamp flashed in her eyeglasses but did not wake her. She began to snore more loudly.

Unwin reached over and pressed the typewriter's carriage release. The platen flew to the end of the line with a clatter, and the bell sounded high and clear. The woman woke and sat straight in her chair. "I don't know any songs for this," she said.

"Songs for what?"

She blinked behind her glasses, which were too big for her girlish face. She could not have been much older than Unwin was on his first day at the Agency. "Are you Detective Unwin?" she asked.

"Yes, I'm Unwin."

She rose and swept her hair back up on her head, fixing it in place— not with a pin, Unwin now saw, but with a sharpened pencil. She said, "I'm your assistant, Emily Doppel."

She straightened her blue woolen dress, then began clearing the crumpled pages off her desk and into a wastepaper basket. Her hands were shaking a little, and Unwin thought he should leave the room and give her the chance to recover, but she spoke quickly and without pause as she worked, so he was unable to excuse himself. "I'm an excellent typist, and I practice as much as I'm able," she said. "I've studied the Agency's most important cases, and I'm not averse to working extra hours. My greatest fault is my susceptibility to unpredictable bouts of deep sleep. The irony of my condition, in light of the Agency's foremost motto, is not lost on me. But the work I've done to make up for my weakness has strengthened my resolve beyond normal expectations. I apologize in advance for the snoring."

All that remained on her desk—aside from the typewriter, telephone, and lamp—was a shiny black lunch box.

Emily came around the desk and reached to take Unwin's hat, but he held tightly to the brim. She clutched it and tugged until he relented, then she brushed off the trilby and hung it on the coatrack.

She stood very close, and the room felt suddenly small for them both. He could smell her perfume in the air: lavender. She reached for his briefcase, and he drew it against his chest, shielding it with both arms.

"It's okay," she said, her smile revealing her crooked teeth. "That's what I'm here for."

So his assistant knew what she was here for, even if Unwin did not. But what to do with her? Were he at his desk on the fourteenth floor, he might have been able to think of something. There were always labels to be typed, folders to be sorted: alphabetically, in chronological or reverse-chronological order. But Unwin took pleasure even in those minor tasks and would not soon have parted with them.

He freed one arm from his coat and transferred his briefcase to the other hand while Emily slipped the coat off and away and hung it below the hat. She had also taken possession of his umbrella without his seeing how it was done.

"I have a lot of work to do," he said.

She folded her hands in front of her. "I'm prepared, of course, to hear all about our case, assuming you've already been contacted by your watcher."

"I have . . . conferred with the gentleman," Unwin said.

There was a knock at the door, and Emily opened it before Unwin could stop her. In the hall stood a man in a crisp white shirt and yellow suspenders. His age was unapparent: the unkempt blond hair belonged on the head of a boy of thirteen, but he entered the room with the unhesitant calm of someone much older. He was holding a shoe-box-size package wrapped in brown paper.

"Messenger for you, sir," Emily announced, as though Unwin were not in the room with her.

Unwin accepted the package and unwrapped it while the two watched. Inside was an Agency identification badge for Charles Unwin, Detective. Beside it was a pistol. Unwin snapped the box shut. "Who sent this?"

"That information is not within the bounds of my message," said the messenger, running his thumbs along the undersides of his suspender straps.

Unwin had parlayed with messengers before. He found them, on the whole, a rascally lot, prone to twist the rules governing their profession to their own advantage. This one was clearly no exception.

"Can you tell me when it was sent?" Unwin tried.

The messenger only looked at the ceiling, as though to acknowledge the question would shame them both.

"Are you free to take a message, then?"

With that, Unwin knew he had snared the man. Messengers were obliged to deliver only what they were given, whether packages or words, but they had to take a message whenever asked. This one let go of his suspenders and sighed. "Spoken or typed?" he asked.

"Typed," said Unwin. "Emily, you told me you are an excellent typist."

"Yes, sir." She returned to her typewriter and loaded a fresh sheet of paper bearing the Agency seal. She held her hands suspended over the keys and tilted her head a little to the left. Her eyes went unfocused, as though she were gazing into some distant, tranquil place.

Unwin began, "To colon Lamech comma Watcher comma floor thirty-six return from colon Charles Unwin comma capital C capital L capital E capital R capital K comma floor fourteen comma temporarily floor twenty-nine return.

"Now for the body of the text. Sir comma with all due respect comma I must request your immediate attention to the matter of my recent promotion comma which I believe has been given in error point."

Emily's typing was confident and somewhat brash—she threw the carrier to each new line with a flourish, as one might turn a page of exquisite piano music, and her fingers danced high off the keys at the end of each sentence. Her style lent Unwin even greater resolve.

"As you may know comma I am solely responsible for the case files of Detective Travis Tee point Sivart point. Naturally comma I hope to return to that work as soon as possible point. If you are unable to reply to this message comma I will assume that the matter has been settled comma as I would not wish to trouble you any further than is necessary point. I will of course make sure that you receive a copy of my report point."

Emily plucked the page from her typewriter, folded it into thirds, and slipped it into an envelope. The messenger put it in his satchel and left.

Unwin wiped his brow with his shirtsleeve. The messenger would go directly to Lamech's office on the thirty-sixth floor and discover Lamech dead. That relieved Unwin of the responsibility of reporting the fact himself.

"A clerk," said Emily thoughtfully. "It's the perfect cover, sir. Criminals will naturally underestimate a common clerk, never suspecting that he could be their undoing. And you already look the part, if you don't mind my saying. Since your subterfuge must prevail within the Agency, as well as without, I assume this is an internal affair. No wonder you're the one they got to replace Detective Sivart."

Emily rose from her chair and gestured toward the back of the room. Her nervousness was gone now—her virtuoso performance at the typewriter had restored her confidence. "Sir," she said, "allow me to conduct you to your private office."

There was a door behind the desk, painted the same drab color as the walls—Unwin had failed to notice it before. Emily led the way into a room sunk in greenish gloom. Its dark carpeting and darker wallpaper gave the impression of a small clearing in a dense wood, though it smelled of cigar smoke.

The single window offered a much better view than those on the fourteenth floor. Through it Unwin could see the rooftops of the tightly packed buildings in the old port town and beyond them the great gray splotch of the bay, where smoke from ships mixed with the rain. This was the view Sivart would have turned to gaze upon while writing up his case notes. Down there, near the water, Unwin could just make out the dilapidated remains of Caligari's Carnival, which had served for years as Enoch Hoffmann's base of operations. Strange, Unwin thought, that the detective could see the lair of his adversary from the comfort of his own chair.

But then, Hoffmann had not been heard from in a long time—not once in the eight years since The Man Who Stole November Twelfth— and the carnival was in ruin. Could it be that Sivart was gone as well? Unwin remembered discovering, in some of the detective's reports, inklings of plans for retirement. He had been careful to excise them, of course—not only were they extraneous, they were tendered gloomily, when a lull between cases put Sivart in a dour mood. They appeared with greater frequency after November twelfth, and Unwin supposed he was the only one who knew the toll that case had taken on Sivart. *I was wrong about her,* he had written, meaning Cleopatra Greenwood. And it was true—he had been.

Sivart's plan involved a home in the country somewhere and the writing of his memoirs. Unwin had been surprised at the detail of Sivart's description: a little white cottage in the woods, at the north end of a town on a river; a slope covered with blackberry briars; a tire swing; a pond. Also a trail that led to a clearing in the woods. *A nice place to take a nap,* he had written.

Unwin knew that Sivart might never have found his way to that cottage. Something terrible could have happened—why else a corpse on the thirty-sixth floor?

As though sharing in Unwin's thoughts, Emily said, "There's no official explanation regarding his disappearance."

"Is there an unofficial explanation?"

Emily frowned at that. "Sir, there is no such thing as an unofficial explanation."

Unwin nodded, swallowing against the dryness in his throat. He would have to be careful with his words, even when speaking to his assistant.

Emily switched on the desk lamp, and now he could see a wooden filing cabinet, chairs for visitors, empty bookshelves, and a decrepit electric fan in the corner. He set his briefcase on the floor and sat down. The chair was too big for him, the desk absurdly expansive. He put the box containing his badge and pistol next to the typewriter.

Emily stood before him, her hands clasped behind her back, waiting. What would she do once she perceived that his clerk's identity was not a cover? The scent of her lavender perfume, mingled with that of Sivart's cigars, tickled Unwin's nostrils, made him dizzy. He tried to dismiss her with a polite nod, but Emily only nodded in reply. She had no intention of leaving.

"Well," he said, "I trust you have undergone standard Agency training, as well as any training requisite to your particular position."

"Of course."

"Then you can tell me what I might expect from you at this time?"

She frowned again, only now the look was darker, more wary. Unwin understood that his assistant had been looking forward to this day, her first on the job, for a long time. He risked disappointing her. It would be dangerous, Unwin thought, to disappoint her.

She changed her mind about what was happening, though, and appeared suddenly pleased. "You're testing me!" she said.

She closed her eyes and tilted her head back, as though to read something imprinted on the backs of her eyelids. She recited, " 'On the first day of a new case, the detective shares with his assistant whatever details he feels the assistant ought to know. Typically this includes important contacts and dates, as well as information from related cases called up from the archives.' "

Unwin sat back in the enormous chair. He thought again of that corpse upstairs, bloated with mystery. He felt as though the thing had crawled onto his back and would drag him into the grave with it if he did not throw it off. What was the case Lamech had meant for him? Whatever it was, Unwin wanted nothing to do with it.

He said, "I see that you have a subtle mind, Emily, so I can trust you. As you suspected, this is an internal affair. The case before us, number CEU001, concerns the very reason for my presence here. Our task is simple: to find Detective Travis T. Sivart and convince him to return to his job as quickly as possible." He was forming a plan even as he spoke it. With Emily's help, perhaps, he could pretend to be a detective just long enough to bring Sivart back to the Agency. Then *he* could make sense of the watcher's corpse, of Miss Truesdale's long-stemmed roses, of the phonograph record he had found in Lamech's office.

Emily was all business now. "Clues, sir?"

"No clues," Unwin said. "But then, this *was* Sivart's office."

Emily checked the filing cabinets while Unwin searched the desk. In the top drawer, he found, forwarded according to Lamech's demands, his personal effects: magnifying glass for small type, silver letter opener presented to him upon the completion of his tenth year of faithful service to the Agency, spare key to his apartment. The second drawer contained only a stack of typing paper. Unwin could not resist: he withdrew several sheets and rolled one of them into the typewriter. It was a good model, sleek and serious, with a dark green chassis, round black keys, and type bars polished to a silvery gleam. Thus far the typewriter was the only thing Unwin liked about being a detective.

"Empty," Emily said, "all empty." She had finished with the filing cabinets and was moving on to the shelves.

Unwin ignored her and checked his margins, adjusted the left and right stops (he liked them set precisely five-eighths of an inch from the edges of the page). He tested the tension of the springs by depressing, only slightly, a few of the more important keys: the E, the S, the space bar. They did not disappoint.

He pretended to type, moving his fingers over the keys without pressing them. How he wanted to begin his report! *This*, he might start, and lead from there on into *morning*, yes, *This morning, after having purchased a cup of coffee*, but no, not the coffee, he could not start with the coffee. How about *I*? From *I* one could really go anywhere at all. *I am sorry to have to report* would be nice, or *I was accosted by one Detective Samuel Pith at Central Terminal*, or *I am a clerk, just a clerk, but I write from the too-big desk of a detective*, no, no, *I* would not do at all, it was too personal, too presumptuous. Unwin would have to leave *I* out of it.

Emily was standing in front of him again, out of breath now. "There's nothing here, sir. The custodian did a thorough job."

That gave Unwin an idea. "Here," he said, "let me show you an old clerk's trick. It's something of a trade secret among the denizens of the fourteenth floor."

"You have done your homework, sir."

He was happy for a chance to impress her, and perhaps to win her confidence. "In an office as busy as the one on the fourteenth floor," he explained, "a document occasionally—very occasionally, mind you—goes astray. It is lost under a cabinet, maybe, or accidentally thrown out with someone's lunch. Or, as you have just reminded me, cleared away by the overzealous custodian."

Unwin opened the lid of the typewriter and gently prised loose the spools of ribbon. "In cases such as those," he went on, "where no carbon copy is available, there is only one method for recovering the missing document. Impressed upon the surface of the typewriter ribbon, so faintly that only close examination under a bright light will reveal them, are all the letters it has ever marked on paper. This ribbon here is only slightly used, but Sivart must have done some work with it."

He put the ribbon into Emily's hands. She drew a chair closer to the desk and sat down, while Unwin angled the lamp to provide her with the best possible illumination. She held a spool in each hand and stretched the ribbon between them, her big glasses shining in the lamplight.

Unwin removed the paper he had just rolled into the typewriter and took a pen from his briefcase. "Read them to me, Emily."

She squinted and read, " 'M-U-E-S-U-M-L-A-P-I-C-I-N-U-M.' Muesum Lapicinum? Is that Latin?"

"Of course not. The first letter on the ribbon is the last Sivart typed. We'll have to read it backward. Please proceed."

Emily's nervousness returned (better that, Unwin thought, than her suspicion), and her hands shook as she continued. Twenty minutes later those hands were covered with ink. Unwin typed a final copy, separating the words where he imagined spaces ought to be.

Wednesday. I'm putting aside my designated case in favor of something that's come out of left field, even though it's probably a load of bunkum. As for protocol, stuff it. I think I've earned the right to break the rules now and then, assuming I know what they are. So, clerk, if you ever see this report, may it please you to know I've been contacted by atypical means—over the telephone for cripes sake—by a party previously unbeknownst to me, to whom I am apparently beknownst. I mean, he knew my name. How did he get my number? I don't even know my number. He said, "Travis T. Sivart?" And I said, "Okay." And he said, "We have much to discuss," or something of that bodeful ilk.

He wants me to meet him at the cafe of one of our finer civic institutions. Maybe Hoffmann's behind it. Maybe it's a trap. One can hope, right? Thus concludes my report for the day. I'm off to the Municipal Museum.

Once he had read the report twice, Unwin handed it to Emily. She read it and asked, "Could the telephone call have had something to do with The Oldest Murdered Man?"

Unwin ought to have guessed that she would be familiar with Sivart's cases, but to hear his own title spoken aloud by someone he had only just met—someone not even a clerk—caused him to shudder. Emily seemed to take this as discouragement and lowered her eyes.

Still, he had to consider the possibility that Emily was correct, that the telephone call did have something to do with the ancient cadaver in the museum, with the case consigned to the archives thirteen years ago. He thought of the note to Lamech he had found in the dumbwaiter: *Let sleeping corpses lie.* What if the Miss P. who had offered that advice meant *that* corpse, *that* file?

It did not matter. All Unwin had to do was find Detective Sivart, and now he knew where Sivart had gone. He picked up his new badge and rubbed its face with his sleeve. In the burnished Agency eye he could see his own distorted reflection. *Charles Unwin, Detective.* Who had inscribed those words? He took the clerk's badge from his jacket pocket (no gleaming frontispiece there, only a worn, typewritten card) and replaced it with the detective's. That, at least, would help him if he encountered Screed again. And the gun? The gun went with his old badge into the desk drawer. The gun he would not need.

Emily followed him to the outer office. He took his coat, hat, and umbrella from the rack, waving off her assistance.

"Where are you going?" she asked.

"I'm off to the Municipal Museum," he said, but the situation seemed to call for some words of encouragement, so he adapted something he had seen in Agency newspaper advertisements. "We have a good team here, and the truth is our business."

Emily said, "But we haven't rehearsed and codified any secret signals, for use in times of duress."

He glanced at his watch. "I'll let you choose something, if you think it's necessary."

"You want me to come up with something right now?"

"It was your idea, Emily."

She closed her eyes again, as though better to see her own thoughts. "All right, how about this? When one of us says, 'The devil's in the details,' the other must say, 'And doubly in the bubbly.' "

"Yes, that will do nicely."

Still she squinted behind those enormous lenses, out of worry or irritation or both. Unwin would have to find something for her to do, an assignment. The phonograph record in his briefcase was a Sivart file of some kind and could be of some use to him in his search. He said, "I have a job for you, Emily. I want you to find a phonograph player. The Agency must have one somewhere."

He did not wait to see if this was enough to placate her, and turned to go. His hand froze on the doorknob, however, at the sound of movement on the other side of the door. A shadow loomed in the window, but no knock came. An eavesdropper. Or worse: they had already found Lamech's body and come to question him.

Unwin cautioned his assistant with a nod and set his briefcase down. The interloper was tapping the glass now, very lightly, as though to send a secret signal of his own. Unwin raised his umbrella saberwise over his head and threw the door open.

The man on the other side toppled backward onto the floor. Black paint spilled from a bucket in his hand, splattering over his clothes, his chin, and the polished wood floor. He held his paintbrush over his head, to protect himself from the anticipated blow.

Unwin lowered his umbrella and looked at the freshly painted words on his office window. DETECTIVE CHARLES UN, it read, and that was all it would ever read, because the painter stood, stabbed his brush into the bucket, and walked back toward the elevator, muttering.

Detective Screed's door opened. He saw the puddle of paint, saw the black boot prints that trailed down the hall. He yanked the hand-kerchief from his jacket pocket as though to begin cleaning the mess but put it to his forehead instead. He slammed his door closed again.

"Emily," Unwin said, "send a message to the custodian, please."

He stepped over the paint and went down the hall, his shoes squeak-ing. Other office doors opened, and other detectives peered out at him. Among them were the two he had seen in the elevator with Detective Screed. Peake was the name on one door, Crabtree the other. They shook their heads at him as he passed, and Peake—still scratching the rash at his collar—whistled in mock admiration.

FIVE

On Memory

Imagine a desk covered with papers. That is everything
you are thinking about. Now imagine a stack of file
drawers behind it. That is everything you know. The trick
is to keep the desk and the file drawers as close to one
another as possible, and the papers stacked neatly.

Unwin pedaled north along the dripping, shadowed expanse of
City Park. There were fewer cars on the street now, but twice he
had to ride up onto the sidewalk to pass horse-drawn carriages, and a
peanut vendor swore at him as he swerved too close to his umbrella-
topped stand. By the time Unwin arrived at the Municipal Museum,
his socks were completely soaked again. He hopped off his bicycle and
chained it to a lamppost, stepping away just in time to avoid the spray
of filthy water raised by the tires of a passing bus.

The fountains to either side of the museum entrance were shut off,
but rainwater had overflowed the reservoirs and was pouring across
the sidewalk to the gutter. The place had a cursed and weary look
about it—built, Unwin imagined, not to welcome visitors but to keep
secrets hidden from them. He fought the urge to turn around and go
home. With every step he took, the report he would have to write
explaining his actions grew in size. But if he were ever going to get his

old job back, he would have to find Sivart, and this was where Sivart had gone.

Unwin angled his umbrella against a fierce damp wind, climbed the broad steps, and passed alone through the revolving doors of the museum.

Light from the windowed dome of the Great Hall shone dimly over the information booth, the ticket tables, the broad-leafed potted plants flanking each gallery entrance. He followed the sound of clinking flatware to the museum café.

Three men were hunched over the lunch counter, eating in silence. All but one of the dozen or so tables in the room were unoccupied. Near the back of the room, a man with a pointed blond beard was working on a portable typewriter. He typed quickly, humming to himself whenever he had to stop and think.

Unwin went to the counter and ordered a turkey and cheese on rye, his Wednesday sandwich. The three men remained intent on their lunches, eating their soup with care. When Unwin's food came, he took it to a table near the man with the blond beard. He set his hat upside down next to his plate and put his briefcase on the floor.

The man's stiff beard bobbed while he worked—he was silently mouthing the words as he typed them. Unwin could see the top of the page curl upward, and he glimpsed the phrases *eats lunch same time every day* and *rarely speaks to workfellows*. Before Unwin could read more, the man glanced over his shoulder at him, righted the page, and frowned so that his beard stuck straight out from his face. Then he returned his attention to his typewriter.

Despite all that Unwin had read of detective work, he had no idea how to proceed with this investigation. Whom had Sivart met with, and what had transpired between them? What good did it do to have come here now? The trail might already have "gone cold," as Sivart would have put it.

Unwin opened his briefcase. He had sworn not to read *The Manual of Detection*, but he knew he would at least have to skim it if he were going to play at being a detective. He told himself he would read only enough to help him along to the first break in the case. That would come soon, he thought, if he only knew how to begin.

He turned the book over in his hands. The edges of the cloth were worn from use. *It's saved my life more than once,* Pith had said to him. But Unwin had never even heard of the book, so he was sure the Agency did not wish for non-employees to learn of its existence. Instead of setting the book on the table, he opened it in his lap.

THE MANUAL

OF

DETECTION

A Compendium of Techniques and Advice
for the Modern Detective,
Representing Matters Procedural, Practical, and Methodological;
Featuring
True Accounts of Pertinent Cases
With Helpful Illustrations and Diagrams;
Including an Appendix of Exercises, Experiments,
and Suggestions for Further Study.

FOURTH EDITION

He turned to the table of contents. Each chapter focused on one of the finer points of the investigative arts, from the common elements of case management to various surveillance techniques and methods of interrogation. But the range of topics was so broad that Unwin did not know what to read first.

Nothing in the index seemed entirely appropriate to his situation, except perhaps one entry: "Mystery, First Tidings of." He turned to the corresponding page and began to read.

> The inexperienced agent, when presented with a few promising leads, will likely feel the urge to follow them as directly as possible. But a mystery is a dark room, and anything could be waiting inside. At this stage of the case, your enemies know more than you know—that is what makes them your enemies. Therefore it is paramount that you proceed slantwise, especially when beginning your work. To do any-thing else is to turn your pockets inside out, light a lamp over your head, and paste a target on your shirtfront.

The iciness that had settled in Unwin's wet socks climbed up his legs and began melting into his stomach. How many blunders had he al-ready committed? He read the next few pages quickly, then skimmed the beginnings of those chapters that dealt with the foundations of the investigative process. Every paragraph of *The Manual of Detection* read like an admonishment tailored specifically for him. He should have developed an alternate identity, come in disguise or through a back door, planned an escape route. Certainly he should have remained armed. In one case file after another he had seen these techniques used, but detectives employed them without any apparent forethought. Was Sivart really so deliberate? Everything he did—whether throwing some-one off his trail or throwing a punch—he did as though the possibility had only just occurred to him.

Unwin closed the book and set it on the table, set his hands on top of it, and took a few deep breaths. The man with the blond beard was working quickly now. Unwin saw the phrase *habits suggesting a dull but potentially dangerous personality, empty or clouded over,* and then, just as he typed it, *if he is in contact with the absentee agent, he does not know it.*

Maybe he had stumbled into a lucky spot after all. Unwin got the man's attention with a wave of his hand.

The man turned in his seat, his beard a pointed accusation.

"Begging your pardon," Unwin said, "but are you the person who met here with Detective Sivart recently?"

The typist's frown deepened, his eyebrows drooping even as his beard rose an inch higher. He ground his teeth and said nothing, then plucked the page from his typewriter, stuffed it into his jacket, and rose from the table with his fists clenched. Unwin straightened, almost expecting the man to come at him, but he walked past Unwin's table and stomped off to the very back of the room, where a pay phone was mounted to the wall. He lifted the transceiver, spoke a number to the operator, and dropped a dime into the slot.

The three men at the lunch counter had turned from their bowls of soup. They looked on with tired expressions. Unwin could not tell if they were suspicious of him or thankful for the reprieve from the man's typing. Unwin nodded at them, and they swiveled back to their lunches without a word.

He took up the *Manual* again. His hands were shaking. He fanned the pages, breathing in the scent of old paper, and caught a whiff of what might have been gunpowder. He could begin to count the things he had done wrong, was perhaps even now adding to the list, but he still did not know where to begin.

"He still does not know where to begin," said the man on the telephone.

Unwin turned. Had he heard correctly? The man with the blond beard stood with his back to the room, one arm resting on top of the telephone, his head bent low. He spoke quietly, then listened and nodded.

Unwin took a deep breath. This was his first hour in the field, and already his nerves were getting to him. He turned back to his book and tried to focus.

"He is trying to focus," said the man at the telephone.

Unwin set down the *Manual* and rose from his seat. He had not misheard: somehow the man with the blond beard was speaking Unwin's thoughts aloud. His hands shook at the thought; he had begun to sweat. The three men at the lunch counter swiveled again to watch Unwin walk to the back of the room and tap the man on the shoulder.

The man with the blond beard looked up, his eyes bulging with violence. "Find another phone," he hissed. "I was here first."

"Were you speaking about me just then?" Unwin asked.

The man said into the receiver, "He wants to know if I was speaking about him just then." He listened and nodded some more, then said to Unwin, "No, I wasn't speaking about you."

Unwin was seized by a terrible panic. He wanted to run back to his seat or, better yet, back to his apartment, forget everything he had read in the *Manual,* everything that had happened that day. Instead, without thinking, he snatched the telephone out of the man's hand and put it to his own face. He was still shaking, but his voice was steady as he said, "Now, listen here. I don't know who you are, but I'd appreciate it if you'd keep to your own affairs. What business is it of yours what I'm doing?"

No response came. Unwin held the receiver to his ear, and he heard something, a sound so quiet he could barely tell it from the prickle of static on the line. It was the rustling of dry leaves, or sheets of paper, maybe, blown by a mild wind. And there was something else, too—a sad warbling that came and went as he listened. The cooing, he thought, of many pigeons.

He set the telephone back in its cradle. The man with the blond beard stared at him. His jaw was moving up and down, but he made no sound. Unwin met his eyes for a moment, then returned to his table, sat, and hurriedly began to eat his sandwich.

One of the men at the lunch counter got off his stool. He wore the plain gray uniform of a museum attendant. His white hair was thin and uncombed, and his dark eyes were set deep in his pale face. He shambled toward Unwin, breathing through his whiskers while crumpling a paper napkin in his right hand. He stood in front of the table and dropped the napkin into Unwin's hat. "Sorry," he said. "I mistook your hat for a wastepaper basket."

The man with the blond beard was on the telephone again. "He mistook his hat for a wastepaper basket," he said. But as the museum attendant left the café, he knocked into the table where the man with the blond beard had been sitting. A glass tipped and spilled water on the papers stacked beside the typewriter. The man with the blond beard dropped the receiver and came running over, cursing under his breath.

Unwin took the napkin out of his hat; something was written on it in blue ink. He uncrumpled the paper and read the hastily scrawled message. *Not safe here. Follow while he's distracted.* He stuffed the napkin into his pocket, gathered up his things, and left. The man with the blond beard was too busy shaking wet pages to notice him go.

THE MUSEUM ATTENDANT GRABBED Unwin by the arm and directed him north into the first of the museum galleries. The name on his pin was Edwin Moore. He leaned close and spoke into Unwin's ear. "We must choose our words carefully. You especially. Everything you say to me I must spend precious minutes unremembering before I sleep. I apologize for waiting as long as I did to intercede. Until I heard you speak, I thought you were one of them."

"One of whom?"

Moore breathed worry through his whiskers. "I cannot say. Either I never knew or I have purposefully forgotten."

Their route took them through the halls of warfare, where empty suits of mail straddled horse's armor empty of horses. Gold and silver

weapons gleamed in their cases, and Unwin knew them each, knew the
slim-bladed misericord, the graceful rapier, the double-barreled wheel
lock pistol. They were all in the Agency's index of weapons, though the
pages dedicated to such antiquated devices were less useful than those
covering the more popular implements of the day: the pistol, the gar-
rote, the cast-iron skillet.

Moore looked in Unwin's direction as he spoke but would not meet
his eyes. "I have been an employee of the Municipal Museum for thirteen years, eleven months, and some-odd days," he said. "I always follow the same path through these corridors, altering my course only
when necessary, as when a lost child begs my assistance. I like to keep
moving. Not to see the paintings, of course. After all this time, I no
longer see the paintings. They may as well be blank canvases or windows onto white sky."

A dull but potentially dangerous personality, the man with the blond
beard had typed, *empty or clouded over.* Was it Moore he had been describing? What sort of man worked to forget everything he knew?
Doubtless he was a little mad. Unwin, mindful of the commandment
to choose his words carefully, chose none for now.

Soon they came to a broad, circular chamber. Unwin knew the
place. Light entered through a small window at the top of the domed
ceiling, entombing in gray light the coffin of glass on a pedestal below.
The Oldest Murdered Man was surrounded by schoolchildren, out
on a field trip. The more brave and curious among them stood close,
and some even pressed their faces to the glass. Unwin and Moore
waited until their chaperone, a stooped young man in a tweed coat,
counted the children and shepherded them away. Once the patter of
their feet had receded, the only sound was that of the rain on the
window high above.

They went closer, the squeaking of Unwin's shoes echoing in the
vast room. A plaque set in the floor at the base of the pedestal declared,
To DETECTIVE TRAVIS T. SIVART, WHO RETURNED THIS TREASURE TO ITS

RIGHTFUL PLACE OF REST, THE TRUSTEES OF THE MUNICIPAL MUSEUM
EXPRESS THEIR UNDYING GRATITUDE.

The Oldest Murdered Man lay curled on his side, his arms folded
over his chest. His flesh was yellow and sunken but intact, preserved
by the bog into which he had been thrown, all those thousands of
years ago. Had he been a hunter, a farmer, a warrior, a chieftain? His
eyes were not quite closed, his black lips drawn back over his teeth in
an expression that suggested merriment rather than terror. The
hempen cord with which he had been strangled was still twisted
around his neck.

"I always found the name imprecise," Unwin said. "He may be the
first victim of murder we've discovered, but surely he wasn't the first
man to be killed by another. He may even have been a murderer himself. Still, he is our oldest mystery, and an unsolved one at that. We have
the weapon, but not the motive."

Edwin Moore was not listening. He looked at the ceiling while
Unwin spoke. "I hope there is enough light," Moore said.

"For what?"

The sun, though partly obscured by clouds, crested the window at
the top of the dome, and the room suddenly brightened.

"There we are," Moore said. "Did I tell you that I always keep to
the same route when making my rounds? That is why I reach this room
at the same time every afternoon. There was a woman, I think. She
wanted to draw my attention to something, to this. Who was she? Did
I only dream of her? I try not to notice things, Detective. I know a story
or two. I know the days of the week. That is enough to help eclipse the
rest. But look, look there. Can you fault me for noticing that?"

Moore pointed at the glass coffin, at the dead man's parted lips.
Unwin saw nothing at first, just the grim visage that Sivart had described, in his reports, as *a sad sorry face, laughing because it has to—a
face you'd like to buy a drink*. Then he noticed a glinting at the back of
the man's mouth, like that of the gold lettering on *The Manual of*

Detection. He knelt, using his umbrella for balance, and drew as close to the corpse as he could bear. He and the mummy peered at one another through the glass. Then the light shifted, and the dead man gave up his secret.

In one of his teeth, a gold filling.

Unwin dropped his umbrella and jerked upright, tripping over his own feet as he backed away from the mummy. He had the odd impression that his breath had escaped with his umbrella and gone skittering over the floor with it, out of reach. He needed them both, but he could not go and fetch them. He was still standing only because Edwin Moore was propping him up.

Let sleeping corpses lie, the note in the dumbwaiter had read. The gold filling twinkled in the mouth of the Oldest Murdered Man, and to Unwin it was as though the corpse were silently laughing at him. The implications extended deep into the Agency archives, all the way down to Unwin's own files. He said it aloud as he realized it: "The Oldest Murdered Man is a fake."

"No," Moore said. "The Oldest Murdered Man is real. But he is not in this museum."

Footsteps at the edge of the room caused Unwin and Moore to turn. The man with the blond beard stood in the doorway, his portable typewriter in his hand.

"We must continue," Moore whispered. "I've never seen that man before, but I don't like the looks of him."

Unwin was standing on his own now. "He was in the café not ten minutes ago," he said.

"No time to argue," said Moore. He picked up Unwin's umbrella and pressed it into his hands. They left the way the schoolchildren had gone, through an arched doorway and into a dim hall between galleries.

"Please understand," Moore said. "I tried hard to forget the whole thing. Succeeded, perhaps, many times. But every day there is the tooth again, the filling. And that woman, who keeps insisting that I see it. It itches at my brain. The filling may as well be set in my own head. I need to forget about it. Knowing much of anything is a danger to me. I need you to fix your mistake."

"My mistake?"

"Yes. I did not want to be the one to break it to you, Detective Sivart. But the corpse you retrieved from *The Wonderly* the night you first confronted Enoch Hoffmann—it was the wrong corpse. A decoy." Moore looked sad as he spoke, his breath whistling through bunched whiskers. "He tricked you, Detective. He tricked you into helping him hide a dead body in plain sight."

"Whose dead body?"

"Either I never knew—"

"Or you've purposefully forgotten," Unwin said.

Moore seemed surprised to have his sentence finished for him, but he took Unwin's arm without comment and guided him from the corridor. They passed through rooms of medieval paintings. Knights, ladies, and princes scowled from their gilded frames. Then a lighted place: shards of pottery on marble pillars, urns of monstrous size, miniatures of long-dead cities. Moore moved faster and faster, dragging Unwin on while the man with the blond beard followed. They caught up with the schoolchildren in a room of statues. These were of men with elephants' heads, the wise and quiet gods of a strange land sequestered in one dim and narrow gallery. Jewels glinted in the shadows, and the air was heavy and warm.

"Not my mistake," Unwin said at last.

Moore glared at him. "If not yours, whose?"

"You called Sivart a week ago. You must have met with him and forgotten. You showed him what you showed me. What did he do when you told him? You have to remember. You have to tell me where he went."

"But if you're not Sivart, then who are you?"

Those weird, elephant-headed gods fixed Unwin with their impassive eyes, and he found he could not speak. *I am Sivart's clerk,* he wanted to say. *I am the one who set down the details of his false triumph. It is my mistake, mine!* But they would trample him when they heard, those elephant people, and gore him with their jeweled tusks, strangle him with their trunks. *Remember,* they said to him, in a dream he could not entirely wake from. *Try this time, would you? Remember something.*

"Chapter Elephant," Unwin said.

"What was that?" Moore asked. "What did you say?"

"Chapter Eighteen!" Unwin corrected himself. He took *The Manual of Detection* from his briefcase and flipped through the pages, searching for Chapter Eighteen, for the chapter Sivart, in the dream, had told him to remember.

Moore's whole body was trembling, and the snowy hair on his head shook with each wheezing breath. He stared at the book in Unwin's hands. "*The Manual of Detection* has no Chapter Eighteen," he said.

Some of the schoolchildren were ignoring the exhibits now. They gathered instead around these two men, who were possibly the strangest things they had seen in the museum.

Unwin flipped to the last pages of the book. It ended with Chapter Seventeen.

"How did you know?" he asked.

Moore leaned forward, his face contorted, his eyes terrible. "Because I wrote it!" he said, and collapsed.

SIX

On Leads

Follow them lest they follow you.

I've got just enough to go on, Sivart had written in his first report on the theft of the Oldest Murdered Man. *That's what makes me nervous.*

On the night of the heist, a museum cleaning woman had spotted an antique flatbed steam truck, color red, lurking under the trees behind the Wonders of the Ancient World wing. In her thirty-seven years of employment, she told Sivart during questioning, she had seen many strange things, had seen the portraits of certain dukes and generals turn their eyes to watch her as she mopped, had seen the marble statue of a nymph move its slender right leg two inches in the moonlight, had seen a twelve-year-old boy rise sleepily from the settee of an eighteenth-century boudoir and ask her why it was so dark, and where his parents had gone, and whether she had a sandwich for him. But never had the cleaning woman seen anything so strange as the steam truck, which had the smokestack of a locomotive and the hulking demeanor of a story-book monster.

A thing like that tends to stick out, so it wasn't too hard to track it down. Caligari's Travels-No-More Carnival was closed up for the night: nothing on the midway but the smell of stale popcorn. I found the truck parked beside a pavilion near the boardwalk and pressed my thumb to the smoke-stack over the engine. Still warm.

I thought I'd have a peek inside, but somebody was coming from the docks, and I had to scram. The tent flap was hanging open by the entrance, so I wrapped myself in that and hoped nobody would spot my hat. In the end, though, I couldn't help but risk a look.

What I saw was a tall fellow with one very odd mug. It looked like it was made out of clay, all pocked and pale, but his eyes were bright green. He peered into the cab, his breath fogging up the glass. Then he sighed and walked on.

I came out in a hurry, meaning to get out of there, and nearly walked straight into a second man. The weird thing, clerk? It was the same guy I'd just seen go in the opposite direction. Turns out this model of goon comes in sets of two.

He called to his brother, and they got hold of me quick, then gave me a very professional roughing over. Our walk down to the pier was less than romantic. A rusting smuggler's ship, The Wonderly, *was docked down there. The whole thing reeked, like maybe they'd just raised it off the filthy bottom of the harbor.*

The man in charge was a squat little fellow in a rumpled gray suit. The Man of a Thousand and One Voices is more impressive in the carnival posters, with his face lit green by hocus-pocus. In the flesh he looks more like an accountant who's had a bad day and stumbled into the wrong part of town. He was shaking his head, looking sad about the whole thing. I was sad about it, too, and I let him know, in so many words.

We talked for a while. His real voice (if that's what it was) sounded soft and high-pitched, like a kid's. He explained how the Oldest Murdered Man had been the carnival's main attraction for years, that they had been search-ing for the mummy for a long time. "I'm only bringing him back home," he said.

"Why the boat, then?" I asked.

Enoch Hoffmann grinned. "The boat is for you," he said, and that's when his two buddies threw me into the cargo hold.

The story of the detective's escape—how he found the corpse on board, commandeered a lifeboat, and rowed it ashore through the night—was in the newspapers the next morning. Agency representa-tives returned the Oldest Murdered Man to the museum that day, amid shouted questions and the popping of flashbulbs.

But if the mummy was not in the museum now, where was he? And whose corpse was here in his place?

WITH HELP FROM SOME of the schoolchildren, Unwin carried Moore into a back room. The place served as a holding area for pieces of exhibits on their way into or out of the museum. Objects that might have seemed momentous in the galleries languished here like junk-sale leftovers. Paintings leaned in piles against the walls, sarcophagi gathered dust in the corners, marble statues lay half buried in packing material. The children put Edwin Moore on a worn blue chaise longue, and he lay with his arms over his face, shivering and mumbling.

"Is he a knight?" one of the children asked.

"He's an artist," another one said.

"He's a mummy," insisted a third.

Unwin corralled them back into the museum and set them in line behind their chaperone, who had failed to notice them leave. The chil-dren waved good-bye, and Unwin waved back. When they were gone, he walked partway down the hall and peered around the corner. He did not see the man with the blond beard.

From his sickbed Moore called out for water. Unwin searched

though the crates and found a bowl, dark clay with a black crisscross pattern around the exterior. It was, he supposed, ancient, priceless, and difficult to drink from, but it would have to do. He filled it from the drinking fountain in the hall and carried it to the chaise longue with both hands.

Moore sipped the water, spilling some onto his jacket. Then he lay down and sighed, but immediately began to shiver again. "There is no keeping it back," he said. "I had bound it so tightly, it came undone all at once."

"You did meet with Sivart," Unwin said.

"Yes, oh, yes." He took his arms from his face; it was as white as his hair. "But I never should have spoken to him. He left here in a passion. I thought he would chew his cigar in two. And you! Who are you?"

Unwin considered showing the man his badge, then thought better of it. "I'm Charles Unwin, Agency clerk. My detective's gone missing, and I'm trying to find him. Mr. Moore, you have to tell me where he went."

"Do I? I have already remembered too much, and they are sure to come for me now." He gestured for the bowl of water, and Unwin raised it to his lips. He drank, coughed some, and said, "Not even the Agency wants every mystery solved, Mr. Unwin."

Unwin set the bowl aside. "I'm not trying to solve anything," he said.

Moore's gaze appeared focused now, and the color was returning to his face. He looked at Unwin as though seeing him for the first time. "If you are Sivart's clerk, then you ought to know where he went. The sight of the gold tooth left him baffled. He needed information, the most reliable he could find." He added quietly, "Whatever the price."

Some of the places mentioned in Sivart's reports were as foreign lands to Unwin—he came upon their names often enough to be convinced of their existence, but it was preposterous to think he could reach them by bicycle. For him there were two cities. One consisted of the seven blocks between his apartment and the Agency office building. The other was larger, vaguer, and more dangerous, and it intruded upon his imagination only by way of case reports and the occasional uneasy dream. In a shadowy corner of that other city was a certain taproom, an unofficial gathering place frequented by the enterprising, the scheming, and the desperate. Sivart went there only when every supposition had proved false, when every lead had dead-ended. And because the place rarely had any direct bearing on a case, Unwin usually excised its name from the files.

"The Forty Winks," he said.

Moore nodded. "If you insist on tracking him down, Mr. Unwin, then I suggest you work quickly. I fear I've started the timer on an explosive, but I do not know when it will go off." He rose suddenly from the chaise longue. He was light on his feet and seemed a little giddy.

"What about the woman you mentioned?" Unwin asked. "The one you said showed you the tooth?"

Moore grimaced and said, "I took you at your word when you said you aren't trying to solve anything."

Unwin clenched his jaw. Without thinking, he had started asking questions he did not want to ask. After this, he thought, he would have to put down *The Manual of Detection* for good.

"This way, then," Moore said. "There is a back door—that will be the safest route."

The exit was no taller than Unwin's waist. It was blocked by empty crates, so they worked together to move them aside. The door opened onto the park. Here the trees grew thickly about the back of the museum, and the path was matted with oak leaves, orange and red. Unwin crouched to go through and opened his umbrella on the other side.

Moore bent down to look at him.

"Tell me one thing," Unwin said. "Is it true, what you said? That you wrote *The Manual of Detection*?"

"Yes," said Moore. "So take it from me—it is a bunch of rubbish.

They should have asked a detective to write it. Instead they asked me, and what did I know?"

"You weren't a detective?"

"I was a clerk," Moore said, and he closed the door before Unwin could ask him anything else.

HE RODE SOUTH THROUGH the city, his umbrella open in front of him. He ignored the blare of horns and the shouts of drivers as he wove through the midday traffic, keeping his head tucked low.

He passed the narrow green door of his own apartment building, then the grime-blackened exterior of Central Terminal. There he caught sight of Neville, the boy from the breakfast cart, standing just out of the rain, smoking a cigarette.

At the next block, Unwin veered east to avoid the Agency offices. He did not want to risk seeing Detective Screed again, or even his own assistant, not yet. The noise of the traffic receded as the cast-iron facades of warehouses and mill buildings rose up around him, rain pouring in torrents from their corniced rooftops. Unwin's arms and legs were shaking now, but not from the exertion or from the cold. It was that dead face he had seen behind the glass in the museum. He felt as though it were still mocking him with its awful gold-toothed grin. The thread, the one that connected mystery to solution, that shone like silver in the dark—Sivart had picked the wrong one, and Unwin had strung it up as truth. What did the false thread connect?

In the old port town, Unwin slowed to navigate the winding, crowded streets. Business carried on in spite of the rain, with deals being made under awnings and through the windows of food stalls. He felt he was being watched, not by one but by many. Was there something that marked him as an employee of the Agency? An invisible sign that the people here could read?

He pedaled on, easing his grip on his umbrella. The rain fell softly now. In the maze of old streets that predated the gridding of the city, he passed timbered warehouses and old market squares cluttered with the refuse of industry. Machines—the purpose of which he could not guess—rusted in red streaks over the cobblestone.

The crowds thinned. From chimneys, crooked fingers of smoke pointed at the clouds. Barren clotheslines sagged dripping over the street, and a few windows glowed yellow against the day's persistent gloom. Unwin quickened his pace, his memory of Sivart's descriptions serving as map, and came at last to the cemetery of Saints' Hill, a six-acre tangle of weeds, dubious pathways, vine-grappled ridges, and tumble-down mausoleums.

The Forty Winks was beneath the mortuary, a low-slung building of crumbling gray stone at the southeast corner of the block. He had half hoped that the place did not really exist, but the chipped steps leading from the sidewalk down to the basement level were real enough. He chained his bicycle to the cemetery fence, under the eaves of the building.

From the top of the stairs, he could hear the smacking of pool balls, the clinking of glasses. He could still go home, if he wanted. Sleep off the day and wait for the next one, hope that everything would right itself somehow. But a window level with the sidewalk creaked open, and someone looked up at him, wrinkling his nose as though trying to catch Unwin's scent. A pair of wide, reddish brown eyes blinked behind the glass.

"In or out?" the man called from below.

It was too late to go back. Unwin descended the stairwell, collapsing his umbrella just enough to make it fit. At the bottom of the steps was a slow drain, cigarette butts floating in the puddle that had formed. Unwin pushed the door open with the tip of his umbrella, then stepped over the water and into the Forty Winks.

The tables were lit only by candles, while the bar, on the cemetery side, had the benefit of several windows near the ceiling, through which a greenish light dribbled over bottles of liquor. Most of the bottles were arranged on shelves in a tall, oblong cabinet, its door gaping.

Not a cabinet, Unwin realized. A coffin.

Near the entrance, two men sat with their hats in front of them, speaking close over a guttering candle. At the back of the room, an electric bulb with a green glass shade hung low over the pool table. Two other men, very tall and dressed in identical black suits, were in the midst of a game. They played slowly, taking a great deal of care with each shot.

Sivart was nowhere to be seen. Unwin took a seat at the bar and set his briefcase in front of him. The man who had spoken through the window cranked it shut, made a show of dusting off his hands, and hopped down from the barrel he had climbed to reach. He ran a hand along the bar as he approached, sweeping up a folded newspaper. "Newsman says there's foul play at the Agency," he said. "An internal affair, they say. The eyes up top suspect one of their own."

A single black curl made an upside-down question mark in the middle of the man's forehead. This was Edgar Zlatari, the caretaker of the cemetery and its only gravedigger. So long as no one was in need of burying, he served drinks to the living. He was someone who knew things, a collector of useful information.

"New faces bring new woes, that's what they say," Zlatari went on. "What about you? You call your troubles by name? Or maybe they call you by yours?"

Unwin did not know how to reply.

"Leave your tongue on your pillow this morning? What's your line, friend?" Zlatari cast a suspicious look at the briefcase, and Unwin slipped it onto his lap.

"Okay, tight-lips. What'll it be, then?"

"Me?" Unwin said.

The bartender looked around, rolling his eyes. He smelled of whiskey and damp earth. " 'Me?' he says. That's a laugh."

The two at the table snickered, but the men at the pool table were unamused. At the sight of this, Zlatari's grin vanished. "Come on, pal," he said to Unwin. "A drink. What do you want to drink?"

There were too many bottles stacked in that coffin, too many choices. What would Sivart have ordered? A hundred times the detective must have named his drinks of choice. But Unwin had stricken them from the reports, and now he found he could not remember even one. Instead the response to Emily's secret phrase came uselessly to mind: *And doubly in the bubbly.*

"Root beer," he said at last.

Zlatari blinked several times, as though maybe he had never heard of the stuff. Then he shrugged and moved away down the bar. On the wall beyond the register was a tattered velvet curtain. In the moment Zlatari drew it aside, Unwin glimpsed a tiny kitchen. A radio was playing back there, and he thought he recognized the song—a slow melody carried by horns, a woman singing just above them, voice rising with the swell of strings. He was sure he had heard the tune somewhere before and had almost placed it when Zlatari pulled the curtain closed behind him.

Unwin shifted on his stool. In the mirror he could see the men at the booth behind him. One tapped his hat excitedly as he said, "Have I got a story!" and the other man leaned forward to listen, though the man with the story told it loudly enough for everyone in the room to hear.

"I saw Bones Kiley the other night," he said, "and we were just talking business, you know? Then suddenly, out of nowhere, he started talking *business.* So I said to him, 'Wait, wait, do you want to talk about *business?* Because if it's *business* you want to talk about, then we shouldn't be talking about business, because there's business and there's *business.*'"

"Ha," said the other man.

"So then I asked him, 'Just what sort of business are you in, Bones, that you want to talk about *business?*'"

"Ha ha," said the other.

"And Bones gets serious-looking, kind of screws up his eyebrows like this . . ."

"Ha."

". . . and he looks at me with his eyes squinty, and he says in this really deep voice, 'I'm in the business of blood.' "

The other man said nothing.

"So I said to him," and the man with the story raised his voice even higher as he finished his story, " 'The business of blood? The business of blood? Bones, there is no business but the business of blood!' "

Both men laughed and tapped their hats in unison, and the candle flickered and flared, making their shadows twitch on the uneven stone wall.

While the man with the story was telling it, the two at the pool table had set down their cue sticks. Identical faces, lips pale gray, eyes bright green: Unwin wondered if these could be the Rook brothers, Jasper and Josiah, the twin thugs who had aided Enoch Hoffmann in the theft of the Oldest Murdered Man, and in countless other misdeeds during the years of his criminal reign. *The worst thing that can happen,* Sivart often wrote, *and the other worst thing.*

Shoulder to shoulder the two approached, leaning toward each other with every step. It was said that the Rooks had once been conjoined, but were separated in an experimental operation that left them with crippled feet—Jasper's left and Josiah's right. Each wore two sizes of boots, the smaller on the side of that irrevocable severance. This was the only sure way to tell them apart.

The twins stood over the table with their backs to Unwin, obscuring his view of the men seated there. He felt a great heat coming off the two, drying the back of his neck. It was as though they had just come out of a boiler room.

"My brother," said one in a measured tone, "has advised me to advise you to leave now. And since I always take my brother's advice, I am hereby advising you to leave."

"Yeah, who's asking?" said the man who had told the story.

"In point of fact," said the other, in a voice that was deeper but otherwise identical to his brother's, "my brother is not asking, he is advising."

"Well, I don't know your brother," said the man with the story, "so I don't think I'll take his advice."

In the silence that followed, it seemed to Unwin that even the dead in their graves, just behind the wall where the mirror was hung, were waiting to hear what would happen.

One of the twins licked the tips of his thumb and forefinger and leaned over the table. He pinched the candle flame, and it went out with a hiss. From the dark of the booth came a muffled cry. Then the two men walked to the door with the storyteller between them, his feet kicking wildly a few inches above the ground. They deposited him outside, facedown in the puddle over the slow drain. He lay slumped amid the floating cigarette butts and did not try to pick his face up out of the puddle.

The brothers returned to the back of the room. One chalked his cue stick while the other considered the table. He took his next shot, sinking one ball, then another.

The man still in the booth blinked, his eyes not yet adjusted to the change in light. He put his hat on and went outside. After a moment's hesitation and a glance back into the bar, he lifted his friend out of the puddle and dragged him up the stairs.

Zlatari came out from behind the curtain, muttering as he went to close the door. Once he was back behind the bar, he uncorked the bottle in his hand and slid it across to Unwin.

The two men at the back of the room had finished their game, and were seating themselves side by side at the booth nearest the pool table.

One of them nodded at Zlatari, and Zlatari raised his hand and said, "Yes, Jasper, just a moment."

Eight years had passed since the names Jasper and Josiah Rook had appeared in Sivart's reports—like Hoffmann, the twins had gone into hiding following the events of The Man Who Stole November Twelfth. There were times when Unwin had hoped to see them come back—but only on paper, not in the flesh.

"Well," Zlatari said to him, "it's your lucky day. We're about to play some poker, and we need a fourth."

Unwin raised one hand and said, "Thank you, no. I'm not very good at cards."

Josiah whispered something into Jasper's ear—it was Josiah, according to Sivart's reports, who served as counsel, while Jasper was generally spokesman. The latter called to Unwin, "My brother has advised me to advise you to join us."

Unwin knew enough to know he had no choice. He took his bottle and followed Zlatari to the table, seating himself at the gravedigger's right. The Rooks regarded him unblinkingly. Their long faces, molded as though from the same mottled clay, could have been lifeless masks if not for the small green eyes set in them. Those eyes were very much alive, and greedy—they caught the light and did not let it go.

Zlatari dealt the cards, and Unwin said, "I'm afraid I don't have much money."

"Your money is no good here," said Josiah, and Jasper said, "To clarify, my brother does not mean that you play for free, as the expression may commonly be interpreted. Only that we do not play for money, and thus yours is literally of no value at this table."

Zlatari whistled and shook his head. "Don't let Humpty and Dumpty here spook you, tight-lips. That's just their version of gentlemanly charm. Mine is traditional generosity. The bank will forward you something to start with. And like he said, we don't play for money at this table. We play for questions."

"Or rather," said Jasper, "for the right to ask them. But only one question per hand, and only the winner of that hand may ask."

Unwin did know a thing or two about poker. He knew that certain combinations of cards were better than others, though he could not say for sure which beat which. He would have to rely on poker-facedness, then, which he knew to be a virtue in the context of the game.

"Ante is one interrogative," said Zlatari.

Unwin placed a white chip beside the others on the table and examined his cards. Four of the five were face cards. When his turn came, he raised the bet by one query, though under the guise of hesitancy. Then he traded in his single non–face card and received another face card, a king, in its place. A handful of royalty, then. What could be better? Minding his poker face, however, he made sure to frown at his hand.

There ensued a whirl of bets, calls, and folds, until finally only Unwin and Josiah were still in the game. Josiah set his cards on the table, and Jasper said for him, "Two pair."

Unwin revealed his own cards, hoping that someone would interpret.

"Three kings," Zlatari said. "Tight-lips takes the pot and keeps his nickname for now."

Unwin tried not to look pleased as he claimed the pile of chips. "I may ask my question now?"

"Sure," said Zlatari. He seemed cheerful at the Rook brothers' loss.

"But you just asked it," said Josiah, "and now you are down one query." As he said this, he blinked for the first time since they had started playing, though it was less a blink than a deliberate closing and reopening of the eyes.

"Shouldn't you have told me the rules before we started?" Unwin said.

"The laws of the land are not read to us in the crib," was Josiah's reply. "And you just expended another query, though you are allowed only one."

"It was rhetorical," said Unwin, but he tossed aside the two chips anyway.

Zlatari said, "Hell, we should be fair to the new guy," and he told Unwin how to trade up: two queries for a single inquiry, two inquiries for a perscrutation, two perscrutations for a catechism, two catechisms for an interrogation, and so on.

Unwin's next hand did not look to him as strong as the first, and he folded early, assuring himself there were better cards to come. Worse hands followed, however, and the other players directed their questions at one another, ignoring him. He listened carefully to their answers, but they were of little use because he hardly understood the questions. He heard names he did not recognize, references to "jobs" that were "pulled" rather than worked, and a lot of talk that sounded more like code than speech.

Zlatari asked, "Would putting the hat on the uptown bromides win dirt or be a fishing expedition?"

"A few rounds of muck could show ghost," was Josiah's reply.

At the end of the next hand, it was Jasper who threw in enough chips for a perscrutation and said to Zlatari, "Tell me about the last time you saw Sivart."

Zlatari shifted in his seat and scratched the back of his neck with grimy fingernails. "Well, let's see, that would have been a week ago. It was dark when he got here, and he did a lot of things he doesn't usually do. He was nervous, fidgety. He didn't ask me any questions, just took a seat in the corner and read a book. I didn't know the man could read. He stayed until his candle burned down, then left."

The Rooks appeared dissatisfied with the account. Apparently a perscrutation was a rather weightier kind of question and required a more thorough disclosure. Zlatari drew a breath and went on. "He said I might not see him again for a while. He said that Cleo was back in town, that he had to go and find her." Zlatari glanced at Unwin when he said this, as though to see if it meant anything to him. Unwin looked down at his chips.

Cleo could only be Cleopatra Greenwood, and Unwin had long ago come to fear—even loathe—the appearance of her name in a report. She had first come to the city with Caligari's Traveling Carnival and for years was one of Sivart's chief informants. But to file anything regarding her motives or aims was to risk the grueling work of retraction a month later. Mysteries, in her wake, doubled back on themselves and became something else, something a person could drown in. *I had her all wrong, clerk:* how many times had Unwin come upon that awful admission and scurried to fix what had come before?

The others were waiting for Unwin's next bet. His winnings were largely depleted, so he traded an inquiry for two queries but quickly lost both. The Rooks, as though sensing that Unwin would soon leave the table, turned their attention on him. Jasper used a query to learn his name, and Josiah spent an inquiry to ask what kind of work he did.

Unwin showed them his badge, and the Rook brothers blinked in tandem.

Zlatari's brow wrinkled behind his question-mark curl. "Well," he said, "it wouldn't be the first time I've had an Eye at my table. Detective Unwin, is it? Fine. Everyone's welcome here." But on this last point he seemed uncertain.

Unwin lost and lost again. All the questions came to him now, and he gave up answers one after another. His opponents were disappointed at the spottiness of his knowledge, though Zlatari licked his lips when Unwin told what he knew about Lamech's murder, about the bulky corpse at the desk on the thirty-sixth floor, its bulging eyes, its criss-crossed fingers.

Zlatari dealt new hands, and Unwin's was unremarkable: no face cards, no two or three of any kind. His beginner's luck had run out. This would be his last hand, and he had learned so little.

Zlatari folded almost immediately, but the Rook brothers showed no sign of relenting. They eagerly took up their new cards and just as eagerly counted out their bets. Unwin was going to lose. So he said to Zlatari, "A two, three, four, five, and six of spades: is that a good hand?"

Again that slow, sleepy blink from the twins.

"Yes," said Zlatari. "That is a good hand."

The brothers tossed their cards onto the table.

Unwin set his own cards facedown and collected his winnings, quickly, so they would not notice how his hands were shaking. He traded in all his chips, which was enough, Zlatari told him, for the most severe sort of question the game allowed. The inquisition would be answered by everyone at the table.

Unwin looked at each of them carefully. The Rooks were silent, imperious. But their questions had revealed that they, like him, were looking for Sivart. And Sivart was looking for Greenwood. So Unwin cleared his throat and asked, "Where is Cleopatra Greenwood?"

Zlatari looked over his shoulders, as though to make sure no one else had heard, even though the bar was otherwise empty. "Hell!" he said. "Hot stinking hell! You want to bury me, Detective? You want us in the dirt today? What's your game, Charles?"

Josiah whispered something in Jasper's ear, and Jasper said, "Those questions are out of turn, Zlatari. You're breaking your own rules."

"I'll break more," Zlatari said. He flicked his hands at Unwin. "Up, let me up!"

Unwin got to his feet, and Zlatari shoved past, knocking chips off the table and onto the floor. "You get your answers from them," he said, "but I don't want to know what they are. I've got enough graves to dig without having to dig my own." He went muttering to the farthest table and sat facing the door, twisting his mustache between thumb and forefinger.

The Rooks were still in their seats. Unwin sat back down and tried not to look directly at those green, unblinking eyes. He felt again the strange heat of the two men, dry and suffocating. It came over the table in waves; his face felt like paper about to catch.

Jasper took a card from his jacket pocket. Josiah gave him a pen, and Jasper wrote something and slid the card across the table.

Unwin's nose tingled with the scent of matchsticks as he read what Jasper had written: *The Gilbert, Room 202.*

Without having to look, he knew it was the same address written on the piece of notepaper in his pocket. Unwin had already met Cleo Greenwood, then. She had called herself Vera Truesdale and told him a story about roses in her hotel room.

He put the card in his pocket and stood up. He had asked only one question, and the Rooks had answered it—was he not entitled to a second, since there were two of them at the table? There were plenty of questions on his mind: about the identity of the corpse in the Municipal Museum, the meaning of Cleopatra Greenwood's visit to the Agency that morning, whether any of it meant that Enoch Hoffmann had come out of hiding. But the Rooks were looking at him in a way that suggested their business was concluded, so he stood and gathered his things.

At the door Zlatari grabbed his arm and said, "The price of some questions is the answer, Detective." He glanced back at the Rooks, and Unwin followed his gaze. They might as well have been a pair of statues, the original and a copy, though no one could have said which was which.

"I suppose you saw Cleo Greenwood since she got back to town," Zlatari said. "Heard her singing at some joint a little classier than this one. Maybe she looked at you from across the room. Time stopped when you heard her voice. You'd do anything for her, anything she asked, if only she asked. Am I right? Or maybe you imagined all that. Try to convince yourself that you imagined all that, Detective. Try to forget."

"Why?"

"Because you'll always be wrong about her."

Unwin put on his hat. He would have liked to forget, forget every-thing that had happened since he woke up this morning, forget even the dream of Sivart. Maybe someday Edwin Moore could teach him how it was done. In the meantime he had to keep moving.

He went to the door and hopped over the puddle on his way up the stairs. The Rooks' red steam truck was parked down the street—he was surprised he had failed to notice it before. It was just as the cleaning lady at the Municipal Museum had described it all those years ago: red and hunched and brutal-looking. Had he fallen into his files, or had his files spilled into his life?

He hurried to his bicycle, wanting to be as far from the Forty Winks as possible by the time the Rooks understood the extent of his poker-facedness. When they flipped over his last hand, they would see various numbered cards there, none of them concurrent, and of four different suits.

SEVEN

On Suspects

They will present themselves to you first as victims, as
allies, as eyewitnesses. Nothing should be more suspicious
to the detective than the cry for help, the helping
hand, or the helpless onlooker. Only if someone
has behaved suspiciously should you allow
for the possibility of his innocence.

An empty hat and raincoat floated at the center of the diagram in
Unwin's mind. Beside them was a dress filled with smoke. A pair
of black birds with black hats fluttered above, while below lay two
corpses, one in an office chair, one encased in glass. The diagram was
a fairy tale, written by a forgetful old man with wild white hair, and it
whirled like a record on a phonograph.

The rain fell heavily again, and Unwin pedaled against the wind.
These were unfamiliar streets, where unfamiliar faces glared with seeming menace from beneath dripping hats. A small dog, white with apri-
cot patches, emerged from an alley and followed him, barking at his
rear tire. No amount of bell ringing could drive it away. When it
rained like this, these city dogs were always lost, always wandering—the
smells they used to navigate were washed into the gutters. Unwin felt
he was a bit like one of those dogs now. This one finally left him to

investigate a sodden pile of trash at the corner, but once it was gone, he found that he missed it.

His umbrella technique worked best over short distances and at reasonably high speeds. Now he was soaked. His sleeves drooped from his wrists, and his tie stuck to him through his shirt. If she saw him like this, Cleopatra Greenwood would laugh and send him on his way. That she knew something was a certainty—she always knew something, was always "in on it." But what was she in on? Why had she come back to the city now?

Even after all his work at maintaining consistency, Unwin knew that a careful examination of the Agency's files would reveal perhaps a dozen versions of Cleopatra Greenwood, each a little different from the others. One of them, at the age of seventeen, renounced her claim on her family's textile fortune and ran off to join Caligari's Traveling Carnival. The carnival, in the autumn of its misfit life and haunted by odd beauties and ill-used splendors, made of the girl a sort of queen. She read futures in a deck of old cards and suffered a man with a handlebar mustache to throw daggers at her.

During one performance a blade pierced her left leg, just above the knee. She removed the dagger herself and kept it. The wound left her with a permanent limp, and the blade would appear again in many of Sivart's reports. When she found him in the cargo hold of *The Wonderly*, that night out on the bay, it was already in her hand.

I'd been trying to remember something I'd read about escaping from bonds, Sivart wrote. It's easier if you're able to dislocate certain bones at will, but that's not in my job description. I was about as useful as a jack-in-the-box with his lid glued shut. So I was happy to see her, even though I didn't know what she was doing there.

"I'm going to help you get what you came for," she said. "And you're going to get me out of here."

So she was in trouble, too. She was always in trouble. I wanted to tell her she could do better than old twiddle-fingers back there, but I still needed her to cut those ropes, so I played nice and kept it to myself.

We found the crate with Mr. Grim inside and carried it to a lifeboat. It was tough going, she with her limp and me with sore feet, but with a pair of ropes to lower them we managed to get corpse and crate down onto the dinghy. She sat at the prow and rubbed her bad knee while I rowed. It was dark out there on the water, no moon, no stars, and I could barely see the seven feet to her face. She wouldn't tell me where she would go after this. She wouldn't tell me where I could find her. Truth is, I still don't know where she stands. With Hoffmann? With us? She seems like a good kid, clerk, and I want to trust her. But maybe I'm getting her wrong.

For years, over the course of dozens of cases, Sivart was never sure whose side she was on, and neither was Unwin, until the theft of November twelfth, when Sivart caught her red-handed and did what he had to do.

If what Edwin Moore had said was correct, then it might have been Greenwood who made the switch that night and tricked Sivart into returning the wrong corpse to the museum. And if Sivart had failed to get the truth out of her, what hope did Unwin have? He was no threat to her; he was nothing at all: DETECTIVE CHARLES UN, as it said on his office door.

Ahead of him a black car rolled from an alleyway, blocking his route. Unwin braked and waited. No traffic prevented the car from taking to the street, but it stayed where it was. He tried to look in at the driver; all he could see was his own reflection in the window. The engine let out a low growl.

What would the *Manual* have to say about this? Clearly, Unwin was meant to be intimidated. Should he pretend that he was not? Act as though this were all a misunderstanding, that he was only a little embarrassed by so awkward an encounter? No such cordiality was forthcoming from the driver of the vehicle, so he dismounted and walked his bicycle to the opposite side of the street.

The vehicle sprang from the alley and came straight at him. Unwin leapt back as it rolled onto the curb. Two steps farther and he would have been pinned against the brick wall. In the driver's window, distorted by streaks of rain, his own reflection again.

Unwin mounted his bicycle and pedaled back across the street. He tried to keep calm, but his feet slipped from the pedals, and he wobbled. He heard the screech of the car's tires as it turned in the street, its engine roaring as though it sensed its prey's weakness. Unwin regained control and slipped into the alley from which the car had come. Then the beast was behind him, filling the narrow passage with its noise. He pedaled faster. The car's headlights glared, turning the rain into a solid-seeming curtain. He thought he could reach the far end, but on the street beyond, the car was sure to overtake him.

He held his umbrella behind him as he emerged, and the wind tore it open. With his free hand, he yanked the handlebar to the left. The umbrella gripped the air, and the bicycle veered sharply onto the sidewalk, teetering at the gutter's edge.

The car dashed directly into the street, nearly colliding with a taxicab. Unwin did not stop to look. He was off and pedaling again, head ducked low over the handlebars, rainwater sloshing in his shoes. Then a second car, identical to the first, emerged from the cross street and halted in the intersection, blocking his escape. Unwin did not stop—he had forgotten how. He collapsed his umbrella and hefted it on his forearm, cradling it like a lance.

The driver's door opened, and Emily Doppel poked her head over the roof. "Sir!" she said.

"The trunk!" Unwin cried.

Emily got out and raised the trunk lid, then stood with arms open. Unwin hopped off, and the bicycle soared straight to his assistant, who lifted it into the air with surprising strength and dropped it into the trunk. She tossed him the keys, but he tossed them back.

"I don't know how to drive!" he said.

She got back into the driver's seat just as the other car halted beside them. Detective Screed stepped out. He spit his unlit cigarette into the street and said, "Unwin, get in the car."

"Get in the car!" Emily screamed at him.

Unwin got in beside Emily and closed the door. She threw the vehicle into gear, and his head snapped against the seat back. In the rear window, he saw Screed run a few steps after them. Then the detective stopped, bent over, and put his hands on his knees. The man with the blond beard was standing beside him, his portable typewriter in his hand.

"Where did you get this?" Unwin asked.

"From the Agency garage," she said.

"The Agency gave you a vehicle?"

"No, sir. It's yours. But under the circumstances I didn't think you'd mind."

Emily drove with the same gusto she put into her typing, her small hand moving quickly between the wheel and the gearshift. She rounded a corner so fast that Unwin nearly fell into her. Her shiny black lunch box tipped over between their seats, and its contents rattled.

How had his assistant found him? She knew he had gone to the Municipal Museum, but she could not have learned of his trip to the Forty Winks unless she spoke to Edwin Moore—or to other contacts of her own.

"I shadowed Detective Screed," she said, as though guessing his thoughts. "I knew he was up to no good when I saw him slink out of the office."

She took a winding route through the city, using tunnels and side streets Unwin had never seen. He felt the cold now, felt the dampness of his clothes against the seat. He took off his hat and squeezed the water out of it, took off his jacket and tie, squeezed those, too. The address on the card was still legible; he gave it to Emily, and she nodded.

"Did you find a phonograph?" he asked.

Emily's cheeks turned red. "I fell asleep," she said, keeping her eyes on the road.

Unwin opened the heating vents and settled back into the seat. They were headed uptown now, and through the gray drifts of rain to the north, beyond the farthest reaches of the city, he could see green hills, distant woods. Had he been there once, as a child? He seemed to remember those hills, those woods, and a game he played there with other children. It involved hiding from one another; hiding and then waiting. Hide and wait—is that what the game was called? No, it involved seeking, too. Watch and seek?

"Screed thinks you're guilty of murder," said Emily.

Unwin remembered his conversation with the detective on the twenty-ninth floor, how he had given Lamech's memo to him. Screed must have gone upstairs soon after. He probably found the corpse before the messenger did.

"What do you think?" Unwin asked.

"I think you're going to clear your name," she said. Her cheeks were still red, and there was something very much like passion in her voice. "I think you're going to solve the biggest mystery yet."

Unwin closed his eyes as the air from the vents slowly warmed him. He listened to the sound of the windshield wipers sweeping over the glass. Watch and follow? Hide and watch? Follow and seek?

Maybe he was confused. Maybe he had never played a game like that at all.

IT WAS DARK WHEN UNWIN WOKE, and his clothes were dry. Through the passenger window, he saw a low stone wall. Behind it a copse of red-leafed maple trees dripped in the light of a streetlamp. He was alone. He reached down and found his briefcase by his feet, but his umbrella was gone.

He opened the door and clambered out onto the sidewalk, jacket and tie over his arm. The air from City Park was cool and smelled of soil, of moldering things. A row of tall buildings stood opposite, the light from their windows illuminating shafts of rain over the street. Emily was gone. Had she finally seen through his facade and abandoned him?

A man in a gray overcoat emerged from the park with two small dogs on leashes. He paused when he saw Unwin, and both the dogs growled. The man seemed to approve and let them go on growling. A minute passed before he pulled them away down the block.

Unwin put on his tie, slipped into his jacket and buttoned it. He considered hailing a taxicab—not to take him to the Gilbert Hotel but to take him home. No cars moved on the block, however, and now he saw Emily, coming toward him from across the street. Her black raincoat was cinched around her waist, and she walked with one hand in her pocket. She did not look like a detective's assistant. She looked like a detective.

Without a word she handed him his umbrella, took the keys from her pocket, and opened the trunk. Together they lifted the bicycle out, and Unwin set it against the lamppost.

"Everything's set," Emily said. "There's a little restaurant in the back, but Miss Greenwood isn't in there. You'll have to go straight to her room. I've already spoken to the desk clerk. No one will stop you from going up."

Unwin looked across the street and noticed the sign over the door from which she had come. The cursive script was lit by an overhanging lamp: *The Gilbert*.

"You've done great work, Emily. I think you should take some time off now. Lie low, as they say."

Emily stood with him under his umbrella. She moved in very close and reached a hand up to his chest. He felt as he had that morning, in the office on the twenty-ninth floor—that the two were shut in together, without enough space between them. He could smell her lavender perfume. She was unbuttoning his jacket.

Unwin stepped away, but Emily held to his jacket. Then he saw why. He had put the buttons in the wrong holes, and she was fixing his mistake. She undid the rest of the buttons, then straightened the sides and refastened them.

When she was finished, she closed her eyes and tilted her head back, lifting her face toward his. "Those closest to you," she said, "those to whom you trust your innermost thoughts and musings, are also the most dangerous. If you fail to treat them as enemies, they are certain to become the worst you have. Lie if you have to, withhold what you can, and brook no intimacy which fails to advance the cause of your case."

Unwin swallowed. "That sounds familiar."

"It ought to," she said. She opened her eyes and patted his briefcase. "Don't worry, I put your book back where I found it. And I only took a peek. I think that page is especially interesting. Don't you?"

Emily closed the trunk and went around the car. He followed her with the umbrella, holding it over her head until she was inside. She rolled down her window and said, "There's something I've been wondering about, Detective Unwin. Say we do find Sivart. What will happen to you?"

"I'm not sure. This may be my only case."

"What about me, then?"

Unwin looked at his feet. He could think of nothing to say.

"That's what I thought," Emily said. She rolled up the window, and Unwin stepped aside as she pulled away from the curb. He watched the car veer down a street into the park and vanish among the trees, heard its gears shifting. When it was gone, he walked his bicycle across the street to the hotel, found an alleyway beside it, and left it chained to a fire escape.

Not until he had entered the hotel lobby and exchanged nods with the desk clerk did he realize that Emily had admitted to knowing his reason for coming here, even though he had never mentioned Miss Greenwood's name.

THE WOMAN WHO HAD introduced herself as Vera Truesdale answered her door on the second knock. She wore the same old-fashioned dress, black with lace collar and cuffs, but it was wrinkled now. Her hair was down, wavy and tousled. There were streaks of white in it that Unwin had failed to notice that morning. In the room beyond, the little lace cap lay folded on the pillow, and a black telephone was sunk in the folds of the untidy bed.

Her red-rimmed eyes were wide open. "Mr. Lamech," she said. "I didn't expect you to come in person."

"All part of the job," Unwin said.

She took his coat and hat, then closed the door behind him and went into the kitchenette. "I have some scotch, I think, and some soda water."

What had he read in the *Manual*, about poisons and their antidotes? Not enough to take any chances. "Nothing for me, thanks."

Unwin glanced around the room. An unfastened suitcase lay on a chair, and her purse was on the table beside it. In Lamech's office she had said she arrived in the city about three weeks ago—that much may have been true. But in a corner of the room, on a table of its own, was an electric phonograph. Had she brought this with her, too, or purchased it after she arrived? A number of records were stacked beside it.

She came back with a drink in her hand and pointed to one of the two windows. Both offered dismal views of the building beside the hotel, an alley's width away. "That's the one that's always open in the morning," she said, "even though I lock it at night."

The window gave out onto the fire escape. Unwin examined the latch and found it sturdy. He wondered how long he could get away with this impersonation. Miss Greenwood might already have found him out and was only playing along. He would have to take risks while he still could.

"Do you mind if I put something on the phonograph?"

"I suppose not," she said, nearly making it a question.

Unwin took the record from his briefcase and slid it out of its cover. He set the pearly disk on the turntable, switched on the machine, and lowered the needle. At first there was only static, followed by a rhythmic shushing. Then a deeper sound, a burbling that was almost a man's voice. The recording was distorted, though, and Unwin could not make out a word.

"This is horrid," she said. "Please shut it off."

Unwin leaned closer to the amplifier bell. The speechlike sound continued, stopped, started again. And then he heard it. It was the same thing he had heard on the telephone at the museum café, when he snatched the receiver from the man with the blond beard.

A rustling sound, and the warbling of pigeons.

Miss Greenwood set down her drink and came forward, nearly catching her foot on the rug. She lifted the needle from the record and gave Unwin an angry, questioning look. "I don't see what this has to do with my case," she said.

He put the record back in its sleeve and returned it to his briefcase. "That sleepiness routine disguised your limp this morning," he said.

She flinched at the mention of her injury. "I read the late edition," she said. "Edward Lamech is dead. You're no watcher."

"And you're no Vera Truesdale."

Something in her face changed then. The circles under her eyes were as dark as ever, but she did not look tired at all. She picked up her drink and sipped it. "I'll call hotel security."

"Okay," Unwin said, surprised at his own boldness. "But first I want to know why you came to Lamech's office this morning. It wasn't to hire Sivart. He went looking for you days ago."

That made her set her drink down. "Who are you?"

"Detective Charles Unwin," he said. "Edward Lamech was my watcher." He showed her his badge.

"You're a detective without a watcher," she said. "That's a unique position to be in. I want to hire you."

"It doesn't work that way. Detectives are assigned cases."

"Yes, by their watchers. And you don't have one. So I wonder what you're working on, exactly."

"I'm trying to find Detective Sivart. He went to the Municipal Museum, but you know that. Because it was you, wasn't it, who showed that museum attendant the Oldest Murdered Man's gold tooth?"

She considered this with obvious interest but did not reply. "What time is it?" she said.

He checked his watch. "Nine thirty."

"I want to show you something, Detective." She led him back to the doorway but did not open it. She pointed to the peephole and said, "Look there."

Unwin leaned in to look, then thought better of turning his back on Cleopatra Greenwood. She took a few steps away and opened her hands, as though to show that she was unarmed. "I trusted you enough to let you in, didn't I?"

He hesitated.

"Hurry," she said, almost whispering. "You'll miss it."

Unwin looked through the peephole. At first he had only a fish-eyed view of the door across the hall. Then a red-coated bellhop appeared with a covered tray in his hand. He set it on the floor in front of the opposite door, knocked twice, and went away. No one came for the food.

"Keep watching," Miss Greenwood said.

The door opened slowly, and an old man wearing a tattered frock coat peered into the hall. He had an antique service revolver in his hand and was polishing it with a square of blue cloth. He looked each way, and when he was satisfied that the hall was empty, he slid the revolver into his pocket. Then he picked up the tray and went back inside.

Miss Greenwood was grinning. "Do you know who that was?" she said.

"No," Unwin said, though the man did seem vaguely familiar. This game, whatever it was, was making him nervous.

"Colonel Baker."

"Now you're deliberately trying to rattle me," Unwin said.

"I'm trying to do good by you, Detective Unwin. You ought to realize by now that things are rather more complicated than you may have believed. Everyone knows that Colonel Baker is dead. Everyone knows that Sivart walked away victorious, case closed. Nonetheless, Colonel Baker is living across the hall from me. He orders room service every night. He likes a late dinner."

If not for the revolver, Unwin might have gone over there to prove that what Miss Greenwood had said was a lie. The Three Deaths of Colonel Baker was one of Sivart's most celebrated cases, and Unwin's file was a composition of the first order—no clerk could deny it.

Colonel Sherbrooke Baker, a decorated war hero, had become famous for the secret battlefield tactic that made him seem to be in two places at once. But in his later years, he was best known for his unparalleled collection of military memorabilia. In addition to several pieces of interest to historians of the ancient world, the collection contained numerous antique rifles and sidearms, some of which had belonged to the country's founding fathers. Others, experts agreed, were the weapons that had fired the first shots of various wars, revolutionary, civil, and otherwise. Few were allowed to study or even view these extraordinary items, however, for Colonel Baker spoke of them with pride but guarded them with something very much like jealousy.

In the colonel's will, he left all of his possessions to his son Leopold. But there was a stipulation: the colonel's precious collection was to remain in the family and remain whole.

A businessman who was not very good with business, Sivart had written of Leopold Baker. When the colonel died, his son was happy to accept the considerable sum his father had left him. He was less happy to learn that he had inherited the collection as well. All too vivid in Leopold's mind was the afternoon, as a boy of twelve, when he had interrupted his father's polishing to ask him to play a game of catch. "This," the colonel had told him, holding a long, thin blade before his eyes, "is the misericord. Medieval footmen slipped it between the plates of fallen knights' armor, once the battle was over, to find out who was dead and who was only pretending. Think of that while you sleep tonight."

The will contained no consequence for disobeying the colonel's wishes, so he was only three days in the grave when the auction commenced. Attendance was good, the hall filled with the many historians, museum curators, and military enthusiasts the colonel had spurned through the years. Once the bidding began, however, lot after lot was won by the same strange gentleman, seated at the back of the room with a black veil over his face. It was whispered through the hall that this was a representative of Enoch Hoffmann, whose taste for antiquities was by then well known. Leopold suspected it, too, but he was not displeased, for the stranger's pockets seemed bottomless.

At the end of the auction, the gentleman met with Leopold to settle their accounts. It was then that he pulled back his veil and revealed himself as Colonel Baker. The old man had not died, only faked his death to test his son's loyalty. The colonel declared his will invalid—he was very much alive after all—and reclaimed all that Leopold had thought was his.

That was when Sivart became involved. His report began: *The assignment was on my desk first thing this morning. Truth is, I'd expected it. A man plays a trick like that and word gets around. Word gets around enough, someone gets into trouble. To wit, the body of the colonel was discovered on the floor of his library early in the a.m., stab wounds eight in number. The weapon was the misericord from the colonel's own collection. The fallen pretender has been found out.*

My client? Leopold Baker, primary suspect.

It was the first time Sivart had been tasked with proving someone's innocence, and Unwin sensed that the job made him grumpy. Sivart took his time getting to the Baker estate, and his examination of the corpse was cursory.

Yes, he wrote, *dead.*

I told them to leave the body where it was and went for a walk. So many secrets in that place it gave me a headache. Through the trapdoor under the statue in the foyer, up a set of stairs behind a rack in the wine cellar, down the tunnel under the greenhouse. All this just to find a comfortable chair, probably the only one in the place.

That was in the colonel's study, which was where I found the whiskey, and also the first interesting thing about this case.

In the desk Sivart discovered the colonel's own writings about his military days. There the colonel revealed the secret behind the battlefield technique that had won him his glory. He seemed to appear in two places at once because he had a double, a brother named Reginald, whose identity was kept a secret from military command.

What almost got them caught was the matter of which hand to use when firing their weapons: Sherbrooke was left-handed and Reginald right-handed. A general noticed the discrepancy once, and Sherbrooke said, "In the trenches, sir, I am ambidextrous. In the mess hall, I use a fork." That made so little sense that it worked.

I took the whiskey with me and finished it before I could get back to the library. They'd left the body like I'd asked, though the coroner was getting prickly. I became intensely earnest with him, a tactic that usually works with men of his disposition. Is it wrong of me, clerk, to imagine sometimes that I am living in a radio play?

Detective: Here, on the victim's right hand, between his thumb and forefinger. What do you see?

Coroner: Why, those are ink stains. What of them?

(Arm thumps against floor.)

Detective: Colonel Sherbrooke Baker was left-handed. Sinister, if you will. Don't you think it strange that a left-handed man would hold a pen with his right hand?

Coroner: Well, I—

Detective: And those wounds. The angle of the thrusts. Did your examination reveal whether the killer was left- or right-handed?

(Papers leafed through.)

Coroner: Let me see. Ah. Ah! The dagger was held in the left hand!

Detective: Precisely right, because Sherbrooke Baker is the killer, not the victim. This body is that of Reginald, his brother.

(Cue the strings.)

Reginald had learned of his brother's death and came to claim his rightful share of the loot, only to find the colonel still alive. The two men had not spoken in years, and neither was happy to see the other. Their estrangement, necessitated by the deception committed in their youth, was lodged deeply. Sherbrooke had reaped the majority of the benefits from their scheme, but this did not make him generous. The misericord was one of his favorite pieces, and he had always wanted an excuse to use it.

Sivart tracked the colonel to a hideout in an old fort in City Park. *He was half mad when we found him, and his retreat was quick. We lost his trail in the woods east of the fort. Then, an hour later, we got the report about the man in military uniform standing on the bridge over the East River. He'd jumped by the time I arrived.*

The final report in the case, a few days hence, was the shortest in the series.

A jacket washed up today, though with so many medals pinned to it, it's a wonder it didn't sink to the bottom and stay there. No doubt about whose it was. The Colonel had to die three times before it would stick. Leo's name is cleared, and I'm told that he's paid the Agency in full. Not a word of thanks from him, though, and my paycheck, I see, is in the same amount as usual.

"THE BODY WAS NEVER recovered," Unwin admitted, "but no conclusion could be drawn, other than the death of Colonel Baker. The case file is seamless, every clue set down in perfect detail. . . ." He trailed off, and saw in his mind the glint of gold in the mouth of the Oldest Murdered Man. He and Sivart had been wrong once; could they have been wrong again?

Miss Greenwood was watching him.

"The Oldest Murdered Man a fake," he said. "Colonel Baker alive despite three deaths. Is that what you're telling me, Miss Greenwood? And what about Sivart's other cases? You cannot dispute his success on The Man Who Stole November Twelfth."

"I'm sorry I lied to you," she said. "I did come to the Agency for help, but I knew what sort of reception I would receive if I used my real name. Please sit with me, Detective."

Unwin disliked the way she used his title. It sounded like encouragement. Still, he followed her back into the room. She moved her suitcase off the chair for him and sat down on the edge of the bed.

"I did look for Sivart when I first arrived in town," she said. "I needed his help. But by the time I saw him, about a week ago, he was shabby and a bit out of his head. It was here, in the lobby of the hotel. He said he couldn't stay. He said he'd seen something he couldn't believe."

"The gold filling," Unwin said. "I saw it, too. And Zlatari told me Sivart was at the Forty Winks about a week ago. He was reading something." Unwin heard in his mind a warning like a typewriter bell and stopped himself. He was giving information he did not have to give.

But Miss Greenwood only shrugged. "Probably his copy of the *Manual.* He was getting desperate."

"You're familiar with *The Manual of Detection?*"

"Know thy enemy," she said.

Unwin looked at his lap. Miss Greenwood was his enemy, of course. But now that they were speaking plainly, he found himself wishing it could be otherwise. Was this how Sivart had felt, each time he got her wrong?

She said, "I went to Lamech because I thought he would know what had happened to Sivart. I was concerned. Naturally, I was surprised when I found you sitting there."

"You hid it very well."

"Old habits," she said.

The telephone rang. It gleamed black against the stark white sheet and seemed louder for the contrast.

Miss Greenwood looked suddenly tired again. "Too soon," she said.

"If you have to answer it—"

"No!" she said. "Don't you answer it either."

So they sat staring at the telephone, waiting for the ringing to stop. Miss Greenwood swayed a little and breathed deeply, as though fighting off nausea. Unwin counted eleven rings before the caller gave up.

Miss Greenwood's eyes fluttered closed, and she fell back onto the bed. The quiet of the room was total. He could not hear the move-

ments of the other hotel guests, could not hear their voices. Where was
the noise of automobile traffic? He wished idly for any sound at all, for
even a cat to call out from the alleyway.

Unwin rose from his chair and said Miss Greenwood's name, but
she did not stir. He shook her shoulder—no response.

At a time like this, he thought, Sivart would take the opportunity to
investigate. Perhaps he ought to do the same. He lifted Miss Greenwood's drink and sniffed it, but for what, he was not sure. The ice had
nearly melted—that was all he could deduce. With his foot he raised the
lid on her suitcase and saw that the clothes inside were neatly folded.

He brought the glass into the kitchenette, left it in the sink. Was
Miss Greenwood, like his assistant, the victim of some sleeping sick-
ness? Nothing of the kind had ever been mentioned in Sivart's reports.
Perhaps her exhaustion had simply overtaken her. But what could have
made her so tired?

He watched her lying on the bed—her breaths came slowly, as
though her sleep were a deep one. He wondered whether he should
cover her with the sheet or remove her shoes. Miss Greenwood had
seemed, for a moment, generous with him. He would have to wait for
her to wake up, and hope she would still be willing to talk.

He sat beside her and, without thinking, drew *The Manual of Detection* from his briefcase and opened it on his lap. He found the section
Detective Pith had recommended to him that morning at Central Terminal, on page ninety-six.

> If the detective does not maintain secrets of his own—if he does not
> learn firsthand the discipline required to keep a thing hidden from
> everyone he knows, and pay the personal costs incurred by such an
> endeavor—then he will never succeed in learning the secrets of others,
> nor does he deserve to. It is a long road that stretches from what a
> person says to what a person hides by saying it. He who has not mapped
> the way for himself will be forever lost upon it.

Unwin could picture himself on that road: a narrow avenue between tall rows of tenements, just a few lights on in each building, and all the doors locked. In both directions the road went all the way down to the horizon.

Did Unwin have any secrets of his own? Only that he was not really a detective, that he had been making unofficial trips for unofficial reasons—that he had considered, for a moment long enough to buy the ticket, abandoning everything he knew. But those secrets were liabilities. `

When he glanced from the book, he was startled to find Miss Greenwood sitting up in bed. She carefully smoothed the front of her dress with her hands.

"You're awake," he said.

She did not reply. Her eyes were open, but she did not seem to see him as she rose from the bed. She went across the room without speaking.

"Miss Greenwood," he said, getting up again. He put the *Manual* back in his briefcase.

Ignoring him, she went to the window and unlatched it. Before he could reach her, she had thrown the window open. The chill autumn air pervaded the room immediately, and rain blew in from the alley, dampening everything.

EIGHT

On Surveillance

It is the most obvious of mandates, to keep one's eyes
open, but the wakefulness required of the detective is not
of the common sort. He must see without seeming
to see, and watch even when he is looking away.

M iss Greenwood climbed out onto the fire escape and balanced
on the toes of her high-heeled shoes as she descended the pre-
cipitous steps. Unwin was about to call her name again when he remembered something he had heard about the dangers of waking a
sleepwalker. He imagined her eyes popping open, a moment of confusion, a foreshortened cry. . . .

He dreaded the thought of going back into the rain, but he gathered
his things and followed her down two flights of steps, past the dark
windows of other hotel rooms. At the bottom he found his bicycle
chained to the base of the fire escape. He did not have time to unlock
it and bring it with him—Miss Greenwood was already on her way
out of the alley. He caught up with her on the sidewalk and opened
his umbrella over both their heads.

Was this what she had in mind when she said she wanted to hire
him? On the next block he followed her past the sweeping limestone

facade of the Municipal Museum as the rain dampened the cuffs of his slacks and the wind wrestled with his umbrella. She turned right at the next corner and led them away from City Park, then headed north. On that block a man came out of an apartment building with a sack over his shoulder. He drew up alongside them, and Unwin saw he was dressed only in his bathrobe. His eyes, like Miss Greenwood's, were unreadable. From within his sack—nothing more than a pillowcase—came the ticking of clocks, maybe a hundred of them.

Other sleepers joined them as they walked, women and men of varying ages in varying states of disarray, pajamaed, underdrawered, dripping. All bore sacks of alarm clocks over their shoulders, and all seemed to know where they were going.

Unwin felt he had stumbled into the mystery he was supposed to be solving, the one to which Lamech had planned to assign him. He suddenly hated that smug, silent corpse on the thirty-sixth floor. He wanted nothing to do with this mystery, but all he could do was allow himself to be dragged along by its current.

They walked ten, twelve, fifteen blocks. At the north end of town, they came to a part of the city that did not seem to belong to the city at all. Here a broad stone wall girded a wide, hilly expanse. A pair of iron gates, two stories tall, had been left open to allow the sleeping congregation through. The sycamores lining the drive beyond dropped samaras that spun in the rain as they fell.

At the top of the hill crouched a grand, high-gabled house. Lights shone in every window, illuminating stretches of wild gardens all around. The place seemed familiar to Unwin—had Sivart described it in one of his reports? Above the door was a sign depicting a fat black cat seated with the moon at his back, a cigar in one paw and a cocktail glass in the other. Written in an arc over the moon were the words CAT & TONIC. Unwin was sure he had never heard of it.

Beneath the portico a line of sleepers awaited admittance into the club. Unwin's group joined the line, and others gathered behind them.

A butler ushered them inside, welcoming each guest with a sleepy nod.

"What is this?" Unwin asked him, collapsing his umbrella. "What's going on?"

The butler did not seem to understand the question. He blinked a few times, then squinted at Unwin as though from a great distance.

The crowd pushed forward, and Unwin was driven into the club. The entry hall was dominated by a wide staircase. Most of the guests proceeded into a room on the right. It was a gambling parlor, and attendants and players alike were sleeping. There were no chips. Instead the players pushed heaps of alarm clocks over the tables. When the house had won enough of the clocks, butlers carted them away in wheelbarrows.

Emily was here among the players, dressed in yellow pajamas. Her face looked smaller without her glasses, and the rain had turned her hair a dark copper color. She had her own sack of alarm clocks, and for the moment she seemed to be winning. She laughed aloud, revealing her small crooked teeth. Others in the room, after a delay, laughed with her. Unwin felt as though he were looking into an aquarium: everyone in it breathed the same water, but sound and sense moved slowly among them.

Emily rolled the dice, won again, and a shirtless man with thick eyebrows put his arm around her shoulder. Unwin went toward them, thinking to shake Emily awake if he had to, but Miss Greenwood was suddenly at his side, her arm linked with his. She drew him away, back into the entry hall and through a curtained doorway opposite the gaming room.

Here dozens of guests were seated at tables, some smoking, some muttering, some laughing, all of them asleep. Sleepwalking waiters went among them, bringing fresh drinks and cigars. On a tasseled stage was a quartet of washboard, jug, rubber-band bass, and accordion. Unwin recognized the accordion player. It was Arthur, the custodian he had seen that morning. He had been sleeping when Unwin and Detective Pith were with him at Central Terminal, and he was still sleeping, still dressed in his gray coveralls.

Miss Greenwood did not search for an empty seat; instead she went toward a door at the right of the stage. Guarding it were Jasper and Josiah Rook. The twins were not asleep. They stood with their hands in their pockets, scrutinizing the crowd with their trapdoor eyes. Unwin half closed his own eyes to blend in, and let go of Miss Greenwood's arm.

Jasper (or was it Josiah?) opened the door for her, and Josiah (Jasper?) greeted her by name. They went with her through the door and closed it behind them.

Unwin wandered back to the tables. The guests went on with their dream-party, and he was invisible to them. He looked for an empty seat, thinking he should conceal himself in case the Rooks returned.

Then he saw her. The woman in the plaid coat was seated alone at a table in the center of the room. Beneath her coat she wore a blue nightgown. She tapped her glass of milk and stared toward the stage with glassy gray eyes.

What was she doing here? First she had taken his place on the fourteenth floor, and now she was ensnared by whatever madness had claimed Emily and Miss Greenwood. Could it be that the fault was Unwin's, that his unofficial trips had embroiled her in this dilemma of his? Detective Pith must have seen him watching her at Central Terminal, must have thought she was a secret contact. Perhaps the Agency had hired her to keep her close, promoted him to keep him closer.

Unwin went toward her, thinking that he had to explain, had to apologize for all the trouble. Assure her that everything would be set right again, as soon as he found Sivart. He stood to her side and took off his hat. "Are you waiting for someone?" he asked.

She perked one ear, though she did not look at him. "Someone," she said.

"Of course. I can't imagine you'd be here alone."

"Alone," she echoed.

Unwin checked his watch. It was nearly two o'clock. On a normal day, in only a matter of hours, he would be at Central Terminal. She would be there, too, and he would watch her and say nothing.

"I still remember the first day I saw you," he told her. "I got out of bed and took a bath, ate oatmeal with raisins. I put my shoes on in the hallway because they squeak if I wear them in the house and that bothers the neighbors. I don't blame them, really."

He could not tell if she understood what he was saying, but she did seem to hear. So he sat with her and laid his umbrella on his lap. "I ride my bicycle to work," he said. "I've perfected a technique to keep my umbrella open while riding. The weather . . . well, you know how it is. Sometimes I think it will never stop. The rain will fill up the bay, and one day the city will be gone, just like that. The sea will take it."

He looked around; no one was listening. He was the only person awake, but he might as well have been alone and dreaming. He wanted, suddenly, to tell her everything.

"That morning," he said, "the morning I first saw you. Something was different. No one was on the streets. At first I couldn't understand why. Then I realized that I hadn't turned off my alarm clock. I hadn't needed to. I'd woken hours before it was set to ring, hours before I should have been awake. The day hadn't started yet, and there I was, ready for work.

"I didn't know what to do with myself. I'd already made it halfway to the office by the time I figured out what had happened. I was standing outside Central Terminal. I've never had to take the train anywhere, because I've lived in this city my entire life. But suddenly I knew I could never go to work again. I really don't know why."

"Why," said the woman in the plaid coat.

"Well, because Enoch Hoffmann was gone," Unwin said. "The

Rook brothers, Cleopatra Greenwood, they'd all left. Sivart's reports were—only reports. I could tell he didn't care about the work anymore. What was the point?"

"The point."

"Yes, I'm coming to it. I went into the terminal. I bought a cup of coffee and drank most of it. It was awful. I took a schedule of trains from the information booth, and I even bought a ticket. I was going to go into the country, and I was never coming back. Sivart had imagined his cottage in the woods—why shouldn't I have mine? By then it was twenty-six minutes after seven in the morning. That's when I saw you. You came through the revolving doors at the east end of the terminal, and you went to Gate Fourteen and waited. I watched you. I pretended to look at my train schedule, but all I could do was watch you. And when the train arrived, and no one came to meet you, and you turned around and went back into the city, I knew—just as certainly as I had known a moment before that I could never go back to work—that I *would* go back to work, that I could not leave the city. Not while you were in it, left alone to wait."

"Wait," said the woman in the plaid coat.

"I will," Unwin said. "I have a bicycle that I clean and oil every day, and I have a hat that I'll never part with. My umbrella does everything it's supposed to do. I have a train ticket, and I keep it in my pocket, just in case that person you're waiting for ever gets back. But what am I supposed to do in the meantime? I still don't know your name."

The woman in the plaid coat was applauding—all the guests were. Unwin turned to look at the stage. Miss Greenwood had joined the musicians. She went to the microphone, and the music struck up, slow and somber. Arthur leaned into his accordion as he played, and in his hands it breathed like a living thing. The words Miss Greenwood sang were unfamiliar to Unwin, except for the refrain, which he knew from somewhere. Maybe he had heard it on the radio. Yes, it might have been the song that was playing in Zlatari's kitchen, behind the curtain in the Forty Winks.

> *Still I hear that old song*
> *And I'm sure I belong*
> *In my dream of your dream of me.*

Applause rose up again, and several guests threw long-stemmed roses onto the stage. She caught a few of the flowers and let the others fall at her feet. Unwin clapped, too.

"Mr. Charles Unwin?"

He turned in his seat. Detective Pith, very much awake and still in his herringbone suit, stood at his shoulder. "You," growled Pith. "Outside. Now."

Unwin rose from his chair and followed the detective from the room. They went outside and stood under the portico, where a few sleepwalkers were quietly puffing on cigars and mumbling insensibly to one another. Pith swung his hat as though he were going to hit him. "Damn it, Unwin, are you trying to get us both killed? What are you doing here? You came with Greenwood, didn't you? This is no good, Unwin, no good at all. Screed's trying to pin a murder on you, and now you're hanging around with Greenwood."

"I'm trying to find Sivart," Unwin said. "I thought she might know where he went."

"The Agency's through with the guy. If word gets out that you're looking for him, it could bother people high up, and I mean very high up. People you don't want to bother."

Unwin fiddled with his umbrella; he could not get the clasp buttoned.

"Now, I didn't expect to see you out in the field yet. That takes guts, Unwin, I'll give you that. But it doesn't take brains. You should have spent a day or two with your copy of the *Manual.* Have you read a word of it yet? If you want my advice, you'll get out of here and forget about the Cat & Tonic, forget about Cleo Greenwood. Talking the way you were in there! Do you know how long it took to set up this sting?"

The door burst open, and the Rook brothers stepped outside. Unwin immediately closed his eyes, then opened them enough to see what was happening. Pith was doing the same. But Jasper and Josiah went straight to him.

"My brother," Jasper said to Detective Pith, "has advised me to advise you to quit the somnambulism act."

Pith opened his eyes, and Unwin sidled over to where the others were smoking cigars. A sleepwalker offered him one, and he took it.

"Good evening, gents," said Pith. "I thought I was having a bad dream. Looks like I'm having two at once."

Jasper pointed toward the sycamores, and Pith started walking. They went two dozen paces from the house, and then Jasper told him to stop. Pith looked directly at Unwin and said loudly enough for him to hear, "You're done for, you louts. We have our best people working on this. Our very best."

Josiah drew a pistol from his coat, and Detective Pith took off his hat and held it over his heart. Josiah put the gun against the hat and fired once. Pith fell face-up in the rain.

AT THE SOUND OF THE SHOT, the cigar smokers started walking in circles and muttering but did not wake. The Rooks carried Pith's body to where their steam truck was parked. The bed was loaded with ticking clocks, and the alarm bells clinked sullenly under Pith's weight.

The Rooks had Edwin Moore, too. He was still in his gray museum attendant's uniform and lay beside Pith, bound at the wrists and ankles. The old man was unconscious and shivering. How long had they kept him out in the rain?

The Rooks were coming back up the drive now. Unwin ran inside.

A crowd of sleepwalkers was streaming through the curtained door, troubled and confused by the sound of the gunshot. He pushed through them and climbed the stairs, looking for a place to hide. He opened the first door he saw and went through it.

The room was wallpapered in a dark red pattern. A fire burned in the hearth, crackling and warm. On the back wall was hung an array of antique weapons, swords and sidearms rivaling the collection at the Municipal Museum. Now he understood why he had recognized this place. It was the mansion that had once belonged to Colonel Sherbrooke Baker, and this the very room where he had murdered his brother. Here was the precious hoard, complete and perfectly maintained. Had his son Leopold kept it through the years?

No: one object did not belong with the Baker estate. In a glass case on its own table, small and shriveled and yellow, lay the Oldest Murdered Man, the real one. Unwin had stumbled upon the trophy room of Enoch Hoffmann.

Two wingback chairs were angled toward the hearth. In one of them sat a short man in blue pajamas with red trim. He turned his squarish face toward Unwin and with lidded eyes seemed to see. He held a brandy snifter in one hand and gestured for Unwin to sit, then poured a second glass and set it on the pedestal table.

What a fool Unwin had been, mourning for all those years the disappearance of the nefarious biloquist. No report could be worth this encounter.

Hoffmann offered him a cigar cutter, and Unwin realized he was still holding the cigar the sleepwalker had given him outside. He set it down on the table. "Mr. Hoffmann," he said, "I really don't want to be your rival."

Hoffmann chuckled to himself, or maybe snored. He picked up a cigar and clipped it.

"I don't want to know if you killed Edward Lamech," Unwin went on. "Or whose body is in the museum, or what you want with Edwin

Moore. I don't even want to know what you're planning to do with all those alarm clocks. I just want to find Detective Sivart so I can have my old job back."

Hoffmann shrugged. He lit the cigar and puffed at it. Then he raised his glass as though in toast and waited until Unwin raised his own. The glasses met, and they drank. The brandy was hot on Unwin's lips.

"If you can't tell me where he is," Unwin said, "then maybe you can tell me something about one of your guests. She always wears a plaid coat."

Hoffmann leapt out of his chair and threw his brandy snifter into the fire. The glass exploded, and the flames burst from the hearth. Then Hoffmann leaned against the mantelpiece, head cradled in his arms, shoulders heaving.

Unwin rose and went to him. He wanted to stop himself but found he could not. He put one hand on the magician's shoulder. Hoffmann spun and glared at him with unopen eyes.

The brandy was still burning its way toward Unwin's stomach. "Please," he said, and what he wanted to say was, *Please, don't wake up,* but the words were stuck in his throat and the brandy erased them. Unwin stumbled backward, and the fire leapt again, and the music of accordion and rubber band swelled from below.

Gagging on brandy and smoke, Unwin fled from the room, following the music.

Downstairs everyone was dressed so well. He loosened his collar and took a few deep breaths, feeling his pulse slow. He was glad he had finally joined the party. Emily Doppel came from the gaming room, and the man who accompanied her was no longer shirtless; in fact, he wore a double-breasted suit of a very fine cut. When she saw Unwin, she pushed her escort away and came up to him. "What do you think of the dress?" she asked.

It was black, cut low in the front, and reached nearly to the floor. It was, Unwin meant to say, very flattering. The words failed him, but she smiled, took his hand, and led him to the dance floor. He still had his umbrella, so he hooked it over his wrist while they waltzed.

Emily laughed at him. "Admit it," she said. "You need me. You wouldn't be able to do any of this without me. You don't have to lie, Detective Unwin. You can trust me with your innermost thoughts and musings." She laughed again and added, "I'm a trustworthy gal!"

"I wouldn't lie to you," Unwin lied.

"I'm so glad we can finally say these things. It's different here, don't you think? Different from the office? And the car?" She was leading him in the dance, and he was thankful for it, because he was no better at dancing than he was at driving.

"Do you come here often?" he asked.

She looked around. "I'm really not sure."

"We're dreaming," he said. "I wasn't before, but now I am. We both are."

"You're sweet," Emily said. "Listen. Why don't you tell me why you're so interested in Cleopatra Greenwood? What's she got that's so special? Is she in on it, do you think? How do you know I'm not in on it? Don't ignore me, Detective Unwin."

He had caught sight of the woman in the plaid coat, still alone at her table. Unlike everyone else in the room, she wore the same clothes as before: a plain blue nightgown, blue slippers. Unwin noticed these kinds of things. He was a meticulous dreamer. "Excuse me," he said to Emily, and walked off the dance floor.

"Hey!" his assistant called after him.

He went up to the woman in the plaid coat. She was sitting with her legs crossed, watching the dancers. Her eyes were open now, gray and cool. They took Unwin in as he approached, and he struggled to keep balanced. It felt as though he were walking on sand while waves crashed about his legs.

"I don't remember inviting you," said the woman in the plaid coat.

"Isn't this Hoffmann's party?"

She sipped her milk. "Is that what he told you?"

The woman in the plaid coat seemed to know more than he knew. The revelation left him feeling helpless and strangely betrayed. "I thought I'd dragged you into something dangerous," he said, steadying himself with his umbrella. "But it's the other way around, isn't it? Who are you?"

She was starting to look annoyed with him. "It's too soon for us to speak," she said. "You haven't finished your report."

"My report?"

She sighed and looked at one of her slippered feet. "I am your clerk, you know."

The music had climbed to a new pitch, and the dancers swerved wildly over the floor. Arthur, the accordionist, bellowed while he played. Unwin turned to see the bassist's rubber band snap and fly across the room—with that, the set was over.

When he looked back, the woman in the plaid coat was gone. The party was ending, everyone was saying goodbye. What had happened to Emily? He had been rude to leave her on the dance floor alone.

Miss Greenwood found him and took his arm. "A few of us are headed back to my place," she said.

The butler nodded to them as they went out the door, and a dozen people congratulated Miss Greenwood on her performance. The man in the double-breasted suit was among them, but Emily was not. They went down among the sycamores together, and a bald man in a tuxedo grabbed a handful of fallen samaras and threw them into the air. They spun down around their heads, and he shouted, "Crazy little propellers!"

They returned to the Gilbert Hotel and climbed the fire escape to Miss Greenwood's room. The man in the tuxedo popped open a bottle of champagne, and they drank. Miss Greenwood laughed and dropped long-stemmed roses everywhere. Then the man in the tuxedo and the man in the double-breasted suit started fighting about which of them had given Miss Greenwood more flowers. After the first sloppy punches were thrown, she kicked them both out.

"I'm going to forget all of this," she said to Unwin. "He uses me, uses my voice, but keeps me in the dark. So you'll have to remember for both of us. That's why I hired you. To remember."

Unwin left. It was cold outside, and the walk was a long one. He could not tell if he was awake or asleep now—shadows fell at the wrong angles, and the streets curved where they should have been straight. The cold was real enough, however. His hand was a ball of ice around the handle of his umbrella. At last he found the narrow green door of his own apartment building and went upstairs.

A trail of red and orange leaves led from the door all the way into the bathroom.

Detective Sivart was in the tub. The water looked cold and was covered with leaves: a dark little pond. "This channel's closed to us now, Charlie. That woman, I was wrong about her. She broke my heart. Look." He pulled a torn leaf out of the water and slapped it onto his chest. It stuck fast.

When Unwin woke, he was on his bed, still wearing his clothes. His head throbbed, his alarm clock was missing, and someone was in the kitchen, making breakfast.

NINE

On Documentation

It is not enough to say that you have had a hunch.
Once written down, most such inklings reveal
themselves for what they are: something to be
tossed into a wishing well, not into a file.

The theft of November twelfth: who can think upon that black patch of the mind, lingering where a memory might be, and not feel cold, lost to it? It seeps like ink along the grooves of the fingertips. Who has not tried to scrub it away?

I was like the rest of you, Sivart wrote in his report. *Hoodwinked. Taken in. But then I had a hunch that morning, over breakfast. So what if hunches are against policy? I had one, clerk, and I acted on it. Lucky thing, too—for all of us.*

No one hired the Agency to solve the crime, because no one knew that it had been committed. Unwin went to sleep on Monday, November eleventh, and woke up on Wednesday, November thirteenth. He rode his bicycle the seven blocks to the Agency offices. He had been a faithful employee for eleven years, four months, and some-odd days, and it had never occurred to him, at this point in his career, to make unofficial trips for unofficial reasons.

On the fourteenth floor, the messengers brought no new assignment for him, so he passed the morning putting the finishing touches on a case from the previous week. It still needed a title. Unwin liked titles, even though the Agency filing system did not require them. Each case was numbered, and only the numbers were used in the official logs. Still, naming cases was a small and harmless pleasure, and occasionally useful, too. If a fellow clerk had a question about one case or another, using the name could save them both time.

Unwin was still pondering the possibilities over lunch. He had brought a sandwich with him in his briefcase. It was turkey and cheese on rye, his Wednesday sandwich. No better way to pass a Wednesday, he thought, than pondering titles over turkey and cheese on rye.

Nothing about this case had made it into the papers, so the clerks at neighboring desks had their eyes on Unwin's work whenever they thought he was not paying attention. He was always paying attention, though. Only when the file was completed, and for Unwin that meant titled, would his colleagues become privy to its contents.

As he finished his lunch, he became aware of an unusual number of telephone conversations taking place on the floor. Most of the other clerks were hunched over mouthpieces, mumbling. He sensed in their voices a mixture of fear and incredulity.

Were the families and friends of his colleagues calling to find out about his case? This was unprecedented. Unwin crushed his lunch bag and dropped it into the wastepaper basket. He knew by then what he was going to call the file—The Episode of the Facing Mirrors, after the case's most significant clue—but this show of discourtesy convinced him to delay the final processing for at least another hour.

More telephone calls came in while Unwin sorted papers and vetted old notes. Those who received the calls began to confer with one another, leaning over the aisles to whisper. If he had been deep in a case, Unwin would have found this immensely distracting.

The noise reached a crescendo when Lorraine, one of the most recent hires on the floor, slammed her receiver onto its cradle, flung back her head, and emitted a long, thin wail. As though in response, other clerks knocked stacks of pages off their own desks, rattled drawers, slammed typewriter keys, or went to the windows for air. Unwin, appalled and bewildered, threw himself over his files to protect them.

What had happened?

The overclerk's door opened, and Mr. Duden materialized for the first time that week. He jogged between the desks toward the center of the room, clutching his hair. "Stop!" he cried.

Unwin could see in the overclerk's eyes the same panic that had seized the others. Mr. Duden had not come to calm them; he had come to join them. "Stop everything you're doing!" he cried. "Everything is wrong! It isn't Wednesday, it's Tuesday!"

Unwin clutched his files more tightly. Mr. Duden was right—it *was* Tuesday, only two days since Unwin had woken to the ringing of the city's church bells. Yesterday's lunch had been cucumber and horseradish: his Monday sandwich.

He counted the number of times he had written the date since arriving that morning. *November thirteenth:* it was everywhere, in his notes, in memoranda, entries of at least four indices, the master log, the ancillary log, in the final sections of The Episode of the Facing Mirrors. He tried to multiply in his mind the number of errors he alone had committed by the number of people on the floor, and that by the number of floors in the Agency office building, but his calculative powers failed him. It would take weeks to undo the damage, and traces of the calamity were sure to abide indefinitely.

The story trickled in over the course of the afternoon, and the clerks gathered in circles at one desk or another, sharing new tidbits of information. Calls came in from people out of town who had noticed the discrepancy—Wednesday in the city and Tuesday everywhere else. There was chaos in the harbor: ships held in port or turned away by bewildered customs officials, goods piled on the wharf with no one to accept them, longshoremen brawling with sailors, radio officers trading insults on every frequency. Traffic on the major bridges halted as delivery trucks choked both lanes and drivers left their vehicles to huddle confused and indignant amid the mayhem. Appointment desks at beauty salons, employment bureaus, doctors' offices, and the courts were overwhelmed. At the schools children wept over examinations for which they had not studied.

Unwin remained in his own seat, trying not to listen to this news, working instead to list the corrections he would have to make. (He lost the list by the end of the day and would have to start over the next morning.)

That Hoffmann was responsible came as no surprise to anyone on the fourteenth floor, though it added to Unwin's dread the weight of impending responsibility. Evidently, the magician's criminal network extended well beyond the rickety sprawl of the Travels-No-More Carnival. His agents had somehow infiltrated all the major newspaper offices, radio stations, and civic departments, just to set the calendars ahead one day. But that did not explain how an additional *X* appeared on wall calendars in homes throughout the city. The biloquist might imitate any one of us, Unwin thought, but surely we are not all working for him.

Though the effects of the disruption were pervasive, it was at the Central Bank that the true purpose of Hoffmann's gambit was discovered. There a convoy of armored cars with a cargo of gold was slated to arrive midmorning. But because it was expected on Tuesday, and not Wednesday, no members of the bank staff were there to greet them. Hoffmann's own agents, dressed for the part, were ready to fill in. The gold went from one set of cars to another and would have left in them had Sivart not intervened.

It was all in the early edition the next day, the second issue of the city paper to bear the date of Wednesday, November thirteenth. Unwin skimmed the article in the elevator and went quickly to his desk. He had come to the office early and was the first to arrive on the fourteenth floor, except for Mr. Duden, who peeked through his office door and nodded gratefully. From the circles beneath the overclerk's eyes, Unwin guessed he had stayed through the night.

Sivart's report was already on Unwin's desk. It was improbably thin and, according to the cover page, the first and last in the series.

I don't think I really have to file a report on this one, Sivart began, *because I wasn't working on the Agency's dime. Call it a sick day if you like. Still, I'll give you a few of the details, and you can do what you want with them.*

There was little in the report that had not already appeared in the papers. Sivart said he had no idea how Hoffmann managed the trick; furthermore, he did not intend to find out. Unwin was dizzied by the implication—to file a case with no true solution!—but he read on.

Sivart, acting on that hunch of his, had alerted several other detectives from his floor and called them all down to the parking lot behind Central Bank. They staked out the place and waited for an hour. Hoffmann's agents arrived, not in their usual carnival remainders but driving a column of black trucks and dressed as bank staff. Sivart paid attention to one of them in particular.

The limp, he wrote, *was familiar.*

I had my men circle the place, just to be safe. Then I shimmied up to the lead vehicle and opened the door. The driver was picking his teeth in the mirror. I hit him as hard as was necessary and rolled him under the cab. Then I took his place and waited.

They were quick about their work. They had rehearsed. The one in charge got in beside me and let the hair out of her hat. "Okay," she said, "that's all of it."

"Not by a long shot," I said.

Greenwood wasn't happy to see me. And I saw a look on her face, one I'd never seen there before. I think it was surprise, but we might need a new name for it, just because it was hers.

"That's a lot of gold, honey. What's your cut?"

"I'll show you," she said, but I was ready for the dagger and got hold of the wrist on the other side of it.

I told her about my friends outside. I told her the game was up, goose cooked, et cetera. Eventually she came around, though neither of us was feeling good about it.

Listen, clerk. I wasn't on the job. Nobody assigned me to this case. What I did next I did as a citizen of this unfair land. I think I broke a law or two. If someone wants to come and arrest me for it, fine. I'm too tired to care.

I said, "We're going to round up your helpers, here, and we're going to bring the shiny stuff inside. But you, lady, you're going to leave. I don't ever want to see you in this town again."

"After this," she said, "you won't be the only one."

I left with her and let the others clean up. They're a decent bunch of yahoos, and none of them tried to stop me. I walked her to Central Terminal. We had pretzels on the way, just like old times, except we didn't have any old times, so we had to make them up. The whole town had gone mad, but the trains were still running. I paid for her ticket, one way, and we stood together awhile down on the platform. I won't tell you what we talked about. I won't tell you what happened just before I put her on the train. What business is it of yours, what we said?

I watched the train until the tunnel ate it.

Now I'm in my office. It's dark in here, and I'm choking on my own smoke. I'm starting to wonder about early retirement. I was wrong about her, clerk. As per usual. All wrong.

Unwin scoured the report again, searching for some better explanation. How did Sivart know what had happened that morning, when everyone else was fooled? The best explanation he could find, and the only conclusion the file would ever have, was Sivart's assertion that he had simply *remembered*.

UNWIN'S UMBRELLA WAS FOLDED on the bed beside him, droplets of water clinging to the black fabric. The bed was made, though the blankets were soggy and rumpled, as were his clothes. His briefcase was on the floor by the bed. From the kitchen came the sound of the icebox door clinking open and closed. A woman was humming to herself, and Unwin recognized the tune from Miss Greenwood's performance the night before.

It hurt too much to move his head, so he raised his wristwatch to his eyes. Six thirty-two—still early. But early for what? For work? They would apprehend him as soon as he brought his bicycle through the lobby door. For coffee at Central Terminal? They could be waiting for him anywhere: in line at the breakfast cart, next to the information booth, beneath the arch of Gate Fourteen. Even the woman in the plaid coat, it seemed, was in on it.

Then he remembered Edwin Moore, remembered how he had looked in the back of the steam truck, shivering among all those alarm clocks. *They will find me,* Moore had told him in the museum storeroom, and he was right—they had found him. Would the Rooks murder him, as they murdered Detective Pith?

"Breakfast is ready," Emily called from the kitchen.

He sat up slowly. What was his assistant doing in his apartment? The sleep drained out of his head and pooled sickeningly in his stomach. He peeled the damp socks off his feet and dropped them onto the floor next to his shoes. He would have to find Edwin Moore, and quickly.

He rose shakily and went to the kitchen. Buttered toast was piled at the center of the table, and a pair of eggs, sunny side up, were set on a plate for him. Emily was swirling more butter over the hot surface of a skillet. It had been a late night for her, but she appeared rested, dressed now in a gray skirt and pinstripe blouse. The pencils in her hair were freshly sharpened.

"I hope you don't mind that I let myself in," she said. "I found the spare key in your desk yesterday. And since I couldn't go back to the office, I came right here. I figured you'd want to start on your case first thing."

"You stole my spare key?"

" 'Stole' is unfair," she said. She selected an egg from the open carton, cracked its shell, and spilled it into the skillet, all with one hand.

"Emily, we don't have time for breakfast. One of my . . . primary contacts. He's been kidnapped."

"Kidnapped? Who is he?"

Unwin wondered whether her question was genuine. Emily always seemed to know more than she let on. Still, she had only helped him thus far, so he would have to trust her for now. "He's a museum attendant. He—"

"Eat while you talk, Detective. I won't consider it rude."

It was more a command than a suggestion. Unwin helped himself to his plate from the table, took some toast, and ate standing up. He was hungrier than he thought, and the eggs were perfect, the whites cooked through but the yolks still runny. "His name's Edwin Moore," he said between bites. "He told me he used to work for the Agency."

She thought that over for a moment. "He could be valuable, then— if he's telling the truth. Where is he?"

"The Rook brothers took him."

She stood still, running the tip of her tongue along her crooked teeth. Then she sprinkled pepper over the eggs in the pan. "Nobody's seen the Rooks since Hoffmann went into hiding," she said.

"Emily, do you remember anything about last night? About the Cat & Tonic?"

He saw a twitch at the corner of her eye, magnified by her glasses. Some part of her knew what he was talking about, but she said, "I went

straight home after I dropped you off at the Gilbert. I worked on a
crossword puzzle and went to sleep. Cat, tonic. It *sounds* familiar. Did
you do the same puzzle? I think maybe 'cat' was one of the answers,
and so was 'tonic.' They might have shared their letter *t*. I'm not sure,
though. I don't remember what the clues were."

She would not remember their dance, then, or anything else she
had seen.

Unwin sat down. "Enoch Hoffmann's back," he told her. "The
Rooks are working for him again, and they're up to something. Something big, I think. If we're ever going to find Sivart, we'll have to figure
out what he was investigating when he disappeared."

She was quiet a moment. Then she flipped her eggs onto a plate and
said, "In that case, you'll have to go to the Travels-No-More."

Unwin knew she was right. The Rooks had always operated out of
the carnival—they arrived in the city with it thirteen years before. They
would not have taken Moore to the Forty Winks: too many questions
to answer there. But in the lightless center of Caligari's, they could carry
on with their plans undisturbed.

Emily brought her plate to the table and sat down, then unfolded a
napkin on her lap. "I just hope he's worth it," she said.

THEY WALKED TOGETHER UNDER Unwin's umbrella. Neither of
them had seen the morning papers yet, but they knew that Unwin's
photograph would likely have made front page by now. They kept to
the alleyways and side streets, and Emily went ahead to peer around
the corners. She took his hand, pulling him along while he kept the
umbrella low over his face.

"Aren't we going the wrong way?" he asked.

"I think the closest entry point is a block north of here."

He knew better than to ask what she meant, and besides, Emily was
doing a good job of keeping them out of sight. They passed no one on

the sidewalks, and no vehicles moved on the streets. Still, Unwin felt they were being watched. He tried to remind himself that Sivart considered that a good thing. *Means I'm doing my job,* he often wrote.

She waved him into a subway station and produced a pair of tokens from her skirt pocket. As she passed through the turnstile, she raised her lunch box in the air. Unwin did the same with his umbrella. He had left his briefcase in his apartment: safer there than with him.

When the train arrived, Emily ushered him into an empty car. He moved to take a seat, but she grabbed his arm and pulled him over to a door on the opposite side. With a swift movement, she snatched the umbrella out of his hand and wedged it between the doors, forcing them open. Then she gave the umbrella back and led him onto the platform beyond. They went along the narrow walkway to a gate at its end—the entrance, Unwin thought, to a place only the city's transit workers could ever need to access. Emily lifted the padlock in her hand. "I know a few of the codes," she said, and added bashfully, "in case of emergencies."

She turned the dial a few times, and the lock popped open. Once they were in, she closed the gate and reached through the bars to lock it again. The air was cold and musty here, and Unwin could hear a low electrical hum. They took a flight of stairs downward, switching back at a landing, moving slowly until their eyes adjusted to the dimness of the place.

They had come to a second subway platform below the first. Water dripped from leaky pipes in the ceiling and formed grimy puddles amid bits of trash. Emily took only a few steps before turning to face the tracks. She grabbed hold of his left arm, lifting it to bring his wristwatch close to her face. The scent of her lavender perfume nearly blocked out the stench of the place.

"The eight train always arrives on time," she said.

"You mean the A train?"

Emily pursed her lips, then said, "I mean the *eight* train. I suppose they didn't cover that in your orientation. It's an old line, decommissioned by the city years ago. The Agency made arrangements. Only detectives are allowed to ride it."

He nodded as though to say that yes, of course, he remembered all that now.

"Not even assistants are permitted on board," she went on. "Really, we're not even supposed to know about it."

Unwin refrained from asking the obvious question.

The rails began to warble, and then the light of the approaching train appeared in the tunnel. Unlike the station, the train itself looked clean and well maintained. It glided into place alongside the platform, and the doors hissed open. Unwin got on, then turned to face his assistant.

"They say every detective has a dagger-sharp understanding of the human mind," she said to him. "Do you have a dagger-sharp understanding of the human mind, Detective Unwin? Can you tell me what I have in my lunch box?"

He had tested her; now she was testing him. Unwin wondered whether some part of *The Manual of Detection* might have prepared him for a question like this. Looking at the lunch box, he could not even tell if it was a detail or a clue. Finally he made his guess. "Your lunch?"

The doors closed. Through the window, behind her thick glasses, Emily's eyes were unreadable. She stood unmoving at the platform's edge as the train left the station.

He was the only passenger in the car—maybe the only passenger in the train. He took a seat and watched the tunnel walls slide past the windows.

It was seven o'clock now, and on a normal day he would already be on his way to Central Terminal. He thought of the woman in the plaid coat. Had she gone to wait at Gate Fourteen as usual? What if the person she was waiting for chose this day to arrive? Unwin would never see her there again, never know what happened. Who was she, to have taken his job on the fourteenth floor? To have sipped milk at the Cat & Tonic? Enoch Hoffmann was enraged at the mention of her. Did they know each other?

The train screeched as it rounded a bend. Unwin saw abandoned stations go by—not real places anymore, just forgotten hollows, decaying in the dark under the city. The train halted at one of them and opened its doors. It was not his stop.

All this was happening, he imagined, not because Sivart was gone, or because Lamech promoted him, or because Hoffmann was stealing the city's alarm clocks. It was happening because the woman in the plaid coat had dropped her umbrella and he failed to pick it up. If he *had* picked it up, she would have spoken to him. They might have left the terminal together, before Detective Pith could find him. They might have walked side by side and talked, he pushing his bicycle along the sidewalk.

His bicycle! It was still chained to the fire escape outside the Gilbert Hotel. Its chain would rust badly in this weather.

The door at the back of the car opened, and a gray, coveralled figure shuffled in, pushing a wheeled bucket in front of him. It was Arthur, the custodian. The man seemed to be everywhere—first in Central Terminal, then on the stage of the Cat & Tonic, and now in the subway. The train rounded another bend, and he stumbled. Unwin rose to offer assistance, but Arthur hopped to keep his balance, then resumed his advance.

The custodian's eyes were closed; he was still snoring. Yet he came toward Unwin as though with conscious design, squeezing the handle of the mop with his big hands, his knuckles white with the effort. They were very clean, those hands, and his fingernails were wide and flat.

The lights went out, and the darkness was total. Unwin could hear the creaking of the bucket's wheels draw closer. When the lights came back on, Arthur was only a few paces away, his teeth clenched behind parted lips.

Unwin backed away and knocked into a pole, nearly falling, then spun himself around to the other side of it. What did Arthur want with him? He blamed Unwin for Samuel Pith's death, perhaps; or worse, he was in league with those who had murdered the detective. Unwin fled, but this was the lead car—he had nowhere to go. The window at the front offered a view onto the tunnel, tracks gleaming in the train's single headlight.

Arthur drew closer, his face set in a rictus. Unwin could not make out the words he was muttering, but they sounded disagreeable at best. He pounded a fist against the door to the motorman's compartment. The only reply was the static from a two-way radio, and he thought he heard in it those familiar sounds—the rustling of paper, the cooing of pigeons.

The train slowed as it entered another station. Unwin brandished his umbrella in front of him as he circled the custodian and went to the door. For a moment he could see into Arthur's bucket. It was full of red and orange leaves.

When the train stopped, he ran along the platform toward the exit. The walls of the station were decorated with a tile mosaic depicting carousels and tents with pennants at their peaks. This was the stop he wanted. At a row of broken turnstiles, he paused to look back.

The train was leaving the station. The custodian had not followed.

TEN

On Infiltration

**The hideout, the safe house, the base of operations:
you may assume that your enemy has one, but not
that it is to your advantage to find it.**

An enormous plaster clown stood bowlegged at the entrance of the
Travels-No-More Carnival. The colors of its face and suit were
chipped and faded to shades of brown and purple, and the arch of its
legs were the gates through which visitors were compelled to pass. The
clown's smile was welcoming, but in a hungry sort of way.

Beyond was the flooded labyrinth of the Travels-No-More. Planks
of wood lay over wide pools of muddy water between the remaining
attractions—though "attractions" was hardly the word. Great machines
that had once swayed and wheeled and swerved now lay rusting, their
broken arms sprawled amid collapsed tents and decrepit booths. The
place was full of lost things, and Edwin Moore was one of them now.
Looking at it, Unwin felt lost himself. He knew he could not leave the
old clerk to this place.

He had gone no more than a few steps beyond the gate when the window of a nearby booth shot open. A man with a cigarette clenched in his teeth peered at him through a cloud of yellow smoke. He had a thick white mustache, stringy shoulder-length hair, and he wore an oilskin duster buttoned tight at his throat. From out of the collar, angular black tattoos like the roots of an overturned tree spread up his leathery neck to his jawline.

"Tickets," he said.

Unwin approached the booth, and the man folded his hands in front of him. The same tattoos extended from under his sleeves and down to his knuckles.

"How much?" Unwin asked him.

"Exactly," he said.

"Exactly what?"

"It'll cost you."

"Yes, but how much?"

"That's right," the man said, disclosing a yellow grin.

Unwin felt he had gotten himself into some kind of trouble, but he could not tell what kind.

The man was puffing at his cigarette, saying nothing. Then he squinted and looked past Unwin toward the entrance.

Someone else was walking under the legs of the enormous clown. She held a newspaper over her head as she limped toward them through the rain. It was Miss Greenwood, wrapped in a red raincoat. She insinuated herself beneath Unwin's umbrella and tossed aside the sopping newspaper. She looked more tired than ever—the revelries of the night before had deepened her exhaustion.

The man in the booth unbuttoned the front of his jacket. He had on a shoulder belt of worn leather, lined by a dozen or more gleaming daggers. He removed one and held it lightly by the blade end. Unwin checked its appearance against his memory of the Agency's index of weapons: small, slim, with a pommel weighted for balance. It was a throwing knife.

"Mr. Brock," Miss Greenwood said, "surely you're not troubling anyone for tickets on a day like this."

Unwin recognized the name from Sivart's reports. This was Theodore Brock, who had arrived in the city as Caligari's knife thrower and remained in it as one of Hoffmann's lieutenants. It was his stray throw, all those years ago, that had left Cleo with her limp. He spit his cigarette at their feet and said, "Well, if it isn't the enchantress Cleopatra Greenwood, come down to visit her old friends."

"I'm not here for a reunion, just a little outing with my new friend, who seems to have gotten ahead of me somehow." She shot Unwin a playfully angry look.

"And that's why you need a ticket. It costs money to see the freaks." He smiled again. "But you ought to know that, Cleo. How's the leg doing? Still hurt when it rains?"

She drew close to the window. "My guest is an Agency Eye," she said. "It's on business of his that we've come here. I think I can convince him not to see too much while we stroll the grounds, but for that you'll have to be nice."

"Agency?" Brock said. "But the hat's all wrong."

Miss Greenwood raised one hand, cupping it to her lips as though to whisper something in his ear. He leaned forward, then started and brandished his dagger, eyes going wide. She said something Unwin could not make out, and Brock's eyelids fluttered closed. The dagger fell from his hand and embedded itself in the ticket table; his head dropped hard beside it. The knife thrower was asleep.

Miss Greenwood looked around, then pulled the window shut. "Quickly," she said.

They went along paths strewn with broken bottles and toys, feathers, illegible playbills. The old fairground pavilions along the midway were constructed to look like the heads of giant animals, their mouths agape to allow access to the exhibits installed in the domes of their skulls. A pig's snout was a tunnel into fetid darkness, the eyes of a fish served as bulging windows, a cat's fangs were stalactites.

They passed them by and came to a causeway of wooden planks set on cinder blocks. Miss Greenwood went first, and Unwin followed.

"What did you do to Brock?"

"I told him to go to sleep," she said.

In some of his reports, Sivart had hinted that Cleo Greenwood possessed certain strange talents, picked up during her days with the Traveling Carnival. Unwin had assumed that the detective was being fanciful, or even poetic (*truly*, he had once written, *the lady is a knockout*), so Unwin cut those details. Perhaps he had been wrong to do so.

They stepped off the plank and walked along a row of junk stalls and shooting galleries. Mechanical ducks were perched on rusted rails, punched through with holes from real bullets. The rain pattering on abandoned popcorn carts and unmoving carousels made for a melancholy kind of music. "So different from the carnival I arrived with," Miss Greenwood said.

It was true: sixteen years ago Unwin had seen the sputtering caravan of red, orange, and yellow trucks passing through his neighborhood on their way to the fairgrounds. A west-side bridge had been closed that morning, to allow for the safe conduct of the elephants, and the newspapers ran photographs of the animals rearing on their hind legs. Posters were everywhere in the city, promising strange and stirring delights: Nikolai the mind reader, the giantess Hildegard, and Isidoro "The Man of Memory." But the show's main attraction was the biloquist Enoch Hoffmann.

Unwin never saw his performance, but he heard plenty about it in those weeks. The Man of a Thousand and One Voices was an unlikely magician, eschewing cape and hat in favor of the baggy, ill-fitting gray suit he wore with sleeves rolled. He gestured indifferently with little fingers while performing his feats and was quickly upstaged by his own illusions, the magic working almost in spite of him. Those who saw the show described the impossible—phantoms onstage, or animals, or inanimate objects, speaking to them in the voices of people they knew: relatives and friends, living and deceased. Those specters were privy to secret knowledge, and some who heard fainted at the revelations.

"The trick I used on Brock just now came in handy while I worked here," Miss Greenwood said. "Enoch and I had our own sideshow. Hypnosis, fortunetelling—that kind of thing. Of course, all that's changed. The remnants are no longer in the habit of entertaining."

The remnants of Caligari's were mentioned in numerous reports that Unwin had filed over the years. They were a crooked cabal, the progeny of a crooked line—plotters, scoundrels, and thieves, each one. Without them Hoffmann could not have seized control of the city's underworld. Unwin had seen them spying since the moment he and Miss Greenwood left the ticket booth. They stood in tattered coats beneath the eaves of game booths or skulked in the shadows of defunct rides, cooking breakfast over open fires: scowling roustabouts, disgruntled clowns, arthritic acrobats. They spoke together in whispers and guffaws or paced alone and spit. Unwin could smell sausage frying, could see the smoke of it threading the rain.

"They hate the Agency," Miss Greenwood said. "But you're safe with me, so long as I want you to be."

She had scarcely bothered to veil the threat—she was Unwin's captor as much as his guide. And here, in the den from which Hoffmann had recruited his every agent and thug, he knew he would need her. How many of the remnants had been apprehended due to the Agency's work? More than he cared to count. He clenched his teeth and tried not to sound bitter as he said, "That story you told me, about the open windows and the roses. You knew the cause from the beginning."

"I wasn't the only one playing tricks, Detective Unwin. It was Ed Lamech I'd wanted to see, remember?"

"But you meant for me to be there, at the Cat & Tonic."

"I needed someone to be my eyes."

"What did you expect me to see?"

"Strange things," she said. "The beginnings of a great and terrible crime. Hoffmann himself, maybe."

"And a murder."

Miss Greenwood lost her balance a moment, and Unwin put his hand under her elbow to steady her. She was flexing her bad leg. "Murder?" she said.

"Samuel Pith. The Rooks shot him."

She looked away. "That's horrid. Don't get me wrong. Sam was always a bit of a stuffed shirt. And he knew the risks. But he was an innocent, when it comes down to it. The rules must be changing."

"There are rules?"

"The Agency isn't the only organization requiring discipline, Detective Unwin. Now, tell me what else happened last night."

"You sang a song or two," Unwin said.

She stopped and turned, her face close to his under the umbrella. "You're sounding like a detective," she said. "Just when I was beginning to like you."

Some of the remnants had followed and were lurking now at the edge of the hall of mirrors. There were a dozen of them, maybe, or just a few, accompanied by their distorted reflections. They stood with their arms crossed in front of them, watching.

"What do you want to know?" Unwin asked her.

"What you're doing here, to begin with."

"I want to see the Rooks."

"No one *wants* to see the Rooks, Detective Unwin. They were sweet little boys when they came here with the carnival. But they were still attached then. After Enoch paid for the operation, they got to walk on their own, but it changed them in other ways, too."

"What do you mean?"

"They lost something," Miss Greenwood said. "I don't know what to call it. 'Conscience' isn't quite the word. Some people do cruel things, but the Rooks are cruelty itself, monsters under any moon. And they never sleep."

"Never?"

"Not in seventeen years."

Unwin thought that explained something, but he was not sure what. "You haven't slept in a long time either," he said.

"That's a very different story. The Rooks are no more than their master's hands. Now, I want you to tell me what happened last night."

When he hesitated, she turned to signal to the men by the fun house. They took a few steps forward, their reflections multiplying. Sivart might have seen a way out of this, but Unwin did not.

"I'll tell you what I saw," he said, and she signaled again for the remnants to wait.

Unwin described the gambling tables, the alarm clocks, her own performance, which seemed somehow to draw the sleepwalkers to the party. He told her how the Rooks were overseeing the operation and how the custodian had played accordion while she sang.

All of it interested her, but he could tell she was after something else. "I want us to be honest with each other," she said. "I must seem like a bully to you. The truth is, I only came back to the city because I'm trying to help someone. You were wrong when you accused me of showing your friend the truth about the Oldest Murdered Man. That must have been my daughter."

Unwin did not have to think long about the Agency's files on Cleopatra Greenwood to assure himself that there was nothing in them about a daughter. Either Miss Greenwood was lying to him or she was revealing something Sivart had failed to discover.

"I'm afraid she's gotten herself into some kind of trouble," Miss Greenwood went on. "She's turned out too much like her mother, that's the problem."

"You think she's wrapped up in Hoffmann's plans."

She glanced over her shoulder to make sure the remnants could not hear, then said quietly, "I'll help you stop him."

"Miss Greenwood, I don't want to stop Enoch Hoffmann."

Her exhaustion was showing again. A strong, sea-smelling wind hurled rain from the direction of the bay, and she squinted against it. "Hasn't it occurred to you that Travis might be dead by now?" she asked, her voice rising as the wind picked up. "Your only way out of this thing is to do what he failed to do."

A sound like thunder caused them both to turn. It was the clattering rumble of a heavy vehicle on a pitted road. Unwin looked for it, but a row of ragged sideshow tents blocked his view. The remnants were coming toward them now. Even with their reflections left behind, there were still a lot of them.

"Sivart was too stupid to see he'd been beaten," Miss Greenwood said. "Don't make the same mistake."

Unwin collapsed his umbrella and ran. In a moment the remnants were only a few strides behind him; they whooped into the rain, thrilling to the pursuit. Unwin headed for the nearest tent and slipped inside. The air smelled thickly of mold, and rainwater poured in through tears in the canvas. He ran to the back and swung his umbrella, rending the fabric, then split it to the ground with one downward stroke.

The Rooks' steam truck was approaching on the road beyond. It bounced over potholes and tossed black clouds from its smokestack, its headlights throwing twin yellow beams into the rain. He ran along behind until the truck slowed to round a corner. Then he hopped onto the rear bumper, opening his umbrella and swinging it over his head. He kept hold of the tailgate with his free hand.

Behind him Miss Greenwood stood in the middle of the road with the remnants, her raincoat bright amid those drab, disheveled men. She watched him go until the truck turned again, passing a row of old theaters on its way into the heart of the Travels-No-More.

DETECTIVE SIVART'S FIRST BRUSH with Caligari's occurred soon
after the carnival arrived, months before the events surrounding the
Oldest Murdered Man case. Reports coming into the Agency at the
time indicated that the ringmaster might have represented a threat to
the city. He was wanted in over a dozen states for crimes ranging from
robbery to smuggling, blackmail to fraud. It was said that even his
name was stolen—from a forebear in the trade, one who retired in
infamy.

Sivart was one of several information gatherers assigned to investigate. He had taken a leisurely stroll along the midway, then slipped into
a small pavilion in a remote corner of the fairgrounds. There an eight-
foot-tall woman was bent over a worktable, measuring and mixing
foul-smelling powders from barrels and bowls.

They need to get this gal a bigger room, Sivart wrote in his report.
Hildegard, he discovered, oversaw the troupe's pyrotechnic displays and
also served as the resident giantess. *We got along like old pals, and after
a while we were sharing a drink. Well, "sharing" isn't the right word, since
she emptied my flask with one swig. I went to find something more and
brought back a cask of fancy stuff, paid for with Agency funds, thank you.
If I have to drink on the job, I'm not going to pay for it.*

The two sat together for hours. She seemed to know what he was
doing there but did not mind telling him about her time with the
carnival, where they had traveled, the sights she had seen. While they
talked, she poured her black-powder mixtures into the tubes of rockets
and fixed fuses to them. When Sivart got too close to her work, she just
pushed him back with one huge hand.

Nicest girl I've talked to in months, Sivart wrote. *The air must be
clearer up there.*

Only when Sivart tried to turn the conversation to Caligari himself
did the giantess grow reticent. The cask was almost empty, so he had

to try a more direct approach. Was it true that the carnival served as a haven for criminals and outlaws? That Caligari was responsible for corruption and ruination wherever he went?

The giantess was silent. She went back to work, ignoring him.

That's when I put a cigar in my mouth, tore the end with my teeth, and raised a lighter to the tip. Before I could spark the flint, she had my fist closed up in hers. I showed her my best grin and said, "I can understand your not wanting to talk about it, angel. So maybe I should speak to the man himself?"

Though Sivart's report from this investigation belonged to no particular case, it was significant as the only documented account of an agent's meeting with Caligari. The ringmaster was in the tent where the elephants were stabled. According to the detective's description, he was a quick-moving, gray-bearded man in an ancient, moth-eaten suit, his eyes blue behind round, wire-rimmed spectacles. He told Sivart he had come just in time to help with the cleaning.

A little girl, about seven years old, handed the detective a brush and said, "They like it when you scrub them behind the ears."

From the report:

Apparently, Caligari and his young assistant do the dirty work themselves, almost every day. It is not fun and does not leave you smelling wholesome. If I'm ever feeling down, clerk, remind me not to run away and join the circus.

"The ears," the girl reminded me. I'd been sudsing the big guy's back, and she held my ladder steady while I worked, which was a good thing, what with my belly full of swill.

"Yeah, sure," I said to her. "The ears."

The three of us talked, and Caligari fed me a nonsense sandwich or two. He told me he took special care of the elephants because their dreams were so expansive, and clear as crystal.

That got a chuckle out of me. "What do you do," I said, "peel back their eyelids and shine a light in there?"

"*Everything I tell you is true,*" he said, "*and everything you see is as real as you are.*"

I'd read that on one of the posters they'd pasted around town. It was this fellow's catchphrase, and I didn't need it. Later, while we were getting fresh water from the cistern, I finally got him to say something interesting. "The people who stay put don't trust the people who don't," he said. "My carnival's been the subject of many wild accusations over the years, all of which have proved groundless. I'm getting tired of having to listen to the same old stories."

"Stories are what I'm here for," I told him. "Are you saying we have nothing to worry about?"

Clerk, you should have seen the sparkle in his eye. "You have plenty to worry about, Detective. Make no mistake, I am *your enemy.* You think you can control what is known and what is unknown? I tell you the unknown will always be boundless. This place thrives on mystery; we revel in it here. All the world's a rube, and he who tries to prove otherwise will be the first to wake onstage, victim of our just ridicule."

He'd worked himself up a bit and had to sit down and catch his breath. The little girl ran off and came back a minute later with a cup of cocoa. He sipped, watching the elephants. The animals were eating now, fetching clumps of hay with their trunks.

"They remember everything," Caligari said quietly. "I don't know what I'd do without them. And their dreams, Detective. A minute in one of their dreams is a month on the open plain, unfettered, unchartable."

I don't know what he meant by that, or whether he meant anything at all. But this much I know: we need to keep an eye on this character.

The carnival had closed up by then, and lights were going off all around us. The girl took my hand and led me away, back to the front gate. There she turned my hand over and looked at the palm. "You'll live a long life," she said, "but a long part of it won't be your own. Good night, Travis."

That bugged me some—not the fortune, which is malarkey. But the *fact that she knew my first name. I hadn't mentioned it, not to anyone in the place.*

Five months later Caligari vanished. His employees never left the city, and in the end the carnival was shut down by force. But the workers, despite numerous arrests, refused to go. They found other ways to provide for themselves, and like-minded souls were welcomed into their gang. The gates were shut against all others, and the Traveling Carnival became the Travels-No-More.

Many wondered: What about the elephants? What happened to them?

For years some reported hearing, on especially quiet nights, a trumpeting call out there in the dark, like a reminder, or an omen.

What troubled Unwin now was that little girl, Caligari's assistant, who had known Sivart's name and had spoken like some kind of sibyl. Could she have been the daughter of Cleopatra Greenwood?

IN THE BED OF the Rooks' steam truck, the ticking of the alarm clocks was the hum of a thousand insects. They jangled and buzzed when the truck went over bumps, and Unwin imagined they were about to burst free in a great tick-tocking swarm. Peering under the canvas, he saw that Moore was not in there, and neither was Pith's body. How many truckloads of clocks had the sleepwalkers stolen?

In time they came to the farthest corner of the carnival. Here at the edge of the bay, the tents were still striped with color, and electric lights along the waterfront shone red, blue, and orange. Most of the little makeshift structures had been converted into cottages, and shacks had sprung up among them. It looked less like a carnival here and more like a shantytown into which a carnival had erupted. The truck halted beside the largest of the pavilions, and almost immediately a group of men with shovels emerged.

Unwin hopped off the bumper and went around the passenger side. The men went straight to work, shoveling the alarm clocks into the tent, where thousands more were already piled. The noise of them was a second storm. Down at the docks, tractors swept heaps of clocks onto the deck of a waiting barge.

The steam engine of the truck spluttered and halted, and one of the Rooks climbed from the cab, a clipboard in his hand. Unwin knelt behind the rear tire. Looking beneath the truck, he saw a dockworker's shoes draw up to the big, uneven boots—Josiah's.

"What's Hoffmann want with it all anyway?"

"I believe there was something in your contract about questions and whether they ought to be asked," said Josiah.

"Right, right," the dockworker said. He flipped open a cigarette lighter and followed Josiah in the direction of the tent. "So long as I get paid."

The truck was parked not far from a row of cottages. They were built close to one another, some leaning nearly to the point of touching. Unwin took to the paths between them, crouching low under the windows, though all were dark. He moved as quickly as he could, keeping his umbrella closed in his hand, searching for some sign of Edwin Moore.

Rounding a corner, he nearly collided with an enormous animal—a real one, not one of those plaster simulacra. It was an elephant, gray and wild-looking in the rain, its eyes bright yellow in their dark, wrinkled sockets. Unwin slipped and fell in the mud at its feet. Startled, the elephant reared on its hind legs and raised its trunk in the air.

Unwin froze as the beast's forelegs churned over his head. He could smell the musky scent of the animal, could hear its wheezing breath. Finally the elephant held still, then slowly returned the columns of its legs gently to the ground.

Unwin got to his feet and picked up his umbrella. There were two other elephants here in a makeshift pen. These were older and lay with their bellies flattened to the muck. All three were chained to the same post, and their tethers had become tangled and knotted. The largest elephant, its hide sagging with age, raised its head and spread its ears but was otherwise still. The other rolled its eyes in Unwin's direction and lifted its trunk from the mud. Its searching snout moved toward him through the rain, issuing steam as it sniffed the air. The youngest began to rock impatiently, its great round feet squelching in the soft earth.

The beasts must have been evicted from their pavilion to make way for the alarm clocks. Unwin remembered the affection with which Caligari had spoken of the beasts, and he felt sick at the sight of them now. He would have liked to set them free, but even if he were able to remove the stake, it seemed unlikely that the elephants' condition would be improved. If those in charge cared little enough about the animals to leave them here, would they hesitate to kill them if they were set loose into the carnival? Unwin would have to return for them later; for now he had to concentrate on finding Edwin Moore.

The windows of one nearby cottage were lit with a flickering, rosy glow. Smoke streamed from a crooked length of stovepipe at the back, and Unwin thought he heard music playing within. He went to the window and peered through. Inside was a coal-burning stove, a table covered with books, and buckets of dirty plates and cups. A phonograph was on, and Unwin recognized the song. It was the same one Cleopatra Greenwood had sung the night before, at the Cat & Tonic.

At the back of the single room were two beds, perfectly made and barely an inch apart. More books were scattered over the beds, and the pillows were undented. Propped against the foot of the bed on the right was Edwin Moore. He was bound at the wrists and ankles by lengths of tough-looking rope, and his uniform was dirty.

The elephants seemed to have lost interest in Unwin. The youngest had gone to huddle against the eldest, and the other laid its trunk on the ground again.

Unwin tried the door and found it unlocked. The air inside was warm and smelled faintly of grease. He set his umbrella by the door, then opened his coat to rid himself of the chill he had carried with him all morning. On the table was a backgammon board, abandoned in midgame. White and brown playing pieces were grouped in sets of twos and threes, and the dice revealed the last roll as a double three. From what Unwin knew of the game, it looked as though each player had the other in a deadlock, with pieces captured and escape routes blocked.

Unwin knelt beside Moore and shook him. The old clerk mumbled in his sleep but did not waken.

Outside, the elephants were moving again; one of them sent up an aggrieved lament. Unwin moved around the beds, thinking to hide beneath one of them, but he stubbed his foot against a tin bucket and sent it clattering over the floor, strewing coal briquettes in a wide arc.

The door opened, and one of the Rooks came into the room. It was Jasper: left boot smaller than the right. He looked at Unwin, looked at the toppled bucket, then blinked once and closed the door behind him. He went to the phonograph and shut it off.

Unwin stepped over the coal, upsetting a stack of books in the process. He mumbled an apology and quickly began to gather them, blowing coal dust off the covers as he set them in a pile.

Jasper reached into his coat and withdrew a pocketwatch, checked the time, and put the watch away. His hand came back with a pistol in it. Even with the gun in his hand, Jasper seemed only vaguely interested in the fact that Unwin was there.

Unwin set the last few books into place and stood up. He thought of his own pistol, still in his desk drawer in Room 2919, but knew it would not have been of any help to him. Pith surely carried a pistol, and he had not even bothered to draw.

Talk. He had read that in the *Manual* somewhere. *When all seems lost, start talking, keep talking. People do not kill people they think have something useful to say.*

"Is it true?" Unwin said. "Seventeen years without a minute of sleep?"

Jasper's face was a dull mask, his eyes green stones. He raised the pistol, pointing it at Unwin's heart.

What would the shot feel like? Like a hole punch, Unwin thought, when it punctured a small stack of pages. He took a step toward the gun and said, "That's a tiredness beyond tiredness. Everything must seem like a dream." He glanced at the pair of identical beds at the back of the room. "When was the last time you even bothered to try?"

Jasper blinked again, and Unwin waited for the blast.

It did not come. "I wonder how it happened," Unwin said. "Did you even want the operation? Or was that Hoffmann's idea? He needed the two of you to be in different places at the same time, I suppose. But he didn't know how much he was cutting. You weren't really two people to begin with. There was a time when you could see each other's dreams, hear each other's thoughts. But they were the same dreams, the same thoughts."

He was guessing now, imagining a role for them in the earlier days of Caligari's carnival: those boys Cleo Greenwood had described, clothed in a single wide coat and set on a double stool, put onstage to sing a duet, maybe. He must have come close to the truth, because Jasper slowly lowered his pistol.

"One plus one does not equal one," Jasper said.

"No," Unwin agreed. "That man you have there, Edwin Moore, is a lot like me. Or I'm a lot like him, maybe. We don't know each other very well, but I understand him, I think. We were both clerks once. So you see why I had to come looking for him."

Jasper seemed to consider this.

"I'm going to carry him out of here," Unwin said. "I won't ask you to help me. I won't ask you to open the door. I won't even ask you not to shoot me, but if you don't, I'll take it to mean that you understand, and I'll thank you for that."

Unwin lifted Moore by the arms. Taking care not to upset any of the books or to look at Jasper, Unwin dragged the man slowly toward the door. There he set Moore down and picked up his umbrella. It was shaking in his hands.

Just then the door opened and Josiah came in, still carrying his clipboard. He did not take his hat off, did not even blink. He looked at Unwin, looked at Moore, and looked at his brother. Then he set his clipboard on the table and whispered something in Jasper's ear.

The fire in the coal stove brightened, and Unwin felt the room grow suddenly hotter. Moore began to mumble in his sleep. The muscles of his skinny arms convulsed, and he slid back to the floor as Unwin lost his grip on him.

Jasper drew close and said, "My brother has advised me to advise you to hold very still." He raised the gun over his head and brought it down hard. With it came sleep—sleep, and a very strange dream.

IN THE DREAM, Unwin stood with his head against a tree, hands cupped around his face, counting out loud. When he finished counting, he had to go find some people who were hiding from him. His socks were wet, because he had been running around in the grass without any shoes on.

He stood on a hill near a little cottage, and at the bottom of the hill was a pond. The cottage was the one Sivart had written about in his reports, the one he wanted to retire to.

"Ready or not," Unwin called, but the words dropped like stones into the pond and fell to the bottom. A tire swing moved back and forth over the water, spinning as though someone had only just climbed off it. That, Unwin thought, was not a detail. It was a clue.

At the bottom of the hill, past a tangle of blackberry briars, he found footprints in the mud. He followed them around the edge of the pond, then down a trail leading into the woods, kicking red and orange leaves as he walked. In the middle of a clearing, the leaves were piled higher than everywhere else, just high enough to conceal a small person.

Unwin smelled something burning. A thin stream of smoke rose up from the leaves. Poking out of them was the tip of a lit cigar. He knelt beside it and cleared away some of the leaves, revealing the face of a young boy. The boy blinked at Unwin, then took the cigar out of his mouth and said, "Okay, Charlie. You got me."

The boy sat up and brushed the rest of the leaves off his body, off his gray raincoat. Then he stood and put his hat on. "I'll help you get the others," he said.

Unwin followed the boy back down the trail. His feet were getting cold. "Detective Sivart?" he said.

"Yeah, Charlie," said the boy.

"I can't remember the name of this game."

"It's an old game," the boy said. "Older than chess. Older than curse words and shoeshine. Doesn't matter what you call it, so long as you know how to play. Everyone's in on it, except one guy, and that guy's 'it.' Okay?"

"Detective Sivart?"

"Yeah, Charlie."

"I'm 'it,' aren't I?"

"And quick, too," the boy said.

They stood together at the edge of the pond, the boy puffing at his cigar. Up in the cottage, someone had turned the radio on. Unwin could hear the music, but he could not make out the words. The sun was going down behind the hill.

"Some birthday." The boy sighed. "So who's next?"

"We have to find the magician," Unwin said.

"They hired a magician? What kinds of tricks can he do?"

"All kinds," Unwin said.

"Then how do you know you haven't found him already?"

Unwin looked down. The boy's face had changed. It was squarish now, and his eyes had turned a dull brown color. He still had the cigar in his hand, but both his sleeves were rolled up, and the coat looked too big on him.

Enoch Hoffmann grinned. "See?" he said. "He could be anyone."

ELEVEN

On Bluffing

**Answer questions with questions. If you are caught
in a lie, lie again. You do not need to know the
truth to trick another into speaking it.**

Unwin waited for the world to stop swaying, but it did not stop
swaying, because the world was a barge, and the barge was out
on the rolling waters of the bay. He tried to check the time, but his
arms were tied behind his back. Anyway, he did not need his watch.
He was surrounded by alarm clocks—hills, mountains of them. On a
dozen of their rain-spattered faces, he read the same time. It was only
ten of eight.

Curled at his feet was Edwin Moore, still bound, still sleeping. In
this light, Unwin could see the lump at the top of the old man's forehead. He knew from the throbbing at his own temple that he had one
to match.

Next to Moore was the plump body of Detective Pith, his suit wa-
terlogged and bloodstained. Unwin glimpsed the ashen, jowly face
above the collar of the herringbone suit. He looked away.

Unwin's hat was still on his head, and his umbrella was open above him, fixed in place by the same ropes that bound his aching arms. He wondered which of the Rooks had afforded him this kindness. There was no sign of the twins here. In every direction he could see nothing but piles of alarm clocks. All the alarm clocks in the city, maybe even his.

"Wake up," he said to Moore. "Wake up, will you?"

He slid himself forward, bringing his feet close to the other man's, and tapped the sole of one of his shoes. "Wake up!" he shouted.

"Hush," said someone behind him. "The Rooks will hear you. You're lucky they prefer to watch their victims drown."

Unwin recognized Miss Greenwood's voice. "How did *you* get here?"

She knelt behind him and tugged at the ropes. "More easily than you did," she said. She reached into her coat, and Unwin looked over his shoulder to see a dagger appear in her hand. It was identical to those that Brock carried—it must have been the one that pierced her leg during his knife-throwing act, all those years ago.

"I don't like being left in the rain without an umbrella, Mr. Unwin."

"Those elephants back there," he said. "Something ought to be done about them, too."

She sighed. "Caligari would be furious."

Unwin waited, listening. He felt the edge of the blade against his spine. Then a sudden pressure, and the fibers of the rope started snapping. He held the umbrella over Miss Greenwood while she cut the cords around his ankles. When they both were standing, she said, "I know you're not a detective."

That passage from page ninety-six of the *Manual* returned to his mind. Without any secrets he was lost forever. But what was he now, if not lost already? "No," he admitted. "I'm not a detective."

"Not a watcher either. Something else, some new kind of puppet. I know you're working for him. I know he sent you to taunt me."

"Working for whom?"

She narrowed her eyes at him. "That phonograph record, those sounds. You have no idea what it's like, Mr. Unwin. To always find him there waiting for you. To have his eyes in the back of your skull."

"Whose eyes? What are you talking about?"

She stared at him, still disbelieving. "The Agency's overseer," she said. "Your boss."

It had never occurred to Unwin that the Agency had an overseer, that one person could be in charge. Where, he wondered, was that man's office?

Miss Greenwood must have seen that his surprise was real. "He and I . . . we know one another," she said. "Hoffmann is dangerous, Mr. Unwin. But you ought to know that your employer is something worse. Whatever happens, he can't find out about my daughter." The barge shifted, and she stumbled on her bad leg. Unwin moved to steady her, but she pushed him away. "There's a boat tied up on the starboard side," she said. "Go, take it."

He gestured at Moore. "Will you cut him free?"

"There's no time," she said. "The Rooks aren't far."

He held out his hand. "Give me the dagger, then. I'll do it myself."

Miss Greenwood hesitated, then turned the handle over to him. "I hope this rescue goes better than your first," she said.

Unwin knelt and started cutting. These ropes were thicker, and he made slow progress.

"I didn't want to come back to the city," Miss Greenwood said. "I was through with all of this. With the Agency, with Hoffmann; I can hardly tell the difference between them anymore. But I had to come back."

Unwin cut through the last cord around Moore's wrists and started working to free his ankles.

"These clocks remind me of a story I used to read to my daughter," she said. "It was in her favorite book, an old one with a checkered cover. It was the story of a princess who'd been cursed by an old witch—or was it a fairy? In any case, the curse meant she would fall asleep—forever, maybe—if she were pricked by a spinning needle. So the king and queen did what any good parents would do, and piled up all the spindles in the land and burned them, and everyone had to wear worn-out old clothes for a very long time."

The last of the ropes fell away. He swung Moore's arms up over his shoulders and with Miss Greenwood's help lifted him onto his back. She put the umbrella into his hand, and for a moment they stood looking at one another.

"How did the story end?" he asked.

It was not a question she had expected. "They missed one of the spindles, of course."

UNWIN TRUDGED TOWARD THE starboard side of the barge, following a narrow trail between mounds of alarm clocks. His shoes squeaked with every labored step over the slick metal deck. He would have taken them off, but shards of glass from the broken faces of clocks were everywhere.

He paused often to catch his breath and to reposition Moore's limp body over his back. Finally he saw the edge of the barge. Bobbing over the green-gray swells was the little rowboat Miss Greenwood had promised. But one of the Rooks was nearby, leaning over the water with his big left boot on the rail: Josiah. He gazed across the bay at the mist-shrouded city, smoking a cigarette while the rain poured over the brim of his hat, which was nearly the size of Unwin's umbrella.

Unwin thought he could reach the boat without Josiah's seeing, but not without his shoes betraying him. So he crouched and waited for Josiah to finish smoking.

Somewhere amid the hills of clocks, a bell began to ring, a futile attempt to wake some sleeper a mile or more away. To Unwin the sound was a hook in his heart: the world goes to shambles in the murky corners of night, and we trust a little bell to set it right again. A spring is released, a gear is spun, a clapper is set fluttering, and here is the cup of water you keep at your bedside, here the shoes you will wear to work today. But if a soul and its alarms are parted, one from the other? If the body is left alone to its somnolent watches? When it rises—if it rises— it may not recognize itself, nor any of brief day's trappings. A hat is a snake is a lamp is a child is an insect is a clothesline hung with telephones. That was the world into which Unwin had woken.

While he listened, the one bell was joined by another, and then another, and soon a thousand or more clocks were sounding all at once, a chorus fit to rouse the deepest sleeper. He glanced at his watch. It was eight o'clock; many in the city had meant to wake up now. Instead they had given him a chance to reach the rowboat undetected. The squeaking of his shoes was nothing compared to that thunderous proclamation of morning.

His sleeping companion's feet dragged bumping behind him as he ran, and the umbrella wobbled above. He leaned against the rails, heaving Edwin Moore up and over. The old man landed hard and the rowboat shuddered beneath him. One of his arms flopped into the water, and his bruised face turned up to the rain.

Josiah looked over—he had felt the rail shift under Unwin's weight. He flicked his cigarette into the water and came toward Unwin, an expression of mild disappointment on his face.

Unwin clambered up onto the rail, collapsing his umbrella. In his haste he caught the handle on the sleeve of his jacket, and the umbrella popped open again. The wind pulled at it, and Unwin pitched back onto the barge.

Josiah took him by the collar and swung him to the deck, his coat flapping in the rain as he fell upon Unwin. The heat coming off the man was incredible—Unwin thought he saw steam rising from the Rook's back. Josiah put one enormous hand behind Unwin's head, as though to cushion it, and the other flat over his face. His hand was dry.

He covered Unwin's nose and mouth and did not take it away. "Let's both be very quiet now," he said.

The bells were ringing all around them—some stopping as others started. The ringing joined with the ringing in Unwin's ears, and a darkness rose up as though from the sea. It seemed to him that he stood on a street in the dark. Children had left chalk drawings on the pavement, but there were no children here. It was the avenue of the lost and secretless: empty tenement buildings all the way to the bottom of the world.

Detective Pith emerged from the shadows and stood in the cone of light from a streetlamp. "Papers and pigeons, Unwin. It's all papers and pigeons. We'll have to rewrite the goddamn manual."

"Detective Pith," he said, "I saw them shoot you."

"Aw, nuts," said Pith. He took off his hat and held it over his chest. There was a bullet hole in the top of it. "Damn it, Unwin. Do something!" he said, and when he moved the hat away his shirt was covered with blood.

Unwin tried to hold the wound shut, but it was no use; the blood seeped between his fingers and spilled everywhere.

When the darkness receded, the blood was still there, pouring down Unwin's arms and over his chest. Not Detective Pith's, though. Miss Greenwood's dagger was in his hands again—he had slipped it into his pocket without thinking—and now the blade was stuck deep in Josiah's chest. Unwin had stabbed him.

Josiah took his hand from Unwin's face and sat down next to him, staring at the handle there between the third and fourth buttons of his shirt.

Unwin got to his knees. He reached to take the knife but stopped himself. Had he read in the *Manual* that removing the weapon will worsen the wound? "Don't move," he said.

Josiah closed his eyes. From below came the whirring of machinery, and the deck of the barge began suddenly to lift. Unwin grabbed Josiah's hand and tried to pull him toward the rowboat but could not budge him. The deck angled higher, and Unwin's shoes slipped. It was too late. He let go of Josiah and grabbed his umbrella, then scrambled under the rail and into the rowboat. He swiftly undid the knot securing them to the barge and started to paddle.

Josiah Rook tipped, then tumbled across the tilting barge. The hills of alarm clocks collapsed and slid with him. Many were still ringing as they spilled into the bay, going mute as the water took them.

Edwin Moore sat up and blinked. "I don't know any songs for this," he said.

Unwin did not know any either. He was thinking of the backgammon board he had seen in the Rooks' cottage, of the game left unfinished there.

UNWIN ROWED WHILE Edwin Moore held the umbrella over their heads. It swayed and bobbed above them while the boat bobbed beneath. They sat close to keep dry, facing one another with knees nearly touching. Someone had left a tin can under the seat, and Moore used it to bail water. Sometimes the wind dragged the umbrella sideways and they both were drenched.

Moore shivered and said, "I tried to forget as much as I could, but I couldn't forget enough. They knew me the instant I fell asleep."

The world was two kinds of gray—the heavy gray of the rain and the heavier, heaving gray of the water. Unwin could barely tell them apart. Reaching through both was the yellow arm of a lighthouse beacon. He rowed toward it as best he could.

"Who knew you?" he asked.

"The watchers, of course." Moore squinted, and drops of water fell from his thick eyebrows. "They watch more than the detectives, Mr. Unwin. They are detectives themselves, in a manner of speaking. Of

course, I didn't know who would catch me first: Hoffmann's people or
the Agency's. Some of your colleagues must still be using the old channels, the ones the magician knows to monitor."

Unwin understood that no better than he understood how to keep
the boat pointed in the right direction. It veered as soon as he rowed
on one side, then spun the other way when he tried to compensate.

Moore set the tin can on the seat between them and wiped his face
with his hand. "I owe you an apology," he said. "I lied when I told you
there is no Chapter Eighteen in *The Manual of Detection.*"

"But I saw for myself," Unwin said. "It ends with Chapter
Seventeen."

Moore shook his head. "Only in the later printings. In the original,
unexpurgated edition, there are eighteen chapters. The last chapter is
the most important. Especially to the watchers. And to the Agency's
overseer." He set his elbows on his knees, looked down, and sighed. "I
thought you knew all this. That you were a watcher yourself, maybe,
and had been sent to toy with me. I'm the architect of an ancient tomb,
Mr. Unwin. I was to be buried inside my own creation, the better to
keep its secrets. I will not tell you more, for your sake. But if you ask,
I will answer."

The rain drummed on the umbrella as water splashed against the
sides of the boat. Unwin's arms were sore, but he kept rowing. Their
little craft was taking on water. He watched it swirl around his shoes,
around Moore's shoes. The water was red. There was a stain on his shirt,
and his hands had stained the oars.

"I killed a man," Unwin said.

Moore leaned close and set his hand on Unwin's shoulder. "You killed
half of a man," he said. "It's the other half you have to worry about."

Unwin rowed faster. He was getting the hang of it now. The trick
was to play each side off the other, but gently. Still, it would take a long
time to reach the shore.

"Tell me about Chapter Eighteen," Unwin said.

WHEN THEY REACHED THE harbor, it was far from the pier of the Travels-No-More. Unwin rowed in the shadows of cargo ships, and each splash of the oar echoed in the vastness between the towering hulls. It was dark, and the air smelled of rust and brine. They landed in a small cove at the base of the lighthouse, where bits of junk had collected among the rocks and seaweed. Together they dragged the boat out of the water.

Unwin noticed something gleaming at the fore of the craft as the light swept past. It was an alarm clock, and it looked a lot like the one that had vanished from his own bedside. Unwin put the clock to his ear, heard its machinery still at work, and wound it. The clock just fit inside his coat pocket.

They walked together through abandoned dockyards. What Unwin understood of Moore's description of Chapter Eighteen he would have disbelieved entirely if not for the events of the last two days. *Oneiric detection,* Moore had whispered to him. *In layman's terms: dream surveillance.*

This is was what Miss Greenwood must have meant when she spoke of another's eyes in the back of her skull. Dream spies. Had the Agency's overseer done this to her? Hounded her through her sleep so she never rested? She said she did not want him to know about her daughter. Would a dream of the girl be enough to betray Miss Greenwood's secret? Unwin wondered whether he himself could ever sleep easily again.

Edwin Moore, his feet back on solid ground, seemed to have discovered new stores of vitality. He walked with a jaunty step, his cheeks reddening from the exertion. He was still trying to explain how dream detection worked. "You've heard the story of the old man who dreamed he was a butterfly," he said. "And how, when he woke, he wasn't sure if he really was an old man who had dreamed he was a butterfly or if he was a butterfly dreaming it was an old man."

"You'd say there's truth to it?"

"I'd say it's a lot of nonsense," Moore snapped. "But the mind struggles with the question nonetheless. How often have you tried to recall a specific memory—a conversation with an acquaintance, maybe—only to determine that the memory was a delusion, spawned in dream? And how often have you dreamed a thing, then found that it spoke some truth about your waking life? You solved a problem that had been impenetrable the day before, perhaps, or perceived the hidden sentiments of someone whose motivations had baffled you.

"Real and unreal, actual and imagined. Our failure to distinguish one from the other, or rather our willingness to believe they may be one and the same, is the chink through which the Agency operatives conduct their work."

"But what do they do, exactly?" Unwin asked. "Lie down next to someone who's sleeping? Rest with their heads touching?"

"Don't be ridiculous. You don't have to be near your subject; you only need to isolate that person's frequency. It's work a watcher can do from the comfort of an office chair." Moore winced and touched the lump on his forehead, which had assumed a purple hue. He sighed and went on. "You know of course that signals from the brain may be measured, even charted. There are electrical waves, devices to read them, people who study these things. Different states have been identified, cataloged, analyzed. What our people figured out is that one brain may be entrained to another, 'tuned in,' so to speak. The result is a kind of sensory transduction. Not so different, really, from listening to the radio.

"That's my metaphor, at least. Those who practice dream detection describe it as a kind of shadowing, only they tail their suspect through his own unconscious mind rather than through the city. If they are after some specific piece of information, they may even influence the dreamer in subtle ways, nudging him toward the evidence they need."

They left the dockyards a few blocks from the cemetery. They would have to keep to the shoreline now—Unwin did not wish to draw too close to the Forty Winks and be spotted by someone who might inform Jasper Rook of his whereabouts. He led his companion north, and Moore seemed content to carry on with his lecture, following wherever Unwin directed his umbrella.

"Some in the Agency believe that this technique has been practiced for a long time but called different things through the centuries. It was easier to do, they say, when people lived in small tribes spread over the earth. Fewer signals to sift through then, and a greater willingness to allow them to mingle. The omens, visions, and prophecies of shamans and witch doctors: these might have been rooted in what we call dream detection.

"But I don't care much for the history, and in any case things are different now. In our city, each night is an enormous puzzle of sensation, desire, fear. Only those who have trained extensively can distinguish one mind from another. At the Agency their training is put to use on behalf of the organization's clients. The watchers, whose work is coordinated by the overseer himself, investigate the unconscious minds of suspects while the detectives seek out clues of a more tangible nature. It is this technique that gives Agency operatives their unprecedented insight."

"What if someone tried to use the technique with only a little training?" Unwin asked.

Moore glared at him. "Assuming he succeeded at all, he would put himself and others in danger. There are reservoirs of malevolence in the sleeping city, and you would not want to tap them accidentally." He paused, then added quietly, "There are, however, some who can assist in the process. Who can induce the focused states necessary to employ oneiric detection—or be more easily subjected to it. Their talents, when used, might appear as hypnosis to the uninformed."

Unwin recalled what Miss Greenwood had done to Brock that morning, at the carnival ticket booth. Something whispered in his ear and the man had fallen immediately into a kind of trance. "Cleopatra Greenwood is one of those people," he said.

Moore grunted. "The power of Greenwood's voice has been observed on several occasions. Sivart knew of it, though he didn't know what it was. You remember she had a brief career as a singer? When I left the Agency, the overseer was experimenting with recordings of her music, to see if they could help expand the uses of dream detection. To what end I'm not entirely certain. But Hoffmann, of course, is also aware of her talent. In fact, I no longer consider it a coincidence that one of Cleo Greenwood's songs was first played on the radio almost eight years ago, on the night of November eleventh."

Of course: Unwin had heard it, too. That was why he recognized the tune when he heard it performed at the Cat & Tonic the night before. The questions that Sivart had left unanswered in his report on The Man Who Stole November Twelfth returned to Unwin's mind: the day skipped on calendars across the city, the mysterious operatives—never identified or apprehended—who changed the date at all the government offices and news agencies. But maybe there had been no operatives, at least not conscious ones.

"Could Hoffmann have influenced us somehow?" Unwin asked. "Infiltrated our dreams and made agents out of us while we slept? We might have altered the calendars ourselves."

Moore frowned, his lips disappearing behind his whiskers. "He knows the technique of dream detection. Years ago the secret was leaked to him—the work of a double agent, probably. And he is more powerful by far than any of the watchers, because his mastery of disguise and ventriloquism makes him untraceable as he moves from one dream to another. But how he could have planted suggestions, fooled us into stealing a day from ourselves—that I cannot imagine. And if he had done it once, wouldn't he have done it again? Why stop with one day if he could take so much more? Every night, his sleeper agents would be doing his work."

"Last night the alarm clocks were stolen by a gang of sleepwalkers," Unwin said. "I saw one or two people emerge from every building we passed—they must have broken in to each apartment and taken the clocks. They thought they were going to a party to drink and gamble, but really they were delivering their plunder to the Rooks. Miss Greenwood was there, singing to them, and Detective Pith was shot because he discovered the operation."

Moore shook his head. "There's something we're missing, then. Some tool the enemy has acquired. A battle is under way, Mr. Unwin. The last, maybe, in a long and quiet war. I don't understand the meaning of the maneuvers, only the stakes. Hoffmann's desire for vengeance has grown in the years since his defeat on November twelfth. The gambling parlors, the protection rackets, the black markets—these have always been means to an end, a web from which to feed through the long years of his preparations. His true goal is the destruction of the boundary between the city's rational mind and the violent delirium of its lunatic dreams. His ideal world is a carnival, everything illusory, everything in flux. We'd all be butterflies dreaming we were people if he had his way. Only the Agency's rigorous adherence to the principles of order and reason have held him in check. Your work, Mr. Unwin, and mine."

From the north came the sounds of traffic, of the city awakening. Unwin's clothes were torn and bloodstained. How many people would have seen his name in the papers by now? It would not be good for his defense, he thought, to be found covered in another man's blood. He wondered whether there was a subway station nearby, one with access to the eight train.

"You realize by now that your search for Sivart is hopeless," Moore said. "He is probably dead."

"He contacted me," Unwin said.

"What? How?"

"He appeared in my sleep two nights ago. And again, I think, last night. He told me about Chapter Eighteen."

"Impossible. Sivart knows nothing about dream infiltration. None of the detectives do; they're given expurgated editions of the *Manual*, like yours."

"But the watchers—"

"The watchers never reveal the true source of their knowledge. It is disguised as intelligence gleaned from mundane informants. This is standard protocol; it's all in the Agency bylaws. The unabridged edition, of course."

"Someone told him, then. Zlatari saw him reading at the Forty Winks, just before he disappeared. It must have been a complete version of the *Manual*."

"Who would have given it to him?"

"The same person who showed you the gold tooth in the mouth of the Oldest Murdered Man," Unwin said. He stopped and took Moore's shoulder. "I thought you were only being forgetful when you said you dreamed her. But maybe it really did happen in your sleep."

Moore appeared suddenly dazed. He closed his eyes, and Unwin saw them darting back and forth under the lids. "It was Cleopatra Greenwood, I think."

"Are you sure?" Unwin said. "Describe her."

"You're right," Moore said, his eyes still closed. "She was younger than Miss Greenwood. Just as pretty, though. And very quiet, as if she thought someone else might be listening. Brown hair under her gray cap. Eyes gray, almost silver, like mirrors. She was dressed for bad weather. She was wearing, I think, a plaid coat."

The act of remembrance had left Moore in a stupor. Unwin stood with his hand still on his shoulder. The woman in the plaid coat had broken in to the old clerk's dream and shown him the thing he could not forget. She had unveiled Sivart's gravest of errors.

Little surprise that Moore had mistaken her for Cleopatra Greenwood. The resemblance, now that Unwin considered it, was obvious. The woman in the plaid coat was Miss Greenwood's daughter. And she was most certainly "in on it." But what did she have to gain from revealing the fake in the Municipal Museum? Or from stealing a copy of the *Manual* and giving it to Sivart?

Moore's eyes popped open. "We have a ride," he said.

A taxicab was approaching from a narrow side street farther up the block. Moore stepped out from under the umbrella to signal it with both hands. The taxicab lurched to the curb and idled there, its checkered chassis shuddering.

"We'll go to my place," Moore said to Unwin, "and plan our next move."

The driver of the cab was a slouched, thin-faced man. He lowered his window a few inches and watched them cross the street. Unwin drew his coat tighter over his shirt, trying to conceal the stains.

"You're available?" Moore called.

The driver took this in slowly, refusing to meet Moore's gaze. At last he muttered, "Available."

Moore nodded sharply and reached for the handle of the door. He tugged at it a few times, but the door held fast. "It's locked," he said.

The driver ran his tongue over his teeth and said, "Locked."

"Will you take us?" Moore demanded. "Yes or no?"

"No," the driver said.

Unwin lowered his umbrella over his face and searched for an escape route. Had the cabbie recognized him? He wondered if the newspapers had used the photo on his clerk's badge.

Moore was insistent, however. "Why did you stop when I waved for you if you did not plan to take on a fare?"

The driver mumbled inaudibly, then reached back, found the lock with his hand, and unfastened it. Moore threw the door open and slid across the seat. Unwin hesitated, but Moore beckoned for him to follow, so he closed up his umbrella and got in.

Moore gave an address just a few blocks from Unwin's own, then settled back into the seat. "Soon after I completed the *Manual*," he said, "it was decided that only a few specially trained agents would be privy to the secrets of Chapter Eighteen, and a shorter edition was quickly printed for general use. Enormous changes were under way at the Agency at this time: a new building, the construction of the archives. Controls had to be tightened. Every copy of the original edition was cataloged and accounted for. But what the overseer and I both knew was that one copy of the book could not be so easily repressed."

Moore tapped his own head and gave Unwin a meaningful look.

"But you would not have betrayed the Agency's trust."

"Of course not. I had been with the organization from the beginning, when fourteen of us shared one office heated by a coal stove. But the world had changed since then. The enemy had changed. Caligari's Traveling Carnival had arrived, and with it the nefarious biloquist Enoch Hoffmann. The old boundaries were already eroding, and to know a thing was to put it in jeopardy. The overseer had dictated to me his profoundest secrets, and he knew that Hoffmann, if he chose, could break the lock on my brain as easily as a child tears the wrapping from a birthday present. I was a danger to the Agency, loyal or not."

"The overseer threatened you?"

"He didn't have to."

"So you left. Made yourself forget everything."

"It was easier than you might think. I had been the Agency's first clerk. For years, I was its only clerk. I had developed memory exercises to retain all the information entrusted to me. Imaginary palaces, archives of the mind. They were structural; I could feel their weight in my head. The supports had been bending and groaning for a long time. I had only to loosen a brick or two, and let the rest collapse." Moore leaned forward and said to the driver, "You there, can't you go a bit faster?"

Unwin peered through the window. The streets were uncrowded, but despite Moore's insistence the driver maintained his pace, keeping always to one lane, never hurrying to beat a traffic signal.

Moore fell back into the seat, shaking his head. "I can't pretend to understand your role in all this, Mr. Unwin. But I think whoever has you on this case put you there because you know so little. How else to explain it? The enemy would not suspect your importance, even were he to search every corner of your mind."

"That's changing, though."

Moore nodded. "You know the dangers, but the dangers know you, too. We will have to act swiftly, now. Our investigation depends upon it."

"Investigation": it was just the word Unwin had been trying to avoid. How long now had he been doing the work of a detective, in spite of himself? Ever since he had stolen the phonograph record from Lamech's office. Or longer: since he first began to shadow the woman in the plaid coat.

"There's a document," Unwin said. "A phonograph record. I've played it, but I can't understand the recording—it's just a lot of garbled noises. I think Lamech intended to give it to me before he was killed."

Moore's face darkened. "It must have come from the Agency archives. That's where the overseer was experimenting with the new methodologies. You'll have to bring the record down there if you want to learn what it is."

Moore stopped talking and turned to rub condensation from the window with his sleeve. He gazed out at the street, frowning. Unwin saw the problem, too: their driver was headed the wrong way. Where was the man taking them? Perhaps a reward had been posted for Unwin's capture, and the cabbie meant to collect.

"I'm not paying you to take the scenic route," Moore said. "Left, man. Turn left!"

The driver turned right. On the next block, they saw a car that had swerved off the road and struck a fire hydrant. Water shot in torrents into the air, cascading over the vehicle, flooding the gutter and part of the street. A man in a suit sat on the crumpled hood of the car, scratching his head and trying to speak, but his mouth kept filling with water and he could only gurgle and spit. People walking by did not even look at him.

"This is outrageous," Moore said. "Has someone alerted the authorities? You," he said to the driver, "use your two-way radio, would you?"

The cabbie ignored him and drove slowly past the scene. Moore's face went red, and the bruise on his forehead grew a darker shade of purple. He seemed too angry to speak.

A police cruiser was parked at the next corner. Moore rolled down his window, and Unwin sank deeper into his seat as the old man shouted into the rain, "Officer! Officer!"

The driver's door was open. Seated behind the wheel with her feet on the dashboard was a girl of twelve or thirteen, dressed in her school uniform, twirling a billy club in her left hand. Imprisoned in the back of the car were seven or eight people, packed so tightly that one man—a policeman to judge from his hat, and maybe the rightful owner of the car—was stuck with his face pressed up against the glass.

Moore gasped. "The wicked truant!" he said to Unwin.

At the next block, the cabbie parked in front of a flower shop, where a few people stood beneath a blue-striped awning. He took the car out of gear and let the engine idle.

"I won't pay you a dime," Moore said. "Furthermore, I demand your registration number."

"Quiet," Unwin said to him.

Moore touched the lump on his head and looked at Unwin as though he had been struck.

"He's asleep," Unwin said. "They're all asleep. The whole city— everyone."

The people under the awning of the flower shop had noticed the taxicab. Moore peered through the window as they approached, then looked at Unwin. "You're right," he whispered.

A woman wearing a yellow housecoat opened the front passenger-side door. She leaned down and said to the driver, "Something to do."

The driver tapped his palm against the gear stick. "Someplace to be."

This was apparently the reply the woman was looking for, because she got in beside him and shut the door.

Unwin leaned close to Edwin Moore. "How could Hoffmann have done it?"

Moore was shaking his head and rubbing the white bristles on his chin. Quietly he said, "The alarm clocks."

Unwin thought again of the nighttime parade he had marched with, of that strange troupe with their thieves' sacks over their shoulders. Hoffmann had needed the help of only a few to steal the clocks. But then what? The entire city oversleeps and is susceptible to his influence?

"There is still something we're missing," Moore said. "But the clocks were implements of order, ones we've long taken for granted, and Hoffmann drowned them in the bay. These people outside, they may have dreamed of waking to phantom alarms, when in truth they were waking into a second sleep, one that Hoffmann had prepared for them. The city nearly fell to pieces on November twelfth. Now Hoffmann's cracked open the madness in its heart and spilled it into the streets."

"I don't see what he gains."

"Anything he wants," Moore said. "The dissolution of the Agency. The gold he thought was his on November twelfth, with interest. Who knows what he'll demand? We are beaten—and he has left us awake so that we may witness the manner of our defeat."

A sleepwalking boy in a green poncho opened the rear door and looked into the cab, his eyes dull behind drooping lids. Startled, Moore scooted across the seat, closer to Unwin. The boy climbed in and said to no one, "Have to get there soon."

Without turning, the driver of the taxi said, "Have to get it done."

Others were gathering around the vehicle now. They stood silent in the rain, swaying a little while they waited to take their places inside.

"There's more than plain madness here," Unwin said.

Moore pursed his lips. His eyes for a moment were those that Unwin had seen at the museum the morning before—blank in the dark caves of his eye sockets—and Unwin wondered how long the rebuilt frame of the man's mind would hold. But light quickly returned to them, and Moore said, "Yes, this group of sleepwalkers is different from those others. Special operatives of some kind, perhaps. It's as though they've been recruited for a particular task."

Unwin opened his door. "I don't think we want to be in this taxi," he said.

Moore shook his head. "One of us should stay with them, see what they're up to. And you already have a burden of your own. Get that record to the archives, Mr. Unwin. Let no one take it from you."

Unwin climbed out of the car. As soon as he was on his feet, a man in a red union suit slipped by and took his place. Now Moore was sandwiched between two sleepwalkers. For him there was no turning back.

Unwin reached in and handed him his umbrella. "You may need this."

Moore took it. "We have a good team here," he said.

Before Unwin could reply, the sleepwalker in the red union suit closed the door, and the taxicab rolled slowly away down the block.

Moore turned in his seat to gaze out the rear window, one hand open in grim salute.

"And the truth is our business," Unwin said quietly.

IT WAS DARK AS midnight now, though according to Unwin's watch it was barely eleven in the morning. The storm had worsened, and inky clouds blotted out every trace of the sun. He pulled his jacket tight over his chest as he walked, though it meant baring one hand to the cold.

Sleepwalkers, dozens of them on every block, ignored him as he passed. Some, like the girl who had stolen the police car, were enacting their strange whims in the streets, transforming the city into a kind of open-air madhouse. One man had dragged his furniture onto the sidewalk and was seated on a soggy couch, tugging anxiously at his beard while listening to the news from a silent, unplugged radio. A woman nearby shouted up at an apartment building, arguing with no one Unwin could see or hear—there was a disagreement, it seemed, about who was to blame for ruining the pot roast.

Other sleepwalkers moved in small groups, stepping around Unwin as he passed. They were silent, their eyes open but unfathomable. They were headed east, the same direction Moore had been taken.

By the time Unwin drew near to his apartment, his clothes were soaked through but his hands were clean. A black Agency car was parked at the end of the block. He cupped his hands against the glass to peer through, expecting to find Screed's scowling face, but the car was empty. He returned to his building and went inside, climbed the stairs to the fifth floor.

His apartment door was open, his spare key still in the lock. He put that in his pocket and went in, closing the door behind him. In the kitchen he found himself again at the barrel end of a gun—his own this time. Emily Doppel's eyes were half closed, but her aim seemed true enough. She carried her lunch box in her other hand.

Testing her, Unwin walked toward his bedroom. Emily followed, keeping the pistol trained on her target. He considered going into the bathroom to change, but Emily would probably have followed him there, too. So he undressed in front of her, leaving the damp and bloody clothes in a heap on the floor. Naked, he wondered if there were Agency bylaws regarding detectives and their assistants and whether this violated any of them.

Once he had put on dry clothes, he set the alarm clock he'd taken from the rowboat on his nightstand, then changed his mind and tucked it into his jacket. "I'm sure I was wrong about your lunch box," he said to Emily. "This might be my last chance to learn the truth."

After a moment she seemed to understand. She shook the pistol at him, directing him into the kitchen, then put the lunch box on the table and flipped it open.

Inside were dozens of tin figurines. Unwin set them on the table, lining them up like soldiers. They were not soldiers, though—they were detectives. One crouched with a magnifying glass in his hand, another spoke into a telephone, another held out his badge. One stood as Emily stood now, arm outstretched with pistol in hand. Another resembled Unwin in his current stance, bent over with his hands on his knees, an expression of mild astonishment on his face.

Only flecks of paint remained on the figurines; they had seen a lot of use through the years. Unwin imagined a little red-haired girl, alone at the playground, sitting cross-legged in the grass, surrounded by her dreamed-up operatives. What adventures they must have had under her authority! Now the game had become real for her.

"You understand that the memo I asked you to type was not a ruse," Unwin said. "You deserve better. You deserve a real detective."

Emily swept the figurines back into her lunch box. She kept the gun pointed at him and gestured toward his briefcase, which was lying on the floor near the door. He picked it up and she directed him out of the apartment and back down the stairs.

No one was on the street to witness the sleepwalker conduct him at gunpoint to the black car at the end of the block. He got in on the passenger side and set his briefcase between his feet.

"Are you sure you can drive?" Unwin asked.

For answer, Emily put the car into gear and turned out onto the street. She drove very carefully the seven blocks to the Agency office building, though no one else was on the road now. They parked right outside the lobby, and when Unwin got out of the car, he saw that lights were on in all forty-six floors.

TWELVE

On Interrogation

**The process begins long before you are alone in
a room together. By the time you ask the suspect your
questions, you should already know the answers.**

The fortieth floor, like the fourteenth, was a single enormous room,
but it was empty except for a square metal table and two chairs
at its center. Emily stood to one side, at the edge of the bright yellow
light aimed at the table from above. She still held the gun but had left
her lunch box in the car and taken Unwin's briefcase instead.

The man with the pointy blond beard was seated opposite Unwin.
Of all the people who lived in the city, this man was one who Unwin
wished were among the sleeping. But it seemed that Hoffmann had left
the Agency's employees to go about their work unhindered—Emily's
sleep was probably just a result of her condition. Whatever the magician was up to, he did not want anyone from the Agency's ranks involved. Or was it simply as Moore had said, that Hoffmann wanted
them to see how he had triumphed?

If so, the man with the blond beard revealed no concern for what
was happening outside. Without looking at Unwin, he set his portable

typewriter on the table. He snapped his fingers at Emily, and she gave him the briefcase. He began removing its contents.

"Two pencils," he said, and put them side by side. "In need of sharpening."

Next he took out Unwin's copy of *The Manual of Detection*. "Standard issue," he said, and sneered as he flipped it open to the title page. "Fourth edition, utterly useless."

Next were some file folders, all empty—Unwin liked to keep a few spares handy.

Last was the phonograph record. This he examined more carefully, holding it up to the light and gazing at its grooves, as though he could hear it if he looked closely enough. "A watcher-class file, Sivart-related. Recorded by the late Mr. Lamech, pressed by Miss Palsgrave on Agency premises. Not logged in any official registry. Most suspect." He slipped it back into its cover and set it on the table, then turned the briefcase upside down and shook it. It was empty.

"I think the Agency has bigger worries than what I keep in my briefcase," Unwin said.

"Quiet," snapped the man with the blond beard. He put everything back, set the briefcase aside, and loaded a sheet of paper into his typewriter. "It took me hours to polish the keys after your accomplice spilled water on them." He sat very straight in his chair and closed his eyes, then rubbed his temples with the tips of his fingers. Next he stretched out his arms and flexed his hands. He seemed to be getting ready for some kind of performance.

"Maybe you should take notes about what's going on outside," Unwin said.

The man with the blond beard said to Emily, "If he speaks again, shoot him."

Unwin sighed and looked at the table while the man went through his stretching routine again. Then, with his eyes partly closed, he began to type. He worked quickly, just as he had done at the museum café.

He seemed to be drawing words out of the air, typing them as he breathed them in.

He reached the bottom of the first page, set the sheet aside, and loaded another. Unwin looked at his watch to time the man's progress. He finished the second page in just under three minutes.

When the third page was done, the man with the blond beard stacked them together, folded them, and slid them into an envelope. He put the envelope inside his jacket, then closed the typewriter case and stood.

"That's it?" Unwin asked.

The man picked up Unwin's briefcase and went toward the door.

"Sir," Unwin said, getting to his feet, "I'd like my briefcase now."

"We have what we need," the man said to Emily. "And you have your orders."

Emily frowned in her sleep. It would not be easy for her to shoot him, Unwin thought. But she was angry. He had deceived her, disappointed her, made her believe he was something he was not. She must have drifted off to sleep sometime after she put him on the eight train that morning. Then she fell victim to the same plague that had infected the rest of the city, and her anger was shaken awake.

She pushed her glasses back on her nose and took aim. Did the *Manual* include advice appropriate to situations like these? No, Unwin thought, it was not *The Manual of Detection* he needed. It was his assistant's own good planning.

"Emily," he said. "The devil's in the details."

Her aim faltered a little.

He repeated the phrase, and Emily swayed on her feet as though the ground had shifted beneath her. "And doubly in the bubbly," she said, opening her eyes. She looked with alarm at the gun in her hand.

Unwin gestured to the man with the blond beard. "There," he said. "There!"

Emily swung the gun around, and the man with the blond beard stopped walking.

"Sir," Unwin said again. "My briefcase."

The man gave Emily a withering look and returned to the table. He dropped the case in front of Unwin.

"Your typewriter as well," Unwin said.

He set the typewriter down.

"Now sit."

Audibly grinding his teeth, the man with the blond beard sat. Emily kept the gun trained on him while Unwin removed the man's necktie and used it to bind his hands behind his back. It would not hold for long, Unwin thought, but it was the best he could do for now.

"Quickly," he said to Emily. "I need you to write a memo."

She put the pistol away, then sat and opened the typewriter, loaded a fresh sheet of paper.

The man with the blond beard snorted at all this but said nothing. Indeed, as Unwin began to dictate, he leaned forward a little, listening with apparent interest.

"To colon Benjamin Screed comma Detective comma floor twenty-nine return from colon Charles Unwin comma capital D capital E capital T capital E capital C capital T capital I capital V capital E comma floor twenty-nine comma temporarily floor forty return.

He took a deep breath and continued. "Sir comma despite the unhappy beginning of our association comma it is my hope that we may still find a way to work together as colleagues to our mutual satisfaction point. To that end comma I offer you the opportunity to assist me—"

But here Unwin frowned and said, "Emily, strike that. Resume: To that end comma I offer to assist you in solving a very important case comma or rather several important cases all at once point. In addition to delivering to you the killer of Edward Lamech comma I intend also to shed new light on cases now at rest in the Agency archives comma including The Oldest Murdered Man comma The Three Deaths of

Colonel Baker comma and The Man Who Stole November Twelfth point. I trust this will be of interest to you comma as you are no doubt aware that our organization is in need of a new star detective comma and I can tell you I have no interest in the job point. If you find this satisfactory comma I leave it to you to choose our place of meeting point. I will come unarmed full stop."

Emily snatched out the page, quickly typed a final draft, and said, "I'll go and find a messenger."

"No messengers, Emily. I don't think they can be trusted. This remains, as you once put it, an internal affair."

The man with the blond beard was grinning now. Straining against the bonds, he turned in his seat to watch them go. Unwin avoided the man's eyes, glancing back only once while he and Emily waited for the elevator to arrive. He had not even bothered to look at the document the man with the blond beard had typed. Whatever it contained—a false confession, a memory somehow plucked from his brain—it could not possibly matter after this. They believed he was a renegade, and now he was acting like one.

Unwin had worried that the elevator attendant might recognize him, that even he might have been notified of Unwin's fugitive status. But the white-haired little man only hummed to himself as the car descended, seemingly oblivious to his passengers.

Emily drew close to Unwin and whispered, "Do you really know who killed Lamech?"

"No," he said. "But if I don't find out soon, I think it won't matter anyway."

Emily looked at her shoes. "I haven't been a very good assistant," she said.

They both were quiet, and the only sounds in the car were the elevator attendant's tuneless humming and the grating of the machinery above. Unwin knew that it was he, not Emily, who had failed. She had saved him from Detective Screed, had chosen the secret signal that saved him a second time. But outside the Gilbert Hotel, when she asked him what would happen to her once they found Sivart, he had failed to give her an answer.

Maybe he should have told her that he would remain a detective, that she would still be his assistant. Better yet, they could act as partners: the meticulous dreamer and his somnolent sidekick. Together they would untangle the knots Enoch Hoffmann and his villainous cohorts had tied in the city, in its dreams. Their suspects would be disarmed by his clerkly demeanor; she would ask the tough questions and do most of the driving. They would track down every error Sivart had committed, re-solve all the great cases, set the record straight. Their reports would be precise, complete, and timely: the envy of every clerk on the fourteenth floor.

But he had not even cleared his name yet, and Emily now would also be hunted.

She was still looking at her shoes when Unwin put a hand on her shoulder. "You are the finest assistant a detective could wish for," he said.

With a swift movement, as though the floor had tilted or the elevator slipped its cable, Emily fell fully into him and laid her head against his chest, wrapping her arms around his middle. Unwin stifled a gasp at the sudden and complete materialization of this young woman in his arms. He could smell her lavender perfume again, and beneath that the sharpness of her sweat.

Emily raised her lips close to his ear and said, "It's really something, don't you think? We have so much work to do, but we can't trust anyone. And when you get right down to it, we can barely trust each other. But it's better that way, I suppose. It keeps us thinking, keeps us guessing. Just a couple of shadows, that's what we are. Turn the light on and that's the end of us."

The elevator attendant had stopped humming, and Unwin caught himself wondering about bylaws again.

"Emily," he said, "do you remember anything of the dream you were having earlier?"

She moved back an inch and adjusted her glasses. "I remember birds, lots of them. Pigeons, I think. And a breeze. Open windows. There were papers everywhere."

The elevator attendant cleared his throat. "Floor twenty-nine," he said.

Emily slowly let go of Unwin, then stepped out onto the polished wood floor. The custodian had cleaned it to a shine—not a trace of black paint remained.

"Emily?" Unwin said.

"Sir?"

"Do try to stay awake."

The attendant closed the door, and Unwin told him to take him to the archives. Clerks, and even detectives, were technically prohibited from entering, but the little man made no protest. He threw the lever and sat on his stool. "The archives," he said. "The long-term memory of our esteemed organization. Without it we are nothing but a jumble of trivialities, delusions, and windblown stratagems."

A bulb on the attendant's panel lit yellow, and he brought the car to a halt. Unwin found himself looking into the broad office of the fourteenth floor. His overclerk, Mr. Duden, stood in front of him. The round-faced man took a step back when he saw Unwin. "I'll get the next one," he said.

THAT ONLY UNDERCLERKS were permitted access to the Agency archives had instilled in Unwin a simmering resentment of his inferiors. He sometimes daydreamed about catching one of the affable little men on his way to lunch and accompanying him to the booth of a local eatery. There he would buy the man a sandwich, pickles, a glass of what-have-you, and gradually turn the conversation to the topic of their work—forbidden, of course, between employees of different departments. In time the underclerk's caginess would give way to happy disclosure; he was as proud of his work as Unwin was of his, after all. And so Unwin would come to learn the secrets of that place to which his completed case files, and the files of a hundred other clerks, were delivered each day, to be housed in perpetuity. All for the price of a roast beef on rye.

Of course Unwin never did anything of the sort. He was not a faker, not a sneak. At least he had been neither of those things until recently.

The elevator attendant had left him in a corridor one level below the subbasement. It ended at a small wooden door. Slowly, but not so slowly he would appear to be trespassing, Unwin opened it and stepped through.

The heart of the archives (for what else could this be?) smelled of cologne, of dust, of the withered-flower sweetness of old paper. Its ceiling, high as Central Terminal's sweeping vaults, was hung with clusters of electric lamps shaded in green glass, and the walls were made entirely of file drawers. The drawers were of the older sort, with bronze handles and paneling of dark wood. Rolling library ladders, each seven times the height of a man, provided access throughout. Eight massive columns spanned the room, and these, too, were lined with file drawers and equipped with ladders.

Dozens of underclerks were at work here, browsing open drawers, jotting notes on index cards, ascending and descending ladders, wheeling them into new positions. They went back and forth between the files and a squat booth at the center of the room. Meanwhile, messengers in yellow suspenders appeared and disappeared through doors disguised to look like stacks of file drawers, some of them high in the walls. To access one of these, the messenger would climb a ladder, open the door with a telescoping pole he drew from his sack, then leap through the opening.

Unwin closed the door behind him—it, too, was disguised as a stack of file drawers—and walked along the wall searching for some indication of an organizational scheme. But the drawers were not labeled, nor were they divided into sections, alphabetical or otherwise. He chose one at waist height and opened it. The files were all dark blue, not the light brown he was accustomed to seeing. He removed one and found a card pasted to its front. Typed on the card were a series of phrases:

Stolen Journal
Jilted Lover
Vague Threats
Long-Lost Sister
Mysterious Double

The documents inside were formatted according to some method that was wholly unfamiliar to him. Pages of handwritten notes identified a client, described his meeting with an Agency representative, and gave an account of his suspicions and fears. But where were the clues? Who was the detective assigned to the case? How had the matter been resolved?

A nearby drawer slid open, and Unwin looked up to see an underclerk just a few steps away. The man grinned at him. He had round cheeks and wore a bowler hat and a scarlet cravat. Unwin returned the file and ran his fingers over the folder tabs, pretending to search for another.

But the underclerk came closer and bowed, and when Unwin did not look up at him, he bowed again, more deeply this time, and with the third bow he made a dispirited little huffing sound. Finally the underclerk spoke. "You must be the new fellow, yes, the new fellow?"

Unwin avoided answering by patting his palms against the folders and smiling.

"Why don't you tell me what you're looking for?" The underclerk's cheeks reddened. Apparently, the prospect of assisting someone else was a great embarrassment to him.

"You're too kind." Unwin did not want to ask this man about the phonograph record, but he had to tell him something, so he said, "I'm looking for the Sivart case files. The Colonel Baker case would be a good start."

The underclerk frowned at that. "Sounds like you've got too many modifiers. What's the primary correlative?"

Unwin considered. "Faked death," he said.

The underclerk tapped one finger against his round, clean-shaven chin. "Now, I've been here almost two years, and I don't recall . . ." His cheeks went redder, until they matched the color of his cravat. "What did you say your name was?" he asked.

Unwin coughed and waved his hand, and pretended to study the files again. The underclerk went away very quietly and quietly closed the drawer he had opened a minute before. Then he started off toward the center of the room with a quick, resolute pace, more like a messenger than an underclerk.

Unwin closed the drawer and followed. The underclerk saw him pursuing and walked faster, so Unwin began to run. The underclerk ran, too, and by this time most everyone in the archive was watching them. Unwin could see the booth more clearly now. At its peak was a four-faced clock, nearly identical to the one at Central Terminal. Unwin checked his watch and saw that it matched to the very second the clock at the heart of the Agency archives. It was seventeen minutes after one o'clock in the afternoon. The underclerk drew up to the booth, pushing others aside to reach the front. There was a lot of jostling and grumbling, but the others went quiet as he began to speak to someone inside the booth. Then they all turned to watch Unwin's approach. Some removed their hats and started fidgeting with the brims. They parted to let him through, and the one in the red cravat stood aside.

A woman was seated in the booth, surrounded by card catalogs. She was younger than Unwin, though older than Emily. She had straight brown hair and a wide, frowning mouth. She looked him over carefully, paying special attention to his hat.

"You're not an underclerk," she said.

"My apologies," said Unwin. "It is not my intention to deceive. I am a clerk of the fourteenth floor."

Now the underclerks began to chatter all at once. "Clerk!" they said, and, "Fourteenth floor!" They repeated the words until the woman hushed them with a wave of her hand.

"No," Unwin said, shaking his head, "I *was* a clerk. I am hardly accustomed to the change myself. Just yesterday I was promoted to the rank of detective. In fact, I'm here on business of a detectorial nature." He showed her his badge.

Again the underclerks started talking, their voices rising higher as they pushed and pulled at their hats, nearly tearing them in half. "Detective!" they said, and one among them wailed, "What's a detective?"

"Quiet!" the woman shouted. She glared at Unwin. "This is highly irregular. You'd better come in."

She opened a door to the side of her window and ushered Unwin into the booth; some of the underclerks made as though to follow, but the woman closed it before any could slip through. Then she closed green shutters over her window. Unwin could still hear the pleas of the underclerks outside: "What's a detective?" they cried, and then, "What's promoted?" The few near the window scratched at the shutters with their fingernails; one was brazen enough to tap his knuckles against the door.

Unwin now saw that the card catalogs replicated in miniature the archives themselves. Each stack of file drawers outside had a corresponding stack within the booth; even the columns were replicated by eight freestanding pillars. This explained the lack of references to content or indexing in the archive proper. The only key was here.

The woman reached under her desk, took a silver flask from its hiding place, and set out two tin cups. She poured a little brown liquid into each and pressed one into Unwin's hand. She drank. Unwin was unaccustomed to drinking whiskey straight, from a flask or otherwise. And though he did not find it altogether unpleasant, each sip was a keen surprise to his tongue.

The underclerks were silent now. They had either dispersed or agreed to stay quiet and listen in.

"You must forgive them," the woman said. "They've had a very trying week. We all have." She offered him her hand; her palm was cool and papery against his own. "Eleanor Benjamin," she said, "Chief Clerk of Mysteries."

"Charles Unwin, Detective."

"And, I suppose, the reason I lost my best staffer to the fourteenth floor yesterday. To promote someone from one department to another is atypical. To promote two people at once is absurd. I'm afraid we're all a little rattled down here."

"The woman who has taken my place used to work for you?" Unwin asked.

"Yes," said Miss Benjamin. "Only two months into the job and she was already the best underclerk I had."

This was a surprise even sharper than the whiskey. The woman in the plaid coat, Cleo Greenwood's daughter, had started working at the Agency long before the first time Unwin saw her at Central Terminal. She must have used the time to find and steal an unabridged copy of the *Manual*. But what else had she been up to?

"I hardly know what to do without her," Miss Benjamin went on. "She went about her work so calmly that she kept everyone else calm, too. I'm certain one of these twittering old men will fall from his ladder someday. And they haven't even assigned a replacement yet. The whole archive could fall into ruin."

She paused and looked up at the shutters, seeming to see through them and into an archive in flames, sheets of burning paper falling out of the sky, columns of file drawers collapsing under their own weight. Unwin wondered if she knew that the world outside the Agency office was already in the process of disintegrating.

"Why was she promoted?" Unwin asked. "Did anyone inform you?"

Miss Benjamin blinked away her vision. "I hardly see the relevance of that," she said, and poured more whiskey into their cups. "You know perfectly well that detectives are barred from the archives, Mr. Unwin. Only messengers are permitted to move freely from one floor to another. And under no circumstances should a detective be caught drinking whiskey with a chief clerk. So what are you doing down here?"

Answer questions with questions, he reminded himself—he had read that in the *Manual.* "How many chief clerks are there?"

Miss Benjamin smiled. "I'm not unwilling to help you, Detective. I'm just saying that there's a price. Now, what were you looking for out there in my archive?"

Unwin found that he liked this chief clerk's plainspokenness, but he was not yet sure if he could trust her. "I was looking for my old case files," he said. This was not completely a lie—seeing those files would have been of interest, especially after all he learned since his first meeting with Edwin Moore.

Miss Benjamin laughed, and from outside the booth came the sound of shuffling feet.

"Are you surprised?" Unwin asked. "I've done plenty of case files. The Oldest Murdered Man, The Three Deaths of Colonel Baker."

"Yes, yes," said Miss Benjamin. "But you're talking post-detection, Mr. Unwin. Solutions. This"—she gestured to the card catalogs around her and, by extension, the file drawers beyond—"is Mysteries."

"Only Mysteries?"

"*Only* Mysteries! What did you expect, everything jammed into one archive? That would be an organizational nightmare. I am Chief Clerk of Mysteries, and the underclerks out there are familiar only with mysteries. It's why they don't know what a detective is—they don't need to. The vicissitudes of detection aren't part of their work. As far as they know, mysteries come here and stay here. It's why they're so nervous. Imagine having all the questions but none of the answers."

"I don't have to imagine it," Unwin said.

"Three."

"What?"

"You asked me how many chief clerks there are. There are three. Miss Burgrave, Miss Palsgrave, and myself. Miss Burgrave is Chief Clerk of Solutions. It's her archive you meant to infiltrate, not mine." She lowered her eyelids and added, "Though it isn't a terrible thing, having someone to talk to. Your average underclerk doesn't know a woman from a pile of paper clips."

Unwin sipped from his whiskey—just as little as he could, because he already felt dizzy from it. "What about Miss Palsgrave's archive?" he asked. "What is kept there?"

"What I want to know is why a clerk, promoted though he may be, would want to see his own files. Don't you fellows know your cases back to front?"

"Yes," Unwin said. "But it's less a matter of content than of cross-referencing."

She was silent. He would have to give her at least part of the truth. "The case files are categorized as solutions, and rightly so. They are the finest, most thorough solutions imaginable. But what if an error, a purposeful error conceived for some dark purpose, had been inserted into one of those files? What if an aspect of a solution were thus rendered a mystery? What then, Miss Benjamin?"

"You would not have done such a thing."

"I have, Miss Benjamin. Many times, perhaps, though without realizing it. I believe that a man was murdered to keep it a secret. Somewhere in these archives are mysteries that have been passed off as solutions, so they belong here, Miss Benjamin, in your archive. And they are deliberately being kept from you.

"Under normal circumstances, I could work through the messengers, calling up one file after another, checking references, piecing the puzzle together. But that would take time. And I don't know if I can trust the usual channels. Will you help me, Miss Benjamin? Will you tell me the way to the Archive of Solutions?"

He was not sure what he was getting himself into, but Moore had told him that the key to understanding the phonograph record was here in the archives. If not in the first, then maybe in the second.

Miss Benjamin stood, and Unwin saw that she was tall, perhaps a foot taller than he was. She crossed her arms and looked worried. "There are several paths to the Archive of Solutions," she said, "but most will be too dangerous." She pushed her chair aside and lifted an edge of the frayed blue rug. A trapdoor was beneath. "This passage is reserved for the use of the chief clerks. I don't think anyone but the three of us remembers it's here."

She lifted a brass ring and pulled the trapdoor open. A stairwell spiraled downward into the gloom.

"Thank you," he said.

Miss Benjamin took a step closer to him. With the shutters over the window, the air in the booth had grown warmer, and now Unwin found it difficult to breathe, especially when each breath carried with it the sweet aroma of the whiskey on Miss Benjamin's lips.

She said, "I do know a thing or two about detectives, Mr. Unwin. I know that with a few words you could have won my heart. But you're one of the noble ones, aren't you?"

Unwin did not contradict her, though he doubted that even the *Manual* would contain the few words—whatever they were—to which Miss Benjamin was referring.

"What about the third archive?" he said. "You didn't tell me about Miss Palsgrave."

Miss Benjamin stepped back. "I won't," she said. "This is Mysteries, after all, and Miss Palsgrave's work is her own."

Unwin put on his hat and started down the stairs. Miss Benjamin had seemed tall to him, and now, waist-deep in the floor, he looked up and found her terrible and magnificent, a towering, sulky idol in a brown wool skirt. "Good-bye, Miss Benjamin."

She capped her silver flask and sighed. "Watch out for the ninth step," she said, and Unwin had to duck as she kicked the trapdoor closed over his head.

THE STAIRS WERE LIT only by dim lamps that flickered as though to relay a coded message. There was no banister. The wooden steps creaked underfoot, and Unwin felt each with the toe of his shoe before stepping down. Was it a trick of the whiskey, that the walls of the passage seemed to narrow as Unwin descended? Or had he always been a claustrophobe and only needed an experience like this to find out?

The ninth step appeared as sturdy as the others, but he skipped it as Miss Benjamin advised. Unwin found it difficult to stop counting anything once he had begun. Counting sheep, in fact, was his surest route to insomnia—by morning he could fill whole pastures with a vast and clamorous flock. Now he counted steps, and by the twentieth he felt certain the walls really were narrowing, and the ceiling was getting lower, too. How deep did the stairway go? Maybe Miss Benjamin had tricked him into an oubliette. She could have locked the trapdoor and sent a message to Detective Screed by now—but then, perhaps Mr. Duden already had.

The lamps were fewer in number here, and dimmer. He hoped Edwin Moore had known what he was talking about. Could the old man's memory be trusted at all? Unwin had to bend low to take the last several steps. The fifty-second was the last.

Here was a plain wooden door no more than four feet tall. From beyond it came a sound—a wild, incessant clattering, as of many people typing without pause. Unwin felt for a doorknob but could not find one. When he pushed, the door swung open on silent hinges. He ducked through and had to remain crouched on the other side because the ceiling was so low.

The room was barely larger than the desk in his own office, though finished all in dark wood that gleamed in the light from a chandelier. Where Unwin had expected a legion of underclerks, he saw one tiny woman, her silvery hair pinned in a mound atop her head, seated at a desk at the center of the room. He stooped over her, an uncouth giant in a too-small cave, but she did nothing to acknowledge his presence. Her typing was the quickest Unwin had ever seen—quicker than Emily's, quicker, even, than the man with the blond beard's. The sound of one key-clap was indiscernible from the next, and the carrier bell never ceased to reverberate, chiming the end of each line in rapid succession.

"Miss Burgrave?" Unwin said.

The woman stopped typing and peered at him, the wrinkles at the edges of her mouth and eyes fixed in severe concentration. She wore red lipstick, and her cheeks, soft and sagging, were the pink of pink roses. "Oh, it's you," she said, then went back to her work.

Her little hands were a hundred-fingered blur. The paper went into her typewriter from a single great roll that had been mounted to the front of her desk, then onto a second roll mounted just above the first. This system freed her of the need to pause and insert fresh sheets.

Unwin bent over to read what she was typing, but Miss Burgrave stopped again and stared at him, causing him to withdraw so quickly that he bumped his head against the ceiling.

"This will not do," Miss Burgrave said. "You know what it means to be on a schedule, of course, so I will not rebuke you unnecessarily, as that would be tantamount to redundancy, which I already risk by speaking to you at all, and risk again by observing the risk, and so again by observing the observation. In this we could proceed endlessly. Will you not relent? Are you really so stubborn? I ask these questions rhetorically, and thus degrade further the value of my speech."

"I'm not sure I follow you, Miss Burgrave, but if perhaps you'd allow me into the archives—"

"*If perhaps,*" she repeated, her wrinkles deepening. "Mr. Unwin, we shall brook no degree of mysteriousness on this floor. So that weak-kneed naïf allowed you entrance through the trapdoor, and you believe that entitles you to further transgression—and with my assistance, at that."

Unwin kept quiet now. In spite of himself, he glanced again at the typescript mounted to the desk.

"Facts," Miss Burgrave explained. "Dead facts, all questions beaten out of them, all lines of inquiry followed to their termini. Answers and answers to answers, the end of the road, of the world, maybe. Yes, that is how I feel sometimes, as though the world has already ended, the shades drawn over every window, the stars burned down to little black beads, the moon waned beyond waning, all life a dollop of ash, and still I remain at work, trying to explain what happened."

"Explain to whom?"

"Ah, now we come to something." Miss Burgrave rose from her chair, and Unwin saw that she stood no taller than a child. She waved Unwin out of her way and opened a panel hidden in the wall. From there she drew a book about the size of *The Manual of Detection* but bound in red rather than green. She turned to a certain page and, without having to search, read aloud a single paragraph:

Solutions, as distilled by the clerks so Entrusted, from the Reports of detectives so Assigned, and borne by messengers to the aforementioned Dominions, are there to be studied and Linked each to the other according to common significance, and so prepared for Review by the

Overseer. It is solely to the Chief Clerk of Solutions to whom this Task falls, so let him work alone, unhindered by his subordinates in their Courses and his Seniors in their many Doings.

"Where are your underclerks, then?" Unwin asked.

Miss Burgrave sighed. She seemed to have abandoned something: a conviction, maybe, or a hope. She replaced the book and closed the panel, then gestured for Unwin to follow her through a door behind her desk. In the passage beyond, Unwin was able to stand straight again. He heard the quiet commotion of clerkly work: the whisperings, the pen scratchings, the hurried footfalls. But those who made these sounds were nowhere visible in the long hall, nor in the many branches extending from it. Out of the walls protruded two rows of file drawers, one near the floor and the other at waist height, situated so that all their contents were visible. Now and then these drawers would disappear into the walls, only to return a moment later.

As they walked, Miss Burgrave explained, "We are now between the walls of the Archive of Solutions. My underclerks are without, accessing what files they require, according to the instructions I give them by various means, including notes, bellpulls, and color-coded signals. They do not know me, nor would I recognize them, except by the way each clears his throat."

She took a stepstool from a shadow, climbed it, and switched on a light that extended over one of the drawers. She squinted and adjusted the glasses on her nose. "This is what you are here for, no doubt."

Unwin perused the titles quickly. There they were, in chronological order—all the work he had done in his twenty years, seven months, and some-odd days at the Agency, every word of every case file, the great works and the lesser-known, the grand capers and the minor mysteries. They barely filled the single drawer.

Miss Burgrave watched attentively as Unwin drew out the file for The Oldest Murdered Man. A long card was fixed to the back of the file, covered with typed references to files elsewhere in the archives. Here was the original mystery, upstairs with Miss Benjamin, here the case files of other detectives overlapping with this one. And below them references to another archive, a third.

He said to Miss Burgrave, "These refer to files kept by Miss Palsgrave. What are they?"

Miss Burgrave winced. "For a Chief Clerk of Mysteries," she said, "that Miss Benjamin has a great deal to say. How I long for the days of Miss Margrave, who preceded her in the position. Now, there was a woman who knew how to keep a thing to herself. She died just a few days after she retired. Nothing unusual in that. Some people have little in them except the work. But it's something of a syndrome here at the Agency. Clerks and underclerks are immune, mind you. But anyone who knows anything about anything is granted a very short retirement. I will have my own before long, I suppose. And if laws of proportion apply, then my retirement shall be very short indeed. And your own watcher—which is to say your detective's watcher—is due to retire soon. A nice man, Ed Lamech. I'll miss him."

Unwin understood then that Miss Burgrave knew nothing about his recent promotion. And why would she? His promotion was a mystery even to him, and Miss Burgrave knew only the solutions. So she had not heard of Lamech's murder either.

"You hesitate to speak," Miss Burgrave said, "and I warned you once about our tolerance for mysteriousness on this floor."

He chose his words carefully. "It was the discovery of Lamech's death, among other mysteries, Miss Burgrave, that brought me here."

She covered her mouth with one small hand, steadying herself against the file drawer with the other. After a moment she said, "Now, Ed Lamech, he and I used to play cards together. That was before all this, of course. Miss Margrave and I shared a desk, and the archive was just two cardboard boxes at the back of the room: one for mysteries, one for solutions. Edwin Moore kept the files in order. There was a big table at the center of the room where the detectives would lay out mug shots and maps of the city. They smoked and talked big and planned stings; Ed was the loudest of the bunch, but he always had something nice to say. He knew how to make a person feel a little taller. Some nights we'd clear off the table and play a few hands, all of us together. Yes, I always thought Ed Lamech and I might sit down and play cards again, when we found the time."

She switched off the light and said, "Help me down the stepladder, Mr. Unwin," and he did, but when she reached the floor, she did not let go of his hand. "This way."

Unwin's eyes did not have time to adjust as Miss Burgrave pulled him more and more quickly through the darkness between the walls. When a drawer opened or closed, a band of light from the archive swept momentarily across the floor, but that was all, and Unwin knew he would not find his way back on his own. They came to a corridor that was almost entirely dark, from the walls of which no file drawers extended.

"You go that way," Miss Burgrave said, "and you tell Miss Palsgrave that I sent you, though I doubt she cares anymore about what I have to say."

She took her hand back and added, "She works here, but she's never been like the rest of us; not really. Her curriculum vitae is a curious one, to say the least. Be wary of her. Be polite."

Unwin said, "I will, Miss Burgrave. But please, tell me one thing. If you know your underclerks only by their coughs, how did you know me?"

"Oh, Mr. Unwin, don't you know you're one of my own children? Your work has given me some pleasure through the years. When you leave a thing, you leave it where no doubt can touch it. I will not wish you luck. Of your success or failure I will hear in due course."

Unwin heard her footsteps receding, glimpsed the silver of her hair as it passed an open file drawer. And then Miss Burgrave was gone.

He went alone into the dark. The passage sloped downward and curved to the left, tracing a spiral through the earth. Sometimes he kept his eyes open and sometimes he shut them; it made little difference. Miss Burgrave had been right about him: he left matters where no doubt could touch them. But that had been his flaw, to bind mystery so tightly, to obscure his detective's missteps with perfect files. Somehow Unwin had made false things true.

At last his hands found something solid. He felt around the wall, found there the cool roundness of a doorknob and beneath it the gap of a keyhole. He knelt and peered through.

At the center of a vast, dark room were two velvet chairs set on a round blue rug. A blue-shaded floor lamp was set between them, and in its light a phonograph was playing. The music was all drowsy strings and horns, and then a woman began to sing. He knew the melody.

It may be a crime,
But I'm sure that you're mine
In my dream of your dream of me.

The doorknob turned in his hand, and Unwin entered the third archive of the Agency offices.

THIRTEEN

On Cryptography

The coded message is a lifeless thing, mummified and
entombed. To the would-be cryptologist we must
offer the same advice we would give the grave
robber, the spelunker, and the sorcerer of legend:
beware what you dig up; it is yours.

A distance of perhaps fifty paces separated him from the chairs, one
pink, the other pale green. Unwin felt drawn to the warmth of
the electric light, to the languid music playing there, to the voice that
could only have been Miss Greenwood's. It looked to him as though a
cozy parlor had been set down in the middle of a cavern. He went
toward it, feeling alone and insubstantial. He could not see his arms or
his legs, could not see his own shoes. All he could see were the chairs,
the lamp, and the phonograph. All he could hear was the music.

The floor was flat and smooth. A floor like that should have set his
shoes squeaking, but they were muffled—by the darkness itself, Unwin
thought. He kept his mouth shut tight. He did not want to let any of
the darkness in.

He stopped at the edge of the blue rug and stood very still. Here
was a boundary between worlds. In the one were chairs, and music, and

light. In the other there were none of these things, nor even the words for chair, or music, or light.

He did not cross over, only observed from the safety of his wordless dark. Phonograph records were stacked in a cabinet near the green chair, and on top of the cabinet stood a row of books. One of the books looked exactly like the red volume that Miss Burgrave had taken from the secret panel in her office. But everything in the parlor was subjugated to that pink chair. It was nearly three times as large as the green one. Anyone sitting in it would seem a child in proportion. It was the most sinister piece of furniture Unwin had ever seen. He could not imagine sitting in it. He could not imagine sitting in the one that faced it.

He took a step back. The chair would spring upon him if he gave it the chance, devour him whole. If only he could call it by name, he thought, then it might be tamed. Or if he had not given his umbrella to Edwin Moore, he could open it and shield himself from the sight.

From the farthest recesses of the room came a flash of light, bright and brief as the death of a little sun, and for the moment in which it burned, Unwin saw the walls in that region of the archive—saw that they were lined, not with filing cabinets but with shelves of phonograph records. The source of the light was a gigantic machine, a labyrinth of valves and pipes and pistons. It hissed and coughed steam into the air, resembling nothing so much as an oversize waffle iron. The light burst from the space between two great plates, pressed together by the machine's operator. She had wide shoulders and thick forearms, and it might have been a trick of light or perspective, but she appeared impossibly large, a titanic blacksmith at her infernal forge.

Unwin knew that this was the chief clerk Miss Palsgrave. The pink chair could only have been hers.

By the time the vision faded, the song on the phonograph had come to an end. The needle reached the lead-out and rose by itself, and the record stopped turning.

The darkness was no longer oppressive to him, nor was Miss Palsgrave's colossal chair. Worse was the thought that Miss Palsgrave herself would come closer, to put on a new record.

He retreated farther into the darkness, and the air grew warmer as he walked. There was a stale, burning odor in the air, like electrical discharge or the breath of the oversleeping. From all around came coughing sounds, rasps, weird mumblings. Unwin was not alone. But did those who made the sounds know that he was among them?

Something snagged his foot, nearly tripping him. He knelt and searched with his hand, found a rubberized cord stretched over the floor. This he followed several feet to the leg of a table. The table was knee-high, and there was a lamp on top of it. He found the switch and flipped it.

The shaded bulb cast its dim yellow light over a low, narrow bed. Its occupant was an underclerk—he wore an unfashionable gray suit and lay with his bowler perched on his chest. The bed was made up with drab, olive-colored blankets, but the underclerk slept on top of them rather than beneath. His little mustache trembled with each softly whistled exhalation, and his feet were bare. On the floor beside the bed were a pair of furry brown slippers, like two rabbits.

A little machine whirred softly on the table beside the lamp. It was a phonograph, though of a simpler, more utilitarian design than the one at the center of the archive. A ghost-white record, like the one Unwin had found in Lamech's office, revolved under the needle. The phonograph produced no sound that he could hear; it had no amplifying bell. Instead it was equipped with a pair of bulbous headphones, which the underclerk wore as he slept.

Other beds nearby were arranged, like the desks of the fourteenth floor, in three long rows. In each of them an underclerk lay sleeping. Some made use of their blankets, some did not. Some slept in their suits, some in pajamas, and some had black sleeping masks strapped over their eyes. All wore identical headphones plugged in to quietly humming phonographs.

Unwin leaned close to the underclerk's head, gently lifted the earpiece, and listened. All he heard was static, but the static was richly patterned, rising and falling in waves, cresting, breaking, receding. In time other sounds became apparent. He heard a muted honking, like traffic at a distance of several city blocks or birds circling over the sea. He heard animals calling from the depths of that sea and smaller animals scuttling over the sand at its bottom. He heard someone turning the pages of a book.

The underclerk opened his eyes and looked at him. "They've sent extra help, have they? Not a moment too soon."

Unwin let go of the earpiece and stood straight.

The underclerk's eyes closed, and for a moment it seemed he might fall asleep again, but then he shook his head and removed the headphones. "It's unprecedented," he said. "What is it, almost two in the afternoon? And they're still sending fresh recordings."

He sat up and rubbed his face with both hands. "It's as though no one is waking up. But the subjects lack culpability modulations of any kind, and the delineations are too vivid to be self-generated. And then there's the smaller bunch, all sharing the same image array—a whole subset with nearly identical eidetic representations, and it's a juvenile construct to boot." He raised the arm of the phonograph and switched off the machine.

"What is it?" Unwin asked.

"What is what?"

"The repeated . . . eidetic representation," Unwin managed.

"Oh. It's a carnival." The underclerk smirked and rolled his eyes.

There was another flash of light from Miss Palsgrave's machine, and both men turned to look at it.

"At first I thought it was a transduction error," the underclerk said,

whispering now. "But try telling that to *her.*" He removed the phonograph record and slid it into its slipcase, slid his feet into the slippers
beside the bed. Then he stood, tightened the blankets over the edges of
the mattress, and fluffed the pillow. "Well," he said, "it's all yours. Feel
free to recycle my report if you get one from the circus crowd. You'll
grow tired of hearing it: 'Something to do, someplace to go.' What kind
of liminal directive is that?"

The underclerk clapped Unwin on the shoulder, then shuffled away
into the dark. A minute later Unwin heard a door open and close, and
he was alone again with the sleeping underclerks.

Unwin sat on the edge of the bed. He should have been exhausted,
but his brain was moving as quickly as his feet had been. The underclerk had repeated the phrases the taxi driver and his passengers had
used to identify one another. They were swimming in the same strange
dream—but for what purpose had Hoffmann devised it? Hopefully,
Moore had made progress with his investigation.

Unwin looked back toward the center of the archive and saw Miss
Palsgrave seated in her pink chair. She wore a lavender dress, and her
hair was all soft brown curls. From this distance her eyes appeared as
dark hollows. She seemed to be watching him.

Unwin stood and began to speak over the distance. "Miss Palsgrave,
I—" but she immediately put a finger to her lips.

The nearest underclerks turned in their beds, and some mumbled
in their sleep. One adjusted his headphones and said, "Trying to
work here."

Miss Palsgrave began to turn the crank on her phonograph. When
she finished, she set the needle down and Cleo Greenwood's voice, accompanied by an accordion, filled the archive again. Those underclerks
who had been disturbed were perfectly quiet now, and Unwin, too, felt
the effects of the music.

He set down his briefcase, switched off the light, and settled back
onto the bed. It was comfortable despite its small size. He kicked off

his shoes without bothering to untie them and swung his legs up onto the mattress. The pillow was very soft, and the blanket, once he had slipped beneath it, was the finest, most luxurious blanket in the world. It might have been made of silk, he thought.

He took off his hat and dropped it beside his shoes. He would never need any of those things again. He would stay down here where no one knew him and sleep through the rest of his days, and when he died, they could tuck him away into a long file drawer, write his name on the label, and close it up forever. His mind lingered for a time in the hinterlands of sleep, words drifting over the border as though on a warm wind, unfastened from their meanings. He had almost let the wind take him when a few of the words appeared in boldface and he woke himself by speaking aloud.

"Papers and pigeons," he said, and knew he had forgotten something important.

Fighting the effects of Miss Greenwood's mesmeric voice, he reached over the side of the bed and undid the clasp on his briefcase, found the record from Lamech's office, and drew it from its sleeve. He fitted it onto the turntable of the electric phonograph by the bed, fumbled with the machine's controls, and set it playing. Then he found the headphones and put them on.

Miss Greenwood's voice faded, and with it the somber strains of the accordion music. He heard the familiar static, the shushing, the cadenced crackling. It was a language of sorts, but Unwin understood none of it. Then he stopped hearing the sounds and began instead to see them. The static had shape to it, dimensions; it rose like a waterfall in reverse and then froze in place. More walls leapt up, and in the one before him was a window, in the one behind him a door, and lining the other two were rows of books with blue and brown spines. The static spilled over the floor and made a carpet, made shadows of chairs and then made chairs.

The crackling sound was rain tapping against the window. The shushing was the shushing of secrets in a desk, and on the desk were a green-shaded lamp and a typewriter. A man was seated behind it with his eyes closed, breathing very slowly.

"Hello, Mr. Unwin," Edward Lamech said.

"Sir," said Unwin, but Lamech raised his hand.

"Do not bother speaking," he said. "I cannot hear you. Nor, for that matter, can I be certain that it's you, Mr. Unwin, to whom I am speaking. In recording this session, I am merely preparing for one of many contingencies. I hope that I'll have the opportunity to place this file directly into your hands. If I do not, or if it falls instead into the hands of our enemies, then . . ." Lamech wrinkled his considerable brow. "Then they will already have understood my intentions, I think, and none of it will matter anymore."

Lamech opened his eyes. How different they were from those Unwin saw the previous morning. They were watery and blue, and very much alive. But they were blind to his presence.

Lamech rose from his seat, and a hat appeared in his hand. When he put it on, a matching raincoat fell over his shoulders. "I don't know whether I've been able to explain very much to you," he said. "But since you're seeing this, then you've likely received my instructions and taken this file to the third archive. So you may understand a great deal. Time moves differently here, and that can be confusing to the uninitiated, but it will work to our advantage. I will tell you what more you need to know while we walk together. I have a few errands to run before I go to my appointment."

He walked toward the door, and Unwin jumped aside to avoid him.

"In case you're wondering," Lamech went on, "I almost always begin with my office. We watchers work best when we stick to certain patterns. Some prefer a childhood home for their starting point, others a wooded place. One woman uses a subway station with countless intersecting tracks. My office is familiar to me, and I can reconstruct it with relative ease. These are only details, though, meaningless unto themselves. If you are seated, I suggest you stand at this time."

Lamech opened the door. Instead of the hallway of the thirty-sixth floor, with its yellow light fixtures and bronze nameplates, Unwin saw a twisting alleyway, dark and full of rain. They stepped outside, and the door closed behind them. Unwin wished for his hat and found that he was wearing it. He wished for his umbrella, and that, too, was with him, in his hand and open. But as they walked the maze of high brick walls, he remained partly aware of the warmth of the blankets on the bed and of the softness of his pillow.

"All this is representational," Lamech said. "And arbitrary, for that matter. But it takes years of practice to achieve this degree of lucidity. Think of the alley as an organizational schematic. It's one I find especially useful. Here are as many doors as I need, and they serve logically as connecting principles. Some watchers work more quickly than I do, because they don't bother with such devices. But they have forgotten how to take pleasure in their vocation. There is something good about it, don't you think? The night, and the splash of the rain around us? We move unseen through the dark, along back ways and side streets. Forgive me if I indulge in the particulars, Mr. Unwin. A lot has happened very quickly, and I'm working this out as we go."

The moon emerged from behind the clouds, and Lamech gazed up at it, grinning a little. Then it was gone again, and he drew his coat more tightly about his body. "Miss Palsgrave's machine in the third archive is a wonder—we tell her when we're close to something important, something we may need to document, and she'll tune it to the correct frequency. She can even check in on you herself and follow you from one mind to another if necessary. The truth is, it's one of the few advantages we have over Hoffmann: the ability to record, review, correlate, compare. We don't always know what he's up to, but we can spot Hoffmannic patterns in the recordings of the city's dreams, then act to thwart his next move.

"This recording," he added, "may turn out to be especially valuable, and more than a little dangerous—to you as well as to me, I'm afraid."

In the shadow of a junk pile, they came to a shabby door, blue paint peeling from its worn wooden surface. Lamech leaned close to it and listened. "Here we are," he said.

He opened the door, and bright light shone into the alleyway, gilding the wet bricks. Over Lamech's shoulder Unwin saw the impossible: a broad beach, the sea deep and boundless, and the sun, high and bright at the top of the sky. He followed Lamech out onto the sand. On this side, the door served as the entrance to a rickety beach house.

The heat was terrible. Unwin removed his hat and wiped his brow with his sleeve. He kept his umbrella over his head, shielding himself from the sun as they trudged toward the water.

Near the edge of the waves' reach was a heap of smooth black rocks. A round woman in a ruffled blue bathing suit leaned against them, watching the sea. When she saw Lamech coming toward her, she turned and waved at him. She wore a string of imperfect-looking pearls around her neck, and a few strands of gray hair protruded from under her white bathing cap.

"Edward," she said. "When are you coming home? I polished the silverware while I waited. Twice. You know how tired I get when I polish. Did you unplug your telephone again?"

Unwin remembered the cord left disconnected on Lamech's desk. So it was the watcher himself who had been responsible for that. He had wanted to make sure nothing would wake him during the recording.

Lamech removed his hat and bent to kiss the woman on her cheek. "Working late tonight," he said.

"Can't you bring your work home?"

He shook his head. "I just came by to say good night."

She looked at the sea, a trace of a scowl on her face. Her cheeks were red from the sun and the wind. "The strange thing is," she said, "I don't even know if this is the real Edward I'm speaking to. I wanted so badly to see you that I may very well have dreamed you up."

"No, ladybug, it's me. I have an appointment, that's all."

"Ladybug?" she said. "You haven't called me that in years."

Lamech looked at his feet and tapped his hat against his leg. "Well, I've been thinking a lot about the old times. You know, a couple of kids in the big city, working bad jobs, dancing to the radio at night, drinks at the corner bar. What was that place called? Larry's? Harry's?"

The woman fingered the roughly formed pearls of her necklace.

"Sarah," he said, "there's something else. I just want you to know—"

"Stop. We'll talk about this in the morning."

"Sarah."

"I'll see you in the morning," she said, her voice firm.

Lamech frowned and took a deep breath through his nose. "All right," he said.

The wind was picking up; it made the ruffles of Sarah's bathing suit flutter and teased the gray curls at the edge of her cap. She was looking at the sea again. "This dream always ends the same way," she said.

"How's it end?" Lamech asked.

She was quiet for a while. "Edward, there are leftovers in the icebox. I have to go now." She stood straight and ran her hands down her sides. Then, without looking back, she jogged away toward the water, her pearls swinging back and forth around her neck. Clouds had risen up over the edge of the horizon, and the sea appeared choppy and dark.

"Come on," Lamech mumbled. He turned and starting walking back toward the beach house.

Unwin stayed where he was, watching as Sarah strode nimbly into the water. When she was in above her knees, she dove forward over a wave and began to swim.

"Come on," Lamech said again, as though he had known that Unwin would stay.

Unwin folded his umbrella to keep the wind from taking it and hurried up the beach after Lamech. He could feel the softness of the sand beneath his feet, but his shoes left no impression.

Lamech's raincoat billowed and snapped in the wind. He stuck his hands in his pockets and drew his coat close about him. His shoulders were hunched, his head down. He did not look back.

Unwin looked back. He could no longer see Sarah—she had vanished into the water. A great wave was forming on the horizon. It churned and swelled and boiled, gathering the sea to itself as it rolled toward the shore. Unwin quickened his pace, but he could not take his eyes off the wave. It was tall now as any building, its roaring louder than the traffic of citywide gridlock. Gulls flew over its crest and screamed. In the smooth window of its broad face Unwin could see animals swimming—fish, and starfish, and great heaving squid. They went about their business as though nothing strange were happening, as though they were still deep in the ocean instead of hurtling toward dry land. The wind was saturated with the stink of their briny world.

Lamech was at the faded blue door now. He opened it, and Unwin followed him back into the alleyway, opening his umbrella over his head. Lamech left the door open long enough to watch the wave's shadow blanket the beach. Then he closed it.

"I try not to peer too often into her sleeping mind," Lamech said. "It is an occupational hazard of ours, to learn too much about the people we love. But on those occasions when I have met my wife on her own territory, so to speak, I have always been amazed at the vastness of events under way there. I admit that it frightens me a little."

He stuck his hat back on his head and walked off down the alley. Unwin went after him, fighting the urge to stop and shake the sand out of his shoes.

FOURTEEN

On Nemeses

**There is no better way to understand your own
motives and dispositions than by finding
someone to act as your opposite.**

Their route along the worn brick pathways of Lamech's dreaming mind grew ever more strange and circuitous. They ducked beneath rusting fire escapes, passed through tunnels that smelled of algae and damp earth, hopped gutters brimming with filth. Twice they crossed deep ravines on makeshift bridges of steel grating. Down below, Unwin could see other alleyways, other tunnels, other gutters. The place was built in layers, one maze stacked upon another—a peculiar choice, Unwin thought, for an organizational system. Why not a house, or even an office building, if anything were indeed possible? If Lamech could use doors to travel from one dream to another, could he not also use file drawers?

But the watcher appeared perfectly at home here; he traversed the convoluted byways of his phantom city with a prowess that belied his age and his girth. How terrible that Unwin could not warn him of what was ahead. But even if he could speak to Lamech, even if he could bend time as these alleys bent space, he would not know what to say. The engine of the watcher's destruction was still veiled to Unwin. Could a dream kill a man? Could it strangle him where he sat sleeping?

Ventilating fans churned over their heads, drawing air into edifices housing unknowable visions. Or knowable, Unwin reminded himself. To Lamech and his fellow watchers, these dreams were as rooms to be entered, books to be opened and perused.

As though Unwin's own thoughts were before Lamech's eyes, the watcher said, "Not all surveillance is as easily accomplished as what you just witnessed, Mr. Unwin. My wife desired my presence, so I was granted passage. But some of these doors are shut tight or locked. Others are too well hidden to be found. And the minds of a certain few are simply too dangerous to enter. We watchers wield some influence in the dreams of ordinary sleepers, but the visions of one practiced in the arts of dream detection are entirely his own. You could stumble into such a place and be driven mad by the monstrosities lurking there, summoned with perfect lucidity to taunt and cajole.

"You know, I'm sure, of whose methods I speak."

Ahead, Unwin glimpsed a part of the landscape that was different from the rest: a patch of bright, sparkling light the size of several city blocks. The buildings nearby reflected its glow, and the entire thing swelled and flexed as though breathing. For a moment Unwin thought it was the sea—that the water had poured, still shining, straight from Sarah Lamech's dream to flood this part of the city. But Unwin could hear the thing as well as see it, and it was not the crash of waves that reached his ear. A droning music emanated from the place: a haunting, repetitive tune.

It was a carnival, and Lamech was leading them toward it.

"In most cases," the watcher went on, "the greatest challenge is to remain undetected by one's subject. In order to exist in another's dream—and that is different from observing a recording—one must be *part* of the dream. How, then, is the watcher to keep from revealing himself? The trick is to keep to the dreamer's own shadow, to the darker places of his mind, to the nooks and crawl spaces into which he dare not cast his gaze. There are usually plenty of such places."

In front of them, the alleyway split in two. Lamech stopped walking and peered down each passage. To Unwin they were perfect mirror images. His guide hesitated, then shrugged and chose the one on the left.

"But the watcher is limited in his investigations by what the suspect dreams," Lamech continued. "A man may dream of a closet door, but unless he opens it, the watcher cannot see inside the closet. That is why we learn to nudge our suspects a little. 'Don't you want to see what's in there?' we might whisper. And the suspect does wonder, and opens the door, and lo, there is the memory of the murder he committed just last Tuesday."

Unwin looked back the way they had come, troubled by the doubt Lamech had shown at the split in the alley. Until then the watcher had chosen his route without hesitation. If he was unfamiliar with a feature of his own creation, was he exposing himself to some risk? Could they have taken a wrong turn?

"Curiously," Lamech said, "Miss Palsgrave's device somehow pushes those boundaries a bit. When you review a recording, you can see outside the suspect's immediate perspective: peer around corners, open books, search under beds. The machine seems to pick up low registers emanating from deep in the subconscious. It has a kind of peripheral vision and sees things neither the dreamer nor the watcher thinks he can see. Another advantage we have over Hoffmann."

Unwin, still looking over his shoulder, saw something that astonished him. A door opened, and a woman slipped quietly into the alley. She followed after Lamech, keeping close to the walls, a shadow among shadows, quick as the rain. When a stray beam of moonlight caught her face, Unwin nearly startled awake. Back in the third archive, his legs twitched and his feet became tangled in the blanket.

It was Miss Greenwood's daughter, her plaid coat belted around her waist, her hair pinned tightly beneath her gray cap.

Lamech failed to notice that his dream had been infiltrated. Unwin shouted at him, tugged at his coat, pointed at their pursuer, all to no effect. The woman in the plaid coat trailed only a few steps behind them. Unwin was invisible to her—she was part of the recording—but she watched Lamech intently, pausing only to adjust the gray cap over her hair. Unwin thought, *She is asleep, it is the night before last, and hours from now she will go to Central Terminal and drop her umbrella, and I will fail to pick it up.*

They were drawing close to the carnival. The streets were suffused with hazy white light, and Unwin could hear the music clearly now— it was that of a hurdy-gurdy or a barrel organ. The watcher rounded a corner, wiping his eyes and blinking a little. Unwin followed him, and the woman in the plaid coat came after.

"For the first time since the Agency adopted dream detection as standard practice," Lamech said, "unauthorized operatives have learned the truth of what we watchers do. If you are indeed seeing this, Mr. Unwin, then you are one of two. I'm sure you can guess who the other is."

At the mention of Unwin's name, the woman in the plaid coat narrowed her eyes and looked around. Seeing no one else, she continued on, but at a greater distance than before. So the daughter of Cleopatra Greenwood knew his name. Had she known who he was when she dropped her umbrella at Central Terminal? Somehow she had contrived to be hired as an underclerk and then promoted to Unwin's own desk. But her talents were such that she could infiltrate even an experienced watcher's dream. Cleo may have been concerned for her daughter's well-being, but to Unwin she seemed able to take care of herself.

"A week ago," Lamech said, "someone stole my copy of *The Manual of Detection* and gave it to Detective Sivart. He had seen the book before, of course, knew it front to back. But there was something different about this edition. It included an eighteenth chapter, detailing the technique termed oneiric detection by its author. Sivart was furious. Why had this technique been denied to him all these years? Why hadn't someone told him? Why hadn't *I* told him? That's what he asked me when he stormed into my office first thing that morning.

"I had to tell him something. So I told him the truth. I told him oneiric detection was deemed too dangerous by the overseer to be included in editions beyond the first. Only watchers were to be trusted with its secrets. Detectives, while benefiting from its existence, would remain in the dark, if you will. Sivart didn't like being in the dark. He told me he was going to win the war.

" 'What war?' I asked him.

" 'The war against Enoch Hoffmann,' he said.

"He thought that by breaking in to the sleeping mind of his enemy he could somehow learn his secrets. Forget that Hoffmann had been in hiding for years, kept always in check by our efforts. And forget that none of our finest operatives would risk half a minute in that man's mind. Sivart felt there was something unfinished between them.

"I couldn't stop him from going, so I helped him break some rules instead. First, I told him who his clerk was. He's built up a lot of respect for you over the years, Mr. Unwin, and he thinks you're the one to help him. He said you know things no one else knows about him—details from his reports that didn't make it into the files because they weren't relevant to the case. Things you would have cut, but which matter now. He wouldn't tell me what they were, of course.

"Second, I notified Miss Palsgrave I'd need a new recording made and that I didn't want it cataloged in the third archive. I asked her to send it to me directly, so that I could give it to you. I just hope it's enough."

The carnival bore a likeness to Caligari's Travels-No-More, with buildings shaped like enormous animal heads, striped tents topped with pennants, and row upon row of gaming booths. This carnival, however, appeared to be in perfect working order: no flooded causeways, no broken rides, no collapsed pavilions. The place had an ethereal quality, its every part emanating that pale glow and seeming to swell and shiver as though touched by a wind Unwin could not feel on his own dreamed skin. The music came from everywhere at once, and the clouds above were lit like B-movie ghosts.

Lamech walked more slowly now, taking care with every step. "This place isn't what you think it is," he said. "At least not exactly. We've been unable to pinpoint the precise location of Hoffmann's mind, so each of these structures marks only one possibility. He leaves echoes of himself wherever he goes, to throw us off his trail. The people represented here may be among the remnants of Caligari's. Or worse, they are ordinary folk who don't know they've been touched by the magician's hand. In recent weeks, especially since Sivart's departure, this area has expanded dramatically."

They were nearing what must have been the center of the carnival. The cars of the nearby big wheel groaned on their axes as they slowly revolved. Lamech stopped walking and spun in a circle, surveying his surroundings. The woman in the plaid coat retreated around the edge of a ticket booth but kept the watcher in sight.

"I am loath to admit that its appearance is not of my choosing," he said. "Hoffmann's power is such that he determines his own semblance, even in the minds of others. Believe me, it's a damn annoyance. And I don't much care for the music either."

The warmth of the bed in the third archive was gone from Unwin's senses—only the cold light of the carnival was real to him now; that, and the rain thumping against his umbrella and spattering his shoes. His socks were getting wet. His socks were always getting wet, even in his sleep.

"There," Lamech said.

Unwin followed his gaze to a squat building with a wide set of stairs leading to a windowed gallery. Inside, the carnival landscape appeared reflected and fractured along seemingly endless corridors—a hall of mirrors. Lamech himself was replicated dozens of times over, his body distorted or broken into pieces: an arm here, a leg there, his gut over there. Unwin had no reflection, but for a moment he glimpsed another form moving among the panels: a hat, a gray raincoat, the ember of a cigar.

Lamech jogged quickly toward it, puffing a little, and Unwin was at his side. By the time they reached the building, the image was gone. Lamech put one foot up on the bottom step and leaned on his knee. They waited.

"Hoffmann probably caught him as soon as he set foot in there," Lamech said. "All he has to do now is stay asleep to keep him prisoner. But it's worse than that, much worse. The longer Sivart is trapped, the less his mind is his own. Hoffmann will learn all that he knows, subsuming his identity along with his thoughts. In the end, Sivart will be nothing, a vegetable. Or a witless pawn subject wholly to the magician's will."

Sivart reappeared. There were many copies of him, all tiny—he must have been deep inside the hall of mirrors, and what they saw was an image a dozen times reflected. He seemed to see them, too, because he crouched and tilted his hat back.

"Travis!" Lamech called. "Can you hear me?"

The miniature Sivarts all stood straight and took their cigars out of their mouths. Unwin thought he could see the mouths moving, but he heard nothing except the rain and the creaking of the big wheel. He and Lamech leaned closer. Something changed in the glass then, and Unwin's vision blurred. He closed his eyes and opened them, but the problem was not with his eyes.

The reflection of the carnival at their backs was moving, fading in some places as it brightened in others. Parts of the landscape receded into the distance, while other parts zoomed closer.

Unwin no longer heard the sound of the rain on his umbrella. The hall of mirrors had enclosed them. Lamech, in his confusion, spun around once and stepped backward into a transparent wall. "What?" he said, and then, as though he were on a telephone with a bad connection, "Hello?"

"Ed Lamech," the many Sivarts called, moving again, some of them disappearing as others materialized. "What brings you down here at this time of—" He stopped a moment. "Aw, heck, buddy. Is it day or night? I lose track."

"It's good to see you alive, Travis. I'm giving someone a tour, that's all."

"They'll pay you for anything, huh?" The Sivarts ducked around corners, and some of them grew. He was drawing closer. "Who you got with you?"

"Someone who can help us, I think. Help you, Travis—maybe get you out of here."

"That's great, Ed." Sivart's tone had turned suddenly sour. "I'm glad you've still got my back."

Lamech swept his hat off. "I told you not to go. You've put us all in jeopardy. Here in Hoffmann's mind, one of the Agency's top men!"

"Now you're just flattering."

"We made a good team, Travis. But I'm in some pretty deep water here. Deeper than you know. It's dangerous for me to be in this place." Lamech was feeling the walls with his hands, batting at them with his hat. He found an opening between two mirrors and moved through it; Unwin followed him.

"They call this a fun house," Sivart said. "But I tell you it's worse than anything we've sent the crooks to. He comes in now and then to check up on me. And when he does, it's like having the top of my skull screwed off and a flashlight shone in. It hurts, Ed. You should have told me what I was up against."

"I tried, Travis. I tried."

Several more of the Sivarts vanished. There were only a few of them now. He was close, but Lamech could not find his way to him.

Sivart and his reflections said, "You know how he did this? He learned it from Caligari, that crazy little guy who brought the carnival here. You remember: 'Everything I tell you is true, and everything you see is as real as you are.' What did that mean anyway?"

"No," Lamech said, "the technique came out of the Agency. Somebody stole the secret and brought it to Hoffmann. Greenwood, probably."

"That's just the story. Bunch of smoke. Truth is, we're dabbling in something a hell of a lot older. This goes back, back to the beginning, maybe. It came in with the carnival, and your boss got hold of it some-how. We'd all have been better off without it."

"How do you know this?"

"You don't think I got caught right away, do you? I saw it first-hand. Not the way the *Manual* said to, though. I jumped in at the deep end, went right for the spooky stuff. I wanted to know what makes him tick."

Lamech was out of breath. He stopped walking and put his hands on his knees. "Well?"

"Nobody taught him to do the voices," Sivart said. He was pacing back and forth, his reflections multiplying and converging while he spoke. "He was born like that. Grew up in a little village out in the country, immigrant family, hardworking folks. He stole bread by im-personating the baker's wife, calling him out of the shop with her voice. Clever boy, see? Later he hid in a church balcony and pretended to be an angel, tricked the minister into altering his sermons. Convinced him to put in strange things about overturning the order of the world, no salvation but in topsy-turvydom, et cetera. When they figured out what was going on, they put the kid down as some kind of devil. Prob-ably would have killed him if the carnival hadn't taken him in."

Something was wrong. Sivart was shaking as he spoke, and when the face of one reflection was visible for a moment, Unwin thought he saw tears. Lamech noticed, too. "Travis," he said, "we don't have time for this."

Sivart tore the cigar out of his mouth and threw it on the floor. "It could be important, Ed. Will you listen to me for once? Hoffmann was just a boy when his mother gave him to the carnival. And that monster Caligari taught him but never taught him enough. So Hoffmann thought he'd figure it out on his own. He sneaked into the old man's mind one night, trying to learn his secrets. Caligari caught him and kept him there. Tortured him, wouldn't let him wake up. Worst of all, he knew that Caligari had kept something from him, would always keep something from him. He would never share the secret that made him powerful."

Lamech looked calm now, as though he had arrived at an understanding of some kind. "Sounds to me like Hoffmann needed a lesson, Travis. Sounds like he was getting ahead of himself."

There were only two Sivarts now. They both turned away and threw their hands in the air. "What do you know? You haven't seen what I've seen. Anyway, you better let me in on the plan. Who is it you're recruiting? I hope he's good."

"Under the circumstances," Lamech said, "it's probably better that I not tell you."

The Sivarts were quiet for a time. Then they stood straight, stretching to crack their necks. When they turned around, their eyes were closed and they were grinning. "What circumstances, exactly?"

"I know who you are," Lamech said.

The Sivarts took a deep breath. There was a squelching sound as the face of the nearer loosened and crinkled around the edges. It slid off and fell to the floor, folding like an omelette where it landed.

Unwin stepped back. Down in the third archive, he heard himself whimper into the pillow.

The face that had been masked was squarish, dull, bored-looking. Enoch Hoffmann opened his eyes and rolled up his sleeves. The biloquist was wearing his pajamas now, blue with red trim.

The real Sivart fell back against a transparent wall, a marionette whose strings had been cut. He looked groggy, exhausted, invisibly bruised. Had his mind already turned to dust? No: he coughed and grimaced at Lamech, managing a little wave.

"I ought to strangle you," Hoffmann said to the watcher. His regular voice was as Sivart had described it in his reports—high-pitched and whispery, barely a voice at all, empty of feeling even when it threatened.

"You'd have to wake up first," Lamech said. "And you're not going to do that, are you? Now that you've finally caught him, you can't bear to let him go. You're as much a prisoner as he is."

The magician was ignoring him; his gaze was fixed on the spot where Unwin stood. Hoffmann came toward him, and Unwin felt as though his damp clothes had frozen solid. The corridors stretched, so that the magician seemed to approach from a great distance, with the inevitability of a nightmare. The look on his face was unreadable—it might as well have been carved into a block of wood. "Who is it you've brought with you?" he asked.

Unwin stepped aside at the last moment, and Hoffmann walked past him. He reached around a mirrored wall and came back clutching the wrist of the woman in the plaid coat. Hoffmann yanked her to her feet; she let out a cry and stumbled forward, her cap coming loose. She regained her balance, then stood straight and straightened her coat.

"Hey, kiddo," Sivart said, getting to his feet.

Lamech put his hat back on. "Where did she come from?"

Sivart snorted. "She followed you, fancy-boots. Ed Lamech, meet Penelope Greenwood. She's better at what you do than you are, knows everything you're thinking, and can hurt your feelings without saying a word. Self-taught, too—a real wunderkind. Enoch, I believe you're already acquainted."

Hoffmann, for the first time since he made his presence known, appeared shaken. His lower lip was trembling as he gazed at the woman in the plaid coat.

"Dad," she said to him, "we need to talk."

Lamech was looking at Sivart. "Greenwood? She and Hoffmann? Travis, why didn't you ever report this?"

Hoffmann gestured vaguely toward Lamech. The watcher put up his hands and started to speak, but whatever he said was lost as his hat grew to twice its size and swallowed his head. He tore at it with both hands, but the brim was stuck under his chin and his shouts were muffled by the heavy felt.

Hoffmann took a step toward the woman in the plaid coat, arms outstretched. "I searched for you," he said. "I tried so hard to find you."

"Maybe I didn't want to be found." She picked a piece of lint off her coat, avoiding his eyes.

"Your mother took you from me."

"You let her get caught," Penelope said. "The job was more important to you."

Sivart knelt down to pick up his cigar, listening to their argument as though to a story he already knew. And Unwin realized that Sivart did know this story, because he had played a role in it. Hoffmann and his daughter were talking about November twelfth, about the day Sivart caught Cleopatra Greenwood at Central Bank and sent her out of the city. *I won't tell you what we talked about,* he had written. *I won't tell you what happened just before I put her on the train.* This is what they had talked about: Miss Greenwood's little girl. They were making arrangements that day in the terminal. They were deciding how to get Penelope out of the city, away from her father.

"That isn't what I came here to talk about," Penelope said. "I want to tell you about my new job. It's all underground, more than you know about. They have you beat, Dad. You remember Hilda Palsgrave? She used to do the fireworks for the carnival?"

Unwin drew a breath, a real one. Hilda, the giantess Hildegard: Sivart had met her the same day he met Caligari, had spoken to her while she mixed black powder for her rockets. Now she was chief clerk of the third archive. How had one of Caligari's old employees come to be with the Agency?

Hoffmann was incensed. "You're both working at the Agency? Working for *him*?"

The overseer, Unwin thought. The man Miss Greenwood had said was something worse than Enoch Hoffmann.

Though that was hard to imagine just now, as Lamech fell to the floor, rolling and twisting, beating at his hat with his fists. This, Unwin thought, was how Lamech's life was to end: suffocated by his own hat. He could not stop it from happening. And when Lamech died, the recording would end. He did not have much time.

"Penny, Penny," the biloquist whispered, almost singing her name. "We lost each other so long ago. Where have you been? Your eyes, when you were born, like little mirrors; terrifying! Caligari saw you and claimed you for his own. But you've come back to me just in time. I need your help. We'll work together, like we did before."

Sivart laughed. "Sure. We all know how well that went."

"November twelfth was a fluke," Hoffmann snapped.

Sivart waved his hand dismissively, but the woman in the plaid coat was listening with evident interest. She and Hoffmann stood looking at one another. He was nearly a foot shorter than she was, almost forlorn in his rumpled pajamas.

"Kiddo," Sivart said to her. "Don't listen to him."

Penny ignored him. "We need to talk," she said again to her father. "Alone."

With a nervous glance at Lamech, Sivart snatched his own hat off his head. But Hoffmann was not preparing any new tricks. "I'm not taking my eyes off him," he said.

"What do you think he'll do?" Penelope asked. "Rummage through the junk in the back of your brain? Find out you're one of the bad guys? Let him wander for a minute." She gave Sivart a meaningful look and added, "We'll have him back here soon enough."

Hoffmann was frowning, but he sighed and said, "All right." He snapped his fingers, and behind him a single mirror dissolved into mist. The stairs down to the carnival were just beyond.

Sivart shrugged and put his hat back on. Then he puffed at his cigar a few times, until the ember burned red again. "You kids have fun," he said, and with a last look at Lamech's writhing form he went briskly from the hall of mirrors.

Unwin followed him. Outside, the eldritch light of the carnival had grown brighter, almost fiery, and the rides were chugging and whirling at breakneck speeds. The air smelled of popcorn and fresh sawdust, and the music of the hurdy-gurdy roared. Sivart leapt onto the turning platform of a carousel, and Unwin hurried after him, grabbing hold of a horse's reins to steady himself. Sivart debarked on the other side and jogged away into the outer reaches of the carnival.

The detective was moving purposefully, as though according to some prearranged plan. Could he and Penelope Greenwood have conspired in advance to allow him this reprieve? Unwin did not know how far he could follow. He was already pushing at the boundaries of what Miss Palsgrave's machine had recorded, and he felt a tug at the back of his skull. This dream was nested like one of those dolls that contain themselves a dozen times over. But if the chief clerk of the third archive had been observing the dream, might she have shifted the focus from one mind to another, changing frequencies as Lamech said she could? Yes: the closer Unwin kept to Sivart, now, the better the recording maintained its coherence.

Sivart had reached the edge of the carnival. There at its border was a small, almost perfectly square building, its windows reflecting the fairground's glow. The detective went up to the steps and put his hand on the doorknob, then shut his eyes and wrinkled his brow. "Okay," he said to himself, "easy as spinning a radio dial." He turned the knob and threw the door open with a flourish.

On the other side was Unwin's bathroom.

Sivart went in and looked around. He yawned, stretched, then took his coat off and flung it over the shower curtain. "This is more like it," he said. He turned on the hot-water faucet and undressed, then reached up into his coat pocket and pulled out a small bottle of smoked glass. This he unstoppered, sniffed, and emptied into the water. The tub filled with bubbles. When the bath was ready, he tested the water with one toe and got in. With his hat down over his face, he began puffing on his cigar, dropping ashes into the tub. The only spot of color in the room was the ember of the cigar, and it burned so hot it made the steam over the tub glow red.

Unwin stretched his legs beneath the covers of an underclerk's bed in the third archive of the Agency offices. In his dream of Lamech's dream of Hoffmann's dream of Sivart's dream, a dreaming Unwin opened his bathroom door, a fresh towel over his arm, his robe cinched tight around his waist. Sivart scrubbed his feet with a long-handled brush, and the other Unwin said, "Sir, what are you doing in my bathtub?"

Sivart told the other Unwin not to use his name. Somebody could be listening in. He accused him of being forgetful. He said, "I'm going to tell you something that you're going to forget. Ready?"

"Ready," the other Unwin said.

"Okay, here it is. You're awfully worried about getting everything right. I've seen what you've done to my reports. I've read the files. You edit out the good parts. All you care about are details, and clues, and who did what and why. But I'm telling you, Unwin, there's more to it than that. There's a . . . I don't know"—he waved his cigar in the air— "there's a spirit to the whole enterprise. There's mystery. The worse it gets, the better it is. It's like falling in love. Or falling out of love, I forget which. Facts are nothing in comparison. So try, would you? Try to leave the good parts alone?"

"Sorry," Unwin said, "what were you just saying? I was thinking of something else."

"Never mind. Just remember this: Chapter Eighteen. Got it?"

"Yes."

"Say it back to me: Chapter Eighteen."

"Chapter Elephant," Unwin said.

FIFTEEN

On Skulduggery

**If you are not setting a trap, then you
are probably walking into one. It is the
mark of the master to do both at once.**

Somewhere an elephant trumpeted. Somewhere else an alarm clock
rang. And back in Lamech's city, someone was screaming.

The cord that had tugged at the back of Unwin's brain grew taut
and wrenched him from the nested dreams, out of his bathroom, out
of the carnival, back into the hissing static of the rain. A dark shape
rolled on the ground at his feet. It was Lamech, still pulling at his hat,
which was shrunk tight over his face now, so that his nose and brow
were visible through the felt. Unwin crouched over him, wanting to
help somehow, trying to get hold of the hat, though he knew it was
impossible.

Lamech kicked his shoes against the cobblestones and bellowed. He
twisted and rolled, his shirt coming untucked. Finally the hat popped
off. His face was red and sweaty, his mouth a perfect O as he gulped
the air.

The hat had lost its shape and lay on the ground, a dead little animal. Lamech slapped it into the gutter, where the water carried it away. He rose slowly to his knees and watched it go, his breath coming in hoarse wheezes. Then he got to his feet, brushing himself off with his hands. So it was not Enoch Hoffman who had murdered the watcher.

He looked nowhere in particular and said, "All right, end of the tour. There's little else I can do to help you. We're pickles in our own jars, Mr. Unwin. That's how it has to be now."

He wiped his brow with his sleeve. He was breathing easier, but his voice was quiet. "I could have done better. I could have shown you more. We're in trouble, the whole lot of us. Read your copy of the *Manual*. Find Sivart if you can, and get him out of there before he makes things worse."

Lamech thrust his hands into his pockets and looked around. "Well?" he said. "Wake up, already."

Unwin woke up.

BENEATH THE HEAVY COTTON BLANKET, his feet were damp in their socks. His head was heavy, and the pillow felt heavy beneath it. He had the odd impression that his skull had been magnetized. There was an unpleasant metallic taste in his mouth.

No music played in the third archive, and Miss Palsgrave had left her machine. Hilda, the Giantess Hildegard, the Chief Clerk of—of all this, Unwin supposed—was nowhere to be seen. Around him her underclerks carried on with their slumberous labors. What strange visions had Hoffmann and his daughter contrived for their perusal? Only the ever-wakeful Jasper Rook could remain immune to them forever— and Jasper, Unwin reminded himself, was probably back in the city by now, searching for the man who killed his brother.

The phonograph needle had reached the lead-out on the record of Lamech's final dream and was traveling an endless, soundless loop.

Unwin stopped the machine and flipped the record over, found more grooves on the B-side. Lamech had told him there was nothing more to see, but the watcher did not seem to understand everything that was happening. Unwin needed more; he put the needle down and closed his eyes.

Again the sounds formed patterns, the patterns shapes, and this time he sank into the dream from above. For a moment he had a dizzying view of Lamech's city beneath him. He descended quickly, matching speed with the rain, so that each long drop appeared to hang unmoving in front of him. He looked up. More drops hovered like daggers over his eyes; he wished for his umbrella, had it, opened it. The umbrella parachuted over his head, and he swung below it like a pendulum while the rain drummed over his head.

Lamech was headed for the entrance of a building, the tallest in this part of the city, in all of the city, maybe. It stood a little apart from those nearby, a dark obelisk. There was something familiar about the place. Just as Unwin's feet touched the ground, he realized why. It was the Agency office building.

Unwin followed, slipping through the lobby doors before they closed behind Lamech, then collapsed his umbrella on his way toward the elevator, just as he had done many hundreds of times before in that other lobby, the real one. If Hoffmann's mind was represented by a hall of mirrors, whose dreaming thoughts were housed here?

Lamech went past the elevator doors, mumbling to himself as he walked. "Stupid, stupid," Unwin heard him say—to himself, apparently. Then he shook his head, as though to clear his thoughts. At the back of the lobby, he angled his watch in the dim light. Someone called out, "Come in, Ed, you're right on time." Unwin did not recognize the voice; it came from behind a door stenciled in black letters: CUSTODIAN.

When Lamech went in, Unwin heard a noise that was immediately familiar. It was the rustling of paper and the cooing of pigeons. The sounds froze him for a moment, and he barely had time to squeeze through, ducking under Lamech's arm as the watcher closed the door.

The room was small, and smaller for its contents. Piles of paper, some bundled into files, some floating free, were stacked floor to ceiling. Filing cabinets stood in rows and at odd angles, forming a kind of maze. A living breeze inhabited the place, lifting pages from one pile and dropping them onto another or discarding them on the floor. Some of the file drawers stood open, and in most of them pigeons had roosted, with nests of twigs and paper and bits of trash. The birds regarded Lamech familiarly, puffing with disdain when his coat brushed their drawers.

"Won't you ever clean this place up?" Lamech said. He rounded a filing cabinet and stood with his hands in his pockets. "Arthur, there used to be a chair here."

The custodian was seated at a little desk that had fallen to the same disarray plaguing the rest of the room. His accordion was hung on the wall behind him, over the wide basin sink from which a mop handle extended. Hanging beside it was a pistol in its holster. The place must have been a replica of the custodian's real-life office, though surely the original was not equipped with so many file drawers. And hopefully the custodian did not have all these pigeons, either—nor that gun.

Arthur looked up from the file he was studying, stared at Lamech a moment, then removed his spectacles. It was the first time Unwin had seen the man's eyes. They were pale and attentive. "Emily," he said. "Find our guest a place to sit, please."

Unwin had to stop himself from speaking her name aloud as Emily Doppel, wearing a yellow peignoir and blue slippers, emerged from behind a stack of papers at the back of the room. She stuck her pencil into her hair and came around the custodian's desk. Waving her arms, she evicted the pigeons nesting on a chair, then moved a pile of papers off it and onto the top of another pile.

"Elaborate," Lamech said, watching her.

"She's real," Arthur said. "I have her come in to keep things tidy, but mostly she does crossword puzzles. Imagine the devotion, to do crossword puzzles in your sleep."

Emily sniffed at this.

"I hope he pays you enough," Lamech said to her.

"He doesn't pay me," Emily said. "I have a condition. I fall asleep when I mean to be awake, and he takes advantage by bringing me here. Nights, too. I've always wanted to be an Agency operative, but this is not what I imagined."

"Tell him to get you a day shift," Lamech said.

"Get me a day shift," she said to Arthur.

"What, and have you nodding off on the job? Sweetie, you know it wouldn't work."

"I quit, then," she said. The two men watched as she gathered her things: black lunch box, newspaper, a pillow. She brushed past Lamech and went out of the room, slamming the door behind her. The pigeons fussed and warbled.

"She does this every day," the custodian assured Lamech. "It's the only way she knows how to leave. I do have plans for her, though. Just waiting for the right assignment to come along. Now sit, sit."

Lamech shrugged and sat down, letting his coat droop open. His face was still red from the struggle with his hat. He probably could have dreamed up a new one, but maybe he could not bear to.

Arthur ran his tongue along his teeth and looked at the ceiling. "Those memos of mine," he said.

Lamech waved his hand. "You know, Arthur, it gets hard to keep track of all the rules. It's getting to be like the bylaws need bylaws."

The custodian sat upright and tossed his spectacles onto the desk. He stared straight at Lamech, his face reddening. "These are the basics, Ed. You keep track of your copy of the *Manual*. You know that."

Lamech hung his head.

"Who took it?"

"I don't know."

"The whole thing makes me tired," Arthur said. "Imagine that: tired in your sleep."

Lamech said nothing for a moment. Then he asked, "What are you, three days in?"

"Three, four, maybe," Arthur said, shaking off a laugh. "Shows, does it? I'm trying to keep up on Cleo, that's all."

Unwin recalled what Miss Greenwood had told him, out on the barge, about the eyes in the back of her skull. Not just a watcher's eyes, but this man's. Who was the Agency custodian, that he should be conducting dream surveillance?

"Most I ever went was six hours," Lamech admitted, "and that was by accident. Strangest thing, too. My subject dreamed she woke up, and I thought she really was awake. Went about my day for a while, but it turned out I was still in her head."

"Hah," said Arthur.

"But listen, Greenwood's back in town, isn't she? Maybe she's the one who nabbed my book. I'll get after her myself. I'll—"

Arthur stopped him by slapping a sheaf of papers against the desk. He stacked the pages even, his big fingers moving with an accordionist's quickness. "You don't ever quit, do you, Ed? You could have retired—what, seven years ago? It's a dangerous job. I don't have to tell you that. You have a wife, children."

"A grandchild, too," Lamech added. "Little girl, four years old. Wants to be like her grandpa when she grows up."

Arthur clicked his tongue against his teeth, signaling approval. He set his hands down on the square of desk he had cleared. "But something has to go wrong, eventually."

"Eventually," Lamech agreed.

Just then a pigeon came in through a window, and Lamech ducked as it landed on the desk in an uproar of scattered feathers and paper.

Arthur steadied the bird with one hand and got hold of its leg with the other. A tiny canister was fixed to the pigeon's leg; Arthur opened it and withdrew a rolled slip of paper.

Carrier pigeons, Unwin thought. The dreamed equivalent of the Agency's messengers.

Relieved of its charge, the pigeon flapped off and found its nest among the file drawers.

"It's from your pal down the hall, Alice Cassidy," Arthur said, reading the note. "Her agent's been busy lately."

Lamech leaned closer. "Sam Pith? What's he up to?"

"Got him staking out the old Baker place. We think it might be where Hoffmann's holed up these days. Time we got to the bottom of whatever all the chatter's about." He set the note down, and it curled again. "How's the weather out there?"

Lamech sat back in his chair. "Clear skies and a balmy breeze," he lied. "Sunshine, warm on the face. Piles of red leaves. Children run, laugh at themselves. Laugh at the whole damn thing."

Arthur frowned and scratched the side of his face with one big fingernail. "What about your case, Ed?"

"Sivart," Lamech began.

"Taken a powder, has he?"

The watcher got to his feet. He moved his jaw from side to side, as though he wanted to spit. "Well, you already know. You always already know. Why do you bother with these appointments? I'll send a bird next time. I've got work to do."

"Sit down."

Lamech cursed under his breath and sat with his arms crossed.

Arthur smiled peaceably. "I wanted to hear about it, straight from the source. Was he angry? Was he furious? How furious was he? Tell me about it."

"Whoever took my copy of the *Manual* turned around and gave it to him. Unexpurgated edition."

A phone rang. Arthur dug through the papers on his desk while Lamech looked on, incredulous. The telephone was identical in appearance to every other telephone Unwin had seen in the Agency offices, but there was something different about the sound of this one's bell. It echoed as though from the far end of a tunnel.

Arthur snatched up the receiver. "Yes. . . . What? . . . No, listen. Listen to me. . . . Hey, listen! I don't care if he eats the same thing all next week, too. Keep on him, he's your man. Check your frequencies. . . . Recheck them, then. I'll do it myself next time." He hung up.

"Funny," Lamech said.

Arthur sucked his teeth and said, "That Miss Palsgrave is a wizard with the gadgetry. This is our latest development. Turns out the recording thingum can be plugged into the transmission gizmo, then spliced to a telephone's domajig. Means instant communication between the oneiric mind and a mundane pay phone. Connection's a little spotty, still."

Lamech shook his head at all this.

"Nikolai there," Arthur went on, nodding at the phone, "was at the Municipal Museum today. He thinks he's found Edwin Moore. And it looks like our old friend was in touch with Sivart just before he went AWOL."

"What, you think it's connected?"

"Listen, Ed, I need help here. If Hoffmann gets too deep into Sivart's head, it's trouble for all of us. We need to find him."

"Hoffmann's keeping himself checked out. Even if we found him, we wouldn't be able to wake him. Sivart's trapped."

"Who said anything about waking him?" Arthur said.

Lamech shifted uncomfortably in his chair. Then he looked around, as though something had startled him.

"What's wrong?" Arthur said.

"Thought I heard—"

"Focus, Ed."

Lamech grumbled. "Hoffmann's up to something, something big, November twelfth big. But it sounds like Cassidy and Pith know more than I do. I hear Sam's been working with you directly. With Sivart stuck where he is, we need to throw off the opposition, keep them guessing. So we do something we've never done before—and that means breaking some rules, Arthur. We promote someone. Someone completely incapable of solving a mystery. That should buy us the time we need to find Sivart. The harder their agents work to follow our guy, the farther off course they'll be."

Arthur looked at him like he thought he was kidding. Then his face went red and his whole body shook with his laughter. It was an angry, wheezing laugh. "I like it," Arthur said, crying a little.

"Good," said Lamech. "Because I've already sent the memo."

That got Arthur going again, and Lamech laughed, too. They went on like that until the custodian was wiping tears from his eyes. Then he sighed his whistling sigh and started playing with the papers on his desk.

"Strangest thing, though," Lamech said.

"Oh, yeah?"

"I saw Hoffmann just now."

"Just now?"

"Came from his place directly."

"No kidding. What'd he have to say?"

"A lot of nonsense, mostly. One thing that caught my ear, though. About our standard procedures. He said the Agency didn't come up with Chapter Eighteen. That dream detection predated our work. He said he didn't steal it from us but that we stole it from him."

Arthur put his spectacles back on.

"Got me thinking," Lamech said. "Maybe we're not just worried about Hoffmann getting too far into Sivart's head. Maybe we're worried about Sivart getting too far into his."

Arthur nodded slowly. "Well, Ed, you're no slouch. See, I met

Greenwood in the early days of the carnival, long before the Oldest Murdered Man case, when she and Hoffmann had their own little sideshow. You'd go into their tent expecting your fortune to be told, but then Cleo would put you to sleep and Hoffmann would hop in and see what you had on your mind."

"Sure, I see," Lamech said. "A little blackmail operation. You telling me they got you with that scam?"

"It was just after I took over this outfit. That's why I made all those changes, wrote all those rules—had to keep as much as I could hidden."

Lamech's jaw was clenched. "Hoffmann would have learned everything about our operations otherwise."

"I know I should have told you, Ed. But it's more personal than business. See, Cleo and I got to know each other after that. We were kids. We fell in love. But the only way we could see each other without Hoffmann catching on was if we met sleepside, in the old Land of Nod. What a courtship that was! I convinced her to teach me how it was done, so I could go over to her place, too, if you follow me.

"Hoffmann told you the truth, Ed. That Caligari fellow taught him dream detection, though he'd have called it something different. Then Hoffmann taught Cleo, and she's the one who brought it to me. To the Agency. She and I didn't last, of course. Too complicated, once we found ourselves in opposite trenches."

Lamech took all this in. "Must be strange for her now," he said. "Her old boyfriend on full-time surveillance duty."

"I'm wearing her down, Ed. She's hiding something from me. I don't know what it is, but she can't keep it up much longer. I've got the lights turned up bright, and she's getting tired."

Lamech looked around the room and said, "There it is again."

"What?"

"I heard something. Not here. In my office."

Arthur waved his hand. "That's just me."

Lamech gave him a careful look, and after a moment Arthur shrugged.

"Ed, I'm in your office." He looked put out by having to explain. "All the time I've been spending in here these days, I've had to work on my sleepwalking. There are a lot of places I have to be, you know."

"Just stopping in to empty the wastepaper basket, I guess?"

"That's right," Arthur said. "Coming by to clean things up a little."

Lamech put his hat on. "I may as well go, then. I'll shake your hand topside, on my way out."

"Door's locked," Arthur said. "You don't wake up until I do."

Lamech was moving his jaw again, though he looked more thoughtful than angry.

"You've been like an uncle to me," Arthur said. "Showed me the ropes when I first came on staff. Remember me in my messenger's suspenders? I'd still be wearing them if it wasn't for you. You pretended like I knew what I was doing before I knew a damn thing. That's what makes it all so difficult."

"Makes what difficult?"

"The lying, Ed. I've lied to you. So much. But the best way to fool a monkey is to fool his trainer. Sivart's the monkey, Ed. You've always known that. I just want to come clean about the rest of it."

"Why bother?" Lamech said.

"Ed, listen to me. Sivart's cases were all bogus."

"His cases," Lamech said.

"Your cases. Bunkum. Hooey. Everything you solved, you solved wrong. The both of you, together. You made a good team. That's how we needed things. Kept the important stuff hidden that way. Except November Twelfth. He got that one right somehow."

"That your hand on my shoulder, Artie?"

"Listen to me. You've done great work, Ed. The most important work anyone in this outfit has done for me. Just not in the way you

think. That night at the carnival, when I realized Hoffmann had me—
had us all—I knew I had to make a deal. One hand washes the other."

"Dirties it, more like."

"Easy now, Ed."

"How's it work?" Lamech asked. "You let him get away with the
crimes and you do cover-up? The Agency makes its dollar, your puppet
looks like a hero, he gets anything he wants."

Unwin thought it over and was sickened when he saw how it fit together. The phony mummy, Colonel Baker alive and well—Hoffmann
and Arthur must have orchestrated each of those cases in advance.
Hoffmann kept the priceless trophy he wanted, kept Colonel Baker's
inheritance as well. And the Agency had its star detective and its front-
page stories. Sivart had been tricked every time, and Unwin along with
him—the whole city, too.

"I had to come clean with you, Ed. Had to let you know how
it was."

Lamech touched his own throat. He danced his fingers around his
collar, grasping for something he could not get hold of. He was fighting
the hands of a ghost. Unwin thought he could feel them, too.

"Could be something," Lamech said, gasping.

Arthur was calm as he watched the man opposite him. "Something you haven't told me yet? Something I need to know that I don't
know already? Probably not, Ed. I'm the overseer. I'm the man who
sees too much."

But there was something, Unwin knew. Penelope. Her existence was
the thing Miss Greenwood was fighting to keep hidden from Arthur,
and the fight had exhausted her. Would Lamech trade what he knew
for his life?

"You were supposed to watch him," Arthur went on. "That was
your job, Ed. But this isn't happening because you failed. It's happening
because you've done so well."

Unwin went to Lamech, tried to feel for the hands that were choking him. His fingers blurred with the watcher's, passing through them as though through a mist. Unwin was seized by cold panic. He screamed and grabbed at the air, punched at it.

"I just have to clean your office," Arthur said. "Tidy up a little."

Unwin closed his dreaming eyes, but he could not occlude the vision of the man thrashing where he sat. The dream insisted. In the watcher's office on the thirty-sixth floor, Lamech had died as he died here. His convulsions formed a weird geometry amid the fluttering papers. The pigeons were mesmerized.

Lamech was still trying to speak, but Arthur had begun sorting papers again. Unwin's senses went gray as the watcher's body stilled.

He felt himself lifted from the bed, felt the blanket falling off his body. He tried to catch it, but something snatched him upward and away. The earphones landed on the pillow. He saw below him a great lavender dress and knew he lay in the arms of Miss Palsgrave. She cradled him like a child while she slipped his shoes onto his feet. Her breath was warm on his forehead. She put the record back in his briefcase and gave it to him; his arms were shaking as he took it.

At the far end of the archive, near the place where Unwin had entered, a pair of flashlight beams swept through the dark, casting broad ovals of light over the floor. Miss Palsgrave sighed to herself when she saw them, then tapped Unwin's hat back onto his head. She started walking. Underclerks slept undisturbed all around them.

How cold Unwin was! Through chattering teeth he said, "You used to work for the carnival. For Hoffmann."

Miss Palsgrave's voice sounded metallic and thin; it was a voice from a string-and-tin-can telephone. "For Caligari," she said. "Never for Hoffmann. After he staged his coup, I left."

"And defected to the Agency."

"The problem is not belonging to one or the other, Mr. Unwin— and there is always an Agency, always a Carnival to belong to. The problem is belonging for too long to either of them."

Unwin thought of the little square building that represented his own mind in Lamech's final dream. It had stood right at the edge of the carnival; might it be annexed in time? "Have I—" he said, but he did not know how to finish the question.

Miss Palsgrave looked down at him. In the dark he could see only the dull gleam of her eyes. "The sleeping king and the madman at the gates," she said. "On the one side a kind of order, on the other a kind of disorder. We need them both. That's how it's always been."

"But your boss—my boss. He's a murderer."

"The scales have tipped too far," Miss Palsgrave agreed. "When Hoffmann made a deal with the overseer, he stopped working for the carnival and started working for himself. Their deal fell apart on November twelfth because Sivart solved that case correctly and Hoffmann imagined he had been betrayed by his conspirator. Now the Agency oversteps its bounds while the carnival rots in the rain. Hoffmann's grown desperate over the years. He'll drown the city in nightmare just to have it for his own again."

They came to the enormous machine at the other end of the archive. Here the air smelled of wax and electricity. On a wheeled cart nearby was a row of freshly pressed phonograph records. Now that Unwin knew the truth of the Agency's overseer, he saw this place in a new light. A repository of the city's most private thoughts, fancies, and urges, all in the hands of a man who would coerce and torment to learn what he wanted to know, who would murder an old friend to keep his secrets safe. Unwin's own dreams were out there, he thought, along with those of anyone who had ever drawn the attention of the Agency's unblinking eye.

"How could you allow Arthur such . . ." He struggled to find the right word. ". . . such trespass?"

"There was a time when I thought it necessary," Miss Palsgrave said. "Hoffmann was too dangerous, and we needed every tool to fight him."

"And now?"

She seemed, for a moment, uncertain. "Now a lot of things must be changed."

The two detectives Unwin had seen on the elevator with Detective Screed—Peake and Crabtree—had arrived at the middle of the archive. They cast grim glances at the huge pink chair, the lamp, the rug. Peake smacked his flashlight against his palm and said, "Forgot my spare batteries."

"Hush up," said Crabtree, even louder.

The detectives were limping. Peake had cuts and bruises on his face, and Crabtree's green jacket was torn along one shoulder: Miss Benjamin must have neglected to warn them about the ninth step. They aimed their flashlights deeper into the archive. A few of the underclerks sat up, removed their headphones, and blinked into the light.

"Enoch and Arthur have both grown stupid and hungry," Miss Palsgrave said to Unwin. "Someone will have to see them unseated. Someone will have to restore the old balance."

"Not me," Unwin said.

Miss Palsgrave sighed. "No," she said. "I suppose not."

Behind the cart of phonographs was a caged platform—the dumbwaiter. Miss Palsgrave opened the wire mesh door with her free hand and gently set Unwin inside.

"Where do I go now?" Unwin asked.

She leaned close and said, "You go up."

She took hold of the rope that hung from the ceiling and began to pull. Unwin fell against the floor of the little car as it shot into the air. He was treated to a brief view of the archive from above, of the pink chair glowing under its lamp, of the underclerks waking and sitting up in their beds, and of Miss Palsgrave, formidable in her lavender dress, drawing him into the air by the force of her great arms as the detectives closed in on her.

Unwin had to remind himself to breathe as the pulley far above creaked under the strain. In that nothing-place between here and there, time slowed, hiccupped, leapt forward. He felt he was still separated from his body, an invisible specter in someone else's dream. Seams of light marking the secret doors into offices throughout the building flitted past. Unwin heard voices on the other sides of the walls, heard typewriters, footsteps. He was seeing the world from the other side now—from the center of mystery, out into the lighted place he had once inhabited.

The ascent ended abruptly, and his arrival was announced by the ringing of a little bell. Unwin tapped the wall in front of him, and a panel flew open. When he clambered out of the dumbwaiter, he found himself once again on the thirty-sixth floor, in the office of Edward Lamech.

The watcher's body was gone now, but Unwin was not alone. Detective Screed stood beside the desk, a few papers in his hands. When he saw Unwin, he stuffed the papers into his jacket pocket and drew his pistol, then shook his head as though to say that now, at last, he had seen it all.

"They always come back to the scene," he said.

SIXTEEN

On Apprehension

**Woe to he who checkmates his opponent at last,
only to discover they have been playing cribbage.**

Screed looked Unwin up and down, his thin mustache bending with pleasure, or disdain, or both. "You look terrible," he said. "And again that hat on the thirty-sixth floor."

Screed's suit, navy blue, was identical to the one Unwin first saw him in. It had been cleaned and pressed, or exchanged for a pristine duplicate. If Emily had succeeded in bringing him the memo, Screed did nothing to acknowledge it. He patted Unwin down, keeping the pistol trained on him. He was thorough in his search, but all he came up with was the alarm clock from Unwin's jacket pocket. This he held gently for a moment, as though he thought it might explode. He shook it, put it to his ear, and stuffed it into his own pocket.

"I'm not much of a tough guy," he said, relaxing his grip on his pistol. "And we're both gentlemen, as I see it. So I'm going to put this away now, and we'll talk like gentlemen. Agreed?"

Without waiting for a reply, Screed put his pistol back in its shoulder holster. Then he closed his hand and struck Unwin in the jaw with a quick jab. Unwin fell back against the wall.

"That," Screed said, "was for getting into the wrong car yesterday."

Screed grabbed him by the shirt and pulled him out into the hall. The place was silent, the other watchers' doors all closed. They took the elevator to the lobby, and Screed led him around the corner to where his car was parked. With an unlit cigarette in his mouth, the detective drove them uptown, along the east side of City Park.

The somnambulists were all around them, on every block. They went insensibly through the streets, playing the lead roles in their own delirious dramas. A man in a business suit stood at the edge of the park throwing seeds over his head while a flock of pigeons descended upon him to feed. His face was covered with scratches, his suit soiled and torn. A nearby tree was full of young boys, all of them throwing paper airplanes made of newspaper pages. While Unwin watched, one of the boys leaned too far off his branch and fell.

Screed hit the horn and swerved to avoid an old woman crouched in the middle of the street, her hands covered in dirt. She had relocated a pile of soil onto the pavement and was planting flowers in it.

"People these days!" Screed said.

The detective seemed to think that nothing was out of the ordinary—that this was simply the chaos of the everyday. *An enemy to messiness in all its forms,* he had called himself. Maybe Hoffmann's version of the world was how Screed already imagined it to be. When they stopped at a traffic signal, he took the cigarette from his mouth and leaned forward to pick his teeth in the rearview mirror.

Unwin rubbed his jaw where Screed had struck it. He considered the many accounts he had read of the wild assertions made by suspects after they were apprehended. Protestations of his own would only sound like the pleas of a desperate man, but he had to try to convince Screed of his innocence. "I sent you a memo," he told him. "Part of it was about Sivart's cases."

"Uh-huh," Screed said.

"I found out he was wrong about a lot of things. That most of his cases have never been solved correctly. You could be the one to fix the record, Detective Screed. We can still help one another."

"Oh, we are going to help one another," he said, accelerating through the intersection.

Screed reached into his jacket pocket and removed the pad of paper he had taken from Lamech's office, holding it so Unwin could see the top sheet. It had been rubbed with the flat of a pencil to reveal the impression left by words written on the previous page. Unwin recognized his own handwriting. *The Gilbert, Room 202.*

They parked across the street from the hotel. Screed directed him through the lobby to the restaurant, a dim, high-ceilinged room, crystal chandeliers coated in dust. The wallpaper, patterned with curlicues of gold specks, was stained yellow from years of tobacco smoke. On each table was a vase of withering lilies. They sat themselves in the back of the room.

"Your accomplice," Screed said, "has been under surveillance since shortly after she returned to the city two weeks ago. We lost track of her for a day here and there, but we know it's become her habit to take her meals at the Gilbert, where, as you know, she is currently lodged."

The restaurant was all but empty. A few old, well-dressed men sat at a table near the center of the room, speaking quietly. When Unwin could hear what they were mumbling, he heard only numbers. They were arguing about an account of some kind, or the dream of an account. Seated to Unwin's left, alone with his napkin tucked into his shirt collar, was the man with the pointy blond beard. He scrutinized an omelette while cutting small bites from it and chewing with measured care. When he saw Unwin look in his direction, he flashed him a glance of smug triumph.

"We will wait here for Miss Greenwood's arrival," Screed went on, "and you will greet her without rising from your seat. When she sees you, you will urge her to join us. When you speak of me, you will speak of me—in whatever sly, insinuating terms with which the two of you are accustomed to communicating—as one who has been brought into your plot to infiltrate the Agency."

Unwin had no choice but to play along. "She'll suspect something," he said. "Even if she does sit with us, she won't tell us anything."

"That's in your hands," Screed said. "I'm giving you a chance to help, Unwin. You should be grateful. Now drink some more, your glass is too full."

Screed had insisted on whiskey sours for both of them. There was no waiter in the place, but a red-jacketed bellhop—or a boy dreaming he was a bellhop—had filled in, taking the order and returning with the drinks. Unwin sipped from his glass and winced.

"Yes," Screed said, answering a question he must have silently posed to himself, "my biggest case yet." He took the maraschino cherry from his drink and plucked it from its stem with his teeth.

Just then the bellhop came back into the restaurant. The boy was oddly alert, and his actions more precise than those of the other sleep-walkers Unwin had seen. He went to the man with the blond beard and gestured with his thumb and pinkie open over his ear: a telephone call. The man with the blond beard looked annoyed but set down his fork, a bit of omelette still stuck to it, and rose from his chair. His napkin was dangling from his collar when he followed the bellhop into the lobby.

Unwin wondered whether it was the overseer on the phone, impatient for an update from his agent.

A minute later the bellhop came back. This time he had on his arm an old man in a tattered frock coat. He directed him to a table nearby, and the old man was about to sit when he saw Screed. He looked at Unwin, then at Screed again, then nodded and closed his eyes in solemn resignation.

It was Colonel Sherbrooke Baker. Like them, he was perfectly awake.

"So you have me at last," he said. "Battered, world-weary, a lowly fugitive, and a threat to no one. But you have me, and now you demand my surrender."

Screed glowered at Unwin, as though he were somehow responsible and had better not try anything.

The colonel went on, "Once in the poor dregs of his life, the old wretch determines to take his meal in the company of his fellow men, and that is when you nab him. So be it. Better this than to die alone in my cell, wondering how long before I am found by room service, stiff in my chair, eyes gone to jelly."

Screed's mustache was twitching as Colonel Baker sat with them at their table.

"My name is Sherbrooke Thucydides Baker," he said. "I am eighty-nine years old. I am going to tell you the story of my first three deaths and how I was undone at last by the wiles of a madman and his treacherous agents."

Screed recognized the name—he knew Sivart's case files as well as anyone, if only out of envy. Slowly grasping the situation, he said, "You've made the smart choice, Baker. Why don't you start from the beginning?" He took the notepad from Lamech's office out of his pocket and gave it to Unwin. "You're a clerk," he said. "Write this down."

Unwin took a pencil from his briefcase and waited.

"She came late one night to my home," Baker began, "uninvited, unexpected. That Greenwood woman, from the carnival. I was busy at my polishing and would have shot her where she stood, if not for the plan she proposed. For a modest price, Enoch Hoffmann would oversee the faking of my death. It would be, she told me, the simplest of feats for the master illusionist. I saw immediately the advantages of such an arrangement."

Screed leaned forward, his elbows on the table. "Okay," he said, "so Hoffmann helped you with the phony funeral. I read the rest of it in the papers. All to fool your son."

The colonel took hold of the napkin and crushed it in his hand. His voice cracked as he said, "Leopold. My boy!"

"Easy now," Screed said, looking to make sure Unwin was getting it all down. "What about your second death?"

The colonel dropped the napkin onto his plate. "Hoffmann betrayed me. He was the one who contacted my brother, told him where I was, what I'd planned. Reginald came to stop me, to claim my treasures."

"You killed him," Screed said. "You stabbed him with that dagger, eight times."

"What a bore he was. How dreadful to see living boredom spilled from lips identical to yours. Forget the war, forget our childhood on the hilltop. Forget the hedgehog hunts; I despised them! Where was that, where?"

"You fled," Screed said, trying to keep him on track.

"I was dead again, and a murderer besides. I went to City Park, to that old fort. It pleased me to go there sometimes, in the autumn. I took my son, once, to show him the view from the battlements." The colonel chuckled to himself and drummed his hands against the edge of the table, as though to beat out the march of an approaching regiment.

Screed was at a loss. He sipped from his drink again, shaking his head.

"Sivart found you," Unwin tried. "You fled to the bridge."

"No, not to the bridge! To Hoffmann, to that carnival sideshow. He was in his tent at the fairgrounds, looking smug. There was a party going on. He invited me in, introduced me to the other guests. I remember there was a man who stood no taller than my knees, and some lascivious acrobats, and a woman with a hairless cat on a leash. I hated them all and showed them my teeth. He took me outside, sat me next to a fire, gave me a glass of brandy. I told him not to put on airs—anyone could see how lowly and mean were his circumstances. They say a magician never reveals his secrets, but out of spite he told me how he had encompassed my ruin."

"They found your coat in the river," Screed said.

"My son!" the colonel cried again, taking up the napkin and twisting it. "Greenwood found him. She was still working to finish Hoffmann's trick."

The man with the blond beard had come back into the restaurant, his napkin still tucked in his collar. He took in the scene instantly and came toward them with his beard thrust forward.

"Poor, poor Leopold," the colonel said. "He thought his father was dead. Everyone suspected him. Greenwood found him and told him he was done for, gave him my old coat to wear. There was no escape for him. A little lion, my son, he always was. He put the coat on. I should have been the one to go to the bridge. Not he!"

"Stop this!" cried the man with the blond beard. He grabbed Screed by the shoulder. "You must end your investigation, close the case. Orders from up top."

The three older gentlemen at the other table were looking around, troubled by all the noise but blind to its source. They spoke nervously in streams of inexplicable digits, their voices rising.

The colonel said, "Hoffmann would pose as my son, you see. It was the simplest of tricks for the master illusionist. I was dead, my brother was dead, and he would inherit everything. My collection, my home—he was going to throw nice parties there, he said. Not so lowly and mean anymore. He said he would drink brandy at my fireside."

The man with the blond beard circled the table and tried to snatch Unwin's pencil. Unwin kept hold of it until it snapped in two.

"He let me keep one thing," the colonel said. "Any one thing of my choosing." He withdrew the antique service revolver from his pocket. It shone from constant polishing and was worn to perfect smoothness, like an object come back from the sea. It was the brightest thing in the room.

"Cease, desist!" shouted the man with the blond beard, lunging at him.

The colonel responded to these words as though to a battle cry. He growled and locked arms with his adversary, spittle flying from his lips. Neither of the men was very strong; they circled one another in a jerky dance, the colonel straining backward to keep the beard from brushing his face. He fell, and the man with the blond beard fell with him. Then came the shot.

Colonel Baker rose to his knees. He took hold of the edge of the table and pulled himself up. The man with the blond beard remained on the floor. His teeth were chattering. It sounded, Unwin thought, like coins falling through a pay phone.

"Just the one thing," the colonel said. The old service revolver was still in his hand. He looked surprised to see it there. "I took only what I needed."

Screed had his pistol out, but there was nothing he could do to stop the colonel from turning the gun on himself. Unwin looked away just before the shot that signaled the fourth and final death of Colonel Baker.

Screed dropped his pistol on the table and picked up the napkin. He put it to his face and breathed quickly, making little sounds into the fabric. A minute later he put the napkin down and drank his whiskey sour. When that was gone, he started drinking Unwin's.

Unwin stood with his back against the restaurant's dappled green wallpaper. He could not remember when he had risen from his chair. Screed was saying something to him, but Unwin could only see the detective's lips moving. Gradually his hearing returned.

"You were telling the truth," Screed said. "About Sivart's cases."

On the floor the man with the blond beard had stopped chattering.

"Yes."

"I don't want the cases," Screed said. "I want Enoch Hoffmann."

Unwin allowed himself a few more breaths, taking time to think that over. "And in exchange you'll let me go."

Screed's mustache twitched, but he said, "Yes, I'll let you go."

A plan was forming in Unwin's mind. It was full of holes, and he did not have time to check it against the recommendations of the *Manual*. Still, it was all he had. "Okay," he said. "I'll make the arrangements."

"What do you need?" Screed asked.

"I need my alarm clock."

Screed fished it out of his jacket and thrust it at him, its alarm bell jangling.

"Go to the Cat & Tonic at six tomorrow morning," Unwin said. "Go to the room that was Colonel Baker's study and wait."

"Why?" Screed asked.

"Hoffmann will be there, and he won't be ready for you. You have to wait for the right moment, though. You'll know it when it comes." It was the sort of bold statement Sivart would have made in order to buy himself more time. Sometimes the detective delivered, sometimes he changed the rules enough that his promise no longer mattered. Unwin would be lucky, he thought, if he managed to survive the night.

He put the alarm clock in his briefcase and left through the front door. In the alley he found his bicycle chained to the fire escape, right where he had left it the night before. He had been correct about one thing. The chain would need a good deal of oiling.

SEVENTEEN

On Solutions

A good detective tries to know
everything. But a great detective knows
just enough to see him through to the end.

Unwin walked his bicycle toward the street but found the Gilbert's bellhop at the entrance of the alley, blocking his way. The boy stood under a broad black umbrella. He held it out to Unwin and said, "This was in lost and found. I thought you might need it." The boy's voice was perfectly clear, but his eyes were half closed and unfocused.

Unwin approached slowly, then ducked under the umbrella with him. "Tom," he said, reading the name tag on his red jacket, "what makes you think I need this more than anyone else?"

Without looking at him, the bellhop said, "It's a long ride from here to the Cat & Tonic."

Unwin felt suddenly colder. In spite of himself, he stepped back into the rain, rolling his bicycle with him. He remembered his vision of that morning—the game at the cottage, Hoffmann's blank stare: *The magician could be anyone.*

"Tom, how do you know about the Cat & Tonic?"

The bellhop frowned and shook his head, struggling with the words. "I don't," he said. "I'm just the bellhop. But Dad says I might get promoted to desk clerk if I keep my head screwed on straight."

While the bellhop was talking, Unwin began to circle slowly around him. But Tom grabbed his wrist and held him there. The boy's grip was strong. "I don't know anything about the Cat & Tonic," he said. "But I'm good at getting messages to people."

"You have a message for me? From whom?"

Unwin could see the boy's breath as he spoke. "She's on the fourteenth floor right now, asleep with her head on your old desk. Mr. Duden is trying to wake her, and he might succeed soon. In the meantime she and I are in . . ." Tom trailed off, frowning again. "We're in direct communication."

Unwin looked around. He saw no one on the street, no one looking down from the windows above. He moved back under the umbrella and whispered, "Direct communication? With Penelope Greenwood, you mean."

"No names," Tom said. "Don't know who—"

"Don't know who might be listening in," Unwin said. "That's fine, Tom. But what's the message?"

"She and her dad are in the mist. No, the midst. Of a contest of wills. She's trying to stop him. She says she's on your side."

"But I saw their reunion," Unwin said. "Her father said they would work together. He said it wasn't the first time."

Tom tilted his head, as though his ears were antennae and he was trying to improve reception. "She was eleven years old on November twelfth. He . . . conscripted her."

"Into what, exactly?"

Tom closed his eyes and breathed slowly, swaying a little. A minute passed, and Unwin thought that he had lost him, that the connection to Penelope—whatever its nature—was broken. Then the bellhop said quietly, "Her father is no puppeteer. But she had another teacher.

From him she learned to . . . to let herself in, but also to leave things behind."

"What sorts of things, Tom?"

"Instructions," he said.

This was the part of Hoffmann's scheme that had boggled Edwin Moore that morning. The magician did not know how to plant suggestions into a sleeping mind—but his daughter did. Caligari had taught her how.

"Instructions," Unwin repeated. "To get up in the night and cross tomorrow off your calendar. Or to steal your neighbors' alarm clocks. Or worse, to abandon all sense and help turn the world upside down." Unwin gestured toward a man who had exited the hotel with a suitcase. He was going along the sidewalk, leaving his clothes draped over everything he saw. He had already dressed a letterbox and a fire hydrant. Now he was trying to button a jacket around a lamppost.

"She says that's not her doing," Tom replied. "They went together through the sleeping minds of the city last night, and she did what he asked. She opened up their deepest selves and jammed them open. But she made sure you and everyone at the Agency were left alone. And in some people she planted the . . . seeds of resistance. A limin . . . a liminal . . ."

"A liminal directive," Unwin said, recalling the words of the underclerk in the third archive: *something to do, someplace to go.* So the sleepwalkers Moore had gone off with *were* special operatives. But they were working for Penelope Greenwood, not Enoch Hoffmann. "She tricked him, then. But what was the directive? What were her instructions?"

Tom tightened his grip and shook Unwin's arm. "You have to stop him, Charles. Her father's onto her, and she doesn't have much time."

"What about Sivart?"

"There's barely anything left of him." Tom was looking directly at Unwin now, his eyes nearly open. "He's been broken. None of us can help him."

"I have a plan—"

"There isn't time. Get back to the Cat & Tonic, quickly. Finish this."

The bellhop thrust the umbrella at him, and Unwin took it, but Tom left his arm extended, hand palm up. A moment passed before Unwin realized that the boy was waiting for a tip. He fished a quarter out of his pocket and gave it to him.

They turned at a chugging, rattling sound, just audible over the patter of rain on the umbrella. To Unwin the sound was unmistakable—it was the Rooks' steam truck. The vehicle was not far off, and running hot, to judge from the high-pitched whine that accompanied the thunderous clamor of its engine. Jasper was coming for him.

"Charles," the bellhop said. "Go!"

Unwin collapsed the umbrella and tucked it under his arm. He turned his bicycle onto the street, pedaling hard despite the stiffness in his legs. He rode north along the park, following as best he could the route Miss Greenwood and the other sleepwalkers had taken the night before. Cold water dripped off his hat brim and trickled past his collar, down his spine. His pants were flecked with grime from the street, and his socks squelched in his shoes.

No one drove on the avenue. Some cars and taxicabs were left in the middle of the road or driven up onto the curb and abandoned. In that strange quiet, the sounds of the steam truck grew steadily louder. The rumbling seemed to come from every direction at once, echoing off the facades of buildings and through the twilit park.

Unwin braked in front of the Municipal Museum. Edwin Moore was seated on the bottom step, shivering beneath the umbrella Unwin had given him. The old clerk saw Unwin's reflection in the puddle he was staring at and looked up, squinting under his thick white eyebrows.

"Mr. Moore," Unwin said. "What happened?"

"Do I know you?" Moore said. He studied Unwin's face, shaking his head. "I can't recall. I know that I knew, and yet . . . Mr. Unwin, that's your name, isn't it? Did we work together?"

"I'm Charles Unwin. We were in the rowboat together, and then the taxi—"

"The taxi," Moore said, his eyes brightening a little. "Yes, I was a passenger in one of many taxis, and we joined others who had walked the whole way. They were bound for the fairgrounds, Mr. Unwin—an army of somnambulists, all set to one great task. We have been beaten, I'm certain of it now. Hoffmann has won."

"Why?" Unwin asked. "What did they do?"

"They gathered tools. They brought ladders and saws and drills. The remnants of Caligari's were terrified at first and tried to keep them out, tried to wake them. But once the old carnies comprehended the invaders' objective, they let them be, and then they joined them, even helped to direct their work. I had to pitch in, too, or be found out!" Moore was trembling harder now. "Caligari's Carnival is remade, Mr. Unwin, in all its iniquity. Hoffmann's lair of old is restored. He is laughing at us—laughing."

Unwin set his bicycle down and knelt beside the old clerk. He put a hand on Moore's knee and said, "Mr. Moore, I'm not sure it was Hoffmann who did this."

"Who then?"

"The woman in the plaid coat. The same woman who showed you the gold tooth of the Oldest Murdered Man, that night in your sleep."

Moore stood and moved back a step. "Who are you, to have seen into my dreams?"

"No, it's nothing like that," Unwin said. "We have a good team here. Remember?"

Moore was moving farther up the steps. He surveyed the street as the sound of the approaching steam truck grew louder. "You're one of *them,*" he said. "I remember nothing. Nothing! You may put that in your report if you like." He threw the umbrella to the ground and hurried back up the steps. Unwin watched him go, hoping he would stop, but the old clerk scurried between the massive columns and through the revolving door of the museum.

What good would it do to go after him? Moore would walk the halls of the museum alone, keeping to his usual route. There would be no guests today, no tearful children seeking their parents. After a while he might come to the chamber where the Oldest Murdered Man was housed. There, he would notice the glinting of a gold tooth at the back of the corpse's mouth. And then he would telephone the Agency, to let Detective Sivart know that he had been tricked, that he had better come see for himself and fix his mistake.

The discarded umbrella was already filling with rainwater. Unwin left it and pedaled on.

IN THE LIGHT of day, Unwin saw that the wall of the Baker estate was in disrepair; stones had long ago come loose in places and lay in mounds over the sidewalk. The iron gates, which he had thought left open for Hoffmann's sleeping guests the night before, were simply rusted open on their hinges. He pedaled up the long drive, his legs aching, the bicycle tires scattering wet sycamore seeds behind him.

At the top of the hill, the mansion lay in partial ruin. It had appeared stately the night before, lit from within and shining like a magic lantern. Now Unwin saw its sickly old face, its slumping porches and teetering balconies, its broken windowpanes and gapped shingles. He dismounted and walked his bicycle the rest of the way up the hill, left it leaning against a column of the portico.

The front door was unlocked. He went into the foyer, his clothes dripping on the hardwood. In the room where Miss Greenwood had performed the night before, highball glasses crusted with milk lay strewn over the tables and ashtrays overflowed with cigarette butts and stubbed cigars. The floors were covered with muddy footprints, most from bare feet.

He took to the stairs, and the creaking of the steps was the only sound in the place, aside from the rain pattering on the roof. He went down the hall to Hoffmann's room and opened the door.

The hearth was cold. A draft from the chimney played with the ashes, tracing small spirals over the floor. Hoffmann was still in his chair, asleep. Someone had left him with a blanket, but it had fallen off him and lay twisted around his ankles. He mumbled and shook, his hands trembling in his lap. He looked like nothing more than a harmless old man in blue pajamas.

Penelope had given up on Sivart, but Unwin could not. *You're the best chance I've got,* the detective had told him in the dream Unwin twice dreamed, first in his own bed and then in the third archive. *Try this time, would you?* And so he would try. It was possible that Penelope had underestimated Sivart's stubbornness.

Unwin took the alarm clock from his briefcase, wound it, and turned the hands to match those on his wristwatch. It was six o'clock exactly. He set the alarm as far in advance as he could and carefully placed the clock on the table, next to the near-empty bottle of brandy.

Eleven hours, fifty-nine minutes: that was how long he had to set everything in place. It was just a matter of timing now. If his plan worked, it would be like Miss Greenwood's story about all those spindles, and the one the king had missed. Only in this version of the story, instead of someone falling asleep, someone was going to wake up. A few people, actually.

A shadow moved over the floor. Unwin turned to see Cleo Greenwood standing by the window, her red raincoat dripping on the rug. She had been watching from a corner of the room—had come in, maybe, through one of Colonel Baker's old secret passages. The pistol in her hand was steady in spite of her exhaustion. It was another one of Baker's antiques; she had taken it from the wall.

"You're standing in my way," she said.

Unwin stood straight and kept himself in front of the magician. "Hoffmann is already spoken for, Miss Greenwood. And anyway, he's only half of the problem. If you'll give me the chance, I can deliver the overseer to you." Unwin was making bold promises again. He knew that it was more likely he would soon find the overseer's fingers at his own throat the next time he slept—if he ever slept again. But he went on talking.

"Those eyes at the back of your skull," he said. "You've had to work hard to keep your secret hidden from them. I understand now why you don't want him to know about your daughter. He would torment her as he's tormented you. And if she were turned to his side, nothing would be safe from the Agency's eye. Arthur thinks he's close to breaking you."

"He is," she said.

"Then let me help you."

"What do you get out of it?"

"Sivart. My old job back, maybe."

She held still a moment, then covered her face with her free hand. "You're a clerk," she said, her shoulders shaking. "Oh, God, you were his clerk."

"Not a very good one," Unwin said. "My files are full of errors. I'm just trying to make corrections now."

Hoffmann mumbled in his sleep again. On the table beside the magician, Unwin's alarm clock ticked faintly.

"All those years you played the magician's assistant," Unwin said. "I know how you tricked Colonel Baker out of his fortune. And you were there that night on *The Wonderly*, to make sure Sivart took the wrong corpse back to the museum." He gestured toward the display case at the back of the room. "There's the real Oldest Murdered Man there. And it's Caligari's corpse in the museum, isn't it?"

She did not deny it, and Unwin knew that his guess was right.

Hoffmann would have needed the old man's carnival to seize control of the city's underworld. And he needed it more after striking his deal with the Agency: where else to find so dependable a supply of performers to act as the agents, goons, and spies who would be thwarted by Travis T. Sivart? Getting Caligari out of the way, and hiding his body in plain sight, must have been the first scheme on which the magician and the overseer colluded.

"I got out when I could," Miss Greenwood said at last.

"But now you're back in. Hoffmann needed you to make everyone sleep. Just as he did on November twelfth. Your song was on the radio that time. We all heard it, we all slept. But putting people to sleep wasn't enough. He could get into their dreams, but that wasn't enough either. He needed to plant a single suggestion in all their minds, all *our* minds: cross that one day off the calendar. That's where your daughter came in."

"It was Caligari who realized what she could do," Miss Greenwood said. "He took an interest in her from the beginning. He said that she was a natural hypnotist, that it would be dangerous to allow her talents to develop unschooled. Once, when she was only six or seven, I caught her watching me in my own dreams—just standing there, staring. Those eyes of hers, Mr. Unwin. When I saw them, I knew that my daughter no longer belonged to me, would never belong to me again. I was frightened. So was Enoch."

"Not too frightened to put her talents to use."

A sound from outside: the Rooks' steam truck had arrived. It spluttered to a halt, and the door opened and slammed closed.

Miss Greenwood heard it, too. She squeezed the handle of the gun. "I would have stopped him if I'd known how he intended to use her. It's why I'm here now."

"And why is Penelope here?" Unwin asked. "Why would she want to rebuild Caligari's Carnival?"

The ancient pistol shook in her hand. Unwin could not tell if she was surprised by the question or by the fact that Unwin knew her daughter's name. "To give it back to her father," she said, "or to take it from him." Miss Greenwood swayed slightly, struggling to stay awake even as she stood there. The front door opened, and heavy footsteps sounded on the stairs.

Unwin glanced down at Hoffmann, saw the magician's eyes darting behind their lids. A fever rose up from him, and Unwin thought he detected the sickly burning odor of kettle corn. Sivart was still in there—trapped in that other carnival, the spectral one Hoffmann had built in the dream of the city. What would happen to Sivart if Miss Greenwood pulled the trigger?

"Cleo," Unwin said. "Please."

The door slammed open, and Jasper Rook burst in, his green eyes feverish under the brim of his immense hat. With every step he seemed to grow in size, until they were all gathered up in the great black heat of his shadow. Unwin opened his umbrella to shield himself, but Jasper flung it aside, and Unwin stumbled backward, landing hard on the floor.

Jasper reached for him with those enormous, suffocating hands. They filled Unwin's vision, and he felt himself drowning in the monster's shadow, which was bottomless and the color of headache.

Then Miss Greenwood was there, her arms around Jasper's shoulders. She had her lips to his ear as she embraced him. Jasper's eyelids fluttered, his body slackened, and he staggered back. Miss Greenwood eased him down, until finally he lay across the rug with his head in her lap. She took off his hat and smoothed his hair with her hand, still whispering sleep into his ear.

"He's tired," Miss Greenwood said to Unwin. "He'll sleep for a very long time, I think."

Unwin stood and found his umbrella, then leaned himself against the back of Hoffmann's chair. The air in the room was cooling again. "I will too, when this is over."

Miss Greenwood said nothing, but through her exhaustion Unwin saw something else, something she could not speak of, even now. She had loved those two men, and both had tried to destroy her— Hoffmann when he let her take the fall for November twelfth, Arthur when he began to besiege her dreams. *A kind of order and a kind of disorder:* Miss Greenwood had suffered in the tempest between the two.

In the refuge of her lap, Jasper Rook started to snore.

TOGETHER THEY dragged the sleeping body out of the room and down the stairs. Nothing woke Jasper—not the steps striking the back of his head when Unwin lost his grip for a moment, not the rain falling full on his face outside. With much effort they managed to get him up into the bed of his truck. Miss Greenwood found an oilcloth tarp and laid it over him. It was just after seven o'clock when they left the grounds of the Baker estate.

Miss Greenwood was familiar with the peculiar controls of the steam truck. She kept her eye on a row of gauges over the dashboard while regulating the engine with a row of levers under the wheel, which was enormous and had the spokes of a ship's wheel. The boiler thumped and hissed at their backs.

Unwin gazed silently out the passenger window. On one corner a young boy was shaking a woman's arm and crying, "Wake up, Mom! Wake up!" Lights were on in some apartment buildings, and Unwin glimpsed nervous, confused faces in the windows. Some people had woken and gone home. Was Hoffmann's grip beginning to loosen?

"It will come in waves now," Miss Greenwood said. "He can't keep them asleep all the time, so some will get a reprieve. But most who do will doubt whether they're really awake."

It was hot inside the cab, and sometimes the needles on the dials strayed into the red. Miss Greenwood drove south past the Agency office building and into the old port town. They left Jasper and his truck in front of the Forty Winks, where someone from the carnival was sure to find them. At eight twenty-seven, Unwin and Miss Greenwood went together into the cemetery.

Unwin read the names on tombstones they passed: Two-Toe Charlie, Theda Verdigris, Father Jack, Ricky Shortchange. Saints' Hill had always been the place where criminals went to bury their own, and these were the outlaws, thieves, and grifters of an earlier era. It ended with the rise of Enoch Hoffmann and was familiar to Unwin only through the oldest of the Agency's files.

"Caligari took Hoffmann in when he was a boy," Unwin said. "It couldn't have been easy for him to plot the old man's murder."

"They always disagreed on how the carnival should be used," Miss Greenwood said. "I think Caligari saw it as a tool for stirring up trouble—but only for those he felt deserved it. He would go ahead to each town we visited, get a room somewhere, and 'scout things out,' as he used to say. He was delving into the dreams of the people there."

"Looking for what?"

"He never really explained, and there wasn't always a logic to it. But most of time he found people who had something to hide. Caligari could be ruthless once he'd chosen his subject. Sometimes, though . . ." She paused and rested with one hand against a tombstone, catching her breath.

Unwin waited, and for the first time since he had met her, Miss Greenwood smiled. "Sometimes the carnival was just a carnival," she said.

She led him through the door of one of the mausoleums. Together they strained against the lid and moved it aside, revealing a set of tiled stairs where a cadaver should have been. There were lights on down there. Miss Greenwood climbed in first, and Unwin followed after her, sliding the lid back into place behind them.

At the bottom of the stairs was a dank subway platform. Roots grew through the cracked and dripping ceiling. The eight train was already in the station, its doors open. Unwin and Miss Greenwood were its only passengers. Once the train was moving, he said, "What about Hoffmann? He saw the carnival as a means for profit?"

"That's what he saw when he met Arthur: the potential for profit, for control. What Enoch's doing now resembles a plan he used to talk about sometimes. A way to seize the city entirely if his deal with the Agency ever went sour. The understanding he'd had with Arthur fell apart on November twelfth. Then, when Sivart bumbled into his head, he must have assumed the worst."

"Which is what your daughter expected," Unwin said. "That's why she gave Sivart the stolen copy of the *Manual.*"

"I understand now what she's doing. She always considered Caligari her true father and wanted to follow in his footsteps. There was a saying of his she liked to repeat, about those who belong to the carnival. 'We're just some people who lost their house keys, and everyone who loses their house keys are neighbors.'

"You see, Mr. Unwin, she intends to give the carnival back to the remnants. To steal it from the man who bent it from its true purpose."

The train squealed on its tracks and swayed as it rounded a corner, and they both held tightly to the straps.

If Penelope succeeded, Unwin thought, then part of Miss Palsgrave's changing of the guard would be complete.

"Well," Miss Greenwood said after a while, "don't you think it's time you told me your plan?"

Unwin was figuring parts of it out as he described it to her, but Miss Greenwood listened patiently. When he was finished, they were both quiet a moment.

"It's not a very good plan," she said.

THEY GOT OFF at Central Terminal and went up the stairs to the concourse. Some of the trains from Central Terminal were still running on time. The one they boarded moved into the tunnels a few minutes after ten o'clock: less than eight hours, now, before the alarm at Hoffmann's side would ring. When the conductor reached their booth, Miss Greenwood paid for her ticket and Unwin handed him the one he purchased nine days before, on the morning he first saw the woman in the plaid coat. The conductor punched it without looking and moved on.

It was dark, but Unwin did his best to memorize everything he saw outside the windows: the city thinning and then giving way to trees, the bridges spanning the river, the rise and fall of the mountains on the far side. He tried to imagine what it would look like in the daytime.

Miss Greenwood read magazines to stay awake. Whenever Unwin caught her drifting off, he reached under the sleeve of her red raincoat and pinched her. She swore at him, though they both knew that even a momentary slip could cost them everything.

They reached the end of the line with less than five hours left. No one met them at the station. The town was just as Unwin had imagined, and seeing it was like remembering. Maybe he *was* remembering. Maybe this was where he had come once, as a boy, to play that game with the other children. Seek-and-find? Call-and-hide?

They walked north along the town's only street, and Unwin counted his steps, noting everything: the gray cat moving between the slats of a picket fence, the colors of the mailboxes, the breeze coming off the river. They followed a dirt path into the woods. It was cooler here, and Unwin paused to button his jacket. He smelled the pond before he saw it.

"I cut all mention of this place from Sivart's reports," he said. "I'd always assumed he made it up."

"You overestimate his imagination," Miss Greenwood said.

The water, patched with oak leaves, was dark and cold-looking in the moonlight. A tire swing hung from a tree at its edge. Anyone kicking hard enough could swing far over the water. He could let go if he wanted; he could let himself fall right in.

Beyond the swing a slope covered with blackberry briars and, at the top of the slope, the cottage where Miss Greenwood and her daughter had lived for the seven years of her exile. A rubberized electrical cord snaked down from one of the windows. They followed it east into the woods, away from the water. Unwin recalled his dream of footprints in the mud, of the meeting with the boy who had been Enoch Hoffmann, and shivered.

The clearing was just as Sivart had described it. But there at its center a narrow brass bed instead of a pile of leaves, and on a table beside it a green-shaded lamp and a typewriter. The lamp was plugged in, and the bulb glowed yellow. Sivart was asleep under a yellow cotton blanket, on top of which was spread a second blanket of leaves. He snored with his hat down over his eyes, and his face was stubbled.

A dozen open umbrellas were hung in the tree above the bed, forming a makeshift canopy. He must have used to stepladder to get them arranged that way.

"I told him he could use the place but that I didn't want him sleeping in my room," Miss Greenwood said. "I thought he'd understood I meant for him to use the couch, or the spare room in the back. Instead he drags my bed all the way out here."

Unwin recalled what Sivart had written about this spot: *A nice place to take a nap.* He removed Sivart's hat from his head and peered at the man's eyelids. They were purple and bruised-looking. "Wake up," he said quietly. "Wake up."

Miss Greenwood already had hold of the detective's ankles. "You get his wrists," she said.

They lifted Sivart off the bed and carried him across the clearing, where they leaned him against the trunk of an oak tree. Unwin put the detective's hat back on his head, then returned to the bed. The sheets were still warm from Sivart's body. He settled into the pillow and closed his eyes, listening to the sound of the rain on the umbrellas above.

"Four hours and a half," Miss Greenwood said. "You'll be able to keep track of the time?"

"I'm more worried about falling asleep," he said. "I should be tired, but I'm not."

Miss Greenwood leaned close and whispered something into Unwin's ear. The words fit like a key into a lock he had not known was there, and he fell asleep so quickly he had forgotten what the words were by the time he started dreaming.

EIGHTEEN

On Dream Detection

Among the many dangers associated with this technique—
if it may be so characterized—is the possibility that its
practitioner, upon waking, may wonder whether
everything he has seen was real or simply a construct
of his own fancy. Indeed, the author of this manual
cannot claim with certainty that the technique
described in these pages actually exists.

U nwin dreamed that he woke in his own bed, that he got up and
put on his robe. He dreamed himself a nice hot shower (no time
for a bath), and because he was a meticulous dreamer, he took care to
tie the right tie this morning and to turn off the stove before his oatmeal burned. He did not want to be late. He carried his shoes to the
door and put them on in the hall, just as he always did. He almost
picked up his umbrella, then remembered that he had dreamed the sun
out and the clouds gone.

Outside, the streetlights were still on, and the only vehicles moving
were delivery trucks bringing bottles of milk and soda water. The bakery across the street had its door open, and he could smell the bread on
the cool air.

Everything was pretty much the way it was supposed to be, but his
bicycle was still at the Cat & Tonic, so he walked. At the corner he felt
for a moment that someone was watching him. Had he glimpsed a

figure standing in the bakery door? He tried to recall what advice *The Manual of Detection* had for those who suspected they were being tailed. Something, he thought, about being friendly to your shadow. Well, it hardly mattered—he was going only a few blocks.

At Central Terminal there was no line at the breakfast cart, but he did not need a cup of coffee. If someone asked him why he came to Central Terminal, he would tell the truth—that he was taking the first train out of town, all the way to the end of the line.

The old schedule was still in his pocket. He checked it against the four-faced clock above the information booth. His train would board in just a few minutes.

He dreamed he still had the ticket he purchased the morning he first saw the woman in the plaid coat, then dreamed he sat at the front of the train. As the conductor punched his ticket, he turned in his seat, fighting the feeling that someone was watching him. He was one of only a few passengers in the car, and everyone else was either reading a newspaper or napping.

The train began to move. Unwin settled back in his seat as it emerged from the tunnels into a brightening morning. The city rose up on either side of the tracks, then gradually thinned. They passed under a bridge and veered north along the river. In the valley the leaves on all the trees had turned red and yellow. The colors reflected on the surface of the water made him dizzy. He closed his eyes against them and dozed.

He took the train as far into the country as it would go. The terminal at the other end of the line was small and made of red brick, with a door painted green. Seeing it all reminded him again of that game he had played with the other children.

Hide-and-seek: that is what the game was called. It had been somebody's birthday, he thought.

He walked north on the town's one road. A gray cat moved between the slats of a picket fence, following him without looking like it was following him. Beyond the last mailbox, he found the dirt path leading into the woods. It was cool in the shade there, and he buttoned his jacket. The ground was soft but not too damp.

Again the feeling that made him turn, expecting a pair of eyes in the shadow. There was no one there, just a small animal darting into the ferns. Two days as a detective and already he was suspicious of everything.

He came to the pond, to the tire swing. Unwin followed the electric cord into the woods, to the clearing where Sivart had moved the narrow brass bed. The lamp was on, and some leaves had fallen onto the typewriter. Sivart was under the covers, his hat down over his eyes.

Unwin stood at the foot of the bed and shook it. Sivart did not stir, not even a little. Back at the Cat & Tonic, the magician was still asleep, still keeping him prisoner. Unwin checked his watch. He had just a few minutes before the alarm would ring.

"Move away, Mr. Unwin."

Arthur, still in his gray coveralls, appeared at the end of the path. He had a pistol in his hand. "I knew I'd have to take care of this myself eventually."

Unwin stepped aside. "You knew I'd come here."

"I didn't know where 'here' was, but I knew you had nowhere left to go. And I understood the same thing Lamech did, when he promoted you. That if anyone knew where Sivart had gone, it was you."

The overseer walked up to the foot of the bed. A breeze stirred the leaves on the blanket and brought a few more down out of the trees. Unwin could just hear the creaking of the tire swing over the pond.

Arthur said, "I was trying to tell you something yesterday morning, when I saw you on the eight train. I was trying to tell you that I got your memo. The one you sent to Lamech, knowing it would reach someone in charge. Your request is granted, Mr. Unwin. You're not a detective anymore. Which means you don't have to watch this."

"I'll stay," Unwin said.

"Suit yourself." Arthur raised the pistol and closed one eye to aim.

"You're going to miss," Unwin said. "Are you sure it's even loaded?"

Arthur's arm shook a little. He opened the cylinder to check and gave Unwin a weary look. Then he snapped it closed and readied himself.

"You're going to miss," Unwin said again. "You aren't even pointing the gun at Sivart. You're pointing it at me."

"You're an odd one, Mr. Unwin." He let out his breath and dropped his arm. "Why is this gun so damn heavy?"

"I don't think it's a gun," Unwin said. "I think it's your accordion. You must have grabbed the wrong thing on your way out of your office."

Arthur whistled through his teeth. "A total loon."

"It's nothing to be ashamed of," Unwin said. "It would be easy to mix them up while you were sleepwalking."

"I didn't sleepwalk," Arthur said. "I waited for you outside your apartment building. I was hiding in the bakery across the street. I followed you those few blocks to Central Terminal. I bought a ticket and rode one car behind you, all the way to the last stop. I've been awake the entire time."

"But I'm still asleep, sir, so you are, too. That's the way it works, isn't it? Door's locked. You don't wake up until I do."

Arthur leveled the gun. "You're talking nonsense."

"Actually, I got the idea from something Lamech said, in his last dream. The one he was having when you killed him."

Arthur moved his jaw while he thought about that. "Oh, yeah? What did he say that gave you this idea of yours?"

"He said that once, during an investigation, his subject dreamed she woke up, and Lamech thought she really had. He went about his day for a long time before he figured out he was still asleep, still in the dream he had infiltrated."

"What makes you think I'd fall for a thing like that?"

"I'm a meticulous dreamer, sir. Always have been. I took a train out of town last night, and Miss Greenwood came with me. I made note of everything I saw on the way. I knew I'd have to dream it later, make it perfect. I came out here and found Sivart asleep in this bed, in the moonlight with that lamp on. I dragged him out and took his place.

"Miss Greenwood helped me sleep. I dreamed that I was home, that I woke up there. I dreamed that I went down to the street and smelled the bread baking, and that's when you started following me. I went to Central Terminal and took the first train into the country. I dreamed it well enough for you to follow me. You've been asleep for so long, I think you don't remember what it feels like to be awake. I'm still asleep. You're asleep, too. And I'm pretty sure that's just your accordion in your hand. With your eyes closed, you must have taken the wrong thing off the wall. Still, I wish you'd stop pointing it at me."

Arthur had grown more agitated while he listened, and his whole body was shaking now. "I don't believe any of this," he said.

"I saw you murder Lamech," Unwin said. "Miss Palsgrave recorded the dream—she knows you killed him, too. Do you think she'll stay loyal to you after this? Do you think any of your watchers will?"

With a growl Arthur pulled the trigger, and the gun leapt in his hand. The shot shook the bed, shook more leaves out of the trees. It was so loud it woke Unwin and Arthur both.

Unwin sat up and felt his chest—no wound, only wet leaves. He brushed them away and checked his watch: it was just after six o'clock. Back at the Cat & Tonic, the alarm clock he left had woken Enoch Hoffmann.

Woken Sivart, too. The detective was standing beside the bed, hat low over his brow, his gun aimed at the overseer. Arthur looked down at his accordion. He was holding it by the bass strap with the bellows unlatched and dangling, so that the other end nearly touched the ground.

"I don't know any songs for this," Arthur said.

Sivart rubbed the back of his neck. "I am so tender. Charlie, couldn't you at least have given me a pillow?"

Miss Greenwood stepped into the clearing, limping badly on her bad leg. She went to stand next to Sivart. Her exhaustion had developed into something else, something hard and cracked. The look in her shadowed eyes, when she saw Arthur, was full of a strange fire.

Unwin leaned over the edge of the bed and started putting on his shoes.

"Idiots," Arthur said. "You know what that madman's doing to my city. To our city. You need me."

"Like hell," Sivart said.

"Mr. Unwin, you saw the third archive. What the Agency always needed was an honest-to-goodness record, not just of our work but of the city's work. Its secrets, its thoughts, its dreams—good and bad. They're down there in our basement, the whole shebang. It's only because of Hoffmann that any of it's necessary. He'll twist the world out of whack if we don't keep a watch on things."

For a moment Unwin found himself wanting to be convinced. It would be safer for everyone, he thought, to keep those records, to make more of them, to document everything they could see, to possess forever the solutions to those mysteries for which each person was treasury, keeper, and key.

But if everything is knowable, then nothing is safe, and the sentinels are unwelcome guests, mere trespassers. Not an antidote to the enemy—only his mirror.

"Hoffmann's taken care of," Unwin said. "Screed has him by now."

Sivart looked furious when he heard that. He came over to Unwin and said, "Ben Screed? That jokester? It isn't his case, Charlie, never was. You shouldn't have done that."

Arthur seemed to have given up on them and was watching Miss

Greenwood attentively. He righted his accordion and held it with both hands. "How's that one go, darling?" he said, running his fingers over the keys. "The one we used to play when it was almost time to go?"

She drew a gun from the pocket of her red raincoat. It was the antique pistol she had taken from Hoffmann's trophy room. "Almost time to go," she said.

Arthur filled the bellows and played a few chords. "Wait, wait," he said. "I've almost got it."

He and the others turned at the sound of another person coming up the path. Something glinted in the shade—a pair of eyeglasses, Emily Doppel's. She must have followed the sleepwalking overseer, maybe even sat next to him on the train. She had Unwin's pistol in one hand and her lunch box in the other.

She took a long look at everyone in the clearing. Unwin wondered whether she could have created the same scenario with those figurines in her lunch box. Investigator, suspect, informant, criminal: there were only so many ways to arrange them.

Unwin stood and went to her. "We did it, Emily. We found Sivart."

"Did we?" she said, her voice flat. "And what now?"

"Now—well, I was thinking about it. I was thinking we should keep working together. I don't know what the rules are, exactly, but what's to stop us from solving more mysteries together? I think I'm getting the hang of this. And I think I can't do it without you."

She met his gaze, but only for a moment. "You know, Detective Unwin, I applied three times to work at the Agency. I was twelve the first time. I wanted to be a messenger, but I fell asleep in the middle of the interview. A year later I tried again, but they remembered who I was and they didn't even ask me to come in. The last time was about a year ago. I thought maybe I'd ask for a spot at a clerk's desk. But I changed my mind at the last minute and told them I wanted to be a detective, that I wouldn't be happy with anything less. They still remembered me. And they knew, somehow, what I had in my lunch box. 'Little girl,' they said, 'why don't you just go home and play with your toys.'

"I was so mad I almost went down to the carnival, to see if the remnants would take me in. But before I could, Arthur visited me in my sleep." She was looking at the overseer now. "He gave me a chance when nobody else would. He said, 'Come and be my assistant. I'll teach you everything.' I thought maybe it was just a delusion, something I'd invented to make myself feel better. But it wasn't. Every time I drifted off, I was back in his office. And cases I heard about there would show up in the papers a few days later. It was real. And the head of the Agency was teaching me everything."

Emily's gaze had settled on Cleo. "Miss Greenwood," she said, "you have to drop that gun now."

Arthur wheezed until his wheezing became laughter. "Attagirl," he said, still teasing a tune from the bellows. "I knew I could count on you."

Miss Greenwood showed no indication that she had heard any of this, and Emily took a step closer to her.

"Lady," Sivart said to Emily, "put the gun down."

Emily pointed the gun at Miss Greenwood as Sivart took aim at Emily. Did the *Manual* contain a name for this, for what was happening? These three could stand that way forever, no one making a move, because there was no good move to make. Miss Greenwood shook her head—barely conscious, it seemed, of what was going on around her. She knew the gun, knew the man at whom she aimed. That was all, maybe.

The overseer was still wheezing. He looked at Emily and said, "What are you waiting for?"

She ignored him and said to Unwin, "I convinced Arthur to assign me to you, after your promotion. The plan was to keep an eye on you. Make sure you stayed on track. Make sure you found Sivart for us."

Unwin felt cold as he recalled one of the first assignments he had given his assistant—to contact the Agency's custodian and ask him to clean the paint spilled in the hall. But they had discussed more than spilled paint—as they must have every time she fell asleep.

"You did a good job of it, then," Unwin said.

"Not good enough," she said. She was shaking her lunch box as she spoke, rattling the tin figurines inside. "It shouldn't be like this. . . ."

Arthur had stopped laughing. "That's right, Emily," he said. "There are protocols."

Emily did not seem to hear him. "I stole Lamech's copy of *The Manual of Detection*," she said.

The accordion sagged in Arthur's hands, emitting a dissonant sigh. "Emily," he said quietly.

"At first I just wanted it for myself," she said. "But once I'd read the whole thing, I saw what it could do, what it could . . . incite a person to do. So I left it in Sivart's office, where he was sure to find it. I couldn't stand the waiting anymore. I wanted someone to make a move, a real one. I wanted Hoffmann back, and the Agency ready to fight him."

Unwin took a step away from her, closing his eyes as he considered his mistake. Penelope Greenwood was not the thief of the unexpurgated copy of *The Manual of Detection*. Though in revealing the gold tooth of the Oldest Murdered Man, she had worked in concert with Emily, and toward the same end. The two of them, without apparent knowledge of one another, had together rekindled the old war between the Agency and the carnival.

The leaves, when the breeze took them, rustled like paper. Emily looked at the ground, shaking her head. "What a mess I've made. I could have done a better job."

"Don't be too hard on yourself," Sivart said.

She half closed her eyes, then recited, " 'To the modern detective, truth is rarely its own reward; usually it is its own punishment. And if you cannot track mystery to the back of its ugly cave, then be content to stand at the edge of the dark and call it by name.' "

She looked at Arthur as she lowered her gun.

The overseer, as though a spring in him were suddenly loosed, leaned into his accordion and began to play. The bellows strained and crumpled between his hands, and his big fingernails danced over the keys. "That's how it goes, isn't it, darling?" he said.

Miss Greenwood went closer to him. "Stop calling me that," she said.

Arthur's song was the opposite of a lullaby, thunderous and brash. "Sure," he said, stamping the time with his foot. "That's it. What are the words? 'Between you and me, All the way to the sea, In my dream of your dream—' "

Miss Greenwood's shot sent him tumbling backward. He tripped over the roots of the old oak and fell cradled against its trunk. His arms were still moving as he lay there, but the air went in and out through the two holes the bullet had made in the bellows, and the notes were just ragged whispers now.

Detective Sivart took his hat off and sat on the edge of the bed. He looked at the ground and waited until it was quiet again. Then he switched off the light.

THE DINING TABLE was big for the cottage, and Unwin had to walk with his back against the wall to reach his seat. He looked around while Sivart fussed in the kitchen. There were shelves of old books and photographs on the walls. The pictures were hung with their frames nearly touching, so that the wallpaper—a faded pattern of carts and haystacks—was all but obscured. In one yellowing image, the giantess Hildegard sat on a tree stump, boxes of fireworks open all around her. Aloof and queenly on her bower throne, she regarded the camera with her chin raised and her eyes downturned.

In another picture a young Miss Greenwood was seated at a dime-store counter, straw in her soda glass. Her smile was careful. A little girl sat on the stool beside her, legs dangling with her ankles crossed. Penelope, her hair tied back in a braid, gazed mistrustfully at the camera.

"Be there in a minute," Sivart called from the kitchen.

Unwin realized he had been drumming his fingers against the table and stopped himself. Through the window he had a view of the pond at the bottom of the hill. Emily and Miss Greenwood were walking around the water together, talking.

Sivart came into the room with a blue dish towel draped over his shoulder. He had taken off his jacket and shirt, leaving his black suspenders strapped over his undershirt. "Hope you're hungry," he said. He set down a tray covered with strips of bacon and fried eggs, most of the yolks broken. He went away and came back with plates and forks, a pile of toast, pancakes, a bowl of blackberries, butter.

The detective looked at everything, frowning. He left again and came back with a pot of coffee and a creamer. "Haven't eaten in days," he said, tucking a napkin into his collar.

Unwin was hungry, too. He helped himself to pancakes and a handful of blackberries. Sivart forked a stack of bacon onto his plate and said, "It took you long enough to figure out where I was."

"You could have told me right from the start."

"Nah, you would have screwed it up if I'd done that. Like today, except our friend out there would've been awake, and he would've remembered to bring his gun."

Outside, Emily and Miss Greenwood had arrived at the tire swing. They were still speaking, and they seemed to have come to an agreement of some kind. Miss Greenwood was nodding, her arms crossed over her belly, while Emily stood with one foot up on the tire.

"That Emily's a firecracker," Sivart said as he ate. "Reminds me a little of Cleo's girl. Now, Penny, she was an odd kid. Barely ever talked, listened to everything like she was taking notes. I used to see her down there on the swing. It never seemed like she was playing, really. More like she was just—I don't know—*waiting*."

Unwin spread butter over his pancakes. "Hoffmann looked almost afraid of her when I saw them together in Lamech's dream."

Sivart grinned and stabbed another piece of bacon. "He should've been. I wish you'd seen him when he realized what she was doing with *his* sleepwalkers. I thought his skull would break open and we'd both fall out.

"You know, Penny caught me at Central Terminal the day I was headed out here. We talked it all through in advance, about you being our agent in the field. We needed radio silence through the whole thing after that. Between Arthur and Enoch, there were no safe channels."

"That's why she's at Central Terminal every morning," Unwin said. "She's waiting for you to come back and let her know it's over."

Sivart chewed thoughtfully, washed it down with coffee. "I'm not going back, Charlie," he said.

The two women came inside, and Miss Greenwood went straight for the coffee. Emily stood in the doorway until Sivart gestured at her and said, "Sit. Eat." Then she reluctantly found a chair and put her lunch box on the table.

Sivart looked at it and said, "Do you have one of an old detective, ready to retire, a respectable gut under his coat?"

"No," Emily said. "They're all active-duty."

"Well, those days are over for me," he agreed. Then he turned to Miss Greenwood. "How about you, honey?"

"I'm going to get some sleep," she said.

"Here? Or in the slammer?"

"Here," Emily said. "But that depends on Detective Unwin, really. He'll be the one writing the report."

Miss Greenwood looked at Unwin over the rim of her cup.

"I'll have to include everything I know," he said. "But I'm a clerk again, so it's my job to determine what's relevant and what isn't."

Sivart shook his head and snickered. "Spoken like a true-blue spook," he said.

For a while the only sounds were the clatter of forks on plates and spoons in coffee cups and the ticking of a clock in another room. Sivart, sated, leaned back in his chair and raised his arms over his head. "Still," he said, "I wish we all could have sat down and talked about it. The three of you, me, Hoffmann. Even Arthur down there."

Miss Greenwood had begun to doze in her chair, but now she was listening again. Her voice was cold when she spoke. "It would have been helpful for your memoirs," she said.

Sivart shifted uncomfortably in his chair. Unwin knew they were all thinking the same thing—that those memoirs, if Sivart ever wrote them, would have to tell the story as it was in the files, not as they knew it now. The detective was looking to Unwin for help, but it was Emily who spoke first.

"Maybe we can open the archive to you," she said. "For your research."

Sivart took the napkin out of his collar and said, "Fine. That would be fine." He got up and started gathering the dirty dishes.

Later Sivart and Miss Greenwood walked Unwin back to the station while Emily returned to the clearing. ("Someone has to start cleaning up," she said.) A cool breeze was blowing off the river, and Unwin noticed details he had failed to include in his dream of the place: the second church steeple at the south end of town, bits of trash floating along the shore, some old railroad ties in the weeds beside the tracks. If Arthur had not been asleep for so long, he might have sensed that something was wrong when he followed Unwin here. But waking and dreaming must have been a blur to him by the end.

One part of Unwin's dream had carried over to the real world some-how. The rain was gone, and the sun was rising into a clear sky. It was as though no one trusted it yet—all the people climbing into the train still wore raincoats and carried umbrellas.

The conductor called for them to board. Sivart, suddenly sheepish, rubbed the bristles on his chin and said, "I think I promised you a drink once, Charlie."

"Another time," Unwin said. "Maybe next month, for your birthday."

"What, you figured it out?"

What Unwin had figured out was that Sivart did not have a hunch on the morning of November twelfth, as he wrote in his report. It was just that Arthur and Hoffmann chose the one day of the year that the detective would notice had gone missing.

Sivart handed Unwin the typewriter that had been at his bedside, closed up in its case now. "It's just my old portable," he said. "I don't think I'll need it anymore. And there's no telling how the chips are going to fall, back at the home office. Might be good to keep a little nimble, you know?"

Unwin hefted the case to test its weight. It was lighter than he expected, but he noticed a keyhole by the latch. Sivart saw what he was looking at.

"Let's see," the detective said. Then, with a swift, graceful movement, he reached behind Unwin's ear. The key was in his hand when he brought it back.

Sivart's grin fell away, and his face went pale. "I didn't even mean to do that," he said. "A week ago I didn't know how. More Hoffmann's style, really. You don't think there are side effects, from all that time we spent cooped up together? Like maybe there's a bit of old twiddle-fingers still left in here?"

Unwin recalled what young Penny Greenwood, all those years ago, had said to Sivart when she read his palm. That he would live a long life but part of it would not be his own. Unwin took the key. "Thank you," he said. "The typewriter is perfect."

The detective, something like fear on his face, stared at his own shaking hand. Miss Greenwood took it in her own and held it. "Don't worry," she said to Unwin. "I'll take care of him."

Unwin boarded and chose a seat on the side facing the shore. As the train pulled away, he glimpsed Sivart trudging back up the road, toward the cottage. He and Miss Greenwood were walking arm in arm.

Unwin opened the typewriter on his lap. One of the oak leaves was stuck between the type bars. He put that in his pocket, loaded a fresh sheet of paper, and began to work on his report. "I," he decided, would have to be part of it after all.

Lest details be mistaken for clues, note that I ride my bicycle to work every day, even when it is raining. That's how I came to be at Central Terminal last Wednesday morning with my hands full and my umbrella under my arm. So encumbered, I found it impossible to recover the umbrella dropped to the floor by a certain party, whose role in all this I will, over the course of this report, attempt to explain. She was, as they say, "in on it" from the beginning, whereas I was merely "it," and I use the word as children do when playing games that involve running and hiding, and seeking those who are hidden.

We have been playing a game like that, a great many of us for a great many years. Some of us did not know we were playing, and some of us were not told all the rules.

Now that I have the opportunity to begin this report, I do not know how best to categorize it. I am both clerk and detective, but due to the circumstances of the case at hand I am also neither of those things. A train will bring you back to the place you came from, but it will not return you home.

Dozens more black raincoats boarded the train at each stop on its descent through the valley. The clattering of the wheels kept time with the rhythm of Unwin's typing, and newspapers rustled all around. He caught sight of one of the headlines: RETURN OF THE CARNIVAL THAT NEVER LEFT.

He wrote, *At least I know who I am writing this report for. Miss Greenwood's daughter is my clerk, after all, and she will want every detail, every clue, from top to bottom.*

The seven twenty-seven train arrived at Central Terminal one minute late as usual. Unwin put the typewriter away and slipped the pages of his first report into an empty folder from his briefcase. He waited for the last of the black raincoats to pour out the doors, then followed them through Gate Fourteen. The woman in the plaid coat stood on her toes. She stopped searching when she saw him, and he went to her. She had been waiting a long time.

HE DID NOT see Emily again for several days. When he did, it was on the Agency elevator. She was wearing the same blue woolen dress she had worn the day they started working together. At first it seemed as though she were going to ignore him. "I'm sorry," she finally said. "It's just that it's against policy for us to speak."

"You've been promoted."

"Yes."

"High up in the ranks, I hope."

"Very," she said, and touched the pencil in her hair. "Some of the watchers, I guess, have had their eyes on me. And then, you know, there was a vacancy."

Unwin recalled Miss Palsgrave's words about the changing of the guard and knew that it was not Edward Lamech's place Emily had taken. She had been the overseer's only assistant—no one knew the job better than she did. He wondered whether she kept those figurines on her desk while she worked: totems of the agents whose efforts she now directed. Better that, he supposed, than those blank-eyed pigeons.

"There must be a lot of changes under way," Unwin said.

Her gaze grew suddenly hard. "Well, change takes time. And there are only a few people who know as much about this place as you do, Mr. Unwin, so I'm trusting you to keep it that way. Do you follow me?"

"I'm not sure that I do."

"Please try, Mr. Unwin. You're very valuable to us." Her voice softened. "To me, I mean. It would be terrible, you know, if you put me in a difficult position."

"A difficult position," Unwin said.

She took his hand and pressed something into it. He recognized its shape against his palm: it was the figurine from her collection that he thought looked like him. The one with his hands on his knees and a look of astonishment on his face. She kept her hand in his until they reached the twenty-ninth floor. Then Unwin pocketed the figurine and stepped off the elevator, turning to say good-bye. Emily's smile was sad, and Unwin thought for a moment that the sight of her crooked teeth would break his heart—and then it did, a little. He could not even tell her why, not now, though she might understand once she received his report.

Emily looked away as the attendant closed the door.

He packed his things quickly: silver letter opener, magnifying glass, spare spools of typewriter ribbon. He took some typing paper, too. It could be a long time before he had fresh supplies at hand again.

He closed the office door behind him and found Screed waiting in the hall.

"I need your help getting this thing lit," Screed said. His right arm was in a cast, and he was fumbling with the lighter in his left hand. Unwin took it from him, struck the flint, and raised the flame to the cigarette dangling from the detective's lips. It was the first time Unwin had actually seen him smoking.

"Everything was just as you said it was," Screed said. "The Cat & Tonic was empty, and there was Hoffmann, asleep in his chair. Wasn't he surprised to see me, after your alarm went off! I had him, Unwin."

"You had him," Unwin repeated.

"I wanted to take my time, you know. Get in touch with the right people at the newspaper. I figured that everyone should know about the historic occasion. I left him locked in my closet while I made the arrangements."

"But you forgot about his voice," Unwin said.

Screed looked at the floor and coughed smoke through his nose. "I was only gone a minute. When I got back to my office, Peake and Crabtree were waiting in the dark. They jumped me. Hoffmann had called them over using my voice and convinced them that Hoffmann had stuck me in the closet and was coming back to kill me. By the time we'd figured out what happened, he was gone."

Screed would not look Unwin in the eyes. They both knew that Hoffmann might never be caught again, that he could already be anywhere, any*one*. But if Sivart really did have a bit of Hoffmann still in his brain, might the opposite also be true? It pleased Unwin to imagine a fragment of the detective in the magician's mind, shadowing his every move.

After a while Unwin said, "At least you got the Oldest Murdered Man."

Screed sighed. "There's one old museum attendant down there who was pretty pleased about it. Not sure anyone else cared. I think they're even going to keep the plaque with Sivart's name on it."

Screed was still smoking when Unwin left, flinching each time he had to move his arm.

The fourteenth floor was Unwin's next stop. The clerks pretended not to see him, which made the walk to his old desk a little easier. Even now the sounds of the place tugged at him. He would have liked to sit for a while with his eyes closed, just listening to those typewriters and file drawers.

Penelope Greenwood had packed her things into a cardboard box. When she saw Unwin, she tucked it under her arm and put on her gray cap. Mr. Duden was watching as they returned to the elevator together. Unwin glanced behind him and caught the overclerk wringing his hands.

Out on the sidewalk, Unwin stood with Penny in the sunlight and waited. After the third time he checked his watch, she took his wrist gently and said, "Charles, this isn't the kind of thing it's possible to be late for."

She had returned to the city to revenge the murder of Caligari—but revenge, Unwin had come to understand, was not her only motive. She felt it was her duty to reclaim the thing that was lost when the carnival passed to her father. "The unknown will always be boundless," Caligari had said, and Unwin believed that Penelope Greenwood meant to keep it that way.

Some at the Agency, he thought, would be pleased to hear that the organization had a proper adversary again.

Caligari's Carnival rounded the corner. It was restored in full and traveling again, the mud of the old fairgrounds washed away, its every part repainted red or green or yellow, flinging streamers and music in all directions. The remnants had taken to their trucks; they waved and honked horns at the children who shouted from the sidewalks. The parade heaved itself in starts and stutters up the avenue, and at the front were the elephants, walking trunk to tail. Penelope had cleaned and fed them and scrubbed them behind their ears. Even the oldest of the three looked lively again.

As the parade drew close, a series of deep thudding sounds shook the sidewalk. Unwin and Penny held each other's arms as cracks appeared in the cement at their feet and a gust of hot, acrid air erupted from the Agency lobby. They turned to see black smoke streaming out the door, and with it a crowd of bewildered, red-faced men clutching bowler hats to their heads. Whistling sounds and the cracks of explosives followed.

Unwin and Penny drew closer as the underclerks tumbled past them, shouting and coughing, some still pulling jackets over their pajamas. The crowd merged with the parade in the street, bringing the procession to a halt. Clowns and underclerks toppled over one another as drivers shouted from their seats and hats, pillows, and balloons flew into the air. Up and down the avenue, people huddled at open windows to watch the spectacle. The youngest elephant, out of delight or indignation, reared on its hind legs and trumpeted.

The tremors ceased as Hildegard Palsgrave ducked out through the lobby door, her arms and face covered in soot. She dragged her enormous pink chair behind her, and on it was her phonograph. "My first fireworks display in years," she said.

Penelope shook soot from the dress of the giantess. "You haven't lost your touch," she said.

Unwin gazed up the facade of the Agency office building and saw windows opening on every floor. Clerks looked down from the nearest rows, taking turns at the view. Detectives watched from their higher floors, shaking their heads at the scene. Farther up, so far that Unwin could not make out the expressions on their faces, the watchers observed everything from the comfort of their private offices, and above them, fewer in number, were operatives whose titles and functions he did not know.

Emily's first week on the job, and changes were under way more quickly than she had anticipated. The watchers would be asking their new overseer what to do, now that the chief clerk of the third archive had destroyed what she helped to create.

Edgar Zlatari was driving the Rooks' truck. He navigated slowly through the crowd and drew up to the curb with the steam engine sputtering. Theodore Brock, the knife thrower, was in the cab beside him, and Jasper was still in the back, still sleeping. Miss Palsgrave set her chair beside Jasper and climbed in.

"What about the Forty Winks?" Unwin asked Zlatari. "What about your work?"

"Show me a place where nobody's drinking and nobody's dying, and

I'll show you a man ready to stay put," he said. "Besides, there's an old crook in need of burying. Seems his funeral's been long delayed."

Unwin looked at Penelope, and she smiled. They must have smuggled Caligari's remains out of the museum somehow, after the real mummy was returned.

Miss Palsgrave smacked the roof of the cab to signal that she was ready. She had a traveling bag with her, and inside were more recordings of Miss Greenwood's songs, to make sure Jasper Rook stayed sleeping.

Unwin was tired, too. He had worn himself down—to nothing, nearly—with his cuts and corrections, his erasures and emendations. He was awake now, but was there still time for him? His mind had wearied of its appointed rounds, of the stream of typescript and transcript, and now he wondered what might have been different, what might still be different, if only the day would hold and not abandon him to sleep.

The carnival had disentangled itself from the knot of baffled underclerks and was preparing to move on. The elephants stamped impatiently, the drivers returned to their trucks, and Penny left Unwin's side to join the front of the line.

Zlatari offered him a ride. He turned down the offer but set his portable typewriter and his briefcase in the cab. He had found the time, that week, to oil the chain of his bicycle.

Maybe Penny was correct, and this was not the kind of thing he could be late for. He glimpsed Caligari's old motto emblazoned across the side of another truck: EVERYTHING I TELL YOU IS TRUE, AND EVERYTHING YOU SEE IS AS REAL AS YOU ARE.

If that was right, then nothing Unwin saw was real and the ticking of his watch was just another magician's trick. He had time, so much time. He had all the time he needed.

Some of the underclerks wrapped themselves in the blankets they had brought with them from the archive and stood watching the parade withdraw, dumbfounded. A few of them, confused by all the sights and sounds, or just because they had no place to go, went with it. Other people joined the carnival as it moved west between the office buildings—those who, no doubt, had been among Penelope's sleepwalkers, the members of her resistance. They had helped rebuild the carnival in their sleep and recalled enough that it mattered. The carnival was twice as large as it had been by the time it left the city.

He allowed himself a last glimpse of the Agency office building, and it appeared to him as it had many times before: a watchtower, a tomb. Not his, now, though someone there—the overseer herself, probably—would be expecting his report. If Unwin dispatched a copy from afar, would its recipient be surprised to find that it originated in the camp of the enemy? He smiled at the thought of it, and the smile surprised him into laughter. He was still laughing when a wind rose up from the river, nearly taking his hat. He held it to his head and steered his bicycle with one hand.

It would be hours at least before they halted long enough for him to set out his typewriter, so he carried on with his work as best he could, drafting in his mind the report that was the last of one series and the first of another.

I rode alongside the steam truck for a while, then overtook it and wove my way to the front of the column. Penelope Greenwood walked with the reins of the lead elephant in her hand, and the big beast flapped its ears in the wind. What frightens us about the carnival, I think, is not that it will come to town. Or that it will leave town, which it always does. What frightens us is the possibility that it will leave forever, and never come back, and take us with it when it goes.

It is taking me now, and I am frightened and alive and very much awake.

Where are we going next? With what purpose? Penny says she will carry on with Caligari's work, and whatever happens, someone is going to have to write it all down. So I have my job back, in a way, but the words mean nothing, all is mystery, and always there's room enough for more.

I'll try to record it as we go, but that's for another report. This one ends here, on a bridge over the river with the elephants leading us toward what routes they remember, and Hoffmann still out there with his thousand and one voices, and Agency operatives already on our tail, and the city waking, and the river waking, and the road waking under our feet, and every alarm clock ringing at the bottom of the sea.

Acknowledgments

Thanks first to my family: Sean, Caitlin, and Kellin Bliss, Kevin, Debbie, and Michael Berry, Michael Bliss, and Robert Boolukos. Cara Parravani, Dorothy Strachan, and Frank, Ellen, and Kyle Berry, each greatly missed, are everywhere in this novel. I am deeply indebted to Kelly Link, Gavin Grant, Sabina Murray, Mira Bartók, and Holly and Theo Black for their friendship and advice. Thanks also to Chris Bachelder, Brian Baldi, Robert N. Casper, Cecil Castellucci, Ellen Datlow, Miciah Bay Gault, Noy Holland, Shahrul Ladue, Leigh Newman, Jon Sequeira, and Terri Windling for all their help and sound criticism; to Esmond Harmsworth for his guidance and great insight; to Eamon Dolan for his encouragement and general brilliance; to Jason Arthur for his support, and for bringing this book to the UK in style; to Mimi Di-Novo for her generosity; to Deirdre d'Albertis for Chesterton, to William Weaver for Calvino, to Bradford Morrow for Carter and most everyone else; to Christa Parravani for lending me her dream of the sea.

This book is dedicated to my mother, Maureen Berry Bliss, who is always looking for a good mystery.

THE TROJAN WAR

By the same author

Salamis: The Greatest Naval Battle of the Ancient World, 480 B.C.

THE TRO

JAN WAR

A New History

BARRY STRAUSS

HUTCHINSON
LONDON

Published by Hutchinson 2007

2 4 6 8 10 9 7 5 3 1

Copyright © Barry Strauss 2007

Barry Strauss has asserted his right under the Copyright, Designs
and Patents Act 1988 to be identified as the author of this work

First published in Great Britain in 2007 by
Hutchinson
Random House, 20 Vauxhall Bridge Road,
London SW1V 2SA

www.randomhouse.co.uk

Addresses for companies within The Random House Group Limited can be found at:
www.randomhouse.co.uk/offices.htm

The Random House Group Limited Reg. No. 954009

A CIP catalogue record for this book is available from the British Library

ISBN 9780091799809

The Random House Group Limited makes every effort to ensure that the papers used in
its books are made from trees that have been legally sourced from well-managed and cred-
ibly certified forests. Our paper procurement policy can be found at:
www.randomhouse.co.uk/paper.htm

Printed and bound in Great Britain by William Clowes Ltd, Beccles, Suffolk

Map of Troy on page xxvi from *Celebrating Homer's Landscapes: Troy and Ithaca Revisited* by
J. V. Luce, Yale University Press, page 94, © 1998, used by permission.

For Scott and Karen, Judy and Jonathan,
Larry and Maureen, and Ronna and Richard

CONTENTS

AUTHOR'S NOTE

Most of the quotations from the *Iliad* and the *Odyssey* are from Alexander Pope's translation. A few have been translated by the author for greater accuracy.

Homer never uses the word "Greeks," referring instead to Achaeans, Danaans, Argives, and, occasionally, Hellenes. Modern scholars refer to the Greeks of the Late Bronze Age as Mycenaeans. This book generally refers to them as Greeks.

All dates in this book from the Bronze Age (ca. 3000–1000 B.C.) are approximate unless otherwise stated.

TIMETABLE OF EVENTS RELATING TO THE TROJAN WAR

Bronze Age	3000–1000 B.C.*
Height of Mycenaean civilization	1450–1180
Linear B writing	1450–1180
Submycenaean Period	1180–1050
Troy VI a–h	1740/1730–1300
Troy VIi (formerly known as Troy VIIa)	1300–1210/1180
Troy VIj (formerly known as Troy VIIb1)	1210/1180–1130
Troy VIIb2	1130–1050
Trojan War	1210–1180
Hittite Empire	1380–1180
Egyptian New Kingdom	1550–1070
Battle of Megiddo	1479
Amarna Letters	1382–1334
Battle of Qadesh	1274
Height of Assyria's Bronze Age power	1300–1200
Ugarit destroyed	1187
Greek palaces destroyed	1180
Sea Peoples	1200–1100
Greek Dark Ages	1150–750
Greek Renaissance	800–700
Greek alphabet invented	750
Homer	700s
Iliad and *Odyssey* written down in Athens	560–527

*All dates are approximate.

A NOTE ON ANCIENT HISTORY
AND ARCHAEOLOGY

Ancient Greek history traditionally begins in the year 776 B.C., when the first Olympic Games are supposed to have been held. By coincidence, the earliest example of the Greek alphabet dates to about 750 B.C. So both tradition and scholarship would agree in labeling everything that happened before the early eighth century B.C. in Greece as "prehistory." But thanks largely to archaeology, we know a great deal about the history of the "prehistoric" Greeks. And some of our knowledge even comes from written sources, because centuries before the Greek alphabet, scribes used a primitive writing system for record-keeping in Greek. Called Linear B, it was in use from about 1450 to about 1180 B.C., after which it disappeared. Much more sophisticated writings also survive from other so-called prehistoric cultures, and they offer important historical information about prehistoric Greece.

But more on that later. First, let us quickly scan the historic period of ancient Greece. The Greek city-states reached their heyday in the centuries between about 750 and 323 B.C. The period between 750 and 480 is known as the Archaic Age, while the years from 480 to 323 are called the Classical Period. At the end of the Classical Period, King Alexander III of Macedon, known today as Alexander the Great, conquered all of Greece as well as the Persian Empire to the east. Alexander's conquests began a new era of Greco-Macedonian kingdoms known as the Hellenistic Age, 323–30 B.C. That gave way, in turn, to the Roman Empire, which lasted until A.D. 476, when it split into barbarian kingdoms in the West and the Byzantine Empire in the East.

Almost all ancient written testimonies about the Trojan War date to the 1,200-year period from the start of the Archaic Age to the end of the Roman Empire. But in order to understand what really happened, we must look backward. The four centuries before the start of the Archaic Age are known collectively as the Greek Dark Ages (ca.1150–750 B.C.). "Dark" refers to the absence of writing, but the physical evidence uncovered by archaeologists sheds light on that era.

Another important term is Iron Age, used for the millennium from about 1000 B.C. to A.D. 1. In this epoch, new technology made iron the most durable metal for tools and weapons. The earlier two millennia, from about 3000 to about 1000 B.C., are known as the Bronze Age, after that era's most widespread metal for tools and weapons; iron was known but rare. The Bronze Age is the setting for this book.

In Greece, the Bronze Age is commonly divided into three periods, Early (3000–2100 B.C.), Middle (2100–1600), and Late (1600–1150). Naturally, it is difficult to assign dates to events that took place so long ago. Most dating is relative and approximate rather than absolute: that is, we can say that A is older than B or even that A comes from the period of, say, 1600–1500 B.C., but rarely can we be more specific.

Sometimes we get help from surviving written records, such as lists of Egyptian kings and their reigns (although even in that case we are not completely sure about dating). On occasion we hear of an eclipse, which can be dated by astronomers. In rare instances, it is possible to find samples of once-living material (from bone to shells to minerals) that can be dated by laboratory testing through radiocarbon dating, neutron activation analysis, or dendrochronology (counting tree rings, based on tree physiology as well as on rainfall and other environmental factors). By the last technique, for example, the tremendous volcanic explosion that destroyed most of the island of Thera has been dated to 1627–1600 B.C.

But these cases are few and far between because they depend on the quality of the sample and because testing is very expensive. Dendrochronology requires having both a number of comparative ancient tree samples as well as having nearby living trees with identical ring patterns to the sample in question. And radiocarbon testing can narrow dating to about a century but not a year.

So most dating of material dug out of the earth has to be done by more rough-and-ready methods. Fortunately for historians the remains of past civilizations tend to be deposited in layers. For example, if a house is built in A.D. 1700 and then torn down and replaced in 1800, the remains of the old house will be located below the remains of the new house. Any glass, wood, bricks, artwork, or other material found together with the foundations of the old house can be dated to the period 1700–1800. If we could take a "slice" of history in the soil of an ancient land, like Greece, we would find layers of history stacked up one above the other. The technical name for these layers is strata, and the careful study of them is called stratigraphy. Stratigraphy is one of the most important tools in the archaeologist's kit for assigning dates.

The city of Troy, for example, consists of a dozen separate levels in the Bronze Age. Each corresponds to the city during a particular era. Troy I, for example, is the city as it was ca. 3000–2600 B.C., while Troy VIi (formerly called Troy VIIa) is the city of ca. 1300–1180 B.C. The division between two layers is sometimes sharp and sometimes barely distinct. For example, there is relatively little difference between Troy VIh (ca. 1470–1300 B.C.) and Troy VIi but Troy VIj (ca. 1180–1130 B.C. and formerly called Troy VIIb1) was very unlike Troy VIi, which it followed.

The most common item found in the layers of ancient civilization is pottery. By carefully tracing changes in the shapes and styles of pottery, and by vigilantly recording the layer in which a particular potsherd is found, experts can date archaeological strata, sometimes fairly narrowly, to as little as a generation.

Through a combination mainly of pottery analysis and stratigraphy, scholars have devised a system of relative dating for the Greek

Bronze Age. Anchored by a few absolute dates, the periods known as Early, Middle, and Late Helladic are the building blocks for dating Greek prehistory. They are subdivided in turn into such subperiods as Middle Helladic III, Late Helladic IIB1.

Pottery dating is sometimes specific to a particular region, and these periods apply mainly to the Greek mainland and islands. In Anatolia, where Troy is sited, pottery dating is based on locally produced pottery, much of it imitations of the popular and widely traded pottery of Greece. So Trojan pottery dating differs from Greek.

Archaeology is mostly a matter of digging in the soil, but it can also mean going beneath the sea. Underwater archaeology in the Mediterranean has exploded with dramatic discoveries in the last few decades. For the background to the Trojan War, three Bronze Age shipwrecks, two off the coast of Turkey and one off the coast of Greece, stand out in importance. The Ulu Burun wreck (Turkey), a ship of about 1300 B.C., the Cape Gelidonya wreck (Turkey), and the Point Iria wreck (Greece) each date to about 1200 B.C.; all offer intriguing evidence.

With so many factors involved, dating events in the Bronze Age is complicated and often controversial. Consider these as rough guides: From about 2000 to 1490 B.C., civilization flourished on the island of Crete. Organized around several great palaces, this civilization is known today as Minoan. The Minoans were great farmers, sailors, traders, and artists. Although their ethnicity is not clear, we do know that they were not Greek.

The first speakers of Greek arrived in Greece from points east around 2000 B.C. They were a warlike people and took over the Greek peninsula from its earlier inhabitants. In the Late Bronze Age (ca. 1600–1150 B.C.) the newcomers' civilization dominated Greece in a series of warrior kingdoms, of which the most important were Mycenae, Thebes, Tiryns, and Pylos. We call their civilization Mycenaean. Linear B (a writing system representing syllables) shows that their language was Greek, and that they worshipped the same gods as their Archaic and Classical Greek descendants. In short, they were

Greek. Evidence suggests that the Mycenaeans called themselves Achaeans or Danaans, the two terms which, along with Argives, Homer uses for them. New Kingdom Egyptian texts refer to the kingdom of "Danaja" and to such cities in it as Mycenae and Thebes. This is independent confirmation of Homer's political framework.

The Mycenaeans were sailors, soldiers, raiders, and traders. Around 1490 B.C. they conquered Minoan Crete and took over its former colonies in the eastern Aegean islands and on the Anatolian mainland (present-day Turkey) at Miletus. Over the next several centuries, they engaged in war, diplomacy, commerce, cultural exchange, and dynastic intermarriage with the great kingdoms of the eastern Mediterranean. At least one king of Ahhiyawa was addressed as an equal in diplomatic correspondence from the Hittite king. Although Linear B texts do not allow the identification of specific events, they provide an abundance of data about weapons and warfare. If the Trojan War really happened, it was an event in the Mycenaean Age—one of the last great events before the decline and fall of Mycenaean civilization in the 1100s B.C.

The Mycenaeans' main rival was the greatest kingdom in Anatolia, Hatti, also known today as the Hittites. The Great King of the Hittites was important enough to correspond on an equal footing with the rulers of Assyria, Babylon, Mitanni, and Egypt and powerful enough to make war on them. These six kingdoms were the perennial powers of the region in the Late Bronze Age.

From their stronghold high in the central Anatolian plateau, the big city of Hattusha, the Hittites looked down and competed for the rule of what was then the world. Their main interest was in expanding southward to the Mediterranean coast of Anatolia and eastward into Syria. But they found themselves drawn willy-nilly into the ever-shifting politics of western Anatolia. Thanks to the evidence of archaeology and epigraphy, this story is much richer than most people would guess—but largely untold.

The most important source is the Hittite royal archives from Hattusha, from which thousands of clay tablets survive, as do hundreds of similar tablets from other Hittite cities. Most of them are written in the Hittite language, in a writing system called cuneiform, which employs about five hundred wedge-shaped symbols. We also have Hittite inscriptions from various places carved on stone or inscribed on metal. Some of these are written in hieroglyphics, a rebuslike system of picture-writing, but not in the famous Egyptian hieroglyphics: rather, they are written in a language called Luwian. Luwian is closely related to Hittite and was spoken widely in southern and western Anatolia. Luwian survived the Bronze Age, and we have Luwian inscriptions as late as the 200s A.D. Another related Bronze Age Anatolian language is Palaic, spoken in northwestern Anatolia. Little Palaic writing survives.

Other writing systems also existed in the eastern Mediterranean in the Bronze Age. Akkadian, originally a language used in Mesopotamia (modern Iraq), was the international language of diplomacy. Akkadian tablets survive from Cyprus; from Ugarit, a merchant city on the coast of northwest Syria; from Amurru, a border state between the Hittites and Egypt; and from Egypt itself. In addition, texts from the powerful city of Mari (1800–1750 B.C.) abound in information about warfare, although they predate the Trojan War by about five hundred years, so they should be used cautiously. Akkadian inscriptions from the Assyrian Empire of the 1200s B.C. are also a big source of evidence about conflicts and combat, and they are roughly contemporaneous with the Trojan War.

Turning to the Levant, the so-called Amarna Letters (most from 1382–1334 B.C.) are a collection of communications among eastern Mediterranean princes, especially between Pharaoh and his Canaanite vassals. These letters amply document diplomacy and war, especially small wars and low-intensity conflicts. The letters show that the years between about 1450 and 1250 mark the first international system of states in history. For their part, the warrior-pharaohs of New Kingdom Egypt (1550–1070 B.C.) have left a trove of information about military matters.

Finally, various epic poems, myths, and prayers survive from the ancient Near East, from the Sumerian *Gilgamesh* to the Ugaritic *Kirta*, and many are relevant to our story. Although some date to

2000 B.C. or earlier, they reveal continuing behaviors and technologies.

There were various kingdoms in western Anatolia in the Late Bronze Age, but for us, by far the most important was Wilusa. The subject of international conflict and civil war, Wilusa is accepted by many scholars as the place the Greeks called first Wilion and then Ilion—that is, Troy.

Troy was a great city for the two thousand years of the Bronze Age, from about 3000 to 950 B.C. After being abandoned near the beginning of the Iron Age, Troy was resettled by Greek colonists around 750 B.C. and remained a small Greek city throughout antiquity. Wave after wave of different peoples lived in Bronze Age Troy. None of those populations is easily identifiable today, but all left signs of wealth, power, and sometimes tragedy. The city was destroyed from time to time by fire, earthquake, and war, and then rebuilt. The ruins have yielded gold, artistic treasures, and palatial architecture. In the Late Bronze Age, Troy was one of the largest cities around the Aegean Sea and a major regional center—even if not nearly as large as the great cities of central Anatolia, the Levant, or Mesopotamia. Late Bronze Age Troy controlled an important harbor nearby and protected itself with a huge complex of walls, ditches, and wooden palisades. If any period of Troy corresponds to the great city of the Trojan War, this was it.

The most important texts about the Trojan War are two long poems, called epics because they tell of the heroic deeds of men long gone. The *Iliad* is set near the end of the Trojan War, and it covers about two months of the conflict. The *Odyssey* relates the hero Odysseus's long, hard trip home from Troy; it adds only a few additional details about the Trojan War. Both of these texts are attributed to a poet named Homer.

Other poems about early Greece were also written down in Archaic Greece. Known as the "Epic Cycle," six of these poems narrate the parts of the Trojan War missing from the *Iliad* and *Odyssey*. These poems are the *Cypria*, on the outbreak and first nine years of the war; the *Aethiopis*, which focuses on Troy's Ethiopian and Amazon allies; the *Little Iliad*, on the Trojan Horse; the *Iliupersis*, on the sack of Troy; the *Nostoi*, on the return of various Greek heroes, especially Agamemnon; and the *Telegony*, a continuation of the *Odyssey*. Unfortunately, only a few quotations from the Epic Cycle as well as brief summaries survive today. Many, many later writers in ancient times used these and other sources to comment on Homer.

Finally, there is ancient art, both painting and sculpture, which often illustrates details of the Trojan War, sometimes in invaluable ways for historians.

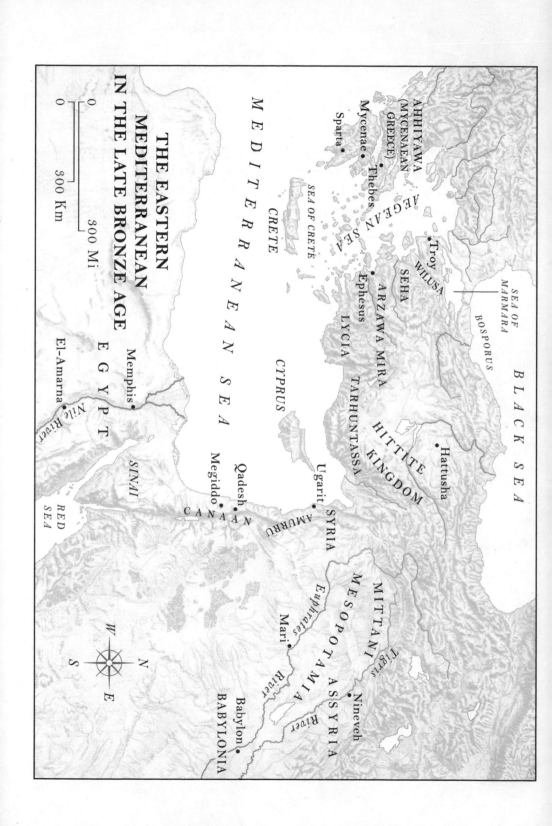

THE EASTERN
MEDITERRANEAN
IN THE LATE BRONZE AGE

0   300 Mi

0   300 Km

MEDITERRANEAN SEA

BLACK SEA

SEA OF MARMARA

BOSPORUS

AHHIYAWA
(MYCENAEAN
GREECE)

Sparta

Mycenae

Thebes

SEA OF CRETE

CRETE

AEGEAN SEA

Troy

WILUSA

SEHA

ARZAWA MIRA

Ephesus

LYCIA

TARHUNTASSA

HITTITE
KINGDOM

Hattusha

CYPRUS

Ugarit

SYRIA

AMURRU

Qadesh

Megiddo

CANAAN

Memphis

EGYPT

El-Amarna

Nile River

SINAI

RED SEA

MESOPOTAMIA

MITTANI

ASSYRIA

Nineveh

Mari

Euphrates River

Tigris River

Babylon

BABYLONIA

N
W   E
S

BRONZE AGE GREECE

PELOPONNESUS

IONIAN SEA

ITHACA

EPIRUS

MACEDONIA

Mt. Olympus ▲

THESSALY

PHTHIA

Mt. Parnassus ▲

BOEOTIA

Thebes • Aulis

GULF OF CORINTH

Corinth •

Mycenae • Tiryns

ARGOLIS

Sparta •

ARCADIA

LACONIA

ATTICA

Athens •

EUBOEA

SCYROS

AEGEAN SEA

LESBOS

CHIOS

LEMNOS

TENEDOS

SAMOTHRACE

IMBROS

• Troy

DARDANELLES

Scamander River

SEA OF MARMARA

THRACE

Hebrus River

Strymon River

BOSPORUS

BLACK SEA

SAMOS

• Ephesus

Hermus River

• Miletus

Maeander River

• Halicarnassus

ANATOLIA

DODECANESE

RHODES

CYCLADES

SEA OF CRETE

CRETE

Knossos •

Scale: 0 – 150 Mi

0 – 150 Km

N W S E

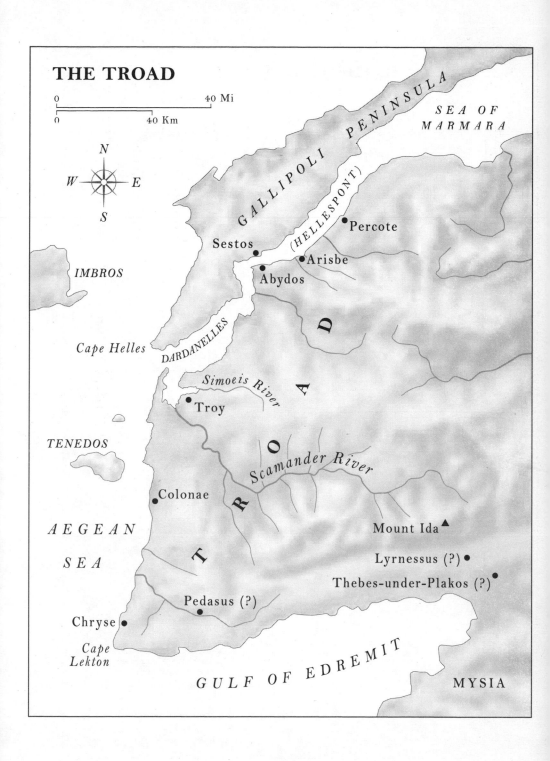

THE TROAD

0 ———————— 40 Mi
0 ———————— 40 Km

N
W   E
S

GALLIPOLI PENINSULA

SEA OF
MARMARA

(HELLESPONT)

Percote

Sestos

Arisbe

IMBROS

Abydos

Cape Helles

DARDANELLES

Simoeis River

Troy

T R O A D

TENEDOS

Scamander River

Colonae

Mount Ida ▲

AEGEAN

Lyrnessus (?) ●

SEA

Thebes-under-Plakos (?) ●

Pedasus (?)

Chryse ●

Cape
Lekton

GULF OF EDREMIT

MYSIA

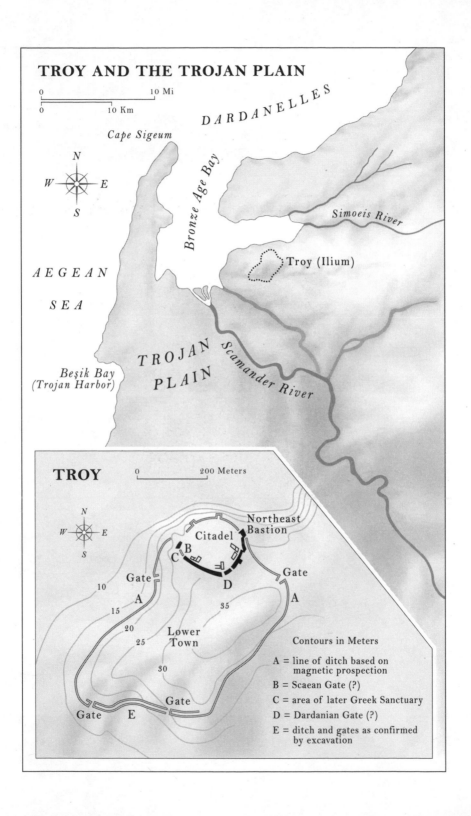

TROY AND THE TROJAN PLAIN

0 ——— 10 Mi
0 ——— 10 Km

Cape Sigeum

D A R D A N E L L E S

N
W — E
S

Bronze Age Bay

Simoeis River

Troy (Ilium)

A E G E A N

S E A

Beşik Bay
(Trojan Harbor)

T R O J A N
P L A I N

Scamander River

TROY

0 ——— 200 Meters

N
W — E
S

Northeast
Bastion

Citadel

B
C

D

Gate

A

10

15

20

25

30

35

Lower
Town

Gate

A

Gate

E

Gate

Contours in Meters

A = line of ditch based on
    magnetic prospection

B = Scaean Gate (?)

C = area of later Greek Sanctuary

D = Dardanian Gate (?)

E = ditch and gates as confirmed
    by excavation

THE TROJAN WAR

INTRODUCTION

Troy invites war. Its location, where Europe and Asia meet, made it rich and visible. At Troy, the steel-blue water of the Dardanelles Straits pours into the Aegean and opens the way to the Black Sea. Although the north wind often blocked ancient shipping there, Troy has a protected harbor, and so it beckoned to merchants—and marauders. Walls, warriors, and blood were the city's lot.

People had already fought over Troy for two thousand years by the time Homer's Greeks are said to have attacked it. Over the centuries since then, armies have swept past Troy's ancient walls, from Alexander the Great to the Gallipoli Campaign of 1915.

And then there are the archaeologists. In 1871 Heinrich Schliemann amazed the world with the announcement that a mound near the entrance to the Dardanelles contained the ruins of Troy. Schliemann, who relied on preliminary work by Frank Calvert, was an inspired amateur, if also something of a fraud. But the trained archaeologists who have followed him by the hundreds in the 130 years since have put the excavations on a firm and scientific basis. And they all came to Troy because of the words of a Greek poet.

But are those words true? Granted that ancient Troy really existed, was it anything like the splendid city of Homer's description? Did it face an armada from Greece? Did the Trojan War really happen?

Spectacular new evidence makes it likely that the Trojan War indeed took place. New excavations since 1988 constitute little less than an archaeological revolution, proving that Homer was right

1

about the city. Twenty years ago, it looked as though Troy was just a small citadel of only about half an acre. Now we know that Troy was, in fact, about seventy-five acres in size, a city of gold amid amber fields of wheat. Formerly, it seemed that by 1200 B.C. Troy was a shabby place, well past its prime, but we know now that in 1200 the city was in its heyday.

Meanwhile, independent confirmation proves that Troy was a byword in the ancient Near East. This outside evidence comes not from Homer or any Greek source but from Hittite texts. In these documents, the city that Homer calls Troy or Ilion is referred to as Taruisa or Wilusa—and in the early form of the Greek language, "Ilion" was rendered as "Wilion."

A generation ago scholars thought that the Trojans were Greeks, like the men who attacked them. But new evidence suggests otherwise. The recently discovered urban plan of Troy looks less like that of a Greek than of an Anatolian city. Troy's combination of citadel and lower town, its house and wall architecture, and its religious and burial practices are all typically Anatolian, as is the vast majority of its pottery. To be sure, Greek pottery and Greek speakers were also found at Troy, but neither predominated. New documents suggest that most Trojans spoke a language closely related to Hittite and that Troy was a Hittite ally. The enemy of Troy's ally was the Greeks.

The Greeks were the Vikings of the Bronze Age. They built some of history's first warships. Whether on large expeditions or smaller sorties, whether in the king's call-up or on freebooting forays, whether as formal soldiers and sailors or as traders who turned into raiders at a moment's notice, whether as mercenaries, ambassadors, or hereditary guest-friends, the Greeks fanned out across the Aegean and into the eastern and central Mediterranean, with one hand on the rudder and the other on the hilt of a sword. What the sight of a dragon's head on the stem post of a Viking ship was to an Anglo-Saxon, the sight of a bird's beak on the stem post of a Greek galley was to a Mediterranean islander or Anatolian mainlander. In the 1400s B.C., the Greeks conquered Crete, the southwestern

Aegean islands, and the city of Miletus on the Aegean coast of Anatolia, before driving eastward into Lycia and across the sea to Cyprus. In the 1300s they stirred up rebels against the Hittite overlords of western Anatolia. In the 1200s they began muscling their way into the islands of the northeastern Aegean, which presented a big threat to Troy. In the 1100s they joined the wave of marauders, known to us as the Sea Peoples, who descended first on Cyprus, then on the Levant and Egypt, and settled in what became the Philistine country.

The Trojan War, which probably dates to around 1200 B.C., is just a piece in a larger puzzle. But if the resulting picture builds on Homer, it differs quite a bit from the impression most readers get from his poems. And "impression" is the right word, because much of the conventional wisdom about the war, from Achilles' heel to Cassandra's warnings, is not in Homer at all.

Consider what Homer does say: He tells the story in two long poems, the *Iliad* or Story of Ilion (that is, Troy) and the *Odyssey* or Story of Odysseus. According to Homer, the Trojan War lasted ten years. The conflict pitted the wealthy city of Troy and its allies against a coalition of all Greece. It was the greatest war in history, involving at least 100,000 men in each army as well as 1,184 Greek ships. It featured heroic champions on both sides. It was so important that the Olympian gods played an active role. Troy was a magnificent city and impregnable fortress. The cause of the war was the seduction, by Prince Paris of Troy, of the beautiful Helen, queen of Sparta, as well as the loss of the treasure that they ran off with. The Greeks landed at Troy and demanded the return of Helen and the treasure to her husband, Sparta's King Menelaus. But the Trojans refused. In the nine years of warfare that followed, the Greeks ravaged and looted the Trojan countryside and surrounding islands, but they made no progress against the city of Troy. Ironically, the *Iliad* focuses on a pitched battle on the Trojan Plain, although most of the war was fought elsewhere and consisted of raids. And the *Iliad* concentrates on only two months in the ninth year of the long conflict.

In that ninth year the Greek army nearly fell apart. A murderous epidemic was followed by a mutiny on the part of Greece's greatest warrior, Achilles. The issue, once again, was a woman: this time, the beautiful Briseis, a prize of war unjustly grabbed from Achilles by the Greek commander in chief, Agamemnon. A furious Achilles withdrew himself and his men from fighting. Agamemnon led the rest of the army out to fight, and much of the *Iliad* is a gory, blow-by-blow account of four days on the battlefield. The Trojans, led by Prince Hector, took advantage of Achilles' absence and nearly drove the Greeks back into the sea. At the eleventh hour, Achilles let his lieutenant and close friend Patroclus lead his men back into battle to save the Greek camp. Patroclus succeeded but overreached himself, and Hector killed him on the Trojan Plain. In revenge, Achilles returned to battle, devastated the enemy, and killed Hector. Achilles was so angry that he abused Hector's corpse. King Priam of Troy begged Achilles to give back his son Hector's body for cremation and burial, and a sadder but wiser Achilles at last agreed. He knew that he too was destined to die soon in battle.

The *Iliad* ends with the funeral of Hector. The *Odyssey* is set after the war and mainly describes the hard road home of the Greek hero Odysseus. In a series of flashbacks, it explains how Odysseus led the Greeks to victory at Troy by thinking up the brilliant trick of smuggling Greek commandos into Troy in the Trojan Horse, an operation which he also led. Achilles did not play a part in the final victory; he was long since dead. The *Odyssey* also shows Helen back in Sparta with Menelaus. But Homer leaves out most of the rest of the war. One has to turn to other and generally lesser Greek and Roman poets for additional detail.

Aeneas is a minor character in the *Iliad*, but the hero of a much later epic poem in Latin, written by Vergil, the *Aeneid*. Vergil makes Aeneas the founder of Rome (or, to be precise, of the Italian town that later founded Rome). But in Homer, Aeneas is destined to become king of Troy after the Greeks depart and the Trojans rebuild.

Now, consider how new evidence revises the picture: Much of what we thought we knew about the Trojan War is wrong. In the old view, the war was decided on the plain of Troy by duels between champions; the besieged city never had a chance against the Greeks; and the Trojan Horse must have been a myth. But now we know that the Trojan War consisted mainly of low-intensity conflict and attacks on civilians; it was more like the war on terror than World War II. There was no siege of Troy. The Greeks were underdogs, and only a trick allowed them to take Troy: that trick may well have been the Trojan Horse.

The *Iliad* is a championship boxing match, fought in plain view at high noon and settled by a knockout punch. The Trojan War was a thousand separate wrestling matches, fought in the dark and won by tripping the opponent. The *Iliad* is the story of a hero, Achilles. The Trojan War is the story of a trickster, Odysseus, and a survivor, Aeneas.

The *Iliad* is to the Trojan War what *The Longest Day* is to World War II. The four days of battle in the *Iliad* no more sum up the Trojan War than the D-day invasion of France sums up the Second World War. The *Iliad* is not the story of the whole Trojan War. Far from being typical, the events of the *Iliad* are extraordinary.

Homer nods, and he exaggerates and distorts too. But overly skeptical scholars have thrown out the baby with the bathwater. There are clear signs of later Greece in the epics; Homer lived perhaps around 700 B.C., about five hundred years after the Trojan War. Yet new discoveries vindicate the poet as a man who knew much more about the Bronze Age than had been thought.

And that is a key insight because Bronze Age warfare is very well documented. In Greece, archaeologists showed long ago that the arms and armor described by Homer really were used in the Bronze Age; recent discoveries help to pinpoint them to the era of the Trojan War. Like Homer, Linear B documents refer to a Greek army as a collection of warrior chiefs rather than as the impersonal institution of later Greek texts.

But the richest evidence of Bronze Age warfare comes from the ancient Near East. And in the 1300s and 1200s B.C., Bronze Age civilization was international. Trade and diplomacy, migration, dynastic marriage, and even war all led to cultural cross-fertilization. So the abundant evidence of Assyria, Canaan, Egypt, the Hittites, and Mesopotamia puts in perspective the events of the *Iliad* and *Odyssey*.

Some things in Homer that may seem implausible are likely to be true because the same or similar customs existed in Bronze Age civilizations of the ancient Near East. For example, surprise attacks at night, wars over livestock, iron arrowheads in the Bronze Age, battles between champions instead of armies, the mutilation of enemy corpses, shouting matches between kings in the assembly, battle cries as measures of prowess, weeping as a mark of manhood—these and many other details are not Homeric inventions but well-attested realities of Bronze Age life.

Besides recording Bronze Age customs, Homer reproduces Bronze Age literary style. Although he was Greek, Homer borrows from the religion, mythology, poetry, and history of the Near East. By composing in the manner of a chronicler of the pharaohs or the Hittites or Babylon's King Hammurabi, Homer lends an air of authenticity to his poem. For instance, Homer portrays champions on both sides carving paths of blood through the enemy as if they were supermen—or as if they were pharaohs, often described by Egyptian texts as superheroes in battle. Ironically, the more Homer exaggerates, the more authentic he is as a representative of the Bronze Age. And even the prominence of the gods in Homer, which drives most historians to distraction, is a Bronze Age touch, because writers of that era always put the gods at the heart of warfare. Belief in divine apparitions on the battlefield, conviction that victories depended on a goddess's patronage, and faith that epidemics were unleashed by offended deities are all well documented.

Could Homer have preserved the truth about a war that preceded him by five centuries? Not in all its details, of course, but he could have known the outline of the conflict. After all, a remarkably accurate list of Late Bronze Age Greek cities survived to Homer's day and appears in the *Iliad* as the so-called Catalog of Ships. And it survived even though writing disappeared from Greece between about 1180 and 750 B.C.

As for Trojan memories, writing did not disappear from the

Near East, and trade routes between Greece and the Near East survived after 1200. Around 1000 B.C., Greeks crossed the Aegean Sea again in force and established colonies on the coast of Anatolia. Tradition puts Homer in one of those colonies or on a nearby Aegean island. If so, the poet could have come into contact with records of the Trojan War—maybe even with a Trojan version of the *Iliad.*

In any case, writing is only part of the story. The *Iliad* and *Odyssey* are oral poetry, composed as they were sung, and based in large part on time-honored phrases and themes. When he composed the epics, Homer stood at the end of a long tradition in which poems were handed down for centuries by word of mouth from generation to generation of professional singers, who worked without benefit of writing. They were bards, men who entertained by singing about the great deeds of the heroic past. Often, what made a bard successful was the ability to rework old material in ways that were new—but not too new, because the audience craved the good old stories.

We can presume that the Trojan War indeed happened: that is, that a Greek coalition attacked and eventually sacked Troy. But if the Trojan War really happened, how was it fought? What caused it? To answer these questions we will start with Homer and then scrutinize all details in light of what we know about the Late Bronze Age.

Take, for instance, the war's length. Homer says that the Trojan War lasted ten years; to be precise, he says that the Greeks at Troy fought and suffered for nine years and finally won in the tenth. But these numbers should not be taken literally. Among many other reasons, consider that in the ancient Near East, there was an expression "nine times and then a tenth," which means "over and over until finally." It was a figure of speech, much as in today's English the phrase "nine times out of ten" means "usually" rather than the literal numbers. In all likelihood, Homer uses a time-honored expression to mean that the Trojan War lasted a long time. We should not understand it literally. Either that, or the meaning of the phrase was garbled by the time it reached Homer.

So how long did the Trojan War really last? We don't know. All we can say is that it lasted a long time but probably considerably less than ten years. Since they had limited resources, Bronze Age kingdoms are unlikely to have mounted a ten-years' campaign. It was a protracted war. But then, Troy was a prize worth fighting for.

Troy's fortune lay in its location. "Windy Troy," as Homer calls it, was not merely gusty, it was a meteorological miracle. The city rose because it was located at the entrance to the Dardanelles, the water link between the Aegean and the Black Sea. In its prime, Troy covered seventy-five acres and held 5,000–7,500 people, which made it a big city in Bronze Age terms and a regional capital.

The Troad, the hinterland of Troy, was a blessed land. There was fresh water in abundance, the fields were rich with grain, the pastures were perfect for cattle, the woods were overrun with deer, and the seas were swarming with tuna and other fish. And there was the special gift of Boreas, the Greek god of the north wind: Boreas usually blows in the Dardanelles for thirty to sixty days during the summer sailing season, sometimes for weeks at a time. In antiquity, when boats lacked the technology to tack, that is, to zigzag against the wind, Boreas stopped shipping in the Dardanelles. For much of the sailing season, ship captains were forced to wait in Troy's harbor until the wind fell. As lords of the waterfront, Trojans got rich, and they owed it to Boreas.

The Trojans were among the world's great middlemen. Middlemen are rarely beloved, especially if they get rich on bad weather. With the possible exception of textiles, the Trojans had only one good to sell, their famous horses. Horse dealers were the used-car salesmen of the ancient world. The fast-talking Trojans probably found ways to cheat other men that outdid anything thought up in Thebes or Mycenae.

Troy may not have been popular, but with its natural advantages and business savvy, Troy was peaceful and prosperous—or it would have been, had it been wrapped in a bubble. Unfortunately, Troy stood exposed on the bloody fault line where two empires met. There was no more dangerous piece of real estate in the ancient world. To the east lay the Hittites, great charioteers who rode out of the central highlands and dominated Anatolia as well as much of the Near East. To the west lay the Greeks, a rising power whose navy exerted pressure across the Aegean Sea. These two warlike peoples were cousins of a sort. Both spoke an Indo-European language, and both had arrived in the Mediterranean from farther east around 2000 B.C. Although these two rivals never invaded each other's heartland, they took out their fury on the people stuck between them.

Western Anatolia was the Poland of the Late Bronze Age: wealthy, cultured, and caught between two empires. In a region of about forty thousand square miles (roughly the size of Kentucky or about four-fifths the size of England), an ever-shifting set of countries struggled for power—with the Hittites and the Greeks always ready to stir the pot. There was a never-ending series of wars among the dozens of kingdoms that came and went over the years, vying for power in a turbulent no-man's-land.

To the Greeks, who laid claim to the Aegean islands and who held a foothold in Anatolia, the Troad was a threat and a temptation, both a dagger pointed at the Greek heart and a bridge to the Hittites' heartland. It was also the richest source of booty on the horizon. A major regional hub, Troy was a way station for goods from Syria and Egypt and occasionally even from the Caucasus and Scandinavia. How could the predatory hearts of the Greeks not have yearned to plunder it? But it was not a fruit to be easily picked.

Troy was a sturdy fortress. The plain of Troy was broad but, otherwise, it was no place for a bloody brawl. It was soggy for much of the year, which was bad for chariots. It may have been malarial—the evidence is unclear. Add to these factors the Trojan army and Troy's wide network of alliances. But though the city was strong, Troy had weak spots. Twenty-eight towns lay in Troy's rich hinterland, not to mention more towns on the nearby islands, and none of them had fortifications to match the walls of the metropolis. These places overflowed with the material goods and the women whom the Greeks coveted.

Practiced and patient raiders, the Greeks were ready for the challenge of protracted conflict. Living in tents and shelters between the devil and the wine dark sea would be miserable, but no one becomes a "Viking" in order to be comfortable. The Trojans enjoyed all the rewards of wealth and sophistication. But the Greeks had three advantages of their own: they were less civilized, more patient, and they had strategic mobility because of their ships. In the end, those trumped Troy's cultural superiority. And so we come to the Trojan War.

The war probably took place sometime between 1230 and 1180 B.C., more likely between 1210 and 1180. At that latter date the city of Troy was destroyed by a raging fire. The presence of weapons (arrowheads, spearheads, and sling stones) as well as unburied human bones points to a sack—that is, a sudden and violent attack. The towns in the Troad, according to a recent survey by archaeologists, may have been abandoned around 1200, consistent with an invasion.

Yet some skeptics deny the veracity of the Trojan War because few weapons have been found in the ruins of Troy compared to other ancient cities that had been sacked. But we must remember that Troy is no undisturbed site. It was the premier tourist attraction of the ancient world; its soil was dug up in search of relics for such VIP tourists as Alexander the Great and the Emperor Augustus. And later "urban renewal" flattened the citadel for terraces for Greek and Roman temples, a process that destroyed layers of Bronze Age remains. The archaeological evidence fits the picture of a city that was sacked, burned, and, in later centuries, picked through by eager tourists.

The date of the Trojan War sticks in some historians' craws. Around 1180 B.C. the great palaces of mainland Greece, from Mycenae to Pylos, and many places in between, were themselves destroyed. With their own ruin looming, could the Greeks have possibly attacked Troy between 1210 and 1180? Yes. History is full of sudden reversals. For example, most Japanese cities were rubble in 1945, yet only four years earlier, in 1941, Japan had attacked the United States. Besides, the Greek myths say that the Trojan War gave way to civil war and chaos within the Greek homeland, and that might just fit the archaeological evidence. Finally, unrest in Greece in the period 1210–1180 might have made the Trojan War *more*, not less, likely, because it might have tempted Greek politicians to export violence abroad.

History is made up not of stones or words but of people. Was there ever a queen named Helen and did her face launch a thousand ships? Was there a warrior named Achilles who in a rage killed thousands? Did Aeneas suffer through a bitter war only to have the last laugh as a king? What about Hector, Odysseus, Priam, Paris, Hecuba, Agamemnon, Menelaus, and Thersites? Did they exist or did a poet invent them? We don't know, but names are some of the easiest things to pass down in an oral tradition, which increases the likelihood that they were real people. Besides, we can almost say that if Homer's heroes had not existed, we would have had to invent them. There may not have been an Achilles, but Greek warriors used his tactics of raiding cities and of fighting battles by attacking chariots on foot. Whether Helen's face launched a thousand ships or none, queens of the Bronze Age wielded great power and kings made war over marriage alliances. Priam may never have ruled Troy, but Kings Alaksandu and Walmu did, and Anatolian rulers lived much as Homer describes Priam, from his dealings with uppity nobles to his practice of polygamy. So this book will refer to Homer's characters as real-life individuals. The reader should keep in mind that their existence is plausible but unproven. Descriptions of them are based on Homer and, whenever possible, on details drawn from archaeology, epigraphy, art, etc.

And with that, let us meet our leading lady. She is a character who sums up the spirit of her age, and new evidence increases the chances that she really did exist. And that she ran away from home to go to the windy city, blown by Boreas, and the fatal waterway by which it sat, where soldiers stole cattle and hunted men.

CHAPTER ONE

WAR FOR HELEN

She is the spark that ignited the war. Helen is dressed in a flowing, woolen gown, deftly woven by slave women, in black, taupe, and crimson stripes, and soft and shimmering from the oil with which it has been treated. The sleeves cover her upper arms but leave exposed the pearl skin of her lower arms. The winding bands of a gold bracelet cover each of her bare wrists. Two matching gold brooches hang from the garment's neckline. A tight-fitting bodice and a gold belt emphasize her full breasts. Her face is framed by her long hair, oiled to prevent dryness, and held in place by an elaborate, jeweled headband. Her elegant coiffure consists of pin curls and tendrils about her forehead, and long, glossy curls that fall below her waist. Her maids arrange her tawny hair every morning and night with ivory combs. Her cheeks are glowing with health and rouge, and her shining eyes are lined with carefully applied kohl. She wears a delicate perfume scented with oil of iris and carnation. Love runs after her like puppies, to quote a Hittite proverb.

But on this night, it is a man who pursues her. Paris, prince of Troy, has come to Greece, having commissioned new ships especially for the occasion. He knows that he has to put his best foot forward, because Troy and Greece are rivals, and the Greeks would seize on any sign of weakness. By the same token, Paris is supposed to be at

13

his diplomatic best. By accepting the hospitality of the king of Sparta, Menelaus, Paris has an unspoken obligation to behave like a gentleman. But all's fair in love and war.

Imagine the first meeting of Helen and Paris at a state banquet in his honor, no doubt in Menelaus's palace, which was surely set among the pines in the rich hills of Lacedaemon, the countryside around Sparta. The company sits in the throne room, a large, high-roofed hall with four columns surrounding a central hearth, whose smoke is drawn up and out through an opening in the ceiling. Armed sentries stand along walls frescoed with scenes of lions attacking deer and griffins standing guard. After a procession and offerings to the gods, the guests sit down, in silver-studded chairs. Paris sits in a place of honor, between the king and queen.

Paris and Menelaus are probably each wearing a linen tunic and below it a belted kilt of finely woven wool, possibly made into patterned panels and with a fringed edge and a tassel. Menelaus probably wears a diadem in the sign of royalty favored by the Greeks, while Paris might have the horned tiara of royalty common in Anatolia. Each is likely to have a gold signet ring. Menelaus probably has shoulder-length hair and a trimmed beard but no mustache. Paris might be clean-shaven in the Hittite fashion, but with long hair tied in a knot at the nape of his neck. Greek royalty and nobles all wore leather sandals, while Paris might have worn the boots of an Anatolian king.

Barefoot servants hurry to and fro with oil lamps and silver-and-gold pitchers and bowls for the ritual washing of hands. Then comes the meal. There would be honey, figs, and bread, and a selection of the finest meat from the royal stock: lamb, kid, pork, hare, venison, or wild boar. For a special guest from a royal house, there would be fish. In Greece meat was available even to ordinary people, but fish was food for a king. Fishing was labor-intensive, transport overland was expensive, and fish was not as easy to preserve as meat.

The food would be washed down with plenty of alcohol. The preferred beverage was a cocktail, mixed in a large bowl, of wine, beer, and honey mead, possibly with a taste of pine resin; resinated wine was already popular in Bronze Age Greece. The partygoers drank out of two-handled cups with a wide, shallow bowl above a stem, and made of either the finest painted pottery or of silver or gold. A bard playing the lyre would have entertained the banqueters with heroic song. In between the figs and the lamb, Helen and Paris might have exchanged their first words.

They might well have spoken Greek. Troy's language was probably either Luwian, the main tongue of southern and western Anatolia, or Palaic, the main language of the north. Both were Indo-European tongues, closely related to Hittite. But foreign languages were surely widespread in an entrepôt like Troy, especially Greek, which was spoken by traders and potters as well as nobles who had married into the Anatolian nobility. It seems that Troy's elite were bilingual in their own language and Greek; they had dual names, such as Paris—itself perhaps just Homer's rendition in Greek of a Luwian name, *Pari-zitis*, whose Greek name was Alexander. Troy's elite moved easily in and out of the Greek world, including Menelaus's palace.

In fact, Greeks and Trojans are likely to have forged friendships and kept them going across the generations, because these ties were good for business and they were prestigious. Consider the Greek kingdom of Pylos, west of Sparta, where Linear B texts record a military commander named "Trojan" and a leaseholder of a plot of land named "Trojan Woman." These names may have been bestowed to mark an international friendship, just as in later Greek times an Athenian friend of Sparta named his son "Lacedaemonius," that is, the Spartan.

Some ancient sources insist that Menelaus was about to go abroad: urgent business was calling him away to Crete. If he indeed left Helen alone with Paris, then Menelaus was the most foolish husband since Cronus had trusted Rhea, and *she* took advantage of him by helping their son Zeus overthrow the old man. Menelaus should have paid more attention to Helen's feelings: others surely were doing so.

An indiscreet remark by a Greek ambassador, a letter from a spy, a bawdy song in a Trojan tavern: one or all of these hints of Helen's unhappiness might have spurred Paris to action. The queen of Sparta had a wandering eye and Paris wanted to fill its field of vision. He loved the ladies, whom he handled with the same skill as his famous bow. But in Helen, he had met his match.

According to Homer, Helen was passionate, intelligent, and manipulative. He gives her a pair of hands speedy enough to slip a drug into a man's drink without him noticing. She had a way of leaning back in her chair and resting her feet on a stool, as if she were a judge about to pronounce sentence or a cat getting ready to pounce. She might have been the favorite of Aphrodite, goddess of love, but Helen was nobody's plaything. Although she was young—perhaps still in her early twenties—Helen was not without experience. She was a royal princess, daughter of King Tyndareus of Sparta or, in some versions of the myth, of Zeus himself; her mother was Leda or Nemesis.

That is myth, but the power of certain Bronze Age queens is a historical fact. And nowhere was this truer than in Anatolia. Land of the mother goddess, it was the veritable homeland of strong women. Archaeology may yet document a mighty queen in Greece, but in the current state of the evidence, we have to look eastward for that. And perhaps Helen did so too. Perhaps she was ambitious and saw Troy as a place offering her freedom and power.

Homer's Paris is handsome and amorous. He is stylish, lithe, athletic, and a talented bowman. History lends credibility to the picture. Anatolians were famous as archers. Troy was older than any city in Greece, so Trojans may have found it easy to pour on Old World charm when on the far side of the Aegean. But the other side of the scale held Greek stereotypes about effete easterners and, indeed, Homer makes Paris just a little cowardly in battle. No doubt the real Paris was charming and a hustler, the latter surely not an uncommon figure in a country of horse traders.

But charm is not a word that comes to mind in the case of Menelaus. Helen praised his intelligence and good looks, but that was only after she had been dragged home from Troy to Sparta and was eager to get back in Menelaus's good graces, not that he was fooled. No doubt the *Iliad*'s description of Menelaus is closer to the truth. He was a well-built warrior with distinctive red hair. As a speaker he was no-nonsense. We hear nothing of his skill at the lyre or the figure he cut on the dance floor, as we do of his rival Paris. As a soldier Menelaus was second-rate, incapable of going for the enemy's jugular, let alone fighting the Trojan champion Hector—as he would later have pretensions of doing. He was the kind of warrior who is dismissed again and again in Egyptian texts as "feeble" or "despicable." The god Apollo offers a withering put-down: Menelaus is a "soft spearman." He was, in fact, faintly ridiculous.

She blamed uncontrollable passion for her decision to leave home, husband, and daughter, Hermione, for Paris. But that is what gamblers say when they look back afterward. The real Helen, one suspects, knew just what she was doing.

Paris was no fool for love either. His abduction of Helen may have had less to do with lust than with power politics. By capturing Helen, Paris carried out a bloodless raid on enemy territory. He may have been a knave but he was no pawn: he aimed to use Helen to advance his own position in the royal house of Troy and his country's position in the international arena. Ultimately, her aim was to use him too, so the adulterous couple was less like Romeo and Juliet than Juan and Eva Perón.

The modern reader is skeptical of Homer. Surely, something as big as the Trojan War was about more than a case of wife-stealing. In ancient times others felt similarily, and the Greek historian Herodotus (ca. 485–ca. 425 B.C.) quoted the opinion that the Greeks were fools to make a fuss about Paris and Helen and go to war. And so they would have been if the only reason for the Trojan War had been the beautiful wife of Menelaus. In fact, the Greeks had many reasons to make war on Troy, involving both domestic politics and foreign policy.

Yet Homer is not mistaken but merely authentic. The Bronze Age was an era that preferred to put things in personal terms rather than in abstractions. Instead of justice, security, or any of the other issues that would be part of a war debate today, the Bronze Age tended to speak of family and friendship, crime and punishment. Near Eastern kings proclaim in their inscriptions that they fought to take vengeance on their enemies and on rebels; they fought those who boasted or who transgressed their path or who violated the king's boundaries or raised their bows against royal allies; they fought to widen their borders and bring gifts to their loyal friends. A Hittite king says that his enemies attacked him when he came to the throne because they judged him young and weak—their mistake! Allies are royal vassals, obliged to have the same friends and enemies as the king.

Consider an example from Canaan in the 1300s B.C. When the sons of the ruler of Shechem asked the mayor of Megiddo to join their military campaign against the city of Jenin, they personified the matter: the cause of the war, they said, was the murder of their father by citizens of Jenin. Failure to help would also be personal, as it would turn the sons into Megiddo's enemy.

We would, therefore, expect the Bronze Age to put the causes of the Trojan War in personal terms—murder, rebellion, or even wife-stealing—rather than the aggression, competition, resentment, covetousness, and insecurity that underlay the conflict. But these latter factors were there. They can be traced in Greek and Trojan archaeological finds and in Hittite and other Near Eastern documents. Let's begin with the texts.

Both sides saw conflict looming between Troy and Greece. Hittite texts trace a rising tide of troubles in the 1200s B.C. Around 1280 B.C., Troy gave up its traditional policy of splendid isolation to make an alliance with the Hittites. The king of Troy, Alaksandu, had great wealth but not enough military power to protect his lands, cities, vineyards, threshing floors, fields, cattle, and sheep, not to mention his wife, concubines, and sons—to use the terms of Hittite treaties. The Hittites, in turn, were always looking for allies in turbulent western Anatolia, a region that distracted them from their main interests to the south and east.

So Troy became what the Hittites called a "soldier servant," that is, a Hittite vassal state with military responsibilities, with a promise of Hittite military protection in return. But as the century progressed, Hittite power declined, probably because of a civil war among the various branches of the ruling dynasty. And the Greeks put pressure on Troy, as shown by a letter ca. 1250 B.C. from the king of Ahhiyawa—that is, Greece—to the king of the Hittites. The addressee was probably Hattushilish III (1267–1237 B.C.). The name of the Greek king who sent the letter is unknown. It is possible that he ruled in Thebes. One scholar finds in the text a reference to a famous name of Greek mythology: Cadmus, legendary first king of Thebes. Most scholars, however, reject this reading.

The subject of the letter is the control of the islands off the Anatolian coast, possibly the northeastern Aegean islands of Lemnos, Imbros, and Samothrace. Long ago, the letter says, Cadmus had married off his daughter to an Anatolian king who owned these islands. So according to the Greek king, the islands belonged to him and not to the Hittites. Note that, in typical Bronze Age fashion, the matter is expressed in terms that are personal and familial. The issue is not international law but inheritance.

Note too that any conflict between Greece and Hatti over these islands would pass straight through Troy. And there was other trouble brewing to the south. The brother of the Greek king, a man named Tawagalawa—Eteocles, in Greek?—was pushing out in force from Miletus, aiding a Hittite rebel and trying to make Hattushilish III give Tawagalawa/Eteocles a fief in western Anatolia. Not long afterward, another king of Troy, Walmu, had been forced to flee the city, apparently after a coup. Because Walmu was his vassal, Hittite King Tudhaliya IV (1237–1228 B.C.) wanted to restore him to his throne. But Walmu was stuck in the hands of another king near Troy. We don't know how things turned out and we can only wonder what was at issue in the coup d'état at Troy. Was it simply a power struggle or was some principle at stake? And might that principle have concerned Trojan relations with the Greeks?

Paris's Greek name—Alexander—might mean that he was descended from King Alaksandu, who forged Troy's alliance with the Hittites. Certainly, Paris's mission faced a similar problem: how could Troy achieve maximum security at minimum cost and without undue risk? His answer was to treat the enemy like a rival gang leader, whose power depended on his honor and whose honor meant controlling his woman, at a minimum. Dazed and caught off-guard, the squabbling Greeks would either have to unite—in itself no small thing—and wage a very tough war or they would have to accept one very big but cheap triumph for Troy. Paris had played the game well.

But Menelaus knew the rules too. He went to war not because his bed was cold but because his future was shaky. Paris had not only cuckolded the king but abused his hospitality. The Trojan was like a high roller who openly cheats in front of the casino owner. Unless he punished Paris, Menelaus would be branded as an easy mark. Since he ruled Sparta by marriage and not birth, unless he forced the return of his wife, he would eventually face someone wanting to knock him off his throne. But Menelaus had an immediate problem: his treasury was lighter thanks to Helen's decision to take a queen's ransom with her to Troy.

Just what Helen took is unknown; it was certainly not cash, since coinage had not yet been invented. At a minimum, the hoard included her dowry, which must have been substantial because she was a royal princess. Who knows what other loot she and Paris helped themselves to as they left. The treasures surely gleamed. Greek goldsmiths were famous for their craft, and their masterworks were matched by the pick of the world's imports. Greek kings and queens enjoyed gold and silver vases and cups, bronze daggers inlaid with gold decoration, solid gold earrings, solid gold rings with inlaid amber or lapis lazuli, silver pins with decorated gold heads, ivory plaques and combs, gold diadems and bracelets, gold necklaces with precious-stone pendants. Their shapes were a forest of swirls and rosettes, and decorated with a gallery of ivy leaves, crocuses, figure-eight shields, bulls, lions, hunters, gods, and priests. It was a collection built up over generations, and it was a thief's dream.

Paris not only made off with Sparta's queen, therefore, but with its Fort Knox. Later, Paris describes the Trojan War as a fight

For beauteous Helen and the wealth she brought.

Agamemnon echoes these words. Homer was much too pragmatic to reduce war to romance.

Regional politics also played a role. Agamemnon's Mycenae was the strongest kingdom in Greece, but the other Greek states could and did go their own ways, and in the age's warrior culture, that meant blood. Around 1250 B.C., the great city of Thebes had been sacked by an army that, although largely from other Greek kingdoms, had its roots in a Theban dynastic dispute. Agamemnon would surely rather have the Greeks unite against Troy than turn on one another.

In short, if the question about the Trojan War is, "What's love got to do with it?" the answer is probably, "Nothing."

In later ages Helen was worshipped as a goddess in Sparta, but opinions were mixed elsewhere. The Athenian classical tragedian Aeschylus no doubt spoke for many when he wrote off the woman who had caused the Trojan War with the puns of Helen the "Helandros" and "Helenaus"—Helen the Man-Killer and Ship-Destroyer. Yet the royal princess of Sparta had been an extraordinarily eligible bride. Her dowry was the kingdom.

Like Helen, Menelaus was born royalty, brother of King Agamemnon of Mycenae, but Menelaus did not inherit the kingship. In Hittite society it was possible for a man to marry into the royal family and so win a throne, and the same may have been true for Greece. This usually happened only when a king had no sons, but Helen had two brothers, Castor and Polydeukes. Perhaps they, like Telemachus in the *Odyssey*, were too young to inherit, or more likely, Tyndareus decided it was worth passing them over in order to ally his family with the powerful dynasty nearby. Menelaus became king of Sparta.

Sparta was wealthy and comfortable. Laconia (as the valley in which Sparta lies is known) has yielded many Bronze Age treasures, such as the elegant pair of solid gold cups found in a tomb at a village called Vapheio. These fifteenth-century B.C. masterpieces show scenes of bull-chasing. At Amyclae, near Sparta, stood a Bronze Age mansion; here, centuries later, there rose a structure called the

Menelaion, a shrine to Menelaus and Helen. Many scholars think the palace of Menelaus and Helen once stood there too. Meanwhile, recent excavations in northern Laconia, outside the village of Pellana, have uncovered a Bronze Age cemetery, complete with big and imposing beehive *(tholos)* tombs—the largest such tombs found anywhere. Nearby is a hill on which the excavator believes that he may have found the palace of Menelaus and Helen. This theory is still unproven, but the big tombs of Pellana add to the impression of Bronze Age Laconia's prosperity.

But Laconia was not Troy. Menelaus was a provincial warrior, while Paris was a cosmopolitan prince. Troy was the city of light and life at the meeting place of the world. And it was a good place to be a woman. Women in Bronze Age Anatolia had more freedom and power than their sisters in Mycenaean Greece. The evidence of archaeology, epigraphy, and Homer all agree on this point. Consider a recent and remarkable discovery by the excavators of Troy: a bronze disk, which is convex on both sides, not quite an inch in diameter and just a half inch thick. It weighs only four ounces. Yet it offers an important insight into the society of Troy. Each side of the disk is incised with writing, which shows that it was a seal. The Trojan seal was last used ca.1150–1100 B.C., but it was probably an heirloom. Its style went out of fashion after 1200 and its worn surface suggests long use. So the seal may well tell us about the world of Priam.

The practice of sealing was common in the ancient Near East, including Anatolia. Seals were used to stamp land deeds, court decisions, treaties, royal pronouncements, and even clay "envelopes" in which contracts were stored. Seals were also an important part of commerce, used to mark containers and other merchandise. If the seal was broken, the container had been opened. A respected merchant's seal on a product, then as now, was a guarantee of quality.

The Trojan seal catches the eye for two reasons. First, it is the only writing ever found in Bronze Age Troy. Second the seal is inscribed on both sides. One side bears the name of a man, who was a scribe, while the other side bears the name of a woman, presumably his wife. The writing system is Luwian hieroglyphic, as was standard for Late Bronze Age Anatolia. The bronze is too worn for us to read either name but the signs for "man" and "woman" are each clear. In short, the seal testifies to a degree of freedom and equality for women.

That is not unusual for Bronze Age Anatolia. In the Hittite kingdom, for instance, there was nothing remarkable about married couples, whether royalty or commoners, using seal stones with the husband's name on one side and the woman's on the other. A Hittite woman might even have a seal of her own.

The Greek world had nothing similar to Troy's husband-wife seal. While seals were tools of commerce in Anatolia, in Greece they were used mainly as ornaments. Although Greek bureaucrats stamped goods in the warehouse with seals, in general the Greeks treated their seals as jewelry, as signs of wealth and display, meant to be worn around the neck. Greek seals were not inscribed with writing. Women were sometimes depicted but men predominated, and that seems to fit Mycenaean culture.

In Homer, Trojan men, such as Hector, worry about the opinion of the women of Troy. When Hector's wife, Andromache, asks him to leave the battlefield for her sake and for the sake of their child, Hector replies:

> *How would the sons of Troy, in arms renown'd,*
> *And Troy's proud dames, whose garments sweep the ground*
> *Attaint the lustre of my former name,*
> *Should Hector basely quit the field of fame?*

Homer's Greeks display no corresponding concern for what their women thought.

Hittite history is punctuated by the careers of powerful royal women. Yes, the Hittite Great King, like other Anatolian monarchs, practiced polygamy. But the power of the chief wife was potentially enormous, especially if she was in charge of raising and marrying off all the royal children. The greatest Hittite queen had those pow-

ers and many others: she was Queen Puduhepa, wife of King Hattushilish III. Puduhepa came from a noble family of high priests in
southern Anatolia and went on to play a pivotal role in Hittite religion. She also took a hand in law and diplomacy. She had both a
joint seal with her husband and her own independent seal. When,
for example, Egypt and the Hittites negotiated a peace treaty, which
was recorded on a silver tablet, the seal of King Hattushilish appeared on one side of the tablet and the seal of Queen Puduhepa appeared on the other. She corresponded as an equal with Pharaoh
Rameses II.

Bronze Age Greece offers the occasional image of a powerful
queen like the *Odyssey*'s Queen Arete of the probably fictional kingdom of Phaeacia, but otherwise it had no room for Puduhepas or for
gender equality. It was a world whose captains and kings called their
bedmates "prizes" and traded them like bric-a-brac. Helen's response
was neither to accept nor to protest; Helen's response, one might
posit, was to opt out.

From Sparta the lovers fled to Paris's ships, loaded with treasure. They were in a hurry, but found time to stop at Cranae, an island
off the coast, where they consummated their passion, or so tradition
says. Then came the Aegean crossing. As they neared the Anatolian
coast, Helen could hardly have helped noticing the light gleaming on
Troy's towers. After disembarking at Troy's harbor, she might have
seen, as she rode to town, the wheat fields on the low hills in the distance. Unlike their ancestors, who lived on barley and lentils, the
prosperous Trojans of Paris's day grew an abundance of wheat.

As she reached the city, Helen surely found it as foreign as she
did exciting. At the gates of the city stood steles, standing stones
honoring the gods, a common Anatolian custom but not Greek. Another typical Anatolian feature was the layout awaiting her inside
the wooden walls: a lower town around a fortified citadel. Inside
Troy's imposing gates, Helen would have found a bustling city of
narrow alleys around paved streets with inset drains, a city of
shrines, markets, courtyards, ovens, and houses built of stone, mud
brick, and wood.

At dawn and sunset the town would have echoed with the din of cattle and sheep and the herders who brought them out to graze and back. The day was filled with the cries of merchants, the talk of slaves and housewives heading out to the springs to do laundry, and the laughter of children. The night rang with the clatter of pottery at the evening meal, the footsteps of the night watch, and the twang of the lute mixed with the whistle of pipes. And on a hot summer afternoon, when anyone sensible was taking a siesta, the city heard nothing at all.

The lower city was so thickly settled that its buildings reached right up to the wall of the citadel, or Pergamos, as Homer calls it. Pergamos rose about one hundred feet above the plain, a half-acre stronghold protected by an 1,150-foot circuit of walls standing 30 feet high. The serpentine path that led up from the lower city would have brought Helen to the royal palace atop the hill.

Helen is likely to have formally divorced Menelaus. Hittite law allowed a woman to initiate divorce proceedings, and society would not have looked kindly on ongoing adultery. The Amarna Letters, for example, consider a woman without a husband as a symbol of desolation, neglect, and futility—like a field without a cultivator. Paris saved Helen from such a fate. The two of them lived in style: Their beautiful house on Pergamos was built by the best craftsmen in the Troad. There they slept in a high-vaulted, perfumed bedroom. She was attended by a group of Trojan handmaids, whom she directed in such household chores as weaving. She enjoyed all the freedom of an Anatolian princess as well as the cosmopolitan pleasures of life in a big city on the crossroads of international trade. Some of Troy's nobles grumbled about her presence, but King Priam was her champion and she called him father. There was only one problem: the long arm of her rightful husband.

Arranged dynastic marriage was a staple of Bronze Age diplomacy. A marriage was, in effect, a treaty. Take, for example, Madduwatta, a wily Hittite vassal king in western Anatolia around 1400 B.C. Madduwatta married off his daughter to King Kupanta-Kurunta of the nearby land of Arzawa. This was the beginning of an alliance between two former enemies, as the Hittite Great King recognized, with no little annoyance. How could he trust Madduwatta to uphold Hittite interests against Kupanta-Kurunta now that the latter was Madduwatta's son-in-law?

If a royal marriage was an alliance, a royal seduction was an act of war. Hittite law uses this striking image for a man who runs off with a woman without her family's consent: "You have become a wolf." It meant, in effect, that he was banished. Adultery was considered an even worse crime, and Hittite law pardoned a husband for killing his wife and her lover if he caught them in the act. But while a man who raped another man's wife got the death penalty, a man who seduced another man's wife got off; in that case, only the wife was executed. If Greek or Trojan law were similar, Helen would have known that she had put her life on the line by running off with Paris. Either she didn't care or she expected to get away with it.

This was not just wishful thinking. It may seem incredible that Helen or Paris thought they could attack the institution of royal marriage without war. But there was precedent. Pharaoh Ay of Egypt had lived down the murder of Hittite prince Zannanza, en route to Zannanza's arranged marriage with Ankhesenamun, the widowed queen of the young Pharaoh Tutankhamun. The murdered prince's father, King Shuppiluliuma I (1344–1322), was one of the strongest of all Hittite kings. Yet his response was a routine attack on Egyptian possessions in southern Syria. Thousands of prisoners were hauled back to Hattusha, but this was no showdown. Shuppiluliuma did not even take part in the campaign, perhaps because he faced other threats on the northern and eastern borders. In short, the Hittite response was little more than a punitive raid, the Bronze Age equivalent of lobbing a few cruise missiles over the border. Pharaoh must have breathed a sigh of relief.

As for the Greeks, it was one thing to threaten to invade Troy and quite another to pull off an invasion. Imagine Priam's reaction to the news of Helen's abduction: whatever his worries, Priam might well have doubted that a Greek army would ever dare appear before Troy's fortifications. If the Greeks did come it would be too late for regrets because backing down would have destroyed Priam's prestige. But Priam surely believed that between Troy's allies and its walls, the city was impregnable. The Greeks would be hard-pressed to carry out more than a few raids, then they would fight over the booty and turn on each other. Surely the expedition would go home after a few months, while Paris kept Helen. Like Pharaoh Ay in the Zannanza affair, Priam might have expected to pay a price for misbehavior but not a very big price.

In any case, Agamemnon would have no easy time persuading the other Greeks into a big and risky war against Troy. A tradition, not mentioned in Homer, records an oath supposedly sworn by all the princes of Greece to uphold Menelaus's claim to Helen, said to be the most beautiful woman in the world, not to mention Greece's premier heiress. The hard-nosed historian Thucydides dismisses this story. He says the other Greeks followed Agamemnon not as an act of grace but because they feared his power.

No doubt Agamemnon was able to twist arms, but Thucydides' analysis is one-sided. The king of Mycenae had the gods on his side. The Bronze Age generally thought of war as a divine drama of law enforcement: war punished criminals who had offended the gods. The Hittites gave this conception a twist and imagined war as a lawsuit before the gods, who would favor one of the plaintiffs with victory. To the Greeks, Paris had twice violated the gods' laws, first by committing adultery and second by abusing his host's generosity. Menelaus's fellow rulers had a clear responsibility to avenge the gods by going to war against Troy unless Helen and the treasures were returned. Anything less would expose themselves to divine punishment.

Even the most pious Greek might have balked at throwing himself against the mighty walls of Troy, but there were compensations. The Greek kings no doubt knew that war would keep their fighting men busy and out of trouble at home. And the potential for plunder outside Troy's walls sweetened the deal. Bronze Age invasions usually included raids, like those carried out under the Hittite King Hattushilish I (1650–1620 B.C.), whose armies plundered the cattle and sheep of an Anatolian enemy's farmers. The Greeks surely relished the chance of doing likewise to the Troad and nearby islands.

They were not likely to have had second thoughts about the pretext for the war, because the Bronze Age was not finicky about the *casus belli*. Conquest was its own reward. It brought glory, honor, and an occasion for king and commoner alike to display what the Hittites referred to as "manly deeds." The victors also got loot, both inanimate and human, including slaves, both male and female. In the reign of Hattushilish III, to cite an example, seven thousand Hittite subjects were transplanted from Lycia (in southwestern Anatolia) to Greece.

In the Bronze Age, women were often regarded as a commodity. The victorious King Zimri-Lin of Mari (in Syria, 1789–1752 B.C.), brought back women captives to serve as weavers and harem mates. In the 1300s, a pharaoh ordered one of his vassals in Canaan to buy him forty "extremely beautiful" female cupbearers; he sent silver weighing sixteen hundred shekels, forty per woman, as well as an escort of archers to bring them back to Egypt. In the Greek kingdom of Pylos, women played a big role in the woolen industry, for instance, as weavers, spinners, and sheep shearers. Linear B tablets from around 1200 B.C. identify about fifteen hundred women and children in these jobs. Some came from places located up and down the coast of Anatolia as well as from the Aegean islands. Others are labeled as "captives," and it is a good guess that they had been seized by Greek raiders. No wonder that, centuries later, the Greek historian Herodotus commented that when Paris ran back to Troy with Helen wife-stealing was an old custom.

Helen was not the cause but merely the occasion of the war. By seducing a Greek princess, Troy had interfered in the politics of the Greek kingdoms and humiliated a powerful man. It was dangerous to hurt an enemy without destroying him; as one of the Amarna Letters says, when an ant is struck it bites back, and on the hand of the man who struck it. And there remained the underlying causes of war: resentment, greed, and power lust. Troy had everything that was dear to the Greeks' rapacious hearts. If Paris had come from

Dogpatch instead of Troy, then the king would have found few tak-
ers for the mission to avenge the gods and uphold Menelaus's honor.
But Agamemnon rallied the Greeks to attack a gold mine.

And so the harbor of Aulis filled up with the black ships in which
the Greeks planned to sail off to war.

CHAPTER TWO

THE BLACK SHIPS SAIL

The king of all Argos and of many an isle stands on the rocky soil and surveys his fleet. Before him in the harbor lie hundreds of wooden ships, their hulls coated with black pitch, their hollow interiors carrying men and supplies, preparing to bring ruin to King Priam and the people of Troy. Or so we might imagine King Agamemnon, son of Atreus, on the eve of the Greeks' departure for war.

The hills echo with the shouts of the harbormaster and the cries of the captains. Horses are whinnying, low, fast, and urgently. Sailors call out curses and every now and then there comes the crack of a stick on the back of some slacking menial. The priests are mumbling something to each other, the oxen bellow, and in the distance, through the noise, there is the sound of the salt sea slapping against the ships.

Agamemnon towers above his servants. He is a big man, healthy and muscular. Homer gives him the broad shoulders of a javelin champion, and as a king he is likely to be well fed and tall—nearly six feet tall, to judge from the skeletons found in the royal graves of Mycenae. That was a great height then, when the average Greek male stood only about five feet five inches. He is a veteran warrior, but if Agamemnon has a broken bone or two from past battles, it doesn't show, because the fractures would have been set by the palace physician and so would have healed perfectly. He has long hair and fiery eyes that offer, in turn, hints of passion, brutality, and resignation. His lips border a beard, his teeth shine gleaming white. He is dressed in a soft, newly made tunic underneath a big, sleeveless cloak. He wears fine leather sandals. A silver-studded sword hangs from an oxhide strap around his shoulders. On sleepless nights, says Homer, when the cares of office weigh, Agamemnon is in the habit of replacing the cloak with a lion skin, a reminder of his power.

He was the greatest king in Greece. Potential rivals ruled in Pylos and Tiryns, but Sparta was in the hands of his younger brother and the power of Thebes had been broken in a civil war the generation before. No wonder Homer reserves for Agamemnon the title *anax*, harkening back to the Bronze Age term for king: *wanax*. Agamemnon was rich and had a big army and navy. His domain was centered in the northeastern Peloponnese but it extended to the islands of the Aegean, perhaps as far east as Rhodes.

Homer's Agamemnon is arrogant, which makes him similar to the many Bronze Age kings whose monuments invited the mighty to look upon their works and despair. Take the king of Mari, Iahdun-Lim (1820–1798 B.C.), who describes himself in an inscription as "opener of canals, builder of walls, erector of steles proclaiming [his] name, provider of abundance and plenty for his people, who makes whatever [is needed] appear in his land, mighty king, magnificent youth." No doubt Agamemnon had an equally high opinion of himself. But he was no autocrat.

Agamemnon's kingdom was typical of its times; it was less a state than an estate, that is, it was essentially a big household. The royal palace had grand staterooms but most of its space was devoted to workshops, storerooms, and armories. It was a manor that produced luxury goods for the *wanax* to trade or give as gifts. Raw materials for the workshops were siphoned off the king's subjects as taxation.

More important, from the military point of view, the palace produced bronze breastplates and arrowheads, manufactured and maintained chariots, and stabled horses. The *wanax* controlled a corps of charioteers and bowmen and possibly one of infantrymen too. In any case, as powerful as he was, the *wanax* probably had no monopoly on the kingdom's military force.

The royal writ was strongest on the king's landholdings, concentrated around the palace. The rest of the territory was run by local big men or *basileis*, each no doubt with his own armed followers. The *wanax* could muster an army and navy out of his own men, but for a really big campaign he would need the support of the *basileis*. In short, the *wanax* was only as strong as his ability to dominate the *basileis*, be it by persuasion or force.

And he had better things to do with his time than learn the rebuslike system for recording Greek that we call Linear B. Homer takes a lot of criticism from scholars who cite the total absence from the epics of the Linear B tablets. But Linear B was used strictly for administrative convenience. Unlike Hittites or Egyptians, Mycenaean Greeks did not put writing on their monuments, boundary markers, wall paintings, or seal stones. So a *wanax* such as Agamemnon was no more likely to know Linear B than Queen Victoria was to know shorthand.

But one text the king might have learned was lines of poetry sung by bards at palace feasts; Mycenaean art shows that bards predated Homer by centuries. Poetry offered the possibility of immortality. Agamemnon already had honor, power, and glory as a "scepter-bearing king"—the term is Homer's, but the royal scepter was already a symbol of power in Sumer, two thousand years before the Trojan War. Agamemnon was a man of many possessions, but now he wanted more.

Greece's pulse quickened as the heralds of the *wanax* made their rounds to call the other kings into action. Agamemnon's peasantry had to look enthusiastic as the king's men rounded them up to serve. The Greek monarchs were no doubt blunter: Troy was an impregnable fortress and only a fool would try to take it. No wonder Homer says that Odysseus kept Agamemnon and Menelaus cooling their heels on rocky Ithaca before he agreed to join the expedition. But in the end, fear, greed, glory, and the gods won out. So they came to Aulis, the best of the Greeks, as perhaps they had never come together before.

There was Nestor, the grand old man of Pylos and most eloquent of the Greeks; Odysseus, the canny lord of Ithaca, Zacynthus, and other islands; Philoctetes, great archer from the rugged country around Mounts Ossa and Pelion; Menelaus, Agamemnon's brother and king of Sparta; Diomedes, the champion "of the great war cry" and the youngest general in the Greek army, who led a contingent from Argos and Tiryns; Ajax son of Telamon of Salamis, the so-called Greater Ajax, known as the Greeks' bulwark if not their brains; Ajax son of Oïleus of Locris, called Lesser Ajax, a hot-blooded bruiser who was spoiling for a fight; and the fearless Protesilaus of Thessaly. A different group of men testifies to the prior Greek penetration of the Aegean: Idomeneus of Crete, the island that Greek arms had grabbed from the Minoans; Tlepolemus son of Heracles, a thug who had murdered his great-uncle on the mainland and moved to Rhodes; and men from the other Dodecanese islands of the southeastern Aegean Sea. Finally, to return to the mainland, there was Greece's greatest warrior, a man known as the best of the Greeks, prince of the central Greek region of Phthia, leader of the fearsome unit of warriors called the Myrmidons: Achilles.

Maybe they are all fiction, but as a group they represent the Bronze Age art of war. Their hands were battle-wise with blood and calloused from stealing cattle. They could trample the enemy like a carpet under their feet or calm the heart of a nervous army under attack. They knew horses like a stable hand and ships like a boatswain, but most of all they knew men and how to lead them. They could be as smooth as the ghee-and-honey paste with which Assyrians cemented rows of mud brick or as rough as the gnarled limbs of an old olive tree. They knew which soldiers to reward with silver rings and which to punish with prison or mutilation. They could inspire the men to follow on foot while they rode in their chariots and to compete for the honor of fighting bravely in their presence.

They could break an enemy's lance or deceive him with words.

They knew how much flour it took to feed an army and how much wood was needed to burn a corpse. They knew how to pitch camp or launch a fleet, how to debrief a spy or send out an informer. They could draw a bow and split a copper ingot like a reed or hurl a spear and pierce the seam in an enemy's armor. They shrugged off mud and snow, towering waves or buckets of rain. They could appraise lapis lazuli with a jeweler's eye or break a merchant's neck with a hangman's hands. They could court a milkmaid or rape a princess. They relished ambushes after dark and noontime charges. They feared the gods and liked the smell of death.

They knew war in all its bloody ways, but they shared a single dream: to set sail home from Troy in ships with timbers creaking from the weight of plunder. Achilles says that he plundered no fewer than twenty-three cities in the Trojan War and Odysseus proudly calls himself "sacker of cities." It was a fitting motto for the Bronze Age way of war, and an inspiration for Agamemnon's commanders. Odysseus and Achilles echoed centuries of predecessors in Late Bronze Age Anatolia. Shortly before 1400 B.C. a Greek called Attarissiya in Hittite—in Greek, perhaps Atreus—landed on the Anatolian coast. He went on a spree of war and plunder through southwest Anatolia with one hundred chariots and a force of infantrymen. Then he crossed the sea to carry out raids on Cyprus. Agamemnon's father was also called Atreus, so perhaps the men were kin. Nearly two hundred years later, ca. 1250, a Luwian general named Piyamaradu continually raided the territory of Hittite vassal kings in western Anatolia. Piyamaradu had the tacit consent and perhaps the help of a Greek royal prince in Miletus called Tawagalawa in Hittite. This Greek might have been Eteocles, a Theban prince of myth, or maybe Teucer, as Greater Ajax's brother was called.

Each of Agamemnon's generals was the leader of a band of warriors; Greek for warrior band is *laos*, a common term in Homer. The warriors were bound by strongly personal ties. We see this, for example, in Homer's emphasis on the loyalty of the Myrmidons to Achilles. Linear B tablets refer to a group of royal officials as "followers" and to the commander of the *laos* as the "man who assembles the warrior band." This latter is, possibly, *lawagetās* in Mycenaean Greek, and some scholars think that the name Laertes, Odysseus's father, is just a contraction of that word. Whereas we, and later Greeks, tend to think of an army as an institution and war as a deployment of men and material, Homer and Bronze Age Greeks tended to think of both in personal terms. For example, the classical Greek word for army, *stratos*, means "encampment," and for war, *polemos* means "engagement of opposing warriors or troops." But both Homer and Linear B avoid these terms, preferring instead "warrior band" and "war spirit" or "war god" (Ares). The army that gathered at Aulis, therefore, was in a real sense, a collection of warrior bands and their chieftains.

It was also a collection of soldiers. Bronze Age documents tend to refer to the army as "the infantry and the chariotry," but that oversimplifies. A well-equipped army around 1200 B.C. had a variety of fighting men, including both heavy and light infantry, charioteers, archers, slingers, specialists in siege warfare (ladder men, sappers, and operators of battering rams and siege towers), scouts, spies, trumpeters, and standard-bearers. As a naval power, the Greeks also had ship's pilots, boatswains, and a variety of seamen as well as marines able to wield long pikes in sea fights.

The support personnel were not small in number. Elite positions were held by priests, diviners, physicians (who also doubled as veterinarians), scribes, and heralds. The masses were made up of carpenters, shipwrights, wainwrights, grooms, stable hands, herdsmen, butchers, cooks, wine stewards, smiths, metalworkers, tinkers, and slaves to handle tasks of every variety, from farming to sewing to maintaining latrines. There might have been a few concubines and prostitutes, but with new sources of women beckoning to the east, it might have seemed unself-confident to bring many bedmates to Aulis.

Aulis sits in the rocky hills at the foot of Mount Messapion, which rises 3,350 feet over the Gulf of Euboea. Watchmen looked down from the mountain, and one day they would light one of the

(Above) THE WINDY DARDANELLES. The north wind whips up whitecaps on the water in summer. The Gallipoli Peninsula is in the foreground and the Asian shore lies across the straits. *(Barry Strauss)*

BOREAS. The north wind is personified as a powerful man, winged, flying, and blowing through a shell, in this sculptured relief on the Tower of the Winds in Athens (150–125 B.C.). *(Barry Strauss)*

THE NARROWS. At Çanakkale (foreground), north of Troy, the Dardanelles narrow to a width of less than a mile. In the center the Koca River (Rhodius in Homer) flows into the straits; the Gallipoli Peninsula stretches on the far shore. *(Murat Kiray)*

KARABEL RELIEF. Carved on a cliff about 200 miles south of Troy, this Late Bronze Age sculpture shows a warrior, possibly a king, armed with bow and spear. Might the Trojan prince Paris have dressed like this? *(Sevim Karabiyik Tokta)*

MYCENAE. With its huge blocks and sculpted lions (or lionesses) the Lion Gate of the citadel symbolizes power. Soldiers manning the walls above would have hemmed in attackers on three sides. *(Barry Strauss)*

(Below) PHTHIA. The olive groves that fill the plain illustrate the fertility of the supposed homeland of Achilles. *(Barry Strauss)*

LEMNOS. The harbor of Mirina, the island's capital, lies on the west coast of Lemnos, near the site of the ancient city of Myrina. *(Barry Strauss)*

KNOSSOS. After the Mycenaean Greeks conquered Crete in the 1400s B.C., they ruled this palace, whose throne room complex (reconstructed) and central court are shown here. *(Barry Strauss)*

LACEDAEMON. The Menelaion, or shrine to Menelaus and Helen, stands on a hill east of the valley of Lacedaemon. In the distance, snow-covered Mount Taygetos rises. *(Barry Strauss)*

MYCENAEAN WOMAN. Fragment of a fresco from a house in Mycenae, 1200s B.C. *(National Archaeological Museum, Athens/ Hellenic Republic, Ministry of Culture)*

HITTITE GODS. This sculptured relief, carved on the side of a cliff near Hattusha, is a detail of a larger work. Note the figures' conical hats and sickle-shaped swords. *(Barry Strauss)*

TROY FROM THE WEST. This aerial view shows the ridge on which Troy stood. The ruins are visible in the foreground, and farmland stretches toward the hills in the distance. *(Hakan Öge)*

TOWARD TROY'S HARBOR. Troy's harbor has been identified as a cove just beyond the Beşik Promontory in the center of the photo. The island of Tenedos lies to the right. *(Barry Strauss)*

GREEK CAMP? A view from Troy toward the ridge on which the Greeks might have camped. At the time of the Trojan War, most of the fields seen here would have been underwater, covered by a bay of the Dardanelles. *(Barry Strauss)*

SEAL FROM TROY. Three views of the only Bronze Age writing found at Troy: a small, double-sided bronze seal, written in Luwian, bearing the names of a scribe and his wife. *(Troia Project Archives)*

BRONZE FIGURINE. This four-inch-high statuette from the Lower City of Troy VIi shows a man standing in a gesture of prayer. The workmanship appears to be Hittite. *(Mehmet Gülbiz/Dogan Burda Magazine)*

chain of beacon fire messages from Mount Ida to Argos, announcing the fall of Troy. At the shoreline below, at Aulis, a Mycenaean town stood on a rocky ridge separating two harbors. Between them they made Aulis the best port in northern Boeotia, and Boeotia was the logical meeting place for the Greek fleet. The region sits midway between Mycenae, home of Agamemnon, and Phthia, home of Achilles. Boeotia was a wealthy land, rich in warriors for the Trojan expedition. And Aulis faces east, where it looked out on a three-day sail to Troy, when the wind was fair.

But the wind was famously not fair for the Greeks. Aulis was sacred to Artemis, goddess of the hunt. The royal Agamemnon was used to giving commands and thinking later; he had neither the cunning nor the patience of a good hunter. It is not surprising that he fell afoul of the deity.

Homer says nothing about the incident; in fact, he implies that it never happened. But the tale of Iphigenia is preserved in other sources. Like the other Olympians, the goddess Artemis is named in Linear B texts; more intriguing, so is a certain "priestess of the winds," keeper of a cult that might have been important to mariners like the Greeks.

Stories differ as to how Agamemnon offended Artemis, whether by killing one of her sacred animals, by going back on a promise of a special sacrifice, or simply by bragging. The Greeks, like other Bronze Age nations, made substantial offerings to their gods, from oxen, sheep, and pigs to wine, wheat, and wool. In any case, Artemis was angry, so she kept the Greek fleet bottled up in port by making the north wind, Boreas, blow. It is not unusual for Boreas to bluster for a two-week spell in the summer. There is a powerful riptide at Aulis, which would have multiplied the effect of the wind.

In order to appease the goddess and make the wind stop, Agamemnon is said to have coldly consented to the murder of his daughter, Iphigenia. While unverifiable, the tale is plausible. Greece's trading partners in Syria and Canaan practiced child sacrifice, especially in moments of extreme stress. Mycenaeans borrowed many customs from the Near East, as did the Minoans, and the

Greek myths are full of stories of child sacrifice. Archaeology does not prove the myths true but it has found impressive circumstantial evidence.

On Crete, near the palace of Knossos, excavators discovered the bones of four children, all in perfect health. Two can be identified, by their teeth, as having been around ten years old. Their bones had been cut by knives much as animal bones are cut by a butcher's cleaver. Is this a case of cannibalism? And if so, was it part of a religious ritual? Another case comes from four miles away, on the slopes of a mountain south of Knossos, near the village of Arkhanes. Here a temple was discovered and inside were three human skeletons, two men and a woman. Some evidence, such as a bronze dagger and bone discoloration (a sign of death by blood loss), points to human sacrifice. Although not proof positive, the facts suggest human sacrifice on Bronze Age Crete. Admittedly, this evidence is Minoan and not Mycenaean, but the Mycenaeans borrowed heavily from their predecessors. Did Agamemnon?

Agamemnon desperately needed to regain the gods' favor, because he faced a problem that was as much political as meteorological. He knew as well as his men did that a good general has to have good luck. The longer the wind blew, the clearer it was that Agamemnon was unlucky. To galvanize his men and get the attention of the gods, Agamemnon might have wanted to do something bold. Enter Iphigenia.

Legend has her come from Mycenae, riding with her servants on a mule cart—a common Bronze Age conveyance—and thinking that she had been summoned to her wedding. A different kind of altar awaited her. No doubt the girl had expected the feasting, music, and dance that marked a royal wedding. Imagine her, instead, heading for the sacrificial table, white-armed, veiled, dressed in the shimmering gown of a bride, as lithe as Artemis herself, and terrified by the sight of the empty space where there should have been an animal for the slaughter. By killing his own daughter, Agamemnon gave notice of his ruthless dedication to the cause, thereby inspiring and terrifying others. Did he feel remorse as he first washed his hands, then pulled out the knife that hung by his sword scabbard, next lifted the bronze blade to his girl's throat, and finally saw the blood spurt out? Or did Artemis save Iphigenia at the last minute and substitute a deer, as some versions of the story go? All we know is that the wind stopped blowing.

And so the king of Argos and of many an isle inspected his navy. The thought may not have occurred to him, but Agamemnon was looking at one of the glories of ancient Greek civilization. It was technological, it was bloody, and it was new: it was as revolutionary in military affairs as that other Bronze Age invention, the chariot. The 1300s and 1200s were a great age of innovation at sea. The Greeks of that era were the first sea power in history on the continent of Europe. They may have picked up the know-how of shipbuilding and sailing from Aegean islanders, especially the Minoans on Crete, themselves great seafarers, but the Greeks established a navy in the harbors of the mainland and they invented a new ship: the galley.

The galley is an oared, wooden ship, built for speed, and used mainly for war or piracy. Mycenaean galleys were light and lean. The hull was narrow, as hydrodynamics dictated, and straight and low, to cut down on wind resistance and to ease beaching. A pilot stood in the stern and worked a large-bladed single steering oar. (Incidentally, Homer gets this Bronze Age detail right: in his day galleys used the double-oared rudder.) The hull was decorated with a painted set of eyes in the bows and probably also with an image of the ship's name, such as a lion, griffin, or snake. On the stem post was a figurehead in the shape of a bird's head.

The galley was so successful that its form remained standard in the Mediterranean throughout Roman times. But Bronze Age galleys lacked one refinement that marked their classical Greek and Roman descendants: the ram. The ram wasn't invented until centuries later, possibly by Homer's day. Bronze Age naval battles were decided not by ramming but by crews wielding spears, arrows, and swords and engaging the enemy either from a cautious distance or up close in a hand-to-hand free-for-all.

The galley could be sailed, but the most reliable way to go fast was to row. The most common galley at Aulis was probably the penteconter, a fifty-oared ship about ninety feet long, with twenty-five rowers sitting along each side of the hull. At Aulis there would also have been twenty-oared ships, each with two files of ten rowers on a hull estimated at thirty-five feet long.

Bronze Age Greeks had an advantage in sea battles because of their navies and their know-how. Like today's missiles, airplanes, or tanks, the galley provided strategic mobility. As in modern warfare, the key to much of Bronze Age fighting was to "get there firstest with the mostest." A well-run fleet allowed a king to dominate a theater of war by rapidly moving his men and materiel from place to place before the enemy did likewise.

And Mycenaean fleets were well run indeed. The king's men drafted rowers from the towns of the realm. The rowers were paid, sometimes in land allotments, and their families were looked after while they were at sea. They deserved it, because in addition to rowing, these men also doubled as marines and, once the ships landed, as infantry. If we may judge by Bronze Age Egyptian Nile boats, Greek rowers had to endure harsh discipline: in Egypt, the whip and the stick were routinely used aboard ship.

Greek kingdoms also maintained professional seamen, such as pilots and pipers (who kept time for the rowers), as well as sail weavers and other specialists. Naval architects supervised teams of skilled woodworkers in building and taking care of galleys. It took six months for a team of a dozen carpenters, supervised by an architect, to build a Bronze Age galley, as an expert estimates.

This frenzy of naval activity left the Greeks ship-crazy. They gave their sons names like "Famous Ship" and "Fine Sailing." Linear B tablets record the names of more than five hundred rowers. Idle scribes doodled sketches of ships, while artists created more sophisticated images of the same on gems, pots, and pillars. And then there is Homer. If he composed his poems in the 700s B.C., the maritime world that he describes—and describes in detail—is closer to that of the Bronze Age. The *Iliad* is an epic of land war, but sea power runs through the story like a golden thread: without it, the whole fabric of the poem would unravel.

Without the hollow ships, the Greeks could not have resupplied their army at Troy, nor raided the enemy's cities around the coast of the Troad and on the islands of Tenedos and Lesbos; they never could have gone to war with Troy at all. And the watery truth about Greece, that seafaring land, is brought home again and again by the most humble reminders in the least expected places. Like this ghostly image: one of the men found on Crete, who might have been the victim of human sacrifice, was wearing a seal on a thong around his wrist, and carved into the stone was an illustration—of a ship.

There were a lot of ships and men at Aulis. But were there really 1,184 ships, the huge number cited by Homer? Or 102,000 men aboard, as calculated by Thucydides (ca. 460-397 B.C.), the Athenian historian who was himself an admiral? And did the Trojans and their allies have 50,000 men, as Homer states?

Hardly. The Hittites had 47,500 men at the battle of Qadesh in 1274 B.C., which is one of the largest Bronze Age armies mentioned in historical texts. No such figures for navies survive, but the great naval power of Ugarit was said in 1187 B.C. to have had considerably more than 150 ships. If true, then a Greek coalition around 1200 might well have mustered hundreds of ships at Aulis—but not 100,000 men. Fielding an army that big in a protracted war seems beyond the means of a Bronze Age society.

A more modest figure is in order, and here is a way to an educated guess: Troy's excavators estimate a total population for the city of 5,000–7,500 people. In preindustrial societies, typically a little more than 20 percent of the population is males of military age (18–49): so, 1,125–1,700 Trojans. Combine this with Agamemnon's statement in the *Iliad* that the Greek army greatly outnumbers the Trojan soldiers who lived in the city of Troy—in fact, the ratio is greater than ten to one. The problem is, continues Agamemnon, that the Trojans have allies at their disposal, "who knock me far off my path and keep me from capturing the well-peopled fortress of Ilion, no matter how much I want to." On that reckoning, the Greek army was greater than 11,250–17,000 men. So a conservative estimate might calculate armies of about 15,000 men per side.

To carry 15,000 men to Troy the Greeks would have required three hundred penteconters, assuming every man rowed. Some of the ships might have been smaller than penteconters, that is, twenty-oared ships, and some might have been larger, that is, merchant vessels, so "around 300" is a plausible estimate of the number of Greek ships that left Aulis for Troy.

It is possible that the Greeks had some merchant ships at Aulis, in spite of their apparent willingness to leave trade in the hands of Canaanite ships and captains. The Ulu Burun shipwreck is suggestive of Greek priorities. When the ship sank off the southwest coast of Anatolia around 1300 B.C. it carried everything from copper ingots to hippopotamus teeth, but only one Greek product: weaponry (two sets of spears, swords, and knives). Yet merchant ships were so well suited for transporting men, animals, and supplies that the Greeks may well have bought or built some for the Trojan expedition. A Bronze Age merchant ship could carry as many as 250 men, which is no doubt why Pharaonic Egypt used merchant ships to transport soldiers, horses, and chariots. Homer's Eumelus of Thessaly (in central Greece) brought his peerless mares to Troy, and he would surely have found a merchant ship convenient.

Perhaps merchantmen were also used to carry arms and armor as well as a limited supply of food and water. But no more than a limited supply, because ancient armies expected to live off the enemy's land. The ideal was to fare like the army of Egypt's King Thutmose III (1504–1450 B.C.) in northern Syria. After victory, his men found fruits on the trees, grain on the threshing floors, and vats overflowing with wine. They got as drunk as at a party at home in Egypt.

Whether sobriety reigned or not, the day finally came to leave Aulis. At dawn, a favorable wind was blowing. The pitch-black hulls had been eyed and pawed and checked by hand for any holes. The gear was stowed, the horses brought on board, the fodder was found, and the men were ready. All that remained was for the chiefs to sacrifice to the gods. They set up an altar at a spring under a plane tree and led the bulls to the slaughter.

Then, when everything was done, an ill omen appeared—this one, reported in Homer. A snake crawled up the altar and onto the tree, where it found a sparrow and her eight chicks in a nest on a branch, and killed them. Then the snake turned to stone. A rational explanation of the phenomenon might be that the beast died on the spot. In any case, only Zeus could have done it: everyone knew it, and they were terrified.

It took the seer Calchas, son of Thestor, to break the spell. Imagine him wearing a long robe, with a bay-leaf wreath in his hair, and carrying a staff tied with the ribbons of the god Apollo, whom he served. He carried himself with the dignity of someone close to the gods and with the caution of the man who had given King Agamemnon the bad news that his child would have to be sacrificed.

Divination—predicting the future on the basis of natural phenomena—was common in the Bronze Age. Birds were important omens, especially in Anatolia, and so were snakes. The portent at Aulis meant, Calchas explained, that a long, hard war lay ahead. For nine years they would struggle but in the tenth, absolute victory would be their reward. The chiefs chose to accentuate the positive: final victory.

And so, at last, the chiefs boarded their vessels, and the fleet was off. The size of the expedition was extraordinary, but the act of setting sail was common. Homer describes such a scene well:

> Then launch, and hoist the mast: indulgent gales,
> Supplied by Phoebus, fill the swelling sails;
> The milk-white canvas bellying as they blow,
> The parted ocean foams and roars below:
> Above the bounding billows swift they flew. . . .

When the wind fell the men would row. They sat on benches in the long ships along two open, well-ventilated galleries, with leather screens to protect their heads, which stuck out over an open bulwark.

They averaged twenty-five men on a side, and each of them pulled an oar. The men's grain was stored in leather bags; their water and wine were in clay jars or skin bottles. Their gear was under the benches. If challenged, the men would have to grab a shield, spear, and sword and take on the enemy's boarding party, but they would not be challenged: they had the greatest navy in the world.

After leaving Aulis, the sleek hulls would have passed through the channel between the Greek coast and the island of Euboea and then turned eastward, island-hopping from the Sporades to Lemnos to Imbros. From there, it took only twenty miles on the bright sea for the black ships to reach Troy.

The Greeks would have a great deal to worry about when they got there: finding the right landing ground; protecting themselves from the slings and spears and arrows of the Trojan army that would surely be there to await them; securing local sources of food, fodder, and water; and winning some easy loot in order to keep the men happy. But there was one thing the Greeks would not have to worry about—the Trojan navy. Amazingly, despite its location by the sea and its economic dependence on maritime trade, Troy had no navy, or at least no significant one.

This was more than a passing weakness; it was a major vulnerability for the Trojans. Because they had command of the sea, the Greeks were able to raid the enemy coast at will. If it had similarly possessed competitive naval power, Troy could have brought the war to the enemy with an offensive across the Aegean Sea into the Greek heartland. Without a fleet, however, the Trojans were continually stuck on the strategic defensive. Agamemnon might have felt like the Hittite King Hattushilish III, who said that he could "cast a glance" at the enemy's country but the enemy could not cast a glance back at him.

Here is a paradox: Troy was a seaport that did not fight at sea. Founded by continentals looking *outward* to the sea, it became rich by offering sailors a foothold in the wind, but without developing its own navy. The Trojans fit the description of Bronze Age peoples of whom Thucydides says "although they inhabited the lowlands they were not sea-goers"—at least not when it came to fighting at sea. The Trojans no doubt had boats but not of the quality of the Greek warships nor in large enough number to compete.

For example, when Paris went to Sparta to bring back Helen, he had ships specially made for the trip. The builder was Phereclus son of Tekton and grandson of Harmon. Phereclus was a superb crafts-man, described by Homer as someone who "knew how to make, with his hands, many elaborate and skillfully crafted things." Indeed, his name means Famous, son of the Builder and grandson of the Joiner. Homer says:

> Thy father's skill, O Phereclus! was thine,
> The graceful fabric and the fair design;
> For loved by Pallas, Pallas did impart
> To him the shipwright's and the builder's art.
> Beneath his hand the fleet of Paris rose,
> The fatal cause of all his country's woes. . . .

Phereclus built Paris "well-balanced ships" for his getaway. The implication is that the ships on hand in Troy were no match for Menelaus's fleet.

Troy had little incentive to build a navy. Middlemen have no need to go abroad for plunder. Warships had little appeal to men who could garner wealth, glory, and security by breeding horses.

Archaeology as well as myth makes the Trojans latecomers to the horse. Myth considers Troy's horses a gift from Zeus. Excava-tion shows that the horse was not native to Troy but arrived around 1700 B.C., late, by Near Eastern standards, after which horse bones abound in the ruins. Trojans took to horses with the zeal of con-verts. Homer's Priam has royal stables in Troy and a horse farm near the city of Abydos on the Dardanelles. Andromache feeds her husband Hector's horses grain and wine, while Pandarus goes one better, by fighting on foot in order to spare his mounts from miss-ing mealtime.

These were princes who could have rubbed shoulders with any

age's bluebloods, including the horsey Hittites, Troy's powerful ally. And like the Hittites, the Trojans couldn't see beyond a silken mane. Landlocked in central Anatolia, the Hittites tended to imagine the coast as the edge of the world. Hittite kings boasted of extending their realm to "the border of the sea," as if nothing lay beyond. Their treaty with Troy, for example, says nothing about ships, while it specifically mentions Troy's obligation to send infantry and chariotry to Hatti when needed. The horse was king, or so it seemed, but danger came by sea.

According to Homer, a generation before the Trojan War, King Laomedon of Troy promised horses to Heracles in exchange for ridding Troy of a sea monster. Heracles killed the beast but Laomedon reneged. The angry hero attacked the city and "filled the streets with widows."

True, Heracles had only six ships at his disposal, but Heracles's son Tlepolemus brags that his father destroyed Troy, and evidence from Ugarit supports his boasting. In a letter from around 1200 B.C. the last king of Ugarit, Ammurapi, complained that an enemy did serious damage to his country with only seven ships. The crews of Heracles' six ships would have amounted to just several hundred men, and they could not have taken a walled city like Troy, but the harbor town, farmhouses, and other unwalled settlements in the Troad would have all been at their mercy. And who knows? Pushed by Heracles' famous hot temper, they might even have found a weak point in the walls.

Nor should we discount help from their friends within Troy. They needn't have been many; in fact, most Trojans might have winced at the sight of Mycenaean ships, given the tide of violence in Mycenaean culture. How many Mycenaean traders turned into raiders when, like Heracles, they were hoodwinked?

Yet there were indeed Mycenaean merchants at Troy. In fact, the archaeologists have found so much Mycenaean pottery at the site, both imports and imitations made of local clay, that if we didn't know better, we might have thought the place was a Mycenaean colony and not Troy. One of the most eloquent signs of Mycenaean commerce comes from a grave in a cemetery at Troy's harbor: it is a seal stone with a stylized face, mouth open in a wide grin. The style is typically Mycenaean, and perhaps the seal was a trader's device, used to mark his wares. Somebody at Troy did business with men like him. Someone—perhaps a Trojan, perhaps an immigrant—traded with the Mycenaeans for horses or textiles or slaves. And that person might have opened the gates to Heracles' men. Consider the *Iliad*'s Antenor, a Trojan elder who was well-disposed to the Greeks and who proposed that Helen be returned to them. When Troy was sacked, he was spared—some say because he in fact opened the city gate to the enemy.

By developing land power to the exclusion of sea power, the Trojans made the smart choice—or so they thought. It may well be that the Trojans had enough warships to project their power into the nearby islands, but they could not fight off an armada like the Greeks'. Trojan strategists might have reasoned that their land defenses were sufficient to repel any invasion from the sea.

Troy would not be history's only example of a state located on the sea but without a strong navy. Japan, for example, is an island nation that had superb infantry and cavalry but never had a navy before the late 1800s. Japan was not a trading state, but history records commercial powerhouses whose forte was maritime trade and yet had no navy. Consider the cities of the Hanseatic League of the late Middle Ages: at its core about sixty great merchant cities in northern Europe, mainly Germany. They dominated trade in the Baltic Sea but they had no permanent army or navy. Only in the face of a serious threat from Denmark in the 1360s did they put together a fleet, but that lasted only for a few years, until Denmark was defeated. In the 1400s, the new nation-states of northern Europe, such as Sweden and Poland, easily outmatched what little naval power existed in the disorganized League. Another case is the Netherlands: it was a giant of maritime trade in the 1650s, but it had only a small navy, and so it was battered by the English fleet. If the Dutch had strengthened their navy in time, New York might still be New Amsterdam, as it was until the English fleet seized it in 1664.

Like Troy, the Netherlands and the Hanseatic cities were rich and unrealistic. They all faced a similar temptation of putting their resources into productive or prestigious things instead of necessities. They were wrong.

Agamemnon did not make the same mistake. The king of Argos and many an isle built a war machine for all seasons. Argos, a land that Homer calls "horse-nourishing," was a hothouse of chariots, while the islands were guarded by the Greek fleet. The Greek way of war was versatile and it had been for centuries. Now, as Agamemnon sat in his flagship, his fleet of black ships crossed the billowing waves. On every stroke, as we may imagine, calloused hands of rowers strained at the wooden oars, while grooms whispered to the tethered horses not to fear the sea. Slaves checked the chariots against any loosening by the waves, and the surge made one man sick while lifting another to reveries of gold. Warriors missed their wives, seers prayed to Poseidon, and a veteran seaman reached for a goatskin's slug of wine. As the ships advanced, the Harpies of Death flew ahead to scout the plain of Troy.

CHAPTER THREE

OPERATION BEACHHEAD

elios the Sun, who sees everything and knows the gods, is beginning his ride in his four-horse chariot, turning the sky a gauzy blue and the sea the color of widows' tears. Gulls fly toward the cliffs of the Gallipoli Peninsula across the Dardanelles to the north, framed by the barren peaks of the islands of Imbros and Samothrace. The scene is completed by the brown hills of the island of Tenedos in the west and, in the east, the rolling Trojan Plain, with the long ridge of Mount Ida rising ghostlike in the distance. A pastoral scene, as we might imagine it, then the Greek fleet appears.

The black ships fill the sea like horses at the starting gate. The land, in turn, is unclear at first and as the ships come closer, it reveals fields and scrub. The morning fragrance invigorates the men aboard ship. If they weren't working at the oars, the Greeks might shout, echoing the cry of a Hittite king on the warpath: "Behold, the troops and chariots of the land of Greece are coming!" Across the water, even the toughest Trojan in his bronze armor might shiver at the flutter of the polished firwood oars, driving the armada like birds of prey onto the Anatolian shore. It is the moment of decision.

But not of surprise: the Trojans have had plenty of warning and their troops are poised to stop the enemy from landing on the

49

fertile soil of Ilion. They were waiting, just as a large number of Cypriot troops waited for the seaborne Hittite invaders of King Shuppiluliuma II (1207–? B.C.) when they disembarked on the island. The beach is thick with defenders. What Homer says of a later rallying of the Trojan forces would surely apply that day as well:

> *Nations on nations fill the dusky plain,*
> *Men, steeds, and chariots, shake the trembling ground:*
> *The tumult thickens, and the skies resound.*

Offshore lies part of the small Trojan fleet; the rest is guarding another possible Greek landing ground. The rowers sit ready, while archers and shield-carrying spearmen prepare for the unequal battle ahead. Although they have no hope of defeating the Greek navy they can at least slow it down and ease the task of the Trojan shore defense.

As they watch the enemy ships grow larger on the horizon, the Trojans on shore get ready too. The priests might have been doing what Hittite priests did before battle: hosting the enemy's gods at a ritual meal, of wine and slaughtered sheep, at which they blame the war on enemy aggression. The soldiers no doubt have more mundane tasks. Veterans may be checking their bow or tightening their shield straps while the new men joke as if on an outing. Some might wish that they could reach under their breastplate and wipe off the sweat, while others don't even notice how sore their hands already are from clenching a spear.

The battle of the beach is about to begin. Of this key event, Homer says only that a Trojan killed the first Greek to jump ashore. But the historian Thucydides, writing centuries later, reasoned that the Greeks must have fought and won a battle on their arrival on Trojan territory; otherwise they could not have set up camp. Hector son of Priam struck the first blow, as we learn from the Epic Cycle, those non-Homeric early Greek poems about the Trojan War.

Hector was a great warrior but a mediocre husband. He was strong, agile, fearless, dogged, and by turns self-centered and sensitive. Hector could remember how he had lifted his bride's veil on their wedding night to tenderly offer her a cup of wine but could shrug his shoulders at the thought of the widowhood that awaited her thanks to his aggressive pursuit of glory in battle.

Homer makes Hector an expert spearman who could handle a sword if need be, but he was probably an archer as well. Around 1225 B.C. the ruler of a western Anatolian kingdom not far from Troy had his portrait carved in relief on a cliff. The king strides boldly with a spear in one hand, a bow slung over his shoulder, and a dagger tucked into his belt. What was good enough for him was probably good enough for Hector.

Homer's Hector is tall and imposing, with a streaming mane of black hair and a handsome face, and eyes that no doubt flash from time to time with his reckless and aggressive spirit. He was probably clean-shaven and he might have kept his hair in a ponytail. He probably wore gold earrings, an embroidered kilt, and Hittite-style shoes with upturned toes. If Hector was uncomfortable beneath a bronze breastplate, he lacked the odor of someone permanently stained with sweat since, unlike commoners, royalty took daily baths.

Hector is a type well attested in the ancient Near East, the crown prince burning to prove himself as a warrior. He knew that the only way to show that he was no longer a boy was to lead armies and give commands. A Hittite king told his young Babylonian counterpart that unless he led an armed raid into enemy territory and soon, people would say that, like his father, the Babylonian was all talk and no action. Hector, by contrast, had an old fighter for a father, who advised caution.

Old King Priam, white-haired and scratchy-voiced, confined to the city rather than the battlefield he once strode, still had the power of command. Priam was shrewd, self-controlled, and an old hand at the ways of war as it was waged in the Bronze Age. It was under his leadership, no doubt, that Troy had put together an alliance and a strategy. Priam knew that Troy's best policy was defense and that the farther the Trojans fought from the city's walls the better. Priam might have known the words of the Hittite king who said that the alternative to fighting in the open was risking suffocation in the crushing embrace of an enemy siege. The preferred option was to defeat the enemy on the beach as he tried to land. Should that fail, the Trojans would fight the Greeks on the plain of Troy, keeping them away from the city. If that tactic should not work in turn, then they would fall back to the anti-chariot trenches and palisades that protected the lower city—with the great walls of the citadel themselves as the final refuge. But it would never come to that, not if the gods showed Priam the favor that they always had in the past.

The Storm God—Zeus, to the Greeks—held Priam and his people closer to his divine heart than he did any other king or country on earth. Known in Anatolia by such names as Tarhunt or Teshub, the Storm God was one of the chief deities of the Trojan pantheon. Priam was a favorite of his in no small part because the king knew that the gods help those who help themselves. Priam was not only intelligent but brave out of all proportion to his years. He was so bold and decisive that even an enemy marveled at Priam's "iron heart." No one in the region was more blessed with wealth or sons than Priam. And then the Greeks came.

The Trojans would surely have learned about the Greeks' approach from signal flares sent up by their friends on the nearby islands of Imbros and Tenedos. Allies were expected to serve as "border guards" and "watchmen," as Hittite treaties often state. The use of torches for military signaling goes back at least as far as Mesopotamia in the 1700s B.C. That same era is full of references to the importance of intelligence to warfare. The city of Mari had an intelligence bureau and it may have been headed by an official with the wonderful name of "Little Gnat."

The Trojans may well have taken a leaf from the same book. Homer has the Trojans employ lookouts, perhaps like the "coastal watchers" of the kingdom of Pylos attested in the Linear B tablets. One of the Trojan lookouts was Hector's brother Polites. He was a fast runner and no doubt had excellent vision. Information that he provided would surely have been welcome, even though the Greeks had hardly kept their approach a secret.

On the way to Troy from Aulis, the Greeks seem to have stopped first at the island of Scyros and sacked it. If there is anything to the epic tradition that Achilles' mother had forced him as a boy into a humiliating hiding place on Scyros in girl's clothing in order to dodge the war, which she foresaw, then this would have been sweet revenge for him. When the Greeks attacked en route to Troy, the Scyrians would not have had a chance against so big a force. In addition to settling Achilles' private score, the attack would have been a morale builder for the men, who could thrill to their first victory. It was also an experiment, allowing the generals to see how their untested army might perform.

Then, continuing northeastward, the Greeks landed on Lemnos. The rugged island has unexpected bounties, such as its claylike soil with medicinal properties and its sweet red wine. On Lemnos the Greeks lived like Olympians, feasting on beef and chugging wine by the cupful. The more they drank, the more they boasted: each Greek could take on a hundred Trojans, no, two hundred! It was a last binge for the boys, but the generals had to think about strategy. Lemnos was a stepping stone on the route from northern Greece across the Aegean to Troy and the Dardanelles. Lemnos was also a potentially crucial source of supplies for any Greek camp at Troy as well as a potential market for any captives whom the Greeks would want to sell as slaves. It was essential to secure Lemnos before going on.

But the price of doing business on Lemnos was that it gave the Trojans time to prepare. And then some: the epic tradition outside Homer records that after Lemnos the Greeks took a wrong turn. Instead of landing at Troy they ended up about seventy-five miles to the south on the Aegean coast of the region known as Mysia. Mistakenly thinking they had reached Troy, they attacked the forces of King Telephus. The king's army bloodied the Greeks, but in the end Telephus was wounded by Achilles. Myth says that only a scraping of the wood from Achilles' spear could heal the wound—an unusual example of the herbal medicine practiced by the Greeks. Achilles' gigantic spear was made of ash wood, and boiled ash bark makes a good poultice to apply to a wound. In exchange for the medicine, Telephus showed the Greeks the way to Troy.

Whether or not there is any truth in this story, it underlines the fragility of early navigation—and of early military intelligence. If the tale is true, it means that the Trojans had even more time to prepare. They were indeed ready for the invader.

Troy had assembled a grand coalition. Some of the allies came from Europe—Thrace and Macedonia—but most were Anatolian. Alliances were the bread and butter of Anatolian politics, and many figure in Hittite texts, so Homer's list of Troy's Anatolian partners is historically plausible. First come the Trojans or, more accurately, the Trojans and Dardanians, to refer respectively to the populations of the Trojan Plain and, to its south, the fertile middle valley of the Scamander River—Aeneas's country. Next come men from other places in the Troad, such as Abydos, Arisbe, and Zeleia. Then there are Anatolian regions beyond the Troad, namely Mysia and Phrygia due east; Paphlagonia on the Black Sea; Maeonia to the south, in the Hermus River valley; Caria, farther south, in the Maeander River valley; and Lycia, in the southwestern corner of Anatolia. The allied army might also have included Hittites, perhaps referred to by Homer as Halizones from Halube. So just as they had promised in the Alaksandu Treaty, the Hittites might have sent infantry and chariotry in Troy's moment of need—although surely not as many as Troy would have liked, given the Hittites' bigger problems closer to home.

Still, Troy had assembled a formidable alliance. Putting it together was no doubt a tribute to Priam's diplomacy and his purse, because all business between Bronze Age kings had to be greased with gifts. And they had to be top of the line. For example, in the 1300s B.C. the Amarna Letters are full of such gifts as gold and lapis lazuli jewelry, horses, chariots, pieces of silver, and women. Homer cites gold and silver cups or ingots, bronze tripods, embroidered robes, fine jewelry, weapons, armor, heirlooms, vintage wine, mules, horses, and beautiful women. And it was an ancient custom to repay each gift with another gift, to say nothing of the lavish entertainment that had to be offered to ambassadors. All these benefactions were usually given with elaborate courtesy, but sometimes the veil was dropped, and a king just had to pay up, and pay big. Priam might have remembered, bitterly, the Egyptians' claim that the Hittite king had stripped his kingdom of silver to pay the allied troops who fought at Qadesh (1274 B.C.).

Leading Troy's allied army fell to Hector. On the eve of the Greeks' arrival, he probably mustered the men outside the city, perhaps at the hill of Baitieia, which Homer mentions as a place where the alliance drew up its troops. It was a multiethnic force, so varied in fact, that there was a cacophony of languages. As Homer puts it,

Such clamors rose from various nations round,
Mix'd was the murmur, and confused the sound.

The groups camped separately and no doubt fought by national unit, as the Greeks did. Yet, in order to coordinate operations, Troy's commanders must have came up with a few shared words of command or some sort of lingua franca.

Each nation's army was organized by type of troops, size of units, and hierarchy of commanders, as was standard in the Bronze Age. Some details of military groupings survive in Hittite, Mesopotamian, and Linear B texts, but the clearest picture comes from Egypt. There, the army was divided into infantry units ranging from five-thousand-men divisions to ten-men squads. The basic tactical unit was a platoon of fifty men (five squads), in turn grouped into a company (five platoons) and a host (two or more companies). The chain of command ran down from the pharaoh to generals to combat officers to the ordinary men. Alongside infantry units were chariot units and elite soldiers, as well as, when needed, naval units, garrison commands, and foreign troops.

No more than glimpses survive of the force structure of the armies at Troy. The *Iliad* mentions fifty-men Trojan platoons and hundred-men Greek companies, and the Linear B tablets list what may be military units ranging from ten to seventy men, in multiples of ten. Despite differences, no doubt many differences, these armies and Egypt's probably were similarly composed.

Military logic dictated a number of common practices among Bronze Age armies. For instance, several days before the Battle of Megiddo in 1479 B.C., Pharaoh Thutmose III held a war council with a small group of officers, who then passed on the plan to the entire army. On the day the Greeks came, Hector undoubtedly behaved similarly: he talked over the battle plan with the allied commanders, and they in turn sent the word to their men, each in his own language.

That first day at Troy, each general is likely to have rallied his men with a pre-battle speech, which was already an ancient tradition. King Hammurabi of Babylon (1792–1750 B.C.), for example, knew how important it was before a battle to visit his men in camp and make them "happy with words." Whenever his Hana warriors, tough nomadic tribesmen, marched to Babylon, Hammurabi had them enter the city, where he reviewed them in parade and then ate with them personally. Thutmose III addressed his army before Megiddo. Hector's words on a later occasion are typical of such harangues:

> *Death is the worst; a fate which all must try;*
> *And for our country, 'tis a bliss to die.*
> *The gallant man, though slain in fight he be,*
> *Yet leaves his nation safe, his children free;*
> *Entails a debt on all the grateful state;*
> *His own brave friends shall glory in his fate;*
> *His wife live honour'd, all his race succeed,*
> *And late posterity enjoy the deed!*

Courage was another common theme of these speeches, and honor, and the need to prove oneself as a man. "Be men!" is how Hector and Agamemnon each goads his soldiers. They were speaking a language that would have resonated in Anatolia. Hittite soldiers swore oaths to be loyal to their commander—so help them, gods. Otherwise, they swore, they would dress like women and turn in

their arrows for spinning needles. And they often mocked their enemies not only as women but as donkeys, cattle, or dogs.

A good general tailored his talk to the audience. For instance, on
the eve of battle, Agamemnon knew whom to compliment and whom
to shame. To the first group, he said things like:

> *Ah! would the gods but breathe in all the rest*
> *Such souls as burn in your exalted breast. . . .*

Slackers, on the other hand, were blasted in this manner:

> *Inglorious Argives! to your race a shame,*
> *And only men in figure and in name!*

Bucking up the army was easy. The civilians were another matter. As the soldiers poured out of Troy and gathered on the plain, the
news of invasion must have gotten out. The people of Troy no doubt
reacted in various ways. Some of them were determined, some of
them were terrified, and all of them were suddenly alert because the
Greeks were coming. They turned away from their oxen on the plain
or from the wool on their loom and they scanned the horizon, waiting for the black ships to appear. Some of them surely cursed Helen
for bringing an invasion down on them. And some of them swore by
the Storm God of the Army—the first god of Troy, according to a
Hittite text—that they would support their troops until they drove
the invader back into the sea, they, the Trojan men who served King
Priam, who was good at the ashen lance. Others worried that first
the Greeks would pen them up like pigs in a sty, then the enemy
would take the city, killing the Trojans on the spot or dragging them
off as slaves to the islands or to far-off Greece. "Bitter cries" come
from the walls of cities when the land is invaded, as a Mesopotamian
text sums up civilian morale.

The Greeks would not enjoy the advantage of strategic surprise
on their landing, so they had to be certain to choose a good place to
land. One of the keys to executing a successful landing is disem-

barking where the enemy is weak. Geography made this hard to do. There are few beaches on Troy's Aegean shore between Cape Sigeum and the Trojan Harbor at today's Beşik Bay (about seven miles to the south) and those beaches lie under steep cliffs—perfect for defenders. That left the harbor itself and the bay, which, in the Late Bronze Age, stretched southward from the Dardanelles nearly all the way to the city of Troy. Today, that bay no longer exists, having been silted in by the flow of the Scamander and Simoeis Rivers. In the Late Bronze Age the west side of the bay offered a tolerable if not ideal landing ground. The place was marshy and could be reached only by entering the Dardanelles, with its treacherous wind and currents. There was a much better harbor to the south, at Beşik Bay, but it was defended by a fort on an overlooking hill, and surely the Trojans would be dug in there.

Where, then, did the Greeks land? Homer offers no clear answer, but the clues in his text point to the west side of the Bronze Age bay; the best Hellenistic and Roman sources agree; modern experts are divided. Some argue that the Greeks would have gone for the better harbor at Beşik Bay, that is, the Trojan Harbor. But a bloody landing loomed large, and near-term gain usually trumps long-term planning, so the Greek high command is likely to have opted to land at the Bronze Age bay. No matter where they landed, the Greeks surely got command of the Trojan Harbor eventually, and that gave them access to supplies and perhaps income from ships that stopped there, while denying the same to the Trojans.

The Trojans no doubt positioned their army between the two bays and moved when they got the word from their lookouts. If the Greeks were lucky, the Trojans moved slowly. The Greeks sorely needed to be lucky because their leaders had underestimated the enemy. The Greeks so outnumbered the contingent from the city of Troy that Agamemnon was confident of his ability to crush them. But he seems to have grasped neither the size nor the strength of Troy's coalition army, at least to judge by his later complaint about Troy's "unfair" edge in allies. If the dictum is true that in order to win, an attacker needs to outnumber a defender by a ratio of three to one, then the odds favored the Trojans.

But the Greeks had three advantages when it came to grabbing a beachhead. Their ships were, as Homer says, "horses of the sea": fast, mobile, and, even with just their half-decks, serving as raised platforms from which to throw down spears and arrows on the Trojans below. The Greeks were experienced at making fighting runs up onto the beach; the Trojans had little practice in such operations. The Greeks knew how to jump down onto shore rapidly while holding up a shield against enemy arrows, and how to land the ships in a formation that would give their archers maximum protection.

The terror of the ships also gave the Greeks a psychological edge. According to Homer, the unprecedented armada drove Priam's son-in-law Imbrios from his home at Pedaeum back behind the walls of Troy. And, as an ancient Athenian general would note on a later occasion, it was downright terrifying to face the onslaught of enemy ships coming right at you in the surf.

But the most important Greek resource was the quality of their infantry, the backbone of their land power. The spear and the sword were the main weapons. To be sure, Agamemnon was careful to include some contingents of archers and slingers, no doubt remembering Anatolia's reputation as bow country. But his main answer to Anatolian superiority in chariots and archers was the phalanx. It was a primitive phalanx with neither the advanced armor nor the esprit de corps of the classical phalanx. But by the standards of the Bronze Age, it was formidable: in relative terms, cohesive, heavy-armed, and potent.

The Greeks fought in some ways like the Shardana troops whose arresting images stare out at us from Egyptian carved reliefs of the 1200s and early 1100s. The Shardana were foreigners who served in their own units in the Egyptian military—that is, when they weren't busy attacking Egypt in their long ships. As the reliefs show, the Shardana fought with swords and spears but not bows. They wore short kilts, carried round shields, and wore horned helmets—curving horns, sometimes with a disc-topped spike between them. The Shardana served as Rameses II's bodyguard. The Greeks were not Shardana (although just who the Shardana were is unclear), but like them, they were experts in fighting at close range. And it would appear that Greek soldiers too fought in the Egyptian army.

Recently, an exciting discovery was made in the British Museum: a painted Egyptian papyrus from the 1300s B.C. came to light in a storeroom. It had been found in 1936 during the continuing excavations that followed the discovery in 1922 of the tomb of "King Tut" (Pharaoh Tutankhamun, 1334–1325) and then forgotten. Although it is fragmentary and not easy to reconstruct, the painting clearly shows a battle scene. There are at least two Greek warriors fighting, alongside Egyptians, against Libyans. The Greeks can be identified as Greeks because they wear boar's-tusk helmets—a style mentioned in Homer—and because one of them is dressed in an oxhide tunic, a style known to have existed in the Bronze Age Aegean. The Libyans have bows and arrows. We had suspected a Greek presence in Tutankhamun's Egypt because Mycenaean pottery turned up in the 1930s excavation: now we know that it was, at least in part, a military presence.

To speak generally, what Greek infantrymen lacked in chariots and missiles (arrows and slings) they made up for in unit cohesion and speed. Also, unlike the Shardana, the Greeks, or at least some of them, wore heavy armor. They excelled in fighting in thick formation and in letting well-armored champions take the lead.

The Greeks were not deficient in chariot tactics, but their chariotry faced practical limitations. There was little good horse country in Greece, especially compared to Anatolia. There were only so many horses and chariots that could be transported by ship. It would be hard to feed and exercise those horses in the narrow coastal strip of their encampment or to do maintenance on chariots in a camp far from home. Add to this the numerous references in Homer to Greek soldiers like Achilles who were "swift-footed," that is, strong and fast infantrymen who attacked charioteers from the ground with spears and swords, and a picture emerges of a nimble and lethal Greek infantry capable of paying back the Trojans in kind.

The Trojans were great charioteers, which would serve them well on the plain of Troy. The chariot was a multipurpose vehicle, used for transport to, from, and around the battlefield as well as for mobile fire support and for sheer intimidation. The chariot was part tank, part jeep, and part armored personnel carrier. Just as horses were near and dear to the heart of the Hittite Great King—"send me stallions!" writes King Hattushilish III to the king of Babylon—so they were beloved by Priam. In fact, he reared some of his horses with his own hand, just as Pharaoh Amenhotep II (1427–1392 B.C.) did.

But the battle of the beach would not be a chariot battle. It would be a brawl. With ships constantly coming in and men disembarking, with Trojans running forward to stop them and Greeks pushing against the Trojan line, and with missiles flying, neither side could have maintained close order. The result would have been a melee, what Homer calls "a dispersed battle" in which "man took man" and "close combat" was decided by "hand and might."

After all, an amphibious landing on well-defended ground is one of warfare's most difficult maneuvers. The Athenian general Demosthenes reminded his men of this when they had to defend an outnumbered garrison against a Spartan landing by sea. The year was 425 B.C.; the place, an outpost in southwest Greece; and the conflict was the Peloponnesian War. Demosthenes told his men not to fear the Spartans' numbers, because, as experienced seamen, Athenians knew "how impossible it is to drive back an enemy determined enough to stand his ground."

The Spartans failed that day in 425 B.C.; the Athenians pushed them back into the sea. No doubt the Spartans were every bit as tough as Agamemnon's men. But the sandy beach at Troy would be much easier terrain for the invaders than the rocky shore that faced the Spartans. And the Spartans were infamous landlubbers. Seaborne raids, however, were almost run-of-the-mill for Bronze Age Greeks.

Bronze Age galleys could be run right up onto the beach, bow first, and that is surely what the Greeks did at Troy. This procedure generated more speed and power than backing the boat in, stern first. Most defenders would scatter at the sight of a crimson-prowed ship bearing down on them. The discipline of the rowers and the skill of the pilot would be crucial; some ships would hit the target while others would fail. A first-rate pilot, like Phrontis son of One-tor, who served Menelaus, must have been highly prized. Likewise, top-flight rowers, like the Phaeacians of the *Odyssey*, who were strong enough to muscle a ship half its length up onto the beach—perhaps a case of heroic exaggeration.

On each side the commanders would have given the men their orders before battle. Arrows were the best way to cover the distance between ship and shore, so each army would try to get its best archers in position. Slingers could have done damage too, so if possible they would have been positioned within striking distance as well. The Greeks would be particularly vulnerable as they hit the beach, a point the Trojan officers might have emphasized. But Trojans had little experience in the amphibious operations at which the Greeks excelled.

Both sides would have made an effort to get their heroes to the fore: that is, the nobles. This was a sound tactic as well as realistic politics, because the heroes were better armed, better trained, and better fed than the common soldier. On the Trojan side, for example, a man like Euphorbus son of Panthous, whose father was one of Priam's advisors, was taught as a boy the art of fighting from a chariot. The young Achilles, to take another case, was trained (according to Homer) by the hero Phoenix and (according to myth) by the centaur Chiron. The Greek or Trojan infantryman, by contrast, might have been instructed in drill, like the Egyptian conscript, but in combat he might have gotten more use out of what he had learned in scuffles in the barnyard or backstreets.

Before embarking that morning, the Greek chiefs would have had to decide the order in which the ships would come in to shore, because the harbor would be much too small for all the vessels to land at once. The commanders would have wanted elite troops in the first wave, while also saving good men for the later stages of the battle. The Greeks might expect a quick victory over any Trojan ships in their way, but they could count on a tough fight afterward.

As the Greeks jumped off their ships they would have faced what looked like a stockade of spears. The Trojans had the sun in their eyes, but if they could make out the details, they might have seen the images of lions, bulls, or falcons painted on the bows of the Greek ships. They would have heard the thud of timber on the sand and the twang of enemy bows.

Battlefields are rarely quiet as even a king like the Assyrian Shalmaneser I (1274–1245 B.C.) commented. But as he probably knew, noise is a weapon. Homer gives his heroes enormous lung capacities and lionlike roars, and this might not be far from the truth. In the primitive command-and-control conditions of the day, a leader had constantly to think about communicating with his men. The ability to bellow was a practical advantage. And a heroic scream also served as psychological warfare against an impressionable enemy. And so Homer's description of a battle later in the war might be applied to that first day of fighting as well, beginning with Hector:

> *With shouts incessant earth and ocean rung,*
> *Sent from his following host: the Grecian train*
> *With answering thunders fill'd the echoing plain;*
> *A shout that tore heaven's concave, and, above,*
> *Shook the fix'd splendours of the throne of Jove.*

The battle ashore began as the bow of the pine-hulled ship crashed onto the beach and the king of Thessaly leapt down. He turned and faced the enemy. Leadership by personal example is always a key factor in battle but rarely more so than in the hierarchical world of the Bronze Age. If a hero didn't take the lead, no one would. So when Protesilaus son of Iphiclus became the first Greek to set foot on Trojan soil it was not merely a high honor, it was a necessity. But it was a distinction that he had little time to savor, because he was also the first Greek to die. Hector, royal prince and son of King Priam, was waiting for him. He would probably have aimed his spear at a seam in Protesilaus's armor or at his neck or at an unprotected part of his face, all common places for a weapon to penetrate and cause a fatal wound.

The great Achilles had thought about jumping ashore first, but held back because he believed that the first Greek to land at Troy would be killed. He had been warned by his divine mother, Thetis—which may be another way of saying that even tough guys go with their gut feelings sometimes. And so the war had its first combat casualty, which led to the first widow. At home in the city of Phylace, Protesilaus left a wife to tear her cheeks in a sign of mourning.

The men in the Trojan vanguard might have tried to push their way onto the enemy ships or at least to hoist themselves up high enough to grab the ornament off the sternpost as a trophy. Anyone brave enough to try would surely face a rain of enemy arrows and spears and perhaps be hacked at with swords.

It must have been a hard-fought battle and yet we don't hear a word about the role of the ordinary soldier in it. We can be sure that he was in the thick of things. When it comes to the rank and file, the silence of the sources and the clamor of reality are typical of the Bronze Age. Hittite and Egyptian texts, for example, often tell the story of a battle the same way: the Great King or pharaoh single-handedly defeats masses of enemy soldiers. An extreme case is the official Egyptian version of the battle of Qadesh: Pharaoh Rameses II killed so many Hittite soldiers that the plain of Qadesh became impassable from all the blood and corpses. Pharaoh had the help of the gods alone in this victory. In other words, the enemy is a crowd of common soldiers but our side has one divinely inspired hero.

Homer and the other poets of the Epic Cycle take a similar approach. They focus on great warriors and their divine enablers, generally leaving it to the audience to fill in the experience of the masses. Although Homer does little to put a face on the battle experience of the rank and file, other sources of evidence allow educated guesses.

Start with an Egyptian sculpted relief of the early 1100s depicting a sea battle near shore. It shows the damage that could be done by archers, whether aboard ship or posted ashore. The common man in Bronze Age armies was at risk because he had the flimsiest armor or none at all—sometimes he even lacked sandals. The dead fell, as the Egyptians said, as crocodiles fall into the water. Fighting their way ashore, the Greeks would have had to wade through corpses, often their own comrades.

Once he got ashore, the Greek soldier might have aimed at his Trojan counterpart. Well-armored Trojan nobles made poor targets, but a Trojan commoner was a fair foil for the Greek's spear or sword—if the Greek had one, and for his bare fists, if he didn't. If they teamed up, a group of Greek privates might have captured a Trojan hero and held him for ransom, arms tied behind his back, just as one Greek common soldier boasts in one of Homer's rare glimpses of the enlisted men. But surely more ordinary Greek soldiers fell at the hands of Trojan heroes.

The Greeks were not certain of victory until Achilles—by now ashore—killed Cycnus, a Trojan ally who was inflicting big casualties on the Greeks. Cycnus is said to have had the superhuman power of a son of the god Poseidon, to use the Greek name; the Trojans might have known him as the Great Sea God. To declare someone no mere mortal but a god was a Bronze Age gesture of respect to the great and powerful.

Achilles is said to have strangled Cycnus with the leather straps of Cycnus's own helmet. Cycnus appears not in Homer but in the Epic Cycle. It is a less-reliable source, but Cycnus symbolizes both the Bronze Age and the little connection Troy had to the sea.

Cycnus was king of the city of Colonae, located on the Aegean coast of the Troad about fifteen miles south of Troy. The site of Colonae was inhabited during the Bronze Age. It was a maritime location, opposite the island of Tenedos, which, in some myths, was first settled by Cycnus's son. No less intriguing, Cycnus is a Greek word meaning "swan" (compare English "cygnet"), but it also recalls the name Kukkunni, a king of Troy mentioned in a Hittite document. We don't know just when he reigned but Kukkunni was a predecessor of Alaksandu, who sat on the throne ca. 1280 B.C. How appropriate that a name recalling both a Bronze Age Trojan king and the Aegean shore is used for the first man to die for Troy in the war with the Greeks.

Achilles' victory sparked an advance. It encouraged Greece's superb infantry to press forward, while it made the Trojans think about retreating and regrouping. When the Trojans heard their leaders' cry to give up and move back toward the city, the victorious Greeks might have taunted them, calling them weaklings, with legs good for nothing except running away, the kind of men who dropped their bows, their packs, and their water skins for a quick getaway. Then the Greeks would have looted the armor of the enemy corpses.

Meanwhile, the gatekeepers of Troy would have opened the doors wide to let the exhausted soldiers pour back into town. As the news of the dead and missing spread, the sound of wailing would rise. On the citadel, Priam might meet anxiously with his advisors. On the ramparts, the watchmen might anticipate that they would be out that night and for many nights to come. And every time they heard a stranger's voice call out, they would stiffen up.

The Greeks had taken their beachhead. After tending to the wounded, gathering the dead, and praying in thanksgiving to the gods, they would proceed to set up camp. Homer insists that for the next nine years, the camp was left unfortified. The mere presence of heroes such as Achilles and Ajax offered better protection than any wall or trenches could. Only after Achilles quit in a huff did the Greeks get around to fortifying their base. This is implausible but not impossible. For example, encamped before the battle of Qadesh (1274 B.C.), Pharaoh Rameses II's army relied on little more than a barricade of shields for protection. Classical Sparta, to take another case, went without city walls, trusting instead its elite army (and its mountains) to scare off any attacker. But in the Trojan War, the verdict of Thucydides, who knew Sparta, commands respect: after winning a battle upon their arrival, the Greeks fortified their encampment.

Tradition says that the Greeks buried Protesilaus across the straits, near Cape Helles, at the edge of the Gallipoli Peninsula. Excavations at the site find no Bronze Age settlement after 1300 B.C., about a century before the Trojan War, so the authenticity of the tradition is in doubt; the poignancy of the site is not. Looking south from here, the Greeks could have clearly seen the towers of Troy across the straits, crowned by Priam's palace and the temples of the gods, guarded by a double band of walls, all gleaming in the morning light across the blue surface of the Dardanelles.

But long before warlike Protesilaus was turned over to the black earth—wherever he lay—a messenger surely brought word of the battle to Priam. Did the king look his fellow elders in the eye at the news that a hostile army had won a bloody foothold on the Trojan shore? Or was he too ashamed and disappointed to share their judgment of what his family's policy had wrought?

Maybe Priam thought back to his youth, as old men do, to a great battle on the Sangarius River in Phrygia where he fought as an allied soldier. Or maybe he preferred to think ahead, to the idea of a fresh start. In any case, the king would have to face the new facts.

The battle of the beachhead was over. The battle for Troy was about to begin.

CHAPTER FOUR

ASSAULT ON THE WALLS

The bolts are pulled back into their sockets and the double doors—wooden, plated with metal, and tightly fitted together—swing open. The travelers enter the city, passing quickly and quietly through the defenses of Troy. If these walls could talk they would scream. They would cry havoc and let the generals roar for victory and the fugitives shout for ropes to pull them up and the sappers give out war whoops as they hack away with their bronze tools. But today the walls are dead silent: a mass of stone and earth that won't be breached without blood.

The travelers are heading in the opposite direction from the one in which traffic usually moves at this early hour, when the herdsmen head out of town with their goats, sheep, and cattle. But these are unusual times, with an enemy army camped on the rich pastureland of Troy. Homer describes the outcome of the travelers' journey; let us imagine their trip.

Odysseus son of Laertes and king of Ithaca has the build of a boxer and the eyes of a hunter. He wears a trim beard and long hair cut short in front so as not to give the enemy something to grab on to in battle. He is dressed in a glossy tunic beneath a heavy woolen cloak with double folds, colored purple. The folds are clasped by a solid gold brooch incised with an image of a hound killing a fawn. If the expression on his face is a mask, it is no more insincere than the language of brotherhood in which royal scribes couch ultimatums, and no trickier than the nighttime troop movements by which Bronze Age generals steal a march on the enemy. War is deception: no one knows this better than Odysseus. His traveling companion, Menelaus, might dream of avenging his honor, but Odysseus just wants to win.

The expression on his face is a riddle; not so that of Menelaus, whose eyes glow with anger. The two men ride in separate two-horse chariots, driven by trusted friends. They are escorted by a de-tachment of heavy-armed spearmen but not from their own army. The escorts are Trojans, and they are leading a Greek delegation.

The soldiers are elite troops, wearing bronze armor shining for the parade ground. They are protecting the city from the Greeks and the Greeks from the city. Let the long-haired Greeks see the strength of Troy's walls but not the weak spots in need of repair. And don't let the Trojans and their wives, whose garments sweep the ground, see who is suddenly within reach of vengeance. The Greeks have just arrived in the country, but they have already created refugees and mourners.

The two visiting kings are not likely to have reacted in the same way. Menelaus's blood might have been boiling at the thought that he was in Troy, where his adulterous wife was dishonoring his name and her lover was cuckolding him and defying the gods. Paris had violated the laws of Zeus himself, the god of hospitality and strangers. Odysseus was an accomplished sacker of cities and a born scout, the most cunning man in the Greek army. We may imagine him consumed less by anger than by curiosity. The paved streets, the wide court-yards, the exotic statuettes of the bull that represented the army's god, the veiled women, the wind that blew stronger the higher they climbed on Troy's hill—nothing would have escaped the scrutiny of the man of many ways, as Homer calls him.

Ancient Near Eastern etiquette demanded that a king lay down an official challenge to his opponent. It was unmanly, said a Hittite king, to start a war with a sneak attack. The Greeks came, therefore,

to give the Trojans one last chance for peace; the alternative was enmity and death. Or so they said. A razor-sharp Trojan might have
known the Hittite practice of sending an envoy who held two sets of
instructions, a "tablet of war" and a "tablet of peace"; one tablet
threatened the enemy, but the other proposed a deal, should the
enemy refuse to give in. But the Greeks were in no mood for a deal.
It was up to the Trojans to back down and restore peace. Was it
worth dying for Helen?

Odysseus and Menelaus headed for the home of Antenor, their
host. In spite of the circumstances, they would not have forgotten to
bring him gifts, perhaps including a statuette of a god, as a Greek
king once sent to the Hittite monarch. Antenor might have lived in
one of the two-story mansions in a newly fashionable section of the
lower city. When Troy was rebuilt after an earthquake around 1300
B.C., the town's strict class segregation came to an end; no longer did
wealthy people live just on the citadel, and the citadel was no longer
just the preserve of the rich.

Imagine Antenor's house with painted plaster walls and a separate kitchen wing with a dozen large vases sunk into the earth to
provide a kind of refrigerated storage. Inside a house like this
were imported jewelry and seal stones, delicate pottery and silver
bowls, and woven textiles and carved ivories. Perhaps it was even
Antenor who owned a bronze figurine of a man standing in a gesture of prayer: a wide-eyed, straight-nosed piece, apparently of Hittite workmanship. (This figurine has just recently been excavated
at Troy.)

Although a Trojan, Antenor was a friend of the Greeks. He was
an important person in Troy, an elder statesman, noble, and royal advisor. He was married to Theano daughter of Cisseus, who was
priestess of Athena, which is a sign of Antenor's social prominence.
Antenor always took the Greeks' side in Trojan debates, and we
might guess that he had business interests, kinship, and marriage ties
that allied him with Greeks. As for Athena, the Trojan equivalent
isn't known, but we can assume there was one, because Anatolian
cities often had a protector goddess.

Antenor had reason enough to speak for peace without Greek influence: he had many sons whom he no doubt did not wish to sacrifice in war. So when Menelaus and Odysseus spoke up in the Trojan assembly, Antenor supported them. The Greeks demanded that Helen and the stolen treasures of Sparta be returned.

The two Greek speakers made a lasting impression on Antenor. Menelaus was more imposing physically but the lesser speaker. Menelaus said what he had to but he seemed to be in a hurry to get the words out. Just minutes away sat his wife, Helen, under Paris's roof. Menelaus surely knew that every man in the gathering looked at him with scorn. Every word might be taken as a sign of weakness, so no wonder the man kept his speech short.

Odysseus was different. His remarks were delivered with the strategic skill that was his trademark. First, he softened up the audience by playing the hick, too intimidated by the big city to do any more than hold his scepter and look at the ground. But when his turn came, Odysseus let out words that fell on the assembly like a snowstorm. It was a verbal reminder of the man's toughness. War was Odysseus's business. As he reminded Agamemnon when the going got rough:

> *This is what Zeus has given us, from youth to old age:*
> *To fight hard wars to the finish, until we are all dead.*

But the Trojans did not give Odysseus what he wanted. Indeed, things nearly got out of hand in the unruly assembly. The leading hawk was another important Trojan, Antimachus. Like Antenor, he had sons. But the prospect of their corpses on the funeral pyre did not soften his stand: there could be no surrender to the Greeks. Antimachus was a man of fiery temper, but Homer says that something else was afoot: Antimachus had been bought by Paris with especially good gifts, namely, a large amount of gold, no doubt from the hoard brought back from Sparta.

Not only did Antimachus argue against returning Helen or the stolen treasures, he said that the Trojans should kill Menelaus then and there. This would have been "disgraceful" and "an outrage," as Agamemnon later put it. But it would have been a smart move. Killing Menelaus would not only have cost the Greeks a prominent (if not overly effective) leader, but it would also have stripped the war of its logic. The Greeks would have found themselves fighting to return Helen to a dead man and to avenge a murdered king—in fact, two murdered kings, since killing Odysseus would have been a brilliant stroke too. In the long run, no Greek would do more harm to Troy than he did, although the Trojans could not have known that yet.

In the end, the two men were given safe passage back to their camp at the sea. But they returned empty-handed, without Helen or the treasure. And surely Priam approved of that. He had certainly welcomed the adulterous queen to Troy, and he treated her with warmth and chivalry, as Homer shows. While other Trojans blamed the war on Helen, Priam insisted that, as far as he was concerned, it was the gods and not she who were responsible. And he never lifted a finger to return her to the Greeks.

But he couldn't afford to. Priam did not have the luxury of waging war without considering domestic politics. No king did. Civil war lurked in Bronze Age cities, from Canaanite towns to the Hittite capital. One Canaanite mayor confessed his fear of his own peasantry; another was driven into exile by a younger brother who despised him. In Hittite history, a whole population or just part of it could force a city into surrendering. Troy itself had suffered civil war not long before in the 1200s B.C., forcing the exile of King Walmu, a Hittite ally. So Priam and his family had to tread carefully.

Returning Helen would be admitting that it had been a mistake to let her into Troy in the first place. And that admission might well bring the downfall of the house of Priam. It would have been an invitation for a coup by a member of another branch of the royal family, which was not short of pretenders, or even by an outsider like Antenor.

Meanwhile, Priam's supporters in the assembly could argue against appeasement. Give back Helen and the treasures, and the greedy Greeks would ask for more. Accept the ambassadors' demands, and say goodbye to Trojan independence. Let the enemy just try to storm the city: he would stop in frustration soon enough. All that Troy needed was patriotism and patience, the argument might go.

So Priam and his people would face the war and fight to win. That left the Greeks with no choice but to sharpen their spears and wage war with everything they had. Menelaus might have glowed at the thought of vengeance and at the sweet odor of death. But the shadow of Troy's massive walls would have fallen over Odysseus's thoughts, pragmatist that he was.

The question of what the Greeks did next—of how they fought—is much more difficult than it might seem. There is no direct answer in the *Iliad*, focusing as it does on the penultimate part of the war. Another early ancient epic, the *Cypria*, discusses the previous phases of the war. But only a few lines of this poem survive and the *Cypria* is less reliable than Homer. Fortunately, Homer provides clues about the earlier fighting.

The first clue comes from a comment by Poseidon, the god of the sea, horses, and earthquakes. Even mythological figures such as the gods speak to Homer's authenticity. Ancient peoples were deeply religious. In the Bronze Age, for example, Hittite and Egyptian accounts regularly give the gods a role in military campaigns. No Hittite scribe would think of recording a victory without thanking the gods for having marched in front of the army and thereby having granted the king success. No ambassador would swear to abide by a treaty unless an assembly of the various gods had witnessed it. In his poem about the battle of Qadesh (1274 B.C.), Pharaoh Rameses II declares that the god Amun spoke to him and sent him forward.

Even in the rationalistic heyday of classical Greece—and later— gods and heroes were commonly seen in the heat of battle. Sometimes their mere presence provided encouragement to the soldiers. At other times, divinities gave specific military advice. And sometimes they even fought! At the decisive battles of Marathon (490 B.C.), Salamis (480 B.C.), Aegospotami (405 B.C.), and Leuctra (371

B.C.), for example, contemporaries thought that gods and heroes took part.

On the treacherous plain of Troy the only rock of certainty was the gods. Men needed to believe that the deities cared about their fate because the alternative was the loneliness of death. So when Homer sets verse after verse in Olympus, he is not offering mere window-dressing; he is opening a window into the soul of the ancient Greek soldier. And when Homer quotes a god, he may be reporting what men claimed to have heard at the time.

By the ninth year of the war, in an attempt to buck up the Greeks when the battle was going badly, Poseidon cast scorn on the enemy. The ninth year, that is, in Homer's reckoning: we have already seen that the real war was much shorter. How can the Greeks let the Trojans push them back on their ships, he asks, when the Trojans usually behave like frightened deer? The Trojans have been running through the woods as if afraid of the wolves; defenseless creatures without a heart for battle. They were never willing to stand their ground against the armed might of the Greeks.

Achilles makes a similar claim. He says that up to now Hector had never wanted to fight far from the walls, and he would advance no farther than the oak tree near Troy's main or Scaean Gate. There he would have the help of soldiers stationed in the towers at either side of the gate. Even so, the Greek adds, Hector once barely escaped Achilles' charge. And Hera goes one better: she claims that when it came to the Dardanian Gate, Hector wouldn't dare so much as go outside the walls—presumably because this postern gate lacked protective bastions.

This is exaggeration, but the Trojans did indeed spend most of the war on defense, leaving attacks to the Greeks. Perhaps some of the Trojans were cowards, as Poseidon says, but most were sound strategists. Like their brethren elsewhere in the ancient Near East, they knew that coming out and fighting made better rhetoric than strategy.

The Trojans had only limited choices. Tactically, they could have nibbled away at the Greeks with guerrilla raids—and we can fault the Trojans for doing so little of that. But the Trojans were absolutely right to avoid a frontal assault of the Greeks' camp. The Trojans depended on allies and so they had to avoid casualties; high losses would make those allies give up and go home. By staying on the strategic defensive, the Trojans bowed to the realities of warfare at the time.

The Late Bronze Age knew three ways to conquer a fortified city: assault, siege, or ruse. Assault meant either scaling the city walls with ladders, breaking through the walls or through a gate with battering rams or hammers and axes, or tunneling below the walls. Siege meant encircling the city walls, preventing supplies from entering, and starving the defenders into surrender. Ruse meant any trick or tricks, sometimes coordinated with traitors inside the walls, that could gain control of the city.

Each of these tactics was difficult and dangerous. To penetrate the walls at Troy meant you first had to reach them, and that meant either winning a pitched battle against the army that protected Troy or pulling off a surprise attack. During years of intermittent fighting on the plain of Troy, the Greeks reached the walls a few times, but the Trojans always quickly forced them back. The Trojans had taken to heart the Mesopotamian proverb that strong gates alone can't save a city without a strong army to defend them. Chariots were Troy's "secret weapon" and, as Odysseus knew, when men mount swift-footed horses, they could decide the outcome of an equally matched war— and decide it in a flash. No wonder that, when he said goodbye to his wife, Penelope, on the day he left for war, Odysseus told her that he expected many Greeks never to come home.

They had no supply lines from home to sustain them. Instead, large numbers of Greek soldiers had to sail off on food-hunting raids or settle down as farmers on the Gallipoli Peninsula on the other side of the Dardanelles. Thucydides is the source of this insight, and the sober historian may be right because later Greek armies did the same sort of thing when necessary. With the Greeks unable to gather all their men for one big push, the Trojan War could only be bloody and frustrating. No wonder that Odysseus characterized it afterward as "a hateful path decreed by thundering Zeus to lead many men to death."

It is common to speak of the siege of Troy but in fact there was no siege. The Greeks never encircled the city. They built no palisades or ditches to cut off Troy from access to the outside world by land, because they couldn't. They lacked the superiority in numbers to establish a ring around the city without risking an overwhelming Trojan counterattack. The Trojan defenders were, as Odysseus says in another context, "as many as the leaves and flowers that come in spring."

On three occasions before the last phase of the war, the Greeks reached the city walls and nearly took control of them, at a place near the landmark of a particular wild fig tree, near the western gate. If Bronze Age armies had a field manual it would have called for the use of a stratagem to reach the enemy's walls, such as a surprise attack at night or a decoy to lure his army away and leave the walls unprotected. The early Hittite rulers Pithana and his son Anitta (1700s B.C.?) each stormed an enemy city by night. We don't know whether the Greeks used such tactics or took the more direct route of winning a pitched battle and pushing on to Troy. In any case, their probes had found a weak spot in the fortifications, perhaps that point in the northwestern wall where a former gate had been filled in with rubble, a pile that was now sagging. It was there, under the leadership of the two men named Ajax—Ajax son of Telamon and Oilean or "Lesser" Ajax—that Idomeneus, Diomedes, Agamemnon, and Menelaus, the best Greek soldiers, nearly sealed Troy's fate.

The source of this information is not a soldier but a woman: Hector's wife, Andromache. She stood with her husband near the Scaean Gate of the Trojan wall, and the tough-minded lady gave him military advice. If that seems like Josephine telling Napoleon how to invade Russia, it adds to the evidence of the relative freedom of Trojan women. One ancient Greek literary critic even wanted to delete these lines as not really Homer's because he couldn't believe that Andromache would lecture her husband on strategy. But Andromache wasn't Greek. She says:

That quarter most the skilful Greeks annoy,
Where yon wild fig-trees join the wall of Troy;
Thou, from this tower defend the important post;
There Agamemnon points his dreadful host,
That pass Tydides [Diomedes], Ajax, strive to gain,
And there the vengeful Spartan fires his train.
Thrice our bold foes the fierce attack have given,
Or led by hopes, or dictated from heaven.
Let others in the field their arms employ,
But stay my Hector here, and guard his Troy.

A woman like Andromache had perhaps the most to lose in a sack of the city because she would end up a slave and mistress to one of the victors. We can't help but wonder if her statement of three near-breakthroughs isn't another case of heroic exaggeration. But even one attempt to break through the walls would have been frightening enough to the Trojans.

Although the Greeks had much experience storming cities, their forte was attack from the sea. We have to wonder whether they were equal to those experts in land assaults, the Assyrians, Egyptians, and Hittites.

Scaling a city's wall was an elite operation, and Andromache is specific about which Greek champions led the assault. Agamemnon and Menelaus, brothers, kings, and sons of Atreus, have already been introduced. If not the Greeks' greatest warriors, they were nonetheless strong soldiers and key political leaders. Their presence in an attempt to scale Troy's walls is no surprise. The four other attackers (Andromache also mentions Idomeneus and Lesser Ajax as part of the assault), all famous soldiers, represent respectively the Greeks' best hand-to-hand fighter, their most vicious cutthroat, a veteran of their most successful recent assault on a city of the day, and an older man who was as experienced as he was expendable. Surely it also mattered that the latter two had brought the biggest contingents to Troy after Agamemenon and the elderly Nestor. Odysseus, that all-around soldier and well-known sacker of cities, is not recorded as having taken part in the assault on the walls. But the Trojans had a hard time picking Odysseus out of a crowd because he was shorter than some of the other Greek heroes, so perhaps Andromache missed him. Here are the other leaders of the assault team:

Idomeneus was son of Deucalion and king of Crete, the island that, two centuries earlier, had been among the Greeks' first conquests. He was a tough warrior who carried a huge figure-of-eight shield into battle, made of leather, rimmed with bronze, and held together by two rods. Although no longer in the flower of youth, he still loved to fight and was known as a great spearman. Along the wall of his hut stood a barbaric display of spears, shields, helmets, and breastplates stripped from Trojans whom he had killed. It was a modest version of the more than one thousand pieces of arms and armor, including two gilded chariots, that Pharaoh Thutmose III took when he conquered Megiddo in 1479 B.C.

Figure-of-eight shields such as Idomeneus's once seemed anachronistic, since they were thought to have gone out of use around 1500 B.C. But not long ago a painted pottery fragment turned up that shows these shields still in use in the 1300s, so they may well have been a feature of the battlefield at the time of the Trojan War.

Ajax son of Telamon of Salamis was no genius but he was a murderous giant who never passed up a fight. He and Achilles were cousins. Among the Greeks, only Achilles was bigger and stronger than Ajax, and Idomeneus reckoned Ajax could defeat Achilles in a hand-to-hand fight though he could never match Achilles' speed. Ajax would fight Hector, Troy's greatest warrior, to a standstill. Ajax was more like a wall than a man, which is why they called him "the bulwark of the Greeks." He went into battle wearing a full body-suit of armor and carrying a huge, tower-shaped shield made of seven layers of leather and rimmed with bronze. While most tower shields depicted in Mycenaean art are covered with oxhide, some appear to be metallic, so Homer's description might be accurate. Ajax's normal weapon was the spear, but he was strong enough to lift a big piece of marble, swing it above his head, and then bring it down on a Trojan with enough force to smash the man's helmet and crush his skull.

Ajax son of Oïleus of Locris suffered in comparison to the prowess of the comrade whose name he shared, so he was called the Lesser Ajax. But he was in no way deficient when it came to mayhem. He was a foul-mouthed brawler with a short temper and ready fists. He is remembered in the Epic Cycle for dragging Cassandra from the altar of Athena to rape her. Who better than such a brute to lead the first wave over the wall?

Diomedes son of Tydeus was king of Argos. Like Odysseus, with whom he teamed up from time to time, Diomedes was a warrior for all seasons. And, although he was the youngest of the Greek champions in the *Iliad*, Diomedes excelled in pitched battle. Homer details the murderous spree in which Diomedes killed the great Trojan bowman Pandarus son of Lycaon, nearly did the same to Aeneas, and even wounded the gods Ares and Aphrodite—surely a way of saying that he was reckless on the battlefield. Warriors had been wounding goddesses at least since *Gilgamesh*, a Mesopotamian epic with roots in the 2000s B.C.

Diomedes was a favorite of Athena, just as Hattushilish III (1267–1237 B.C.) was a favorite of the goddess Ishtar, whom an Assyrian inscription refers to as the "mistress of strife and battle." In the Hittite king's case, Ishtar was everywhere in battle, now marching in front of Hattushilish, now holding his hand. Diomedes likewise might have felt as if he had Athena's goatskin itself wrapped around his shoulders as he fought.

Diomedes wore a full suit of bronze armor and his helmet was probably bronze with a horsehair plume. His shield was another of the figure-eight style. A combat veteran, he had taken part in the expedition that finally destroyed the city of Thebes; his father, Tydeus, had died trying in an earlier attempt. But he had not died gloriously, as a story in the epic tradition reports. Tydeus killed a Theban warrior, Melanippus, but not without receiving a fatal wound himself. While he lay dying, Tydeus reached over and helped himself to some of Melanippus's brain tissue, which he then ate. The gods approved of warriors who crowed in victory but they drew the line at cannibalism: myth says that Athena punished Tydeus by withdrawing a promise of immortality.

To storm a walled city it was necessary to use ladders, soldiers armed with protective shields, and archers to provide covering fire to the attackers; slingers were also useful. By the Late Bronze Age the art of assault had advanced considerably. Battering rams and siege towers were now common in the ancient Near East. A battering ram was, at its simplest, a long beam tipped with metal. A siege tower allowed the attacker's bowmen to shoot at the defenders on the battlements, thereby protecting the men operating the battering ram below. Another refinement was to put wheels on the scaling ladders, as the Egyptians did. Attackers sometimes built a dirt ramp up to the wall. And it was not unknown to try to tunnel beneath the walls and enter the city from below.

Military architects always tried to keep one step ahead of the latest advance in storming technology, and Troy's walls were up to date. The city had two sets of walls: an outer perimeter protecting the lower town and an inner citadel to which the defenders could retreat. At nearly a mile in circumference, the outer wall was more difficult to defend than the compact circuit of the citadel.

The outer wall consisted of a stone foundation on top of which lay sun-dried mud bricks, better known in North America as adobe. The bricks, made of a mixture of mud, sand, straw, and manure, were cheap and easy to manufacture. Adobe cushions the shock of a battering ram, but unfortunately it is vulnerable to enemy sappers, who can cut right through it; the higher the stone foundation, therefore, the better.

In the *Iliad* the Greeks build a rampart of wood and stone to protect their camp. They surround it with a deep trench, in which they place stakes. Troy's outer wall was similarly surrounded by a wooden palisade and a trench, cut into the bedrock, to eight feet deep and ten to eleven feet wide. At intervals the trench was interrupted for access to the gates. The Greeks' trench was built to stop chariots, and no doubt the Trojan trench was too, but it would also have stopped siege towers and made it difficult to use battering rams anywhere except at the gates.

The trench protected the outer wall before about 1300, but by the 1200s it had been filled with dirt, potsherds, and animal bones. That would have made no military sense except in the unlikely event that the sherds and bones were sharp enough to serve as caltrops (cavalry obstacles). Perhaps the trench was filled in for public-health reasons, since rainwater in it might have represented breeding grounds for mosquitos, leading in turn to outbreaks of malaria. The Trojans would not have known the cause of the illness, but they might have noticed a correlation between the outbreak and the trench. But the likeliest explanation is that the lower town had prospered and grown. A second trench has been discovered, about three hundred feet southeast of the first; it could have replaced the first trench as a defensive barrier.

In any case, the Trojans would not have wanted to concede the lower city without a fight, especially not after the movement of wealthy citizens there in the 1200s B.C. The area could survive attack because of its own fresh water from a well located in the massive Northeast Bastion. Sling stones and metal weapons have been found in the destruction debris around 1200 B.C. of Troy VIi (formerly known as Troy VIIa). All of this may well be evidence of a failed defense. But after breaching the outer wall, the enemy would have to battle through the lower city and its maze of narrow streets. Then would come a bigger challenge: Fortress Troy.

The citadel of Troy, called Pergamos, rose about one hundred feet above the plain, a half-acre stronghold. The defenders could stockpile food and they could also rely on a supply of fresh water from an underground spring, reached via a network of manmade tunnels dug some five hundred feet into the rock.

Pergamos was protected by one of the finest fortifications in the world: a 1,150 foot circuit of walls standing about 33 feet high and more than 16 feet thick. The bottom of the wall was made of stone and stood about 20 feet high with an adobe superstructure about another 13 feet high. A walkway for the defenders crowned the walls, protected by a breastwork. The stone base of the wall sloped outward, thereby denying attackers a blind spot out of reach of a defender's arrow.

The gates were state of the art. The South Gate, probably the main entrance to the city, stood beside an enormous tower built in the 1200s B.C. At a height of more than thirty feet, the tower was a defender's dream. The East Gate had an entrance passage that channeled attackers into a narrow courtyard between two walls and then made them turn a sharp corner before reaching the gate itself. In the 1200s the courtyard was made at least about sixty feet longer and a massive defensive tower and a sort of foregate were added. The imposing Northeast Bastion took advantage of a natural cliff. It stood about forty feet high and was about sixty feet wide. Probably the bastion flanked a gate in the lower town's wall, just as a tower flanked the South Gate in the citadel wall.

Only a punishing and blood-spattered fight could have brought the Greeks over the top at Troy. Imagine, for example, Diomedes in the thick of battle, an angry lion, leading his crack troops in a charge to the ramparts.

The attack on the wall would have been also an assault on the senses: a combination of sights and sounds to terrify defender and attacker alike. We might imagine the twanging of bowstrings, the hum of javelins in motion, the swish of slings, the bang of missiles hitting shields that protected soldiers' backs as they climbed the scaling ladders, the crash of falling ladders, the thud of the battering ram against the doors of the gate, the grunts of the defenders as they tried to absorb the blow and hold the doors in place, the moans of the wounded, the crack of whip on horseflesh and the whinnying of the frightened beasts, the blare of the trumpet ringing out the call to one last charge, and the snapping of the city's standard as it blew in the wind above the walls. Then too, there were surely other sounds that were no less terrifying for their low volume: the pop of a breaking shield strap, the gurgling of a dying man. And imagine, through it all, Diomedes' battle cry, a bellow that came from someplace deep in his heart.

As the Greeks reached for glory and the Trojans made a stand for their homes and families, the cruel war-god, Ares, would have had his fill of victims. A lone Greek warrior might make it up to the battlements, hauling himself up the rungs of the ladder, hand over blistered hand, and then spear a Trojan defender before being stabbed to death himself. Wounded men would tumble down from the ramparts and the scaling ladders. Corpses would lie in heaps of blood, some with their hands cut off, some decapitated, some with their bellies ripped open. Flies would buzz around them in the hot sun and cluster in their mouths and ears.

And yet, the Greeks did not manage to storm the city. Troy stood firm.

CHAPTER FIVE

THE DIRTY WAR

I t is probably a sunny day, but then, it usually is a sunny day on the Gulf of Edremit. Imagine the sky and sea as a cascade of light blue wildflowers, crocuses, windflowers, chicory, and bell-flowers. The meadow is an ocean of grass punctuated by islands of juniper shrubs and an elm tree for shade. Here in the shadow of woody Mount Plakos, the only sounds are the herdsman's pipe and the occasional bleating of the glossy white sheep. The cattle are too intent on eating to make a sound. There are seven herdsmen, all sons of King Eëtion of Thebes-under-Plakos, a city at the head of the gulf. They were half-brothers whose mothers were Eëtion's wives. They are not quite slumming, these princes tending the animals, since the herds are the wealth of the kingdom, but they are blessedly free of the court and its cares. We might imagine that they have nothing on their minds except horseplay, wine, and how to find willing servant girls—when suddenly, an enraged boar comes running out of the woods.

That is, it seems like a boar but in fact it is a man. Brilliant, swift-footed Achilles, the equal of the war-god Ares, is covered with bronze and carrying a shield and a giant spear of ash tipped with bronze. He is massive too, and he is coming at the boys at what seems like an impossible rate of speed. He screams something in Greek—

the words are foreign but the tone is hair-raising—and throws his javelin into the nearest herdsman's neck, and then he pulls out his sword and starts slashing. It is all over before they can take cover or beg or offer ransom or fight back. Seven unarmed princes, seven corpses, and one giant, sweating and panting and smeared with his victims' blood. And he is richer by a very fine herd of cattle and sheep.

Or so Homer tells the tale. The real Achilles was no doubt accompanied on the raid by a platoon of his men, the Myrmidons, his faithful comrades who loved war and fought ferociously.

We would also expect to find Achilles' right-hand man at his side, Patroclus son of Menoetius. Patroclus played a role in the Myrmidons akin to that in the Egyptian army of the top general Horemheb, who was "Sole Companion, he who is by the feet of the lord on the battlefield on that day of killing Asiatics." In other words, Patroclus was Achilles' chief deputy, and no mean commander in his own right. He was murderous on the battlefield but gentle off it, having learned a thing or two since boyhood, when he killed a playmate in a fit of rage during a game of dice. Later Greek writers made Achilles and Patroclus lovers, and perhaps they were, but Homer doesn't say so.

Achilles is the main character of Homer's *Iliad*. The writer focuses our attention on the alternately brooding and bloodthirsty character of the supposed ninth year of the war. But he also offers glimpses of earlier days when Achilles was less emotional, more pragmatic, and more effective.

Homer says nothing about the notorious heel. He does not mention the tale that Achilles' mother, Thetis, dipped her infant son in the River Styx and made nearly all his body invulnerable, except the heel that she held him by. Those details are probably later additions to the story. Homer's Achilles receives a lot of help from the gods but he is mortal.

Like Greece's other great generals, Achilles had an instinct for asymmetry. The Greeks fought war in two dimensions, land and sea, which encouraged them to think creatively. The Trojans acted as if the aim of their policy should be to destroy the enemy's military power. The Greeks' goal was to destroy *all* sources of support for the hostile state, including its economy and even its prestige. And Achilles was the hammer of destruction.

Achilles came from Phthia, a region in central Greece at the raw edge of Bronze Age Greek civilization. He embodied the best and the worst of the era, its talent and its violence. In all the Greek army no one could match Achilles for his looks or physique. He was tall and striking, and his handsome face was crowned with a mane of long, dirty-blond hair. Modesty was not a heroic virtue, and Achilles would have agreed. He calls himself big and beautiful, and further-more, he says:

> *None of the bronze-wearing Greeks is my equal*
> *In war, although some are better than me in the assembly.*

Achilles was temperamental, but when he was in the mood he couldn't get enough of battle. Combat was his road to what every hero wanted: fame, glory, and honor.

In what Homer calls the ninth year of the war, Achilles claimed to have destroyed no fewer than twenty-three cities, which comes to about two and one-half attacks annually. If twenty-three is an exaggeration, it is not out of line with Bronze Age hyperbole. For instance, the eastern Anatolian king Anum-Hirbi (ca. 1800 B.C.) claims that the enemy destroyed twelve of his towns and Hittite texts record similar claims. If the Greeks had originally hoped to terrify Troy into surrender when they landed, they failed. But when Troy made its strategy of forward defense work, the Greeks employed a counterstrategy of slow strangulation. They raided Trojan territory, especially beyond the well-defended plain of Troy, and they carried out two sorts of operations: ambushes of civilians outside Troy's walls and assaults on Trojan settlements and nearby cities friendly to Troy.

The Greek camp at Troy had several functions and one of them was that of naval station: it made a convenient jumping-off place for attacks. Because they enjoyed command of the sea, the Greeks could strike the long Trojan coastline virtually at will. So they ransacked cities; carried off Trojan women, treasure, and livestock; killed some leading men, ransomed others, and sold most of the rest as slaves on the islands of Lemnos, Imbros, and Samos.

The Greeks were not the only sea raiders of the era. Pharaoh Amenhotep III (1382–1344 B.C.), for example, had trouble with Shardana pirates. The Lycians of southwestern Anatolia were another group with a reputation for piracy. Amenhotep's son, pharaoh Akhenaten (1350–1334 B.C.) was plagued by Lycian sea raiders who seized Egyptian towns year after year; Akhenaten accused a Cypriot king of providing aid and comfort to the Lycians.

Greek plundering raids, of which the *Iliad* offers many anecdotes, served several purposes. Loot was a morale booster for wavering Greek soldiers. The raids offered a break from the boredom of camp life. More important, the raids secured food and fodder for poorly supplied Greek forces. For example, Odysseus and his men stormed and sacked the city of Ismarus in Thrace, a Trojan ally. And this was just on their way home.

Livestock loomed large in the Late Bronze Age's list of booty. Egyptian, Mesopotamian, and Hittite texts, for instance, often list it as a coveted prize of war. Among the Greeks, raiding cattle, horses, and sheep was honorable, profitable, and violent. When Attarissiya (Atreus?) attacked the kingdom of Madduwatta in southwestern Anatolia around 1400 B.C. he targeted cattle and sheep. Homer mentions various wars in Greece fought over cattle thieving, and it was not unusual for noblemen to die in the process. Helen's brother, for example, the Spartan prince Castor, was killed in one such raid. And cattle raiding could disrupt an enemy's economy and society. For instance, one Melanippus son of Hicetaon was a kinsman of Hector and an important figure in the town of Percote on the Dardanelles. When the Greeks came after his cattle, he prudently moved to Troy and was put up by Priam. Melanippus saved his skin and lived to fight in the Trojan army, but he was no longer a force of law and order in Percote—assuming that the town survived a visit by the Greeks.

Slaving was lucrative as well. Anatolian slaves were prized in Greece, no doubt in part because of stereotypes about slavish easterners that were common in classical Greece. But Anatolians fetched high prices in the Bronze Age for a more practical reason: in general, they were better-educated, more sophisticated, and more highly skilled than ordinary Greeks. Civilization had deeper roots in the East than in Greece; literacy was more widespread, cities more common. Myth records that Greeks imported engineers from Lycia to build the stunning fortification walls of the city of Tiryns in the Peloponnesus.

Achilles once described the attacks on the cities as a matter of "making war on other men over their women." But he was speaking to Agamemnon then and bitter over their quarrel about a woman. Captive women feature prominently on Egyptian and Hittite booty lists as well as on Linear B tablets that inventory the wealth of Greek kings. And yet women were only a small part of the loot that the Greeks amassed.

Finally, the assaults on other cities hurt Troy, which had connections of marriage and presumably of friendship and alliance with at least some of them. Some had given Troy expensive "gifts" of gold and silver and others might have sold supplies to the beleaguered city. Of the towns that Achilles sacked, eleven were in the vicinity of Troy. Greek attacks harassed civilians and insulted Trojan honor, and they picked off vulnerable allies. Unable to lay siege to Troy, the Greeks inflicted an indirect punishment on it.

How many people—like Melanippus of Percote—left the countryside for safety behind the great city's walls? As a practical matter, only those who, like him, had family in Troy to support them, could have afforded food and shelter in the big city. Most people would probably have needed to rely on local strongholds, which lacked the security of Troy's ramparts, hoping that the Greeks did not come to their corner of the Troad. But there were surely some refugees in Troy, an excess population that could only have increased pressure on the infrastructure of the town.

Needless to say, the Greeks considered it fair game to attack any Trojan civilian who ventured out to do business, even women going to the spring to fetch water. Homer mentions two springs of the Scamander River that flowed into basins

Where Trojan dames (ere yet alarm'd by Greece)
Wash'd their fair garments in the days of peace.

This is reminiscent of the Canaanite *Kirta Epic* (1300s B.C.) in which women flee from the woods, threshing floors, springs, and fountains for shelter in the cities and towns when the enemy invades "like locusts."

We hear nothing about Trojan counter-expeditions to defend the cities that the Greeks attacked. Either they lacked the resources to protect any place except their home territory or Homer has left out the initial details. Archaeology shows that two towns at the southern end of the Trojan Plain were fortified. They were located outside the entrance to a pass that led southward through the hills of the Mount Ida massif. Conceivably, Trojan soldiers manned these forts and sallied out to attack Greeks traveling overland. But the Greeks seem to have had no such worries farther away from Troy, on the periphery of the Troad. Taking Troy was hard work; taking Thebes-under-Plakos was a romp in the meadow.

Years after the war, King Nestor of Pylos remembered Achilles as having shone especially in the sea raids. And well he might have, since Nestor profited from one such raid on the island of Tenedos, from the spoils of which Nestor was awarded the lovely Hecamede, as hostess, servant, and bedmate. She was the daughter of a great man named Arsinous, and she had beautiful hair and divine looks.

A Roman-era collection of myths names seventeen cities that Achilles is supposed to have sacked and adds that there were "many others." But this late source cannot be trusted. Much better to follow the *Iliad*, which specifies six of the cities sacked by Achilles: besides Thebes-under-Plakos, they were Lyrnessus and Pedasus, both in the Troad; and Lesbos, Tenedos, Scyros: all islands, and presumably the main town is meant in each instance, as Homer specifies in the case of Scyros. On the east coast of Lesbos, excavation turned up a Bronze Age city at Thermi that was violently destroyed in the 1200s. Each of the islands supplied a beautiful woman to one of the Greek heroes: in addition to Nestor's Hecamede, there were Iphis, a Scyrian woman who slept with Patroclus, and Diomede daughter of Phorbas of Lesbos, who slept with Achilles (at least in the absence of his favorite female, Briseis). Among the many trophies in Agamemnon's collection were seven beautiful women from Lesbos.

It is a good guess that the weapons used in the attacks on the islands were naval pikes, which the Greeks carried on their ships for sea battles. These were long spears, allegedly forty feet, jointed by iron rings, and tipped with bronze points. Naval battles in the Bronze Age are not well documented, but it is clear that they were mainly attacks on personnel rather than attempts to destroy ships. This is suggested by recently discovered, fragmentary images from Greek vases of the 1100s B.C.

Perhaps the earliest recorded naval battle took place between Hittite and Cypriot ships during the reign of the Hittite King Shuppiluliuma II (1207–? B.C.). But no details survive: around the same time, ca. 1187, there was a battle between Egyptian ships and those of the Sea Peoples and it is well illustrated on a sculpted Egyptian relief. Both sides' vessels carry archers and marines armed with pikes, swords, and shields. The prows of the Sea Peoples' ships have posts ending in duckbill-shaped projections, and these may have served as a kind of ram. The Egyptians are supported by archers on shore as well. A different source, Minoan and Mycenaean images of sieges, shows ships approaching fortified cities and men drowning, presumably battle casualties.

On the mainland, Lyrnessus and Pedasus were taken on the same operation as Thebes-under-Plakos. The order in which the cities were attacked is not known. None of the sites has been securely identified, but Homer does supply some hints, so it is an educated guess that all three cities were on the northern shore of the Gulf of Edremit.

It was no doubt after killing the princes that Achilles led the Greeks to sack Thebes-under-Plakos. In theory the Greeks could have reached the city on foot from their camp at Troy but in between lies rugged country. It would have been easier, faster, and cheaper to go by sea. Safer too, since the Trojans could not stop the Greek navy.

Located in Mysia, the town gave its name to what was then called the Plain of Thebes (today, the Plain of Edremit). Achilles calls the town the "holy city of Eëtion," after the king. Eëtion is probably a non-Greek name; Homer calls the people whom Eëtion rules Cilicians (not to be confused with the better-known Cilicians of southern Anatolia). Plakos, at whose foot Thebes sat, was a wooded mountain, perhaps a spur of Mount Ida.

To conquer Thebes-under-Plakos, Achilles would have needed a detachment of ships and men that was large enough to take on a fairsized town without depleting Greek forces at their beachhead camp and leaving them vulnerable to attack. The Trojans never took advantage of the enemy's temporary weakness. Whether they missed their chance or whether the Greeks carefully kept troop strength high at their camp by sending out only small groups, we do not know. Another possibility is successful deception: for instance, the Greeks might have lit extra fires at night to hide the raiders' absence.

An educated guess is that Thebes-under-Plakos was a city of one thousand people that could muster around three hundred fighting men. Although described as "high-gated," Thebes-under-Plakos's fortifications are not likely to have presented much of a challenge compared to those of Troy. Imagine that the Greeks enjoyed manpower superiority of three to one: a comfortable if not huge advantage. In that case the Greeks would have needed nine hundred men or eighteen penteconters, assuming the soldiers did their own rowing. In addition to spearmen, the Greek force would have required archers and slingers to provide covering fire for the soldiers assaulting the city. They would also have needed ladders, which would be raised and climbed by veterans of earlier assaults. In the best-case scenario they would also have brought a battering ram. In any case, the mission to Thebes-under-Plakos was a success: "we destroyed it and brought everything here [to the camp at Troy]," said Achilles afterward.

It began with the long ships putting out from the shore at Troy and heading south. They would have rounded the rocky coast of Cape Lekton, oars striking rhythmically. Heading eastward along the southern shore of the Troad, they would have had to their starboard the island of Lesbos, its outline shimmering in the day's heat. They would have passed scrub-covered hills and sheer gray cliffs, and heard the distant braying of donkeys. They would have passed the dry gullies of the summer months, when the snow has long disappeared from the slopes of Mount Ida above. Finally, they would have reached Mysia. The Myrmidons would have leaped off the vessels as they were anchoring, following their chief, Achilles, toward the walled acropolis on the hill above.

When the Greeks took Thebes-under-Plakos, Achilles killed King Eëtion. Achilles is said to have shown respect to the man's corpse, which he cremated along with the king's armor and then buried under a mound of earth. Considering the usual practice of stripping an enemy's armor, this showed high respect. Was Achilles' gesture a nod toward Eëtion's in-laws? The king's son-in-law was Hector, who had married Eëtion's daughter, Andromache, and brought her to Troy. "The distant Trojans never injured me," Achilles said in protest to Agamemnon, later on. He spoke out of anger, but his chivalry to the dead Eëtion suggests that Achilles meant it.

As for the other men of Thebes-under-Plakos who survived the battle, the few wealthiest might be ransomed, some of the others would be sold into slavery, and the rest would be slaughtered. The women and children would be enslaved; the beautiful women from noble houses would become mistresses of the Greek heroes, while others, we might guess, were forced to serve as camp whores.

The Greeks took all of the king's treasures, aside from his armor; we know of two items that Achilles kept: a lyre and an iron weight, used in athletic contests—in the Bronze Age, iron was relatively rare and expensive. As for the lyre, Achilles enjoyed sitting in his hut at Troy and playing the clear-toned instrument:

(The well wrought harp from conquered Thebae came;
Of polish'd silver was its costly frame.)
With this he soothes his angry soul, and sings
The immortal deeds of heroes and of kings.

Achilles also acquired a superb horse named Pedasos. The queen of Thebes-under-Plakos was exchanged for a hefty ransom, no doubt paid by her Trojan in-laws. Andromache and Hector took in the ransomed queen but she died in their house "of Artemis's arrows," that is, perhaps of a heart attack or stroke. The Trojan connection gave the Greeks an additional motive for sacking Thebes-under-Plakos: the city was probably a Trojan ally, supplying "gifts" or intelligence or rendering some other service, although apparently it did not send soldiers. The destruction of Thebes-under-Plakos deprived Troy of logistical support and struck a blow against morale.

One of the captive women was a visitor from a nearby city. Chryseis daughter of Chryses came from the city of Chryse in the southwestern Troad, about twenty-five miles from Thebes-under-Plakos. According to an ancient commentary on Homer, she had come to visit the queen of Thebes-under-Plakos for a religious function, which is appropriate, since her father was an important priest of the god Apollo. The unlucky girl was shipped off to the Greek camp, where she was given to Agamemnon as a mistress. It would prove to be a fatal connection, indirectly responsible for the quarrel between Agamemnon and Achilles and its bloody consequences. But at the time, the Greeks might have looked on the capture of Chryseis as a real coup.

Lyrnessus also fell to the Greeks on the Thebes-under-Plakos campaign. As at Thebes-under-Plakos, the assault began with a cattle raid. Achilles almost caught a very big man among the livestock: Aeneas son of Anchises, prince of the junior branch of the royal house of Troy, and a leader in battle and council. We may imagine the scene:

Aeneas had been standing unarmed in the countryside, checking his cattle, the mainstay of his wealth, when the enemy arrived without warning. Suddenly Aeneas might have envisioned his fat heifers and thick-necked bulls slipping through his fingers as weightlessly as gold dust. But there was no time to cry: unless he leapt down the paths of sacred Mount Ida, his linen tunic fluttering out behind him, his leather sandals flying over rocks and tree roots, the massive Greek warrior behind him would have thrust his bronze-tipped spear into the Trojan's back. Normally Aeneas was a lion in battle who could slice through a man's throat with his spear, but with Achilles after him, he had to race down the hill like a runaway slave girl. Miraculously, he outran Achilles, all the way to Lyrnessus. As Aeneas explained afterward:

> *Zeus*
> *Preserved me, He roused my courage and my nimble knees.*

Aeneas escaped Achilles, but the people of Lyrnessus did not. We can imagine their struggle as well. The arms of the Greeks stretched over the countryside and then fell on the town, not that the men who attacked it knew what Lyrnessus was called—or cared. Chances are that they were drunk, scared, homesick, and eager to take it all out on the enemy. The men of Lyrnessus stood before the gate, more steadfast than a row of bricks. The Greeks unleashed a storm of arrows and sling stones that pushed the defenders back. The Lyrnessians prayed to the god Kurunta, Lord of the Stag and their protector, but he had already abandoned them. They could not stop the enemy from hacking at the town gate or from dragging their ladders up against the walls. A blare of horns, a volley of arrows, a roar as the Greeks topped the battlements, and it was over. The defenders died choking on their own blood or staring with terror at a severed arm or curling up beside a dying horse with a spear-torn belly.

The Greeks surely found killing exhausting work, especially after having rowed to Lyrnessus in the hot sun. They also had their own dead and wounded to look after. Some soldiers tended their comrades' injuries with herbs and bandages. A surgeon operated on a man with a grave head wound. The only hope was to drain the swollen cranium by removing a portion of the skull. Known as trepanning, it was an ancient procedure and a desperate one. It rarely worked.

The other Greeks dealt with the defeated. There was livestock to round up and jewels to loot. Any Lyrnessian males who had survived were sold into slavery on the Aegean islands. Some of the women were raped on the spot, and they all were dragged off as prizes of war. The women's future lay in hauling water jugs from Greek wells, weaving wool on Greek looms, and warming the beds of the Greek warriors who had destroyed their lives. Their last memory of home was the sight of their menfolk's corpses stripped naked by Greek scavengers and already attracting flies.

Achilles killed two princes at Lyrnessus, Mynes and Epistrophus, both of whom died fighting in a battle of spears. Their father, Evenus son of Selipiades and king of Lyrnessus, was presumably killed as well. Achilles also slew three brothers of the noblewoman Briseis, who saw them die, as well as Mynes, who appears to have been her husband.

In Homer, Briseis, Helen, Andromache, and Hecuba all watch battles from the walls. Minoan and Mycenaean art also show women doing so. A relief on a silver drinking cup from Mycenae depicts six women looking out at the fighting, waving and gesturing in excitement to the men below. But would real women in the Bronze Age have played such an assertive role, and such a risky one, where they might have been hit by an enemy arrow? Probably yes. When the Pharaoh Kamose (ca. 1550 B.C.) took a fleet up the Nile to attack the city of Avaris, he saw the enemy's women peering out at him from the walls. Better-documented, later periods of ancient Greek history offer a few examples of women spectators during a siege. Nor should we discount the morale value to the defenders of seeing their women on the walls. Indeed, both sides in Homer evoke the women and families for whom they are fighting. The presence of women also served as a taunt to the enemy.

Briseis was taken captive along with the other women of Lyrnessus. She ended up as Achilles' mistress. As she was led off, Briseis wept. She couldn't get over the horror: having witnessed the deaths of her three brothers and her husband she would have to sleep with their killer. But Patroclus comforted her. As she said to him later:

Thy friendly hand uprear'd me from the plain,
And dried my sorrows for a husband slain. . . .

Patroclus promised Briseis a high status, saying that Achilles would bring her to Greece and marry her. This was generous and no doubt astute since Patroclus knew Achilles well enough to recognize a woman who could win the hero's heart.

Achilles' conduct during these raids says a lot about the laws of war, such as they were, in the Late Bronze Age. Achilles might well have nodded in approval at the Hittite King Hattushilish I's description of a victory: "I trampled the country of Hassuwa like a lion and like a lion I slew [it] and I brought dust [down] upon them and I took all their possessions with me and filled Hattusa [with it]." Or, as Pharaoh Seti I (1294–1279 B.C.) put it, an instant of trampling the foe is better than a day of jubilation. For Seti, "trampling" meant slaughter, annihilation, and filling valleys with corpses stretched out in their own blood. And he specifically singles out for the slaughter heirs as well as their fathers. The troops of Pharaoh Merneptah (1212–1203 B.C.) took more than nine thousand hands and penises as trophies in a battle in 1208 with Libyan aggressors: common practice in Late Bronze Age Egypt. The Assyrian king Shalmaneser I (1274–1245 B.C.) boasted of having 14,400 enemy captives blinded or, as some say, just having their right eye gouged out. Judging by such acts, the Greeks were not especially brutal; they were playing by the rules of the day.

By Seti's rules, killing heirs was common sense, and that was reason enough for Achilles to mow down the seven royal brothers outside Thebes-under-Plakos. But they were hardly an immediate threat. The herdsmen princes might have carried daggers for protection, but as far as we know they were otherwise unarmed. Did Achilles and the Myrmidons deliberately attack and kill civilians? By today's standards, Achilles might be judged a war criminal.

But we must remember that the princes of Thebes-under-Plakos were not civilians but potential soldiers who could have put on their armor in minutes. Achilles had every right to round them up or even to kill them if they continued to resist or if no guards were available. No doubt he would have kept the princes alive if possible, since his usual practice was not to kill his enemies but, rather, to ransom them or to sell them into slavery on one of the Aegean islands. As Achilles explains late in the war, after he had turned more brutal:

I used to like to spare Trojans,
And I took many alive and sold them.

A case in point is the Trojan prince Lycaon, one of Priam's sons. Achilles ambushed the lad one night while Lycaon was in the royal orchard outside Troy, furtively cutting young fig wood to use for chariot rails—in other words, Lycaon was on a military mission. Achilles' operation was a stakeout. It brought little glory but potentially a lot of profit, and the great Achilles did not hesitate to stoop to conquer.

Lycaon was a valuable commodity; Achilles spared the boy and sold him for a good price, one hundred oxen as well as a gift to Patroclus of a Phoenician silver mixing bowl. The buyer was a Greek nobleman, Euneus, on Lemnos, son of the famous Jason the Argonaut. But luckily for Lycaon, a family friend stepped in: Eëtion of the island of Imbros ransomed Lycaon for three hundred oxen—which means that the Lemnian made a hefty profit (assuming that a Phoenician silver bowl cost considerably less than two hundred oxen). Once freed, Lycaon took ship for Arisbe, a city on the Dardanelles, and then made his way home to Troy.

Lycaon was not a civilian and he would not have been better off if he had been, since civilians had few rights in Bronze Age warfare. If his city was conquered and he was caught, a civilian would be lucky to suffer mere slavery and not death. But it was better not to be caught, even if that meant heading for the hills. Consider, for example, the people of Apasa (probably the later Ephesus), capital of the western Anatolian kingdom of Arzawa, when it was conquered by the Hittite King Murshilish II around 1315 B.C. Most of the population fled, many of them to nearby Mount Arinnanda, probably today's Samsun Dağ, the classical Mount Mycale. This is a long and high summit, climbing from sea level to four thousand feet. Murshilish reports that the terrain was too rocky and overgrown for as-

cending on horseback. So his army went after the refugees on foot—
allegedly with the king himself in the lead. It was, says Murshilish,
a battle against the mountain, and the king won.

The loser, of course, was not the mountain but the huge mass of
Arzawan refugees, the bulk of whom, says Murshilish, were starved
out. Before winter came, the Arzawans surrendered, even though
they no doubt knew what lay ahead: like other conquered peoples before them, they would be shipped back to Hatti as "deportees," a class
of unfree laborers condemned to menial work—they and their children. Murshilish says that the total number of deportees was beyond
measure, but the royal share alone came to 6,200 people.

Whatever booty the Greeks grabbed on their raids belonged to
the entire army and not to individuals. It was shared according to the
number of men who had participated in the action, with the leader
entitled to an extra cut. Each man's share was known as his *geras*, his
"gift of honor" or "prize." But sometimes it was a poison gift: fights
over the division of the spoils are documented in later Greek history,
and so were mutinies by sailors over their pay. When, toward the end
of the war, a quarrel over plunder broke out in the Greek camp, probably few people were surprised.

Raiding was a mixed blessing for the Greeks. It prolonged the
war, and protracted wars are often as hard on the attacker as on the
defender. The Greeks may have amassed mountains of loot in their
beachhead camp, but the walls of Troy stood as strong as ever. The
result would have been frustration, exhaustion, and anger among the
attackers. Although he is one of the few who remained optimistic,
Agamemnon nicely summarizes the Greek army's gloom:

> *Now shameful flight alone can save the host,*
> *Our blood, our treasure, and our glory lost.*

CHAPTER SIX

AN ARMY IN TROUBLE

Bronze Age soldiers were well-known gripers, and fisticuffs provided an opportunity to let off steam without serious bloodshed. But, as the war dragged on, things were getting out of hand. The supreme commander, Agamemnon son of Atreus, and the best of the Greeks, Achilles son of Peleus, had done something worse than come to blows. They had split the coalition. And the ugliest man who had come to Troy had seen it happen.

So Homer describes him: Thersites was stoop-shouldered, hollow-chested, lame, and his pointy-looking skull was nearly bald—the signs, perhaps, of a congenital disorder in skeletal development. And he had a mouth to match his form. In the manner of a put-down comic, he specialized in insulting men such as Achilles and Odysseus, which was sure to draw a crowd and to make the men laugh.

They needed to laugh, now more than ever. For nine days an epidemic had gripped the camp. It started with the mules and the dogs, then it spread to the men. Infection followed a trajectory like that of anthrax, plague, SARS, avian flu, and the many other diseases spread from animals to human, but no specific illness can be identified from Homer's brief description. It is enough to know that the beach at Troy was crowded with funeral pyres.

When the pyres were lit, smoke billowed out from the softwood used for kindling. It was "evil smelling smoke," as a Bronze Age king put it, because the fumes concentrated the odor of decomposing human flesh. Not until the fire had heated up enough to make the oak logs burn did the billows give way to a red glow and to the aroma of burning meat. Then it was possible to forget that this was a mass cremation in a war zone. But the stink had been unmistakable all the way across the plain, where the wind blew into the city and made the Trojans cry tears of bitter joy.

At the best of times the Greek camp was no rose garden. It smelled of butchered sheep, goats, and cattle; of cooking spices, doused fires, latrines, animal dung, and human sweat. There were flies and mosquitoes, and mice; fleas too. Flea bites became infected from time to time. Lice were everywhere. And there would have been a host of minor illnesses, the sort that always plague travelers (although Homer says nothing of them), from the common cold to diarrhea.

Malaria had been a major problem around Troy until recent years. Did it exist there as early as the Bronze Age? Biomolecular science may one day provide an answer, but we don't yet know. Homer possibly refers to malaria in the *Iliad* when Priam notes how the dog days of summer "bring much fever to wretched mortals." This season was associated with malaria from Roman times on. Imperial Rome managed to achieve grandeur in spite of endemic malaria. Trojans could have survived the disease by adopting so-called avoidance behaviors in malaria season, such as keeping clear of the wet, low-lying areas at night and sleeping with shuttered windows—just as Romans did.

The wind on Troy's hill would have protected the city itself from mosquitoes. But the Greek army, camped in the swampy lowlands, would have been at high risk. The effect on soldiers would have varied widely. For some, malaria would have been devastating, as it frequently was to armies of northerners who attacked Rome. But other Greeks would have shrugged off the illness. Adults who come from areas where malaria is rife are generally immune to the disease, having survived repeated childhood infections.

Whatever the cause of the epidemic, on the tenth day Achilles called an assembly on the beach beside the hollow ships. It was here that the quarrel broke out. The prophet Calchas, no friend of the son of Atreus, made a terrible announcement: Apollo had sent the epidemic to punish the Greeks for having turned a deaf ear to his priest, Chryses, who served at the shrine of Apollo Smintheus in the southern Troad.

Ten days earlier, Chryses had come to the Greek camp to beg for the return of his captured daughter, Chryseis. He offered the Greeks a generous ransom, which would no doubt have been accepted, except that Agamemnon wouldn't give her up. In fact, he threatened to have her father killed if he didn't leave the Greek camp immediately and never return.

The episode typifies Bronze Age religion in western Anatolia, a region with special interest in epidemics and their cure, that is, magical cure. Hittite and other ancient rituals used against disease commonly blame a god, whether local or an enemy's, for making people sick. The Hittites blamed epidemics on the god's anger. Western Anatolians were used to the connection between gods and illness, since the local war-god Iyarri was also the god of pestilence, and he was called "Lord of the Bow"—similar to Apollo "of the glorious bow." In northwestern Anatolia and especially in the Troad, Apollo was worshipped as Apollo Smintheus, a god of mice and plague. A shrine to him stood near the city of Chryse at least as early as 700 B.C. and possibly in the Bronze Age too.

Calchas, backed up by Achilles, put the king on the spot. Bronze Age kings hated bad news and had a tendency to blame the messenger. The Hittite King Hattushilish I, for example, had exploded at the men who reported that their battering ram had broken during a siege: he said he hoped that the Storm God washed them away! Agamemnon in turn snarled at Calchas. But in the end, the king grudgingly agreed to give back Chryseis. Then he upped the ante by demanding compensation with another "prize," that is, another girl. "What girl?" said Achilles, coming right back at him. And with that, the center of gravity moved from the tug-of-war over a woman to the fight between two warrior-kings, a clash that had been a long time coming. The outward problem was the division of loot, but the real issue was honor. Of the various heroes who vied for the right to be called "best of the Greeks," none hated each other more than Achilles and Agamemnon. Achilles found fault with Agamemnon for taking the lion's share of the booty even though Achilles did most of the sacking of cities. Agamemnon found Achilles insolent and uppity. Achilles lacked respect for Agamemnon's preeminence as Greece's leading king, while Agamemnon felt threatened by Achilles' preeminence as a warrior.

So the two men began by calling each other names: Achilles called Agamemnon greedy, shameless, and cowardly. Agamemnon countered by threatening to take Achilles' girl. Then Achilles raised the temperature by threatening to take his ships and men and go home to Phthia, to which Agamemnon responded by making it official: he was coming after Briseis, Achilles' prize girl.

Visibly furious, Achilles gripped the silver hilt of his great sword and started to draw it out of the sheath. For a moment it looked like he was going to rush the king. But after hesitating, he pushed the sword back in again. Out poured another torrent of abuse, and then came an oath. Achilles and his men would not fight for the Greeks any longer. Achilles hurled the speaker's scepter onto the ground.

Agamemnon moved swiftly to return Chryseis. First the whole army had to purify itself by washing and then it had to sacrifice oxen and goats to Apollo. Agamemnon ordered a twenty-oared ship hauled down to the shore to bring Chryseis back to her father. The return of the priest's daughter was a sensitive, high-prestige mission. Agamemnon chose his crew carefully, selecting as captain the shrewd diplomat Odysseus, and picking men, who were, says Homer, "the youths of the Achaeans"—probably, all nobles.

The ship was about thirty-five feet long. Between the two files of rowers, bulls were loaded to be given to Chryses for sacrifice to Apollo. Chryseis sat on the raised quarterdeck, on a chair under a canopy. In addition to her, Odysseus, and the twenty oarsmen, the ship no doubt carried a few seamen, and a herdsman for the cattle; the oarsmen might have stowed their arms below their seats. The mast was up, the sail unfurled, and the ship took advantage of what little breeze there was.

When they reached the harbor of Chryse, the men took down the mast and sail and rowed the ship into a protected corner. Then they moored her, stern first. To hold the ship in place, a pair of stone anchors was dropped from the bows, and stern lines from each quarter were run onto the shore and carefully secured. The crew pulled down a gangplank and disembarked the bulls. Then Chryseis stepped ashore. Escorted by Odysseus she walked to a nearby altar, where she was delivered into the eager hands of her father.

What followed next was, from the Greeks' point of view, the heart of the matter: a sacrifice to Apollo to lift the epidemic that he had called down on them. Archaeology confirms Homer's description, showing that Bronze Age Greeks such as the warriors in the *Iliad* slaughtered bulls as a sacrifice to the gods and then, after cooking the meat, ate most of it in a ceremonial meal. In fact, at Thebes, a sacrifice of about fifty animals—sheep, goats, pigs, and cattle—seems to have been enough to give a taste to each of a thousand people!

Around the altar the men arranged the bulls, a Greek gift that, as a cynic might have noted, had been looted from the people of the Troad. There followed a ritual washing of hands and sprinkling of barley groats on the victims. Then Chryses lifted his hands skyward and prayed to Apollo on behalf of the Greeks. The cattle were slaughtered, flayed, then butchered according to ritual. A fire had been prepared, over which the priest now burned, on a wooden spit, the god's portion—the thighbones plus pieces of raw meat drawn from each leg, all doused with wine. Meanwhile, the innards were roasted and passed around to be eaten by all the worshippers.

So much for the ritual: at this point the rest of the meat was carved up and cooked on five-pronged forks. Wine cups and mixing bowls were brought out. After the wine was mixed with water, every cup was filled to the brim, beginning with a few drops in each cup to be sprinkled on the ground as an offering to the gods.

After feasting, the young Greeks chanted a hymn to Apollo and danced. Homer says they spent the entire day in song and ceremony until night fell. But having traveled about forty nautical miles by ship from Troy to Chryse, after having returned Chryseis, sacrificed oxen, cooked the meat, and having feasted and drunk, they would not have had much daylight left. The song and dance would have lasted an hour or two, until the exhausted men fell asleep beside their ship.

The paean was a prayer for all seasons and occasions, from war to weddings. An appeal for deliverance or a hymn of thanksgiving, a paean could be elaborate or simple but it always included the chant, *Iē Paian, Iē Paian,* which was mysterious and ancient, since the word *Paian* dates back to the Bronze Age.

The paean was no bacchanal; it was meant to be dignified. Perhaps the singing followed the pattern of Hittite music, where singers were divided into two groups, often a soloist and a responding choir. One example is even called "the song of the bulls," which would have fit the scene at Chryse. But twenty-odd tired and drunken young men, deliriously happy at the thought of delivery from an epidemic, were probably not very dignified.

Meanwhile, at the Greek camp, Agamemnon sent two heralds to bring him Briseis from Achilles' hut. Surprisingly, Achilles gave up the girl without a fuss.

But Briseis left Achilles' hut unwillingly. Perhaps she had come to identify with her captor, even to love him, a sort of ancient equivalent of Stockholm Syndrome. Or maybe Briseis simply reasoned that Agamemnon's bed would be worse than Achilles'. Maybe the clear-eyed girl was not a lost soul but a survivor.

Hard-boiled Greek warriors speak of their women as prizes of war. But we might suspect that they formed genuine attachments. Agamemnon says that he prefers Chryseis to his own wife. Among the cattle, cauldrons, and gold, she was flesh. She represented to the son of Atreus the world he missed.

After Briseis left him, Achilles sat on the beach and cried like a baby: tears of rage, to be sure, but perhaps of loss as well. He was not a happy man. Then again, who could be happy knowing as Achilles did that he was fated to die young? Like many other men in the epics, Achilles weeps freely and regularly.

Some philosophers and critics, beginning with Plato, censured Homer for making his heroes crybabies. But in doing so, Homer was following both Bronze Age poetry and Bronze Age life. For example, both the Mesopotamian (and Hittite) hero Gilgamesh and the Anatolian storm god Teshub cry in their respective poems; so does the Canaanite epic hero Kirta (1300s B.C.); so do the Egyptian Wenamun and the Philistine prince Beder of Dor in the Egyptian tale of Wenamun (eleventh century B.C.). And the Hittite king Hattushilish I (1650–1620 B.C.) disinherited his nephew and designated heir because the man failed to cry when Hattushilish lay sick and was expected to die.

Homer describes how Achilles appeals through the tears to his divine mother, Thetis, to have mighty Zeus himself intervene and bring ruin to the Greeks who had dishonored him. Whether or not they believed that divine blood flowed in the veins of the mighty, Bronze Age people expected that great men could lobby the gods for help. After all, a king was the favorite of the gods, as the Assyrian Tukulti-Ninurta asserted. He was a god and the sun, as Abi-Milki of Tyre told Pharaoh. He was the child of heaven and a guardian angel, as the mere governor of the Mesopotamian city of Nippur was addressed by one of his underlings.

Back in the Greek camp, the epidemic ended, but the military situation was worse than ever for the Greeks. The disease had caused a significant number of casualties, and Achilles had withdrawn from the fight. His men muttered about sailing home. The Myrmidons made up about 5 percent of the Greek force. And an oracle had said that the Greeks would not take Troy without Achilles. But we may posit a more practical concern, and that is, the Myrmidons were elite troops. Arguably, their specialty was the same as their leader's: speed. Homer frequently calls Achilles "fast runner." Achilles' strength was multiplied by his ability to outrun others. He was one of those rare warriors who on foot could kill a man on a chariot. Every hero worth his salt was expected to be able to fight both on foot and from a chariot. But few could overwhelm a chariot from the ground: Diomedes, on foot, knocks Phegeus off his chariot; Menelaus and Antilochus son of Nestor, working as a team, pick off a Trojan and his charioteer; Hector and Aeneas planned to overwhelm a Greek pair on a chariot but other Greeks showed up in time to stop them. Old Nestor as a young foot soldier had killed the enemy's best chariot-fighter.

We should expect that in each of these cases the hero(es) received help from his men. Not even swift-footed godlike Achilles could run down a chariot by himself. But ordinary soldiers would not be much help unless they were well equipped and well trained. Leadership was key. Homer notes that the Myrmidons were divided into five battalions and the roll call of their five leaders was: two sons of gods, the third-best spearman among the Myrmidons, a minor king who had taught Achilles the art of war, and a warrior knowledgeable enough to give tips in tactics to Achilles' charioteer. They were a cut above the mere mortals named in the Linear B tablets as commanding companies of soldiers or rowers at Pylos. Unit cohesion mattered as well, and the Myrmidons were solidity itself when they took the field:

> *Ranks wedged in ranks; of arms a steely ring*
> *Still grows, and spreads, and thickens round the king.*
> *As when a circling wall the builder forms,*
> *Of strength defensive against wind and storms,*
> *Compacted stones the thickening work compose,*
> *And round him wide the rising structure grows:*
> *So helm to helm, and crest to crest they throng,*
> *Shield urged on shield, and man drove man along;*
> *Thick, undistinguish'd plumes, together join'd,*
> *Float in one sea, and wave before the wind.*

The withdrawal of such an elite group might have demoralized the rest of the Greek army. Nearly two weeks had passed since Achilles had withdrawn from the war. But Agamemnon had dreamed that Zeus had decided to give the Greeks victory. Bronze Age peoples took dreams seriously as messages from the gods, as did their descendants in the Iron Age. King Naramsin of the Sumerian epic *The Curse of Agade* (ca. 2200–2000 B.C.), for example, saw the ruin of his city in a dream. A thousand years later, Hittite King Hattushilish III (1267–1237 B.C.) had a dream in which the goddess Ishtar promised success in a dangerous court case, and Pharaoh Merneptah (1213–1203 B.C.) received the sword of victory from the god Ptah in a dream. Seven hundred years after that, Herodotus reports how the Persian Emperor Xerxes dreamed during war councils over the planned invasion of Greece in 480 B.C. Agamemnon was so excited that he called a council of his generals to pass on the news. They agreed that it was time to get the men into their armor and onto the field. But Agamemnon suggested a slight delay: he would call an assembly first to test the men's morale.

The men, says Homer, thronged out to assembly like a swarm of insects. The massive gathering required nine heralds to obtain quiet so that the king could speak. Agamemnon stood up. Instead of telling the army the truth, which was that he had dreamt of victory, he pretended that the game was over: Zeus had decided for defeat. The boats were in poor shape, Agamemnon said:

> *Our cordage torn, decay'd our vessels lie,*
> *And scarce insure the wretched power to fly.*

This sad assessment recalls the lament of a Syrian general around 1340 B.C., writing to his overlord, the Hittite king, from a frontier outpost on the border with Egypt:

> *Now, for five months the cold has been gnawing me,*
> *my chariots are broken, my horses are dead, and my troops are lost.*

Agamemnon pretended that the war was lost and the only sensible thing to do was to go home:

> *Fly, Grecians, fly, your sails and oars employ,*
> *And dream no more of heaven-defended Troy.*

Agamemnon hoped to hear the men shout "No!" Instead, the men took him at his word and stampeded for the ships, behaving like conscripts running for their lives at the first sound of the enemy. Every army has its breaking point. The Greeks had turned into a mob—and not just the ordinary Greeks: heroes and kings ran too.

Odysseus's quick thinking saved the day. Borrowing Agamemnon's royal scepter, he ran into the multitude and restored order.

The scepter was part escutcheon and part relic. An ancient symbol, the scepter denoted kingship throughout the ancient world, for the Assyrian King Tukulti-Ninurta (1244–1208 B.C.) as well as for Agamemnon. The scepter stood for divine approval, as Odysseus put it:

> *To one sole monarch Jove commits the sway;*
> *His are the laws, and him let all obey.*

The Greeks did not make a good revolutionary mob, not least because they didn't believe in revolution. They wanted to trust their king.

Homer's account of what follows is amusing, but mutiny was serious business to Bronze Age commanders. With vicious wit Thersites expressed the misgivings that many must have felt about the king who had dishonored Greece's greatest fighting man. Thersites sneered at Agamemnon's arrogance and mocked his fellow soldiers' willingness to tolerate it:

> *Whate'er our master craves, submit we must,*
> *Plagued with his pride, or punish'ed for his lust.*
> *Oh women of Achaia; men no more!*
> *Hence let us fly, and let him waste his store*
> *In loves and pleasures on the Phrygian shore.*

Whether Thersites was a renegade noble, as some think, or simply a common man who was allowed to speak in the assembly, or even a traitor fomenting discontent to help the enemy, he gave voice to the longing for home felt by the ordinary Greeks at Troy. They were the ones who never got the best cuts of meat, if they got meat at all; the ones who never tasted fish; the ones who lived mainly on a diet of beans and barley, which surely left the air thick with foul odor. They washed down the food with young, unseasoned wine, rather than the fine Thracian vintages brought by ship to Agamemnon daily; they mixed their wine and water in wooden rather than silver bowls, and drank from plain pottery cups. They were usually short and wiry, often round-shouldered with bad teeth. They received less care than champion horses. No rubdowns with olive oil after a hot bath for them, no bronze tubs and no soft female hands to wash their backs. Most of their baths were in the salt sea, and they no doubt treasured the occasions when they got to take a dip in a river or a clear mountain spring. They had no perfume to offset the odors of sweat and sheepskin. They did not live in huts made of hewn fir and thatch roofs, as the heroes did. They slept in tents or in the hollow ships or outside on the shore, making it through winter as best they could by huddling around communal fires. The kings had rugs for pillows, the soldiers had leather shields. Their chairs were piles of brush and twigs covered with a goatskin throw, which did double duty as a bed—no lamb's wool rugs for them. They had no beautiful, enslaved princesses as bedmates, only quick trips to the camp whores.

They had come to Troy with one tunic each, as well as a homespun cloak and a pair of rawhide sandals—a basic pair, without the laces that made sandals fit comfortably to the foot. That is, if they were free: slaves were dressed in rags and went barefoot. And once the heroes had taken the pick of the booty, they had whatever was left along with whatever they could steal. Even so this was more than they could ever have hoped to put aside from a lifetime working the thin soil of Greece or herding another man's sheep or goats or cleaning out his pigsty.

They were oarsmen, stewards, cooks, grooms, and perhaps even farmers. They were the men who pulled the wooden chocks out from under the long ships at the moment of departure, the men who cast off the cables and hoisted the pinewood masts. They trooped into the hills to cut oak with axes made of dull bronze rather than sharp iron, gathered firewood, split kindling neatly, built and tended fires, stuffed goat intestines with blood and fat and then roasted them until they were sausage; carved meat; poured wine; gathered jugs of water from the river for drinking, for hand-washing before prayer or sacrifice and for heroes' bathing (loading them onto mules, if they were lucky, but otherwise toting the jugs themselves back to camp). They groomed the horses, dug defensive ditches, cut posts for palisades and hammered them into the ground, repitched the ships, dug trenches for latrines, cleaned the camp of animal dung. They picked up corpses, from which they had to shoo away swarms of flies, and hauled them onto the funeral pyres. They were indispensable to the expedition, but they counted for nothing in battle or council, as their betters were in the habit of telling them.

Some days they fasted until dusk because they worked so hard. A few of them talked back to their lords, like Thersites or the unnamed Trojan commoners who gainsaid Hector in the Trojan assembly, much to his annoyance. But most of them, we may suspect, were more likely to take their lord by the wrist and kiss his hand, whether out of devotion or fear. Agamemnon expected the common people to honor him like a god. Even a high-status noncombatant like Eurybates, Odysseus's herald, had to spend his days following the king and picking up the royal cloak when Odysseus dropped it. Do their job well and the men who counted for nothing could expect a pat on the back. If they were caught misbehaving they could expect a sharp blow, on the back or shoulders, with a stick.

Sometimes in the distance the Greeks could hear the sound of the dogs fighting. The wind carried the insistent, rhythmic, alternating barks and yelps of those bony beasts as they brawled over a bone, perhaps a man's bone that had been left out in the sun from some earlier engagement, or a human limb hacked off in battle. Other times, at night, when they sneaked up in a raid on a Trojan town, the men could hear the sound of prayers to the local god to deliver them from the "visitation of foreign dogs."

Odysseus needed to turn the tide. He said to Thersites,

Have we not known thee, slave! Of all our host,
The man who acts the least, upbraids the most?
Think not the Greeks to shameful flight to bring,
Nor let those lips profane the name of king.

Odysseus showed that Thersites was not the only Greek to know how to work an audience. He threatened that if he ever again heard such cheap sniping at Agamemnon from Thersites, he would strip off Thersites' clothes. He even refers disparagingly to the sight of Thersites' genitals, which strikes a rare and vulgar note for Homer. But soldiers are not known for their delicacy, and what soldier doesn't love to see that the general is just as rough as the next fellow? To finish Thersites off, Odysseus smashed his scepter down on Thersites' back hard enough to raise a welt and to reduce the man to tears.

The audience cracked up. Better to laugh at Thersites as a buffoon than to cry at their own spinelessness. The Hittites knew the value of slapstick humor: they had festivals in which one man hit another over the head three times with a club and another where one man poured hot coals over somebody's head, all for a laugh.

Now that Odysseus had broken the mutiny with some sharp, well-chosen words, it was time to rekindle the men's bellicosity. He had the herald quiet the crowd so he could speak again. The message was brisk and simple. Honor demanded that the Greeks stay and fight. He reminded the men of Calchas's prophecy at Aulis: the war would be long but they would emerge victorious.

Stately, patriarchal Nestor had a smooth voice but when it came to war, he didn't hesitate to pour oil on a fire. He spoke next. Like Odysseus, he pointed out the favor of the gods, in the form of an omen: lightning on the right as the ships first landed at Troy, a sign of Zeus's approval of their mission. Nestor showed that he too understood psychology by offering another answer to the implicit question of "why do we fight?" He said:

Encouraged hence, maintain the glorious strife,
Till every soldier grasp a Phrygian wife,

Till Helen's woes at full revenged appear,
And Troy's proud matrons render tear for tear.

Nestor also offered Agamemnon advice: he should call a muster of the entire army with the men arranged "by peoples and groups." This as a way of judging the quality of the army. Agamemnon got up and readily agreed. He told the men to fill their bellies, sharpen their swords, prepare their armor, feed their horses, and check their chariots: they were going to war.

There was a roar of approval from the men, a rush to the huts, a series of sacrifices to the gods, and the troops got ready for the muster. Agamemnon called his most trusted lieutenants to the ritual: Nestor, Idomeneus, the two Ajaxes, Diomedes, and Odysseus; Menelaus joined them on his own initiative. After the ceremony, these leading commanders fanned out across the camp to supervise, while heralds cried for the men to muster.

They came from their huts and shelters and ships: their polished shields gleamed, their marching shook the ground, and their numbers filled the plain like flocks of cranes or swans. The Greeks rallied, which leads to a famous moment in the *Iliad*, the so-called Catalog of Ships, in which the poet lists all the captains, kings, and countries who took part in the war.

Homer is not, as some critics think, merely exploiting the occasion to roll the credits, as it were. Instead, he is describing sound, simple, and standard military policy. For example, the conquering Hittite King Shuppiluliuma I (1344–1322 B.C.) stopped in southeastern Anatolia to review his troops and chariots before continuing onward to his goal, the siege of the city of Carchemish. From Pharaonic Egypt to Pennsylvania Avenue, parading the troops in review, unit by unit, has been a basic way of building morale. And if there was ever a force that needed its morale reestablished, it was the Greek army at Troy.

No general could have been dressed with more spit and polish, no titan could have bestrode the earth with greater satisfaction than royal Agamemnon did as he moved among his men,

Like some proud bull, that round the pastures leads
His subject herds. . . .

But Agamemnon was not overconfident. He knew that on the far side of the plain, Hector would be mustering his troops.

A smart general knows you cannot suppress a wartime mutiny without shedding blood. Nothing wipes the slate clean like a corpse. Not having executed anyone for the wild dash to the ships, Agamemnon did the only sensible thing he could do: he sent his men out to die.

CHAPTER SEVEN

THE KILLING FIELDS

When the Hittites went to war, they sang hymns to the war-god. Before battle, they would chant an old poem whose refrain asks that they be buried at home with their mothers. When, in the *Iliad*, the Trojans and their allies rush out against an unexpected Greek attack, they shout battle cries to steel themselves. The Greeks are as silent as a boxer conserving his energy for a knockout punch. Two armies approach each other on the Trojan Plain, barely visible through the dust raised by their marching feet.

Suddenly one man steps forward through the ranks on the Trojan side; another man dismounts from his chariot on the Greek side, which makes the Trojans retreat. Then, a third man, a huge figure, appears in the middle of the Trojan ranks and gestures with his long spear. All around him the soldiers sit down, and soon he is the only Trojan standing.

The long-haired Greeks begin to shoot at this perfect target with arrows and slings. The Persians called arrow feathers "messengers of death," and Bronze Age archers could hit a target at 300–400 yards. Estimates are that a top slinger could reach a speed of 100–150 miles per hour and hit a target 150 feet away.

Homer identifies the Locrians and some of the Thessalians as great bowmen among the Greeks. The Cretans were also famous as archers. The Locrians included slingers as well. Most archers and slingers fought without armor or shield and were stationed behind the lines of heavy-armed spearmen. Some were outfitted with composite bows, made of wooden staves reinforced with horn and sinew, much more powerful than the simple wooden bows.

But Agamemnon called for his men to cease their fire. It was clear that Hector wanted a parley. The Trojan proposed that, instead of a general engagement, there be a battle between two champions: none other than Paris and Menelaus, the originators of the war, as it were, and, in fact, the two men who had just stepped forward on each side (it was Paris who had then quickly retreated). If Menelaus killed Paris, the Trojans would return Helen and the Spartan treasure; if Paris killed Menelaus, the Greeks would allow Helen and the treasure to remain in Troy. In either case, the two sides would swear friendship and the Greeks would go home. The Greeks agreed, with the proviso that the Trojans show their good faith by having Priam ride out to the field and sacrifice two lambs while he swore an oath to abide by the outcome of the duel. The Trojans accepted this condition.

Homer shows Paris under pressure from his hard-as-nails older brother, Hector, to prove himself in combat. Hector insults Paris by calling Paris "girl crazy": real men think about war not women. The rebuke was an old one in the Near East. Consider a case around 1800 B.C. involving two Mesopotamian princes, Yashmah-Addu and his older brother, Ishme-Dagan, both sons of King Shamsi-Adad of Ekallatum (1814–1781 B.C.). Ishme-Dagan was the favorite, and chosen to succeed his father, while Yashmah-Addu was made king of nearby Mari.

Shamsi-Adad writes to his younger son with the good news that Ishme-Dagan has triumphed in battle and won a name for himself as a great general. Then comes the kicker: "Here your brother has killed the [enemy] general," writes the old king, "while there you lie about among the women." He then tells Yasmah-Addu to be a man and lead an army against his enemies. Yasmah-Addu might have sympathized with Paris's predicament.

A contest between champions was standard procedure in the

Bronze Age. Two kings could fight it out, or two corporals—a low-risk alternative chosen when the Greek Attarissiya invaded southwestern Anatolia around 1400 B.C. Now, at Troy, champion battle suited both sides' needs. The Greeks had suffered significant manpower losses as a result of disease and defection, and their morale was shaky. The Trojans had hurried out to battle from an assembly, with little time to spare for buckling their war belts.

Priam, accompanied by Antenor, rode out of the city and sacrificed as required. The duelists stepped forward onto a measured field. They would fight with long spears. It was the hero's weapon of choice. The shaft was sometimes ash, sometimes olivewood, and the spearhead was bronze.

Paris drew the right to throw first but his spear broke on Menelaus's shield. Menelaus had better luck on his turn because his spear went clear through Paris's shield and breastplate. But the nimble Paris twisted away and received only a nick to his ribs. Menelaus followed up with a sword blow to Paris's helmet, but the sword shattered. In frustration, Menelaus manhandled Paris by the plume of his helmet and began dragging him back to the Greek ranks. But the leather chinstrap snapped and Paris broke free. It was the work of his patron goddess, who now whisked him to safety in his home in Troy. So Homer says, and no Bronze Age soldier would have reason to doubt it, since every king claimed to have a patron god or goddess on the battlefield.

Then one of the Trojan commanders broke the truce. According to Homer, the gods persuaded Pandarus son of Lycaon, one of Troy's leading allies, to shoot an arrow that wounded Menelaus. Now both sides reached for their weapons. As has often happened in the history of war, a rogue soldier upset the generals' plans.

Pandarus used his magnificent composite bow, which was made from the horns of a wild ibex—presumably set over wooden staves and reinforced with sinew—and tipped with gold. He braced the bow on the ground, took an arrow from his case, and fitted it to the string. Hiding for safety behind his men's shields, he drew the string and the arrow butt to his chest and shot. Pandarus's feathered arrow was tipped with an iron arrowhead, unlike the bronze arrowhead used by the Greeks. Iron weapons existed in Bronze Age Anatolia. But Menelaus escaped with only a flesh wound, because he was protected by his golden belt and his corselet.

But the wound bled enough to worry Agamemnon, who called for the doctor Machaon. In the Bronze Age, medics doubled as veterinarians, so between one thing and another, their linen tunics were usually clotted with blood. Machaon pulled out the arrow, sucked out the blood from the wound, and applied an ointment. It might have been a bitter root, such as Patroclus later used on a similar wound; an ancient commentator suggested Achillea (woundwort) or Aristolochia (birthwort). Or it might have been honey, a natural antibiotic used to dress wounds. A salve of one part honey and two parts grease (either animal fat or olive oil) appears on the Linear B tablets as antiseptic, fungicidal, and antibiotic.

Menelaus did not require surgery, but if he had, a Bronze Age practitioner had cutting tools made of obsidian or bronze as well as such bronze instruments as forceps, probes, spoon, razor, and saw. Opium was available to ease the pain. Linen bandages were known in Egypt, but the only bandage in Homer is a woolen sling doing double duty as a dressing. An unbandaged wound might have been a common sight in the Greek camp.

An expert treated Menelaus's injury, but Menelaus was the supreme leader's brother and so had special access to the scarce supply of physicians. Often in Homer even a champion settles for a companion to remove a spear or arrow, as both the Greek Diomedes and the Trojan ally Sarpedon do later that same day.

Because Pandarus had broken the truce to which Priam had solemnly sworn, a pitched battle ensued. It was unplanned, and yet Agamemnon could not have arranged things better:

> *No rest, no respite, till the shades descend;*
> *Till darkness, or till death, shall cover all:*
> *Let the war bleed, and let the mighty fall;*
> *Till bathed in sweat be every manly breast,*

With the huge shield each brawny arm depress'd,
Each aching nerve refuse the lance to throw,
And each spent courser at the chariot blow.

Agamemnon may emerge as an unappealing personality in Homer, but he could be a good general. He did make a number of mistakes, but he knew how to admit errors and switch course—fast. He gave up Chryseis, for example. He let his colleagues Odysseus and Nestor quell the troops' mutiny. He reviewed the troops and then led them into battle. And he would soon eat his words by apologizing to Achilles and offering him a king's ransom, including the return of Briseis, to rejoin the fight.

One of the strengths of the Greek army was the collective experience of its leaders, from Ajax to Odysseus. Call them an army of forty kings, like the force from the Armenian Plateau that faced the Assyrians under King Tukulti-Ninurta (1244–1208 B.C.). And call them an army of forty counselors, none more impressive than Homer's Nestor. Although he was too old to fight, he had not stayed at home; he was on hand to offer invaluable advice. The Trojan army had no counterpart. Priam stayed on the sidelines and was rarely listened to. Except when he let his emotions get the better of him, as he did with Chryses and Achilles, Agamemnon was careful to consult his colleagues. And he was able to judge who offered the best counsel.

Like modern battle, a Bronze Age engagement was complex. To orchestrate it required accurate information, which made scouts and spies essential. Before clashing, the two sides pushed, tricked, and feinted for the best ground. A Bronze Age army was a combined-arms force of foot soldiers and chariots, skirmishers and linemen, bowmen and spearmen. Each army would try to maximize the deployment of its strengths against the enemy's weaknesses: for example, by raining a cloud of arrows on light-armed troops. If the armies were coalitions, each side had the opportunity to sow discontent in the other by concentrating its attack on the allies while leaving the leader of the alliance relatively untouched.

We can grasp the outline of pitched battle from the daylong engagement that followed Pandarus's bow shot. At a signal the two armies, both thickly massed, marched toward each other. Now came a bombardment of arrows and slings, although archers and slingers are the forgotten men of the *Iliad*. Arrow wounds were frequent and often fatal; merely removing a barbed arrowhead could kill, because of shock or infection, and the pain could be agonizing.

The two phalanxes advanced, perhaps in a crooked line. But advance the Greeks and Trojans did, in close order, and with discipline and speed before coming to blows. Meanwhile, the chariots were coming.

Chariots carried leaders to and around the battlefield. They were light wooden carts, covered with either oxhide or wicker work. Sometimes they were inlaid with ivory and gold, and sometimes they were painted crimson both to stand out and to hide the color of blood. The wheels were also wooden. Each chariot was drawn by a team of two horses, and its crew consisted of a driver and a warrior. The warrior might fight from his chariot but it was more usual for him to dismount and exchange blows on foot. The main advantage conferred by chariots was mobility. Secondarily the chariot was a psychological weapon, since the noise of the wheels and the sight of the horses may have frightened some of the enemy. The tanklike charge of a mass of chariots in order to break the enemy's line may have played a big role in Egyptian and Hittite warfare—the experts disagree—but it was not to be found at Troy. For most of the year the terrain was too wet for that and, besides, neither side had enough chariots for a mass charge: Troy lacked the imperial wealth and Greeks lacked the horse power!

When the infantrymen clashed, the best fighters stood in the front lines, unless the commander had thrown ordinary troops before them to prevent those troops from fleeing. Homer refers to the best soldiers as "fore-fighters" (*promachoi*) or simply "the first men." Elite troops, they inhabited a different world from ordinary soldiers. The elite were professionals, well armed, well trained, and well prepared for the shock of battle. Ordinary soldiers were conscripts, lightly armed, poorly trained, and ill-prepared for bloody combat. It was bad luck for them if they had to step up and replace their comrades, both the fallen and those who simply went to the rear to rest.

The men in the front lines, especially the champions, had a full set of arms and armor. The complete warrior wore bronze greaves (shin guards), a leather kilt, and a crested helmet. He may have worn a loose-fitting bronze breastplate and back plate, which could be extended with pieces to cover his neck, lower face, shoulders, and thighs. An alternative was a linen tunic with bronze scales to serve as a breastplate. An elaborate belt, perhaps red or purple and decorated with gold or silver, would be worn over the tunic or breastplate. The front line fighter carried a big, heavy shield, shaped either like a figure-of-eight or a tower, and composed of multiple layers of leather on a bronze rim. It hung from his shoulder on a strap that may have passed diagonally over his torso. The shield was meant to offer full protection, which is why very few warriors in Homer are described as wearing both a metal breastplate and holding a shield. A scabbard, holding a bronze double-edged sword, lay along his right thigh, suspended by a strap from his left shoulder.

The ordinary soldiers, the majority in either army, consisted of various kinds of light-armed troops. We can imagine them in a linen tunic without armor, leather helmet and kilt, and linen greaves. Most men did not carry a body shield but had to make do with a small, light, round shield. Some men might have had to manage by holding up, as some kind of protection, a simple, unfinished piece of leather without a bronze rim.

When the two phalanxes clashed, the men brought their oxhide shields together and attacked with their spears. The spear was the main close-range weapon at Troy. Swords were only second best because of their tendency to break at the hilt. A few of the heroes may have wielded a type of sword that was new in the Aegean, bronze and about two and a half feet long, much more efficient at inflicting slashing wounds than its predecessors. Because the blade had roughly parallel edges for most of its length, rather than the tapered edges of a dagger, this sword was good at cutting. And with a single piece of metal for both blade and hilt, it was less likely to break than its predecessors. This so-called Naue II sword was of central European origin, and it began to appear in Greece shortly before 1200 B.C. But it was probably a rare import. We hear in the *Iliad* of a few Greeks and virtually no Trojans who wield slashing swords. In any case, a man could do a lot of damage with an ash-wood spear tipped with a six-inch bronze head, its sides bulging outwards like a leaf's—especially if he put his legs and back into thrusting it into the enemy.

Men on each side proceeded to try to slaughter each other by thrusting with a lance or throwing a javelin. When a man went down his comrades tried to drag his corpse back to safety, but the enemy would contest that. Stripping an enemy's corpse gave a man both loot and bragging rights. So a kill was usually followed by knots of men tussling ferociously over the corpse and its armor. Because of encounters like this, however tightly packed the unit had been when it reached the enemy, it could not have stayed that way.

Duels were probably not unusual on the Bronze Age battlefield. But surely they were not nearly as prominent as they are in Homer. Bronze Age battle poetry exaggerates heroic individualism and downplays group effort. Homer's emphasis on duels between heroes is more likely to reflect Bronze Age literary style than actual Bronze Age warfare.

At this point in the encounter, the Trojans gave ground, but they did not flee the field. As was typical, they regrouped for another stand. Meanwhile, the Greeks were not pressing their advantage. In fact, here and there they were slackening: Homer has the goddess Athena buck them up, just as he has Apollo—the war-god Iyarri, no doubt—put some backbone in the Trojans. With the two armies relatively evenly matched, the battle followed a rhythm, with each side taking turns in gaining ground on the other.

But with the Greeks still holding a slight advantage, Homer's attention now shifts to their champion Diomedes. Efficient killer that he was, Diomedes could have accomplished little without the help of his men, but the poet leaves them in the background. First Diomedes defeats, on foot, two noble Trojan brothers in their chariot, killing one and so terrifying the other that he leaves behind both chariot and his brother's corpse. Then Diomedes goes on to slaughter twelve named warriors, including Pandarus, whose arrow started the battle. He nearly kills Aeneas, the Trojans' best warrior after Hector, and he wounds the gods Aphrodite and Ares. He makes most of his kills with lance and javelin, but he also takes out his sword and slashes a man's shoulder off. Apparently, Diomedes is one of the men lucky enough to have a Naue II sword. His squire and charioteer, Sthenelus, followed behind. It was his job to haul away the booty as well as to be ready to give Diomedes a ride to the next target.

Diomedes would have won more booty by taking Pandarus alive and ransoming him. But his comrades had no cause to complain about Diomedes, whose vigorous leadership caused the Trojans to retreat back to the Scamander River. And the Greek offensive inflicted terrible casualties on the allies. Whether the Greeks had purposely targeted them or not, their plight was enough to cause Sarpedon, commander of the key allied division from Lycia, to send a message to Hector: rally the Trojan troops or face a big problem.

Hector responded quickly. He stepped down from his chariot and exhorted the Trojans on foot. They roared their enthusiasm and turned back to give battle. Meanwhile, the Greeks were remobilized by their leaders in turn and they fought fearlessly. But the Trojans steadily pushed them back.

Aeneas then makes a miraculous return to the field. Diomedes had hit him on the hip joint with a huge rock, which tore Aeneas's tendons and broke his socket. But the gods whisked him off to Troy, cured him, and arranged for his wondrous comeback—a case of heroic exaggeration at its finest. In real life, Aeneas would probably have gone into shock. A less serious fracture would not have presented a problem to Bronze Age physicians, because they could set bones so that a fracture healed perfectly.

Directed by Diomedes, the Greeks rediscovered their fighting spirit. They broke through the Trojan ranks and began driving them back toward Troy. But once again, Hector saved the day by rallying the troops. The Greeks pulled back. It was an opportunity for Hector to take the advice of his brother Helenus, Troy's best seer, and dart back into the city where he could have Queen Hecuba organize a special women's appeal to the goddess whom Homer calls Athena. Whether she was worshipped at Troy—ancient peoples often borrowed each other's gods—or whether Athena was actually an Eastern goddess, a prayer to a goddess for military success was not unusual in Anatolia. Hittite King Tudhaliya IV (1237–1209 B.C.), for example, prayed to the Sun-Goddess of Arinna for victory against an unnamed enemy, possibly the Assyrians. We can assume that Troy had a protector goddess even if she cannot be identified.

This religious mission, in the heat of combat, speaks volumes about the nature of this battle. Either Hector was superstitious himself or he knew that his men were. The story demonstrates the awareness that battle would be intermittent. It also underlines the reality that even the doughtiest champion needed to take a break from time to time.

Homer reports how thirsty warriors were after battle. Mesopotamian war poetry called for mind over matter: a soldier needs strength, vigor, and speed; he has to make his mind command his body.

Hector returned to the field with his brother Paris in tow, which gave the Trojans a second wind. Soon it became clear that, far from wanting to continue to fight, Hector sought a graceful way of calling it off. Homer says that Apollo had changed Hector's mind, but the Trojan had good reason to have reached his conclusion without any help from the gods. He needed a respite; he needed time to meet with his commanders and hammer out a fresh plan, as well as to rest the men and to brief them anew. For Hector had received a key piece of intelligence:

The great, the fierce Achilles fights no more.

The best and most honorable way to achieve his goal was for Hector to issue a challenge. Single combat at this point served several purposes. It was a chivalrous way of ending a long day of fighting that had bloodied both sides without a clear outcome. It would strengthen the Trojans' standing in their allies' eyes by showing

Hector's courage. And it would earn Hector political capital in the debate that lay ahead. Before taking his army back to war Hector would have to deal with an urgent issue of morale. As an assembly that very night would show, the nation's will to fight was at question.

Hector was careful not to put as much at stake in this latest duel. When Menelaus fought Paris, Helen and the Spartan treasures were on the line. Hector offered only an honorable funeral for the loser. But he did not have to offer much because the Greeks were equally glad to leave the field.

Ajax won the lottery among the eager Greek champions and he faced Hector with swords. By now it was night. The two champions fought an inconclusive duel. The judges declared a draw, the combatants accepted, and the two made a gallant exchange of gifts. The weary men in each army withdrew.

The long day of battle had rebuilt the morale of the Greeks. Menelaus disgraced Paris, Ajax beat back Hector's challenge, while notable kills were scored by Agamemnon; Idomeneus; Odysseus; the Thessalian leader, Eurypylus; Idomeneus's second-in-command, Meriones; and Antilochus son of Nestor, who teamed up with Menelaus (apparently recovered from his wound in record time). And who could forget Diomedes' bloody rampage through the Trojan ranks? Yet Nestor knew the price of success:

> *How dear, O kings! This fatal day has cost,*
> *What Greeks are perish'd! and what people lost*
> *What tides of blood have drench'd Scamander's shore!*
> *What crowds of heroes sunk to rise no more!*

The Greek dead included many prominent men, most notably Tlepolemus son of Heracles, leader of the Rhodian troops.

Meanwhile, the Trojans and their allies held a stormy assembly outside Priam's palace on the citadel. Antenor proposed the return of Helen and the Spartan treasures. After the day's bloodshed, he would have had plenty of supporters. Antenor was speaking from the heart, and he reminded his audience that they had broken an oath today. By shooting Menelaus after having sworn to resolve the war through a duel of champions, Pandarus had put the Trojans in the wrong. No good could come from this.

Paris responded vigorously by saying the gods must have made Antenor mad. But then he more or less admitted his own failure in the duel with Menelaus that day by offering a major concession: he would give back the Spartan treasures and even add a little extra from his own riches. But Paris refused to return Helen. Then Priam rose to support Paris's plan. He was not optimistic about Greek agreement, and he warned the men to expect no more than a cease-fire for burying the dead. The assembly approved Paris's offer: return of the Spartan treasure and then some, but Helen would stay where she was.

The men dispersed, the soldiers returned to their units. They took their evening meal by companies. After the battle they were exhausted, but they may have had to settle for sleeping in shifts because the watch had to be maintained at all times.

At dawn, the Trojan herald Idaeus delivered the assembly's message to the Greeks. He found the chiefs gathered around Agamemnon's ship. At first, his words were greeted with silence. Then Diomedes spoke for the whole leadership:

> *Oh, take not, friends! defrauded of your fame,*
> *Their proffer'd wealth, nor even the Spartan dame.*
> *Let conquest make them ours: fate shakes their wall,*
> *And Troy already totters to her fall.*

Idaeus returned and reported the defiant rebuff. But the Greeks had at least agreed to a temporary cessation of hostilities.

The Trojans wasted no time sending out cremation parties. One detail went into the hills to gather wood for the pyres while another walked the battlefield to pick up the fallen. Since anything of value had probably already been stripped, the bodies had to be identified by their faces, on which the process of disfiguration would have already begun, since they had been left out overnight on the hot, damp plain.

Whenever they found remains that they recognized, the Trojans washed off the dried blood and lifted the corpse onto a cart. They shed tears but otherwise displayed no emotion, because Priam had forbidden lamenting. This might say something about the shaky state of Trojan morale or it might reveal Priam's determination that the Trojans not show weakness to the enemy.

At the day's end, two sets of pyres were lit at opposite ends of the Trojan Plain. The Trojans returned to town, the Greeks to their ships. Early the next morning, just before the first light of dawn, a battalion of specially picked Greek troops went back to the pyre to heap up a burial mound around it. This work was more than a gesture of respect, for the men immediately built their camp's palisade and trench alongside. If they were taking advantage of the armistice they were surely stretching its spirit, but they might have figured that the enemy's exhaustion guaranteed their safety. According to Homer, the entire defensive work was completed in one day. This would have been a tall order. It is probably more realistic to imagine that the Greeks had already fortified their camp, and now they were strengthening its lines.

In either case, Trojan scouts would surely have seen what the Greeks were now up to. That night, while both armies feasted, Hector and his high command would have time to contemplate yet another change in the balance of power and to make new plans. They might have been forgiven for thinking that they faced a whole new war.

CHAPTER EIGHT

NIGHT MOVES

Kings of the Bronze Age dreamed many dreams, none greater than the hope of undying glory. Only the gods could grant such a wish, and the gods would not be forced. But they did appreciate gifts, so the prudent monarch would cap off his reign with a suitable offering of thanks—an imposing monument, perhaps with an inscription expressing gratitude to heaven for success, long life, prosperity, children, and, of course, victory. Victory was the seed of immortality, and victory was granted by the gods in many ways, from the delivery of a king's enemies into his hands to their destruction beneath his feet. But no victory was sweeter than one that reversed imminent defeat. With the gods' help, he would force the enemy chiefs to stop their boasting.

So Hector might have dreamed that night as the funeral pyres blazed on the Trojan Plain. The Greeks had lost some of their best men and had retreated behind weak walls. If the Trojan prince led his armies out now, they might ride a tide of flames to the Greek ships. Hector might have imagined that long after he had replaced Priam on the throne, and in turn been replaced by his own son Astyanax, he would be remembered by the poets as the king who had saved Troy.

So, when the sun rose the next morning, Hector was on fire. He was at the head of an army that charged out the gates of the city, some on foot and some in chariots, all hungry for a fight. The Greeks had little choice but to leave their camp and meet the Trojans on the plain.

For several hours the battle was evenly balanced, but shortly after noon, in the unforgiving brightness of a sky that stretched from Mount Ida to Samothrace, the tide turned in Troy's favor. The Greeks began to run. Diomedes, however, had the courage to turn his chariot toward the enemy and to hurl a javelin that killed Hector's charioteer.

But the gods were on Troy's side. Homer envisions Zeus himself on Gargaros, the highest peak of Mount Ida, looking down on the battle from the gusty summit. The god thundered against the Greeks, then struck the ground in front of Diomedes' horses with a lightning bolt. Not even the courageous son of Tydeus could resist divine displeasure, so he too turned and fled. The Hittite King Murshilish II had likewise been helped by a divine lightning bolt around 1316 B.C. in his battle against Arzawa, about two hundred miles south of Troy. And a Babylonian prayer to the god of the thunderstorm, found preserved in the Hittite capital of Hattusha, shudders at the god's intervention in combat.

Hector now indulged in one of the oldest traditions of Bronze Age warfare. When they weren't spinning tales about the greatness of the man they had defeated, Bronze Age commanders would demean the enemy as a dog, as the "son of a nobody" or as someone whom the gods should turn into a woman. As Diomedes retreated, Hector shouted after him:

Go less than woman, in the form of man!

Then Hector turned to his own troops:

Trojans and Lycians and Dardanians who fight hand to hand:
Be men, my friends, and remember your valor and might.

Feminization was a threat readily brandished by a Bronze Age commander. Assyrian King Tukulti-Ninurta (1244–1208 B.C.), for example, menaced any man who desecrated his new temple to Ishtar with the curse that "his manhood dwindle away."

Homer does not state exactly where the battle had begun, but by now it had moved far away from Troy. Hector had found a new charioteer and his men surged across the Scamander River and pushed the Greeks all the way back to their camp, a distance across the plain of about two miles from the walls of the city. They had the Greeks penned in behind their ditch and palisade.

Suddenly, inspired by Hera and wrapped in a purple cloak, Agamemnon rallied his men. Purple was the royal color of the Late Bronze Age; the color of the wool, for example, in which Ugarit paid its tribute to the Hittite king and queen. Purple-clad Agamemnon stood on Odysseus's flagship, at the center of the camp, and shouted loudly enough to be heard from one end of the ships to another— from the flank guarded by Ajax's vessels to the ships of Achilles at the other flank (not that *he* was listening).

Roused to action, the Greek champions counterattacked. Teucer's arrows killed ten Trojans, including both a son of Priam and Hector's second charioteer. But the one man whom Teucer could not manage to hit was Hector. He was moving, Teucer complained, like a rabid dog, not knowing where to bite next, as a Mesopotamian saying had it—dogs were the favorite animal for insults in Bronze Age invective. Having found another new charioteer, Hector leaped to the ground and took off with a loud yell after Teucer, throwing a stone that nearly killed him. The Greeks began to fall back once again, to take cover behind their fortifications. Hector's men might have pressed their advantage all the way to the ships but night was now falling. Cursing their luck, they had to give up.

But they were not prepared to fall back tamely behind the city walls. For the first time during the war, they pitched their camp on the Trojan Plain, in an open space free of the bodies of the fallen. By camping on the west bank of the Scamander River, the Trojan army took a calculated risk, but it kept the pressure on the Greeks. Homer calls the place "the bridges of war." The Trojan Plain was marshy, especially in its northern end, and "bridges" possibly refers to an area of solid ground for chariots to cross.

The army was deployed in a line stretching northwest to southeast, which protected the city and covered any retreat. The northern end was anchored by the Carians of Anatolia and the Paeonians of Macedonia, while the Lycians secured the southern tip. In between were various other Anatolian contingents as well as the Trojans and their near neighbors. And a new detachment of Thracians under King Rhesus had just arrived.

The Trojans were busy in the dark. Some companies of men were delegated to feed the horses, others to go back to town to bring sheep, cattle, bread, and wine for the soldiers' meal—more or less the same food served by Syrian towns to Egyptian soldiers in the 1300s B.C. Other companies of Trojans went into the hills to gather firewood. The Trojans would keep their fires burning all night long in order to be able to see any attempt by the enemy to load their ships and sail away. Meanwhile, Hector wasn't taking any chances on the home front, and he put into effect a few simple measures of deception. He sent heralds around the street to order out boys and old men onto the walls and women to light the town with a fire in every house. No doubt he also ordered a herald to be ready to sound the alarm in case of sudden attack.

After sacrificing bulls to the gods and feeding barley to the horses, the Trojans themselves chowed down, a company of fifty men at each fire. Then, away from the city for the first time in years, they fell asleep under the stars. The Greeks, meanwhile, were in a panic.

Agamemnon had ordered a teary-eyed abandonment of the expedition. Diomedes responded with a reckless pledge to stand, conquer, or die, and the men cheered. Nestor came to the rescue with a levelheaded plan: post sentries along the wall and call the chiefs to a council of war. The stakes couldn't have been higher. As Nestor said:

This night will either destroy the encampment or save it.

The Greeks now placed seven hundred spearmen between the wall and the trench, in seven companies of one hundred men each, one of which was led by Nestor's son Thrasymedes. They were sentinels, playing a role well attested in Hittite and other Bronze Age armies. The top commanders gathered in Agamemnon's hut, where the best imported Thracian wine was on offer, along with superb food. This was only the first of many sumptuous spreads for the heroes that night. Even one dinner would be out of place in a modern staff conference, and the whole thing might be a case of epic exaggeration. Or maybe not, since in the Bronze Age Near East, hospitality was standard at *any* gathering under another man's roof. Besides, in the Aegean, then as now, meals were as much a social as a nutritional occasion, and there would have been no need to gorge at any one meal.

Nestor spoke frankly. They were ruined, he said, unless they got Achilles and the Myrmidons back, and that would happen only if Agamemnon returned Briseis to Achilles. Nestor might have saved his words because Agamemnon had already reached the same conclusion. He claimed the gods had blinded him when he offended Achilles. Now that he had his wits about him once more, he would make amends not merely by returning the young woman (untouched by him), but by adding gifts worthy of a king whose property was as wide as the sea: seven women captured when Achilles took Lesbos, seven tripods, ten talents of gold, twenty cauldrons, and twelve prizewinning horses. On top of that, Agamemnon offered to Achilles the lion's share of booty from Troy, including gold, bronze, and the twenty most beautiful women besides Helen, as well as marriage back in Greece to one of Agamemnon's daughters, with a huge dowry, plus a kingdom made up of seven prosperous cities in the western Peloponnese.

It was palm-greasing diplomacy at its finest. Nestor was impressed. Protocol demanded that an ambassador bring the news to Achilles, and the old politician had a three-man team in mind: Ajax, Odysseus, and Phoenix. Ajax was the Greeks' greatest warrior after Achilles, while Odysseus was the Greeks' canniest diplomat. Phoenix was a lesser soul, but he came from the household of Achilles' father

Peleus, where he had tutored the young prince. If anyone could pull at Achilles' heartstrings, it was Phoenix.

Although he welcomed the nighttime ambassadors with all the hospitality that a hut in the field allowed, with wine and meat and seats on couches covered with purple throws, Achilles did not budge an inch. They warned him that Hector planned to burn the ships and kill the Greeks come morning, and they emphasized Agamemnon's enormous generosity. But Achilles wasn't interested. The insult had been too great to forgive. Besides, talk of loot from Troy was just empty words, since Zeus clearly now had decided for the enemy. The Greeks would never take the city. So, if they looked out to sea in the first, gray light of morning, they would see Achilles and all his men sailing home.

The ambassadors tried to reason with the great warrior but the best they could get from him was this: a promise to fight if Hector was foolish enough to attack his huts and ships and the Myrmidons. Otherwise, Achilles would do nothing to help save the camp. Despondently, they trudged back to Agamemnon's hut and relayed the bad news. After a long silence, Diomedes called on them all to eat and drink (again) and to get some rest so that, at dawn, they could fight to save their ships.

The wine helped most of them to sleep. But Agamemnon and Menelaus were kept awake by worry. The supreme warlord was stunned by the sight of so many Trojan fires on the plain. The sound of pipes and whistles rose above the general din. The two sons of Atreus decided that a scouting mission might save the army. They hurried off in separate directions to rouse the commanders, beginning with Nestor.

Agamemnon and a small party then checked that the guards had not dozed off before calling a council of war. Agamemnon needed to instill a sense of urgency in his fellow commanders, who had been awakened from sleep and who did not understand that the army was, as Nestor put it, poised on "a razor's edge." Having galvanized them, Agamemnon needed one or more volunteers for an assignment richer in danger than in glory.

This would be no heroic battlefield performance before a crowd.

The mission was to discover the enemy's battle plans, either by capturing a Trojan straggler or by sneaking around and eavesdropping. The stars had shifted westward in the sky, marking the passage of two of the three "watches" into which the ancients divided the night. The men would have to move fast to enjoy the cover of darkness.

Diomedes volunteered and requested Odysseus as a partner. They were so pressed for time that they borrowed their arms and armor from other men who had come better prepared. Both men took swords, while Odysseus also grabbed a bow and Diomedes a shield. Diomedes wore a plain leather helmet, Odysseus an elaborate, antique, and expensive boar's-tusk helmet. As they made their way toward the enemy lines in the black night, they had to step over corpses, abandoned weapons, and pools of blood.

Unbeknownst to them, the Trojans were organizing a scouting party of their own. But what was serious business for the Greeks was almost comedy for the Trojans. Instead of receiving the service of an Aeneas or Paris, Hector had to settle for the son of a herald, who, like Thersites, was rich but ignoble. Dolon—the name is derived from the Greek *dolos*, trick—was the only boy among his father Eumedes' six children. Although he was outfitted for spying, wearing a wolf skin and carrying a javelin and a curved bow slung from his shoulders, the material of his cap was weasel, which strikes a comic note. When Hector promised the spy a reward of a chariot and two horses from the Greek spoils, Dolon made him swear an oath as a guarantee—as if the commander's word wasn't his bond. Then Dolon claimed the horses and chariots of none other than the great Achilles. When the Greeks ran into Dolon just beyond the Trojan lines, they thought at first that he was a scavenger, stripping the corpses. The one thing in Dolon's favor was his speed, which almost allowed him to escape Diomedes.

Men stripped corpses for many reasons, not all of them reprehensible. Some wanted trophies but others had a practical need for arms and armor. They sought spare parts, extra, better, or new pieces of equipment. Some soldiers might have come to Troy without any weapons at all, advised by their commanders that they would have to pick them up from the battlefield. And then, of course, there were profiteers who stripped corpses out of pure greed.

When Dolon was captured, he begged to be ransomed and readily told the Greeks everything they wanted to know. He was a "man of tongue," as informers were called in a letter of around 1800 B.C. from the city of Mari on the Euphrates. Dolon revealed the disposition of the Trojan and allied troops, the absence of guards around the camp, and the presence of Hector in a war council. He divulged new details about the Thracian reinforcements under their king Rhesus son of Eïoneus, with his magnificent team of white horses (a color especially valued in horses in the Late Bronze Age), as well as his chariot with its gold and silver decoration, and armor with gold details. This last piece of intelligence caught the interrogators' interest, since it offered a chance to add loot and glory to their already successful intelligence-gathering. Dolon's reward was death. Diomedes decapitated him in the act of begging for his life on his knees. Diomedes was not generous, but neither was he entirely wrong. Even nowadays it is no war crime to kill a spy, although today a hearing before a military tribunal is general practice first.

The Greeks stripped Dolon's arms and clothing and hid them under a tamarisk, with a vow to dedicate this booty to Athena. They made no attempt to conceal his body. It was just another corpse in the open. Armed with this latest intelligence, the two Greeks were able to head straight for the Thracians. Undetected, they snuck into camp. Diomedes slaughtered twelve sleeping men in a row, and Odysseus dragged away the bodies in order not to risk frightening horses. There was nothing he could do to mop up the pools of blood. While Odysseus untied the horses, Diomedes killed one last Thracian, King Rhesus himself. With the risk of capture mounting every second they hurried off with the horses, leaving the chariot and the armor behind. By the time the enemy woke up and discovered what had happened, the Greeks had reached the tamarisk where they had stashed Dolon's booty. Then they raced back to their comrades, who welcomed Odysseus and Diomedes with handshakes and honeyed words. After the debriefing, the two heroes washed off their sweat in the sea and each returned to his hut for a proper bath and an oil rub-down.

The account of this expedition is marked in Homer by odd vocabulary, unusual weapons, Greek behavior bordering on the most savage inhumanity, and by more-than-usual bias against the Trojans. Homer lays it on so thick that some scholars see the work of another, lesser poet in this chapter. Maybe—or maybe the episode is remarkable for the insight it offers into another side of the conflict, the Trojan guerrilla war.

Unlike regular warfare, which combines mass, force, and speed, guerrilla warfare consists of dispersed, small-scale operations usually over extended periods of time. Although guerrillas cannot defeat a regular army without a regular army of their own, they can weaken the enemy's will so that the regular army can deliver the knockout blow.

The story of Dolon reveals the road not taken, the road that might have led Troy to victory. Although they were dealt a poor hand the Trojans could have played it better by displaying creativity and adaptability. Instead, they were all frontal assault, focused on a war of attrition, revealing a ponderous lack of maneuverability.

The Trojans should have fought what has been called the "the war of the flea," harassing the Greeks by taking a nip here, a bite there. They were right to stay on the strategic defensive, but they should have engaged in opportunistic tactical offensives. They ought to have used their strength, which was an intimate knowledge of the terrain, to exploit the Greeks' weakness, which was their insecurity in a hostile, foreign land. It would have been easy to use light, agile forces for the continual harassment both of the Greek camp and of parties foraging for supplies.

With their knowledge of the Greek language and Greek mores, the Trojans might also have even been able to infiltrate men into the enemy camp or to feed disinformation. They might have been able to assassinate one or more Greek generals. Infiltration, espionage, and assassination were all staple techniques of Mesopotamian warfare. But the Trojans failed to exploit this guerrilla tactic.

At least, they failed according to Homer. In the epics it is the Greeks who harass Trojan stragglers, murder Trojan allies asleep in camp, carry out reconnaissance, capture enemy propaganda resources, and patiently lie in ambush in spite of miserable weather. The Trojans send out one spy and he is captured almost immediately.

Is Homer playing fair? No doubt the Trojans made more use of guerrilla tactics than he allows, and yet Homer convincingly portrays Hector as a man addicted to a heroic illusion of a decisive victory. That is his tragedy—and Troy's.

Bronze Age propagandists were not subtle. Images of chariot charges, reports of battles involving tens of thousands of infantrymen, royalty holding taut bows, perseverance in single combat, assaulting a fortified city with shock troops mounting ladders and wielding battering rams: these were the stuff of victory monuments and poetry. Commando raids, sabotage, kidnapping, theft, spying, throat-slitting in the dark, and ambushes at the stable door all made poor propaganda, however effective they may really have been. So whatever references to such practices survive may be only the tip of the iceberg.

Homer mentions a number of ambushes, covert operations, raids, sorties, and scouting expeditions in and around Troy, almost all carried out by Greeks. In the *Odyssey* all of Odysseus's actions from his return to Ithaca until the slaughter of the suitors and the maids may be seen as one big exercise in irregular warfare, an armed uprising without an army. The chronicles, law codes, poetry, and art of Egypt and southwest Asia before ca. 1100 B.C. record such low-intensity warfare.

Hittite laws document ingenious and active thieves who make off with slaves and every kind of animal, from bulls to pigs, as well as bees, birds, household goods, grain, plaster, a grapevine's tendrils, plows, carts, chariot wheels, water troughs, lashes, whips, reins, spears, knives, nails, curtains, doors, bricks, and foundation stones. The Sumerians write about breaking and entering, the Babylonians about raids on merchant caravans, while the Egyptians decry those who pilfer a loaf of bread or a pair of sandals from a traveler. Sheep-stealing was a way of life in the Levant and the merchant counted himself lucky if his caravan wasn't picked off.

Near Eastern societies were familiar with personal violence of every sort, from tearing off ears and biting off noses to knocking out teeth and breaking bones, to blinding, rape, and murder. They knew every weapon of interpersonal violence, from fists to clubs, from daggers to bows. Here are three examples: A king of the city of Byblos (in today's Lebanon) in the 1300s B.C. foiled an assassin who came at him with a bronze dagger. An Egyptian tale from before 1200 B.C. involves an elder brother who falsely believed that his younger brother had tried to seduce his wife. Imagine him sharpening his spear and standing behind the stable door, waiting to ambush his younger brother when he returned with the cattle in the evening. A macehead was dedicated to the god Asshur by the Assyrian King Shalmaneser I (1274–1245 B.C.).

Just as coastal dwellers had to deal with pirates, people who lived inland struggled with less civilized raiders from across the border. The farmers of Late Bronze Age Ugarit suffered raids by the men of neighboring Siyannu, who cut their vines. In Egypt during the reign of King Merikare (ca. 2100 B.C.), there was continual trouble from the "miserable Asiatic," that is, Canaanite nomads, who moved their flocks with the seasons and raided the locals wherever they went. One text refers to Canaanites as constantly moving in search of food, constantly fighting, never formally declaring war, and behaving like thieves. Though troublesome, the author says, the group could do only limited damage: like crocodiles, they can grab someone on a lonely road but they are not capable of attacking a town. In short, they fought like guerrillas.

There is less evidence for irregular warfare or covert operations, but there is some. Scouting patrols were a regular feature of Bronze Age warfare, from Mesopotamia in the 1700s B.C. to Hatti in the 1200s B.C. The Hittites sent out spies to gather information about enemy towns. They also employed allies to spread disinformation: on the eve of the Battle of Qadesh, for example, they had two Bedouin purposely captured by the Egyptian enemy who then fed the enemy lies. Meanwhile, concealment of their chariots was the key to Hittite strategy against Egypt in the battle that followed. And as early as around 2000 B.C. a Sumerian poem about a war has one king send out his bodyguard to the enemy in order to confuse and mislead the other king.

If the Trojans had wanted to steal Greek livestock, supplies, and slaves, if they had wanted to waylay individual soldiers and kill or capture them, if they had wanted to send out spies to learn what the Greeks were up to or discharge double agents to spread disinformation, if they wanted to leave the enemy jumpy and worn out, they would have had plenty of contemporary models.

But low-intensity warfare requires tremendous patience, and waiting could not have been easy for the Trojans after all they had endured. Their wealth was dwindling after years of feeding the allies at their own expense and showering the allied leaders with gifts. The mansions of Troy had been emptied of the gold and bronze that once filled them. The people were tired of being shut up inside their walls. And the Greeks were stripping their hinterland of its livestock and luxuries, its field hands and finery, just as they were preventing new wealth from flowing in from the ships of the Trojan Harbor.

Hunger was a by-product of invasion. Describing the situation in the city of Ur besieged by the Elamites around 2100 B.C., a poet said that "hunger contorts [people's] faces, it twists their muscles." Troy was not cut off from the world, but Greek raiders probably took a toll on the food supply. Like the chief magistrate of the Bronze Age city of Byblos when his town came under attack, a Trojan might have bewailed the lack of grain and the loss of livestock. The mayor of Byblos claimed that his citizens had to sell their furniture abroad and sell their children into slavery in order to obtain food when under siege.

Hector had no interest in a victory won by sneaking out of ditches or crawling through the mud; he wanted nothing less than glory "beyond measure, rivaling in height heaven and earth." As he once put it:

My early youth was bred to martial pains,
My soul impels me to the embattled plains!
Let me be foremost to defend the throne,
And guard my father's glories, and my own.

But glory did not come without a price.

CHAPTER NINE

HECTOR'S CHARGE

S he had begged him not to go. Having climbed up to the windy
battlements of Troy, where islands glistened in distant outline,
her eyes were focused on the figures on the plain below. She
scanned the battlefield, searching for her husband, unable to stop
herself from weeping like a widow. And then, suddenly, there he was,
right beneath her in the paved streets of Troy, beside the Scaean
Gate. He had made a quick trip to town to organize a last-ditch appeal to the gods. She ran down the steps of the tower, followed by a
wet nurse, whom she had ordered to bring the baby.

Andromache, daughter of the late King Eëtion of Thebes-under-
Plakos, did not want to lose another man to Achilles' bronze spearhead, no matter how much her husband, Hector, was determined to
prove himself in battle. She took their infant son from the nurse and
held him against her breasts, which were perfumed with oil of iris,
tincture of rose or sage or some other aromatic. Wordlessly, Hector
smiled at the boy. His tearful wife grasped the warrior's arm, and
begged him to take pity on her and their child. She spoke wise words,
telling Hector to stay on the defensive and guard the walls. But the
prince paid no attention. For a moment he held the baby tenderly in
his arms and prayed for the boy's future prowess, then returned him
to Andromache. He stroked her cheek and promised he would hold

his own in combat. Then he sent her back to what he considered women's work. "All males are concerned with war," he said pointedly, "and me most of all."

Two days had passed since that farewell. Hector had returned to battle. At home Andromache worked at her loom, embroidering a purple cloak with flowers, an ancient talisman for bringing back a man. She had the servant women put a cauldron of water on the fire ready to give Hector a warm bath after the battle. But she had already led those same servants in a ceremony of ritual mourning for the man she never expected to see alive again.

Hector had first brought his troops to the gates of the wall in front of the Greeks' ships. Then came the night when the Trojans camped out on the plain. Now, on the second day of battle and at dawn, they would begin the drive that Hector expected would bring them, torches in hand, to the Greek ships.

The events of these second and third days of pitched battle take up fully one-half of the *Iliad*. And that is only right, because they represent high noon in the lives of the poem's two chief protagonists. But when it came to the fate of Troy these two days were almost a sideshow, and so the military story is related more quickly than the personal drama. In Homer, the Olympians play an especially prominent role in these events. We might dismiss this as epic convention but in fact it reflects the psychology of the Bronze Age battlefield. The harder the fighting, the more religious ancient soldiers became.

A direct attack against a well-defended position is never easy, even when the defender is on the ropes. The war in these books of the *Iliad* is bloody and no-holds-barred. The Greeks were determined to defend every inch of ground, and they were disciplined enough to carry out a series of fighting retreats. Although most Greeks were war weary, the Myrmidons were a strong and rested reserve force that would go into action upon the activation of a trip wire. The Trojan commander ignored warnings of the danger because he hungered for glory and shrank from disgrace. Hector's frontal assault on the Greeks was questionable from the military point of view but it did what Bronze Age culture demanded of a king: to throw his army into battle and smash the enemy, as an Assyrian text put it.

The fight began at dawn. The two sides were evenly matched throughout the morning but in the midday heat the Greeks broke through. They pushed the Trojans all the way back across the Scamander to the walls of Troy, only to be repulsed themselves. One by one, many of the best Greek warriors were wounded: Agamemnon, Diomedes, Odysseus, and the lesser but still important Eurypylus and Machaon. The Greeks were driven behind their trench and wall.

Hector wanted to dispatch the chariots across the trench but he was dissuaded by the Trojan seer Polydamas son of Panthous. Reading the omens was standard practice in Bronze Age warfare. Hammurabi of Babylon (1792–1750 B.C.), for example, announced that he would not have launched a major offensive without first consulting the gods. The details of an operation were also matters for consultation. If a seer turned out to be a judicious tactician, as Polydamas did, then all the better. On his advice, the Trojan attack was carried out on foot. Hector divided his men into five battalions and ordered them to breach the Greeks' rampart. In furious fighting the Lycians under Sarpedon and his lieutenant Glaucus almost broke through a gate, but the Greeks under Ajax and his brother Teucer held them off. Then, thanks to what seemed like divine intervention, Hector is alleged to have hurled a huge stone at the gate and smashed an opening through which his men poured. Repair the gate or suffer a heap of corpses, a Mesopotamian priest had advised a city governor—and the Greeks would have known just what the meant.

The Greeks retreated in good order, adopting a tight defensive formation. Men said that Zeus's brother Poseidon had saved them by breathing confidence into the discouraged troops. They regrouped and, with the two Ajaxes as leaders, they demonstrated the Greeks' disciplined excellence:

A chosen phalanx, firm, resolved as fate,
Descending Hector and his battle wait.

An iron scene gleams dreadful o'er the fields,
Armour in armour lock'd, and shields in shields,
Spears lean on spears, on targets targets throng,
Helms stuck to helms, and man drove man along.

   . . .

Thus breathing death, in terrible array,
The close compacted legions urged their way. . . .

The phalanx stopped the Trojans. Furious hand-to-hand fight-ing ensued, in which the Greeks got the better of things, especially against the third Trojan battalion. Its leaders, Priam's sons Helenus and Deïphobus, were both wounded and obliged to retreat to Troy, while the third in command, Asius, was killed, as was his son Adamas. Following Polydamas's advice once again, Hector pulled his troops back to regroup. But earlier he had brushed off Polydamas's interpretation of an omen as cautioning against a Trojan attack on the ships. Nor did Hector really take seriously the seer's warning about Achilles:

> *a man insatiable for war waits*
> *Beside the ships, and I don't think he will hold back for the whole battle.*

Hector was at his best and worst that day. He was as reckless as he was courageous, as arrogant as he was proud, as principled as he was selfish, as intractable as he was firm. Hector was more consis-tent than the Greek commanders, who so lost their nerve that it seemed miraculous when they regained it, but ultimately he was less effective. When he rallied his men for a new charge Hector succeeded only in taking a direct hit on the chest from a stone hurled by Tela-monian Ajax. He blacked out but was saved by a crowd of Trojan champions, who carried him off the field and had him brought quickly to the rear by chariot. Water from the Scamander revived him long enough for him to vomit but then Hector lost conscious-ness again. It was a decisively bad break for Troy.

The resurgent Greeks forced the Trojans into retreat beyond

the wall and trench and followed them out onto the plain. By this
time Hector had recovered and rallied the army. In real life, no man
could have bounced back so quickly from a thoracic contusion, not
to mention a concussion suffered early in the day. But Hector seemed
to enjoy the miraculous intervention of Zeus; as Homer has it, Zeus
had discovered the other gods' tricks and now intervened on the Trojan side. He even had Apollo (perhaps Iyarri to the Trojans) smooth
the ground for an advance by the Trojan chariots. Seeing the Trojans
regroup, the Greeks began an orderly retreat, with the mass of men
falling back to the ships and an elite of champions and their best followers out in front. But once the attack began and the gods gave glory
to the Trojans, the Greeks ran in panic like frightened cattle or sheep.

Scattered duels did little to slow the Trojans' steady advance,
killing Greeks until they had reached the ships again. This time, the
Trojans drove their chariots into the camp. They needed them as
platforms from which to fight those Greeks who took to the ships'
decks and brandished long naval pikes. Meanwhile, on the ground
between the ships, other Greeks formed a solid wall.

The Trojans smelled victory; the Greeks knew that the war
could be lost in an hour. Both sides fought with the ferocity of fresh
troops. This was no long-distance exchange of arrows and javelins
but rather a ferocious brawl where the weapons were swords, pikes,
battle-axes, and everyday hatchets. The earth flowed black with blood.
Ajax refused to give up: he leaped from ship to ship with his pike. But
little by little, Hector's inspired leadership drove the Greeks back
from the first row of ships to the huts that lay beyond.

As Hector grabbed hold of a ship's sternpost he issued a simple
command: "Bring fire!" Could these thrilling words have been spoken
without a shiver? Could they have been followed by any prouder
shout than the battle cry that Hector now commanded his men to
raise in unison? He called out:

Zeus has granted us today, as recompense for everything,
The chance to take the ships that came here against the god's will
And brought us much suffering. . . .

The Trojans pressed forward with renewed force while Ajax lunged with his spear and bellowed to his men to stand and die. Sweating, breathless, and sore from holding up his shield, his ears ringing from the clash of spears against his helmet, Ajax held his ground. But then Hector reached him and sliced through the ash wood of Ajax's spear with his great sword. Ajax was forced to retreat as the Trojan torches began to burn the ship. It was, says Homer, none other than the vessel that had once carried Protesilaus, the first man to fall at Troy.

The long day's battle was a confusion of sounds: human, animal, avian, inanimate, and meteorological (or, as the ancients would have said, divine); a dying cry or the roar of a group of men; piercing or roaring, whistling or thwacking, clanging or thudding, laughing or fulminating; verbal or grunted; shrill or subdued; commanded or uttered in lamentation; words honeyed or harsh, exhortatory or terrified. The field echoed with the thunder of horses' hooves as they drew two-men chariots into battle and, if the driver and warrior fell, rattled with the eerie sound of empty chariots, horses fleeing.

The sights of battle were terrible. As men hacked and lunged at each other, there were lightning-like flashes of bronze. At the Greek ramparts, a storm of stones rained down on the Trojans, followed by a hail of splinters where the wall was breached. The two armies fought in the soft light of dawn, under the hot, midday sun, and in the evening; through clouds of dust, up hills and down muddy river banks, past windy trees and ancient tombs. At the battle's start Zeus sent a rainstorm of blood, which might refer to the real-life phenomenon of showers that deposit red dust carried from the Sahara Desert, still seen in the Aegean today.

The seesaw of battle was dizzying. Soldiers massed and scattered, advanced and retreated as if in some mad dance. The battle raged back and forth half a dozen times over the two-mile-wide plain, forcing the men to cover an exhausting distance. The many ascents and descents of the swale leading up from the plain to the Greek camp would have left men with sore calves and aching lungs. Those who had chariots must have been grateful for the ride.

Between Troy and the Greeks' ship station lay heaps of corpses, horse and human, both fresh corpses and the victims of the fighting the day before, since there had been no truce to retrieve the dead. Many of the human bodies, stripped naked, were covered only by encrusted blood. Some were missing limbs, others had been crushed under chariot wheels. Within twenty-four hours the cadavers would have exuded the pungent odor of death, sweet and sharp. But it would have been a matter only of minutes after death before insects attacked the corpses, and birds and dogs would have followed shortly thereafter. The Trojan Plain would have been thick with vultures and crows, scattering when men approached and returning when they left. Dogs would have grown fat on the abundance of fresh human meat. Swarms of flesh flies would have accompanied the armies on their march. Butterflies and eagles would have fed on the carrion as well. No one on either side would have had any excuse not to know what awaited the fallen.

The Trojans were fighting for their homes, but the Greeks were free to load their ships and leave. No wonder Homer has the day's fighting begin with a visitation to the Greek camp by Eris, the goddess of strife. She emitted such a loud and shrill cry that it goaded the men to think

that war was sweeter than sailing
In their hollow ships to their dear fatherland.

That was an encouraging start but not enough to maintain fighting spirit for the whole long and bloody day. Neither side could have kept going without continual exhortations from the leadership. Battles such as this are won not by materiel but by men. Hector, Agamemnon, Sarpedon, both Ajaxes, Odysseus, Diomedes, and others each addressed the troops from time to time, alternately scolding and encouraging them.

It was vital too for orders to be given clearly. These leaders told the men when to fan out, when to form tight masses, when to attack, and when to fall back. Command and control on the Late Bronze Age battlefield was primitive, depending on speeches from the top, on trumpet calls and hoisted banners. A booming voice was no small advantage; small wonder that the intensity of a man's battle cry was taken as a sign of warrior prowess. Less dramatic but equally important were the subordinate officers who spread the word, especially in the Trojan army, where orders had to be given in a number of different languages.

But all the speeches in the world could not have driven one particular emotion from the soldiers' hearts—and that was fear. The favorable omen of eagle's flight on the right, the feeling of a comrade standing close by, the sound of an enemy in flight: all provided temporary relief. Even so, no one from the sword-bearers to Agamemnon escaped without a moment of terror that day. As a Babylonian hymn says, the war-god shines with a frightening gleam.

The flames of Protesilaus's ship fired Hector's imagination but they also marked the beginning of his end. With an almost mathematical logic, his success entailed his failure because it reawakened Achilles. As the tide began to turn against the Greeks, Nestor planted an idea in the mind of Patroclus: although Achilles had sworn off battle, he, Patroclus, could fight in his behalf. Nestor said:

If thou but lead the Myrmidonian line;
Clad in Achilles' arms, if thou appear,
Proud Troy may tremble, and desist from war.

After the briefest of hesitations Achilles agreed to let Patroclus wear his armor, lead his Myrmidons, and save the ships. In fact, Achilles was so concerned that, as soon as he saw the flames of the burning ship, he told Patroclus to hurry up. The only condition Achilles placed was that he conduct a limited operation. Patroclus could drive the enemy out of the Greek camp but under no circumstances was he to press on to Troy. That might anger some god, Achilles said, and besides, it would diminish Achilles' honor. Patroclus agreed to these terms.

Achilles did everything he could to help his men, except fight. He toured the huts and roused the Myrmidons to arms; he sent them off with a rousing prebattle speech; and he took the precaution of pouring a libation to Zeus. Patroclus also added his own words about the men's glorious reputation and their even more glorious commander, not forgetting to dishonor Agamemnon—not for nothing was Patroclus the perfect second in command:

Think your Achilles sees you fight: be brave,
And humble the proud monarch whom you save.

The Myrmidons attacked the Trojans like ravenous wolves. They drove the enemy back from the burning ship of Protesilaus and put out the fire, but it was a harder fight to clear them from the camp. The Trojans held their ground inside the wall; only after fierce hand-to-hand combat did the Greeks prevail. The Trojans were propelled into a pell-mell flight that left a number of chariots stuck in the trench, the horses having broken free, but the men sitting ducks for Greek bronze.

Back on the plain, Patroclus cut off the Trojans' leading battalions in their retreat to Troy and forced them to stand and fight. The result was bloody but triumphant for the Greeks. Of the many Trojan casualties the most important by far was Sarpedon: a man who claimed to be son of Zeus or the Storm God, king of Lycia, and one of Troy's main allies. His lieutenant, Glaucus, suffered from a hand wound, having been hit by one of Teucer's arrows during the Trojan attack on the walls. But Glaucus knew that his honor depended on the recovery of Sarpedon's body, so nothing could have held him back. He made a blunt approach to Hector: the allies felt abandoned, so he had better help fight for the corpse. And he did. Hector's men engaged in a bitter hand-to-hand battle but the Greeks won. Accepting failure, Hector remounted his chariot and called a retreat. The Greeks stripped Sarpedon's armor while even the heavens sighed; as Homer says, Apollo spirited his corpse back home to Lycia. It was a total triumph for the Myrmidons. In a moment of inspiration, the Trojans had recognized Patroclus's identity, but that wasn't enough to help them stop him.

Then Patroclus got carried away. He disobeyed Achilles' orders and went in thunderous pursuit across the plain to the walls of Troy. There he made three assaults on the wall. Homer says that he climbed the parapet and was pushed back three times before giving up. Presumably a support company had brought ladders with them.

Homer has Apollo call Patroclus down from the walls, just as he talks Hector into rejoining the battle instead of bringing his men to safety behind the walls. Hector ordered his chariot to go after Patroclus, but the Greek was ready. Patroclus killed Hector's latest charioteer, Cebriones. The two men dismounted and fought over the body, joined by their followers. Again, the Greeks won.

By now it was late afternoon. There was still time for Patroclus to make three charges into the Trojan ranks, on which Homer has him kill no fewer than twenty-seven men. Homer mentions by name another twenty-seven Trojans whom Patroclus slew that day, as well as an indeterminate number of others, for a total of more than fifty-four! No single warrior could have carried out all the killing that Homer attributes to Patroclus on his vengeful spree. But with Patroclus at their head, fresh troops like the Myrmidons would have ripped a bloody hole in the Trojan lines.

But now Patroclus's luck had run out. Divine intervention (or a loose strap) caused him to lose his armor, and a young Trojan named Euphorbus son of Panthous took advantage by hurling his spear into Patroclus's back. Seeing his chance for glory, after Euphorbus had removed his javelin, Hector forced his way through the ranks and speared Patroclus in the belly. This was the most vulnerable part of the trunk and a favorite spot in Homer's epic, along with the neck, for administering the death blow. No wonder a Syrian general referred to annihilating an enemy as "smashing his belly"!

The fight for Patroclus's body raged until sunset. Hector had mixed success. He had to suffer charges of cowardice from Glaucus for not having recovered Sarpedon's corpse. He also lost his close friend Podes son of Eëtion, a regular guest at Hector's table. And Hector failed to secure the ultimate prize of Achilles' horses, which had pulled Patroclus's chariot. They escaped. But Hector did manage to claim Achilles' armor and to drive the enemy back across the plain to their camp.

The news of Patroclus's death was a bitter blow to Achilles, but he recovered sufficiently to go to the Greek trench where he boomed in a voice that, like pharaoh's war cry, frightened all the land. According to Homer, Achilles had only to roar three times and the Trojans retreated far enough for the Greeks to retrieve Patroclus's body. By now it was too dark to continue the fight.

The Trojans held an assembly. Once again, Polydamas gave the soundest advice: go back to Troy, camp in the marketplace, and, at dawn, man the walls. They were impregnable, even to Achilles. As Polydamas put it:

> *So may his rage be tired, and labour'd down!*
> *And dogs shall tear him ere he sack the town.*

It was good advice, but Hector rejected it. He scorned retreating now that Zeus or the Storm God had decided to give him glory. Not for the last time in history, a general would claim to have god on his side. The Trojans were convinced; rapturously they cheered Hector's speech and put his plan into effect. They would camp out again on the plain and, at dawn, return to battle, Achilles or not.

Now comes one of the most memorable parts of the *Iliad*. The death of Patroclus gives birth to a new Achilles. Older and wiser, Achilles confesses the error of his past ways and decides to return to battle, although not before accepting the gifts that Agamemnon had offered. The next day, presented by the gods with matchless new armor and a marvelous shield, the hero slaughters a crowd of Trojans. He fights even the Scamander River in a display of the sort of superhuman power attributed to pharaohs. Finally, Achilles hunts down Hector.

The tragic education of an arrogant young hero is one of literature's oldest themes, antique already in Homer's day, and dating back to Mesopotamia's *Epic of Gilgamesh* around 2000 B.C. Could anyone tell the tale more eloquently than Homer does in the latter books of the *Iliad*? Literature aside, in military terms these scenes are important mainly in the negative. With the deaths of Hector and then Achilles, the Trojan War would continue in a different form, with new leaders and new tactics.

Homer narrates a double tragedy: Achilles versus Hector, with Patroclus triangulated between the two. The reality was probably more prosaic. Achilles says that he is avenging Patroclus out of loyalty to a friend who was his soulmate, his very life, and out of shame also for having let him down. However, if Achilles did not kill Hector, he would have been finished as warlord. As even Achilles admits, while Patroclus and many of his other companions had been slaughtered during Hector's offensive, Achilles had sat out the war by the ships, a "useless weight on the ground." The Myrmidons would not long have tolerated a leader who was unable to make good on this failure.

Achilles protests that he knows that by killing Hector he is signing his own death warrant. The fates had decreed that his death would follow fast on Hector's. What else could he have said, given the prophecy? Besides, he loved war; the odor of death was in his nostrils. Achilles had no other way of salvaging his reputation except by killing Hector. He said this clearly to his divine mother—or, as we might put it today, he said it in a moment of honesty:

> *Let me this instant, rush into the fields,*
> *And reap what glory* [kleos] *life's short harvest yields.*

Friendship was fleeting but fame was immortal. Achilles had his priorities clear.

Achilles would have preferred to begin his fight at dawn the next day but the preliminaries could not be overlooked. There had to be a formal reconciliation with Agamemnon, and, afterward, Odysseus prevailed upon Achilles that there be sacrifice and rest before going into battle. War booty also had to be displayed to the men in order to stir up their lust for battle. Then Achilles led them out. The Greeks struck so hard and the enemy ran so fast that after it was over, as soon as a Trojan found safety behind the walls, his first thought was not relief but quenching his thirst.

The old Achilles had disappeared. The amiable buccaneer who preferred ransoming an enemy to slaughtering him was now a killing machine. His victims included two more sons of Priam, Polydorus and his brother Lycaon, a man whom Achilles had earlier spared and sold into slavery. Achilles ignored his pleas for mercy. Most Trojans ran at the mere sight of Achilles; of those who stood their ground, only a rare few, like Aeneas, lived to tell the tale, and then only thanks to divine intervention.

What made Achilles such a successful warrior was that he had strength and speed and superb soldiers to support him. His reputation alone was enough to panic most enemies, which gave him a huge psychological advantage. In an afternoon on the battlefield the *Iliad*'s Achilles kills at least thirty-six Trojans. It was a smaller tally of victims than Patroclus's but it is no less a reminder that the Bronze Age liked its heroes hot.

Achilles' final victim was Hector. Courageous enough to stand and face him when he might have retreated behind his city's walls, Hector nonetheless had second thoughts. But then he thought of the shame that he would face. Hector had to admit that Polydamas had been right about the danger of an enemy led by Achilles. He himself had been a fool, and the Trojan army had paid a terrible price.

In spite of his fears about public dishonor, in the end, Hector ran. Panicked by Achilles' approach, he sprinted off, only to be followed by the great runner. They circled the city three times; indeed, there are indications in Homer that the poet thought of them as circling the entire Trojan Plain three times, a distance of thirty-six miles or more. Finally recovering his courage, Hector stood and fought. Achilles threw his javelin and missed, but recovered it through divine intervention (or a dash to retrieve it). Hector struck Achilles' shield with his javelin. Then he drew his sword and rushed Achilles, but the Greek was ready and drove his spear into Hector's neck. The Trojan fell to the ground, and, with a prophecy of Achilles' approaching doom, he died.

The thrust to the Greek ships was the high-water mark of the Trojan army's resistance. Never again would it pose such a threat. The Trojans followed the wrong strategy. They should have let the Greeks tire themselves out. (In recent times Muhammad Ali brought such a tactic to boxing, the rope-a-dope.) Impatient, arrogant, and hungry for glory, Hector could not accept low-intensity tactics in a defensive strategy; he went after a decisive battle.

The withdrawal of Achilles and the Myrmidons had marked the breakdown of the Greek coalition. Hector should have taken advantage of it by doing precisely nothing. A good rule of warfare is never stop an enemy from trying to withdraw. Instead, Hector did the worst possible thing by launching a frontal attack on the Greek camp. He drove Achilles and company right back into the other Greeks' arms.

The death of Hector might have been a turning point but it did not mean that the war was lost. On the contrary, it might have worked to Troy's advantage. The Trojans still had a lot of fight in them and, what is more, they had a real chance of putting that spirit to good use. They could still inflict casualties on the enemy; they still defended an impregnable fortress; and they still enjoyed the comparative advantage of an urban base. The Greeks were stuck in their wretched camp. The Trojans could wait them out, especially if they replenished their ranks with new allies.

But Hector's family did not see things that way. King Priam and Queen Hecuba watched their son's death from the battlements, where they had earlier called down and pleaded with him not to risk battle with Achilles. Now they were inconsolable in their grief.

Hector's wife, Andromache, was at home, preparing the house for her husband's return when she heard the cries of lamentation. Fearing the worst, Andromache took two servants as escorts and ran to the city walls. From a high tower, she scanned the battlefield for Hector. Achilles had attached Hector's naked body to a chariot by leather thongs cinched through holes in Hector's tendons. Hector's long hair streamed in the dust as Achilles whipped his horses across the plain, dragging the cadaver behind him in triumph.

CHAPTER TEN

ACHILLES' HEEL

Sweet as it was to drive his spearhead through Hector's neck, to spit out taunts—no fewer than three times—about the dogs and birds that would soon eat the dying man's corpse, to strip off his stolen armor from the Trojan's body, to see his comrades poke the still-warm flesh with their spears, and to raise the victory paean among the Greeks, it was not enough for Achilles. Achilles brought the corpse back to his camp and dumped it before Patroclus's bier. It lay there until after his friend's funeral, when Achilles hitched up his chariot and dragged the cadaver around Patroclus's tomb three times. Like Hittite and Egyptian generals, the Greek leader mistreated his enemy's corpse.

At first the gods displayed no objection; presumably they communicated through their priests. In fact, Zeus allowed Hector to be dishonored in his native land. But after nine days, enough was enough, and Zeus insisted that Achilles return the corpse to Troy for burial or suffer divine retribution. Hector's corpse had not begun to rot and the dogs had kept their distance—miracles both, unless "nine days" merely means a long time.

Achilles' behavior shocks us, but perhaps not as much as his cold-blooded slaughter of twelve noble Trojan youths before Patroclus's pyre. The great hero himself had captured them in battle expressly for this purpose.

Meanwhile, a revisionist version of Hector's story began circulating. The real Hector was a self-absorbed, often sharp-tongued martinet whose honor was more important to him than his country's safety; a man who imagined his wife's suffering in captivity but hastened it by his actions; a man who rejected the prudence that would have saved his own life and that of many of his comrades. Now he became a selfless martyr for his homeland.

The *Iliad* tells how Priam journeyed courageously at night across the plain to the Greek camp and, at the risk of his own life, begged Achilles for Hector's corpse. The old man fell to his knees before Achilles and kissed the Greek's murderous hands. It was humiliating, but Priam was engaging in a classic gesture of prostration and self-abasement. And just as an enemy of the Hittite king might signal his surrender by offering valuable gifts (in one example, a throne and scepter, both made of iron), so Priam came laden with treasures. In all of these cases a tit-for-tat exchange was understood on the part of the winner.

The Greeks granted a truce of eleven days so that Hector's funeral could take place; afterward, the war continued. Only a few details of what followed are found in Homer and mainly in the *Odyssey* rather than the *Iliad*. For more the reader has to turn to what is left of the other poems of the Epic Cycle. Only sketchy summaries and a few quotations survive from the *Cypria, Aethiopis, Little Iliad, Sack of Ilium*, and *The Returns*. These accounts were embroidered by such later writers of antiquity as Pindar, the Attic tragedians, Vergil, Statius, Dictys of Crete, Quintus Smyrnaeus, and Apollodorus—not to mention Herodotus and Thucydides. Where Homer is severe and restrained, some of these other authors revel in gossipy details.

The Greek and Trojan generals took the path of least resistance. Each side having failed thus far in its objectives, the generals' recipe, on both sides, was more pitched battle.

The *Aethiopis* tells the story of a woman warrior named Penthesilea. She was an Amazon, a Thracian, and a so-called daughter of

Ares, who came to help the Trojans fight. Penthesilea enjoyed a day of glory on the battlefield until she confronted Achilles, who killed her. Homer does not mention Penthesilea but he offers a few other details about the Amazons. He refers to them as "women who are equivalent to men" and he names two heroes who fought them in battle: King Priam in his younger days and a certain Bellerophontes, who was the grandfather of the Lycian warrior Glaucus, comrade of Sarpedon. These clashes took place years before the Trojan War. Although "Penthesilea" is a Greek name, "Amazon" itself is probably not a Greek word. Priam is said to have fought the Amazons on the Sangarius River in Phrygia, about 350 miles east of Troy. This is far from modern Thrace, which is in southeastern Europe, but the ancients sometimes imagined Thrace as including northwest Anatolia.

It was left to later writers of antiquity to elaborate other details about Amazons: making them man-haters who killed their own husbands, placing them geographically in Anatolia's Black Sea region, having them attack Athens, and pitting them against such Greek heroes as Heracles and Theseus. Penthesilea is said to have come to Troy with twelve other Amazon warriors and to have distinguished herself in action. She is also supposed to have been so beautiful that, after Achilles took off the dead woman's helmet and saw her face, he fell in love.

Women warriors may have seemed outlandish in much of history but not so today when, for example, several hundred thousand women serve in the U.S. military. Nor are women soldiers unknown historically. The best-documented case may be that of the corps of women archers and spear-fighters in eighteenth- and nineteenth-century Dahomey. Good soldiers, they also were trusted as royal bodyguards, and they had a propaganda value to boot, because alpha males felt insulted to be matched in battle with women.

No other all-female units are known in the ancient world, but there were several Joans of Arc, from Artemisia of Halicarnassus, in 480 B.C. the first recorded female admiral, to Boudicca, the British queen who commanded troops against a Roman army in A.D. 61. At sites in southern Russia and Ukraine, archaeologists have found dozens of graves of women buried with weapons. Swords, daggers, bows, quivers, arrowheads, spearheads, horse trappings, and jewelry as well as household objects are among the objects discovered. In some cases, the women's bones demonstrate that they were accustomed to horse riding, heavy use of the bow, and possibly even that they died in battle.

The earliest of such graves dates to around 600 B.C., the latest to about four hundred years afterward. The skeletons represent three Iron Age cultures: Scythian, Sauromatian, and Sarmatian. No archaeological evidence of women warriors has been found for the Bronze Age, but the Iron Age discoveries raise at least the possibility that they did exist.

Thersites resurfaces in the *Aethiopis* to rebuke Achilles for allegedly having fallen in love with Penthesilea. Achilles did not respond well to criticism, and Thersites paid with his life. Later writers claim that Thersites was Diomedes' cousin; but no army could tolerate a warrior who killed one of its own men for so flimsy an offense. Achilles is supposed to have had to make a short trip to the nearby island of Lesbos to be purified before he could fight again. When he did, he found a new enemy.

Memnon, king of the Aethiopians, came to Troy's aid late in the war, perhaps, as Roman-era sources have it, bringing a large contingent of soldiers with him. If so, they surely were not cheap, to judge from one Anatolian ruler under siege who paid up to seven times the normal wage to hire mercenaries. Although Memnon does not appear in the *Iliad*, he is remembered in the *Odyssey* as a great hero. Among other feats, Memnon killed Nestor's son Antilochus before being killed by Achilles in turn. In Homer, Memnon is son of the legendary Tithonus and the goddess Dawn. Other sources claim a marriage tie between Memnon's family and Priam's.

Memnon is too obscure a character for us to be sure that he existed, but it is worth speculating that he might have been black. Memnon came from Aethiopia, a place thought of by the Greeks in various and sometimes vague ways. The term could refer to modern

Ethiopia, to any land south of Egypt—especially Sudan—to any land with dark-skinned inhabitants, or to the East, that is, the land of the morning. But one thing is clear: to the Greeks, Aethiopians had skin burned by the sun. So, to a Greek, an Aethiopian might have been black.

In the late Bronze Age, Nubia, which is roughly today's northern Sudan, was conquered and annexed by Egypt. Nubian mercenaries fought in the pharaoh's army, and sons of Nubian princes were brought northward to be Egyptianized, alongside the sons of Canaanite princes. Some Nubians rose to high positions in Egypt. Nubian nobles began depicting themselves as Egyptians in their tombs and sometimes assumed Egyptian names.

Egypt was no stranger to the politics of western Anatolia. Pharaoh Amenhotep III (1382–1344) had sought an alliance with the kingdom of Arzawa in western Anatolia by marrying an Arzawan royal princess. More recently, Rameses II (1279–1213) corresponded with the king of Mira, a successor state of Arzawa.

But in spite of Memnon's support for Troy, the Greek army led by Achilles routed the Trojans, who streamed back to the city. And Achilles was on the verge of forcing his way into Troy when he was struck down by Paris.

The surviving bits of the Epic Cycle do not specify how Paris killed Achilles but the presence of Apollo (who was lending divine support) points to archery. The heel was supposed to be the only place where Achilles was vulnerable. Another tradition has him shot in the ankle. If either of these stories were true, and since Achilles died right away, it would point to a poison-tipped arrow. An ordinary arrow that penetrated the ankle or heel should not have been instantly fatal; it might have led to a mortal infection, but then Achilles should have lingered for several days before succumbing.

According to the *Aethiopis*, Achilles was shot at Troy's Scaean Gate. The gate was a potentially weak point in the walls, so the attack was usually pressed hard there. Troy's architects compensated by channeling the enemy into a narrow space at the gate where they could be attacked from above by defenders on the battlements or in

a tower. All of the surviving gates of Troy have designs of deadly sophistication, so the challenge facing Achilles is clear (even if the identification of the Scaean Gate is not).

The Trojan gatekeepers had opened the double doors to let the
men back in, which was dangerous with Achilles and his men hot on
their heels. Priam had coached Troy's gatekeepers, on the day of
Hector's last battle, to close the doors in the nick of time, so that
Achilles could not follow the fleeing Trojans back into town. On
this latest occasion Achilles managed to break in, just as the king
had feared. Flung open to let the men stream back to safety, the
gates were not closed until it was too late. Achilles had penetrated
the city's defenses. But not for long. Paris was waiting and with the
help of the god Apollo or Iyarri, he killed Achilles, just as Hector
had foretold with his dying breath.

Paris must have taken up a position on the walls. At an eleva-
tion of twenty-five feet or more, there were few reference points to
judge the distance accurately, which was critical because arrows
shot from a compound bow- follow an arched trajectory in flight.
The ground was also packed with soldiers, so Paris pulled off an
extraordinarily lucky shot.

A battle now raged over Achilles' corpse, as the *Aethiopis* reports. Ajax eventually saved the body and brought it back to the
Greek camp, while Odysseus played the leading role in holding
back the enemy. According to the *Odyssey*, the mourning for
Achilles lasted seventeen days. The *Aethiopis* brings in divine
mourners and funeral games. And the *Little Iliad* mentions a deadly
contest over Achilles' arms, which had been saved along with his
body.

As with Hector, the revisionists were not slow to emerge. If
Achilles had been so glorious, then why did the gods give him such
an ugly, almost random death? Two years after the end of the war,
the ghost of Achilles confessed to Odysseus that he, Achilles, had
made the wrong choice by opting for an early but glorious death instead of a long, dull life. But, Odysseus protested, isn't Achilles
honored as a king in Hades? The ghost replied:

Talk not of ruling in this dolorous gloom,
Nor think vain words (he cried) can ease my doom.
Rather I'd choose laboriously to bear
A weight of woes, and breathe the vital air,
A slave to some poor hind that toils for bread,
Than reign the sceptred monarch of the dead.

Reality was rapidly rejecting the heroic ideal. Nothing was sacred, not even Achilles' arms, at least if the epic tradition is to be trusted. These arms were supposed to go to the Greeks' best remaining warrior, but it would take a contest to choose him. Ajax and Odysseus were the two main contenders; Ajax was all muscle, Odysseus fought with his wits.

The poets agreed that the decision was entrusted to the Trojans, surely a way of avoiding civil war among the Greeks. Homer claims that the "children of the Trojans" made the choice, while the *Little Iliad* offers a delicious if perhaps incredible scheme. Nestor proposed that the Greeks choose the winner by sending eavesdroppers to the walls of Troy. There, they could overhear the enemy discussing the courage and manliness of the Greek heroes. The spies were dispatched and they did indeed hear a conversation but not by Trojan warriors: the speakers were unmarried girls. The first girl sang the praises of Ajax because he had saved Achilles' body, which was more than could be said of Odysseus. The second girl overruled her, arguing that even a woman could drag a corpse to safety, but only a man would have the courage to stand and guard the rear, as Odysseus had. This response was so clever that the poets saw it as the work of Athena.

Indeed, epic sees divine handiwork in the whole affair. The Bronze Age liked to believe that prowess wins battles, but seasoned warriors know that cunning trumps brute force. The best way to state this unpleasant truth was to bring in the gods. According to the *Little Iliad*, Athena willed the outcome.

The Trojan girls' verdict was reported to the Greeks, and Odysseus was declared the victor. Ajax, the original sore loser, went completely mad. Eventually he committed suicide, but not before destroying the cattle of the Greeks. Killing the animals was no small thing, since the cattle represented all the effort that had gone into many raids, usually led by Achilles, and they represented wealth to bring home, sacrifices to the gods, and food for the troops. The *Little Iliad* says that Ajax so angered "the king" (Agamemnon?) that he was denied the usual funeral pyre, and consigned instead to a funerary urn or coffin. Among the Greeks, unlike the Romans, suicide was not considered to be an honorable end.

As for Ajax's burial, cremation was not the norm for Bronze Age kings in Greece but it was for Hittite royalty. And it was obviously an option at Troy. In a cemetery of the 1300s B.C. at the Trojan Harbor, excavators found both cremation burials (that is, the bones and teeth left after cremation) and simple internments (that is, the skeletons left from the burial of unburned bodies). Some of these included Greek artifacts.

Neither side had achieved its objective in the pitched battles that followed the deaths of Hector and Achilles. But it would not be true to say that these battles accomplished nothing. In fact, they were without a doubt the most important confrontations of the war because they were nearly the last. They cleared the decks for one final attempt at an indirect, low-intensity strategy.

From the strategic point of view, the story of the Trojan girls, Ajax's suicide, and Odysseus's triumph sets the stage for the new phase of war. Odysseus was the apostle of unconventional warfare. His moment had finally come. Earlier, Agamemnon had shown good sense by listening to Nestor when it came to the toughest decisions; now, he listened to Odysseus.

Odysseus's first act was to lay an ambush for Helenus, Priam's seer son. Once caught, the seer told the Greeks what he considered to be the secret to success: bring Philoctetes and his bow, which had once belonged to Heracles, and Troy would fall. Philoctetes was a Thessalian warrior who had sailed with the Greeks from Aulis but never reached Troy. He had been bitten by a snake on an Aegean island, either on Lemnos (according to Homer) or Tenedos (according to the *Cypria*) and the venom had left him with a disgusting wound. As a result, the Greeks abandoned him on the island. Now, Odysseus sent Diomedes on a mission to bring Philoctetes.

The physician Machaon was able to heal Philoctetes. Why he was successful this time but not earlier is unclear. But war is often a spur for technology, including the technology of healing, and a process of trial and error on all too many patients might have taught the physician a new herbal recipe or two.

With the bow of Heracles, Philoctetes avenged Achilles by killing Paris. The triumphant Greeks took the body and Menelaus wasted no time in showing his anger by treating the corpse with complete contempt. But the Trojans fought back and recovered what was left of Paris. He was given a decent burial. Trojan custom required that his widow cut short the time spent wearing mournful black. And shortly afterward Helen married his brother Deïphobus. This "levirate marriage" was common ancient Near Eastern practice, found in Ugarit and among the Hittites as well as in the Hebrew Bible. But it was not practiced in Iron Age Greece, which points to the poet's knowledge of non-Greek mores. In levirate marriage a brother is required to marry the widow of his deceased brother. The custom is a reminder that ancient marriage was less about romance than about cementing family alliances and securing male protectors for women.

In Helen's case, her third marriage was either forced on her by the Trojans or it was a sign that she had no desire to return home to face Menelaus—or both. And Helen was still an exceptionally beautiful woman. Ten years later, in the *Odyssey*, she still could be described as looking "like Artemis with her golden arrows."

The generals continued to pay more attention to Ares than to Aphrodite. Both sides were eager for new allies. Homer and the Epic Cycle agree that both parties turned to a new generation of warriors, the sons of the men who had started the conflict. That would have been possible if the Trojan War had really lasted ten years but since it was a much shorter conflict, this detail will have to be ascribed to myth. In any case, the epic tradition says that Odysseus went to the island of Scyros, where he found Achilles' son, Neoptolemus. Having handed over his father's armor, Odysseus convinced the young man to come to Troy to fight in his father's cause. Meanwhile, Priam secured the son of Telephus of Mysia, Eurypylus, as well as the troops under his command. This brought public-relations as well as practical benefit because, like Philoctetes, Eurypylus had a connection to Heracles, who was his paternal grandfather. Priam is also said to have given Eurypylus's mother an exceptionally large gift to win her permission.

Like Neoptolemus, Eurypylus was evidently a very young man, or he would not have required his mother's consent. Such reinforcements came at a very heavy price, since Priam could hardly have been in a mood for largesse at this point in the war, while Odysseus could not have relished giving up the armor that he had competed so hard for. But the stakes were too high to hesitate.

Eurypylus came to Troy and deployed his men on the battlefield, where—naturally—he is said to have fought with distinction. But he was soon to fall to Neoptolemus's spear.

Odysseus was on the verge of a propaganda coup. He sneaked into Troy on what turned out to be the first of two secret missions. The *Odyssey* reports that Odysseus took great pains to camouflage himself, not only exchanging his armor for rags but changing his appearance by striking his face with a whip or a stick until it swelled up. Nobody recognized him in Troy except Helen. Years later, telling the story back in Sparta, she claimed to have helped Odysseus with no less than a bath, a rubdown, and a fresh set of clothes. But she badgered him until he revealed his strategy. As usual, Helen wanted something in return for her attention.

Helen also alleges that, in part thanks to her help, Odysseus killed many Trojans before slipping back out of town. But what was he doing in Troy? Possibly scouting out the target for his second mission. Some sources say Diomedes went along too. Their object was the Trojans' holiest of holies, the Palladium.

In classical Athens, armed Athena was known as Pallas Athena.

Roman-era sources usually describe the Palladium as a wooden statuette of the goddess Athena in arms. Whether the Trojans worshipped Athena is unclear, but the mother goddess was venerated
everywhere in Anatolia, so an image of some female divinity might
well indeed have held a central place in the Trojan pantheon. Stealing the Palladium was a coup that surely gave a lift to the Greeks
while devastating Trojan morale.

In classical times, Greek gods and goddesses commonly had
larger-than-life-size statues. But in Late Bronze Age Anatolia and
Greece, figurines were a familiar way of representing a deity. The
wealthy Hittite capitals had monumental sculptures of the gods, but
figurines made of wood and plated with precious metal were more
common. Or perhaps the Palladium was just a simple pillar or a stele
such as those outside Troy's city gates. Like the sacred medicine bundles carried in animal skins by certain Native American peoples, the
Palladium was considered to contain a power beyond its size.

Stealing the enemy's god could be very successful psychological
warfare. But for some ancient peoples, it was even more: the Hittites
and, many centuries later, the Romans, believed that they could actually bring a particular god over to their side.

The Greeks had tried everything, to no avail. Many of them
might have felt as frustrated as the Hittite commanders who, in spite
of every effort, despaired of having to leave an enemy town unscathed. But rather than despair, Odysseus sought a war-winning
"wonder weapon," to use a modern term of art. Heracles' bow and
Achilles' armor were miraculous objects that led to the deaths of
Paris and Eurypylus; it was thought that the theft of the Palladium
would weaken Troy. That is, if the thieves had been successful: the
Sack of Ilium says that Odysseus did not seize the real Palladium but
rather a fake, set up long before to trick thieves. That would have
been a good story for Priam to put out to steady the Trojans' morale.

The walls of Troy stood firm. But were the Trojans still as committed to defending them? Achilles and Ajax were dead, but Odysseus
had gone from strength to strength, with Philoctetes and Neoptole-

mus now at his side. Meanwhile, Eurypylus, Memnon, and Penthe-silea had all come and gone, Hector and Paris were dead, Priam had demeaned himself before Achilles, Helenus had been captured by the enemy and had given up state secrets, and Helen was treating with the enemy. It was time for the Trojans to pray that Boreas would blow the Greek ships back home.

CHAPTER ELEVEN

THE NIGHT OF THE HORSE

He is the last Greek at Troy. Pale in morning's light, he looks like a weak and ragged runaway. But looks can deceive. Sinon, as he is called, claims to be a deserter—the only Greek remaining when the entire enemy and its cursed fleet had suddenly departed. But can he be trusted? His name, Sinon, means "pest," "bane," or "misfortune" in Greek, leading some historians to consider it a nickname, like "the Desert Fox" for German general Ernst Rommel, or a generic name, like "Bones" for a military doctor. Sinon played a key role in the plot to take Troy, although he is often forgotten, overshadowed by the most famous trick in Western civilization.

The famous horse may be imagined as a tall and well-crafted wooden structure, towering over the wildflowers of the Scamander River plain. Its body is made of the pine of Mount Ida, a tree known today as *Pinus equi troiani*, "Trojan Horse Pine," and renowned since antiquity as a material for shipbuilding. The horse's eyes are obsidian and amber, its teeth ivory. Its crest, made of real horsehair, streams in the breeze. Its hooves shine like polished marble. And hidden inside are nine Greek warriors.

Everyone knows the story. The Greeks are said to have packed up their men, horses, weapons, and booty, set fire to their huts, and departed at night for the nearby island of Tenedos, where they hid their ships. All that they left behind was the Trojan Horse and a spy, Sinon, pretending to be a deserter.

The Trojans were amazed to discover that after all these years, the enemy had slunk home. But what were they to do with the Horse? After a fierce debate, they brought it into the city as an offering to Athena. There were wild celebrations. The Trojans underestimated the cunning of their adversaries. That night, the men inside the horse sneaked out and opened the city's gates to the men of the Greek fleet, who had taken advantage of Troy's drunken distraction to sail back from Tenedos. They proceeded to sack the city and win the war.

Everyone knows the story but nobody loves the Trojan Horse. Although scholars disagree about much of the Trojan War, they nearly all share the conviction that the Trojan Horse is a fiction. From Roman times on, there have been theories that the Trojan Horse was really a siege tower, or an image of a horse on a city gate left unlocked by pro-Greek Antenor, or a metaphor for a new Greek fleet because Homer calls ships "horses of the sea," or a symbol of the god Poseidon, who destroyed Troy in an earthquake, or a folktale similar to those found in Egyptian literature and the Hebrew Bible. There has been every sort of theory about the Trojan Horse except that it really existed.

Many of these theories sound convincing, particularly the horse-as-siege engine, since Bronze Age Assyrians named their siege towers after horses, among other animals. But sometimes a horse is just a horse. Although epic tradition might exaggerate the details of the Trojan Horse and misunderstand its purpose, that the object existed and that it played a role in tricking the Trojans into leaving their city without defenses might just be true.

More about the Horse presently: in the meantime, let us return to the spy whom the Greeks had left behind. Although Sinon is less dramatic than the famous Horse, he was no less effective as an agent of subversion, and he inspires far more confidence as a genuine historical figure. The Trojan Horse is unique and improbable, although not impossible. But Sinon plays a well-attested role in unconventional warfare as it was waged in the Bronze Age.

In Vergil's retelling in the *Aeneid*, Sinon pretends to be a deserter in order to work his way into Troy. He testifies that the Greeks have left for good and argues that the Trojan Horse is a genuine gift and not some trick. Eventually, after a stormy debate, the Trojans decide to bring the Horse into the city.

Deceit is not unique to the Trojan saga; it was a fundamental ingredient in Hittite military doctrine. Consider some examples: A king broke off the siege of a fortress with the approach of winter, only to send his general back to storm the unsuspecting city after it had gone off alert. A general sent agents into the opposing camp before battle, where they pretended to be deserters and tricked the enemy into letting down his guard. Another king attacked a neighbor via a roundabout route to avoid enemy scouts. Nor were the Hittites alone in their use of trickery. For example, the siege of one Mesopotamian city by another involved sneak attacks at night and the impersonation of an allied unit of soldiers in an attempt to lull the besieged into opening their gates. (It failed.)

Think of the fall of Troy not as a myth about a Horse but as an example of unconventional warfare, Bronze Age style. The Trojan Horse might be better known as the Trojan Red Herring. Everyone focuses on the Horse but the real story lies elsewhere. In fact, it would be possible to leave out the Trojan Horse and yet tell a credible and coherent narrative of the capture of Troy much as the ancients told it.

Without the Trojan Horse, the story might go like this: The Greeks decided to trick the Trojans into thinking they had gone home when, in fact, they had merely retreated to Tenedos. Once they had lulled the enemy into dropping his guard, they planned to return in a surprise attack—at night. To know when to move, the Greeks would look for a lighted-torch signal, to be given by a Greek in Troy who had pretended to turn traitor and desert. Signals were used often in ancient battles, most famously at Marathon (490 B.C.), when a Greek traitor in the hills flashed a shield in the sunlight to communicate with the Persians. In the clear skies of the Mediterranean, fire signals could be seen from far off. They were visible as smoke signals during the day and as beacons at night. Tests show that the signals were visible between mountaintops up to a distance of two hundred miles.

At the sign, the Greeks would row back rapidly to Troy. The final part of the plan required a few men inside Troy to open the city gate. These men might either have been Trojan traitors or Greeks who had sneaked into the city. With the emergency supposedly over, Troy's gatekeepers would not have proved difficult to overcome.

Compare the set of tricks by which the south Italian port city of Tarentum was betrayed in turn to Hannibal and then to the Romans. In 213 B.C. a pro-Carthaginian citizen of Tarentum arranged for Carthaginian soldiers to come back with him from a nighttime hunting expedition. The soldiers wore breastplates and held swords under their buckskins; they even carried a wild boar in front, to appear authentic. Once the city gate was opened to them, they slaughtered the guards, and Hannibal's army rushed in. Four years later, the Romans under Fabius Maximus recaptured the city by having a local girl seduce the commander of Hannibal's garrison. He agreed to guide Roman troops over the walls at night while Fabius's ships created a distraction at the harbor wall on the other side of town. Although these events took place a thousand years after the Trojan War, they could easily have been carried out with Bronze Age technology.

The Greek plan at Troy was to trick the enemy into dropping his guard. It worked: the Trojans relaxed. At that point, one Greek inside the city lit a signal fire to bring the Greek fleet back and then others opened a gate.

The island of Tenedos lies about seven miles (six nautical miles) from the Trojan Harbor. The Greeks might have moored their ships in one of the sheltered coves on the island's east coast, near Troy but out of sight. At a rate of about five knots (about that of a thirty-two-oared Scandinavian longship traveling one hundred miles) they could have covered the distance in little more than an hour. That is, in daylight; the trip would no doubt have taken longer at night. But the *Sack of Ilium* claims it was a moonlit night and, anyhow, Bronze Age armies knew how to march by night. So the trip from Tenedos took perhaps no more than two hours. From the Trojan Harbor it was another five miles by land to Troy. It was nighttime and the road was primitive but the Greeks knew it well. They could have covered the distance in three hours. Athenian sources claim the month was Thargelion, roughly modern May. At that time of year, sunrise at Troy is 5:30–6 A.M., sunset 8–8:30 P.M. If the Greeks left Tenedos at, say, 9 P.M., and if everything went without a hitch, they would have arrived at Troy between 2 and 3 A.M., that is, about three hours before sunrise. A forced march may have gotten the Greeks to Troy an hour or so earlier.

To carry out their plan, the Greeks had had to infiltrate a small group of soldiers into the city. But they did not need the Trojan Horse to do so. Odysseus had already sneaked in and out of the city on two separate occasions shortly before. People came and went through the gates of Troy throughout the period of the war, making it all the easier now to trick the gatekeepers into letting in a handful of disguised Greek warriors.

Once inside the city, all the Greeks needed was arms, which a determined man would not have found difficult to get. Hardened commandos could easily have overpowered a few Trojan soldiers and taken their shields and spears.

Ancient cities under attack were also often betrayed from within. Not even weapons could stand up to "dissatisfaction and treachery," says an Akkadian poem. Troy too no doubt had its share of people who preferred dealing with the Greeks to prolonging the misery of war.

But if the Trojan Horse was not strictly necessary to the Greek's plan, it might well nonetheless have been part of it. The Trojan Horse would certainly inspire more confidence if ancient history recorded another occasion on which a similar ruse was employed. But how could it? The Trojan Horse was such a famous trick that it could be used only once.

According to Homer, it was Odysseus who conceived of the idea and Epeius, known otherwise as the champion boxer at the funeral games of Patroclus, who built the Horse. Certainly, the Greeks had the technology to build it. Ancient fleets usually sailed with shipwrights because wooden ships constantly need repairs, and Linear B texts refer both to shipwrights and carpenters as professions. There would have been no shortage of men in the Greek camp to do the job.

And there would have been no question about whether a statue of an animal would catch the Trojan king's fancy. Bronze Age monarchs liked animal imagery. A Babylonian king of the 1300s B.C., for example, had specifically asked the pharaoh for a gift of realistic figures of wild animals, with lifelike hides, made by Egyptian carpenters. But which animal should the Greeks build at Troy? A Trojan Dog would have been insulting; a Trojan Lion, frightening; a Trojan Bull or Cow would have thrown Greek cattle-raids in the enemy's teeth. But a horse symbolized war, privilege, piety, popularity, and Troy itself.

Horses are expensive, and in the Bronze Age they were usually used in military context, rarely as farm animals. Rulers of the era often sent horses as a gift between kings, while ordinary Trojans might cherish a figure of a horse. In the Late Bronze Age, horse figurines, made of baked clay, were collected throughout the Near East. Excavators recently found a clay model of a horse in Troy of the 1200s B.C. Finally, there was the religious connotation: as a votive offering, the Horse was all but an admission of Greek war guilt, a symbolic submission to the gods of the horse-taming Trojans.

The Horse would have been used to smuggle a small number of Greek soldiers into the city, but the chances of detection were very high. Although the traditional story of the Trojan Horse cannot be ruled out, it seems more probable that, if the Horse did exist, it was empty. There were simpler and less dangerous ways of smuggling soldiers into the city. The horse's main value to the Greeks was not as a transport but as a decoy, a low-tech ancestor of the phantom army under General Patton that the Allies used in 1944 to trick the Germans into expecting the D-day invasion in the area of Pas de Calais instead of Normandy.

Epic tradition has some Trojans accepting the Horse as a genuine sign that the Greeks had given up while others remain skeptical. The debate lasted all day, according to Vergil, or three days, according to Homer. The *Sack of Ilium* identifies three camps: those who wanted to burn the Horse, those who wanted to throw it down from the walls, and those who wanted to consecrate it to Athena. The length of the debate was in direct proportion to the stakes. The safety of the city as well as individual careers were hanging on the decision.

Vergil makes much of Priam's daughter Cassandra, an opponent of the Horse who enjoyed the gift of prophecy but suffered the curse of being ignored. This story does not appear in Homer or what we have of the Epic Cycle. One person who does feature in the tradition is the Trojan priest Laocöon, a staunch opponent of the Greeks who wanted to destroy the Horse. In Vergil, the debate over the Horse comes to an end when Laocöon and his sons are strangled by two snakes from the sea. The *Sack of Ilium* apparently places this event after the Horse had already been brought into town. Surely the snakes are symbolic; surely Laocöon and his boys were killed not by a sea-snake but by a member of the pro-Greek faction, and so, therefore, by someone perceived as a tool of a signifier of evil like a snake.

Laocöon's snakes may well be rooted in Anatolian Bronze Age religion, local lore of the Troad, or both. Hittite literature made the snake a symbol of chaos and the archenemy of the Storm God. It makes sense for a snake to foil the Storm God's servant, the Trojan priest who was trying to save his city. The Troad, meanwhile, is rich in fossil remains of Miocene animals such as mastodons and pygmy giraffes, and these objects might have made their way into myth. For example, an Iron Age Greek painter probably used a fossilized animal skull as a model for a monster whom Heracles is supposed to have defeated on the shore of Troy. So the story of Laocöon's murder by monsters from the sea may well have Trojan roots.

Laocöon's fate convinced Aeneas and his followers to leave town; they withdrew to Mount Ida in time to escape the Greek onslaught. Vergil famously tells a different story, in which Aeneas stays in Troy, fights the Greeks, and then at last escapes the burning city while carrying his elderly father, Anchises, on his back. But the account in the *Sack of Ilium,* which records Aeneas's departure, strikes a more credible note. Aeneas would not have been eager to die for Priam, a king who had never given Aeneas the honor that he felt he was due. His homeland was south of the city, in the valley of Dardania beside the northern slopes of Mount Ida. What better place to regroup if Aeneas believed that Troy was doomed?

Helen played a double game. She had helped Odysseus on his mission to Troy and learned of his plan of the Horse. Now she tried to coax the Greeks out of the Horse, but Odysseus kept them silent—or perhaps the Horse was empty. Helen is supposed to have gone back home that night and prepared herself for the inevitable. She had her maids arrange her clothes and cosmetics for her reunion with Menelaus.

Whether or not there was a Trojan Horse and whether or not the Trojans brought it into town and dedicated it to Athena, it is easy to imagine them celebrating the end of the war. They treated themselves to a night of partying, according to the *Sack of Ilium.* It was now, when the Trojans were occupied, that Sinon supposedly gave the prearranged torch signal. Once watchers on Tenedos saw it, the expedition to take Troy rowed rapidly back to the mainland.

Surprise, night, and Trojan drunkenness would have given the Greeks substantial advantages, but taking Troy would require hard fighting nonetheless. Experienced warriors, the Trojans would have scrambled quickly after their initial shock. If the battle began in darkness, it no doubt would have continued well into the daylight hours. The epic tradition offers a few details of Trojan resistance. The Greek Meges, leader of the Epeans of Elis, was wounded in the arm by Admetus son of Augeias. Another Greek, Lycomedes, took a wound in the wrist from the Trojan Agenor son of Antenor.

But what the tradition highlights, of course, is Greek victory. Admetus and Agenor, for instance, did not savor their successes, because that same night one was killed by Philoctetes and the other by Neoptolemus. A Greek named Eurypylus son of Euaemon killed

Priam's son Axion. Menelaus began his revenge by killing Helen's new husband, Deïphobus, brother of Paris and son of Priam. But the Greek known for scoring the most kills in the sack of Troy is Achilles' son, Neoptolemus. Among his victims, besides Agenor, were Astynous, Eion, and Priam himself, either at the altar of Zeus—no doubt the Storm God, where the Trojan king had sought shelter—or, as some say, at the doors of the palace because, not wanting to violate a god's altar, Neoptolemus was careful to drag his victim away first.

As for the Trojan women, tradition assigns Andromache to Neoptolemus and Cassandra to Agamemnon. Locrian Ajax had attempted to seize Cassandra but violated the altar of Athena or a Trojan goddess, which made the Greeks loath to reward him and thereby earn divine enmity. Prudent Bronze Age warriors knew better than to insult an enemy's god. For example, when Hittite King Shuppiluliuma I conquered the city of Carchemish around 1325 B.C. he sacked the town but kept all his troops away from the temples of Kubaba and Lamma. He bowed to the goddesses instead.

Priam's daughter Polyxena was, according to the *Sack of Ilium,* slaughtered at the tomb of Achilles as an offering to the hero's ghost. Little Astyanax, Hector's son, was murdered by Odysseus—thrown from the walls, in one version—lest he grow up and seek vengeance.

And then there was Helen. The *Little Iliad* states that Menelaus found her at home, in the house of Deïphobus. Menelaus's sword was drawn to seek vengeance on the agent of his humiliation and suffering, but Helen had merely to undrape her breasts to change his mind. It is the sort of story that we can only wish is true.

So much for the epic tradition. What do other Bronze Age texts and the archaeological excavations tell us about the sack of Troy? Bronze Age documents show that however brutal the sack of Troy may have been, it would have conformed to the laws of war. Cities that did not surrender would, if they were captured, be destroyed. This rule goes as far back as the first well-documented interstate conflict, the border wars between the two Sumerian city-states of Lagash and Umma between 2500 and 2350 B.C.

When the Greeks sacked the city, they put Troy to the torch. Archaeology discloses that a savage fire destroyed the settlement level known as Troy VIi (formerly called Troy VIIa). Blackened wood, white calcined stone, and heaps of fallen building material were found in a thick destruction layer of ash and dirt about twenty inches to six feet deep. The inferno can be dated, according to the best estimate, sometime between 1230 and 1180 B.C., more likely between 1210 and 1180.

The flames must have spread fast. One house in the lower city tells the story: a bronze figurine, as well as some gold and silver jewelry, was left abandoned on the floor of a room. The inhabitants had fled in panic.

Imagine Troy's narrow streets clogged, and imagine the rolling cries of disoriented refugees, the wailing of children; the growls and snorts, bleating, high-pitched squeals, and relentless howls and barks of terrified barnyard animals (in the Bronze Age, typically kept within the town walls at night). Imagine too the clatter of arms, the clang and whistle of cold bronze, the soft sound of blood squirting onto paving stones, the cheers of the avengers, the whiz of javelins in flight, the reverberation of a spear that has found its mark, the holler and thud of street fighting, the surge of wails and curses, the gush and choking of pain, and much of it muffled by a fire burning fast enough to sound like a downpour.

Archaeology draws a picture that is consistent with a sack of Troy. Outside the doorway of a house on the citadel, for example, a partial human male skeleton was discovered. Was he a householder, killed defending his property? Other human bones have been found in the citadel, scattered and unburied. There is also a fifteen-year-old girl buried in the lower town; the ancients rarely buried people within the city limits unless an attack was preventing them from going to a cemetery outside town. It was even rarer to leave human skeletons unburied—another sign of the disaster that had struck Troy.

Two bronze spear points, three bronze arrowheads, and two partially preserved bronze knives have been found in the citadel and lower town. One of the arrowheads is of a type known only in the Greek mainland in the Late Bronze Age. The lower town has also yielded a cache of 157 sling stones in three piles. Another supply of a dozen smooth stones, possibly sling stones, was found on the citadel, in a building beside the south gate that looked to the excavators like a possible arsenal or guardhouse.

None of this evidence proves beyond doubt that Troy was destroyed in a sack. The fire that ravaged the city could have been caused by accident and then been stoked by high winds. If Troy was destroyed by armed violence, were the Greeks responsible? The archaeological evidence is consistent with that explanation but does not prove it.

CONCLUSION

On the mountaintop, where the goats forage in the crevices between the rocks and the only sound beside their bleating is a sudden burst of wind in the wildflowers, the sky is the same shade of pale blue and gray as the eyes of the goddess Athena. That's when it happens: not during an afternoon plunge into one of the chilly pools of Ida, the mountain rich in springs, nor in the thickening darkness when the owls appear and the night's first bats take wing. Only here, on the heights, where the light rakes the treeless ridge, does he let the truth come out, and the truth is that he is no herdsman. Only then, when he relaxes his guard, does he remember that he is a soldier who knows the sound of javelins whirring through the air and the sight of the wounded men crawling on the plain.

Aeneas, son of Anchises, would surely like to stay on the mountain. The mountain is his mother. It was here long ago that Anchises slept with the luminous goddess of love. Aeneas grew up on Ida's slopes, hunting deer in the woods and careening down its trails on wild horses. He takes his bearings by the bees that pollinate its flowers and by the star that rises above it, by the Evening Star, Aphrodite herself, or Ishtar, as she was more likely known in the Troad. If anyone can lead him back, the goddess can, since she was a deity not only of love but of war.

If he must come down from Ida, Aeneas would choose to live in the Dardanian Valley that lies in its lap below. The mountain-sheltered valley is as rich as it is wide and well watered: kingdom enough for any man. A river runs through the middle of its grain fields, seemingly as far from the sea as a sinner's heart is far from the gods. But this is the Scamander River, and twenty miles downstream it once ran red with the blood of Achilles' victims. Ida's native son cannot stay in Dardania; Aeneas has to lead the survivors back home. All his life he has complained about his treatment by Priam and his sons, and now that they are gone, Aeneas is heir to the throne. On his broad shoulders lies the fate of Troy. Or so we may imagine him thinking one day, not long after the Greeks had left and the fires had died down in the ruins of the city.

Legend has it that Troy was completely destroyed, but in fact the city was soon rebuilt. The new Troy was once again a great center. It was not as rich or as grand as Priam's city and it was not inhabited by the same people. But there were sources of continuity, and none greater than Aeneas himself.

Epic tradition offers several versions of Aeneas' fate, from captivity under Neoptolemus in Greece, to triumph in Italy near the future site of Rome—after an amorous detour in Carthage. But the *Iliad* is clear. Achilles scoffs at Aeneas for wanting to replace Priam as king, when everyone knows that one of Priam's many sons will inherit the throne. But Poseidon knows better. As the god predicts of Troy after the war,

> *For Priam now, and Priam's faithless kind,*
> *At length are odious to the all-seeing mind;*
> *On great Aeneas shall devolve the reign,*
> *And sons succeeding sons the lasting line sustain.*

The way to the throne of Troy began on Mount Ida, where tradition says that Aeneas gathered together the refugees from the defeated city.

The refugees might have meditated on the irony of Troy's fate. For all their fury, the Greeks never surrounded the city or sealed it off from the outside world. They tried to storm Troy's walls but failed. Nor did pitched battle between armies led by heroes succeed in the conquest of Troy. Only the steady pressure of Greek raids on Troy's hinterland, which lay open to Greek sea power, bled the city white. And in its vulnerable state, Troy fell prey to a fatal act of espionage. It was cunning and not courage that killed Troy.

We in turn may reflect on the ironies of epic. Like a chronicle of the pharaohs or the annals of a Hittite king, the *Iliad* idealizes war. The focus is on divinely inspired heroes who carry out superhuman deeds and suffer only clean wounds. The Greeks crowd the stage and Troy is doomed, although the struggle is so grand that it takes ten years. Yet Homer is honest enough to hint at the real war of far shorter duration; a war of filth and disease, of attacks on civilians, and of ordinary men who died lonely deaths. Helen is not only a beautiful but also a light-fingered cause of war, since she made off with her husband's treasure as well as his honor, and the Greeks wanted the gold back. Besides, they were far more interested in capturing enemy women than in regaining Menelaus's runaway bride.

Both in his exaggerations and his honesty Homer is truer to the Bronze Age than is usually recognized. Bronze Age poets regularly inflate battlefield deeds, but other Bronze Age texts preserve the truth: a way of war that was sometimes low-intensity, often devious, and always squalid. Thanks both to oral tradition and also perhaps to non-Greek written sources, Homer preserves these truths even though Troy fell centuries before his lifetime.

As they returned to their ships from the ruins of Troy, the Greeks would have carried their wounded and the bodies of their dead, and driven a crowd of captive Trojans forward, with cartloads of booty following. The art of the Bronze Age shows many such lines of prisoners, naked as often as not, hands tied behind their backs or locked in wooden beams. Then the plunder and women had to be divided among the army. The chiefs, naturally, got first pick. Neoptolemus, for example, is said to have chosen Andromache, Hector's widow; the other heroes accepted his choice, no doubt glad to have satisfied his considerable ego. The sons of the late, great Athenian hero Theseus, Acamas and Demophon, were content to rescue their mother, Aethra; according to Athenian tradition, she had gone to Troy as Helen's lady-in-waiting. At least they were content according to one story; another version says that Agamemnon gave them "many gifts" as well.

Like many a conquering army, the Greeks fell out with each other as soon as the war was over. The immediate cause of the quarrel was the question of Locrian Ajax and his sacrilege against Athena or her Trojan equivalent, by having inadvertently taken a statue of her when he grabbed Cassandra from the goddess's temple. By violating the goddess's image, Locrian Ajax subjected the whole army to her vengeance. Agamemnon and Menelaus, brothers and now rivals, argued in front of the troops. Agamemnon wanted to put off their departure until he could make amends by carrying out a big sacrifice to Athena; Menelaus wanted to go home. The Greeks had already stoned Ajax, and Menelaus no doubt reminded the men of this punishment. Agamemnon said that wasn't enough.

No ancient army, in any period, would think of making a long journey having incurred the wrath of a god. But Menelaus, Diomedes, and Nestor sailed away with their men the next day anyhow. As Nestor later explained it, Athena's punishment had already started with the royal quarrel; the safest course seemed to be to get far away from Troy. Nestor reached Pylos without incident. Likewise, Diomedes made it home safely to Argos, and Neoptolemus went to his father's ancestral land, Phthia, which he had never seen before, having grown up on the island of Scyros. But he played it safe by avoiding the treacherous sea and traveling overland.

Locrian Ajax escaped Athena, only to run afoul of Poseidon, who let him survive a shipwreck only to drown the man for his blasphemy. Menelaus lost most of his ships in a storm and was blown off course to Egypt with the rest. By the time he finally reached Sparta, the news was waiting of his brother's fatal homecoming. When Agamemnon returned to Mycenae, he was murdered by his wife, Clytemnestra, and the lover whom she had taken in his absence, Aegisthus, who was engaged in a blood feud with Agamemnon.

The sons of Atreus were never lucky in love. Menelaus brought back his prize, Helen. The *Odyssey* depicts the couple reunited and ruling in Lacedaemon, surrounded by war-won trophies in the royal palace. They lived to celebrate the marriage of their daughter to Neoptolemus. So the king was certainly better off than his butchered brother. Yet Helen's practice of slipping drugs into Menelaus's wine suggests that not all was happy in the royal halls.

Odysseus took ten years before reaching home—no doubt another case of the Bronze Age expression for "a long time until finally." In the Bronze Age, being blown off course, being shipwrecked or marooned were not uncommon occurrences, so there is some plausibility in the outline of the *Odyssey*. When Odysseus at last reached Ithaca he found his enemies in charge of his household and battled them to restore his authority.

The tales of trouble in Mycenae and Ithaca perhaps offer a hint of the violence that in fact struck the Mycenaean palaces. Sometime around 1190/1180 B.C. a wave of destruction hit the major centers on the Greek mainland, including Pylos, Tiryns, Athens, and Mycenae itself. Archaeology shows that life continued in the lower towns but the palaces on the citadels were destroyed, and with them went a way of life that included luxury goods, manorial estates, and scribes keeping written records. Greek civilization continued but at a lower level of complexity and wealth.

A similar fate was in store for many of the citadels of Anatolia, Cyprus, Canaan, and Mesopotamia. Egypt weathered the storm but it felt its force nonetheless. Clearly, it was a disastrous time throughout the Bronze Age world of the Eastern Mediterranean and Near East.

The causes of this decline are unclear. Earthquakes appear to have played a role, but they were probably not the only source of trouble. Dynastic disputes, imperial overstretch in adventures like the Trojan War, bad harvests, peasant unrest, may all have contributed. In Anatolia, grain was scarce shortly before 1200 B.C., perhaps suggesting climate change that affected Greece as well.

There is only weak evidence for foreign invasion, whether by the Sea Peoples or the Dorians. The Dorians were Greek-speakers from northwestern Greece. Contrary to popular misconception, they did not come south until much later, so they could not have destroyed the Mycenaean palaces. But the Sea Peoples do fit chronologically. They attacked and destroyed the city of Ugarit around 1190 B.C. They seem to have played a role in the fall of the city of Hattusha around the same time, and they attacked Egypt but were driven back. They were more successful in Canaan, where they settled down as the people known later as the Philistines.

Who were the Sea Peoples? The answer is not yet clear, but we do know that they were a coalition, and there is good reason to think that some of them were Greeks. So, if the Sea Peoples sacked the Mycenaean palaces, they might better be thought of as a faction in a Greek civil war rather than as foreign invaders.

The Hittites, at any rate, had other problems besides the Sea Peoples. Well before the city of Hattusha was sacked, it suffered decline and depopulation. Parts of the Hittite Empire in southern and southeastern Anatolia had become separate kingdoms. Various branches of the Hittite ruling dynasties were enmeshed in intermittent feuds that sometimes turned very nasty. Although Hattusha fell, marking the end of the Hittites' great central Anatolian empire, the Hittite kingdoms in the south managed to survive for centuries more.

We are only beginning to understand why most of the palaces of the eastern Mediterranean were in ruins by not long after 1200 B.C. Future research should shed much new light on the matter. But whatever the truth was, it was probably as complex as the process that left most of the cities of Europe and Japan in ruins by 1945. Just as no single cause can explain World War II, so the Sea Peoples alone cannot explain the end of the palace civilization of the Bronze Age.

Archaeology shows that after the burning and probable sacking of Troy VIi, the city was reconstructed—and in no mean way. Wherever possible, old buildings were repaired and streets were repaved, but new structures went up as well. Troy VIj (formerly known as Troy VIIb1)—to use the archaeologists' ungainly name for this new Troy—was not poor. Gold and bronze jewels, an iron ax, and a carnelian seal have all been found there. And it is to this city, several generations later (ca. 1130 B.C.) that prehistoric Troy's only inscription may be dated, the married couple's seal referred to earlier.

Of course the new Troy was not as rich as the old one. Agriculture provides a clue here. While Priam's Troy produced wheat, Troy VIj subsisted on barley, a poorer grain, which ancient peoples usually fed to animals. And the new Troy was not inhabited by the same people—not after the deaths and deportations. So a new population emerged in Troy VIj: a mixture of old Trojans and newcomers from the Balkans.

Imagine Aeneas back again in Troy. He lives with the din of carpenters, stonemasons, and brick bakers. The dead have been buried, the rubble cleared, the stones replaced. Sheep and cattle have been herded to their pens within the walls. Libations have been poured to the gods.

From his half-built home on the citadel, one evening Aeneas might have looked out on the plain, a tawny sea of grain lying still in the pale blue light. Turning, he would see Poseidon's realm, a silvery ribbon stretching as far as the islands' walls. And as a brisk breeze of Boreas ruffled his hair, he might have looked down on the new town rising. With all the inevitable problems, Aeneas might have been proud of his role in lifting up Troy like a stone out of deep water, to use a Hittite expression. The lofty works of the gods, the peaks of Mount Ida and of Samothrace, would soon be replicated once again by the proud man-made towers of Troy.

GLOSSARY OF KEY NAMES

Achaeans Along with Argives and Danaans, one of the three main names used by Homer for the people we call Greeks.

Achilles Mythical king of Phthia and heroic warrior whose rage is at the heart of the *Iliad*.

Aeneas Mythical figure, son of Anchises and goddess Aphrodite, kinsman of Priam, fights in Trojan War; rules in rebuilt, postwar Troy.

Agamemnon Mythical king of Mycenae, and leader of Greek expedition against Troy.

Ahhiyawa Powerful kingdom referred to by Hittite texts, probably to be identified with the land of Homer's Achaeans.

Ajax son of Oïleus of Locris Mythical figure, an especially rough and impious Greek warrior at Troy, also known as "Lesser Ajax" and "Locrian Ajax."

Ajax son of Telamon of Salamis Mythical character, immensely strong if slow Greek warrior at Troy, also known as "Greater Ajax."

Akkadian Dominant language and culture of Mesopotamia, 2350–1900 B.C., and widespread in its influence throughout Bronze Age Near East.

Alaksandu King of Wilusa, ca. 1280 B.C., made alliance with Hittites; his name recalls Homer's Alexander (Paris).

Amazons Women warriors, referred to by Homer and in Greek myth, vaguely recalled by Iron Age women warriors of southern Russia.

Amenhotep II King of Egypt, 1427–1392 B.C., victorious general in Canaan, Syria, and Mesopotamia.

Amenhotep III King of Egypt, 1382–1344 B.C., reigned at height of New Kingdom's power.

Amyclae Town in Laconia, site of Menelaion (shrine of Helen and Menelaus), possible site of Bronze Age palace.

Andromache Mythical character, wife of Hector, afterward widowed and taken as war-prize by Greeks.

191

Antenor Mythical figure, pro-Greek Trojan.

Antimachus Mythical character, anti-Greek Trojan.

Apasa Probably the later Ephesus, capital of kingdom of Arzawa.

Argives See ACHAEANS.

Arzawa Kingdom in western Anatolia.

Attarissiya Raider from Ahhiyawa, cited in Hittite texts, who attacked Anatolia and Cyprus, ca. 1400 B.C.; possibly to be identified with Atreus of Greek myth.

Aulis Bronze Age (and later) harbor town in east-central Greece; according to Homer the embarkation point of the Greek expedition against Troy.

Beşik Bay Modern name of Trojan Harbor, about five miles southwest of site of city of Troy.

Boreas North wind.

Briseis Mythical princess of Lyrnessus, taken as war-prize by Achilles and appropriated by Agamemnon as compensation for Chryseis.

Bronze Age Era, ca. 3000–1100 B.C., in which bronze was the primary metal for tools and weapons; iron was rare and expensive but it was known.

Cadmus Mythical king of Thebes.

Calchas Mythical Greek seer at Aulis and Troy.

Canaan Region of city-states dominated by Egypt and contested by Hittites, stretching from modern Turkish-Syrian border to Gaza.

Cassandra Mythical figure, daughter of Priam, minor character in Homer, but in Vergil the important but ignored prophetess of Troy's ruin.

Catalog of Ships Lines in which Homer (*Iliad* 2.484–787) lists all the captains, kings, and countries taking part in the Trojan War.

Chryseis Mythical figure, daughter of priest Chryses of city of Chryse in southwestern Troad, taken as war-prize by Agamemnon.

cuneiform Early writing system, widely used in ancient Near East.

Cycnus Mythical character, king of town of Colonae on west coast of Troad, whose name recalls the historical figure Kukkunni, King of Wilusa.

Danaans See ACHAEANS.

Dardanian Valley Fertile region of middle Scamander River in Troad, mythical home of Aeneas.

Dardanians Mentioned in Egyptian text as Hittite allies who sent chariots to fight at Battle of Qadesh.

Deïphobus Mythical figure, Trojan prince who marries Helen after death of his brother, Paris.

Diomedes Mythical king of Argos, the youngest and one of the doughtiest Greek warriors at Troy.

Dolon Mythical figure, vain and incompetent Trojan spy, killed by Diomedes.

Eëtion Mythical king of Thebes-under-Plakos and father of Andromache, killed by Achilles.

Epic Cycle Ancient Greek epics *(Cypria, Aethiopis, Little Iliad, Sack of Ilium, The Returns)* describing Trojan War and aftermath: survives only in a few quotations.

Euphorbus Mythical figure, son of Panthous, young Trojan warrior specially trained in chariot fighting, wounds Patroclus severely.

Eurypylus Mythical figure, son of Telephus of Mysia, brings contingent to fight for Troy.

Gallipoli Fertile peninsula opposite the Troad, on northern shore of the Dardanelles.

Gilgamesh Popular ancient Near Eastern epic poem, ca. 2000 B.C. or earlier, originally in Akkadian but often translated.

Glaucus Mythical warrior, son of Hippolochus of Lycia, leading lieutenant of Trojan ally Sarpedon.

Hammurabi Babylonian king (1792–1750 B.C.), great warrior and codifier of law, conquered Mari.

Hattusha City in central Anatolia, Hittite capital.

Hattushilish I Great Hittite king, 1650–1620 B.C.

Hattushilish III Hittite king (reigned 1267–1237 B.C.), negotiated with Egypt and Ahhiyawa and fought western Anatolian rebel Piyamaradu.

Hector Mythical figure, son of Priam and Hecuba; Troy's crown prince and greatest warrior.

Hecuba Mythical character, wife of Priam and queen of Troy.

Helen Mythical figure, wife of King Menelaus of Lacedaemon; ran off with Trojan prince Paris, sparking the Trojan War.

Helenus Mythical character, brother of Hector and wise seer.

Hellenes In Homer, refers only to inhabitants of part of Thessaly in central Greece, but in Iron Age name for all Greeks.

Hisarlık "Fortified place" in Turkish, the modern-day name for the site of ancient Troy.

Hittites Also known as Hatti, between 1600s and ca. 1180 B.C. ruled an empire in Anatolia and Syria.

Ida Mountain in southern Troad, sacred to inhabitants.

Idomeneus Mythical character, king of Crete and great spearman, fought at Troy.

Ilion Another name for Troy; in early Greek, it was Wilion, but the "W" later dropped out. Source of name of the epic poem the *Iliad*.

Indo-European Language group and culture of its speakers, spread in ancient times from India to Britain; includes Greeks, Trojans, and Hittites.

Iphigenia Mythical character, daughter of Agamemnon and Clytemnestra, victim of human sacrifice at Aulis.

Iron Age First millennium B.C., when iron replaced bronze as main medium for tools and weapons.

Ishtar Near Eastern goddess of love, war, and fertility.

Ithaca Island off western Greece, legendary home of Odysseus.

Iyarri Anatolian god of war and plagues, known as an archer ("Lord of the Bow"), similar to Greek god Apollo.

Kukkunni King of Wilusa at some date before ca. 1280 B.C.

Kurunta Anatolian god, represented by stag; often a city's protector.

Lacedaemon Southern Greek region later also known as Laconia, kingdom of Menelaus and Helen.

Laocöon Mythical figure, anti-Greek priest of Troy, killed along with sons by sea monster.

Levant Region of southwestern Asia roughly equivalent to today's Israel, Jordan, Lebanon, Palestine, and Syria.

Levirate marriage Common ancient Near Eastern custom of a man marrying his deceased brother's widow.

Linear B Bronze Age Greek writing system used by Mycenaean scribes.

Luwian Indo-European language and culture of southern and western Anatolia, closely related to Hittite; possibly the language of Troy.

Lycia Region of southwestern Anatolia, probably the same area as the "Lukka Lands" of Hittite texts.

Lyrnessus In Homer, town in Troad conquered by the Greeks.

Machaon Along with brother Podalirius, mythical physician in Greek army at Troy.

Madduwatta Untrustworthy Hittite vassal in western Anatolia ca. 1400 B.C.

Mari City-state in northwestern Mesopotamia (modern Syria), well documented in decades before being sacked by Hammurabi in 1757 B.C.

Megiddo City in Canaan, site of major battle in 1479 B.C.

Melanippus Mythical character, son of Hicetaeon, fled hometown of Percote on the Dardanelles when the Greeks came; fought for Troy.

Memnon Mythical figure, prince of Aethiopia (possibly Nubia) and kinsman of Priam who brings contingent to fight for Troy.

Menelaus Mythical figure, husband of Helen and king of Lacedaemon as well as brother of Agamemnon.

Miletus City on Anatolia's Aegean coast, colonized by Minoans and Mycenaeans in turn.

Minoan The people and culture of Bronze Age Crete, at its height ca. 1800–1490 B.C.

Mira Western Anatolian state in Late Bronze Age; a successor state of Arzawa.

Murshilish II Hittite king, 1321–1295 B.C., conquered kingdom of Arzawa.

Mycenae Powerful city of mythical King Agamemnon; the adjective "Mycenaean" refers in general to Greeks and Greek civilization of the Late Bronze Age.

Mysia Region in northwestern Anatolia bordering the Troad.

Neoptolemus Mythical figure, son of Achilles and conqueror of Troy.

Nestor Mythical character, elderly king of Pylos and the Greeks' best counselor at Troy.

New Kingdom In both Egypt (1550–1075 B.C.) and Hatti (1400–1180) the Late Bronze Age era of expansion and empire.

Nubia Southern Nile region conquered by Egyptians, inhabited by black Africans, some of whom rose to high positions in New Kingdom Egypt.

Odysseus Mythical figure, king of Ithaca and most cunning and resourceful Greek warrior at Troy.

Old Babylonian literature Body of poetry and prose, ca. 2000–1600 B.C., whose influence may have reached as far as Homer.

Palaic Indo-European language of northern Anatolia, possibly language of Troy.

Palladium Mythical wooden statuette in Troy of goddess Athena.

Pandarus Mythical figure, son of Lycaon and great archer; Trojan ally.

Paris Mythical character, prince of Troy, seduced Helen and thereby caused the Trojan War; also known as Alexander, recalling Alaksandu, historical king of Wilusa.

Patroclus Mythical figure, son of Menoetius; Achilles' chief general and closest comrade.

Pellana Village in northern Laconia, site of Mycenaean buildings and tombs, possibly including palace of Helen and Menelaus.

Penthesilea Mythical figure, Thracian Amazon who brings contingent to fight for Troy.

Pergamos In Homer, citadel of Troy.

Philoctetes Mythical personage, Greek from Thessaly and mighty archer.

Piyamaradu Luwian raider who successfully defied Hittites in western Anatolia ca. 1250 B.C.; allied with Ahhiyawa.

Polites Mythical character, brother of Hector; fast runner and lookout.

Polydamas Mythical personage, son of Panthous of Troy; seer and shrewd tactician.

Priam Mythical figure, king of Troy.

Protesilaus Mythical figure, king of Phylace in Thessaly, first Greek killed at Troy.

Puduhepa Wife of Hattushilish III and one of the Hittites' most powerful queens.

Pylos In Homer, great kingdom in southwestern Greece, well-attested archaeologically by great palace, Linear B texts, and other remains.

Qadesh Canaanite city and site of great battle between Egyptians and Hittites, 1274 B.C.

Rameses II Long-reigning Egyptian King, 1279–1213 B.C., fought Hittites at Qadesh and later made peace with them.

Rameses III Egyptian king, 1184–1153 B.C., defeated Sea Peoples.

Sarpedon Mythical Lycian king and son of Zeus as well as commander of important allied contingent fighting for Troy; killed by Patroclus.

Scaean Gate In Homer, main gate of Troy.

Scamander River Main river of the Troad, flows from Mount Ida past Troy and into Dardanelles.

Sea Peoples Loose and shifting coalition, possibly including Greeks, that attacked eastern Mediterranean lands 1200–1100 B.C. and did great damage.

Shardana Mercenaries in and sometimes pirates against Egypt in 1200s–1100s B.C.

Shuppiluliuma I One of the strongest Hittite kings, 1344–1322 B.C., crushed Mitanni and rebuilt Hattusha.

Shuppiluliuma II Last Hittite king (1207–? B.C.), fought sea battles off Cyprus.

Simoeis River A river of the Troad that flows into the Scamander north of Troy.

CITADEL FORTIFICATIONS. Anyone attacking Troy's citadel from the east would be forced into an alley between the citadel's imposing fortifications (left) and an overlapping wall (right). *(Barry Strauss)*

SOUTH GATE. The main entrance to Troy's citadel featured a paved street (center) and a monumental tower, part of whose foundations are seen here (left). Note the stele in front of the tower (front left). The canopy (rear) protects an early Bronze Age mud brick wall. *(Barry Strauss)*

(Above) TROJAN HOUSE. A large and well-built residence just outside the citadel in the north-west of the Lower City, built in Troy VIi. *(Barry Strauss)*

TROJAN DEFENSE. A part of the defensive ditch around the Lower City, interrupted by a causeway that was protected by a wooden palisade. The stone foundations of later structures are visible on the causeway. *(Troia Project Archives)*

SCAMANDER RIVER. In summer the water level is low in the main river of the Trojan Plain. Note the marshy shores. *(Barry Strauss)*

MOUNT IDA. A spring-fed pool on the south slope of the mountain that overlooks the Troad. Note the deciduous trees. *(Barry Strauss)*

CHRYSE. The cove in the center of the photograph may be the harbor of ancient Chryse. Agamemnon's beautiful captive, Chryseis, was brought back here by ship to her father, the priest Chryses. *(Barry Strauss)*

CAPE LEKTON. A rugged headland at the southwestern tip of the Troad. Raiders heading from Troy to the Gulf of Edremit would have sailed past this spot. *(Barry Strauss)*

GULF OF EDREMIT. A view, through olive trees, toward the mountains above Edremit (ancient Adramyttium), taken from near the presumed site of Thebes-under-Plakos. *(Barry Strauss)*

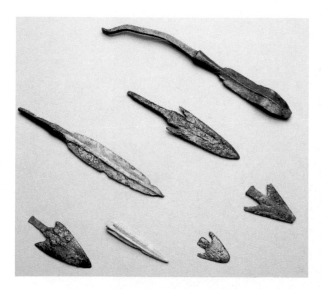

EVIDENCE OF WAR? These arrow- and spearheads were found in the excavations at Troy. *(Troia Project Archives/Dogan Burda Magazine)*

ODYSSEUS. The hero is shown speaking, dressed in a felt cap, cloak, and scabbard, on this chalcedony ring stone from Crete, 400–350 B.C. *(Bildarchiv Preussischer Kulturbesitz/Art Resource, NY)*

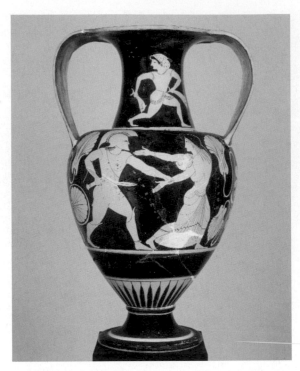

MENELAUS THREATENING HELEN. The king draws a sword on his wayward wife in this red-figure Attic amphora by the Oltos Painter, 525–515 B.C. *(Réunion des Musées Nationaux/Art Resource, NY)*

WARRIORS AT REST. Achilles and Ajax play dice in this black-figure vase from the sixth to fourth centuries B.C. *(Réunion des Musées Nationaux/Art Resource, NY)*

TROY LAID LOW. Achilles drags the body of Hector behind his chariot. Black-figure vase, Diosphos Painter, sixth to fifth centuries B.C. *(Réunion des Musées Nationaux/Art Resource, NY)*

TROJAN HORSE VASE. Detail of the neck of a Cycladic relief vase, depicting the Greek warriors inside the Horse, 675–650 B.C. *(Mykonos Museum/Hellenic Republic, Ministry of Culture)*

MYCENAEAN ARMOR. This suit of bronze body armor was found in a tomb at Dendra, not far from Mycenae, and is dated to the late 1400s B.C. *(Eleutherios Feiler, D-DAI-ATH-Argolis 691, All Rights Reserved)*

MYCENAEAN WARRIORS. This sherd from Tiryns shows parts of two body shields, a spear, and a boar's-tusk helmet. *(D-DAI-ATH-Tiryns-Archiv 1979/015, All Rights Reserved)*

Sinon Mythical figure, duplicitous Greek who tricks Trojans into accepting the Trojan Horse.

Storm God Sky god such as Zeus or Teshub, chief deity of Greeks and Anatolian peoples alike.

Taruisa A kingdom referred to in Hittite documents, possibly to be identified as Troy.

Tawagalawa Brother of king of Ahhiyawa, he aided Piyamaradu's rebellion in western Anatolia against the Hittites; possibly equivalent to Eteocles.

Telephus Mythical king of Mysia.

Teucer Mythical figure, brother of Ajax son of Telamon of Salamis, a great archer among the Greeks at Troy.

Thebes A major Mycenaean city in central Greece, destroyed violently ca. 1250 B.C.

Thebes-under-Plakos Trojan-allied city on Gulf of Adramyttium (Edremit); its site has not been identified.

Thersites Mythical character, malcontent and rabble-rouser in Greek army at Troy.

Tiryns Heavily fortified Bronze Age Greek city near Mycenae.

Tlepolemus Mythical figure, son of Heracles and king of Rhodes, fought with Greeks at Troy.

Troad Region of Troy, about 650 square miles in size.

Trojan Harbor See BEŞIK BAY.

Trojan Plain Broad area west of city of Troy, whose northern part was largely underwater in Bronze Age; in Homer, site of pitched battles of Trojan War.

Tukulti-Ninurta Assyrian king, 1244–1208 B.C.

Tyndareus Mythical personage, king of Lacedaemon, father of Helen.

Ugarit Wealthy and literate Canaanite city, commercial and naval power, Hittite ally, destroyed by Sea Peoples ca. 1187 B.C.

Ur Wealthy city in southern Mesopotamia.

Vergil Also known as Virgil, Roman poet (70–19 B.C.), author of the *Aeneid*, epic of Aeneas's struggles after the Trojan War.

Walmu Exiled king of Wilusa, ca. 1225 B.C.; vassal of Hittites.

wanax Linear B term for "king," perhaps recalled in Homer's use of term *anax* for Greece's leading king, Agamemnon.

Wilusa A kingdom referred to in Hittite documents, thought to be the Greek (W)ilion, that is, Troy.

NOTES

In citing ancient Greek and Roman authors, I follow the abbreviations of the standard reference work, the *Oxford Classical Dictionary*, 3rd edition (Oxford: Oxford University Press, 1999). I cite the titles of Greek and Latin works, however, in English translation. For Near Eastern texts I refer, wherever possible, to common English designations and to easily accessible English translations. EA ("El Amarna") designates a tablet of the Amarna Letters.

INTRODUCTION

1 makes it likely that the Trojan War indeed took place: I follow the arguments set forth by Joachim Latacz in his *Troy and Homer: Towards a Solution of an Old Mystery*, translated by Kevin Windle and Rosh Ireland (Oxford: Oxford University Press, 2004).

2 in its heyday: Manfred Korfmann, "Die Arbeiten in Troia/Wilusa 2003," *Studia Troica* 14 (2004): 17.

3 ninth year of the long conflict: For an argument that the *Iliad* is set in the ninth and not the tenth year of the Trojan War (as is usually thought), see Ernst Aumueller, "Das neunte Jahr. Ilias B 134-295-328," in Joachim Latacz and Heinrich Hettrich with Guenter Neumann, eds., *Wuerzburger Jahrbuecher fuer Die Altertumswissenschaft*, Neue Folge 21 (1996/97): 39–48.

7 "nine times and then a tenth": William L. Moran, ed. and trans., *The Amarna Letters* (Baltimore: Johns Hopkins University Press, 1992), EA 81, l. 24, p. 50, and p. 151 n. 6; cf. EA 82, l. 39, p. 52.

CHAPTER ONE: WAR FOR HELEN

13 Helen is dressed: My description is based on Homer, *Iliad* 3.121–71, 380–447; *Odyssey* 4 *passim*, 15.58, 104–8, 124–30, 171, and Ione My-

lonas Shear, *Tales of Heroes: The Origins of the Homeric Texts* (New York: Aristide D. Caratzas, 2000), 61–72; Elizabeth Barber, *Prehistoric Textiles* (Princeton: Princeton University Press, 1991), 170–73. See the descriptions in Bettany Hughes, *Helen of Troy: Goddess, Princess, Whore* (London: Jonathan Cape, 2005), 42, 65–66, 109–11.

13 Hittite proverb: Billie Jean Collins, "Animals in Hittite Literature," in Collins, ed., *A History of the Animal World in the Ancient Near East* (Leiden: Brill, 2002), 243; Harry A. Hoffner Jr., "The Song of Hedammu," in *Hittite Myths*, 2nd edition (Atlanta: Scholars Press, 1998), 54.

14 Menelaus's palace: That palace has not yet been discovered, so I use features from other Bronze Age Greek palaces such as Pylos and Mycenae.

14 rich hills of Lacedaemon: A region better known today as Sparta, although technically Sparta is only a small part of Lacedaemon. Sparta was not a city yet in the Bronze Age, but the name is much better known than Lacedaemon, so it is used here.

14 the company sits: C. W. Shelmerdine, "Review of Aegean Prehistory VI: The Palatial Bronze Age of the Southern and Central Greek Mainland," *American Journal of Archaeology* 101:3 (1997): 578–80; reprinted with an addendum on the period 1997–99 in Tracey Cullen, ed., *Aegean Prehistory: A Review*, Supplement 1 to *American Journal of Archaeology* (Boston: Archaeological Institute of America, 2001), 370–72.

15 *Pari-zitis:* Calvert Watkins, "Troy and the Trojans," in Machteld J. Mellink, ed., *Troy and the Trojan War*, from a symposium held at Bryn Mawr College, October 1984 (Bryn Mawr, Pa.: Bryn Mawr College, 1986), 57.

15 "Trojan": Michael Ventris and John Chadwick, *Documents in Mycenaean Greek*, 2nd edition (Cambridge, England: Cambridge University Press, 1973), PY 57, p. 190; cf. pp. 103–5.

15 "Trojan Woman": Ventris and Chadwick, *Documents in Mycenaean Greek*, PY 143, pp. 258–59; cf. pp. 103–5.

15 "Lacedaemonius": His father was Cimon son of Miltiades, a leading politician of classical Athens. See J. K. Davies, *Athenian Propertied Families 600–300 B.C.* (Oxford: Clarendon Press, 1971), 306.

16 not that he was fooled: *Odyssey* 4.264.

17 he was no-nonsense: *Iliad* 3.213–15.

17 his rival Paris: *Iliad* 3.54, 393–95.

17 "feeble" or "despicable": For example, James K. Hoffmeier, "The Gebel

Barka Stele of Thutmose III," and K. A. Kitchen, "The Battle of Qadesh—
The Poem, or Literary Record," in W. W. Hallo, ed., *The Context of
Scripture: Canonical Compositions from the Biblical World*, vol. 2 (Leiden:
Brill, 2000), 16, 33.

17 "soft spearman": *Iliad* 17.588.

17 the Greek historian Herodotus: Hdt 1.4.1.

17 Near Eastern kings proclaim in their inscriptions: For the items in this
paragraph, see James K. Hoffmeier, "The Memphis and Karnak Steleae
of Amenhotep II," in Hallo, ed. *Context of Scripture*, vol. 2, p. 20; K. A.
Kitchen, "First Beth Shean Stela, Year 1," in ibid., 25; K. A. Kitchen,
"Karnak, Campaign Against the Hittites," undated, in ibid., 28; Richard
H. Beal "The Ten Year Annals of Great King Muršili II of Hatti," in
ibid., 84; Itamar Singer, "Treaty Between Šupululiuma and Aziru," in
ibid., 93–94; Douglas Frayne, "Rim-Sin," in ibid., 253; Douglas Frayne,
"Iahdun-Lim," in ibid., 260.

18 A Hittite king says: Murshilish II (r. ca. 1321–1295 B.C.); see Beal,
"Ten Year Annals," in Hallo, ed., *Context of Scripture*, vol. 2, pp. 82–83.

18 example from Canaan in the 1300s B.C.: Moran, *Amarna Letters*, EA
250, ll. 15–27, p. 303.

18 king of Troy, Alaksandu: Gary Beckman, "Treaty Between Muwattalli
II of Hatti and Alaksandu of Wilusa," in *Hittite Diplomatic Texts*, 2nd
edition (Atlanta: Scholars Press, 1996), 87–93.

18 "soldier servant": On the expression, see J. D. Hawkins, "Tarkasnawa
King of Mira," *Anatolian Studies* 48 (1998): 14. For the alliance between
the Hittites and Wilusa (Troy), see Beckman, "Treaty," in *Hittite
Diplomatic Texts*, 87–93.

19 Cadmus: The reinterpretation of this letter was announced by Frank
Starke in summer 2003, but a full scholarly version has not yet been
published. See Frank Starke, "Ein Keilschrift-Brief des Konigs von
Theben/Ahhijawa (Griechenland) an den Konig des Hethitischen Reiches aus dem 13. Jh. V. Chr," handout, August 2003, and Michael
Siebler, "In Theben Ging's Los," *Frankfurter Allgemeine Zeitung*, August
12, 2003, p. 31, http://www.faz.net/s/RubF7538E273FAA4006925CC
36BB8AFE338/Doc~EC6CFECB6D44B4344B70010A6675AF6A3~
ATpl~Ecommon~Scontent.html. For an argument against the thesis
that the Hittite document reveals an ancestor of a king of Ahhiyawa
named Kadmos, see Joshua T. Katz, "Review of Joachim Latacz's *Troy
and Homer: Towards a Solution of an Old Mystery*, Version 1.0, December

2005, Princeton/Stanford Working Papers in Classics, http://www
.princeton.edu/~pswpc/pdfs/katz/120503.pdf.

19 Tawagalawa: He appears in a document known as the Tawagalawa Letter or Piyamaradu Letter. See the discussion with translated excerpts in
Trevor Bryce, *Letters of the Great Kings of the Ancient Near East: The
Royal Correspondence of the Late Bronze Age* (New York: Routledge, 2003),
199–212. An English translation of the letter is available online (as "The
Piyama-radu Letter") at http://www.hittites.info/translations.aspx?
text=translations/historical%2fPiyama-radu+Letter.html.

19 Walmu: Gary Beckman, "Letter from a King of Hatti to an Anatolian
Ruler," in *Hittite Diplomatic Texts*, 145.

20 "For beauteous Helen": *Iliad* 3.70.

21 Aeschylus: Aeschylus, *Agamemnon* 687–89.

21 In Hittite society it was possible for a man to marry: Trevor Bryce,
Life and Society in the Hittite World (Oxford: Oxford University Press,
2002), 124.

21 the same may have been true for Greece: Shear, *Tales of Heroes*, 139–40.

23 "How would the sons of Troy": *Iliad* 6.441–43.

24 Queen Puduhepa: See Ekrem Akurgal, *The Hattian and Hittite Civilizations* (Ankara: Republic of Turkey Ministry of Culture, 2001), 101–2;
Trevor Bryce, *The Kingdom of the Hittites* (Oxford: Clarendon Press,
1998), 315–20; Bryce, *Life and Society*, 13–14, 136–37, 174–75.

24 "prizes": For example, *Iliad* 1.185.

25 a woman without a husband: Moran, *Amarna Letters*, e.g., EA 90, ll.
36–47, p. 163.

25 Madduwatta married off his daughter to King Kupanta-Kurunta: Gary
Beckman, "Indictment of Madduwatta," in *Hittite Diplomatic Texts*,
§§16–17, p. 157.

26 "You have become a wolf": Gary Beckman, "Hittite Proverbs," in
Hallo, ed., *Context of Scripture*, vol. 1, p. 215; Harry A. Hoffner Jr., *The
Laws of the Hittites: A Critical Edition* (Leiden: Brill, 1997) §37, p. 44,
plus commentary, 186–87; Bryce, *Life and Society*, 126.

26 Adultery: Hoffner, *Laws of the Hittites*, §197, p. 156; Bryce, *Life and Society*, 128.

26 Zannanza: Bryce, *Kingdom of the Hittites*, 193–99. The Pharaoh Ay
maintained his innocence but he was the chief suspect.

27 Thucydides dismisses this story: Thuc. 1.9.3.

27 war as a lawsuit before the gods: Th. P. J. Van den Hout, "Bellum Ius-

tum, Ius Divinum: Some Thoughts About War and Peace in Hittite Anatolia," in *Grotiana*, New Series 12–13 (1991–92 [1994]): 26.

27 Hattushilish I (1650–1620 B.C.), whose armies plundered: P. H. J. Houwink ten Cate, "The History of Warfare According to Hittite Sources: The Annals of Hattusilis I (Part II)," *Anatolica* 11 (1984): 49.

28 "manly deeds": For example, the ancient title of what is now commonly referred to as the "Comprehensive Annals" of King Murshilish II was "The Manly Deeds of Murshilish"; see Beal, "Ten Year Annals," in Hallo, ed., *Context of Scripture*, vol. 2, p. 82.

28 seven thousand Hittite subjects were transplanted: Tawagalawa Letter §9.

28 King Zimri-Lin of Mari: Barber, *Prehistoric Textiles*, 27–28; cf. W. Heimpel, *Letters to the King of Mari: A New Translation, with Historical Introduction, Notes, and Commentary* (Winona Lake, Ind.: Eisenbrauns, 2003), 27 85, p. 440.

28 "extremely beautiful" female cupbearers: Moran, *Amarna Letters*, EA 369, ll. 15–23, p. 366.

28 "captives": Ventris and Chadwick, *Documents in Mycenaean Greek*, PY 16, p. 161; cf. pp. 156, 579.

28 Herodotus commented: Hdt. 1.3–5.

28 when an ant is struck: Moran, *Amarna Letters*, EA 252, ll., 16–22.

CHAPTER TWO: THE BLACK SHIPS SAIL

31 a big man, healthy and muscular: This hypothetical description of Agamemnon's body, clothing, and arms is based on Homer and the royal skeletons of Mycenae. See Yiannis Tzedakis and Holley Martlew, eds., *Minoans and Mycenaeans: Flavours of Their Time* (Athens: Production Kapon Editions, 1999), 220–27.

32 "opener of canals": Frayne, "Iahdun-Lim," in Hallo, ed., *Context of Scripture*, vol. 2, p. 260.

33 "scepter-bearing king": *Iliad* 1.279.

33 symbol of power in Sumer: J. S. Cooper, "Enmetana," in *Reconstructing History from Ancient Inscriptions: The Lagash-Umma Border Conflict*, vol. 2, fasc. 1 in *Sources from the Ancient Near East* (Malibu, Calif.: Undena Publications, 1983), §v, p. 50.

33 cooling their heels on rocky Ithaca: *Odyssey* 24.118–19.

34 "of the great war cry": *Iliad* 5.855.

34 ghee-and-honey paste: A. K. Grayson, "Erishum I," in *Assyrian Royal*

Inscriptions, vol. 1, *From the Beginning to Ashur-resha-ishi* (Wiesbaden: Otto Harrassowitz, 1972), 7.62 and n. 36, p. 10.

34 prison or mutilation: Heimpel, *Letters to the King of Mari*, 27 161, p. 467; A.486+, p. 508; 26 282, p. 283; 26 257, p. 276.

34 to follow on foot while they rode in their chariots: As Ahmose son of Abana followed three pharaohs in the 1500s B.C.; see Miriam Lichtheim, "The Autobiography of Ahmose Son of Abana," in *Ancient Egyptian Literature: A Book of Readings*, vol. 2, *The New Kingdom* (Berkeley: University of California Press, 1976), 11–15, esp. 12.

35 "sacker of cities": For example, *Odyssey* 8.3.

35 Attarissiya: See Beckman, "Indictment of Madduwatta," in *Hittite Diplomatic Texts*, 153–60.

35 Piyamaradu: See note above on Tawagalawa.

35 Linear B tablets refer: For the points in this paragraph, see Thomas G. Palaima, "Mycenaean Militarism from a Textual Perspective: Onomastics in Context: *Lāwos, Dāmos, Klewos*," in Robert Laffineur, ed., *Polemos: Le Contexte Guerrier en Égée à l'âge du Bronze*, vol. 2, *in Aegaeum* 19 (1999): 367–80.

36 "the infantry and the chariotry": See, e.g., Gary Beckman, "Letter of Hattusili III of Hatti to Kadashman-Enlil II of Babylon," in *Hittite Diplomatic Texts*, 23 §7, p. 141; Itamar Singer, "Mursili's 'Fourth' Plague Prayer to the Assembly of Gods (Arranged by Localities)," in *Hittite Prayers* (Leiden: Brill, 2002), 13 §11, p. 67.

37 chain of beacon fire messages: Aeschylus, *Agamemnon* 293.

37 the tale of Iphigenia is preserved in other sources: It is in the Epic Cycle, in the *Cypria*.

37 "priestess of the winds": Ventris and Chadwick, *Documents in Mycenaean Greek*, 127, 304.

39 the galley: Ugarit also had a navy (as did Egypt and the Minoans) and it is possible that it too had galleys, perhaps even before the Greeks. See Elisha Linder, "Naval Warfare in the El-Amarna Age," in D. J. Blackman, ed., *Marine Archaeology*, Proceedings of the Twenty-third [sic] Symposium of the Colston Research Society Held in the University of Bristol April 4th to 8th, 1971 (London: Archon Books, 1973), 317–25; Paul Johnstone, *The Sea-Craft of Prehistory*, prepared for publication by Seán McGrail (Cambridge, Mass.: Harvard University Press, 1980), 79–82.

39 lion, griffin, or snake: The Minoans decorated their ships thus in the

Acrotiri frescoes (pre–ca. 1625 B.C.); see L. Kontorli-Papadopoulou, "Fresco-Fighting: Scenes as Evidence for Warlike Activities in the LBA Aegean," *Polemos*, vol. 2, p. 333.

40 "get there firstest with the mostest": Confederate cavalry General Nathan Bedford Forrest.

40 the whip and the stick: Steve Vinson, *The Nile Boatman at Work* (Mainz: von Zabern, 1998), 132.

40 sail weavers: F. Tiboni, "Weaving and Ancient Sails: Structural Changes to Ships as a Consequence of New Weaving Technology in the Mediterranean Late Bronze Age," *Nautical Archaeology* 34:1 (2005): 127–30.

40 It took six months: J. R. Steffy, as cited in T. G. Palaima, "Maritime Matters in the Linear B Tablets," *Thalassa: L'Égée Prehistorique et la Mer,* in *Aegaeum* 7 (1991): 288.

40 "Famous Ship" and "Fine Sailing": "Nausikles" and "Euplous" in Ventris and Chadwick, *Documents in Mycenaean Greek,* 95, 97; Palaima, "Maritime Matters," 284.

41 Ugarit was said in 1187 B.C.: J. Hoftijzer and W. H. Van Soldt, "Appendix: Texts from Ugarit Pertaining to Seafaring," in S. Wachsmann, *Seagoing Ships and Seamanship in the Bronze Age Levant* (College Station: Texas A&M University Press, 1998), 336 = M. Dietrich, O. Loretz, and J. Sanmartín, *The Cuneiform Alphabetic Texts from Ugarit, Ras Ibn Hani and Other Places: (KTU: second, enlarged edition)* 2 (Münster: Ugarit-Verlag, 1995), 47.

41 "who knock me far off my path": *Iliad* 2.132–33.

42 Pharaonic Egypt used merchant ships: Donald B. Redford, *The Wars in Syria and Palestine of Thutmose III* (Leiden: Brill, 2003), 204–5; James K. Hoffmeier, "Military: Materiel," in Donald B. Redford, ed., *Oxford Encyclopedia of Ancient Egypt,* vol. 2 (New York: Oxford University Press, 2001), 410.

42 found fruits on the trees: John A. Wilson, "The Asiatic Campaigns of Thut-Mose III, Subsequent Campaigns: Fifth Campaign," in J. B. Pritchard, *Ancient Near Eastern Texts Relating to the Old Testament,* revised edition (Princeton: Princeton University Press, 1969), 239.

43 "Then launch": *Iliad* 1.478–82.

44 "cast a glance": Th. P. J. Van den Hout, "Apology of Hattušili III," in Hallo, ed., *Context of Scripture,* vol. 1, p. 200.

44 "although they inhabited the lowlands they were not sea-goers": Thuc. 1.7.

45 "knew how to make, with his hands": *Iliad* 5.60–61.

45 "Thy father's skill, O Phereclus! was thine": *Iliad* 5.60–64.

45 "well-balanced ships": *Iliad* 5.62.

46 "the border of the sea": Th. P. J. Van den Hout, "The Proclamation of Telepinu," in Hallo, ed., *Context of Scripture*, vol. 1, p. 194.

46 "filled the streets with widows": *Iliad* 5.642.

46 Ammurapi: Hoftijzer and Van Soldt, "Appendix: Texts from Ugarit," RS 1.1, RS 20.238, pp. 343–44.

48 "horse-nourishing": See, e.g., *Iliad* 2.287.

CHAPTER THREE: OPERATION BEACHHEAD

49 "Behold, the troops and chariots": Itamar Singer, "Treaty Between Muršili and Duppi-Tešub," in Hallo, ed., *Context of Scripture*, vol. 2, p. 97.

50 Shuppiluliuma II: Harry A. Hoffner Jr., "The Hittite Conquest of Cyprus: Two Inscriptions of Suppiluliuma II," in Hallo, ed., *Context of Scripture*, vol. 1, p. 193.

50 "Nations on nations fill": *Iliad* 2.808–10.

50 the historian Thucydides: Thuc. 1.11.1.

51 Hittite king told his young Babylonian counterpart: A. L. Oppenheim, "A Letter from the Hittite King," in *Letters from Mesopotamia* (Chicago: University of Chicago Press, 1967), 145–46.

52 the crushing embrace of an enemy siege: Houwink ten Cate, "Annals of Hattusilis I," 66.

52 held Priam and his people closer: *Iliad* 4.45.

52 "iron heart": *Iliad* 24.521.

52 No one in the region was more blessed: *Iliad* 24.546.

52 "border guards" and "watchmen": See, e.g., Beckman, "Indictment of Madduwatta," in *Hittite Diplomatic Texts*, 29, 157.

52 "Little Gnat": J. M. Sasson, *The Military Establishments at Mari*, no. 3 of *Studia Pohl* (Rome: Pontifical Biblical Institute, 1969), 38.

52 "coastal watchers": Ventris and Chadwick, *Documents in Mycenaean Greek*, PY 56, p. 189; cf. p. 544.

53 no, two hundred!: *Iliad* 8.228–34.

54 Halizones from Halube: Watkins, "Troy and the Trojans," in Mellink, ed., *Troy and the Trojan War*, 52–55.

54 Alaksandu Treaty: Beckman, "Treaty Between Muwattalli II of Hatti and Alaksandu of Wilusa," in *Hittite Diplomatic Texts*, 87–93.

54 repay each gift with another gift: *Odyssey* 24.284–85.

55 stripped his kingdom of silver: Miriam Lichtheim, "The Kadesh Battle Inscriptions of Rameses II: The Poem," in *Ancient Egyptian Literature*, vol. 2, p. 64.

55 "Such clamors rose": *Iliad* 4.437–38.

55 fought by national unit, as the Greeks did: *Iliad* 2.362.

56 "happy with words": Heimpel, *Letters to the King of Mari*, 26 366, p. 321.

56 Hana warriors: Heimpel, *Letters to the King of Mari*, A.486+, p. 507.

56 "Death is the worst": *Iliad* 15.494–99.

56 Hittite soldiers: Billie Jean Collins, "The First Soldiers' Oath" and "The Second Soldiers' Oath," in Hallo, ed., *Context of Scripture*, vol. 1, pp. 165–68.

57 "Ah! would the gods": *Iliad* 4.288–89.

57 "Inglorious Argives!": *Iliad* 4.242–43.

57 Storm God of the Army: Beckman, "Treaty Between Muwattalli II of Hatti and Alaksandu of Wilusa," in *Hittite Diplomatic Texts*, §20, p. 92; H. Craig Melchert, ed., *The Luwians*, vol. 68 of *Handbuch der Orientalistik* (Leiden: Brill, 2003), 221.

57 pen them up like pigs in a sty: A Hittite expression; see Van den Hout, "Apology of Hattušili III," 203.

57 "Bitter cries": J. S. Cooper, *The Curse of Agade* (Baltimore: Johns Hopkins University Press, 1983), ll. 166–69, p. 59.

59 "horses of the sea": *Odyssey* 4.708.

59 as an ancient Athenian general would note: Thuc. 4.10.5.

60 a style mentioned in Homer: *Iliad* 10.261.

60 "swift-footed": See, e.g., *Iliad* 1.58; cf. the discussion in Robert Drews, *The End of the Bronze Age: Changes in Warfare and the Catastrophe c. 1200 BC* (Princeton: Princeton University Press, 1993), 141–47, 211.

61 "send me stallions!": Adapted from Beckman, "Letter from Hattušili III of Hatti to Kadasman-Enlil II of Babylon," in *Hittite Diplomatic Texts*, §17, p. 143.

61 he reared some of his horses: *Iliad* 24.279–80.

61 Amenhotep II: Miriam Lichtheim, "The Great Sphinx Stela of Amenhotep II at Giza: The Narration," in *Ancient Egyptian Literature*, vol. 2, p. 42.

61 "a dispersed battle": *Iliad* 15.329, 510.

61 "how impossible it is": Thuc. 4.10.5.

62 Phrontis son of Onetor: *Odyssey* 3.279–83.

62 half its length up onto the beach: *Odyssey* 13.113–15.

62 Euphorbus son of Panthous: *Iliad* 16.811; cf. 3.146.

63 lion, bulls, or falcons: Thera-fresco warships are painted with hunting lions as emblems. See Nanno Marinatos, *Art and Religion in Thera: Reconstructing a Bronze Age Society* (Athens: D. I. Mathioulakis, 1994), 54. "Wild Bull" and "Falcon" are among the recorded names of Egyptian warships; see Lichtheim, "The Autobiography of Ahmose Son of Abana," in *Ancient Egyptian Literature*, vol. 2, pp. 12, 14.

63 Shalmaneser I: A. K. Grayson, "Shalmaneser I," *Assyrian Royal Inscriptions*, vol. 1, *From the Beginning to Ashur-resha-ishi* (Wiesbaden: Otto Harrassowitz, 1972), l. 536, p. 80.

63 "With shouts incessant": *Iliad* 13.833–37.

63 Protesilaus: Possibly just a symbolic name, since in Greek it means "First to Land."

64 Pharaoh Rameses II killed so many: Lichtheim, "The Kadesh Battle Inscriptions of Rameses II: The Poem," in *Ancient Egyptian Literature*, vol. 2, p. 69.

64 Egyptian sculpted relief: At Medinet Habu, 20th Dynasty, Rameses III (1184–1153 B.C.); see Yigael Yadin, *The Art of Warfare in Biblical Lands in the Light of Archaeological Discovery*, vol. 2 (London: Weidenfeld & Nicolson, 1963), 340–41.

64 even lacked sandals: Miriam Lichtheim, "Papyrus Lansing: A Schoolbook," in *Ancient Egyptian Literature*, vol. 2, p. 171.

64 as crocodiles fall: Lichtheim, "The Kadesh Battle Inscriptions of Rameses II: The Bulletin," in *Ancient Egyptian Literature*, vol. 2, p. 62.

65 as one Greek common soldier boasts: Thersites, *Iliad* 2.231. For an image of how Egyptians bound their prisoners, see the Medinet Habu relief, in Yadin, *Art of Warfare in Biblical Lands*, vol. 2, pp. 342–43.

65 Great Sea God: In Near Eastern myth, see, e.g., Itamar Singer, "Mursili's Hymn and Prayer to the Sun-Goddess of Arinna (CTH 376.A)," in *Hittite Prayers*, 51–57.

65 Bronze Age gesture of respect: See, e.g., Rameses II as a god in Lichtheim, "The Kadesh Battle Inscriptions of Rameses II: The Poem," in *Ancient Egyptian Literature*, vol. 2, p. 67.

65 Kukkunni: Beckman, "Treaty Between Muwatttalli II of Hatti and Alaksandu of Wilusa," in *Hittite Diplomatic Texts*, no. 13, §3, p. 87.

66 the watchmen might anticipate: Cf. Miriam Lichtheim, "The Poetical Stela of Merneptah (Israel Stela)," in *Ancient Egyptian Literature*, vol. 2, p. 77.

66 verdict of Thucydides: Thuc. 1.11.1.

67 battle on the Sangarius River: *Iliad* 3.184–90.

CHAPTER FOUR: ASSAULT ON THE WALLS

69 double doors: Cf. Yadin, *Art of Warfare in Biblical Lands*, vol. 1, pp. 21–22.

69 the build of a boxer: *Odyssey* 18.66–74. For clothes, see *Odyssey* 19.225–43; cf. Nestor's clothes at *Iliad* 10.131–34.

70 bull that represented the army's god: The bull was a common Anatolian symbol of the Storm God, see Ann C. Gunter, "Animals in Anatolian Art," in Collins, ed., *History of Animal World in the Ancient Near East*, 90; the Storm God was the symbol of Troy's army, see Beckman, *Hittite Diplomatic Texts*, 92; a bull figure has been found recently in Troy VIi, see Wendy Rigter and Diane Thumm-Dograyan, "Ein Hohlgeformter Stier Aus Troia," *Studia Troica* 14 (2004): 87–100.

70 It was unmanly, said a Hittite king: Hattushilish III (1267–1230 B.C.), as cited in Van den Hout, "Bellum Iustum," 26.

71 a "tablet of war" and a "tablet of peace": Van den Hout, "Bellum Iustum," 17, 25.

71 as a Greek king once sent to the Hittite monarch: *Keilschrifturkunden aus Boghazköi* V (Berlin: Zu beziehen durch die Vorderasiatische Abteilung der Staatlichen Museen, 1921–25): 6, (E. Laroche, *Catalogue des Textes Hittites* ii (Paris: Klincksieck, 1971): 57–64; cf. Bryce, *Kingdom of the Hittites*, 238–40; Bryce, *Life and Society*, 168.

72 "This is what Zeus has given us": *Iliad* 14.86–87.

73 "disgraceful" and "an outrage": *Iliad* 11.142.

73 it was the gods and not she who were responsible: *Iliad* 3.164.

73 One Canaanite mayor confessed his fear of his own peasantry: Moran, *Amarna Letters*, EA 117, ll. 83–94, p. 194.

73 driven into exile by a younger brother who despised him: Moran, *Amarna Letters*, EA 137, ll. 14–35, p. 218.

73 could force a city into surrendering: Houwink ten Cate, "Annals of Hattusilis I," 67.

75 against the armed might of the Greeks: *Iliad* 13.101–6.

75 Hector once barely escaped Achilles' charge: *Iliad* 9.352–55.

75 this postern gate lacked protective bastions: *Iliad* 5.789.

76 three ways to conquer a fortified city: Adapted from Yadin, *Art of Warfare in Biblical Lands*, vol. 1, pp. 16–18.

76 Mesopotamian proverb: John A. Wilson, "Akkadian Proverbs and Counsels," in Pritchard, *Ancient Near Eastern Texts*, 425.

76 when men mount swift-footed horses: *Odyssey* 18.263–64.

76 when he said goodbye to his wife Penelope: *Odyssey* 18.258.

76 Thucydides is the source: Thuc. 1.11.1.

77 "a hateful path": *Odyssey* 14.235–36.

77 "as many as the leaves": *Odyssey* 9.51.

77 Pithana and his son Anitta: Harry A. Hoffner Jr., "Proclamation of Anitta of Kuššar," in Hallo, ed., *Context of Scripture*, vol. 1, pp. 182–83.

77 One ancient Greek literary critic: Aristarchus; see discussion by G. S. Kirk, *The Iliad: A Commentary*, vol. 2, on Books 5–8 (Cambridge, England: Cambridge University Press, 1990), 217–18; cf. ibid., vol. 1, on Books 1–4, pp. 38–43.

78 "That quarter most": *Iliad* 6.433–39.

79 a painted pottery fragment: Shear, *Tales of Heroes*, 29 and fig. 42, p. 31.

79 Ajax could defeat Achilles: *Iliad* 13.324–25.

79 "the bulwark of the Greeks": *Iliad* 7.211.

80 favorite of the goddess Ishtar: Van den Hout, "Apology of Hattušili III," in Hallo, ed., *Context of Scripture*, vol. 1, p. 201.

80 "mistress of strife and battle": A. Kirk Grayson, "Tukulti-Ninurta I," in *Assyrian Rulers of the Third and Second Millennia BC (to 1115 BC)*, Royal Inscriptions of Mesopotamia, Assyrian Periods/vol. 1, (Toronto: University of Toronto Press, 1987), 1.v, 2–22, p. 238.

81 The outer wall: The existence of a wall around the lower city is likely but not certain. For arguments in favor of its existence, see D. F. Easton, J. D. Hawkins, A. G. Sherratt, and E. S. Sherratt, "Troy in Recent Perspective," *Anatolian Studies* 52 (2002): 91–93; for arguments against, see D. Hertel and Frank Kolb, "Troy in Clearer Perspective," *Anatolian Studies* 53 (2003): 77–81.

84 heaps of blood: Lichtheim, "The Kadesh Battle Inscriptions of Rameses II: The Poem," in *Ancient Egyptian Literature*, vol. 2, p. 70.

CHAPTER FIVE: THE DIRTY WAR

86 "Sole Companion": John A. Wilson, "Texts from the Tomb of General Hor-em-Heb," in Pritchard, *Ancient Near Eastern Texts*, 251.

87 no one could match Achilles for his looks or physique: *Odyssey* 11.469–70.

87 big and beautiful: *Iliad* 21.108.

87 "None of the bronze-wearing Greeks is my equal": *Iliad* 18.105–6.

87 Achilles claimed to have destroyed: *Iliad* 9.328–29.

87 Anum-Hirbi: Kemal Balkan, *Letter of King Anum-Hirbi of Mama to King Warshama of Kanish* (Ankara: Türk Tarih Kurumu Basımevi, 1957), 16; Houwink ten Cate, "Annals of Hattusilis I," 69–70.

88 sea raiders: Bryce, *Kingdom of the Hittites*, 368, 369.

88 Egyptian, Mesopotamian, and Hittite texts: Wilson, "The Asiatic Campaigns of Thut-Mose III: The Battle of Megiddo" and "Subsequent Campaigns," in Pritchard, *Ancient Near Eastern Texts*, 234–41 passim; Heimpel, *Letters to the King of Mari*, 27 112, p. 449; Harry A. Hoffner Jr., "Deeds of Šupiluliuma," in Hallo, ed., *Context of Scripture*, vol. 1, pp. 185–92 passim; cf. Bryce, *Life and Society*, 104–7.

88 Attarissiya: Beckman, "Indictment of Madduwatta," in *Hittite Diplomatic Texts*, 27 §19, p. 158.

88 Melanippus son of Hicetaeon: *Iliad* 15.546–51.

89 engineers from Lycia: Pausanias 2.16.5, 25.8.

89 "making war on other men over their women": *Iliad* 9.327.

89 Egyptian and Hittite booty lists: Wilson, "The Asiatic Campaigns of Thut-Mose III: The Battle of Megiddo" and "Subsequent Campaigns," in Pritchard, *Ancient Near Eastern Texts*, 234–41 passim; Hoffner, "Deeds of Šupiluliuma," in Hallo, ed., *Context of Scripture*, vol. 1, pp. 185–92 passim; cf. Bryce, *Life and Society*, 104–7.

89 Linear B tablets: Ventris and Chadwick, *Documents in Mycenaean Greek*, PY 16, p. 161; cf. pp. 156, 579.

89 eleven were in the vicinity of Troy: *Iliad* 9.326.

89 But there were surely some refugees: Dozens of large storage jars were sunk to their full height (up to six and a half feet) beneath the floor of the houses of Troy VIi. This suggests crowding, which was once attributed to a surge of refugees during the Trojan War. Yet the houses date not to Troy VIi's end but to its early years, so they must refer to something other than the Trojan War—they may be a sign of squatters during the rebuilding of the city after the earthquake of ca. 1300 B.C. See P. A. Mountjoy, "Troy VII Reconsidered," *Studia Troica* 9 (1999): 296–97.

90 "Where Trojan dames": *Iliad* 22.155–56.

90 "like locusts": D. Pardee, "The Kirta Epic," in Hallo, ed., *Context of Scripture*, vol. 1, pp. 334–35.

90 Roman-era collection of myths: Pseudo-Apollodorus, *Epitome*, 3.33.

90 Thermi: Excavations in the 1930s dated the destruction to ca. 1250, but the recent redating of Trojan pottery might suggest a later date for the destruction—and hence, a date that fits the Trojan War.

91 naval battle took place between Hittite and Cypriot ships: Hoffner, "The Hittite Conquest of Cyprus," in Hallo, ed., *Context of Scripture*, vol. 1, pp. 192–93.

91 sculpted Egyptian relief: See the illustrations of Rameses III's relief at Medinet Habu in Yadin, *Art of Warfare*, vol. 2, pp. 250–52, 340–41.

92 the "holy city of Eëtion": *Iliad* 1.366.

92 described as "high-gated": *Iliad* 6.416.

92 "we destroyed it and brought everything here": *Iliad* 1.367.

93 "The distant Trojans never injured me": *Iliad* 1.153.

93 "The well wrought harp from conquered Thebae came": *Iliad* 9.186–88.

94 died in their house "of Artemis's arrows": *Iliad* 6.428.

94 According to an ancient commentary: *Iliad* 1.366–69, Scholion on 1.366; see Kirk, *The Iliad*, vol. 1, p. 91.

95 "Zeus / Preserved me": *Iliad* 20.92–93.

95 The arms of the Greeks: For the image, see Cooper, *Curse of Agade,* l. 159, p. 59.

95 fell on the town: Bronze Age Anatolians used the expression "fall on" to mean "invade," e.g., Balkan, *Letter of King Anum-Hirbi*, 1.0, p. 8, comm. p. 14.

95 more steadfast than a row of bricks: Compare Moran, *Amarna Letters*, EA 296, ll. 17–22, p. 338.

96 a silver drinking cup from Mycenae: Commonly known as the Silver Siege Rhyton, the vessel was found in Shaft Grave 4.

96 the Pharaoh Kamose: John A. Wilson, "The War Against the Hyksos (continued)," in Pritchard, *Ancient Near Eastern Texts*, 554.

96 Better-documented, later periods of ancient Greek history: See, e.g., Diodorus Siculus 13.14.5; cf. Aeneas Tacticus, *Siegecraft*, 40.4–5.

96 "Thy friendly hand": *Iliad* 19.295–97.

97 "I trampled the country of Hassuwa": Amelie Kuhrt, *The Ancient Near East: c. 3000–330 BC*, vol. 1 (London: Routledge, 1995), 242.

97 Seti I: John A. Wilson, "Campaigns of Seti I in Asia," in Pritchard, *Ancient Near Eastern Texts*, 254–55.

97 common practice in Late Bronze Age Egypt: Andrea Gnirs, "Military: An Overview," in Redford, ed., *Oxford Encyclopedia of Ancient Egypt*, vol. 2, p. 401.

97 Shalmaneser I: Grayson, "Shalmaneser I," in *Assyrian Rulers*, vol. 1, ll. 56–87, p. 184.

98 "I used to like to spare Trojans": *Iliad* 21.101–2.

98 Lycaon: *Iliad* 21.34–53, 23.740–47.

98 the people of Apasa: On this episode, see Bryce, *Kingdom of the Hittites*, 209–11; Akurgal, *Hattian and Hittite Civilizations*, 82–83; Hawkins, "Tarkasnawa," 24.

99 "Now shameful flight": *Iliad* 2.119–22.

CHAPTER SIX: AN ARMY IN TROUBLE

101 well-known gripers: See the letter to the King of Mari from Bahdi-Addu in ARM 2 118 in Oppenheim, *Letters from Mesopotamia*, 106.

101 softwood: The likeliest woods available around Troy are pine, laurel, juniper, heather-stems, and dried willow. Animal dung too might have been used as kindling.

102 "evil smelling smoke": Balkan, *Letter of King Anum-Hirbi*, 8, p. 16.

102 "bring much fever": *Iliad* 22.31.

103 Hittite and other ancient rituals: See, e.g., Richard H. Beal, "Assuring the Safety of the King During the Winter (KUB 5.4 + KUB 18.53 and KUB 5.3 + KUB 18.52)," in Hallo, ed., *Context of Scripture*, vol. 1, 1.79, §ii. 1–4, p. 210.

103 "Lord of the Bow": Maciej Popko, *Religions of Asia Minor*, trans. Iwona Zych (Warsaw: Academic Publications Dialog, 1995), 93.

103 "of the glorious bow": *Iliad* 15.55.

103 that the Storm God washed them away!: *CTH* 7, obv. 10–18, in Gary Beckman, "The Siege of Uršu Text (CTH 7) and Old Hittite Historiography" *Journal of Cuneiform Studies* 47 (1995): 25.

103 "What girl?": Literally, "prize," *Iliad* 1.123.

104 "best of the Greeks": Literally, "best of the Achaeans," e.g., *Iliad* 1.244.

104 "youths of the Achaeans": *Iliad* 1.473.

105 Archaeology confirms: Shelmerdine, "Review of Aegean Prehistory VI," 577–80 = 369–372.

105 at Thebes a sacrifice: Robin Hägg, "State and Religion in Mycenaean Greece," in R. Laffineur and W. D. Niemeier, eds., *Politeia: Society and State in the Aegean Bronze Age*, in *Aegaeum* 12 (1995). 388.

106 Hittite music: Monika Schuol, *Hethitische Kultmusik: Eine Untersuchung der Instrumental-und Vokalmusik anhand hetitischer Ritualtexxte und von archaeologlogischen Zeugnissen*, Deutsches Archaeologisches Institut

Orient-Abteilung, Orient-Archaeologie, Band 14 (Rahden/Westfalen, Germany: Verlag Marie Leidorf, 2004), 60.

107 Gilgamesh: E. A. Speiser, "The Epic of Gilgamesh," in Pritchard, *Ancient Near Eastern Texts*, 87; cf. M. L. West, *The East Face of Helicon* (Oxford: Clarendon Press, 1997), 231–32.

107 Teshub: "The Song of Hedammu" and "The Song of Ulikummi," in Hoffner, *Hittite Myths*, 51–52, 60.

107 the Canaanite epic hero Kirta: Pardee, "Kirta Epic," in Hallo, ed., *Context of Scripture*, vol. 1, p. 333.

107 Egyptian tale of Wenamun: Miriam Lichtheim, "The Report of Wenamun," in *Ancient Egyptian Literature*, vol. 2, p. 229.

107 Hattushilish I: Kuhrt, *Ancient Near East*, vol. 1, p. 238.

107 Tukulti-Ninurta: Grayson, "Tukulti-Ninurta I," in *Assyrian Rulers*, vol. 1:1.1, 1–20, p. 233.

107 Abi-Milki: Moran, *Amarna Letters*, EA 147, p. 233.

107 governor of the Mesopotamian city of Nippur: Oppenheim, "The Court of the Kassite Kings [BE 17 24]," in *Letters from Mesopotamia*, 116–17.

107 "fast runner": See, e.g., *Iliad* 21.265.

108 companies of soldiers or rowers at Pylos: Ventris and Chadwick, *Documents in Mycenaean Greek*, 183–94.

108 "Ranks wedged in ranks": *Iliad* 16.211–18.

109 Naramsin: Cooper, *Curse of Agade*, l. 86, p. 55.

109 Hattushilish III: Harry A. Hoffner Jr., "Apology of Hattušili III," in Hallo, ed., *Context of Scripture*, vol. 1, p. 200.

109 Merneptah: A. J. Spalinger, *War in Ancient Egypt: The New Kingdom* (Oxford: Blackwell Publishing, 2005), 239.

109 Xerxes: Hdt. 7.12–19.

109 "Our cordage torn": *Iliad* 2.135.

109 "Now, for five months": Shlomo Izre'el and Itamar Singer, *The General's Letter from Ugarit, A Linguistic and Historical Reevaluation of RS 20.33 (Ugaritica V, no. 20)* (Tel Aviv: Tel Aviv University, 1990), 25.

109 "Fly, Grecians, fly": *Iliad* 2.141–42.

110 Tukulti-Ninurta: Grayson, "Tukulti-Ninurta I," in *Assyrian Rulers*, vol. 1: l.i 21–36, p. 234.

110 "To one sole monarch": *Iliad* 2.205–6.

110 serious business to Bronze Age commanders: See, e.g., Sasson, *Military Establishments at Mari*, 41.

110 "Whate'er our master craves": *Iliad* 2.232–38.

110 or even a traitor: For example, see Heimpel, *Letters to the King of Mari*, 62–63.

111 fine Thracian vintages brought by ship to Agamemnon daily: *Iliad* 9.71–72.

111 round-shouldered: *Odyssey* 19.246.

111 the soldiers had leather shields: *Iliad* 10.152.

111 the laces that made sandals fit comfortably to the foot: *Iliad* 10.132.

112 axes made of dull bronze rather than sharp iron: *Iliad* 23.118–19.

112 cleaned the camp of animal dung: Cf. *Odyssey* 17.296–99.

112 swarms of flies: *Iliad* 19.25.

112 fasted until dusk because they worked so hard: Cf. *Odyssey* 18.369–70.

112 gainsaid Hector in the Trojan assembly, much to his annoyance: *Iliad* 12.211–14.

112 kiss his hand: *Odyssey* 24.398.

112 honor him like a god: *Iliad* 10.32–33.

112 picking up the royal cloak when Odysseus dropped it: *Iliad* 2.183–84.

112 "visitation of foreign dogs": *Iliad* 8.526–27.

113 "Have we not known thee, slave!": *Iliad* 2.248–51.

113 The Hittites knew the value of slapstick humor: Harry A. Hoffner Jr., "Daily Life Among the Hittites," in Richard E. Averback, Mark W. Chavalas, David B. Weisberg, *Life and Culture in the Ancient Near East* (Bethesda, Md.: CDL Press, 2003), 112.

113 "Encouraged hence": *Iliad* 2.354–56.

114 "by peoples and groups": *Iliad* 2.362.

114 Shuppiluliuma I: Hoffner, "Deeds of Šupiluliuma," in Hallo, ed., *Context of Scripture*, vol. 1, p. 190; cf. Bryce, *Kingdom of the Hittites*, 192.

115 "Like some proud bull": *Iliad* 2.480–81.

CHAPTER SEVEN: THE KILLING FIELDS

117 hymns to the war-god: Schuol, *Hethitische Kultmusik*, 207–8.

117 buried at home with their mothers: Calvert Watkins, "A Latin-Hittite Etymology," *Language* 45 (1969): 240–41.

117 "messengers of death": Yadin, *Art of Warfare in Biblical Lands*, vol. 1, p. 8.

117 hit a target at 300–400 yards: Yadin, *Art of Warfare in Biblical Lands*, vol. 1, pp. 7–8.

117 a top slinger: Hoffmeier, "Military: Materiel," in Redford, ed., *Oxford Encyclopedia of Ancient Egypt*, vol. 2, 406–12, 410.

118 "girl crazy": *Iliad* 3.39.

118 Yashmah-Addu and his older brother: André Parrot and Georges Dossin, eds., *Archives royales de Mari*, vol. 1 (Paris: Impr. Nationale, 1955), 69.

119 Two kings could fight it out: On Hattushilish III (1267–1237 B.C.), see Van den Hout, "Apology of Hattušili III," in Hallo, ed., *Context of Scripture*, vol. 1, p. 201; Harry A. Hoffner Jr., "A Hittite Analogue to the David and Goliath Contest of Champions?" *Catholic Biblical Quarterly* 30 (1968): 220–25; W. K. Pritchett. *The Greek State at War*, part 4 (Berkeley: University of California Press, 1985): 15–21. Another king who may have fought a champion battle is the Mesopotamian Ishme-Dagan, although perhaps he merely led the army into a battle where the enemy leader was killed; Parrot and Dossin, eds., *Archives royales de Mari*, 69.

119 or two corporals: Richard H. Beal, *The Organisation of the Hittite Military* (Heidelberg: Carl Winter Universitaetsverlag, 1992), 509–13.

119 Attarissiya: Beckman, "Indictment of Madduwatta," in *Hittite Diplomatic Texts*, 27§12, p. 156.

119 every king claimed to have a patron god: See various examples in Grayson, *Assyrian Rulers*, vol. 1, 206; Van den Hout, "Apology of Hattušili III," in Hallo, ed., *Context of Scripture*, vol. 1, pp. 200–1; Lichtheim, "The Kadesh Battle Inscriptions of Rameses II: The Poem," in *Ancient Egyptian Literature*, vol. 2, p. 66; cf. West, *East Face of Helicon*, 209.

120 Iron weapons existed in Bronze Age Anatolia: To be sure, Bronze weapons predominated, but the Hittites produced some iron daggers, knives, axes, spears, and lanceheads, so iron arrowheads are also likely. See J. O. Muhly, R. Maddin, T. Stech, and E. Özgen, "Iron in Anatolia and the Nature of the Hittite Iron Industry," *Anatolian Studies* 35 (1985): 67–84.

120 an ancient commentator suggested: Scholion on *Iliad* 4.218–19.

120 honey: Ventris and Chadwick, *Documents in Mycenaean Greek*, e.g., KN 206, p. 310; cf. Tzedakis and Martlew, eds., *Minoans and Mycenaeans*, 266.

120 "No rest, no respite": *Iliad* 2.385–90.

121 forty kings: Grayson, "Tukulti-Ninurta I," in *Assyrian Rulers*, vol. 1: 5.23–47, p. 244; 18.1–28, p. 266; 20.1–10, p. 268; 23.27–55, p. 272.

122 "fore-fighters" *(promachoi)*: See, e.g., *Iliad* 3.31, 4.354.

122 "the first men": See, e.g., *Iliad* 5.536.

126 Tudhaliya IV: Itamar Singer, "Tudhaliya's Prayer to the Sun-Goddess of Arinna for Military Success (CTH 385.9)," in *Hittite Prayers*, 108.

126 how thirsty warriors were: *Iliad* 22.2.

126 mind over matter: See, e.g., the Old Babylonian poem, Joan Goodnick Westenholz, "Sargon, the Conquering Hero," in *Legends of the Kings of Akkade: The Texts* (Winona Lake, Ind.: Eisenbrauns, 1997), 63, 65, 69.

126 "The great, the fierce Achilles": *Iliad* 4.512–13.

127 "How dear, O kings!": *Iliad* 7.327–30.

128 "Oh, take not, friends!": *Iliad* 7.400–3.

CHAPTER EIGHT: NIGHT MOVES

131 an imposing monument: Among many examples from Bronze Age Mesopotamia, Anatolia, and Egypt, see Kitchen, "First Beth Shean Stela, Year 1," "Second Beth-Shan Stela, [Year Lost]"; Frayne, "Iah-dun-Lim," in Hallo, ed., *Context of Scripture*, vol. 2, pp. 25, 28, 260; Hawkins, "Tarkasnawa," 4–10 (the Karabel Relief).

132 Murshilish II: Beal, "Ten Year Annals," Year 3, in Hallo, ed., *Context of Scripture*, vol. 2, p. 85.

132 Babylonian prayer: Benjamin R. Foster, "IV. Adad (a) Against Thunder," in *Before the Muses: An Anthology of Akkadian Literature*, vol. 2, *Mature, Late*, 2nd edition (Bethesda, Md.: CDL Press, 1996), 540–41.

132 dog: Moran, *Amarna Letters*, EA 76, p. 146.

132 "son of a nobody": A. K. Grayson, "Ashur-Uballit I," in *Assyrian Royal Inscriptions*, vol. 1: 15*.325, p. 50.

132 should turn into a woman: Collins, "The First Soldiers' Oath," in Hallo, ed., *Context of Scripture*, 166.

132 "Go, less than woman": *Iliad* 8.163.

132 "Trojans and Lycians": *Iliad* 8.173–74.

133 "his manhood dwindle away": Grayson, "Tukulti-Ninurta I," in *Assyrian Rulers*, vol. 1: 1.vi 2–22, p. 238.

133 Purple was the royal color: Gary Beckman, "Edict of Suppiluliuma I of Hatti Concerning the Tribute of Ugarit," in *Hittite Diplomatic Texts*, 166–68.

133 Mesopotamian saying: Sasson, *Military Establishments at Mari*, 42.

133 dogs were the favorite animal for insults: Among many examples, consider the Hittite King Shuppiluliuma I's characterization of the tribal chief Huqqana of Hayasa as "a lowly dog" (Beckman, "Treaty Between Suppiluliuma I of Hatti and Huqqana of Hayasa," in *Hittite Diplomatic Texts*, 27) and a Canaanite mayor's assertion that only a dog would disobey the orders of Pharaoh (Moran, *Amarna Letters*, EA 314, ll. 11–16, p. 347).

134 "the bridges of war": *Iliad* 4.371; 8.378, 555; 11.160; 20.427.

134 food served by Syrian towns: Moran, *Amarna Letters*, EA 55, ll. 10–15, p. 127; EA 324, ll. 10–15, p. 352.

134 sound the alarm: Heimpel, *Letters to the King of Mari*, 26 168, p. 239.

134 "This night will": *Iliad* 9.78.

135 sentinels: Beal, *Organization of the Hittite Military*, 251–60.

135 whose property was as wide as the sea: For the phrase, see Moran, *Amarna Letters*, EA 89, ll. 39–47, p. 162.

136 "a razor's edge": *Iliad* 10.173.

138 "man of tongue": Heimpel, *Letters to the King of Mari*, s.v. "informer," 585; S. Dalley, *Mari and Karana: Two Old Babylonian Cities* (New York: Longman, 1984), 150. Cf. Gabriel Lemkin, *My Just War: The Memoir of a Jewish Red Army Soldier in World War II* (Novato, Calif.: Presidio, 1998), 154.

138 white horses: Dalley, *Mari and Karana*, 161; Moran, *Amarna Letters*, EA 16, 9–12, pp. 39, 40 n. 3.

139 guerrilla war: Richard Holmes, ed., *Oxford Companion to Military History* (Oxford: Oxford University Press, 2001), 383–86.

139 "the war of the flea": The phrase comes from Robert Taber, *The War of the Flea: The Classic Study of Guerrilla Warfare* (Dulles, Va.: Brassey's, 2002).

139 staple techniques of Mesopotamian warfare: Sasson, *Military Establishments at Mari*, 39–42.

140 Hittite laws: Albrecht Goetze, "The Middle Assyrian Laws," in Pritchard, *Ancient Near Eastern Texts*, 188–97.

140 breaking and entering: S. N. Kramer, "Lipit-Ishtar Lawcode," in Pritchard, *Ancient Near Eastern Texts*, 160.

140 raids on merchant caravans: Dalley, *Mari and Karana*, 150.

140 Egyptians decry: Miriam Lichtheim, "The Autobiography of Weni," in *Ancient Egyptian Literature*, vol. 1, *The Old and Middle Kingdoms*, 20.

141 merchant counted himself lucky: Dalley, *Mari and Karana*, 150.

141 foiled an assassin: Moran, *Amarna Letters*, EA 81, ll 14–24, p. 150.

141 elder brother: Miraim Lichtheim, "The Two Brothers," in *Ancient Egyptian Literature*, vol. 2, *The New Kingdom*, 205.

141 macehead: Grayson, "Shalmaneser I," in *Assyrian Rulers*, vol. 1: 22, pp. 210–11.

141 farmers of Late Bronze Age Ugarit: Sylvie Lackenbacher, *Textes Akkadiens d'Ugarit: Textes provenants des vingt-cinq premières campagnes* (Paris: Les Éditions du Cerf, 2002), RS 17.341 = PRU IV, 161s. et pl. L, pp. 143–44.

141 "miserable Asiatic": Miriam Lichtheim, "The Instruction Addressed to King Merikare," in *Ancient Egyptian Literature*, vol. 1, *The Old and Middle Kingdoms*, 103–4.

141 Scouting patrols: Sasson, *Military Establishments at Mari*, 18; Heimpel, *Letters to the King of Mari*, 26 156, p. 236; Beal, *Organization of the Hittite Military*, 260–63.

141 two Bedouin: Beal, *Organization of the Hittite Military*, 266–68.

142 Sumerian poem: Dina Katz, "Gilgamesh and Akka," in Hallo, ed., *Context of Scripture*, vol. 1, p. 551.

142 "hunger contorts": Piotr Michalowski, *The Lamentation over the Destruction of Sumer and Ur* (Winona Lake, Ind.: Eisenbrauns, 1989), ll. 390–91, p. 61.

142 the chief magistrate of the Bronze Age city of Byblos: Moran, *Amarna Letters*, EA 125, ll. 14–24, 25–32, pp. 204–5.

142 mayor of Byblos: Moran, *Amarna Letters*, EA 85, ll. 6–15, p. 156.

142 "rivaling in height heaven and earth": The phrase comes from Moran, *Amarna Letters*, EA 29, ll. 16–27, p. 93.

143 "My early youth was bred": *Iliad* 6.444–46.

CHAPTER NINE: HECTOR'S CHARGE

146 "All males": *Iliad* 6.493–94.

146 an ancient talisman for bringing back a man: Barber, *Prehistoric Textiles*, 372–73.

147 as an Assyrian text put it: Grayson, "Shalmaneser I," in *Assyrian Rulers*, vol. 1: 1.88–106, p. 184.

147 Hammurabi: Heimpel, *Letters to the King of Mari*, 26 379, p. 329.

147 details of an operation: See, e.g., Heimpel, *Letters to the King of Mari*, 26 170, p. 240.

147 Repair the gate: Heimpel, *Letters to the King of Mari*, 26 221–bis, p. 263.

147 "A chosen phalanx": *Iliad* 13.126–31, 133–35.

148 "a man insatiable for war": *Iliad* 13.746–47.

149 like frightened cattle or sheep: *Iliad* 15.321–26.

149 "Bring fire!": *Iliad* 15.718.

149 "Zeus has granted us today": *Iliad* 15.719–21.

150 showers that deposit red dust: *Iliad* 16.458; Richard Janko, *The Iliad: A Commentary*, vol. 4, on books 13–16 (Cambridge, England: Cambridge University Press, 1992), 377. The sirocco (ancient Greek Notos or Lips) sometimes brings red rain in the form of dust-laden air from the Sahara. See J. B. Thornes and John Wainwright, *Environmental Issues in the Mediterranean* (New York: Routledge, 2002), 80; cf. Jamie Morton, *The Role of the Physical Environment in Ancient Greek Seafaring* (Leiden: Brill, 2001), 50–51.

151 "that war was sweeter": *Iliad* 11.14–15.

152 As a Babylonian hymn says: Foster, "To Nergal (a) Nergal the Warrior," in *Before the Muses*, vol. 2, p. 612.

152 "If thou but lead": *Iliad* 11.796–800.

153 "Think your Achilles sees": *Iliad* 16.269–74.

154 "smashing his belly": Izre'el and Singer, *General's Letter from Ugarit*, 27, with an argument on 49–50 for this rendition of a difficult original in Akkadian.

155 like pharaoh's war cry: Moran, *Amarna Letters*, EA 147, ll. 9–15, p. 233; John A. Wilson, "The Egyptians and the Gods of Asia," in Pritchard, *Ancient Near Eastern Texts*, 249.

155 "So may his rage be tired": *Iliad* 18.282–83.

156 "useless weight on the ground": *Iliad* 18.104.

156 "Let me this instant": *Iliad* 18.120–21.

157 thirty-six miles or more: Luce, *Celebrating Homer's Landscapes*, 103.

CHAPTER TEN: ACHILLES' HEEL

159 Like Hittite and Egyptian generals: For examples, see Billie Jean Collins, "The 'Ritual Between the Pieces,'" in Hallo, ed., *Context of Scripture*, vol. 1, pp. 160–61. More than one example of this ritual is known: Billie Jean Collins, "The Puppy in Hittite Ritual," *Journal of Cuneiform Studies* 42 (1990): 211–26; Wilson, "The Egyptians and the Gods of Asia," in Pritchard, *Ancient Near Eastern Texts*, 248.

160 a classic gesture: See, e.g., Moran, *Amarna Letters*, EA 64, p. 135; EA 151, p. 238; EA 314, p. 377.

160 signal his surrender: Houwink ten Cate, "Annals of Hattusilis I," 66–67.

161 "women who are equivalent to men": *Iliad* 3.189, 6.186.

161 several hundred thousand women: http://www.womensmemorial.org/PDFs/StatsonWIM.pdf.

162 surely were not cheap: *CTH* 7, rev. 31–32; Beckman, "The Siege of Uršu Text (CTH 7) and Old Hittite Historiography," *Journal of Cuneiform Studies* 47 (1995): 27, comm. 31.

163 Arzawa: Kuhrt, *Ancient Near East*, vol. 1, pp. 250–52, citing EA 31–32.

163 king of Mira: Bryce, *Kingdom of the Hittites*, 308–9.

165 "Talk not of ruling in this dolorous gloom": *Odyssey* 11.488–81.

165 "children of the Trojans": *Odyssey* 11.547.

166 "the king": *Little Iliad*, frag. 3.

167 "like Artemis with her golden arrows": *Odyssey* 4.122.

168 Eurypylus's mother: *Odyssey* 11.519–21; *Little Iliad*, frags. 6–7.

169 figurines were a familiar way of representing a deity: See the illustrations in O. Tashin, *Die Hethiter und ihr Reich: Das Volk der 1000 Götter* (Stuttgart: Theiss, 2002), 227–31, 344–47.

169 wealthy Hittite capitals had monumental sculptures of the gods: Ekrem Akurgal, *The Art of the Hittites*, photographs by Max Hirmer, trans. Constance McNab (New York: H. N. Abrams, 1962), 108–10.

169 sacred medicine bundles: See under "medicine bundle," in Arlene Hirschfelder and Paulette Molin, *The Encyclopedia of Native American Religions: An Introduction* (New York: Facts on File, 1992), 176.

169 the Hittites: Houwink ten Cate, "Annals of Hattusilis I," 70.

169 the Romans: See under "evocatio," *Oxford Classical Dictionary*, 580.

169 leave an enemy town unscathed: Houwink ten Cate, "Annals of Hattusilis I," 73.

CHAPTER ELEVEN: THE NIGHT OF THE HORSE

172 "horses of the sea": *Odyssey* 4.708.

173 Hittite military doctrine: Richard H. Beal, "Le Strutture Militari Ittite di Attaco e di Difesa," in M. C. Guidotti and Franca Pecchioli Daddi, eds., *La Battaglia di Qadesh* (Livorno: Sillabe, 2000), 111, 114–15.

173 siege of one Mesopotamian city: Heimpel, *Letters to the King of Mari*, xxii–xxiii, 67–69; 14 104, pp. 496–97.

173 Marathon: Hdt. 6.115.

174 Tarentum: Appian, *Foreign Wars*, 6.32–33; Plutarch, *Fabius Maximus* 21–22.

174 rate of about five knots: See John Coates, "Power and Speed of Oared Ships," in Christopher Westerdahl, ed., *Crossroads in Ancient Shipbuilding: Proceedings of the Sixth International Symposium on Boat and Ship Archaeology Roskilde 1991*, ISBSA 6 (Oxford: Oxbow Books, 1994), 249–56.

175 Bronze Age armies knew how to march by night: The Mesopotamian city of Kahat was captured at night by the army of Attaya in the 1700s B.C.; see Heimpel, *Letters to the King of Mari*, 26 317, p. 299. On Hittite marches at night, see Beal, "Le Strutture Militari Ittite," 112; Houwink ten Cate, "Annals of Hattusilis I," 68.

175 covered the distance: On marching rates of infantrymen, ancient and modern, see http://carlisle.www.army.mil/usamhi/bibliographies/refer encebibliographies/marching/rates.doc.

175 Thargelion: Dionysius of Halicarnassus, *Roman Antiquities* 1.63.1.

175 "dissatisfaction and treachery": Michalowski, *Lamentation over the Destruction of Sumer and Ur*, ll. 297–99, p. 55.

176 shipwrights and carpenters: Ventris and Chadwick, *Documents in Mycenaean Greek*, 123; KN 47, p. 179; PY 51, p. 182; PY 189, p. 298.

176 realistic figures of wild animals: Moran, *Amarna Letters*, ll. 29–42, EA 8, p. 19; n. 10, p. 20.

176 often sent horses as a gift: See, e.g., Dalley, *Mari and Karana*, 153; Moran, *Amarna Letters*, EA 16, p. 39.

176 found a clay model of a horse: Manfred Korfmann et al., *Traum und Wirklichkeit: Troia* (Stuttgart: Theiss Verlag, 2001), 402.

178 had never given Aeneas the honor: *Iliad* 13.460–61.

179 Shuppululiuma I conquered the city of Carchemish: Cited in Van den Hout, "Bellum Iustum," 27.

179 Lagash and Umma: Cooper, *Lagash-Umma Border Conflict*, 40, 48, 52.

CONCLUSION

184 "For Priam now": *Iliad* 20.306–8.

185 many such lines of prisoners: See, e.g., Royal Standard of Ur War Panel; relief in the tomb of Anta, Deshashe, Upper Egypt, Late Vth Dynasty, each depicted in Yadin, *Art of Warfare*, vol. 1, pp. 132–33, 146;

and relief at Medinet Habu, XXth Dynasty, Rameses III (1192–1160 B.C.), depicted in Yadin, *Art of Warfare*, vol. 2, pp. 342–43.

186 "many gifts": *Sack of Troy*, frag. 4.

189 like a stone out of deep water: Itamar Singer, "Hattusili's Exculpation to the Sun-Goddess of Arinna," in *Hittite Prayers*, 99.

A NOTE ON SOURCES

No one has read everything about the Trojan War. The sheer amount of scholarship on Homer, the archaeology of Troy, Mycenaean civilization, and Bronze Age warfare, not to mention Anatolia and the ancient Near East, is as long as it is exciting. This section lists only the main works used in writing this book. The focus is on scholarship in English and on publications of the last twenty years.

THE TROJAN WAR

Among several recent and important introductions, pride of place belongs to Joachim Latacz, *Troy and Homer: Towards a Solution of an Old Mystery*, translated by Kevin Windle and Rosh Ireland (Oxford: Oxford University Press, 2004). This fundamental work rethinks the historicity of the Trojan War in the light of recent archaeology, Hittite studies, and work on Homer. But it is not always easy going for nonscholars. Some of the same ground is covered, although in much less detail, in Carol G. Thomas and Craig Conant's very good *The Trojan War*, Greenwood Guides to Historic Events of the Ancient World (Westport, Conn.: Greenwood Press, 2005). The volume includes a selection of primary documents. Trevor Bryce, *The Trojans and Their Neighbours* (London: Routledge, 2006), is an excellent introduction to the Late Bronze Age historical context, if debatable on certain points. Slightly out of date but still very good and very readable is Michael Wood's *In Search of the Trojan War*, updated edition (Berkeley: University of California Press, 1996), which scans the subject from Homer to modern archaeology to the Hittites. A shorter survey is available in N. Fields, *Troy c. 1700–1250 BC* (Osceola, Fla.: Osprey Direct, 2004). A number of valuable essays appear in Ian Morris and Barry Powell, eds., *A New Companion to Homer* (Leiden: Brill, 1997). There is much helpful introductory material in Bettany Hughes, *Helen of Troy, Goddess, Princess, Whore* (London:

Jonathan Cape, 2005). Archaeologist and historian Eric Cline has recorded a series of lectures, "Archaeology and the Iliad: Did the Trojan War Take Place?" for Recorded Books/Modern Scholar (2006).

The reader will quickly note that the Trojan War is a story not just of historical data but of the varying ways of interpreting those data. An introduction to the range of scholarly opinion can be found in these collections of essays: Machteld J. Mellink, ed., *Troy and the Trojan War,* from a symposium held at Bryn Mawr College, October 1984 (Bryn Mawr, Pa.: Bryn Mawr College, 1986), and a special issue of the journal *Classical World* 91:5 (1998). A good summary of the state of debate in the early 1990s, before the most recent archaeological discoveries at Troy, is Hans Günter Jansen, "Troy: Legend and Reality," in J. M. Sasson, ed., *Civilizations of the Ancient Near East,* vol. 2 (New York: Scribners, 1995), 1121–34.

Ever since the modern study of history began in the 1800s, there have been two broad schools of thought about Troy. The *positivists* believe that the Trojan War really happened and that there is a kernel of historical truth—and then some—in Homer. The *skeptics* think there is no more truth in Homer than in a fairy tale. Heinrich Schliemann brought the positivists to prominence and they remained active through the mid-twentieth century. Important examples of the argument that there really was a Trojan War and that Homer's narrative reflects the Bronze Age are such books as T. B. L. Webster, *From Mycenae to Homer,* 2nd edition (New York: Norton, 1964), D. L. Page, *History and the Homeric Iliad* (Berkeley: University of California Press, 1959), and J. V. Luce, *Homer and the Heroic Age* (New York: Harper & Row, 1975).

In the decades after World War II, the skeptics gained the upper hand. The excavations of Troy in the 1930s pointed to a small and unimposing place—not the grand city of the *Iliad.* Linguists and students of inscriptions picked holes in the ancient texts that were supposed to provide written confirmation of the truth of Homer's tale. Finally, the bitter experience of the Second World War rendered unfashionable all heroic narratives, such as the Trojan War.

In the English-speaking world, the most prominent postwar skeptic is M. I. Finley, who argued that there is more in Homer of the early Iron Age than of the Bronze Age; see his *World of Odysseus,* revised edition (New York: Viking Press, 1978); his contribution to M. I. Finley, J. L. Caskey, G. S. Kirk, and D. L. Page, "The Trojan War," *Journal of Hellenic Studies* 84 (1964): 1–20; or "Lost: The Trojan War," in his *Aspects of Antiquity: Discover-*

ies and Controversies (London: Penguin, 1991). See also several of the essays and the editors' conclusions in J. K. Davies and L. Foxhall, eds., *The Trojan War: Its Historicity and the Context—Papers of the First Greenbank Colloquium* (Liverpool: Bristol Classical Press, 1981). More recent examples of skepticism about Homer's Bronze Age credentials can be found in several of the chapters of Morris and Powell, eds., *A New Companion to Homer*, as well as in Ian Morris, "The Use and Abuse of Homer," *Classical Antiquity* 6 (1986): 81–138. But for a reassessment in light of the new evidence, see Ian Morris, "Troy and Homer," Version 1.0, November 2005, Princeton/Stanford Working Papers in Classics, http://www.princeton.edu/~pswpc/pdfs/morris/120506.pdf. (For skepticism about the new excavations at Troy, see below.)

Now the pendulum is swinging again. Prominent positivists in the last decade include Latacz in his *Troy and Homer;* Bryce, in his *Trojans and Their Neighbours*, and the late Ione M. Shear, an Aegean–Bronze Age archaeologist, in her *Tales of Heroes: The Origins of the Homeric Texts* (New York: Aristide D. Caratzas, 2000). G. S. Kirk offers a concise and cogent case for positivism in "History and Fiction in the *Iliad*," in his *The Iliad: A Commentary*, vol. 2, Books 5–8 (Cambridge, England: Cambridge University Press, 1990), 36–50. Hughes offers a vivid and well-researched study of Helen as a real-life Bronze Age Greek woman in *Helen of Troy*. She anticipates my conclusions about Helen's lack of passivity and about the personal nature of Bronze Age notions of interstate relations.

Two revolutions have shaped the study of the Trojan War in the last two decades, one in archaeology and the other in epigraphy (the study of inscriptions). For the results of new excavations at Troy since 1988 and for the debate about them, see below, and the overview in W. D. Niemeier, "Greeks vs. Hittites: Why Troy Is Troy and the Trojan War Is Real," *Archaeology Odyssey* 5:4 (2002): 24–35. The latest Hittite epigraphical research increases the likelihood that Troy (Ilion) was the city that the Hittites called Wilusa; that the people whom Homer calls Achaeans and we call Mycenaeans or Bronze Age Greeks were the Ahhiyawa of Hittite texts; that the Achaeans considered themselves equal to the Hittites; that they expanded from the Greek mainland to the southern Aegean islands such as Crete and Rhodes and to the Anatolian mainland; and that they were piratical raiders whose ships struck as far afield as Cyprus and Lebanon. On recent discoveries in Hittite epigraphy, see J. D. Hawkins, "The End of the Bronze Age in Anatolia: New Light from Recent Discoveries," in A. Çilingiroğlu and D. French, eds., *Anatolian Iron Ages 3* (London: British Institute of Archaeology at Ankara, 1994), 91–94; J. D. Hawkins, "Tarkasnawa King of Mira," *Anatolian Studies* 48 (1998): 1–31; Michael Siebler, "In Theben ging's los," *Frankfurter Allgemeine Zeitung*, August 12, 2003, 31, http://www.faz.net/s/RubF7538E273FAA4006925CC 36BB8AFE338/Doc~EC6CFECB6D44B4344B70010A6675AF6A3~ATpl~ Ecommon~Scontent.html; and F. Starke, "Ein Keilschrift-Brief des Königs von Theben/Ahhijawa (Griechenland) an den König des Hethitischen Reiches aus dem 13. Jh. V. Chr," handout, August 2003. Archaeology adds the information that Late Bronze Age Greeks colonized the city of Miletus on Anatolia's Aegean coast. See W. D. Niemeier, "Miletus in the Bronze Age: Bridge Between the Aegean and Anatolia," *Bulletin of the Institute of Classical Studies* 46 (2002–03): 225–27.

The positivists fall into several different categories. Some date the Trojan War to around 1300 B.C. (at the end of Troy VIh) and others to around 1210–1180 (at the end of Troy VIIa—also known as Troy VIi). This book adheres to the latter view, as does Shear in her *Tales of Heroes*. Advocates of a date around 1300 B.C. include Michael Wood and D. F. Easton, "Has the Trojan War Been Found?" *Antiquity* 59 (1985):188–95. Others agree that Homer reflects the genuine historical memory of the Greek people, but deny that there was ever one Trojan War. Instead, they say, Homer took several centuries of wars in Anatolia and turned them into a single conflict. His poems are a smorgasbord of events; most of them really happened but not in any one time or place. The current excavators of Troy tend to this view. Emily Vermeule and Sarah P. Morris date the core material of Homer's poems back to the early Mycenaean era; see E. D. T. Vermeule, "Priam's Castle Blazing: A Thousand Years of Trojan Memories," *Troy and the Trojan War* (Cambridge, Mass.: Harvard University Press, 1986): 77–92, and Sarah Morris "A Tale of Two Cities: The Miniature Frescoes from Thera and the Origins of Greek Poetry," *American Journal of Archaeology* 93:4 (October 1989): 511–35.

This book argues that the Trojan War was caused by a combination of fear, honor, and self-interest: Thucydides' trio of motives underlying international relations. There has been no shortage of other theories. To cite just one category, for clashing economic interests as a cause of war between Greeks and Anatolians (including Trojans), see E. H. Cline, *Sailing the Wine-Dark Sea: International Trade and the Late Bronze Age Aegean* (Oxford: Tempus Reparatum, 1994); Christopher Mee, "Aegean Trade and Settlement in Anatolia in the Second Millennium B.C.," *Anatolian Studies* 28 (1978): 122–55; Christopher Mee, "Anatolia and the Aegean in the Late Bronze Age," in Eric H. Cline and Diane Harris-Cline, eds., *The Aegean and the Orient in the Second Millennium B.C.*, Proceedings of the Fiftieth Anniversary Symposium, Cincinnati, April 18–20, 1997, *Aegaeum* 18 (1998): 137–48; Trevor R. Bryce, "The Nature of Mycenaean Involvement in Western Anatolia," *Historia* 38 (1989): 1–21.

The Trojan War is not just a war but a cultural icon. Films, novels, fashions, and current events shape perceptions of it; there are influences from which not even scholars are immune. Barbara Tuchman saw Homer through the lens of the Vietnam War in *The March of Folly from Troy to Vietnam* (New York: Ballantine Books, 1984): 35–50. In Germany, the debate over the new excavations at Troy takes place against the background of reunification, which may be one reason why discussion has been so bitter; see Johannes Haubold, "Wars of *Wissenschaft:* The New Quest for Troy," *International Journal of the Classical Tradition* 8:4 (Spring 2002): 564–79.

TROY AND ARCHAEOLOGY

Troy was excavated from 1871 to 1891 by Heinrich Schliemann and Wilhelm Dörpfeld, and then again in 1932–1938 by Carl W. Blegen. In 1988, excavations at Troy were resumed after a fifty-year hiatus, having been preceded a few years earlier by a dig about five miles away at Beşik Bay (the Trojan Harbor). These new excavations are directed by Ernst Pernicka, successor to the late Manfred Korfmann, with the cooperation of Brian Rose. In addition to archaeologists, the excavation team includes anthropologists, art historians, chemists, computer scientists, epigraphers, geologists, Hittite specialists, Homerists, students of ancient plant life (archaeobiologists), and others. Reports of "Project Troia," the ongoing excavations at Troy, as well as articles on the archaeology of Troy and the Troad, may be found in *Studia Troica*, a scholarly journal published annually since 1991. Articles appear in English or German, each with a brief summary in both languages. Since 1998, the annual archaeological report has been published in both languages; earlier reports are in German with an English summary. News, bibliography, and other valuable information are also available in English on the Internet at http://www.uni-tuebingen .de/troia/eng/index.html. A summary of the state of the excavations at

Troy, based on a 2003 lecture (in German) by the late director of the excavations, Manfred Korfmann, can be found at http://www.uni-tuebingen .de/troia/deu/trier_deu.pdf. An excellent introduction to the excavations and their meaning for historians is found in Latacz, *Troy and Homer*, 15–100.

The excavators have written a guide to the site, available in English. See Manfred Korfmann, Dietrich Mannsperger, and Rüstem Aslan, *Troia/ Wilusa—Overview and Official Tour* (Istanbul: Ege Yayınları, 2005); it is still hard to find outside of Turkey. In German, there is a highly readable and reliable introduction, with beautiful color photos and remarkable, if hypothetical, reconstructions by Birgit Brandau, Hartmut Schickert, and Peter Jablonka, *Troia wie es wirklich Aussah* (Munich: Piper, 2004). One of the more innovative (and controversial) aspects of Project Troia is the use of computer models to create hypothetical reconstructions of the various ancient cities of Troy. For an introduction on the Internet, see http://www.uni-tuebingen.de/troia/vr/index_en.html. The lavishly illustrated catalog to a 2001 museum exhibit contains fine introductory essays (in German) by leading scholars on a wide range of topics concerning Troy: Manfred Korfmann et al., *Troia: Traum und Wirklichkeit* (Stuttgart: Theiss Verlag, 2001). Two important statements of the Anatolian character of Troy are Manfred Korfmann, "Troia, An Ancient Anatolian Palatial and Trading Center," *Classical World* 91.5 (1998): 369–85 and F. Starke, "Troia im Kontext des historisch-politischen und sprachlichen Umfeldes Kleinasiens im 2. Jahrtausend," *Studia Troica* 7 (1997): 447–87.

On the biconvex hieroglyphic seal found at Troy, see J. David Hawkins and Donald F. Easton, "A Hieroglyphic Seal from Troy," *Studia Troica* 6 (1996): 111–18. On the bronze figurine, see Manfred Korfmann, "Ausgrabungen 1995," *Studia Troica* 6 (1996): 34, 36; Machteld J. Mellink and Donna Strahan, "The Bronze Figurine from Troia Level VIIa," *Studia Troica* 8 (1998): 141–49. On the steles outside the gates of Troy, see Manfred Korfmann, "Stelen vor den Toren Troias, Apaliunas-Apollon in Truisa/Wilusa?" in Güven Arsebük, Machteld J. Mellink, and Wulf Schirmer, eds., *Light on Top of the Black Hill, Studies Presented to Halet Çambel* (Istanbul: Ege Yayınları, 1998), 471–78. An inscribed silver bowl may attest to a victory over Troy by a Hittite king, probably an early one, but the subject is still under debate: J. David Hawkins, "A Hieroglyphic Inscription on a Silver Bowl," *Studia Troica* 15 (2005): 193–204.

For an introduction to the Troad, the region of Troy, in light of Homeric scholarship and recent archaeology, see J. V. Luce, *Celebrating Homer's Landscapes: Troy and Ithaca Revisited* (New Haven: Yale University Press, 1999), 21–164; see Cook's meticulous if now partly outdated *The Troad: An Archaeological and Topographical Survey* (Oxford: Clarendon Press, 1973). A detailed study of the excavations at Beşik Bay (the Trojan Harbor), including the cemeteries, may be found in Maureen A. Basedow, *Beşik Tepe: Das spätbronzezeitliche Gräberfeld* (Munich: Verlag Philipp von Zabern, 2000). On the Mycenaean-style seal stone with smiling face, found in the harbor excavations, see Ingo Pini, "Zu den Siegeln aus der Beşik-Necropole," *Studia Troica* 2 (1992): 157–64, esp. 157–58. Rüstem Aslan and Gerhard Bieg, with Peter Jablonka and Petra Krönneck, "Die Mittel-Bis Spätbronzezeitliche Besiedlung (Troia VI und Troia VIIa) der Troas under der Gelibolu-Halbinsel, Ein Überblick," *Studia Troica* 13 (2003): 165–213, is a fundamental survey of archaeological research in the Middle and Late Bronze Age Troad outside the city of Troy. Fascinating details of the ecology and geology of the region appear in G. A. Wagner, Ernst Pernicka, and Hans-Peter Uerpmann, *Troia and the Troad: Scientific Approaches* (New York: Springer, 2003). For an argument on following Homer when it comes to locating the Greeks' ship station, see J. C. Kraft, "Harbor Areas at Ancient Troy: Sedimentology and Geomorphology Complement Homer's Iliad," *Geological Society of America* 31:2 (2003): 163–66. Botanist Martin Rix offers an appreciation of the plant life of Mount Ida in "Wild About Ida: The Glorious Flora of Kaz Dagi and the Vale of Troy," *Cornucopia* 5:26 (2002): 58–75.

There is a discussion of the fossils of the Troad in A. Mayor, *The First Fossil Hunters* (Princeton: Princeton University Press, 2000). On the winds in the Dardanelles and their impact on Troy's prosperity, see J. Neumann, "Number of Days That Black Sea Bound Sailing Ships Were Delayed by Winds at the Entrance to the Dardanelles Near Troy's Site," *Studia Troica* 1 (1991): 93–100.

A considerable minority of scholars reject a number of the Troia Project's conclusions; that is, they doubt that the lower city has really been found, that Troy was a major center of commerce, that Troy and Wilusa are one and the same—and some question even the identification of Hisarlık with Troy, an equation that goes back to Schliemann. The leading skeptics are the ancient historian Frank Kolb and the archaeologist Dieter Hertel, and they are joined by Hittitologists and experts in the ancient Near East as well as ancient historians and archaeologists. In English, see

Frank Kolb, "Troy VI: A Trading Center and Commercial City?" *American Journal of Archaeology* 108:4 (2004): 577–613, and D. Hertel and Frank Kolb, "Troy in Clearer Perspective," *Anatolian Studies* 53 (2003): 71–88. Christoph Ulf edited a collection of articles (in German) largely critical of the excavators' conclusions in *Der neue Streit um Troia, Eine Bilanz* (Munich: C. H. Beck Verlag, 2003).

But most of these criticisms have been convincingly answered: see D. F. Easton, J. D. Hawkins, A. G. Sherratt, and E. S. Sherratt, "Troy in Recent Perspective," *Anatolian Studies* 52 (2002):1–35, and P. Jablonka and C. B. Rose, "Late Bronze Age Troy: A Response to Frank Kolb," *American Journal of Archaeology* 108:4 (2004): 615–30. In my judgment, the excavators' claims about the lower town stand scrutiny, and likewise their argument that Troy VIi (formerly called Troy VIIa) was probably destroyed by human violence. It is not certain that Wilusa equals Troy or that the Ahhiyawa of Hittite texts are Homer's Achaeans, that is Greeks, but both conclusions are likely. The evidence of Late Bronze Age trade between the Aegean and the Black Seas is stronger than the skeptics allow, although it requires more investigation. See Olaf Höckmann, "Zu früher Seefahrt in den Meerengen," *Studia Troica* 13 (2003): 133–60.

The results of the University of Cincinnati's excavations at Troy between 1932 and 1938 are published in four volumes edited by Carl W. Blegen, John L. Caskey, and Marion Rawson, *Troy: Excavations Conducted by the University of Cincinnati, 1932–1938* (Princeton: Princeton University Press, 1950–53), as well as in three supplementary monographs (1951–63). Blegen summarized his conclusions in *Troy and the Trojans* (New York: Praeger, 1963). Wilhelm Dörpfeld's excavations at Troy are described in an English-language book by Herbert Cushing Tolman, *Mycenaean Troy* (1903). Heinrich Schliemann famously began the modern excavation of Troy in 1871, and he published the pioneering results in volumes called *Ilios* (1881) and *Troja* (1884).

HOMER

Most readers get to know Homer in translation. While they are no substitute for the Greek original, many excellent translations are available. This book uses Alexander Pope's dignified and lapidary *Iliad* of 1720 and *Odyssey* of 1725–26, which render Homer in heroic couplets. Among recent translations, the two outstanding formal renderings of the *Iliad* are

Richmond Lattimore, *The Iliad of Homer* (Chicago: University of Chicago Press, 1951) and Robert Fagles, *The Iliad/Homer* (New York: Penguin Books, 1991). Fagles's *Odyssey* is particularly beautiful: *Odyssey/Homer* (New York: Penguin Books, 1996). But perhaps the outstanding translation is Stanley Lombardo's rendition of Homer in ordinary English: *Iliad/Homer* and *Odyssey/Homer* (Indianapolis: Hackett Publishing Company, 2000).

Indispensable for serious study of the *Iliad* is a six-volume scholarly commentary by G. S. Kirk, Mark W. Edwards, Richard Janko, J. B. Hainsworth, and N. J. Richardson, *The Iliad: A Commentary* (Cambridge, England: Cambridge University Press, 1985–93). A scholarly commentary in English on Books I–XVI of the *Odyssey* is available in A. W. Heubeck, Stephanie Hainsworth, and J. B. Hainsworth, *A Commentary on Homer's Odyssey*, 2 vols. (Oxford: Clarendon Press, 1990). For an introduction to what little survives of the other poems of the Greek Epic Cycle, see M. Davies, *The Epic Cycle* (Bristol: Bristol Classical Press, 1989). M. P. O. Morford and Robert J. Lenardon, *Classical Mythology* (New York: Longman, 1971) is useful.

Scholarly books and articles on Homer are almost innumerable. A good starting point is Barry Powell, *Homer* (Malden, Mass.: Blackwell, 2004), or Mark W. Edwards, *Homer, Poet of the Iliad* (Baltimore: Johns Hopkins University Press, 1987), while Morris and Powell, eds., *A New Companion to Homer*, offers expert essays on topics ranging from poetic meter to the experience of battle. A number of important essays on a variety of related subjects are found in Jane B. Carter and Sarah P. Morris, eds., *The Ages of Homer: A Tribute to Emily Townsend Vermeule* (Austin: University of Texas Press, 1995). On Homer as an oral poet, the basic book remains A. B. Lord, *The Singer of Tales* (Cambridge, Mass.: Harvard University Press, 1960). There is much of value in Gregory G. Nagy, *The Best of the Achaeans* (Baltimore: Johns Hopkins University Press, 1999).

On the impact of the ancient Near East on Homer, see M. L. West, *The East Face of Helicon* (Oxford: Clarendon Press, 1997), and Webster, *From Mycenae to Homer*, 27–64; Walter Burkert, *The Orientalizing Revolution: Near Eastern Influence on Greek Culture in the Early Archaic Age*, trans. Margaret E. Pinder and Walter Burkert (Cambridge, Mass: Harvard University Press, 1992), 1–6, 88–100. Calvert Watkins has done groundbreaking work on the possible Trojan roots of the Homeric poems. See "The Language of the Trojans," in Mellink, ed., *Troy and the Trojan War*, 45–62; "Homer and Hittite Revisited," in P. Knox and C. Foss, eds., *Festschrift Wen-*

dell Claussen (Stuttgart: Leipzig, 1998), 201–11; "Homer and Hittite Revisited II," in K. Alishan Yener and Harry A. Hoffner Jr., eds., *Recent Developments in Hittite Archaeology and History: Papers in Memoriam of Hans G. Güterbock* (Winona Lake, Ind.: Eisenbrauns, 2002), 167–76. On the possible Hittite roots of certain images, verb forms, and similes in the *Iliad*, see Jaan Puhvel, *Homer and Hittite*, Innsbrucker Beiträge zur Sprachwissenschaft, Vorträge und Kleinere Schriften 47 (Innsbruck: Inst. F. Sprachwiss. D. Univ., 1991). Sarah P. Morris's innovative work on the relationship of Greek and Near Eastern art and poetry includes her *Daidalos and the Origins of Greek Art* (Princeton: Princeton University Press, 1992) and her "The Sacrifice of Astyanax: Near Eastern Contributions to the Siege of Troy," in Carter and Morris, eds., *The Ages of Homer*, 221–45.

There are unusual and original insights into the mentality of early poets such as Homer in Elizabeth Wayland Barber and Paul T. Barber, *When They Severed Earth from Sky: How the Human Mind Shapes Myth* (Princeton: Princeton University Press, 2004).

WARFARE

For all his prominence in Western culture, Homer's description of warfare remains highly debated, and poetry is often ambiguous. A fundamental study of the Homeric battlefield is Joachim Latacz, *Kampfparänese, Kampfdarstellung und Kampfwirklichkeit in der Ilias, bei Kallinos und Tyrtaios* (Munich: Beck, 1977). Latacz argues convincingly that pitched battle in Homer is mainly a matter of mass combat rather than individual duels, yet he contends that rather than Homer describing the Bronze Age battlefield, the poet describes Greek warfare of his own day, shortly before 700 B.C. Hans Van Wees wrote a thorough and astute study of the varieties of Homeric warfare, including raiding, although there is more of the Bronze Age in Homer's battles than Van Wees allows. See, among other works, his *Status Warriors: War, Violence and Society in Homer and History* (Amsterdam: J. C. Gieben, 1992) and his "The Homeric Way of War: The 'Iliad' and the Hoplite Phalanx (I)," *Greece and Rome*, 2nd series, 41:1 (1994): 1–18 and "The Homeric Way of War: The 'Iliad' and the Hoplite Phalanx (II)," *Greece and Rome*, 2nd series, 41: 2 (1994): 131–55; also *Greek Warfare, Myths and Realities* (London: Duckworth, 2004), 151–65, 249–52, 290–94. Like Latacz, Van Wees largely removes Homeric battle from the Bronze Age. He differs from Latacz in dating Homer to the 600s B.C. and in taking heroic duels literally. He reconstructs Homeric battle as a matter of the constant ebb and flow of group and individual, which he compares to war in New Guinea. Latacz's reconstruction is more persuasive, but he underestimates the presence of Bronze Age arms and armor in Homer and the existence of mass combat in the Bronze Age. For a corrective, see Shear, *Tales of Heroes*. As Pritchett argues, the phalanx was hardly an invention of Archaic Greece but dates back to the Sumerians: Pritchett, *Greek State at War*, part 4: pp. 5–32. Still useful on raiding is Walter Leaf, *Troy: A Study in Homeric Geography* (London: Macmillan, 1912).

Van Wees and Ralph Gallucci are among those arguing, against the skeptics, that the chariot tactics in Homer are realistic and historical. See Gallucci, "Studies in Homeric Epic Tradition," in Karlene Jones-Bley et al., eds., *Proceedings of the Tenth Annual UCLA Indo-European Conference, Los Angeles 1998* (Washington, D.C.: Institute for the Study of Man, 1999), 165–82. In this same piece Gallucci shows that Bronze Age Assyrians named their siege engines after horses, and suggests that the Trojan Horse is a dim, mythic memory of that.

Skeptics will doubt the relevance of Bronze Age warfare to Homer, but nothing could be more pertinent to the premise of this book. Although four decades old, Yigael Yadin's two volumes are the best introduction to Bronze Age warfare: *The Art of Warfare in Biblical Lands in the Light of Archaeological Discovery* (London: Weidenfeld & Nicolson, 1963). There is much of value in Nigel Stillman and Nigel Tallis, *Armies of the Ancient Near East, 3000 B.C. to 539 B.C.* (Worthington, England: Wargames Research Group, 1984). There are good but brief discussions of Bronze Age warfare in General Sir John Hackett, ed., *Warfare in the Ancient World* (New York: Facts on File, 1989) and in Simon Anglim, Phyllis G. Jestice, Rob S. Rice, Scott Rusch, and John Serrati, *Fighting Techniques of the Ancient World 3000 BC–AD 500: Equipment, Combat Skills, and Tactics* (New York: Thomas Dunne Books, 2002). Robert Drews offers many important insights into conflict in the Late Bronze Age in his *The End of the Bronze Age: Changes in Warfare and the Catastrophe c. 1200 BC* (Princeton: Princeton University Press, 1993); his theories of chariot warfare, the limited role of infantry, and the disconnection between Homeric and Mycenaean society are, however, unconvincing. A. Harding's thoughtful essay considers war and the era's culture: "Warfare: A Defining Characteristic of Bronze Age Europe?" in John Carman and Anthony Harding, eds., *Ancient Warfare: Archaeological Perspectives* (Stroud, England: Sutton Publishing, 1999), 157–74.

Archaeological artifacts, military architecture, and the Linear B tablets are rich in detail about Late Bronze Age Greek warfare. For an overview of the subject, see Sarah Monks, "The Aegean," in R. Osgood, Sarah Monks, and Judith Toms, *Bronze Age Warfare* (Phoenix Mill, England: Sutton Publishing, 2000), 115–37. The first generation of Linear B evidence is discussed in Michael Ventris and John Chadwick, *Documents in Mycenaean Greek*, 2nd edition (Cambridge, England: Cambridge University Press, 1973); for the recent evidence, see Thomas G. Palaima, "Mycenaean Militarism from a Textual Perspective: Onomastics in Context: *Lāwos, Dāmos, Klewos*," in Robert Laffineur, ed., *Polemos: Le Contexte Guerrier en Égée à l'âge du Bronze*, vol. 2, in *Aegaeum* 19 (1999): 367–80. On Mycenaean arms and armor, see Shear, *Tales of Heroes*, 29–60, and A. M. Snodgrass, *Arms and Armour of the Greeks* (Ithaca: Cornell University Press, 1967), 14–34.

For an introduction to Hittite warfare, see P. H. J. Houwink ten Cate, "The History of Warfare According to Hittite Sources: The Annals of Hattusilis I (Part II)," *Anatolica* 11 (1984): 47–83; Richard H. Beal, *The Organisation of the Hittite Military* (Heidelberg: Carl Winter Universitaetsverlag, 1992); Richard H. Beal, "Hittite Military Organization," in Sasson, ed., *Civilizations of the Ancient Near East*, vol. 1, pp. 545–54; Richard H. Beal, "Le Strutture Militari Ittite di Attaco e di Difesa" [in Italian], in M. C. Guidotti and Franca Pecchioli Daddi, eds., *La Battaglia di Qadesh* (Livorno: Sillabe, 2000), 109–21. There is much of importance in these specialized studies: Kemal Balkan, *Letter of King Anum-Hirbi of Mama to King Warshama of Kanish* (Ankara: Türk Tarih Kurumu Basımevi, 1957); H. A. Hoffner, "A Hittite Analogue to the David and Goliath Contest of Champions?" *Catholic Biblical Quarterly* 30 (1968): 220–25; Hans G. Güterbock and Theo P. J. Van den Hout, eds., *The Hittite Instruction for the Royal Bodyguard*, *The Oriental Institute of the University of Chicago, Assyriological Studies*, no. 24 (Chicago: University of Chicago Press, 1991); Gary Beckman, "The Siege of Uršu Text (CTH 7) and Old Hittite Historiography," *Journal of Cuneiform Studies* 47 (1995): 23–32; Schlommo Izre'el and Itamar Singer, *The General's Letter from Ugarit* (Tel Aviv: Tel Aviv University, 1990); T. P. J. Van den Hout, "Bellum Iustum, Ius Divinum: Some Thoughts About War and Peace in Hittite Anatolia," in *Grotiana, New Series* 12–13 (1991–92 [1994]): 13–35.

New Kingdom Egyptian warfare is very well documented, and it is at a minimum suggestive of Late Bronze Age fighting more generally. See Ian Shaw's succinct *Egyptian Warfare and Weapons* (Buckinghamshire, England: Shire Publications, 1991) and A. J. Spalinger's more detailed *War in Ancient Egypt* (Oxford: Blackwell Publishing, 1991), as well as Andrea Gnirs, "Ancient Egypt," in Kurt Raaflaub and Nathan Rosenstein, eds., *War and Society in the Ancient and Medieval Worlds, Asia, the Mediterranean, Europe, and Mesoamerica* (Washington, D.C.: Center for Hellenic Studies, 1999), 71–104. See also J. K. Hoffmeier, "Military: Materiel," in D. B. Redford, ed., *Oxford Encyclopedia of Ancient Egypt*, vol. 2 (New York: Oxford University Press, 2001), 406–12, and D. B. Redford, *The Wars in Syria and Palestine of Thutmose III* (Leiden: Brill, 2003).

On Early Bronze Age warfare in Mesopotamia, see J. S. Cooper, *Reconstructing History from Ancient Inscriptions: The Lagash-Umma Border Conflict*, vol. 2, fasc. 1 of *Sources from the Ancient Near East* (Malibu, Calif.: Undena Publications, 1983). The rich evidence for Middle Bronze Age warfare at Mari can be found in J. M. Sasson, *The Military Establishments at Mari, Studia Pohl* (Rome: Pontifical Biblical Institute, 1969) and W. Heimpel, *Letters to the King of Mari: A New Translation, with Historical Introduction, Notes, and Commentary* (Winona Lake, Ind.: Eisenbrauns, 2003). For an introduction to Mari, see S. Dalley, *Mari and Karana: Two Old Babylonian Cities* (New York: Longman, 1984).

On set battles in the ancient Near East, see, for Megiddo (1479 B.C.), E. H. Cline, *The Battles of Armageddon* (Ann Arbor: University of Michigan Press, 2003), 6–28; and for Qadesh (1274 B.C.), W. J. Murnane, *The Road to Kadesh: A Historical Interpretation of the Battle Reliefs of King Sety I at Karnak* (Chicago: Oriental Institute of Chicago, 1990); and M. Healy, *Qadesh 1300 BC: Clash of the Warrior Kings* (Oxford: Osprey Publishing, 1993).

On chariots, see S. Piggott, *Wagon, Chariot, and Carriage: Symbol and Status in the History of Transport* (New York: Thames & Hudson, 1992), Mary Aiken Littauer et al., eds., *Selected Writings on Chariots, Other Early Vehicles, Riding and Harness*, in *Culture & History of the Ancient Near East*, vol. 6 (Leiden: Brill, 2002) and Juliet Clutton-Brock, *Horse Power: A History of the Horse and the Donkey in Human Societies* (Cambridge, Mass.: Harvard University Press, 1992).

On Bronze Age and Homeric naval history, see S. Wachsmann, *Seagoing Ships and Seamanship in the Bronze Age Levant* (College Station: Texas A&M University Press, 1998); Lionel Casson, *Ships and Seamanship in the Ancient World* (Baltimore: Johns Hopkins University Press, 1971), 30–35, 38–53, 445–46; Lucien Basch, *Le Musée Imaginaire de la Marine Antique* (Athens: Institut Hellénique pour la Préservation de la Tradition Nautique, 1987), 76–202; Shelley Wachsmann, "The Pylos Rower Tablets Reconsidered," *Tropis V, 5th International Symposium on Ship Construction in Antiquity: Nauplia, 26, 27, 28 August 1993, Proceedings*, ed. Harry Tzalas (Nauplion, Greece: Hellenic Institute for the Preservation of Nautical Tradition, 1993), 491–504; T. G. Palaima, "Maritime Matters in the Linear B Tablets," *Thalassa: L'Égée Prehistorique et la Mer*, in *Aegaeum* 7 (1991): 273–310; J. Crouwel, "Fighting on Land and Sea in Late Mycenaean Times," *Polemos*, 455–64. For arguments that the Mycenaeans invented the galley in the Late Bronze Age, see Michael Wedde, "War at Sea: The Mycenaean and Early Iron Age Oared Galley," *Polemos*, 465–78, as well as Michael Wedde, *Towards a Hermeneutics of Aegean Bronze Age Ship Imagery* (Mannheim: Bibliopolis, 2000). On the Egyptian navy, see E. Linder, "Naval Warfare in the El-Amarna Age," in D. J. Blackman, ed., *Marine Archaeology*, Proceedings of the Twentythird [sic] Symposium of the Colston Research Society Held in the University of Bristol April 4th to 8th, 1971 (London: Archon Books, 1973), 317–25; Steve Vinson, *Egyptian Boats and Ships* (Princes Risborough, England: Shire Publications, 1994). On Bronze Age shipwrecks, see George Bass, "Cape Gelidonya: A Bronze Age Shipwreck," *Transactions of the American Philosophical Society* 57, part 8 (1967), cf. http://ina.tamu.edu/capegelidonya.htm; W. Phelps, Y. Lolos, and Y. Vichos, eds., *The Point Iria Wreck: Interconnections in the Mediterranean ca. 1200 BC* (Athens: Hellenic Institute of Marine Archaeology, 1999); on the Ulu Burun wreck, see http://ina.tamu.edu/ub_main.htm.

Health conditions were surely no inconsiderable factor in the Trojan War. On war wounds and battlefield medicine, see Christine Salazar, *The Treatment of War Wounds in Greco-Roman Antiquity* (Leiden: Brill, 2000), 126–58; Guido Majno, *The Healing Hand: Man and Wound in the Ancient World* (Cambridge, Mass.: Harvard University Press, 1975), 142–47; Wolf-Hartmut Friedrich, *Wounding and Death in the Iliad: Homeric Techniques of Description*, trans. Gabriele Wright and Peter Jones (London: Duckworth, 2003); R. Arnott, "War Wounds and Their Treatment in the Aegean Bronze Age," *Polemos*, 499–506. There is much important and comparative information on malaria in Robert Sallares, *Malaria and Rome: A History of Malaria in Ancient Italy* (Oxford: Oxford University Press, 2002). There is an insightful discussion of battle stress in the *Iliad* in J. Shay, *Achilles in Vietnam* (New York: Maxwell Macmillan International, 1994). Poison in Homer is examined in A. Mayor, *Greek Fire, Poison Arrows & Scorpion Bombs* (Woodstock, N.Y.: Overlook Press, 2003).

On Amazons, see J. H. Blok, *The Early Amazons: Modern and Ancient Perspectives on a Persistent Myth* (Leiden: Brill, 1995); Lyn Webster Wilde, *On the Trail of the Women Warriors: The Amazons in Myth and History* (New York: Thomas Dunne Books, 2000); Jeanine Kimball-Davis, *Warrior Women: An Archaeologist's Search for History's Hidden Heroines* (New York: Warner Books, 2002); Renate Rolle, *World of the Scythians*, trans. F. G. Walls (Berkeley: University of California Press, 1989); and browse the archaeology links of the Web site of the Center for the Study of Eurasian Nomads, http://www.csen.org. On the female soldiers of Dahomey, see Stanley B. Alpern, *Amazons of Black Sparta: The Women Warriors of Dahomey* (New York: New York University Press, 1998) and Robert B. Edgerton, *Warrior Women: The Amazons of Dahomey and the Nature of War* (Boulder, Colo.: Westview Press, 2000). For a suggestion that the Amazons were really the female archers (or possibly male archers dressed as women) who took part in Hittite ritual, see Watkins, "The Language of the Trojans," in Mellink, ed., *Troy and the Trojan War*, 53, 55.

War and religion often go together. There are good insights into the religious milieu of Bronze Age Anatolia and its survival in Homer in Christopher Faraone, *Talismans and Trojan Horses* (Oxford: Oxford University Press, 1992). For an introduction to ancient Anatolian religion, see M. Popko, *Religions of Asia Minor* (Warsaw: Academic Publications, 1995); on Luwian religion, see Manfred Hutter, "Aspects of Luwian Religion," in H. Craig Melchert, ed., *The Luwians*, Handbuch der Orientalistik, vol. 68 (Leiden: Brill, 2003), 211–80. There is much on Mycenaean religion in the books below.

THE MYCENAEANS

Among several good and readable introductions to the subject are John Chadwick, *The Mycenaean World* (Cambridge, England: Cambridge University Press, 1976) and W. D. Taylour, *The Mycenaeans*, 2nd edition (London: Thames & Hudson, 1983). A more detailed and scholarly introduction is available in O. Dickinson, *The Aegean Bronze Age* (Cambridge, England: Cambridge University Press, 1994).

For a scholarly survey of fairly recent work, see C. W. Shelmerdine, "Review of Aegean Prehistory VI: The Palatial Bronze Age of the Southern and Central Greek Mainland," *American Journal of Archaeology* 101:3 (1997): 537–85, reprinted with an addendum on the period 1997–99 in

Tracey Cullen, ed., *Aegean Prehistory: A Review,* Supplement 1 to *American Journal of Archaeology* (Boston: Archaeological Institute of America, 2001), 329–82. Elizabeth French, *Mycenae, Agamemnon's Capital: The Site in Its Setting* (Charleston, S.C.: Tempus, 2004) is a succinct introduction to the most important Mycenaean site. An article on the excavations at Pellana and the purported palace of Menelaus and Helen is (in Greek) Theodore G. Spyropoulos, "The Palace of Menelaus and Helen in Mycenaean Lacedaemon," *Aeropos* 54 (March–April 2004): 4–15. An earlier candidate for the site of the palace is Therapne; see Hughes, *Helen of Troy,* 29–33.

On Linear B texts, see Ventris and Chadwick, *Documents in Mycenaean Greek,* and J. T. Hooker, *Linear B: An Introduction* (London: Bristol Classical Press, 1980). For an exciting tale of scholarship in action, see John Chadwick, *The Decipherment of Linear B,* 2nd edition (London: Cambridge University Press, 1967).

Earlier scholarship on the Mycenaeans, especially in light of Linear B texts, tended to regard Late Bronze Age Greek kingdoms as centralized, bureaucratic machines, and therefore utterly different from the ramshackle chiefdoms of the *Iliad.* For a corrective, see D. B. Small, "Surviving the Collapse: The Oikos and Structural Continuity Between Late Bronze Age and Later Greece," in Michael Galaty and William A. Parkinson, eds., *Rethinking Mycenaean Palaces* (Los Angeles: Cotsen Institute of Archaeology, 1999), 283–91; Ione Mylonas Shear, *Kingship in the Mycenaean World and Its Reflections in the Oral Tradition* (Philadelphia: INSTAP Academic Press, 2004). For Linear B texts and the Mycenaean military, see Palaima, "Mycenaean Militarism."

There are tantalizing suggestions of the impact of Anatolia on Mycenaean culture and society in such works as S. Morris, "Potnia Aswiya: Anatolian Contributions to Greek Religion," *Potnia: Deities and Religion in the Aegean Bronze Age,* in *Aegaeum* 22 (2001): 423–34; and Trevor R. Bryce, "Anatolian Scribes in Mycenaean Greece," *Historia* 48:3 (1999): 257–64.

For the possibility of Mycenaean mercenaries in the Egypt of King Tut, see R. Parkinson and Louise Schofield, "Images of Mycenaeans: A Recently Acquired Painted Papyrus from El-Amarna," in W. Vivian Davies and Louise Schofeld, eds., *Egypt, the Aegean and the Levant: Interconnections in the Second Millennium BC* (London: British Museum Press, 1995), 125–26.

On Mycenaean jewelry, see Eleni M. Konstantinidi, *Jewellery Revealed in the Burial Contexts of the Greek Bronze Age* (Oxford: J. & E. Hedges, distributed by Hadrian Books, 2001) and http://www.fhw.gr/chronos/02/ mainland/en/mg/technology/index.html.

On Mycenaean food, drink, and perfume, see Y. Tzedakis and H. Martlew, *Minoans and Mycenaeans: Flavours of Their Time* (Athens: Production Kapon Editions, 1999) and Cynthia W. Shelmerdine, *The Perfume Industry of Mycenaean Pylos* (Göteborg, Sweden: P. Åström, 1985). The possibility of human sacrifice in Minoan Crete is explored in J. A. Sakellarakis and S. E. Sapouna, *Archanes* (Athens: Ekdotike Athenon S.A., 1991).

HITTITES AND OTHER ANATOLIANS

The interaction between man and nature in ancient Anatolia is explored in J. Yakar, *Ethnoarchaeology of Anatolia* (Jerusalem: Graphit Press, 2000). On the animal world, see Billie Jean Collins, ed., *A History of the Animal World in the Ancient Near East* (Leiden: Brill, 2002). For an introduction to archaeological sites in Turkey, see Ekrem Akurgal, *Ancient Civilizations and Ruins of Turkey* (Turkey: Guzel Sanatlar Matbaasi A.S., 2001). There is much of value in Bernard McDonagh, *Blue Guide: Turkey*, 3rd edition (New York: W. W. Norton, 2001). Bilge Umar has written many books on the historical geography of Turkey. It is not necessary to know Turkish to appreciate the photos in his *Türkiye'deki Tarıhsel Anıtlar* (Istanbul: Inkılâp Kitabevi, 1995).

Trevor Bryce, in his *The Kingdom of the Hittites* (Oxford: Clarendon Press, 1998) and his *Life and Society in the Hittite World* (Oxford: Oxford University Press, 2002), provides an excellent introduction to the Hittites, as does J. G. MacQueen, *The Hittites and Their Contemporaries in Asia Minor*, revised edition (London: Thames & Hudson, 1986); see also several good articles in Sasson, ed., *Civilizations of the Ancient Near East*, as well as the lavishly illustrated O. Tashin, *Die Hethiter und ihr Reich: Das Volk der 1000 Götter* (Stuttgart: Theiss Verlag, 2002 [in German]) and the guide to Hattusha by its current excavator, J. Seeher, *Hattusha Guide: A Day in the Hittite Capital*, revised edition (Istanbul: Ege Yayınları, 2002). On new theories about the destruction of Hattusha, see J. Seeher, "Die Zerstörung der Stadt Hattuša," *Akten der IV: Internationalen Kongresse für Hethitologie* (Wiesbaden, 2001), 623–34. H. A. Hoffner, "Daily Life among the Hittites," in R. E. Averbeck et al., eds. *Life and Culture in the Ancient Near East* (Bethesda, Md.: CDL Press, 2003), 95–120, is an excellent overview. There are important recent papers in K. Alishan Yener and Harry A. Hoffner Jr., eds., *Recent Developments in Hittite Archaeology and History: Papers in Memoriam of Hans G. Güterbock* (Winona Lake, Ind.: Eisenbrauns, 2002), and Gary Beckman, Richard Beal, and Gregory McMahon, eds., *Hittite Studies in Honor of Harry A. Hoffner, Jr: On the Occasion of his 65th Birthday* (Winona Lake, Ind.: Eisenbrauns, 2003). There is a great deal of value in the monographs by Gary Beckman, *Hittite Diplomatic Texts*, 2nd edition (Atlanta: Scholars Press, 1999); I. Singer, *Hittite Prayers* (Leiden: Brill, 2002); Harry A. Hoffner Jr., *The Laws of the Hittites: A Critical Edition* (Leiden: Brill, 1997); and Harry A. Hoffner, ed., *Hittite Myths* (Atlanta: Scholars Press, 1998). On Hittite music, see Stefano de Martino, "Music, Dance, and Processions in Hittite Anatolia," in Sasson, ed., *Civilizations of the Ancient Near East*, vol. 4, 2668–69.

For the Hittites' neighbors and the political geography of Anatolia, see H. Craig Melchert, ed., *The Luwians*, with important contributions by Trevor Bryce, J. D. Hawkins, Manfred Hutter, and others; J. D. Hawkins, "Tarkasnawa King of Mira"; Hawkins, "Anatolia: The End of the Hittite Empire and After," in Eva Andrea Braun-Holzinger and Hartmut Matthäus, eds., *Die nahöstlichen Kulturen und Griechenland an der Wende vom 2. zum 1. Jahrtausend v. Chr.: Kontinuität und Wandel von Strukturen und Mechanismen kultureller Interaktion*, Kolloquium des Sonderforschungsbereiches 295 "Kulturelle und sprachliche Kontakte" der Johannes Gutenberg-Universität Mainz, December 11–12, 1998 (Möhnesee: Bibliopolis, 2002), 143–51; M. Benzi, "Anatolia and the Eastern Aegean at the Time of the Trojan War," in Franco Montanari and Paola Ascheri, eds., *Omero Tremila Anni Dopo* (Rome: Edizioni di Storia e Letteratura, 2002), 343–409.

What language or languages did the Trojans speak? There is much of interest on this still-unanswered question in the works by Watkins and Melchert cited above; see also G. Neumann, "Wie haben die Troer in 13. Jahrhundert gesprochen?" *Würzberger Jahrbücher für die Altertumswissenschaften 23* (1999): 15–23; Ruggero Stefanini, "Toward a Diachronic Reconstruction of the Linguistic Map of Ancient Anatolia," in S. De Martino and F. Pecchioli Daddi, eds., *Anatolia antica: Studi in Memoria di Fiorella Imparati, Eothen* 11 (Florence: Logisma editore, 2002), 783–806; Itamar Singer, "Western Anatolia in the Thirteenth-Century B.C. According to the Hittite Sources," *Anatolian Studies 33* (1983): 206–17.

For relations between the Greeks and Anatolia, see H. G. Güterbock, "The Hittites and the Aegean World: Part 1, The Ahhiyawa Problem Reconsidered," *American Journal of Archaeology* 87:2 (1983): 133–38; M. J. Mellink, "The Hittites and the Aegean World: Part 2, Archaeological Comments on Ahhiyawa-Achaians in Western Anatolia," *American Journal of Archaeology* 87:2 (1983): 138–41; E. T. Vermeule, "Response to Hans Güterbock," *American Journal of Archaeology* 87:2 (1983): 141–43. See also Trevor Bryce, "Ahhiyawans and Mycenaeans: An Anatolian Viewpoint," *Oxford Journal of Archaeology* 8 (1989): 297–310; Trevor Bryce, "Relations Between Hatti and Ahhiyawa in the Last Decades of the Bronze Age," in Beckman et al., eds., *Hittite Studies* (2003): 59–72; E. Cline, "A Possible Hittite Embargo Against the Mycenaeans," *Historia* 40 (1991): 1–9; W. D. Niemeier, "Mycenaeans and Hittites in War in Western Asia Minor," *Polemos*, vols. 1–2, in *Aegaeum* 19, pp. 141–56; P. H. J. Houwink ten Cate, "Contact Between the Aegean Region and Anatolia in the Second Millennium B.C." (1973), in R. A. Crossland and Ann Birchall, eds., *Bronze Age Migrations in the Aegean: Archaeological and Linguistic Problems in Greek Prehistory* (Park Ridge, N.J.: Noyes Press, 1974), 141–61.

THE ANCIENT NEAR EAST BEYOND ANATOLIA

A succinct introduction to the ancient Near East is found in B. A. Knapp, *The History and Culture of Ancient Western Asia and Egypt* (Chicago: Dorsey Press, 1988). Two valuable reference books are Sasson, ed., *Civilizations of the Ancient Near East*, and Daniel C. Snell, ed., *A Companion to the Ancient Near East* (Oxford: Blackwell, 2005). Important collections of documents from the region include W. W. Hallo, ed., *The Context of Scripture: Canonical Compositions from the Biblical World*, 2 vols. (Leiden: Brill, 1997–2000); J. B. Pritchard, *Ancient Near Eastern Texts Relating to the Old Testament*, revised edition (Princeton: Princeton University Press, 1969); Amelie Kuhrt, *The Ancient Near East: c. 3000–330 BC*, 2 vols. (London: Routledge, 1995).

A selection of literature from New Kingdom Egypt is available in Miriam Lichtheim, *Ancient Egyptian Literature: A Book of Readings*, vol. 2, *The New Kingdom* (Berkeley: University of California Press, 1976). A good historical introduction can be found in Donald B. Redford, *Egypt, Canaan, and Israel in Ancient Times* (Princeton: Princeton University Press, 1992) while Redford, ed., *Oxford Encyclopedia of Ancient Egypt* (New York: Oxford University Press, 2001) is a valuable reference source. P. H. Newby, *Warrior Pharaohs: The Rise and Fall of the Egyptian Empire* (London: Faber & Faber, 1980) is very readable.

For the royal inscriptions of Assyria, see A. K. Grayson, *Assyrian Royal Inscriptions*, vol. 1, *From the Beginning to Ashur-resha-ishi* (Wiesbaden: Otto Harrassowitz, 1972) and Grayson, *Assyrian Rulers of the Third and Second Millennia BC (to 1115 BC)* (Toronto: University of Toronto Press, 1987). For an introduction to the history of Assyria see H. W. F. Saggs, *The Might That Was Assyria* (London: Sidgwick & Jackson, 1984).

Anthologies concentrating on texts from ancient Mesopotamia include B. R. Foster, *Before the Muses: An Anthology of Akkadian Literature* (Bethesda, Md.: CDL Press, 2005) and A. Leo Oppenheim, *Letters from Mesopotamia* (Chicago: University of Chicago Press, 1967). Two volumes of Mesopotamian poems about war and destruction are Piotr Michalowski, *The Lamentation over the Destruction of Sumer and Ur* (Winona Lake, Ind.: Eisenbrauns, 1989) and J. S. Cooper, *The Curse of Agade* (Baltimore: Johns Hopkins University Press, 1983). Among a number of good introductions to ancient Mesopotamia, one of the best is A. Leo Oppenheim, *Ancient Mesopotamia: Portrait of a Dead Civilization*, revised edition completed by Erica Reiner (Chicago: University of Chicago Press, 1977); for an update on more recent discoveries, see Stephen Bertman, *Handbook to Life in Ancient Mesopotamia* (New York: Facts on File, 2003). Stephanie Dalley and A. T. Reyes write about the impact of Mesopotamia on Bronze Age Greece in Stephanie Dalley et al., *The Legacy of Mesopotamia* (Oxford: Oxford University Press, 1998), 85–94.

For the Amarna Letters, see William L. Moran, ed. and trans., *The Amarna Letters* (Baltimore: Johns Hopkins University Press, 1992). For an analysis of the international relations system illustrated in these letters, see Raymond Cohen and Raymond Westbrook, eds., *Amarna Diplomacy: The Beginnings of International Relations* (Baltimore: Johns Hopkins University Press, 2000). See also Trevor Bryce, *Letters of the Great Kings of the Ancient Near East* (London: Routledge Taylor and Francis Group, 2003) and Mario Liverani, *International Relations in the Ancient Near East, 1600–1100 B.C.* (New York: Palgrave, 2001).

A selection of texts from Ugarit can be found in Michael David Coogan, *Stories from Ancient Canaan* (Louisville: Westminster John Knox Press, 1978); S. Lackenbacher, *Textes Akkadiens d'Ugarit: Textes Provenants des vingt-cinq Premières Campagnes* (Paris: Les Éditions du Cerf, 2002 [in French]). For a brief introduction to Ugarit and Bronze Age Canaan, see Cyrus H. Gordon and Gary Rendsburg, *The Bible and the Ancient Near East*, 4th edition (New York: W. W. Norton, 1998), 82–95.

The identification of the Hittite "Alashiya" as Cyprus is a virtual detective story. See Y. Goren et al., "The Location of Alashiya," *American Journal of Archaeology* 107 (2003): 233–55.

Much new research has been done in recent years on the Sea Peoples, and a good deal of it is available in Eliezer D. Oren, ed., *The Sea Peoples and Their World: A Reassessment* (Philadelphia: University of Pennsylvania Press, 2000). See also the essays in Seymour Gitlin et al., *Mediterranean Peoples in Transition: Thirteenth to Early Tenth Centuries BCE: In Honor of Professor Trude Dothan* (Jerusalem: Israel Exploration Society, 1998). An older but still valuable work is N. K. Sandars, *The Sea Peoples: Warriors of the Ancient Mediterranean, 1250–1150 BC* (London: Thames & Hudson, 1978).

ACKNOWLEDGMENTS

Many people on three continents helped me to write this book. Chapters were generously read in draft and improved by Judith Dupré, Mark Levine, Kim McKnight, Marcia Mogelonsky, Jan Parker, and Meredith Small. My mentor, Donald Kagan, offered valuable advice at the outset of this project. Getzel Cohen opened doors at Troy. I am greatly indebted to him and to the staff of the Troia Project, and in particular to its late director Manfred Korfmann; and to Peter Jablonka, Rüstem Aslam, Gerhard Bieg, and Hans Jansen. Mustafa Aşkin led me through the Troad; Selma and Iskender Azloglu were hosts and guides to Mount Ida; and Scrhan Güngor is Turkey's *guide extraordinaire.* Allen Ward introduced me to Elias and Maria Tomazos, who brought me to a conference on the recent excavations at Pellana, Greece, generously hosted by the local community; there I met Ralph Gallucci, Matthew Dillon, and the excavation director, Theodore Spyropoulos, who offered valuable scholarly advice. My Cornell colleagues John Coleman, Peter Kuniholm, Sturt Manning, Jon Parmenter, Hayden Pelliccia, Pietro Pucci, Hunter Rawlings, Eric Rebillard, Jeffrey Rusten, and James Weinstein shared their knowledge of matters ranging from Thucydides to Anatolian trees to Native American religion. Among scholars at other universities who helped me are Günhan Borekci, Paul Cartledge, Eric Cline, Peter Dorman, Elizabeth S. Greene, Victor Davis Hanson, Simon Hillier, John Lee, Joseph Manning, Michelle Maskiel, Adrienne Mayor, Josiah Ober, Geoffrey Parker, Stephen Radentz, and Katerina Zacharias. Suzanne Lang provided invaluable secretarial and logistical assistance. Elizabeth Shedd did photo research and Susan Dixon designed and produced my Web site.

I would also like to thank Diane Barcelo, Nina Barclay, Stephan Blum, Susanne Bocher, Matthias Cieslak, Çiler Çilingiroğlu, Robert A. Graham, Pavol Hnila, Martin Loicano, Alison Minton, Bill Patterson, Kevin Rooney, Rabbi Eli Silberstein, Sevim Karabiyik Tokta, Sinan Unur, Steffen White, Janis Whitlock, and Chaya Rivka Zwolinksi.

The Department of History of Cornell University granted me leave to write this book. I am grateful to them, to Cornell's Department of Classics, and to the staff of Cornell's John M. Olin Library. I owe a debt to my students past and present, at Cornell and elsewhere, for their stimulation and support.

The people of Greece and Turkey proved as generous as ever.

I am greatly indebted to the wisdom and patience of my editor at Simon & Schuster, Bob Bender. His counsel is present on every page. I would also like to thank his assistant, Johanna Li, as well as Phil Metcalf and Tom Pitoniak. I am greatly indebted as well to my editor at Hutchinson, Paul Sidey, for his thorough, perceptive, and productive reading of the manuscript. I would also like to thank his assistant, Tiffany Stansfield. Without Howard Morhaim, best of literary agents, advisor, and friend, this book would not have come about.

My greatest debts are to my family. My mother continues to encourage me, as does the memory of my late father. The support and affection of my wife, Marcia, and my children, Sylvie and Michael, have made this project an odyssey and not a marathon. My brothers and sisters, both by birth and by marriage, are the greatest of friends, and I dedicate this book to them.

INDEX